Captain Nemo: 20,000 Leagues Under the Sea and The Mysterious Island

Captain Nemo: 20,000 Leagues Under the Sea and The Mysterious Island

by Jules Verne

20,000 Leagues Under the Sea

Table of Contents

SECOND PART

First Part

A Runaway Reef

THE YEAR 1866 was marked by a bizarre development, an unexplained and downright inexplicable phenomenon that surely no one has forgotten. Without getting into those rumors that upset civilians in the seaports and deranged the public mind even far inland, it must be said that professional seamen were especially alarmed. Traders, shipowners, captains of vessels, skippers, and master mariners from Europe and America, naval officers from every country, and at their heels the various national governments on these two continents, were all extremely disturbed by the business.

In essence, over a period of time several ships had encountered "an enormous thing" at sea, a long spindle–shaped object, sometimes giving off a phosphorescent glow, infinitely bigger and faster than any whale.

The relevant data on this apparition, as recorded in various logbooks, agreed pretty closely as to the structure of the object or creature in question, its unprecedented speed of movement, its startling locomotive power, and the unique vitality with which it seemed to be gifted. If it was a cetacean, it exceeded in bulk any whale previously classified by science. No naturalist, neither Cuvier nor Lacépède, neither Professor Dumeril nor Professor de Quatrefages, would have accepted the existence of such a monster sight unseen—specifically, unseen by their own scientific eyes.

Striking an average of observations taken at different times—rejecting those timid estimates that gave the object a length of 200 feet, and ignoring those exaggerated views that saw it as a mile wide and three long—you could still assert that this phenomenal creature greatly exceeded the dimensions of anything then known to ichthyologists, if it existed at all.

Now then, it did exist, this was an undeniable fact; and since the human mind dotes on objects of wonder, you can understand the worldwide excitement caused by this unearthly apparition. As for relegating it to the realm of fiction, that charge had to be dropped.

In essence, on July 20, 1866, the steamer Governor Higginson, from the Calcutta & Burnach Steam Navigation Co., encountered this moving mass five miles off the eastern shores of Australia.

Captain Baker at first thought he was in the presence of an unknown reef; he was even about to fix its exact position when two waterspouts shot out of this inexplicable object and sprang hissing into the air some 150 feet. So, unless this reef was subject to the intermittent eruptions of a geyser, the Governor Higginson had fair and honest dealings with some aquatic mammal, until then unknown, that could spurt from its blowholes waterspouts mixed with air and steam.

Similar events were likewise observed in Pacific seas, on July 23 of the same year, by the Christopher Columbus from the West India & Pacific Steam Navigation Co. Consequently, this extraordinary cetacean could transfer itself from one locality to another with startling swiftness, since within an interval of just three days, the Governor Higginson and the Christopher Columbus had observed it at two positions on the charts separated by a distance of more than 700 nautical leagues.

Fifteen days later and 2,000 leagues farther, the Helvetia from the Compagnie Nationale and the Shannon from the Royal Mail line, running on opposite tacks in that part of the Atlantic lying between the United States and Europe, respectively signaled each other that the monster had been sighted in latitude 42° 15' north and longitude 60° 35' west of the meridian of Greenwich. From their simultaneous observations, they were able to estimate the mammal's minimum length at more than 350 English feet; [Author's Note: About 106 meters. An English foot is only 30.4 centimeters.] this was because both the Shannon and the Helvetia were of smaller dimensions, although each measured 100 meters stem to stern. Now then, the biggest whales, those rorqual whales that frequent the waterways of the Aleutian Islands, have never exceeded a length of 56 meters—if they reach even that.

One after another, reports arrived that would profoundly affect public opinion: new observations taken by the transatlantic liner Pereire, the Inman line's Etna running afoul of the monster, an official report drawn up by officers on the French frigate Normandy, dead–earnest reckonings obtained by the general staff of Commodore Fitz–James aboard the Lord Clyde. In lighthearted countries, people joked about this phenomenon, but such serious, practical countries as England, America, and Germany were deeply concerned.

In every big city the monster was the latest rage; they sang about it in the coffee houses, they ridiculed it in the newspapers, they dramatized it in the theaters. The tabloids found it a fine opportunity for hatching all sorts of hoaxes. In those newspapers short of copy, you saw the reappearance of every gigantic imaginary creature, from "Moby Dick," that dreadful white whale from the High Arctic regions, to the stupendous kraken whose tentacles could entwine a 500–ton craft and drag it into the ocean depths. They even reprinted reports from ancient times: the views of Aristotle and Pliny accepting the existence of such monsters, then the Norwegian stories of Bishop Pontoppidan, the narratives of Paul Egede, and finally the reports of Captain Harrington—whose good faith is above suspicion—in which he claims he saw, while aboard the Castilian in 1857, one of those enormous serpents that, until then, had frequented only the seas of France's old extremist newspaper, The Constitutionalist.

An interminable debate then broke out between believers and skeptics in the scholarly societies and scientific journals. The "monster question" inflamed all minds. During this memorable campaign, journalists making a profession of science battled with those making a profession of wit, spilling waves of ink and some of them even two or three drops of blood, since they went from sea serpents to the most offensive personal remarks.

For six months the war seesawed. With inexhaustible zest, the popular press took potshots at feature articles from the Geographic Institute of Brazil, the Royal Academy of Science in Berlin, the British Association, the Smithsonian Institution in Washington, D.C., at discussions in The Indian Archipelago, in Cosmos published by Father Moigno, in Petermann's Mittheilungen, and at scientific chronicles in the great French and foreign newspapers. When the monster's detractors cited a saying by the botanist Linnaeus that "nature doesn't make leaps," witty writers in the popular periodicals parodied it, maintaining in essence that "nature doesn't make lunatics," and ordering their contemporaries never to give the lie to nature by believing in krakens, sea serpents, "Moby Dicks," and other all–out efforts from drunken seamen. Finally, in a much–feared satirical journal, an article by its most popular columnist finished off the monster for good, spurning it in the style of Hippolytus repulsing the amorous advances of his stepmother Phædra, and giving the creature its quietus amid a universal burst of laughter. Wit had defeated science.

During the first months of the year 1867, the question seemed to be buried, and it didn't seem due for resurrection, when new facts were brought to the public's attention. But now it was no longer an issue of a scientific problem to be solved, but a quite real and serious danger to be avoided. The question took an entirely new turn. The monster again became an islet, rock, or reef, but a runaway reef, unfixed and elusive.

On March 5, 1867, the Moravian from the Montreal Ocean Co., lying during the night in latitude 27° 30' and longitude 72° 15', ran its starboard quarter afoul of a rock marked on no charts of these waterways. Under the combined efforts of wind and 400–horsepower steam, it was traveling at a speed of thirteen knots. Without the high quality of its hull, the Moravian would surely have split open from this collision and gone down together with those 237 passengers it was bringing back from Canada.

This accident happened around five o'clock in the morning, just as day was beginning to break. The officers on watch rushed to the craft's stern. They examined the ocean with the most scrupulous care. They saw nothing except a strong eddy breaking three cable lengths out, as if those sheets of water had been violently churned. The site's exact bearings were taken, and the Moravian continued on course apparently undamaged. Had it run afoul of an underwater rock or the wreckage of some enormous derelict ship? They were unable to say. But when they examined its undersides in the service yard, they discovered that part of its keel had been smashed.

This occurrence, extremely serious in itself, might perhaps have been forgotten like so many others, if three weeks later it hadn't been reenacted under identical conditions. Only, thanks to the nationality of the ship victimized by this new ramming, and thanks to the reputation of the company to which this ship belonged, the event caused an immense uproar.

No one is unaware of the name of that famous English shipowner, Cunard. In 1840 this shrewd industrialist founded a postal service between Liverpool and Halifax, featuring three wooden ships with 400–horsepower paddle wheels and a burden of 1,162 metric tons. Eight years later, the company's assets were increased by four 650–horsepower ships at 1,820 metric tons, and in two more years, by two other vessels of still greater power and tonnage. In 1853 the Cunard Co., whose mail–carrying charter had just been renewed, successively added to its assets the Arabia, the Persia, the China, the Scotia, the Java, and the Russia, all ships of top speed and, after the Great Eastern, the biggest ever to plow the seas. So in 1867 this company owned twelve ships, eight with paddle wheels and four with propellers.

If I give these highly condensed details, it is so everyone can fully understand the importance of this maritime transportation company, known the world over for its shrewd management. No transoceanic navigational undertaking has been conducted with more ability, no business dealings have been crowned with greater success. In twenty–six years Cunard ships have made 2,000 Atlantic crossings without so much as a voyage canceled, a delay recorded, a man, a craft, or even a letter lost. Accordingly, despite strong competition from France, passengers still choose the Cunard line in preference to all others, as can be seen in a recent survey of official documents. Given this, no one will be astonished at the uproar provoked by this accident involving one of its finest steamers.

On April 13, 1867, with a smooth sea and a moderate breeze, the Scotia lay in longitude 15° 12' and latitude 45° 37'. It was traveling at a speed of 13.43 knots under the thrust of its 1,000–horsepower engines. Its paddle wheels were churning the sea with perfect steadiness. It was then drawing 6.7 meters of water and displacing 6,624 cubic meters.

At 4:17 in the afternoon, during a high tea for passengers gathered in the main lounge, a collision occurred, scarcely noticeable on the whole, affecting the Scotia's hull in that quarter a little astern of its port paddle wheel.

The Scotia hadn't run afoul of something, it had been fouled, and by a cutting or perforating instrument rather than a blunt one. This encounter seemed so minor that nobody on board would have been disturbed by it, had it not been for the shouts of crewmen in the hold, who climbed on deck yelling:

"We're sinking! We're sinking!"

At first the passengers were quite frightened, but Captain Anderson hastened to reassure them. In fact, there could be no immediate danger. Divided into seven compartments by watertight bulkheads, the Scotia could brave any leak with impunity.

Captain Anderson immediately made his way into the hold. He discovered that the fifth compartment had been invaded by the sea, and the speed of this invasion proved that the leak was considerable. Fortunately this compartment didn't contain the boilers, because their furnaces would have been abruptly extinguished.

Captain Anderson called an immediate halt, and one of his sailors dived down to assess the damage. Within moments they had located a hole two meters in width on the steamer's underside. Such a leak could not be patched, and with its paddle wheels half swamped, the Scotia had no choice but to continue its voyage. By then it lay 300 miles from Cape Clear, and after three days of delay that filled Liverpool with acute anxiety, it entered the company docks.

The engineers then proceeded to inspect the Scotia, which had been put in dry dock. They couldn't believe their eyes. Two and a half meters below its waterline, there gaped a symmetrical gash in the shape of an isosceles triangle. This breach in the sheet iron was so perfectly formed, no punch could have done a cleaner job of it. Consequently, it must have been produced by a perforating tool of uncommon toughness—plus, after being launched with prodigious power and then piercing four centimeters of sheet iron, this tool had needed to withdraw itself by a backward motion truly inexplicable.

This was the last straw, and it resulted in arousing public passions all over again. Indeed, from this moment on, any maritime casualty without an established cause was charged to the monster's account. This outrageous animal had to shoulder responsibility for all derelict vessels, whose numbers are unfortunately considerable, since out of those 3,000 ships whose losses are recorded annually at the marine insurance bureau, the figure for steam or sailing ships supposedly lost with all hands, in the absence of any news, amounts to at least 200!

Now then, justly or unjustly, it was the "monster" who stood accused of their disappearance; and since, thanks to it, travel between the various continents had become more and more dangerous, the public spoke up and demanded straight out that, at all cost, the seas be purged of this fearsome cetacean.

The Pros and Cons

DURING THE PERIOD in which these developments were occurring, I had returned from a scientific undertaking organized to explore the Nebraska badlands in the United States. In my capacity as Assistant Professor at the Paris Museum of Natural History, I had been attached to this expedition by the French government. After spending six months in Nebraska, I arrived in New York laden with valuable collections near the end of March. My departure for France was set for early May. In the meantime, then, I was busy classifying my mineralogical, botanical, and zoological treasures when that incident took place with the Scotia.

I was perfectly abreast of this question, which was the big news of the day, and how could I not have been? I had read and reread every American and European newspaper without being any farther along. This mystery puzzled me. Finding it impossible to form any views, I drifted from one extreme to the other. Something was out there, that much was certain, and any doubting Thomas was invited to place his finger on the Scotia's wound.

When I arrived in New York, the question was at the boiling point. The hypothesis of a drifting islet or an elusive reef, put forward by people not quite in their right minds, was completely eliminated. And indeed, unless this reef had an engine in its belly, how could it move about with such prodigious speed?

Also discredited was the idea of a floating hull or some other enormous wreckage, and again because of this speed of movement.

So only two possible solutions to the question were left, creating two very distinct groups of supporters: on one side, those favoring a monster of colossal strength; on the other, those favoring an "underwater boat" of tremendous motor power.

Now then, although the latter hypothesis was completely admissible, it couldn't stand up to inquiries conducted in both the New World and the Old. That a private individual had such a mechanism at his disposal was less than probable. Where and when had he built it, and how could he have built it in secret?

Only some government could own such an engine of destruction, and in these disaster–filled times, when men tax their ingenuity to build increasingly powerful aggressive weapons, it was possible that, unknown to the rest of the world, some nation could have been testing such a fearsome machine. The Chassepot rifle led to the torpedo, and the torpedo has led to this underwater battering ram, which in turn will lead to the world putting its foot down. At least I hope it will.

But this hypothesis of a war machine collapsed in the face of formal denials from the various governments. Since the public interest was at stake and transoceanic travel was suffering, the sincerity of these governments could not be doubted. Besides, how could the assembly of this underwater boat have escaped public notice? Keeping a secret under such circumstances would be difficult enough for an individual, and certainly impossible for a nation whose every move is under constant surveillance by rival powers.

So, after inquiries conducted in England, France, Russia, Prussia, Spain, Italy, America, and even Turkey, the hypothesis of an underwater Monitor was ultimately rejected.

And so the monster surfaced again, despite the endless witticisms heaped on it by the popular press, and the human imagination soon got caught up in the most ridiculous ichthyological fantasies.

After I arrived in New York, several people did me the honor of consulting me on the phenomenon in question. In France I had published a two–volume work, in quarto, entitled The Mysteries of the Great Ocean Depths. Well received in scholarly circles, this book had established me as a specialist in this pretty obscure field of natural history. My views were in demand. As long as I could deny the reality of the business, I confined myself to a flat "no comment." But soon, pinned to the wall, I had to explain myself straight out. And in this vein, "the honorable Pierre Aronnax, Professor at the Paris Museum," was summoned by The New York Herald to formulate his views no matter what.

I complied. Since I could no longer hold my tongue, I let it wag. I discussed the question in its every aspect, both political and scientific, and this is an excerpt from the well–padded article I published in the issue of April 30.

"Therefore," I wrote, "after examining these different hypotheses one by one, we are forced, every other supposition having been refuted, to accept the existence of an extremely powerful marine animal.

"The deepest parts of the ocean are totally unknown to us. No soundings have been able to reach them. What goes on in those distant depths? What creatures inhabit, or could inhabit, those regions twelve or fifteen miles beneath the surface of the water? What is the constitution of these animals? It's almost beyond conjecture.

"However, the solution to this problem submitted to me can take the form of a choice between two alternatives.

"Either we know every variety of creature populating our planet, or we do not.

"If we do not know every one of them, if nature still keeps ichthyological secrets from us, nothing is more admissible than to accept the existence of fish or cetaceans of new species or even new genera, animals with a basically 'cast–iron' constitution that inhabit strata beyond the reach of our soundings, and which some development or other, an urge or a whim if you prefer, can bring to the upper level of the ocean for long intervals.

"If, on the other hand, we do know every living species, we must look for the animal in question among those marine creatures already cataloged, and in this event I would be inclined to accept the existence of a giant narwhale.

"The common narwhale, or sea unicorn, often reaches a length of sixty feet. Increase its dimensions fivefold or even tenfold, then give this cetacean a strength in proportion to its size while enlarging its offensive weapons, and you have the animal we're looking for. It would have the proportions determined by the officers of the Shannon, the instrument needed to perforate the Scotia, and the power to pierce a steamer's hull.

"In essence, the narwhale is armed with a sort of ivory sword, or lance, as certain naturalists have expressed it. It's a king–sized tooth as hard as steel. Some of these teeth have been found buried in the bodies of baleen whales, which the narwhale attacks with invariable success. Others have been wrenched, not without difficulty, from the undersides of vessels that narwhales have pierced clean through, as a gimlet pierces a wine barrel. The museum at the Faculty of Medicine in Paris owns one of these tusks with a length of 2.25 meters and a width at its base of forty–eight centimeters!

"All right then! Imagine this weapon to be ten times stronger and the animal ten times more powerful, launch it at a speed of twenty miles per hour, multiply its mass times its velocity, and you get just the collision we need to cause the specified catastrophe.

"So, until information becomes more abundant, I plump for a sea unicorn of colossal dimensions, no longer armed with a mere lance but with an actual spur, like ironclad frigates or those warships called 'rams,' whose mass and motor power it would possess simultaneously.

"This inexplicable phenomenon is thus explained away—unless it's something else entirely, which, despite everything that has been sighted, studied, explored and experienced, is still possible!"

These last words were cowardly of me; but as far as I could, I wanted to protect my professorial dignity and not lay myself open to laughter from the Americans, who when they do laugh, laugh raucously. I had left myself a loophole. Yet deep down, I had accepted the existence of "the monster."

My article was hotly debated, causing a fine old uproar. It rallied a number of supporters. Moreover, the solution it proposed allowed for free play of the imagination. The human mind enjoys impressive visions of unearthly creatures. Now then, the sea is precisely their best medium, the only setting suitable for the breeding and growing of such giants—next to which such land animals as elephants or rhinoceroses are mere dwarves. The liquid masses support the largest known species of mammals and perhaps conceal mollusks of incomparable size or crustaceans too frightful to contemplate, such as 100–meter lobsters or crabs weighing 200 metric tons! Why not? Formerly, in prehistoric days, land animals (quadrupeds, apes, reptiles, birds) were built on a gigantic scale. Our Creator cast them using a colossal mold that time has gradually made smaller. With its untold depths, couldn't the sea keep alive such huge specimens of life from another age, this sea that never changes while the land masses undergo almost continuous alteration? Couldn't the heart of the ocean hide the last–remaining varieties of these titanic species, for whom years are centuries and centuries millennia?

But I mustn't let these fantasies run away with me! Enough of these fairy tales that time has changed for me into harsh realities. I repeat: opinion had crystallized as to the nature of this phenomenon, and the public accepted without argument the existence of a prodigious creature that had nothing in common with the fabled sea serpent.

Yet if some saw it purely as a scientific problem to be solved, more practical people, especially in America and England, were determined to purge the ocean of this daunting monster, to insure the safety of transoceanic travel. The industrial and commercial newspapers dealt with the question chiefly from this viewpoint. The Shipping & Mercantile Gazette, the Lloyd's List, France's Packetboat and Maritime & Colonial Review, all the rags devoted to insurance companies—who threatened to raise their premium rates—were unanimous on this point.

Public opinion being pronounced, the States of the Union were the first in the field. In New York preparations were under way for an expedition designed to chase this narwhale. A high–speed frigate, the Abraham Lincoln, was fitted out for putting to sea as soon as possible. The naval arsenals were unlocked for Commander Farragut, who pressed energetically forward with the arming of his frigate.

But, as it always happens, just when a decision had been made to chase the monster, the monster put in no further appearances. For two months nobody heard a word about it. Not a single ship encountered it. Apparently the unicorn had gotten wise to these plots being woven around it. People were constantly babbling about the creature, even via the Atlantic Cable! Accordingly, the wags claimed that this slippery rascal had waylaid some passing telegram and was making the most of it.

So the frigate was equipped for a far–off voyage and armed with fearsome fishing gear, but nobody knew where to steer it. And impatience grew until, on June 2, word came that the Tampico, a steamer on the San Francisco line sailing from California to Shanghai, had sighted the animal again, three weeks before in the northerly seas of the Pacific.

This news caused intense excitement. Not even a 24–hour breather was granted to Commander Farragut. His provisions were loaded on board. His coal bunkers were overflowing. Not a crewman was missing from his post. To cast off, he needed only to fire and stoke his furnaces! Half a day's delay would have been unforgivable! But Commander Farragut wanted nothing more than to go forth.

I received a letter three hours before the Abraham Lincoln left its Brooklyn pier; the letter read as follows:

Pierre Aronnax

Professor at the Paris Museum
Fifth Avenue Hotel
New York
Sir:
If you would like to join the expedition on the Abraham Lincoln, the government of the Union will be pleased to regard you as France's representative in this undertaking. Commander Farragut has a cabin at your disposal.
Very cordially yours,
J. B. HOBSON,
Secretary of the Navy.

As Master Wishes

THREE SECONDS before the arrival of J. B. Hobson's letter, I no more dreamed of chasing the unicorn than of trying for the Northwest Passage. Three seconds after reading this letter from the honorable Secretary of the Navy, I understood at last that my true vocation, my sole purpose in life, was to hunt down this disturbing monster and rid the world of it.

Even so, I had just returned from an arduous journey, exhausted and badly needing a rest. I wanted nothing more than to see my country again, my friends, my modest quarters by the Botanical Gardens, my dearly beloved collections! But now nothing could hold me back. I forgot everything else, and without another thought of exhaustion, friends, or collections, I accepted the American government's offer.

"Besides," I mused, "all roads lead home to Europe, and our unicorn may be gracious enough to take me toward the coast of France! That fine animal may even let itself be captured in European seas—as a personal favor to me—and I'll bring back to the Museum of Natural History at least half a meter of its ivory lance!"

But in the meantime I would have to look for this narwhale in the northern Pacific Ocean; which meant returning to France by way of the Antipodes.

"Conseil!" I called in an impatient voice.

Conseil was my manservant. A devoted lad who went with me on all my journeys; a gallant Flemish boy whom I genuinely liked and who returned the compliment; a born stoic, punctilious on principle, habitually hardworking, rarely startled by life's surprises, very skillful with his hands, efficient in his every duty, and despite his having a name that means "counsel," never giving advice—not even the unsolicited kind!

From rubbing shoulders with scientists in our little universe by the Botanical Gardens, the boy had come to know a thing or two. In Conseil I had a seasoned specialist in biological classification, an enthusiast who could run with acrobatic agility up and down the whole ladder of branches, groups, classes, subclasses, orders, families, genera, subgenera, species, and varieties. But there his science came to a halt. Classifying was everything to him, so he knew nothing else. Well versed in the theory of classification, he was poorly versed in its practical application, and I doubt that he could tell a sperm whale from a baleen whale! And yet, what a fine, gallant lad!

For the past ten years, Conseil had gone with me wherever science beckoned. Not once did he comment on the length or the hardships of a journey. Never did he object to buckling up his suitcase for any country whatever, China or the Congo, no matter how far off it was. He went here, there, and everywhere in perfect contentment. Moreover, he enjoyed excellent health that defied all ailments, owned solid muscles, but hadn't a nerve in him, not a sign of nerves—the mental type, I mean.

The lad was thirty years old, and his age to that of his employer was as fifteen is to twenty. Please forgive me for this underhanded way of admitting I had turned forty.

But Conseil had one flaw. He was a fanatic on formality, and he only addressed me in the third person—to the point where it got tiresome.

"Conseil!" I repeated, while feverishly beginning my preparations for departure.

To be sure, I had confidence in this devoted lad. Ordinarily, I never asked whether or not it suited him to go with me on my journeys; but this time an expedition was at issue that could drag on indefinitely, a hazardous undertaking whose purpose was to hunt an animal that could sink a frigate as easily as a walnut shell! There was good reason to stop and think, even for the world's most emotionless man. What would Conseil say?

"Conseil!" I called a third time.

Conseil appeared.

"Did master summon me?" he said, entering.

"Yes, my boy. Get my things ready, get yours ready. We're departing in two hours."

"As master wishes," Conseil replied serenely.

"We haven't a moment to lose. Pack as much into my trunk as you can, my traveling kit, my suits, shirts, and socks, don't bother counting, just squeeze it all in—and hurry!"

"What about master's collections?" Conseil ventured to observe.

"We'll deal with them later."

"What! The archaeotherium, hyracotherium, oreodonts, cheiropotamus, and master's other fossil skeletons?"

"The hotel will keep them for us."

"What about master's live babirusa?"

"They'll feed it during our absence. Anyhow, we'll leave instructions to ship the whole menagerie to France."

"Then we aren't returning to Paris?" Conseil asked.

"Yes, we are . . . certainly . . . ," I replied evasively, "but after we make a detour."

"Whatever detour master wishes."

"Oh, it's nothing really! A route slightly less direct, that's all. We're leaving on the Abraham Lincoln."

"As master thinks best," Conseil replied placidly.

"You see, my friend, it's an issue of the monster, the notorious narwhale. We're going to rid the seas of it! The author of a two–volume work, in quarto, on The Mysteries of the Great Ocean Depths has no excuse for not setting sail with Commander Farragut. It's a glorious mission but also a dangerous one! We don't know where it will take us! These beasts can be quite unpredictable! But we're going just the same! We have a commander who's game for anything!"

"What master does, I'll do," Conseil replied.

"But think it over, because I don't want to hide anything from you. This is one of those voyages from which people don't always come back!"

"As master wishes."

A quarter of an hour later, our trunks were ready. Conseil did them in a flash, and I was sure the lad hadn't missed a thing, because he classified shirts and suits as expertly as birds and mammals.

The hotel elevator dropped us off in the main vestibule on the mezzanine. I went down a short stair leading to the ground floor. I settled my bill at that huge counter that was always under siege by a considerable crowd. I left instructions for shipping my containers of stuffed animals and dried plants to Paris, France. I opened a line of credit sufficient to cover the babirusa and, Conseil at my heels, I jumped into a carriage.

For a fare of twenty francs, the vehicle went down Broadway to Union Square, took Fourth Ave. to its junction with Bowery St., turned into Katrin St. and halted at Pier 34. There the Katrin ferry transferred men, horses, and carriage to Brooklyn, that great New York annex located on the left bank of the East River, and in a few minutes we arrived at the wharf next to which the Abraham Lincoln was vomiting torrents of black smoke from its two funnels.

Our baggage was immediately carried to the deck of the frigate. I rushed aboard. I asked for Commander Farragut. One of the sailors led me to the afterdeck, where I stood in the presence of a smart–looking officer who extended his hand to me.

"Professor Pierre Aronnax?" he said to me.

"The same," I replied. "Commander Farragut?"

"In person. Welcome aboard, professor. Your cabin is waiting for you."

I bowed, and letting the commander attend to getting under way, I was taken to the cabin that had been set aside for me.

The Abraham Lincoln had been perfectly chosen and fitted out for its new assignment. It was a high-speed frigate furnished with superheating equipment that allowed the tension of its steam to build to seven atmospheres. Under this pressure the Abraham Lincoln reached an average speed of 18.3 miles per hour, a considerable speed but still not enough to cope with our gigantic cetacean.

The frigate's interior accommodations complemented its nautical virtues. I was well satisfied with my cabin, which was located in the stern and opened into the officers' mess.

"We'll be quite comfortable here," I told Conseil.

"With all due respect to master," Conseil replied, "as comfortable as a hermit crab inside the shell of a whelk."

I left Conseil to the proper stowing of our luggage and climbed on deck to watch the preparations for getting under way.

Just then Commander Farragut was giving orders to cast off the last moorings holding the Abraham Lincoln to its Brooklyn pier. And so if I'd been delayed by a quarter of an hour or even less, the frigate would have gone without me, and I would have missed out on this unearthly, extraordinary, and inconceivable expedition, whose true story might well meet with some skepticism.

But Commander Farragut didn't want to waste a single day, or even a single hour, in making for those seas where the animal had just been sighted. He summoned his engineer.

"Are we up to pressure?" he asked the man.

"Aye, sir," the engineer replied.

"Go ahead, then!" Commander Farragut called.

At this order, which was relayed to the engine by means of a compressed-air device, the mechanics activated the start-up wheel. Steam rushed whistling into the gaping valves. Long horizontal pistons groaned and pushed the tie rods of the drive shaft. The blades of the propeller churned the waves with increasing speed, and the Abraham Lincoln moved out majestically amid a spectator-laden escort of some 100 ferries and tenders. [Author's Note: Tenders are small steamboats that assist the big liners.]

The wharves of Brooklyn, and every part of New York bordering the East River, were crowded with curiosity seekers. Departing from 500,000 throats, three cheers burst forth in succession. Thousands of handkerchiefs were waving above these tightly packed masses, hailing the Abraham Lincoln until it reached the waters of the Hudson River, at the tip of the long peninsula that forms New York City.

The frigate then went along the New Jersey coast—the wonderful right bank of this river, all loaded down with country homes—and passed by the forts to salutes from their biggest cannons. The Abraham Lincoln replied by three times lowering and hoisting the American flag, whose thirty–nine stars gleamed from the gaff of the mizzen sail; then, changing speed to take the buoy–marked channel that curved into the inner bay formed by the spit of Sandy Hook, it hugged this sand–covered strip of land where thousands of spectators acclaimed us one more time.

The escort of boats and tenders still followed the frigate and only left us when we came abreast of the lightship, whose two signal lights mark the entrance of the narrows to Upper New York Bay.

Three o'clock then sounded. The harbor pilot went down into his dinghy and rejoined a little schooner waiting for him to leeward. The furnaces were stoked; the propeller churned the waves more swiftly; the frigate skirted the flat, yellow coast of Long Island; and at eight o'clock in the evening, after the lights of Fire Island had vanished into the northwest, we ran at full steam onto the dark waters of the Atlantic.

Ned Land

COMMANDER FARRAGUT was a good seaman, worthy of the frigate he commanded. His ship and he were one. He was its very soul. On the cetacean question no doubts arose in his mind, and he didn't allow the animal's existence to be disputed aboard his vessel. He believed in it as certain pious women believe in the leviathan from the Book of Job—out of faith, not reason. The monster existed, and he had vowed to rid the seas of it. The man was a sort of Knight of Rhodes, a latter–day Sir Dieudonné of Gozo, on his way to fight an encounter with the dragon devastating the island. Either Commander Farragut would slay the narwhale, or the narwhale would slay Commander Farragut. No middle of the road for these two.

The ship's officers shared the views of their leader. They could be heard chatting, discussing, arguing, calculating the different chances of an encounter, and observing the vast expanse of the ocean. Voluntary watches from the crosstrees of the topgallant sail were self–imposed by more than one who would have cursed such toil under any other circumstances. As often as the sun swept over its daily arc, the masts were populated with sailors whose feet itched and couldn't hold still on the planking of the deck below! And the Abraham Lincoln's stempost hadn't even cut the suspected waters of the Pacific.

As for the crew, they only wanted to encounter the unicorn, harpoon it, haul it on board, and carve it up. They surveyed the sea with scrupulous care. Besides, Commander Farragut had mentioned that a certain sum of $2,000.00 was waiting for the man who first sighted the animal, be he cabin boy or sailor, mate or officer.

As for me, I didn't lag behind the others and I yielded to no one my share in these daily observations. Our frigate would have had fivescore good reasons for renaming itself the Argus, after that mythological beast with 100 eyes! The lone rebel among us was Conseil, who seemed utterly uninterested in the question exciting us and was out of step with the general enthusiasm on board.

As I said, Commander Farragut had carefully equipped his ship with all the gear needed to fish for a gigantic cetacean. No whaling vessel could have been better armed. We had every known mechanism, from the hand–hurled harpoon, to the blunderbuss firing barbed arrows, to the duck gun with exploding bullets. On the forecastle was mounted the latest model breech–loading cannon, very heavy of barrel and narrow of bore, a weapon that would figure in the Universal Exhibition of 1867. Made in America, this valuable instrument could fire a four–kilogram conical projectile an average distance of sixteen kilometers without the least bother.

So the Abraham Lincoln wasn't lacking in means of destruction. But it had better still. It had Ned Land, the King of Harpooners.

Gifted with uncommon manual ability, Ned Land was a Canadian who had no equal in his dangerous trade. Dexterity, coolness, bravery, and cunning were virtues he possessed to a high degree, and it took a truly crafty baleen whale or an exceptionally astute sperm whale to elude the thrusts of his harpoon.

Ned Land was about forty years old. A man of great height—over six English feet—he was powerfully built, serious in manner, not very sociable, sometimes headstrong, and quite ill–tempered when crossed. His looks caught the attention, and above all the strength of his gaze, which gave a unique emphasis to his facial appearance.

Commander Farragut, to my thinking, had made a wise move in hiring on this man. With his eye and his throwing arm, he was worth the whole crew all by himself. I can do no better than to compare him with a powerful telescope that could double as a cannon always ready to fire.

To say Canadian is to say French, and as unsociable as Ned Land was, I must admit he took a definite liking to me. No doubt it was my nationality that attracted him. It was an opportunity for him to speak, and for me to hear, that old Rabelaisian dialect still used in some Canadian provinces. The harpooner's family originated in Quebec, and they were already a line of bold fishermen back in the days when this town still belonged to France.

Little by little Ned developed a taste for chatting, and I loved hearing the tales of his adventures in the polar seas. He described his fishing trips and his battles with great natural lyricism. His tales took on the form of an epic poem, and I felt I was hearing some Canadian Homer reciting his Iliad of the High Arctic regions.

I'm writing of this bold companion as I currently know him. Because we've become old friends, united in that permanent comradeship born and cemented during only the most frightful crises! Ah, my gallant Ned! I ask only to live 100 years more, the longer to remember you!

And now, what were Ned Land's views on this question of a marine monster? I must admit that he flatly didn't believe in the unicorn, and alone on board, he didn't share the general conviction. He avoided even dealing with the subject, for which one day I felt compelled to take him to task.

During the magnificent evening of June 25—in other words, three weeks after our departure—the frigate lay abreast of Cabo Blanco, thirty miles to leeward of the coast of Patagonia. We had crossed the Tropic of Capricorn, and the Strait of Magellan opened less than 700 miles to the south. Before eight days were out, the Abraham Lincoln would plow the waves of the Pacific.

Seated on the afterdeck, Ned Land and I chatted about one thing and another, staring at that mysterious sea whose depths to this day are beyond the reach of human eyes. Quite naturally, I led our conversation around to the giant unicorn, and I weighed our expedition's various chances for success or failure. Then, seeing that Ned just let me talk without saying much himself, I pressed him more closely.

"Ned," I asked him, "how can you still doubt the reality of this cetacean we're after? Do you have any particular reasons for being so skeptical?"

The harpooner stared at me awhile before replying, slapped his broad forehead in one of his standard gestures, closed his eyes as if to collect himself, and finally said:

"Just maybe, Professor Aronnax."

"But Ned, you're a professional whaler, a man familiar with all the great marine mammals—your mind should easily accept this hypothesis of an enormous cetacean, and you ought to be the last one to doubt it under these circumstances!"

"That's just where you're mistaken, professor," Ned replied. "The common man may still believe in fabulous comets crossing outer space, or in prehistoric monsters living at the earth's core, but astronomers and geologists don't swallow such fairy tales. It's the same with whalers. I've chased plenty of cetaceans, I've harpooned a good number, I've killed several. But no matter how powerful and well armed they were, neither their tails or their tusks could puncture the sheet–iron plates of a steamer."

"Even so, Ned, people mention vessels that narwhale tusks have run clean through."

"Wooden ships maybe," the Canadian replied. "But I've never seen the like. So till I have proof to the contrary, I'll deny that baleen whales, sperm whales, or unicorns can do any such thing."

"Listen to me, Ned—"

"No, no, professor. I'll go along with anything you want except that. Some gigantic devilfish maybe . . . ?"

"Even less likely, Ned. The devilfish is merely a mollusk, and even this name hints at its semiliquid flesh, because it's Latin meaning, 'soft one.' The devilfish doesn't belong to the vertebrate branch, and even if it were 500 feet long, it would still be utterly harmless to ships like the Scotia or the Abraham Lincoln. Consequently, the feats of krakens or other monsters of that ilk must be relegated to the realm of fiction."

"So, Mr. Naturalist," Ned Land continued in a bantering tone, "you'll just keep on believing in the existence of some enormous cetacean . . . ?"

"Yes, Ned, I repeat it with a conviction backed by factual logic. I believe in the existence of a mammal with a powerful constitution, belonging to the vertebrate branch like baleen whales, sperm whales, or dolphins, and armed with a tusk made of horn that has tremendous penetrating power."

"Humph!" the harpooner put in, shaking his head with the attitude of a man who doesn't want to be convinced.

"Note well, my fine Canadian," I went on, "if such an animal exists, if it lives deep in the ocean, if it frequents the liquid strata located miles beneath the surface of the water, it needs to have a constitution so solid, it defies all comparison."

"And why this powerful constitution?" Ned asked.

"Because it takes incalculable strength just to live in those deep strata and withstand their pressure."

"Oh really?" Ned said, tipping me a wink.

"Oh really, and I can prove it to you with a few simple figures."

"Bosh!" Ned replied. "You can make figures do anything you want!"

"In business, Ned, but not in mathematics. Listen to me. Let's accept that the pressure of one atmosphere is represented by the pressure of a column of water thirty–two feet high. In reality, such a column of water wouldn't be quite so high because here we're dealing with salt water, which is denser than fresh water. Well then, when you dive under the waves, Ned, for every thirty–two feet of water above you, your body is tolerating the pressure of one more atmosphere, in other words, one more kilogram per each square centimeter on your body's surface. So it follows that at 320 feet down, this pressure is equal to ten atmospheres, to 100 atmospheres at 3,200 feet, and to 1,000 atmospheres at 32,000 feet, that is, at about two and a half vertical leagues down. Which is tantamount to saying that if you could reach such a depth in the ocean, each square centimeter on your body's surface would be experiencing 1,000 kilograms of pressure. Now, my gallant Ned, do you know how many square centimeters you have on your bodily surface?"

"I haven't the foggiest notion, Professor Aronnax."

"About 17,000."

"As many as that?"

"Yes, and since the atmosphere's pressure actually weighs slightly more than one kilogram per square centimeter, your 17,000 square centimeters are tolerating 17,568 kilograms at this very moment."

"Without my noticing it?"

"Without your noticing it. And if you aren't crushed by so much pressure, it's because the air penetrates the interior of your body with equal pressure. When the inside and outside pressures are in perfect balance, they neutralize each other and allow you to tolerate them without discomfort. But in the water it's another story."

"Yes, I see," Ned replied, growing more interested. "Because the water surrounds me but doesn't penetrate me."

"Precisely, Ned. So at thirty-two feet beneath the surface of the sea, you'll undergo a pressure of 17,568 kilograms; at 320 feet, or ten times greater pressure, it's 175,680 kilograms; at 3,200 feet, or 100 times greater pressure, it's 1,756,800 kilograms; finally, at 32,000 feet, or 1,000 times greater pressure, it's 17,568,000 kilograms; in other words, you'd be squashed as flat as if you'd just been yanked from between the plates of a hydraulic press!"

"Fire and brimstone!" Ned put in.

"All right then, my fine harpooner, if vertebrates several hundred meters long and proportionate in bulk live at such depths, their surface areas make up millions of square centimeters, and the pressure they undergo must be assessed in billions of kilograms. Calculate, then, how much resistance of bone structure and strength of constitution they'd need in order to withstand such pressures!"

"They'd need to be manufactured," Ned Land replied, "from sheet–iron plates eight inches thick, like ironclad frigates."

"Right, Ned, and then picture the damage such a mass could inflict if it were launched with the speed of an express train against a ship's hull."

"Yes . . . indeed . . . maybe," the Canadian replied, staggered by these figures but still not willing to give in.

"Well, have I convinced you?"

"You've convinced me of one thing, Mr. Naturalist. That deep in the sea, such animals would need to be just as strong as you say—if they exist."

"But if they don't exist, my stubborn harpooner, how do you explain the accident that happened to the Scotia?"

"It's maybe . . . ," Ned said, hesitating.

"Go on!"

"Because . . . it just couldn't be true!" the Canadian replied, unconsciously echoing a famous catchphrase of the scientist Arago.

But this reply proved nothing, other than how bullheaded the harpooner could be. That day I pressed him no further. The Scotia's accident was undeniable. Its hole was real enough that it had to be plugged up, and I don't think a hole's existence can be more emphatically proven. Now then, this hole didn't make itself, and since it hadn't resulted from underwater rocks or underwater machines, it must have been caused by the perforating tool of some animal.

Now, for all the reasons put forward to this point, I believed that this animal was a member of the branch Vertebrata, class Mammalia, group Pisciforma, and finally, order Cetacea. As for the family in which it would be placed (baleen whale, sperm whale, or dolphin), the genus to which it belonged, and the species in which it would find its proper home, these questions had to be left for later. To answer them called for dissecting this unknown monster; to dissect it called for catching it; to catch it called for harpooning it—which was Ned Land's business; to harpoon it called for sighting it—which was the crew's business; and to sight it called for encountering it—which was a chancy business.

At Random!

FOR SOME WHILE the voyage of the Abraham Lincoln was marked by no incident. But one circumstance arose that displayed Ned Land's marvelous skills and showed just how much confidence we could place in him.

Off the Falkland Islands on June 30, the frigate came in contact with a fleet of American whalers, and we learned that they hadn't seen the narwhale. But one of them, the captain of the Monroe, knew that Ned Land had shipped aboard the Abraham Lincoln and asked his help in hunting a baleen whale that was in sight. Anxious to see Ned Land at work, Commander Farragut authorized him to make his way aboard the Monroe. And the Canadian had such good luck that with a right–and–left shot, he harpooned not one whale but two, striking the first straight to the heart and catching the other after a few minutes' chase!

Assuredly, if the monster ever had to deal with Ned Land's harpoon, I wouldn't bet on the monster.

The frigate sailed along the east coast of South America with prodigious speed. By July 3 we were at the entrance to the Strait of Magellan, abreast of Cabo de las Virgenes. But Commander Farragut was unwilling to attempt this tortuous passageway and maneuvered instead to double Cape Horn.

The crew sided with him unanimously. Indeed, were we likely to encounter the narwhale in such a cramped strait? Many of our sailors swore that the monster couldn't negotiate this passageway simply because "he's too big for it!"

Near three o'clock in the afternoon on July 6, fifteen miles south of shore, the Abraham Lincoln doubled that solitary islet at the tip of the South American continent, that stray rock Dutch seamen had named Cape Horn after their hometown of Hoorn. Our course was set for the northwest, and the next day our frigate's propeller finally churned the waters of the Pacific.

"Open your eyes! Open your eyes!" repeated the sailors of the Abraham Lincoln. And they opened amazingly wide. Eyes and spyglasses (a bit dazzled, it is true, by the vista of $2,000.00) didn't remain at rest for an instant. Day and night we observed the surface of the ocean, and those with nyctalopic eyes, whose ability to see in the dark increased their chances by fifty percent, had an excellent shot at winning the prize.

As for me, I was hardly drawn by the lure of money and yet was far from the least attentive on board. Snatching only a few minutes for meals and a few hours for sleep, come rain or come shine, I no longer left the ship's deck. Sometimes bending over the forecastle railings, sometimes leaning against the sternrail, I eagerly scoured that cotton–colored wake that whitened the ocean as far as the eye could see! And how many times I shared the excitement of general staff and crew when some unpredictable whale lifted its blackish back above the waves. In an instant the frigate's deck would become densely populated. The cowls over the companionways would vomit a torrent of sailors and officers. With panting chests and anxious eyes, we each would observe the cetacean's movements. I stared; I stared until I nearly went blind from a worn–out retina, while Conseil, as stoic as ever, kept repeating to me in a calm tone:

"If master's eyes would kindly stop bulging, master will see farther!"

But what a waste of energy! The Abraham Lincoln would change course and race after the animal sighted, only to find an ordinary baleen whale or a common sperm whale that soon disappeared amid a chorus of curses!

However, the weather held good. Our voyage was proceeding under the most favorable conditions. By then it was the bad season in these southernmost regions, because July in this zone corresponds to our January in Europe; but the sea remained smooth and easily visible over a vast perimeter.

Ned Land still kept up the most tenacious skepticism; beyond his spells on watch, he pretended that he never even looked at the surface of the waves, at least while no whales were in sight. And yet the marvelous power of his vision could have performed yeoman service. But this stubborn Canadian spent eight hours out of every twelve reading or sleeping in his cabin. A hundred times I chided him for his unconcern.

"Bah!" he replied. "Nothing's out there, Professor Aronnax, and if there is some animal, what chance would we have of spotting it? Can't you see we're just wandering around at random? People say they've sighted this slippery beast again in the Pacific high seas—I'm truly willing to believe it, but two months have already gone by since then, and judging by your narwhale's personality, it hates growing moldy from hanging out too long in the same waterways! It's blessed with a terrific gift for getting around. Now, professor, you know even better than I that nature doesn't violate good sense, and she wouldn't give some naturally slow animal the ability to move swiftly if it hadn't a need to use that talent. So if the beast does exist, it's already long gone!"

I had no reply to this. Obviously we were just groping blindly. But how else could we go about it? All the same, our chances were automatically pretty limited. Yet everyone still felt confident of success, and not a sailor on board would have bet against the narwhale appearing, and soon.

On July 20 we cut the Tropic of Capricorn at longitude 105°, and by the 27th of the same month, we had cleared the equator on the 110th meridian. These bearings determined, the frigate took a more decisive westward heading and tackled the seas of the central Pacific. Commander Farragut felt, and with good reason, that it was best to stay in deep waters and keep his distance from continents or islands, whose neighborhoods the animal always seemed to avoid—"No doubt," our bosun said, "because there isn't enough water for him!" So the frigate kept well out when passing the Tuamotu, Marquesas, and Hawaiian Islands, then cut the Tropic of Cancer at longitude 132° and headed for the seas of China.

We were finally in the area of the monster's latest antics! And in all honesty, shipboard conditions became life–threatening. Hearts were pounding hideously, gearing up for futures full of incurable aneurysms. The entire crew suffered from a nervous excitement that it's beyond me to describe. Nobody ate, nobody slept. Twenty times a day some error in perception, or the optical illusions of some sailor perched in the crosstrees, would cause intolerable anguish, and this emotion, repeated twenty times over, kept us in a state of irritability so intense that a reaction was bound to follow.

And this reaction wasn't long in coming. For three months, during which each day seemed like a century, the Abraham Lincoln plowed all the northerly seas of the Pacific, racing after whales sighted, abruptly veering off course, swerving sharply from one tack to another, stopping suddenly, putting on steam and reversing engines in quick succession, at the risk of stripping its gears, and it didn't leave a single point unexplored from the beaches of Japan to the coasts of America. And we found nothing! Nothing except an immenseness of deserted waves! Nothing remotely resembling a gigantic narwhale, or an underwater islet, or a derelict shipwreck, or a runaway reef, or anything the least bit unearthly!

So the reaction set in. At first, discouragement took hold of people's minds, opening the door to disbelief. A new feeling appeared on board, made up of three–tenths shame and seven–tenths fury. The crew called themselves "out–and–out fools" for being hoodwinked by a fairy tale, then grew steadily more furious! The mountains of arguments amassed over a year collapsed all at once, and each man now wanted only to catch up on his eating and sleeping, to make up for the time he had so stupidly sacrificed.

With typical human fickleness, they jumped from one extreme to the other. Inevitably, the most enthusiastic supporters of the undertaking became its most energetic opponents. This reaction mounted upward from the bowels of the ship, from the quarters of the bunker hands to the messroom of the general staff; and for certain, if it hadn't been for Commander Farragut's characteristic stubbornness, the frigate would ultimately have put back to that cape in the south.

But this futile search couldn't drag on much longer. The Abraham Lincoln had done everything it could to succeed and had no reason to blame itself. Never had the crew of an American naval craft shown more patience and zeal; they weren't responsible for this failure; there was nothing to do but go home.

A request to this effect was presented to the commander. The commander stood his ground. His sailors couldn't hide their discontent, and their work suffered because of it. I'm unwilling to say that there was mutiny on board, but after a reasonable period of intransigence, Commander Farragut, like Christopher Columbus before him, asked for a grace period of just three days more. After this three–day delay, if the monster hadn't appeared, our helmsman would give three turns of the wheel, and the Abraham Lincoln would chart a course toward European seas.

This promise was given on November 2. It had the immediate effect of reviving the crew's failing spirits. The ocean was observed with renewed care. Each man wanted one last look with which to sum up his experience. Spyglasses functioned with feverish energy. A supreme challenge had been issued to the giant narwhale, and the latter had no acceptable excuse for ignoring this Summons to Appear!

Two days passed. The Abraham Lincoln stayed at half steam. On the offchance that the animal might be found in these waterways, a thousand methods were used to spark its interest or rouse it from its apathy. Enormous sides of bacon were trailed in our wake, to the great satisfaction, I must say, of assorted sharks. While the Abraham Lincoln heaved to, its longboats radiated in every direction around it and didn't leave a single point of the sea unexplored. But the evening of November 4 arrived with this underwater mystery still unsolved.

At noon the next day, November 5, the agreed–upon delay expired. After a position fix, true to his promise, Commander Farragut would have to set his course for the southeast and leave the northerly regions of the Pacific decisively behind.

By then the frigate lay in latitude 31° 15' north and longitude 136° 42' east. The shores of Japan were less than 200 miles to our leeward. Night was coming on. Eight o'clock had just struck. Huge clouds covered the moon's disk, then in its first quarter. The sea undulated placidly beneath the frigate's stempost.

Just then I was in the bow, leaning over the starboard rail. Conseil, stationed beside me, stared straight ahead. Roosting in the shrouds, the crew examined the horizon, which shrank and darkened little by little. Officers were probing the increasing gloom with their night glasses. Sometimes the murky ocean sparkled beneath moonbeams that darted between the fringes of two clouds. Then all traces of light vanished into the darkness.

Observing Conseil, I discovered that, just barely, the gallant lad had fallen under the general influence. At least so I thought. Perhaps his nerves were twitching with curiosity for the first time in history.

"Come on, Conseil!" I told him. "Here's your last chance to pocket that $2,000.00!"

"If master will permit my saying so," Conseil replied, "I never expected to win that prize, and the Union government could have promised $100,000.00 and been none the poorer."

"You're right, Conseil, it turned out to be a foolish business after all, and we jumped into it too hastily. What a waste of time, what a futile expense of emotion! Six months ago we could have been back in France—"

"In master's little apartment," Conseil answered. "In master's museum! And by now I would have classified master's fossils. And master's babirusa would be ensconced in its cage at the zoo in the Botanical Gardens, and it would have attracted every curiosity seeker in town!"

"Quite so, Conseil, and what's more, I imagine that people will soon be poking fun at us!"

"To be sure," Conseil replied serenely, "I do think they'll have fun at master's expense. And must it be said . . . ?"

"It must be said, Conseil."

"Well then, it will serve master right!"

"How true!"

"When one has the honor of being an expert as master is, one mustn't lay himself open to—"

Conseil didn't have time to complete the compliment. In the midst of the general silence, a voice became audible. It was Ned Land's voice, and it shouted:

"Ahoy! There's the thing in question, abreast of us to leeward!"

At Full Steam

AT THIS SHOUT the entire crew rushed toward the harpooner—commander, officers, mates,

sailors, cabin boys, down to engineers leaving their machinery and stokers neglecting their furnaces. The order was given to stop, and the frigate merely coasted.

By then the darkness was profound, and as good as the Canadian's eyes were, I still wondered how he could see—and what he had seen. My heart was pounding fit to burst.

But Ned Land was not mistaken, and we all spotted the object his hand was indicating.

Two cable lengths off the Abraham Lincoln's starboard quarter, the sea seemed to be lit up from underneath. This was no mere phosphorescent phenomenon, that much was unmistakable. Submerged some fathoms below the surface of the water, the monster gave off that very intense but inexplicable glow that several captains had mentioned in their reports. This magnificent radiance had to come from some force with a great illuminating capacity. The edge of its light swept over the sea in an immense, highly elongated oval, condensing at the center into a blazing core whose unbearable glow diminished by° outward.

"It's only a cluster of phosphorescent particles!" exclaimed one of the officers.

"No, sir," I answered with conviction. "Not even angel–wing clams or salps have ever given off such a powerful light. That glow is basically electric in nature. Besides . . . look, look! It's shifting! It's moving back and forth! It's darting at us!"

A universal shout went up from the frigate.

"Quiet!" Commander Farragut said. "Helm hard to leeward! Reverse engines!"

Sailors rushed to the helm, engineers to their machinery. Under reverse steam immediately, the Abraham Lincoln beat to port, sweeping in a semicircle.

"Right your helm! Engines forward!" Commander Farragut called.

These orders were executed, and the frigate swiftly retreated from this core of light.

My mistake. It wanted to retreat, but the unearthly animal came at us with a speed double our own.

We gasped. More stunned than afraid, we stood mute and motionless. The animal caught up with us, played with us. It made a full circle around the frigate—then doing fourteen knots—and wrapped us in sheets of electricity that were like luminous dust. Then it retreated two or three miles, leaving a phosphorescent trail comparable to those swirls of steam that shoot behind the locomotive of an express train. Suddenly, all the way from the dark horizon where it had gone to gather momentum, the monster abruptly dashed toward the Abraham Lincoln with frightening speed, stopped sharply twenty feet from our side plates, and died out—not by diving under the water, since its glow did not recede gradually—but all at once, as if the source of this brilliant emanation had suddenly dried up. Then it reappeared on the other side of the ship, either by circling around us or by gliding under our hull. At any instant a collision could have occurred that would have been fatal to us.

Meanwhile I was astonished at the frigate's maneuvers. It was fleeing, not fighting. Built to pursue, it was being pursued, and I commented on this to

Commander Farragut. His face, ordinarily so emotionless, was stamped with indescribable astonishment.

"Professor Aronnax," he answered me, "I don't know what kind of fearsome creature I'm up against, and I don't want my frigate running foolish risks in all this darkness. Besides, how should we attack this unknown creature, how should we defend ourselves against it? Let's wait for daylight, and then we'll play a different role."

"You've no further doubts, commander, as to the nature of this animal?"

"No, sir, it's apparently a gigantic narwhale, and an electric one to boot."

"Maybe," I added, "it's no more approachable than an electric eel or an electric ray!"

"Right," the commander replied. "And if it has their power to electrocute, it's surely the most dreadful animal ever conceived by our Creator. That's why I'll keep on my guard, sir."

The whole crew stayed on their feet all night long. No one even thought of sleeping. Unable to compete with the monster's speed, the Abraham Lincoln slowed down and stayed at half steam. For its part, the narwhale mimicked the frigate, simply rode with the waves, and seemed determined not to forsake the field of battle.

However, near midnight it disappeared, or to use a more appropriate expression, "it went out," like a huge glowworm. Had it fled from us? We were duty bound to fear so rather than hope so. But at 12:53 in the morning, a deafening hiss became audible, resembling the sound made by a waterspout expelled with tremendous intensity.

By then Commander Farragut, Ned Land, and I were on the afterdeck, peering eagerly into the profound gloom.

"Ned Land," the commander asked, "you've often heard whales bellowing?"

"Often, sir, but never a whale like this, whose sighting earned me $2,000.00."

"Correct, the prize is rightfully yours. But tell me, isn't that the noise cetaceans make when they spurt water from their blowholes?"

"The very noise, sir, but this one's way louder. So there can be no mistake. There's definitely a whale lurking in our waters. With your permission, sir," the harpooner added, "tomorrow at daybreak we'll have words with it."

"If it's in a mood to listen to you, Mr. Land," I replied in a tone far from convinced.

"Let me get within four harpoon lengths of it," the Canadian shot back, "and it had better listen!"

"But to get near it," the commander went on, "I'd have to put a whaleboat at your disposal?"

"Certainly, sir."

"That would be gambling with the lives of my men."

"And with my own!" the harpooner replied simply.

Near two o'clock in the morning, the core of light reappeared, no less intense, five miles to windward of the Abraham Lincoln. Despite the distance, despite the noise of wind and sea, we could distinctly hear the fearsome thrashings of the animal's tail, and even its panting breath. Seemingly, the moment this enormous narwhale came up to breathe at the surface of the ocean, air was sucked into its lungs like steam into the huge cylinders of a 2,000–horsepower engine.

"Hmm!" I said to myself. "A cetacean as powerful as a whole cavalry regiment—now that's a whale of a whale!"

We stayed on the alert until daylight, getting ready for action. Whaling gear was set up along the railings. Our chief officer loaded the blunderbusses, which can launch harpoons as far as a mile, and long duck guns with exploding bullets that can mortally wound even the most powerful animals. Ned Land was content to sharpen his harpoon, a dreadful weapon in his hands.

At six o'clock day began to break, and with the dawn's early light, the narwhale's electric glow disappeared. At seven o'clock the day was well along, but a very dense morning mist shrank the horizon, and our best spyglasses were unable to pierce it. The outcome: disappointment and anger.

I hoisted myself up to the crosstrees of the mizzen sail. Some officers were already perched on the mastheads.

At eight o'clock the mist rolled ponderously over the waves, and its huge curls were lifting little by little. The horizon grew wider and clearer all at once.

Suddenly, just as on the previous evening, Ned Land's voice was audible.

"There's the thing in question, astern to port!" the harpooner shouted.

Every eye looked toward the point indicated.

There, a mile and a half from the frigate, a long blackish body emerged a meter above the waves. Quivering violently, its tail was creating a considerable eddy. Never had caudal equipment thrashed the sea with such power. An immense wake of glowing whiteness marked the animal's track, sweeping in a long curve.

Our frigate drew nearer to the cetacean. I examined it with a completely open mind. Those reports from the Shannon and the Helvetia had slightly exaggerated its dimensions, and I put its length at only 250 feet. Its girth was more difficult to judge, but all in all, the animal seemed to be wonderfully proportioned in all three dimensions.

While I was observing this phenomenal creature, two jets of steam and water sprang from its blowholes and rose to an altitude of forty meters, which settled for me its mode of breathing. From this I finally concluded that it belonged to the branch Vertebrata, class Mammalia, subclass Monodelphia, group Pisciforma, order Cetacea, family . . . but here I couldn't make up my mind. The order Cetacea consists of three families, baleen whales, sperm whales, dolphins, and it's in this last group that narwhales are placed. Each of these families is divided into several genera, each genus into species, each species into varieties. So I was still missing variety, species, genus, and family, but no doubt I would complete my classifying with the aid of Heaven and Commander Farragut.

The crew were waiting impatiently for orders from their leader. The latter, after carefully observing the animal, called for his engineer. The engineer raced over.

"Sir," the commander said, "are you up to pressure?"

"Aye, sir," the engineer replied.

"Fine. Stoke your furnaces and clap on full steam!"

Three cheers greeted this order. The hour of battle had sounded. A few moments later, the frigate's two funnels vomited torrents of black smoke, and its deck quaked from the trembling of its boilers.

Driven forward by its powerful propeller, the Abraham Lincoln headed straight for the animal. Unconcerned, the latter let us come within half a cable length; then, not bothering to dive, it got up a little speed, retreated, and was content to keep its distance.

This chase dragged on for about three–quarters of an hour without the frigate gaining two fathoms on the cetacean. At this rate, it was obvious that we would never catch up with it.

Infuriated, Commander Farragut kept twisting the thick tuft of hair that flourished below his chin.

"Ned Land!" he called.

The Canadian reported at once.

"Well, Mr. Land," the commander asked, "do you still advise putting my longboats to sea?"

"No, sir," Ned Land replied, "because that beast won't be caught against its will."

"Then what should we do?"

"Stoke up more steam, sir, if you can. As for me, with your permission I'll go perch on the bobstays under the bowsprit, and if we can get within a harpoon length, I'll harpoon the brute."

"Go to it, Ned," Commander Farragut replied. "Engineer," he called, "keep the pressure mounting!"

Ned Land made his way to his post. The furnaces were urged into greater activity; our propeller did forty–three revolutions per minute, and steam shot from the valves. Heaving the log, we verified that the Abraham Lincoln was going at the rate of 18.5 miles per hour.

But that damned animal also did a speed of 18.5.

For the next hour our frigate kept up this pace without gaining a fathom! This was humiliating for one of the fastest racers in the American navy. The crew were working up into a blind rage. Sailor after sailor heaved insults at the monster, which couldn't be bothered with answering back. Commander Farragut was no longer content simply to twist his goatee; he chewed on it.

The engineer was summoned once again.

"You're up to maximum pressure?" the commander asked him.

"Aye, sir," the engineer replied.

"And your valves are charged to . . . ?"

"To six and a half atmospheres."

"Charge them to ten atmospheres."

A typical American order if I ever heard one. It would have sounded just fine during some Mississippi paddle–wheeler race, to "outstrip the competition!"

"Conseil," I said to my gallant servant, now at my side, "you realize that we'll probably blow ourselves skyhigh?"

"As master wishes!" Conseil replied.

All right, I admit it: I did wish to run this risk!

The valves were charged. More coal was swallowed by the furnaces. Ventilators shot torrents of air over the braziers. The Abraham Lincoln's speed increased. Its masts trembled down to their blocks, and swirls of smoke could barely squeeze through the narrow funnels.

We heaved the log a second time.

"Well, helmsman?" Commander Farragut asked.

"19.3 miles per hour, sir."

"Keep stoking the furnaces."

The engineer did so. The pressure gauge marked ten atmospheres. But no doubt the cetacean itself had "warmed up," because without the least trouble, it also did 19.3.

What a chase! No, I can't describe the excitement that shook my very being. Ned Land stayed at his post, harpoon in hand. Several times the animal let us approach.

"We're overhauling it!" the Canadian would shout.

Then, just as he was about to strike, the cetacean would steal off with a swiftness I could estimate at no less than thirty miles per hour. And even at our maximum speed, it took the liberty of thumbing its nose at the frigate by running a full circle around us! A howl of fury burst from every throat!

By noon we were no farther along than at eight o'clock in the morning.

Commander Farragut then decided to use more direct methods.

"Bah!" he said. "So that animal is faster than the Abraham Lincoln. All right, we'll see if it can outrun our conical shells! Mate, man the gun in the bow!"

Our forecastle cannon was immediately loaded and leveled. The cannoneer fired a shot, but his shell passed some feet above the cetacean, which stayed half a mile off.

"Over to somebody with better aim!" the commander shouted. "And $500.00 to the man who can pierce that infernal beast!"

Calm of eye, cool of feature, an old gray–bearded gunner—I can see him to this day—approached the cannon, put it in position, and took aim for a good while. There was a mighty explosion, mingled with cheers from the crew.

The shell reached its target; it hit the animal, but not in the usual fashion—it bounced off that rounded surface and vanished into the sea two miles out.

"Oh drat!" said the old gunner in his anger. "That rascal must be covered with six–inch armor plate!"

"Curse the beast!" Commander Farragut shouted.

The hunt was on again, and Commander Farragut leaned over to me, saying: "I'll chase that animal till my frigate explodes!"

"Yes," I replied, "and nobody would blame you!"

We could still hope that the animal would tire out and not be as insensitive to exhaustion as our steam engines. But no such luck. Hour after hour went by without it showing the least sign of weariness.

However, to the Abraham Lincoln's credit, it must be said that we struggled on with tireless persistence. I estimate that we covered a distance of at least 500 kilometers during this ill–fated day of November 6. But night fell and wrapped the surging ocean in its shadows.

By then I thought our expedition had come to an end, that we would never see this fantastic animal again. I was mistaken.

At 10:50 in the evening, that electric light reappeared three miles to windward of the frigate, just as clear and intense as the night before.

The narwhale seemed motionless. Was it asleep perhaps, weary from its workday, just riding with the waves? This was our chance, and Commander Farragut was determined to take full advantage of it.

He gave his orders. The Abraham Lincoln stayed at half steam, advancing cautiously so as not to awaken its adversary. In midocean it's not unusual to encounter whales so sound asleep they can successfully be attacked, and Ned Land had harpooned more than one in its slumber. The Canadian went to resume his post on the bobstays under the bowsprit.

The frigate approached without making a sound, stopped two cable lengths from the animal and coasted. Not a soul breathed on board. A profound silence reigned over the deck. We were not 100 feet from the blazing core of light, whose glow grew stronger and dazzled the eyes.

Just then, leaning over the forecastle railing, I saw Ned Land below me, one hand grasping the martingale, the other brandishing his dreadful harpoon. Barely twenty feet separated him from the motionless animal.

All at once his arm shot forward and the harpoon was launched. I heard the weapon collide resonantly, as if it had hit some hard substance.

The electric light suddenly went out, and two enormous waterspouts crashed onto the deck of the frigate, racing like a torrent from stem to stern, toppling crewmen, breaking spare masts and yardarms from their lashings.

A hideous collision occurred, and thrown over the rail with no time to catch hold of it, I was hurled into the sea.

A Whale of Unknown Species

ALTHOUGH I WAS startled by this unexpected descent, I at least have a very clear recollection of my sensations during it.

At first I was dragged about twenty feet under. I'm a good swimmer, without claiming to equal such other authors as Byron and Edgar Allan Poe, who were master divers, and I didn't lose my head on the way down. With two vigorous kicks of the heel, I came back to the surface of the sea.

My first concern was to look for the frigate. Had the crew seen me go overboard? Was the Abraham Lincoln tacking about? Would Commander Farragut put a longboat to sea? Could I hope to be rescued?

The gloom was profound. I glimpsed a black mass disappearing eastward, where its running lights were fading out in the distance. It was the frigate. I felt I was done for.

"Help! Help!" I shouted, swimming desperately toward the Abraham Lincoln.

My clothes were weighing me down. The water glued them to my body, they were paralyzing my movements. I was sinking! I was suffocating . . . !

"Help!"

This was the last shout I gave. My mouth was filling with water. I struggled against being dragged into the depths. . . .

Suddenly my clothes were seized by energetic hands, I felt myself pulled abruptly back to the surface of the sea, and yes, I heard these words pronounced in my ear:

"If master would oblige me by leaning on my shoulder, master will swim with much greater ease."

With one hand I seized the arm of my loyal Conseil.

"You!" I said. "You!"

"Myself," Conseil replied, "and at master's command."

"That collision threw you overboard along with me?"

"Not at all. But being in master's employ, I followed master."

The fine lad thought this only natural!

"What about the frigate?" I asked.

"The frigate?" Conseil replied, rolling over on his back. "I think master had best not depend on it to any great extent!"

"What are you saying?"

"I'm saying that just as I jumped overboard, I heard the men at the helm shout, 'Our propeller and rudder are smashed!'"

"Smashed?"

"Yes, smashed by the monster's tusk! I believe it's the sole injury the Abraham Lincoln has sustained. But most inconveniently for us, the ship can no longer steer."

"Then we're done for!"

"Perhaps," Conseil replied serenely. "However, we still have a few hours before us, and in a few hours one can do a great many things!"

Conseil's unflappable composure cheered me up. I swam more vigorously, but hampered by clothes that were as restricting as a cloak made of lead, I was managing with only the greatest difficulty. Conseil noticed as much.

"Master will allow me to make an incision," he said.

And he slipped an open clasp knife under my clothes, slitting them from top to bottom with one swift stroke. Then he briskly undressed me while I swam for us both.

I then did Conseil the same favor, and we continued to "navigate" side by side.

But our circumstances were no less dreadful. Perhaps they hadn't seen us go overboard; and even if they had, the frigate—being undone by its rudder—couldn't return to leeward after us. So we could count only on its longboats.

Conseil had coolly reasoned out this hypothesis and laid his plans accordingly. An amazing character, this boy; in midocean, this stoic lad seemed right at home!

So, having concluded that our sole chance for salvation lay in being picked up by the Abraham Lincoln's longboats, we had to take steps to wait for them as long as possible. Consequently, I decided to divide our energies so we wouldn't both be worn out at the same time, and this was the arrangement: while one of us lay on his back, staying motionless with arms crossed and legs outstretched, the other would swim and propel his partner forward. This towing role was to last no longer than ten minutes, and by relieving each other in this way, we could stay afloat for hours, perhaps even until daybreak.

Slim chance, but hope springs eternal in the human breast! Besides, there were two of us. Lastly, I can vouch—as improbable as it seems—that even if I had wanted to destroy all my illusions, even if I had been willing to "give in to despair," I could not have done so!

The cetacean had rammed our frigate at about eleven o'clock in the evening. I therefore calculated on eight hours of swimming until sunrise. A strenuous task, but feasible, thanks to our relieving each other. The sea was pretty smooth and barely tired us. Sometimes I tried to peer through the dense gloom, which was broken only by the phosphorescent flickers coming from our movements. I stared at the luminous ripples breaking over my hands, shimmering sheets spattered with blotches of bluish gray. It seemed as if we'd plunged into a pool of quicksilver.

Near one o'clock in the morning, I was overcome with tremendous exhaustion. My limbs stiffened in the grip of intense cramps. Conseil had to keep me going, and attending to our self–preservation became his sole responsibility. I soon heard the poor lad gasping; his breathing became shallow and quick. I didn't think he could stand such exertions for much longer.

"Go on! Go on!" I told him.

"Leave master behind?" he replied. "Never! I'll drown before he does!"

Just then, past the fringes of a large cloud that the wind was driving eastward, the moon appeared. The surface of the sea glistened under its rays. That kindly light rekindled our strength. I held up my head again. My eyes darted to every point of the horizon. I spotted the frigate. It was five miles from us and formed no more than a dark, barely perceptible mass. But as for longboats, not a one in sight!

I tried to call out. What was the use at such a distance! My swollen lips wouldn't let a single sound through. Conseil could still articulate a few words, and I heard him repeat at intervals:

"Help! Help!"

Ceasing all movement for an instant, we listened. And it may have been a ringing in my ear, from this organ filling with impeded blood, but it seemed to me that Conseil's shout had received an answer back.

"Did you hear that?" I muttered.

"Yes, yes!"

And Conseil hurled another desperate plea into space.

This time there could be no mistake! A human voice had answered us! Was it the voice of some poor devil left behind in midocean, some other victim of that collision suffered by our ship? Or was it one of the frigate's longboats, hailing us out of the gloom?

Conseil made one final effort, and bracing his hands on my shoulders, while I offered resistance with one supreme exertion, he raised himself half out of the water, then fell back exhausted.

"What did you see?"

"I saw . . . ," he muttered, "I saw . . . but we mustn't talk . . . save our strength . . . !"

What had he seen? Then, lord knows why, the thought of the monster came into my head for the first time . . . ! But even so, that voice . . . ? Gone are the days when Jonahs took refuge in the bellies of whales!

Nevertheless, Conseil kept towing me. Sometimes he looked up, stared straight ahead, and shouted a request for directions, which was answered by a voice that was getting closer and closer. I could barely hear it. I was at the end of my strength; my fingers gave out; my hands were no help to me; my mouth opened convulsively, filling with brine; its coldness ran through me; I raised my head one last time, then I collapsed. . . .

Just then something hard banged against me. I clung to it. Then I felt myself being pulled upward, back to the surface of the water; my chest caved in, and I fainted. . . .

For certain, I came to quickly, because someone was massaging me so vigorously it left furrows in my flesh. I half opened my eyes. . . .

"Conseil!" I muttered.

"Did master ring for me?" Conseil replied.

Just then, in the last light of a moon settling on the horizon, I spotted a face that wasn't Conseil's but which I recognized at once.

"Ned!" I exclaimed.

"In person, sir, and still after his prize!" the Canadian replied.

"You were thrown overboard after the frigate's collision?"

"Yes, professor, but I was luckier than you, and right away I was able to set foot on this floating islet."

"Islet?"

"Or in other words, on our gigantic narwhale."

"Explain yourself, Ned."

"It's just that I soon realized why my harpoon got blunted and couldn't puncture its hide."

"Why, Ned, why?"

"Because, professor, this beast is made of boilerplate steel!"

At this point in my story, I need to get a grip on myself, reconstruct exactly what I experienced, and make doubly sure of everything I write.

The Canadian's last words caused a sudden upheaval in my brain. I swiftly hoisted myself to the summit of this half–submerged creature or object that was serving as our refuge. I tested it with my foot. Obviously it was some hard, impenetrable substance, not the soft matter that makes up the bodies of our big marine mammals.

But this hard substance could have been a bony carapace, like those that covered some prehistoric animals, and I might have left it at that and classified this monster among such amphibious reptiles as turtles or alligators.

Well, no. The blackish back supporting me was smooth and polished with no overlapping scales. On impact, it gave off a metallic sonority, and as incredible as this sounds, it seemed, I swear, to be made of riveted plates.

No doubts were possible! This animal, this monster, this natural phenomenon that had puzzled the whole scientific world, that had muddled and misled the minds of seamen in both hemispheres, was, there could be no escaping it, an even more astonishing phenomenon—a phenomenon made by the hand of man.

Even if I had discovered that some fabulous, mythological creature really existed, it wouldn't have given me such a terrific mental jolt. It's easy enough to accept that prodigious things can come from our Creator. But to find, all at once, right before your eyes, that the impossible had been mysteriously achieved by man himself: this staggers the mind!

But there was no question now. We were stretched out on the back of some kind of underwater boat that, as far as I could judge, boasted the shape of an immense steel fish. Ned Land had clear views on the issue. Conseil and I could only line up behind him.

"But then," I said, "does this contraption contain some sort of locomotive mechanism, and a crew to run it?"

"Apparently," the harpooner replied. "And yet for the three hours I've lived on this floating island, it hasn't shown a sign of life."

"This boat hasn't moved at all?"

"No, Professor Aronnax. It just rides with the waves, but otherwise it hasn't stirred."

"But we know that it's certainly gifted with great speed. Now then, since an engine is needed to generate that speed, and a mechanic to run that engine, I conclude: we're saved."

"Humph!" Ned Land put in, his tone denoting reservations.

Just then, as if to take my side in the argument, a bubbling began astern of this strange submersible—whose drive mechanism was obviously a propeller—and the boat started to move. We barely had time to hang on to its topside, which emerged about eighty centimeters above water. Fortunately its speed was not excessive.

"So long as it navigates horizontally," Ned Land muttered, "I've no complaints. But if it gets the urge to dive, I wouldn't give $2.00 for my hide!"

The Canadian might have quoted a much lower price. So it was imperative to make contact with whatever beings were confined inside the plating of this machine. I searched its surface for an opening or a hatch, a "manhole," to use the official term; but the lines of rivets had been firmly driven into the sheet–iron joins and were straight and uniform.

Moreover, the moon then disappeared and left us in profound darkness. We had to wait for daylight to find some way of getting inside this underwater boat.

So our salvation lay totally in the hands of the mysterious helmsmen steering this submersible, and if it made a dive, we were done for! But aside from this occurring, I didn't doubt the possibility of our making contact with them. In fact, if they didn't produce their own air, they inevitably had to make periodic visits to the surface of the ocean to replenish their oxygen supply. Hence the need for some opening that put the boat's interior in contact with the atmosphere.

As for any hope of being rescued by Commander Farragut, that had to be renounced completely. We were being swept westward, and I estimate that our comparatively moderate speed reached twelve miles per hour. The propeller churned the waves with mathematical regularity, sometimes emerging above the surface and throwing phosphorescent spray to great heights.

Near four o'clock in the morning, the submersible picked up speed. We could barely cope with this dizzying rush, and the waves battered us at close range. Fortunately Ned's hands came across a big mooring ring fastened to the topside of this sheet–iron back, and we all held on for dear life.

Finally this long night was over. My imperfect memories won't let me recall my every impression of it. A single detail comes back to me. Several times, during various lulls of wind and sea, I thought I heard indistinct sounds, a sort of elusive harmony produced by distant musical chords. What was the secret behind this underwater navigating, whose explanation the whole world had sought in vain? What beings lived inside this strange boat? What mechanical force allowed it to move about with such prodigious speed?

Daylight appeared. The morning mists surrounded us, but they soon broke up. I was about to proceed with a careful examination of the hull, whose topside formed a sort of horizontal platform, when I felt it sinking little by little.

"Oh, damnation!" Ned Land shouted, stamping his foot on the resonant sheet iron. "Open up there, you antisocial navigators!"

But it was difficult to make yourself heard above the deafening beats of the propeller. Fortunately this submerging movement stopped.

From inside the boat, there suddenly came noises of iron fastenings pushed roughly aside. One of the steel plates flew up, a man appeared, gave a bizarre yell, and instantly disappeared.

A few moments later, eight strapping fellows appeared silently, their faces like masks, and dragged us down into their fearsome machine.

"Mobilis in Mobili"

THIS BRUTALLY EXECUTED capture was carried out with lightning speed. My companions and I had no time to collect ourselves. I don't know how they felt about being shoved inside this aquatic prison, but as for me, I was shivering all over. With whom were we dealing? Surely with some new breed of pirates, exploiting the sea after their own fashion.

The narrow hatch had barely closed over me when I was surrounded by profound darkness. Saturated with the outside light, my eyes couldn't make out a thing. I felt my naked feet clinging to the steps of an iron ladder. Forcibly seized, Ned Land and Conseil were behind me. At the foot of the ladder, a door opened and instantly closed behind us with a loud clang.

We were alone. Where? I couldn't say, could barely even imagine. All was darkness, but such utter darkness that after several minutes, my eyes were still unable to catch a single one of those hazy gleams that drift through even the blackest nights.

Meanwhile, furious at these goings on, Ned Land gave free rein to his indignation.

"Damnation!" he exclaimed. "These people are about as hospitable as the savages of New Caledonia! All that's lacking is for them to be cannibals! I wouldn't be surprised if they were, but believe you me, they won't eat me without my kicking up a protest!"

"Calm yourself, Ned my friend," Conseil replied serenely. "Don't flare up so quickly! We aren't in a kettle yet!"

"In a kettle, no," the Canadian shot back, "but in an oven for sure. It's dark enough for one. Luckily my Bowie knife hasn't left me, and I can still see well enough to put it to use. The first one of these bandits who lays a hand on me—"

"Don't be so irritable, Ned," I then told the harpooner, "and don't ruin things for us with pointless violence. Who knows whether they might be listening to us? Instead, let's try to find out where we are!"

I started moving, groping my way. After five steps I encountered an iron wall made of riveted boilerplate. Then, turning around, I bumped into a wooden table next to which several stools had been set. The floor of this prison lay hidden beneath thick, hempen matting that deadened the sound of footsteps. Its naked walls didn't reveal any trace of a door or window. Going around the opposite way, Conseil met up with me, and we returned to the middle of this cabin, which had to be twenty feet long by ten wide. As for its height, not even Ned Land, with his great stature, was able to determine it.

Half an hour had already gone by without our situation changing, when our eyes were suddenly spirited from utter darkness into blinding light. Our prison lit up all at once; in other words, it filled with luminescent matter so intense that at first I couldn't stand the brightness of it. From its glare and whiteness, I recognized the electric glow that had played around this underwater boat like some magnificent phosphorescent phenomenon. After involuntarily closing my eyes, I reopened them and saw that this luminous force came from a frosted half globe curving out of the cabin's ceiling.

"Finally! It's light enough to see!" Ned Land exclaimed, knife in hand, staying on the defensive.

"Yes," I replied, then ventured the opposite view. "But as for our situation, we're still in the dark."

"Master must learn patience," said the emotionless Conseil.

This sudden illumination of our cabin enabled me to examine its tiniest details. It contained only a table and five stools. Its invisible door must have been hermetically sealed. Not a sound reached our ears. Everything seemed dead inside this boat. Was it in motion, or stationary on the surface of the ocean, or sinking into the depths? I couldn't tell.

But this luminous globe hadn't been turned on without good reason. Consequently, I hoped that some crewmen would soon make an appearance. If you want to consign people to oblivion, you don't light up their dungeons.

I was not mistaken. Unlocking noises became audible, a door opened, and two men appeared.

One was short and stocky, powerfully muscled, broad shouldered, robust of limbs, the head squat, the hair black and luxuriant, the mustache heavy, the eyes bright and penetrating, and his whole personality stamped with that southern–blooded zest that, in France, typifies the people of Provence. The philosopher Diderot has very aptly claimed that a man's bearing is the clue to his character, and this stocky little man was certainly a living proof of this claim. You could sense that his everyday conversation must have been packed with such vivid figures of speech as personification, symbolism, and misplaced modifiers. But I was never in a position to verify this because, around me, he used only an odd and utterly incomprehensible dialect.

The second stranger deserves a more detailed description. A disciple of such character–judging anatomists as Gratiolet or Engel could have read this man's features like an open book. Without hesitation, I identified his dominant qualities—self–confidence, since his head reared like a nobleman's above the arc formed by the lines of his shoulders, and his black eyes gazed with icy assurance; calmness, since his skin, pale rather than ruddy, indicated tranquility of blood; energy, shown by the swiftly knitting muscles of his brow; and finally courage, since his deep breathing denoted tremendous reserves of vitality.

I might add that this was a man of great pride, that his calm, firm gaze seemed to reflect thinking on an elevated plane, and that the harmony of his facial expressions and bodily movements resulted in an overall effect of unquestionable candor—according to the findings of physiognomists, those analysts of facial character.

I felt "involuntarily reassured" in his presence, and this boded well for our interview.

Whether this individual was thirty–five or fifty years of age, I could not precisely state. He was tall, his forehead broad, his nose straight, his mouth clearly etched, his teeth magnificent, his hands refined, tapered, and to use a word from palmistry, highly "psychic," in other words, worthy of serving a lofty and passionate spirit. This man was certainly the most wonderful physical specimen I had ever encountered. One unusual detail: his eyes were spaced a little far from each other and could instantly take in nearly a quarter of the horizon. This ability—as I later verified—was strengthened by a range of vision even greater than Ned Land's. When this stranger focused his gaze on an object, his eyebrow lines gathered into a frown, his heavy eyelids closed around his pupils to contract his huge field of vision, and he looked! What a look—as if he could magnify objects shrinking into the distance; as if he could probe your very soul; as if he could pierce those sheets of water so opaque to our eyes and scan the deepest seas . . . !

Wearing caps made of sea–otter fur, and shod in sealskin fishing boots, these two strangers were dressed in clothing made from some unique fabric that flattered the figure and allowed great freedom of movement.

The taller of the two—apparently the leader on board—examined us with the greatest care but without pronouncing a word. Then, turning to his companion, he conversed with him in a language I didn't recognize. It was a sonorous, harmonious, flexible dialect whose vowels seemed to undergo a highly varied accentuation.

The other replied with a shake of the head and added two or three utterly incomprehensible words. Then he seemed to question me directly with a long stare.

I replied in clear French that I wasn't familiar with his language; but he didn't seem to understand me, and the situation grew rather baffling.

"Still, master should tell our story," Conseil said to me. "Perhaps these gentlemen will grasp a few words of it!"

I tried again, telling the tale of our adventures, clearly articulating my every syllable, and not leaving out a single detail. I stated our names and titles; then, in order, I introduced Professor Aronnax, his manservant Conseil, and Mr. Ned Land, harpooner.

The man with calm, gentle eyes listened to me serenely, even courteously, and paid remarkable attention. But nothing in his facial expression indicated that he understood my story. When I finished, he didn't pronounce a single word.

One resource still left was to speak English. Perhaps they would be familiar with this nearly universal language. But I only knew it, as I did the German language, well enough to read it fluently, not well enough to speak it correctly. Here, however, our overriding need was to make ourselves understood.

"Come on, it's your turn," I told the harpooner. "Over to you, Mr. Land. Pull out of your bag of tricks the best English ever spoken by an Anglo–Saxon, and try for a more favorable result than mine."

Ned needed no persuading and started our story all over again, most of which I could follow. Its content was the same, but the form differed. Carried away by his volatile temperament, the Canadian put great animation into it. He complained vehemently about being imprisoned in defiance of his civil rights, asked by virtue of which law he was hereby detained, invoked writs of habeas corpus, threatened to press charges against anyone holding him in illegal custody, ranted, gesticulated, shouted, and finally conveyed by an expressive gesture that we were dying of hunger.

This was perfectly true, but we had nearly forgotten the fact.

Much to his amazement, the harpooner seemed no more intelligible than I had been. Our visitors didn't bat an eye. Apparently they were engineers who understood the languages of neither the French physicist Arago nor the English physicist Faraday.

Thoroughly baffled after vainly exhausting our philological resources, I no longer knew what tactic to pursue, when Conseil told me:

"If master will authorize me, I'll tell the whole business in German."

"What! You know German?" I exclaimed.

"Like most Flemish people, with all due respect to master."

"On the contrary, my respect is due you. Go to it, my boy."

And Conseil, in his serene voice, described for the third time the various vicissitudes of our story. But despite our narrator's fine accent and stylish turns of phrase, the German language met with no success.

Finally, as a last resort, I hauled out everything I could remember from my early schooldays, and I tried to narrate our adventures in Latin. Cicero would have plugged his ears and sent me to the scullery, but somehow I managed to pull through. With the same negative result.

This last attempt ultimately misfiring, the two strangers exchanged a few words in their incomprehensible language and withdrew, not even favoring us with one of those encouraging gestures that are used in every country in the world. The door closed again.

"This is outrageous!" Ned Land shouted, exploding for the twentieth time. "I ask you! We speak French, English, German, and Latin to these rogues, and neither of them has the decency to even answer back!"

"Calm down, Ned," I told the seething harpooner. "Anger won't get us anywhere."

"But professor," our irascible companion went on, "can't you see that we could die of hunger in this iron cage?"

"Bah!" Conseil put in philosophically. "We can hold out a good while yet!"

"My friends," I said, "we mustn't despair. We've gotten out of tighter spots. So please do me the favor of waiting a bit before you form your views on the commander and crew of this boat."

"My views are fully formed," Ned Land shot back. "They're rogues!"

"Oh good! And from what country?"

"Roguedom!"

"My gallant Ned, as yet that country isn't clearly marked on maps of the world, but I admit that the nationality of these two strangers is hard to make out! Neither English, French, nor German, that's all we can say. But I'm tempted to think that the commander and his chief officer were born in the low latitudes. There must be southern blood in them. But as to whether they're Spaniards, Turks, Arabs, or East Indians, their physical characteristics don't give me enough to go on. And as for their speech, it's utterly incomprehensible."

"That's the nuisance in not knowing every language," Conseil replied, "or the drawback in not having one universal language!"

"Which would all go out the window!" Ned Land replied. "Don't you see, these people have a language all to themselves, a language they've invented just to cause despair in decent people who ask for a little dinner! Why, in every country on earth, when you open your mouth, snap your jaws, smack your lips and teeth, isn't that the world's most understandable message? From Quebec to the Tuamotu Islands, from Paris to the Antipodes, doesn't it mean: I'm hungry, give me a bite to eat!"

"Oh," Conseil put in, "there are some people so unintelligent by nature . . ."

As he was saying these words, the door opened. A steward entered. He brought us some clothes, jackets and sailor's pants, made out of a fabric whose nature I didn't recognize. I hurried to change into them, and my companions followed suit.

Meanwhile our silent steward, perhaps a deaf–mute, set the table and laid three place settings.

"There's something serious afoot," Conseil said, "and it bodes well."

"Bah!" replied the rancorous harpooner. "What the devil do you suppose they eat around here? Turtle livers, loin of shark, dogfish steaks?"

"We'll soon find out!" Conseil said.

Overlaid with silver dish covers, various platters had been neatly positioned on the table cloth, and we sat down to eat. Assuredly, we were dealing with civilized people, and if it hadn't been for this electric light flooding over us, I would have thought we were in the dining room of the Hotel Adelphi in Liverpool, or the Grand Hotel in Paris. However, I feel compelled to mention that bread and wine were totally absent. The water was fresh and clear, but it was still water—which wasn't what Ned Land had in mind. Among the foods we were served, I was able to identify various daintily dressed fish; but I couldn't make up my mind about certain otherwise excellent dishes, and I couldn't even tell whether their contents belonged to the vegetable or the animal kingdom. As for the tableware, it was elegant and in perfect taste. Each utensil, spoon, fork, knife, and plate, bore on its reverse a letter encircled by a Latin motto, and here is its exact duplicate:

MOBILIS IN MOBILI
N

Moving within the moving element! It was a highly appropriate motto for this underwater machine, so long as the preposition in is translated as within and not upon. The letter "N" was no doubt the initial of the name of that mystifying individual in command beneath the seas!

Ned and Conseil had no time for such musings. They were wolfing down their food, and without further ado I did the same. By now I felt reassured about our fate, and it seemed obvious that our hosts didn't intend to let us die of starvation.

But all earthly things come to an end, all things must pass, even the hunger of people who haven't eaten for fifteen hours. Our appetites appeased, we felt an urgent need for sleep. A natural reaction after that interminable night of fighting for our lives.

"Ye gods, I'll sleep soundly," Conseil said.

"Me, I'm out like a light!" Ned Land replied.

My two companions lay down on the cabin's carpeting and were soon deep in slumber.

As for me, I gave in less readily to this intense need for sleep. Too many thoughts had piled up in my mind, too many insoluble questions had arisen, too many images were keeping my eyelids open! Where were we? What strange power was carrying us along? I felt—or at least I thought I did—the submersible sinking toward the sea's lower strata. Intense nightmares besieged me. In these mysterious marine sanctuaries, I envisioned hosts of unknown animals, and this underwater boat seemed to be a blood relation of theirs: living, breathing, just as fearsome . . . ! Then my mind grew calmer, my imagination melted into hazy drowsiness, and I soon fell into an uneasy slumber.

The Tantrums of Ned Land

I HAVE NO IDEA how long this slumber lasted; but it must have been a good while, since we were completely over our exhaustion. I was the first one to wake up. My companions weren't yet stirring and still lay in their corners like inanimate objects.

I had barely gotten up from my passably hard mattress when I felt my mind clear, my brain go on the alert. So I began a careful reexamination of our cell.

Nothing had changed in its interior arrangements. The prison was still a prison and its prisoners still prisoners. But, taking advantage of our slumber, the steward had cleared the table. Consequently, nothing indicated any forthcoming improvement in our situation, and I seriously wondered if we were doomed to spend the rest of our lives in this cage.

This prospect seemed increasingly painful to me because, even though my brain was clear of its obsessions from the night before, I was feeling an odd short–windedness in my chest. It was becoming hard for me to breathe. The heavy air was no longer sufficient for the full play of my lungs. Although our cell was large, we obviously had used up most of the oxygen it contained. In essence, over an hour's time a single human being consumes all the oxygen found in 100 liters of air, at which point that air has become charged with a nearly equal amount of carbon dioxide and is no longer fit for breathing.

So it was now urgent to renew the air in our prison, and no doubt the air in this whole underwater boat as well.

Here a question popped into my head. How did the commander of this aquatic residence go about it? Did he obtain air using chemical methods, releasing the oxygen contained in potassium chlorate by heating it, meanwhile absorbing the carbon dioxide with potassium hydroxide? If so, he would have to keep up some kind of relationship with the shore, to come by the materials needed for such an operation. Did he simply limit himself to storing the air in high–pressure tanks and then dispense it according to his crew's needs? Perhaps. Or, proceeding in a more convenient, more economical, and consequently more probable fashion, was he satisfied with merely returning to breathe at the surface of the water like a cetacean, renewing his oxygen supply every twenty–four hours? In any event, whatever his method was, it seemed prudent to me that he use this method without delay.

In fact, I had already resorted to speeding up my inhalations in order to extract from the cell what little oxygen it contained, when suddenly I was refreshed by a current of clean air, scented with a salty aroma. It had to be a sea breeze, life–giving and charged with iodine! I opened my mouth wide, and my lungs glutted themselves on the fresh particles. At the same time, I felt a swaying, a rolling of moderate magnitude but definitely noticeable. This boat, this sheet–iron monster, had obviously just risen to the surface of the ocean, there to breathe in good whale fashion. So the ship's mode of ventilation was finally established.

When I had absorbed a chestful of this clean air, I looked for the conduit—the "air carrier," if you prefer—that allowed this beneficial influx to reach us, and I soon found it. Above the door opened an air vent that let in a fresh current of oxygen, renewing the thin air in our cell.

I had gotten to this point in my observations when Ned and Conseil woke up almost simultaneously, under the influence of this reviving air purification. They rubbed their eyes, stretched their arms, and sprang to their feet.

"Did master sleep well?" Conseil asked me with his perennial good manners.

"Extremely well, my gallant lad," I replied. "And how about you, Mr. Ned Land?"

"Like a log, professor. But I must be imagining things, because it seems like I'm breathing a sea breeze!"

A seaman couldn't be wrong on this topic, and I told the Canadian what had gone on while he slept.

"Good!" he said. "That explains perfectly all that bellowing we heard, when our so–called narwhale lay in sight of the Abraham Lincoln."

"Perfectly, Mr. Land. It was catching its breath!"

"Only I've no idea what time it is, Professor Aronnax, unless maybe it's dinnertime?"

"Dinnertime, my fine harpooner? I'd say at least breakfast time, because we've certainly woken up to a new day."

"Which indicates," Conseil replied, "that we've spent twenty–four hours in slumber."

"That's my assessment," I replied.

"I won't argue with you," Ned Land answered. "But dinner or breakfast, that steward will be plenty welcome whether he brings the one or the other."

"The one and the other," Conseil said.

"Well put," the Canadian replied. "We deserve two meals, and speaking for myself, I'll do justice to them both."

"All right, Ned, let's wait and see!" I replied. "It's clear that these strangers don't intend to let us die of hunger, otherwise last evening's dinner wouldn't make any sense."

"Unless they're fattening us up!" Ned shot back.

"I object," I replied. "We have not fallen into the hands of cannibals."

"Just because they don't make a habit of it," the Canadian replied in all seriousness, "doesn't mean they don't indulge from time to time. Who knows? Maybe these people have gone without fresh meat for a long while, and in that case three healthy, well–built specimens like the professor, his manservant, and me—"

"Get rid of those ideas, Mr. Land," I answered the harpooner. "And above all, don't let them lead you to flare up against our hosts, which would only make our situation worse."

"Anyhow," the harpooner said, "I'm as hungry as all Hades, and dinner or breakfast, not one puny meal has arrived!"

"Mr. Land," I answered, "we have to adapt to the schedule on board, and I imagine our stomachs are running ahead of the chief cook's dinner bell."

"Well then, we'll adjust our stomachs to the chef's timetable!" Conseil replied serenely.

"There you go again, Conseil my friend!" the impatient Canadian shot back. "You never allow yourself any displays of bile or attacks of nerves! You're everlastingly calm! You'd say your after–meal grace even if you didn't get any food for your before–meal blessing—and you'd starve to death rather than complain!"

"What good would it do?" Conseil asked.

"Complaining doesn't have to do good, it just feels good! And if these pirates—I say pirates out of consideration for the professor's feelings, since he doesn't want us to call them cannibals—if these pirates think they're going to smother me in this cage without hearing what cusswords spice up my outbursts, they've got another think coming! Look here, Professor Aronnax, speak frankly. How long do you figure they'll keep us in this iron box?"

"To tell the truth, friend Land, I know little more about it than you do."

"But in a nutshell, what do you suppose is going on?"

"My supposition is that sheer chance has made us privy to an important secret. Now then, if the crew of this underwater boat have a personal interest in keeping that secret, and if their personal interest is more important than the lives of three men, I believe that our very existence is in jeopardy. If such is not the case, then at the first available opportunity, this monster that has swallowed us will return us to the world inhabited by our own kind."

"Unless they recruit us to serve on the crew," Conseil said, "and keep us here—"

"Till the moment," Ned Land answered, "when some frigate that's faster or smarter than the Abraham Lincoln captures this den of buccaneers, then hangs all of us by the neck from the tip of a mainmast yardarm!"

"Well thought out, Mr. Land," I replied. "But as yet, I don't believe we've been tendered any enlistment offers. Consequently, it's pointless to argue about what tactics we should pursue in such a case. I repeat: let's wait, let's be guided by events, and let's do nothing, since right now there's nothing we can do."

"On the contrary, professor," the harpooner replied, not wanting to give in. "There is something we can do."

"Oh? And what, Mr. Land?"

"Break out of here!"

"Breaking out of a prison on shore is difficult enough, but with an underwater prison, it strikes me as completely unworkable."

"Come now, Ned my friend," Conseil asked, "how would you answer master's objection? I refuse to believe that an American is at the end of his tether."

Visibly baffled, the harpooner said nothing. Under the conditions in which fate had left us, it was absolutely impossible to escape. But a Canadian's wit is half French, and Mr. Ned Land made this clear in his reply.

"So, Professor Aronnax," he went on after thinking for a few moments, "you haven't figured out what people do when they can't escape from their prison?"

"No, my friend."

"Easy. They fix things so they stay there."

"Of course!" Conseil put in. "Since we're deep in the ocean, being inside this boat is vastly preferable to being above it or below it!"

"But we fix things by kicking out all the jailers, guards, and wardens," Ned Land added.

"What's this, Ned?" I asked. "You'd seriously consider taking over this craft?"

"Very seriously," the Canadian replied.

"It's impossible."

"And why is that, sir? Some promising opportunity might come up, and I don't see what could stop us from taking advantage of it. If there are only about twenty men on board this machine, I don't think they can stave off two Frenchmen and a Canadian!"

It seemed wiser to accept the harpooner's proposition than to debate it. Accordingly, I was content to reply:

"Let such circumstances come, Mr. Land, and we'll see. But until then, I beg you to control your impatience. We need to act shrewdly, and your flare–ups won't give rise to any promising opportunities. So swear to me that you'll accept our situation without throwing a tantrum over it."

"I give you my word, professor," Ned Land replied in an unenthusiastic tone. "No vehement phrases will leave my mouth, no vicious gestures will give my feelings away, not even when they don't feed us on time."

"I have your word, Ned," I answered the Canadian.

Then our conversation petered out, and each of us withdrew into his own thoughts. For my part, despite the harpooner's confident talk, I admit that I entertained no illusions. I had no faith in those promising opportunities that Ned Land mentioned. To operate with such efficiency, this underwater boat had to have a sizeable crew, so if it came to a physical contest, we would be facing an overwhelming opponent. Besides, before we could do anything, we had to be free, and that we definitely were not. I didn't see any way out of this sheet–iron, hermetically sealed cell. And if the strange commander of this boat did have a secret to keep—which seemed rather likely—he would never give us freedom of movement aboard his vessel. Now then, would he resort to violence in order to be rid of us, or would he drop us off one day on some remote coast? There lay the unknown. All these hypotheses seemed extremely plausible to me, and to hope for freedom through use of force, you had to be a harpooner.

I realized, moreover, that Ned Land's brooding was getting him madder by the minute. Little by little, I heard those aforesaid cusswords welling up in the depths of his gullet, and I saw his movements turn threatening again. He stood up, pacing in circles like a wild beast in a cage, striking the walls with his foot and fist. Meanwhile the hours passed, our hunger nagged unmercifully, and this time the steward did not appear. Which amounted to forgetting our castaway status for much too long, if they really had good intentions toward us.

Tortured by the growling of his well–built stomach, Ned Land was getting more and more riled, and despite his word of honor, I was in real dread of an explosion when he stood in the presence of one of the men on board.

For two more hours Ned Land's rage increased. The Canadian shouted and pleaded, but to no avail. The sheet–iron walls were deaf. I didn't hear a single sound inside this dead–seeming boat. The vessel hadn't stirred, because I obviously would have felt its hull vibrating under the influence of the propeller.

It had undoubtedly sunk into the watery deep and no longer belonged to the outside world. All this dismal silence was terrifying.

As for our neglect, our isolation in the depths of this cell, I was afraid to guess at how long it might last. Little by little, hopes I had entertained after our interview with the ship's commander were fading away. The gentleness of the man's gaze, the generosity expressed in his facial features, the nobility of his bearing, all vanished from my memory. I saw this mystifying individual anew for what he inevitably must be: cruel and merciless. I viewed him as outside humanity, beyond all feelings of compassion, the implacable foe of his fellow man, toward whom he must have sworn an undying hate!

But even so, was the man going to let us die of starvation, locked up in this cramped prison, exposed to those horrible temptations to which people are driven by extreme hunger? This grim possibility took on a dreadful intensity in my mind, and fired by my imagination, I felt an unreasoning terror run through me. Conseil stayed calm. Ned Land bellowed.

Just then a noise was audible outside. Footsteps rang on the metal tiling. The locks were turned, the door opened, the steward appeared.

Before I could make a single movement to prevent him, the Canadian rushed at the poor man, threw him down, held him by the throat. The steward was choking in the grip of those powerful hands.

Conseil was already trying to loosen the harpooner's hands from his half–suffocated victim, and I had gone to join in the rescue, when I was abruptly nailed to the spot by these words pronounced in French:

"Calm down, Mr. Land! And you, professor, kindly listen to me!"

The Man of the Waters

IT WAS THE ship's commander who had just spoken.

At these words Ned Land stood up quickly. Nearly strangled, the steward staggered out at a signal from his superior; but such was the commander's authority aboard his vessel, not one gesture gave away the resentment that this man must have felt toward the Canadian. In silence we waited for the outcome of this scene; Conseil, in spite of himself, seemed almost fascinated, I was stunned.

Arms crossed, leaning against a corner of the table, the commander studied us with great care. Was he reluctant to speak further? Did he regret those words he had just pronounced in French? You would have thought so.

After a few moments of silence, which none of us would have dreamed of interrupting:

"Gentlemen," he said in a calm, penetrating voice, "I speak French, English, German, and Latin with equal fluency. Hence I could have answered you as early as our initial interview, but first I wanted to make your acquaintance and then think things over. Your four versions of the same narrative, perfectly consistent by and large, established your personal identities for me. I now know that sheer chance has placed in my presence Professor Pierre Aronnax, specialist in natural history at the Paris Museum and entrusted with a scientific mission abroad, his manservant Conseil, and Ned Land, a harpooner of Canadian origin aboard the Abraham Lincoln, a frigate in the national navy of the United States of America."

I bowed in agreement. The commander hadn't put a question to me. So no answer was called for. This man expressed himself with perfect ease and without a trace of an accent. His phrasing was clear, his words well chosen, his facility in elocution remarkable. And yet, to me, he didn't have "the feel" of a fellow countryman.

He went on with the conversation as follows:

"No doubt, sir, you've felt that I waited rather too long before paying you this second visit. After discovering your identities, I wanted to weigh carefully what policy to pursue toward you. I had great difficulty deciding. Some extremely inconvenient circumstances have brought you into the presence of a man who has cut himself off from humanity. Your coming has disrupted my whole existence."

"Unintentionally," I said.

"Unintentionally?" the stranger replied, raising his voice a little. "Was it unintentionally that the Abraham Lincoln hunted me on every sea? Was it unintentionally that you traveled aboard that frigate? Was it unintentionally that your shells bounced off my ship's hull? Was it unintentionally that Mr. Ned Land hit me with his harpoon?"

I detected a controlled irritation in these words. But there was a perfectly natural reply to these charges, and I made it.

"Sir," I said, "you're surely unaware of the discussions that have taken place in Europe and America with yourself as the subject. You don't realize that various accidents, caused by collisions with your underwater machine, have aroused public passions on those two continents. I'll spare you the innumerable hypotheses with which we've tried to explain this inexplicable phenomenon, whose secret is yours alone. But please understand that the Abraham Lincoln chased you over the Pacific high seas in the belief it was hunting some powerful marine monster, which had to be purged from the ocean at all cost."

A half smile curled the commander's lips; then, in a calmer tone:

"Professor Aronnax," he replied, "do you dare claim that your frigate wouldn't have chased and cannonaded an underwater boat as readily as a monster?"

This question baffled me, since Commander Farragut would certainly have shown no such hesitation. He would have seen it as his sworn duty to destroy a contrivance of this kind just as promptly as a gigantic narwhale.

"So you understand, sir," the stranger went on, "that I have a right to treat you as my enemy."

I kept quiet, with good reason. What was the use of debating such a proposition, when superior force can wipe out the best arguments?

"It took me a good while to decide," the commander went on. "Nothing obliged me to grant you hospitality. If I were to part company with you, I'd have no personal interest in ever seeing you again. I could put you back on the platform of this ship that has served as your refuge. I could sink under the sea, and I could forget you ever existed. Wouldn't that be my right?"

"Perhaps it would be the right of a savage," I replied. "But not that of a civilized man."

"Professor," the commander replied swiftly, "I'm not what you term a civilized man! I've severed all ties with society, for reasons that I alone have the right to appreciate. Therefore I obey none of its regulations, and I insist that you never invoke them in front of me!"

This was plain speaking. A flash of anger and scorn lit up the stranger's eyes, and I glimpsed a fearsome past in this man's life. Not only had he placed himself beyond human laws, he had rendered himself independent, out of all reach, free in the strictest sense of the word! For who would dare chase him to the depths of the sea when he thwarted all attacks on the surface? What ship could withstand a collision with his underwater Monitor? What armor plate, no matter how heavy, could bear the thrusts of his spur? No man among men could call him to account for his actions. God, if he believed in Him, his conscience if he had one—these were the only judges to whom he was answerable.

These thoughts swiftly crossed my mind while this strange individual fell silent, like someone completely self–absorbed. I regarded him with a mixture of fear and fascination, in the same way, no doubt, that Œdipus regarded the Sphinx.

After a fairly long silence, the commander went on with our conversation.

"So I had difficulty deciding," he said. "But I concluded that my personal interests could be reconciled with that natural compassion to which every human being has a right. Since fate has brought you here, you'll stay aboard my vessel. You'll be free here, and in exchange for that freedom, moreover totally related to it, I'll lay on you just one condition. Your word that you'll submit to it will be sufficient."

"Go on, sir," I replied. "I assume this condition is one an honest man can accept?"

"Yes, sir. Just this. It's possible that certain unforeseen events may force me to confine you to your cabins for some hours, or even for some days as the case may be. Since I prefer never to use violence, I expect from you in such a case, even more than in any other, your unquestioning obedience. By acting in this way, I shield you from complicity, I absolve you of all responsibility, since I myself make it impossible for you to see what you aren't meant to see. Do you accept this condition?"

So things happened on board that were quite odd to say the least, things never to be seen by people not placing themselves beyond society's laws! Among all the surprises the future had in store for me, this would not be the mildest.

"We accept," I replied. "Only, I'll ask your permission, sir, to address a question to you, just one."

"Go ahead, sir."

"You said we'd be free aboard your vessel?"

"Completely."

"Then I would ask what you mean by this freedom."

"Why, the freedom to come, go, see, and even closely observe everything happening here—except under certain rare circumstances—in short, the freedom we ourselves enjoy, my companions and I."

It was obvious that we did not understand each other.

"Pardon me, sir," I went on, "but that's merely the freedom that every prisoner has, the freedom to pace his cell! That's not enough for us."

"Nevertheless, it will have to do!"

"What! We must give up seeing our homeland, friends, and relatives ever again?"

"Yes, sir. But giving up that intolerable earthly yoke that some men call freedom is perhaps less painful than you think!"

"By thunder!" Ned Land shouted. "I'll never promise I won't try getting out of here!"

"I didn't ask for such a promise, Mr. Land," the commander replied coldly.

"Sir," I replied, flaring up in spite of myself, "you're taking unfair advantage of us! This is sheer cruelty!"

"No, sir, it's an act of mercy! You're my prisoners of war! I've cared for you when, with a single word, I could plunge you back into the ocean depths! You attacked me! You've just stumbled on a secret no living man must probe, the secret of my entire existence! Do you think I'll send you back to a world that must know nothing more of me? Never! By keeping you on board, it isn't you whom I care for, it's me!"

These words indicated that the commander pursued a policy impervious to arguments.

"Then, sir," I went on, "you give us, quite simply, a choice between life and death?"

"Quite simply."

"My friends," I said, "to a question couched in these terms, our answer can be taken for granted. But no solemn promises bind us to the commander of this vessel."

"None, sir," the stranger replied.

Then, in a gentler voice, he went on:

"Now, allow me to finish what I have to tell you. I've heard of you, Professor Aronnax. You, if not your companions, won't perhaps complain too much about the stroke of fate that has brought us together. Among the books that make up my favorite reading, you'll find the work you've published on the great ocean depths. I've pored over it. You've taken your studies as far as terrestrial science can go. But you don't know everything because you haven't seen everything. Let me tell you, professor, you won't regret the time you spend aboard my vessel. You're going to voyage through a land of wonders. Stunned amazement will probably be your habitual state of mind. It will be a long while before you tire of the sights constantly before your eyes. I'm going to make another underwater tour of the world—perhaps my last, who knows?—and I'll review everything I've studied in the depths of these seas that I've crossed so often, and you can be my fellow student. Starting this very day, you'll enter a new element, you'll see what no human being has ever seen before—since my men and I no longer count—and thanks to me, you're going to learn the ultimate secrets of our planet."

I can't deny it; the commander's words had a tremendous effect on me. He had caught me on my weak side, and I momentarily forgot that not even this sublime experience was worth the loss of my freedom. Besides, I counted on the future to resolve this important question. So I was content to reply:

"Sir, even though you've cut yourself off from humanity, I can see that you haven't disowned all human feeling. We're castaways whom you've charitably taken aboard, we'll never forget that. Speaking for myself, I don't rule out that the interests of science could override even the need for freedom, which promises me that, in exchange, our encounter will provide great rewards."

I thought the commander would offer me his hand, to seal our agreement. He did nothing of the sort. I regretted that.

"One last question," I said, just as this inexplicable being seemed ready to withdraw.

"Ask it, professor."

"By what name am I to call you?"

"Sir," the commander replied, "to you, I'm simply Captain Nemo; to me, you and your companions are simply passengers on the Nautilus."

Captain Nemo called out. A steward appeared. The captain gave him his orders in that strange language I couldn't even identify. Then, turning to the Canadian and Conseil:

"A meal is waiting for you in your cabin," he told them. "Kindly follow this man."

"That's an offer I can't refuse!" the harpooner replied.

After being confined for over thirty hours, he and Conseil were finally out of this cell.

"And now, Professor Aronnax, our own breakfast is ready. Allow me to lead the way."

"Yours to command, Captain."

I followed Captain Nemo, and as soon as I passed through the doorway, I went down a kind of electrically lit passageway that resembled a gangway on a ship. After a stretch of some ten meters, a second door opened before me.

I then entered a dining room, decorated and furnished in austere good taste. Inlaid with ebony trim, tall oaken sideboards stood at both ends of this room, and sparkling on their shelves were staggered rows of earthenware, porcelain, and glass of incalculable value. There silver–plated dinnerware gleamed under rays pouring from light fixtures in the ceiling, whose glare was softened and tempered by delicately painted designs.

In the center of this room stood a table, richly spread. Captain Nemo indicated the place I was to occupy.

"Be seated," he told me, "and eat like the famished man you must be."

Our breakfast consisted of several dishes whose contents were all supplied by the sea, and some foods whose nature and derivation were unknown to me. They were good, I admit, but with a peculiar flavor to which I would soon grow accustomed. These various food items seemed to be rich in phosphorous, and I thought that they, too, must have been of marine origin.

Captain Nemo stared at me. I had asked him nothing, but he read my thoughts, and on his own he answered the questions I was itching to address him.

"Most of these dishes are new to you," he told me. "But you can consume them without fear. They're healthy and nourishing. I renounced terrestrial foods long ago, and I'm none the worse for it. My crew are strong and full of energy, and they eat what I eat."

"So," I said, "all these foods are products of the sea?"

"Yes, professor, the sea supplies all my needs. Sometimes I cast my nets in our wake, and I pull them up ready to burst. Sometimes I go hunting right in the midst of this element that has long seemed so far out of man's reach, and I corner the game that dwells in my underwater forests. Like the flocks of old Proteus, King Neptune's shepherd, my herds graze without fear on the ocean's immense prairies. There I own vast properties that I harvest myself, and which are forever sown by the hand of the Creator of All Things."

I stared at Captain Nemo in definite astonishment, and I answered him:

"Sir, I understand perfectly how your nets can furnish excellent fish for your table; I understand less how you can chase aquatic game in your underwater forests; but how a piece of red meat, no matter how small, can figure in your menu, that I don't understand at all."

"Nor I, sir," Captain Nemo answered me. "I never touch the flesh of land animals."

"Nevertheless, this . . . ," I went on, pointing to a dish where some slices of loin were still left.

"What you believe to be red meat, professor, is nothing other than loin of sea turtle. Similarly, here are some dolphin livers you might mistake for stewed pork. My chef is a skillful food processor who excels at pickling and preserving these various exhibits from the ocean. Feel free to sample all of these foods. Here are some preserves of sea cucumber that a Malaysian would declare to be unrivaled in the entire world, here's cream from milk furnished by the udders of cetaceans, and sugar from the huge fucus plants in the North Sea; and finally, allow me to offer you some marmalade of sea anemone, equal to that from the tastiest fruits."

So I sampled away, more as a curiosity seeker than an epicure, while Captain Nemo delighted me with his incredible anecdotes.

"But this sea, Professor Aronnax," he told me, "this prodigious, inexhaustible wet nurse of a sea not only feeds me, she dresses me as well. That fabric covering you was woven from the masses of filaments that anchor certain seashells; as the ancients were wont to do, it was dyed with purple ink from the murex snail and shaded with violet tints that I extract from a marine slug, the Mediterranean sea hare. The perfumes you'll find on the washstand in your cabin were produced from the oozings of marine plants. Your mattress was made from the ocean's softest eelgrass. Your quill pen will be whalebone, your ink a juice secreted by cuttlefish or squid. Everything comes to me from the sea, just as someday everything will return to it!"

"You love the sea, Captain."

"Yes, I love it! The sea is the be all and end all! It covers seven–tenths of the planet earth. Its breath is clean and healthy. It's an immense wilderness where a man is never lonely, because he feels life astir on every side. The sea is simply the vehicle for a prodigious, unearthly mode of existence; it's simply movement and love; it's living infinity, as one of your poets put it. And in essence, professor, nature is here made manifest by all three of her kingdoms, mineral, vegetable, and animal. The last of these is amply represented by the four zoophyte groups, three classes of articulates, five classes of mollusks, and three vertebrate classes: mammals, reptiles, and those countless legions of fish, an infinite order of animals totaling more than 13,000 species, of which only one–tenth belong to fresh water. The sea is a vast pool of nature. Our globe began with the sea, so to speak, and who can say we won't end with it! Here lies supreme tranquility. The sea doesn't belong to tyrants. On its surface they can still exercise their iniquitous claims, battle each other, devour each other, haul every earthly horror. But thirty feet below sea level, their dominion ceases, their influence fades, their power vanishes!

Ah, sir, live! Live in the heart of the seas! Here alone lies independence! Here I recognize no superiors! Here I'm free!"

Captain Nemo suddenly fell silent in the midst of this enthusiastic outpouring. Had he let himself get carried away, past the bounds of his habitual reserve? Had he said too much? For a few moments he strolled up and down, all aquiver. Then his nerves grew calmer, his facial features recovered their usual icy composure, and turning to me:

"Now, professor," he said, "if you'd like to inspect the Nautilus, I'm yours to command."

The Nautilus

CAPTAIN NEMO stood up. I followed him. Contrived at the rear of the dining room, a double door opened, and I entered a room whose dimensions equaled the one I had just left.

It was a library. Tall, black–rosewood bookcases, inlaid with copperwork, held on their wide shelves a large number of uniformly bound books. These furnishings followed the contours of the room, their lower parts leading to huge couches upholstered in maroon leather and curved for maximum comfort. Light, movable reading stands, which could be pushed away or pulled near as desired, allowed books to be positioned on them for easy study. In the center stood a huge table covered with pamphlets, among which some newspapers, long out of date, were visible. Electric light flooded this whole harmonious totality, falling from four frosted half globes set in the scrollwork of the ceiling. I stared in genuine wonderment at this room so ingeniously laid out, and I couldn't believe my eyes.

"Captain Nemo," I told my host, who had just stretched out on a couch, "this is a library that would do credit to more than one continental palace, and I truly marvel to think it can go with you into the deepest seas."

"Where could one find greater silence or solitude, professor?" Captain Nemo replied. "Did your study at the museum afford you such a perfect retreat?"

"No, sir, and I might add that it's quite a humble one next to yours. You own 6,000 or 7,000 volumes here . . ."

"12,000, Professor Aronnax. They're my sole remaining ties with dry land. But I was done with the shore the day my Nautilus submerged for the first time under the waters. That day I purchased my last volumes, my last pamphlets, my last newspapers, and ever since I've chosen to believe that humanity no longer thinks or writes. In any event, professor, these books are at your disposal, and you may use them freely."

I thanked Captain Nemo and approached the shelves of this library. Written in every language, books on science, ethics, and literature were there in abundance, but I didn't see a single work on economics—they seemed to be strictly banned on board. One odd detail: all these books were shelved indiscriminately without regard to the language in which they were written, and this jumble proved that the Nautilus's captain could read fluently whatever volumes he chanced to pick up.

Among these books I noted masterpieces by the greats of ancient and modern times, in other words, all of humanity's finest achievements in history, poetry, fiction, and science, from Homer to Victor Hugo, from Xenophon to Michelet, from Rabelais to Madame George Sand. But science, in particular, represented the major investment of this library: books on mechanics, ballistics, hydrography, meteorology, geography, geology, etc., held a place there no less important than works on natural history, and I realized that they made up the captain's chief reading. There I saw the complete works of Humboldt, the complete Arago, as well as works by Foucault, Henri Sainte–Claire Deville, Chasles, Milne–Edwards, Quatrefages, John Tyndall, Faraday, Berthelot, Father Secchi, Petermann, Commander Maury, Louis Agassiz, etc., plus the transactions of France's Academy of Sciences, bulletins from the various geographical societies, etc., and in a prime location, those two volumes on the great ocean depths that had perhaps earned me this comparatively charitable welcome from Captain Nemo. Among the works of Joseph Bertrand, his book entitled The Founders of Astronomy even gave me a definite date; and since I knew it had appeared in the course of 1865, I concluded that the fitting out of the Nautilus hadn't taken place before then. Accordingly, three years ago at the most, Captain Nemo had begun his underwater existence. Moreover, I hoped some books even more recent would permit me to pinpoint the date precisely; but I had plenty of time to look for them, and I didn't want to put off any longer our stroll through the wonders of the Nautilus.

"Sir," I told the captain, "thank you for placing this library at my disposal. There are scientific treasures here, and I'll take advantage of them."

"This room isn't only a library," Captain Nemo said, "it's also a smoking room."

"A smoking room?" I exclaimed. "Then one may smoke on board?"

"Surely."

"In that case, sir, I'm forced to believe that you've kept up relations with Havana."

"None whatever," the captain replied. "Try this cigar, Professor Aronnax, and even though it doesn't come from Havana, it will satisfy you if you're a connoisseur."

I took the cigar offered me, whose shape recalled those from Cuba; but it seemed to be made of gold leaf. I lit it at a small brazier supported by an elegant bronze stand, and I inhaled my first whiffs with the relish of a smoker who hasn't had a puff in days.

"It's excellent," I said, "but it's not from the tobacco plant."

"Right," the captain replied, "this tobacco comes from neither Havana nor the Orient. It's a kind of nicotine–rich seaweed that the ocean supplies me, albeit sparingly. Do you still miss your Cubans, sir?"

"Captain, I scorn them from this day forward."

"Then smoke these cigars whenever you like, without debating their origin. They bear no government seal of approval, but I imagine they're none the worse for it."

"On the contrary."

Just then Captain Nemo opened a door facing the one by which I had entered the library, and I passed into an immense, splendidly lit lounge.

It was a huge quadrilateral with canted corners, ten meters long, six wide, five high. A luminous ceiling, decorated with delicate arabesques, distributed a soft, clear daylight over all the wonders gathered in this museum. For a museum it truly was, in which clever hands had spared no expense to amass every natural and artistic treasure, displaying them with the helter–skelter picturesqueness that distinguishes a painter's studio.

Some thirty pictures by the masters, uniformly framed and separated by gleaming panoplies of arms, adorned walls on which were stretched tapestries of austere design. There I saw canvases of the highest value, the likes of which I had marveled at in private European collections and art exhibitions. The various schools of the old masters were represented by a Raphael Madonna, a Virgin by Leonardo da Vinci, a nymph by Correggio, a woman by Titian, an adoration of the Magi by Veronese, an assumption of the Virgin by Murillo, a Holbein portrait, a monk by Velazquez, a martyr by Ribera, a village fair by Rubens, two Flemish landscapes by Teniers, three little genre paintings by Gerard Dow, Metsu, and Paul Potter, two canvases by Gericault and Prud'hon, plus seascapes by Backhuysen and Vernet. Among the works of modern art were pictures signed by Delacroix, Ingres, Decamps, Troyon, Meissonier, Daubigny, etc., and some wonderful miniature statues in marble or bronze, modeled after antiquity's finest originals, stood on their pedestals in the corners of this magnificent museum. As the Nautilus's commander had predicted, my mind was already starting to fall into that promised state of stunned amazement.

"Professor," this strange man then said, "you must excuse the informality with which I receive you, and the disorder reigning in this lounge."

"Sir," I replied, "without prying into who you are, might I venture to identify you as an artist?"

"A collector, sir, nothing more. Formerly I loved acquiring these beautiful works created by the hand of man. I sought them greedily, ferreted them out tirelessly, and I've been able to gather some objects of great value. They're my last mementos of those shores that are now dead for me. In my eyes, your modern artists are already as old as the ancients. They've existed for 2,000 or 3,000 years, and I mix them up in my mind. The masters are ageless."

"What about these composers?" I said, pointing to sheet music by Weber, Rossini, Mozart, Beethoven, Haydn, Meyerbeer, Hérold, Wagner, Auber, Gounod, Victor Massé, and a number of others scattered over a full size piano–organ, which occupied one of the wall panels in this lounge.

"These composers," Captain Nemo answered me, "are the contemporaries of Orpheus, because in the annals of the dead, all chronological differences fade; and I'm dead, professor, quite as dead as those friends of yours sleeping six feet under!"

Captain Nemo fell silent and seemed lost in reverie. I regarded him with intense excitement, silently analyzing his strange facial expression. Leaning his elbow on the corner of a valuable mosaic table, he no longer saw me, he had forgotten my very presence.

I didn't disturb his meditations but continued to pass in review the curiosities that enriched this lounge.

After the works of art, natural rarities predominated. They consisted chiefly of plants, shells, and other exhibits from the ocean that must have been Captain Nemo's own personal finds. In the middle of the lounge, a jet of water, electrically lit, fell back into a basin made from a single giant clam. The delicately festooned rim of this shell, supplied by the biggest mollusk in the class Acephala, measured about six meters in circumference; so it was even bigger than those fine giant clams given to King François I by the Republic of Venice, and which the Church of Saint–Sulpice in Paris has made into two gigantic holy–water fonts.

Around this basin, inside elegant glass cases fastened with copper bands, there were classified and labeled the most valuable marine exhibits ever put before the eyes of a naturalist. My professorial glee may easily be imagined.

The zoophyte branch offered some very unusual specimens from its two groups, the polyps and the echinoderms. In the first group: organ–pipe coral, gorgonian coral arranged into fan shapes, soft sponges from Syria, isis coral from the Molucca Islands, sea–pen coral, wonderful coral of the genus Virgularia from the waters of Norway, various coral of the genus Umbellularia, alcyonarian coral, then a whole series of those madrepores that my mentor Professor Milne–Edwards has so shrewdly classified into divisions and among which I noted the wonderful genus Flabellina as well as the genus Oculina from Réunion Island, plus a Neptune's chariot from the Caribbean Sea—every superb variety of coral, and in short, every species of these unusual polyparies that congregate to form entire islands that will one day turn into continents. Among the echinoderms, notable for being covered with spines: starfish, feather stars, sea lilies, free–swimming crinoids, brittle stars, sea urchins, sea cucumbers, etc., represented a complete collection of the individuals in this group.

An excitable conchologist would surely have fainted dead away before other, more numerous glass cases in which were classified specimens from the mollusk branch. There I saw a collection of incalculable value that I haven't time to describe completely. Among these exhibits I'll mention, just for the record: an elegant royal hammer shell from the Indian Ocean, whose evenly spaced white spots stood out sharply against a base of red and brown; an imperial spiny oyster, brightly colored, bristling with thorns, a specimen rare to European museums, whose value I estimated at ₣20,000; a common hammer shell from the seas near Queensland, very hard to come by; exotic cockles from Senegal, fragile white bivalve shells that a single breath could pop like a soap bubble; several varieties of watering-pot shell from Java, a sort of limestone tube fringed with leafy folds and much fought over by collectors; a whole series of top-shell snails—greenish yellow ones fished up from American seas, others colored reddish brown that patronize the waters off Queensland, the former coming from the Gulf of Mexico and notable for their overlapping shells, the latter some sun-carrier shells found in the southernmost seas, finally and rarest of all, the magnificent spurred-star shell from New Zealand; then some wonderful peppery-furrow shells; several valuable species of cythera clams and venus clams; the trellis wentletrap snail from Tranquebar on India's eastern shore; a marbled turban snail gleaming with mother-of-pearl; green parrot shells from the seas of China; the virtually unknown cone snail from the genus Coenodullus; every variety of cowry used as money in India and Africa; a "glory-of-the-seas," the most valuable shell in the East Indies; finally, common periwinkles, delphinula snails, turret snails, violet snails, European cowries, volute snails, olive shells, miter shells, helmet shells, murex snails, whelks, harp shells, spiky periwinkles, triton snails, horn shells, spindle shells, conch shells, spider conchs, limpets, glass snails, sea butterflies—every kind of delicate, fragile seashell that science has baptized with its most delightful names.

Aside and in special compartments, strings of supremely beautiful pearls were spread out, the electric light flecking them with little fiery sparks: pink pearls pulled from saltwater fan shells in the Red Sea; green pearls from the rainbow abalone; yellow, blue, and black pearls, the unusual handiwork of various mollusks from every ocean and of certain mussels from rivers up north; in short, several specimens of incalculable worth that had been oozed by the rarest of shellfish. Some of these pearls were bigger than a pigeon egg; they more than equaled the one that the explorer Tavernier sold the Shah of Persia for ₣3,000,000, and they surpassed that other pearl owned by the Imam of Muscat, which I had believed to be unrivaled in the entire world.

Consequently, to calculate the value of this collection was, I should say, impossible. Captain Nemo must have spent millions in acquiring these different specimens, and I was wondering what financial resources he tapped to satisfy his collector's fancies, when these words interrupted me:

"You're examining my shells, professor? They're indeed able to fascinate a naturalist; but for me they have an added charm, since I've collected every one of them with my own two hands, and not a sea on the globe has escaped my investigations."

"I understand, Captain, I understand your delight at strolling in the midst of this wealth. You're a man who gathers his treasure in person. No museum in Europe owns such a collection of exhibits from the ocean. But if I exhaust all my wonderment on them, I'll have nothing left for the ship that carries them! I have absolutely no wish to probe those secrets of yours! But I confess that my curiosity is aroused to the limit by this Nautilus, the motor power it contains, the equipment enabling it to operate, the ultra powerful force that brings it to life. I see some instruments hanging on the walls of this lounge whose purposes are unknown to me. May I learn—"

"Professor Aronnax," Captain Nemo answered me, "I've said you'd be free aboard my vessel, so no part of the Nautilus is off–limits to you. You may inspect it in detail, and I'll be delighted to act as your guide."

"I don't know how to thank you, sir, but I won't abuse your good nature. I would only ask you about the uses intended for these instruments of physical measure—"

"Professor, these same instruments are found in my stateroom, where I'll have the pleasure of explaining their functions to you. But beforehand, come inspect the cabin set aside for you. You need to learn how you'll be lodged aboard the Nautilus."

I followed Captain Nemo, who, via one of the doors cut into the lounge's canted corners, led me back down the ship's gangways. He took me to the bow, and there I found not just a cabin but an elegant stateroom with a bed, a washstand, and various other furnishings.

I could only thank my host.

"Your stateroom adjoins mine," he told me, opening a door, "and mine leads into that lounge we've just left."

I entered the captain's stateroom. It had an austere, almost monastic appearance. An iron bedstead, a worktable, some washstand fixtures. Subdued lighting. No luxuries. Just the bare necessities.

Captain Nemo showed me to a bench.

"Kindly be seated," he told me.

I sat, and he began speaking as follows:

Everything through Electricity

"SIR," CAPTAIN NEMO SAID, showing me the instruments hanging on the walls of his stateroom, "these are the devices needed to navigate the Nautilus. Here, as in the lounge, I always have them before my eyes, and they indicate my position and exact heading in the midst of the ocean. You're familiar with some of them, such as the thermometer, which gives the temperature inside the Nautilus; the barometer, which measures the heaviness of the outside air and forecasts changes in the weather; the humidistat, which indicates the degree of dryness in the atmosphere; the storm glass, whose mixture decomposes to foretell the arrival of tempests; the compass, which steers my course; the sextant, which takes the sun's altitude and tells me my latitude; chronometers, which allow me to calculate my longitude; and finally, spyglasses for both day and night, enabling me to scrutinize every point of the horizon once the Nautilus has risen to the surface of the waves."

"These are the normal navigational instruments," I replied, "and I'm familiar with their uses. But no doubt these others answer pressing needs unique to the Nautilus. That dial I see there, with the needle moving across it—isn't it a pressure gauge?"

"It is indeed a pressure gauge. It's placed in contact with the water, and it indicates the outside pressure on our hull, which in turn gives me the depth at which my submersible is sitting."

"And these are some new breed of sounding line?"

"They're thermometric sounding lines that report water temperatures in the different strata."

"And these other instruments, whose functions I can't even guess?"

"Here, professor, I need to give you some background information," Captain Nemo said. "So kindly hear me out."

He fell silent for some moments, then he said:

"There's a powerful, obedient, swift, and effortless force that can be bent to any use and which reigns supreme aboard my vessel. It does everything. It lights me, it warms me, it's the soul of my mechanical equipment. This force is electricity."

"Electricity!" I exclaimed in some surprise.

"Yes, sir."

"But, Captain, you have a tremendous speed of movement that doesn't square with the strength of electricity. Until now, its dynamic potential has remained quite limited, capable of producing only small amounts of power!"

"Professor," Captain Nemo replied, "my electricity isn't the run–of–the–mill variety, and with your permission, I'll leave it at that."

"I won't insist, sir, and I'll rest content with simply being flabbergasted at your results. I would ask one question, however, which you needn't answer if it's indiscreet. The electric cells you use to generate this marvelous force must be depleted very quickly. Their zinc component, for example: how do you replace it, since you no longer stay in contact with the shore?"

"That question deserves an answer," Captain Nemo replied. "First off, I'll mention that at the bottom of the sea there exist veins of zinc, iron, silver, and gold whose mining would quite certainly be feasible. But I've tapped none of these land–based metals, and I wanted to make demands only on the sea itself for the sources of my electricity."

"The sea itself?"

"Yes, professor, and there was no shortage of such sources. In fact, by establishing a circuit between two wires immersed to different depths, I'd be able to obtain electricity through the diverging temperatures they experience; but I preferred to use a more practical procedure."

"And that is?"

"You're familiar with the composition of salt water. In 1,000 grams one finds 96.5% water and about 2.66% sodium chloride; then small quantities of magnesium chloride, potassium chloride, magnesium bromide, sulfate of magnesia, calcium sulfate, and calcium carbonate. Hence you observe that sodium chloride is encountered there in significant proportions. Now then, it's this sodium that I extract from salt water and with which I compose my electric cells."

"Sodium?"

"Yes, sir. Mixed with mercury, it forms an amalgam that takes the place of zinc in Bunsen cells. The mercury is never depleted. Only the sodium is consumed, and the sea itself gives me that. Beyond this, I'll mention that sodium batteries have been found to generate the greater energy, and their electro–motor strength is twice that of zinc batteries."

"Captain, I fully understand the excellence of sodium under the conditions in which you're placed. The sea contains it. Fine. But it still has to be produced, in short, extracted. And how do you accomplish this? Obviously your batteries could do the extracting; but if I'm not mistaken, the consumption of sodium needed by your electric equipment would be greater than the quantity you'd extract. It would come about, then, that in the process of producing your sodium, you'd use up more than you'd make!"

"Accordingly, professor, I don't extract it with batteries; quite simply, I utilize the heat of coal from the earth."

"From the earth?" I said, my voice going up on the word.

"We'll say coal from the seafloor, if you prefer," Captain Nemo replied.

"And you can mine these veins of underwater coal?"

"You'll watch me work them, Professor Aronnax. I ask only a little patience of you, since you'll have ample time to be patient. Just remember one thing: I owe everything to the ocean; it generates electricity, and electricity gives the Nautilus heat, light, motion, and, in a word, life itself."

"But not the air you breathe?"

"Oh, I could produce the air needed on board, but it would be pointless, since I can rise to the surface of the sea whenever I like. However, even though electricity doesn't supply me with breathable air, it at least operates the powerful pumps that store it under pressure in special tanks; which, if need be, allows me to extend my stay in the lower strata for as long as I want."

"Captain," I replied, "I'll rest content with marveling. You've obviously found what all mankind will surely find one day, the true dynamic power of electricity."

"I'm not so certain they'll find it," Captain Nemo replied icily. "But be that as it may, you're already familiar with the first use I've found for this valuable force. It lights us, and with a uniformity and continuity not even possessed by sunlight. Now, look at that clock: it's electric, it runs with an accuracy rivaling the finest chronometers. I've had it divided into twenty–four hours like Italian clocks, since neither day nor night, sun nor moon, exist for me, but only this artificial light that I import into the depths of the seas! See, right now it's ten o'clock in the morning."

"That's perfect."

"Another use for electricity: that dial hanging before our eyes indicates how fast the Nautilus is going. An electric wire puts it in contact with the patent log; this needle shows me the actual speed of my submersible. And . . . hold on . . . just now we're proceeding at the moderate pace of fifteen miles per hour."

"It's marvelous," I replied, "and I truly see, Captain, how right you are to use this force; it's sure to take the place of wind, water, and steam."

"But that's not all, Professor Aronnax," Captain Nemo said, standing up. "And if you'd care to follow me, we'll inspect the Nautilus's stern."

In essence, I was already familiar with the whole forward part of this underwater boat, and here are its exact subdivisions going from amidships to its spur: the dining room, 5 meters long and separated from the library by a watertight bulkhead, in other words, it couldn't be penetrated by the sea; the library, 5 meters long; the main lounge, 10 meters long, separated from the captain's stateroom by a second watertight bulkhead; the aforesaid stateroom, 5 meters long; mine, 2.5 meters long; and finally, air tanks 7.5 meters long and extending to the stempost. Total: a length of 35 meters. Doors were cut into the watertight bulkheads and were shut hermetically by means of india–rubber seals, which insured complete safety aboard the Nautilus in the event of a leak in any one section.

I followed Captain Nemo down gangways located for easy transit, and I arrived amidships. There I found a sort of shaft heading upward between two watertight bulkheads. An iron ladder, clamped to the wall, led to the shaft's upper end. I asked the Captain what this ladder was for.

"It goes to the skiff," he replied.

"What! You have a skiff?" I replied in some astonishment.

"Surely. An excellent longboat, light and unsinkable, which is used for excursions and fishing trips."

"But when you want to set out, don't you have to return to the surface of the sea?"

"By no means. The skiff is attached to the topside of the Nautilus's hull and is set in a cavity expressly designed to receive it. It's completely decked over, absolutely watertight, and held solidly in place by bolts. This ladder leads to a manhole cut into the Nautilus's hull and corresponding to a comparable hole cut into the side of the skiff. I insert myself through this double opening into the longboat. My crew close up the hole belonging to the Nautilus; I close up the one belonging to the skiff, simply by screwing it into place. I undo the bolts holding the skiff to the submersible, and the longboat rises with prodigious speed to the surface of the sea. I then open the deck paneling, carefully closed until that point; I up mast and hoist sail—or I take out my oars—and I go for a spin."

"But how do you return to the ship?"

"I don't, Professor Aronnax; the Nautilus returns to me."

"At your command?"

"At my command. An electric wire connects me to the ship. I fire off a telegram, and that's that."

"Right," I said, tipsy from all these wonders, "nothing to it!"

After passing the well of the companionway that led to the platform, I saw a cabin 2 meters long in which Conseil and Ned Land, enraptured with their meal, were busy devouring it to the last crumb. Then a door opened into the galley, 3 meters long and located between the vessel's huge storage lockers.

There, even more powerful and obedient than gas, electricity did most of the cooking. Arriving under the stoves, wires transmitted to platinum griddles a heat that was distributed and sustained with perfect consistency. It also heated a distilling mechanism that, via evaporation, supplied excellent drinking water. Next to this galley was a bathroom, conveniently laid out, with faucets supplying hot or cold water at will.

After the galley came the crew's quarters, 5 meters long. But the door was closed and I couldn't see its accommodations, which might have told me the number of men it took to operate the Nautilus.

At the far end stood a fourth watertight bulkhead, separating the crew's quarters from the engine room. A door opened, and I stood in the compartment where Captain Nemo, indisputably a world–class engineer, had set up his locomotive equipment.

Brightly lit, the engine room measured at least 20 meters in length. It was divided, by function, into two parts: the first contained the cells for generating electricity, the second that mechanism transmitting movement to the propeller.

Right off, I detected an odor permeating the compartment that was sui generis. Captain Nemo noticed the negative impression it made on me.

"That," he told me, "is a gaseous discharge caused by our use of sodium, but it's only a mild inconvenience. In any event, every morning we sanitize the ship by ventilating it in the open air."

Meanwhile I examined the Nautilus's engine with a fascination easy to imagine.

"You observe," Captain Nemo told me, "that I use Bunsen cells, not Ruhmkorff cells. The latter would be ineffectual. One uses fewer Bunsen cells, but they're big and strong, and experience has proven their superiority. The electricity generated here makes its way to the stern, where electromagnets of huge size activate a special system of levers and gears that transmit movement to the propeller's shaft. The latter has a diameter of 6 meters, a pitch of 7.5 meters, and can do up to 120 revolutions per minute."

"And that gives you?"

"A speed of fifty miles per hour."

There lay a mystery, but I didn't insist on exploring it. How could electricity work with such power? Where did this nearly unlimited energy originate? Was it in the extraordinary voltage obtained from some new kind of induction coil? Could its transmission have been immeasurably increased by some unknown system of levers? This was the point I couldn't grasp.

"Captain Nemo," I said, "I'll vouch for the results and not try to explain them. I've seen the Nautilus at work out in front of the Abraham Lincoln, and I know where I stand on its speed. But it isn't enough just to move, we have to see where we're going! We must be able to steer right or left, up or down! How do you reach the lower depths, where you meet an increasing resistance that's assessed in hundreds of atmospheres? How do you rise back to the surface of the ocean? Finally, how do you keep your ship at whatever level suits you? Am I indiscreet in asking you all these things?"

"Not at all, professor," the Captain answered me after a slight hesitation, "since you'll never leave this underwater boat. Come into the lounge. It's actually our work room, and there you'll learn the full story about the Nautilus!"

Some Figures

A MOMENT LATER we were seated on a couch in the lounge, cigars between our lips. The Captain placed before my eyes a working drawing that gave the ground plan, cross section, and side view of the Nautilus. Then he began his description as follows:

"Here, Professor Aronnax, are the different dimensions of this boat now transporting you. It's a very long cylinder with conical ends. It noticeably takes the shape of a cigar, a shape already adopted in London for several projects of the same kind. The length of this cylinder from end to end is exactly seventy meters, and its maximum breadth of beam is eight meters. So it isn't quite built on the ten–to–one ratio of your high–speed steamers; but its lines are sufficiently long, and their tapering gradual enough, so that the displaced water easily slips past and poses no obstacle to the ship's movements.

"These two dimensions allow you to obtain, via a simple calculation, the surface area and volume of the Nautilus. Its surface area totals 1,011.45 square meters, its volume 1,507.2 cubic meters—which is tantamount to saying that when it's completely submerged, it displaces 1,500 cubic meters of water, or weighs 1,500 metric tons.

"In drawing up plans for a ship meant to navigate underwater, I wanted it, when floating on the waves, to lie nine–tenths below the surface and to emerge only one–tenth. Consequently, under these conditions it needed to displace only nine–tenths of its volume, hence 1,356.48 cubic meters; in other words, it was to weigh only that same number of metric tons. So I was obliged not to exceed this weight while building it to the aforesaid dimensions.

"The Nautilus is made up of two hulls, one inside the other; between them, joining them together, are iron T–bars that give this ship the utmost rigidity. In fact, thanks to this cellular arrangement, it has the resistance of a stone block, as if it were completely solid. Its plating can't give way; it's self–adhering and not dependent on the tightness of its rivets; and due to the perfect union of its materials, the solidarity of its construction allows it to defy the most violent seas.

"The two hulls are manufactured from boilerplate steel, whose relative density is 7.8 times that of water. The first hull has a thickness of no less than five centimeters and weighs 394.96 metric tons. My second hull, the outer cover, includes a keel fifty centimeters high by twenty–five wide, which by itself weighs 62 metric tons; this hull, the engine, the ballast, the various accessories and accommodations, plus the bulkheads and interior braces, have a combined weight of 961.52 metric tons, which when added to 394.96 metric tons, gives us the desired total of 1,356.48 metric tons. Clear?"

"Clear," I replied.

"So," the captain went on, "when the Nautilus lies on the waves under these conditions, one–tenth of it does emerge above water. Now then, if I provide some ballast tanks equal in capacity to that one–tenth, hence able to hold 150.72 metric tons, and if I fill them with water, the boat then displaces 1,507.2 metric tons—or it weighs that much—and it would be completely submerged. That's what comes about, professor. These ballast tanks exist within easy access in the lower reaches of the Nautilus. I open some stopcocks, the tanks fill, the boat sinks, and it's exactly flush with the surface of the water."

"Fine, captain, but now we come to a genuine difficulty. You're able to lie flush with the surface of the ocean, that I understand. But lower down, while diving beneath that surface, isn't your submersible going to encounter a pressure, and consequently undergo an upward thrust, that must be assessed at one atmosphere per every thirty feet of water, hence at about one kilogram per each square centimeter?"

"Precisely, sir."

"Then unless you fill up the whole Nautilus, I don't see how you can force it down into the heart of these liquid masses."

"Professor," Captain Nemo replied, "static objects mustn't be confused with dynamic ones, or we'll be open to serious error. Comparatively little effort is spent in reaching the ocean's lower regions, because all objects have a tendency to become 'sinkers.' Follow my logic here."

"I'm all ears, captain."

"When I wanted to determine what increase in weight the Nautilus needed to be given in order to submerge, I had only to take note of the proportionate reduction in volume that salt water experiences in deeper and deeper strata."

"That's obvious," I replied.

"Now then, if water isn't absolutely incompressible, at least it compresses very little. In fact, according to the most recent calculations, this reduction is only .0000436 per atmosphere, or per every thirty feet of depth. For instance, to go 1,000 meters down, I must take into account the reduction in volume that occurs under a pressure equivalent to that from a 1,000–meter column of water, in other words, under a pressure of 100 atmospheres. In this instance the reduction would be .00436. Consequently, I'd have to increase my weight from 1,507.2 metric tons to 1,513.77. So the added weight would only be 6.57 metric tons."

"That's all?"

"That's all, Professor Aronnax, and the calculation is easy to check. Now then, I have supplementary ballast tanks capable of shipping 100 metric tons of water. So I can descend to considerable depths. When I want to rise again and lie flush with the surface, all I have to do is expel that water; and if I desire that the Nautilus emerge above the waves to one–tenth of its total capacity, I empty all the ballast tanks completely."

This logic, backed up by figures, left me without a single objection.

"I accept your calculations, Captain," I replied, "and I'd be ill–mannered to dispute them, since your daily experience bears them out. But at this juncture, I have a hunch that we're still left with one real difficulty."

"What's that, sir?"

"When you're at a depth of 1,000 meters, the Nautilus's plating bears a pressure of 100 atmospheres. If at this point you want to empty the supplementary ballast tanks in order to lighten your boat and rise to the surface, your pumps must overcome that pressure of 100 atmospheres, which is 100 kilograms per each square centimeter. This demands a strength—"

"That electricity alone can give me," Captain Nemo said swiftly. "Sir, I repeat: the dynamic power of my engines is nearly infinite. The Nautilus's pumps have prodigious strength, as you must have noticed when their waterspouts swept like a torrent over the Abraham Lincoln. Besides, I use my supplementary ballast tanks only to reach an average depth of 1,500 to 2,000 meters, and that with a view to conserving my machinery. Accordingly, when I have a mind to visit the ocean depths two or three vertical leagues beneath the surface, I use maneuvers that are more time–consuming but no less infallible."

"What are they, Captain?" I asked.

"Here I'm naturally led into telling you how the Nautilus is maneuvered."

"I can't wait to find out."

"In order to steer this boat to port or starboard, in short, to make turns on a horizontal plane, I use an ordinary, wide–bladed rudder that's fastened to the rear of the sternpost and worked by a wheel and tackle. But I can also move the Nautilus upward and downward on a vertical plane by the simple method of slanting its two fins, which are attached to its sides at its center of flotation; these fins are flexible, able to assume any position, and can be operated from inside by means of powerful levers. If these fins stay parallel with the boat, the latter moves horizontally. If they slant, the Nautilus follows the angle of that slant and, under its propeller's thrust, either sinks on a diagonal as steep as it suits me, or rises on that diagonal. And similarly, if I want to return more swiftly to the surface, I throw the propeller in gear, and the water's pressure makes the Nautilus rise vertically, as an air balloon inflated with hydrogen lifts swiftly into the skies."

"Bravo, Captain!" I exclaimed. "But in the midst of the waters, how can your helmsman follow the course you've given him?"

"My helmsman is stationed behind the windows of a pilothouse, which protrudes from the topside of the Nautilus's hull and is fitted with biconvex glass."

"Is glass capable of resisting such pressures?"

"Perfectly capable. Though fragile on impact, crystal can still offer considerable resistance. In 1864, during experiments on fishing by electric light in the middle of the North Sea, glass panes less than seven millimeters thick were seen to resist a pressure of sixteen atmospheres, all the while letting through strong, heat–generating rays whose warmth was unevenly distributed. Now then, I use glass windows measuring no less than twenty–one centimeters at their centers; in other words, they've thirty times the thickness."

"Fair enough, captain, but if we're going to see, we need light to drive away the dark, and in the midst of the murky waters, I wonder how your helmsman can—"

"Set astern of the pilothouse is a powerful electric reflector whose rays light up the sea for a distance of half a mile."

"Oh, bravo! Bravo three times over, Captain! That explains the phosphorescent glow from this so–called narwhale that so puzzled us scientists! Pertinent to this, I'll ask you if the Nautilus's running afoul of the Scotia, which caused such a great uproar, was the result of an accidental encounter?"

"Entirely accidental, sir. I was navigating two meters beneath the surface of the water when the collision occurred. However, I could see that it had no dire consequences."

"None, sir. But as for your encounter with the Abraham Lincoln . . . ?"

"Professor, that troubled me, because it's one of the best ships in the gallant American navy, but they attacked me and I had to defend myself! All the same, I was content simply to put the frigate in a condition where it could do me no harm; it won't have any difficulty getting repairs at the nearest port."

"Ah, Commander," I exclaimed with conviction, "your Nautilus is truly a marvelous boat!"

"Yes, professor," Captain Nemo replied with genuine excitement, "and I love it as if it were my own flesh and blood! Aboard a conventional ship, facing the ocean's perils, danger lurks everywhere; on the surface of the sea, your chief sensation is the constant feeling of an underlying chasm, as the Dutchman Jansen so aptly put it; but below the waves aboard the Nautilus, your heart never fails you! There are no structural deformities to worry about, because the double hull of this boat has the rigidity of iron; no rigging to be worn out by rolling and pitching on the waves; no sails for the wind to carry off; no boilers for steam to burst open; no fires to fear, because this submersible is made of sheet iron not wood; no coal to run out of, since electricity is its mechanical force; no collisions to fear, because it navigates the watery deep all by itself; no storms to brave, because just a few meters beneath the waves, it finds absolute tranquility! There, sir. There's the ideal ship! And if it's true that the engineer has more confidence in a craft than the builder, and the builder more than the captain himself, you can understand the utter abandon with which I place my trust in this Nautilus, since I'm its captain, builder, and engineer all in one!"

Captain Nemo spoke with winning eloquence. The fire in his eyes and the passion in his gestures transfigured him. Yes, he loved his ship the same way a father loves his child!

But one question, perhaps indiscreet, naturally popped up, and I couldn't resist asking it.

"You're an engineer, then, Captain Nemo?"

"Yes, professor," he answered me. "I studied in London, Paris, and New York back in the days when I was a resident of the Earth's continents."

"But how were you able to build this wonderful Nautilus in secret?"

"Each part of it, Professor Aronnax, came from a different spot on the globe and reached me at a cover address. Its keel was forged by Creusot in France, its propeller shaft by Pen & Co. in London, the sheet–iron plates for its hull by Laird's in Liverpool, its propeller by Scott's in Glasgow. Its tanks were manufactured by Cail & Co. in Paris, its engine by Krupp in Prussia, its spur by the Motala workshops in Sweden, its precision instruments by Hart Bros. in New York, etc.; and each of these suppliers received my specifications under a different name."

"But," I went on, "once these parts were manufactured, didn't they have to be mounted and adjusted?"

"Professor, I set up my workshops on a deserted islet in midocean. There our Nautilus was completed by me and my workmen, in other words, by my gallant companions whom I've molded and educated. Then, when the operation was over, we burned every trace of our stay on that islet, which if I could have, I'd have blown up."

"From all this, may I assume that such a boat costs a fortune?"

"An iron ship, Professor Aronnax, runs ₣1,125 per metric ton. Now then, the Nautilus has a burden of 1,500 metric tons. Consequently, it cost ₣1,687,000, hence ₣2,000,000 including its accommodations, and ₣4,000,000 or ₣5,000,000 with all the collections and works of art it contains."

"One last question, Captain Nemo."

"Ask, professor."

"You're rich, then?"

"Infinitely rich, sir, and without any trouble, I could pay off the ten–billion–franc French national debt!"

I gaped at the bizarre individual who had just spoken these words. Was he playing on my credulity? Time would tell.

The Black Current

THE PART OF THE planet earth that the seas occupy has been assessed at 3,832,558 square myriameters, hence more than 38,000,000,000 hectares. This liquid mass totals 2,250,000,000 cubic miles and could form a sphere with a diameter of sixty leagues, whose weight would be three quintillion metric tons. To appreciate such a number, we should remember that a quintillion is to a billion what a billion is to one, in other words, there are as many billions in a quintillion as ones in a billion! Now then, this liquid mass nearly equals the total amount of water that has poured through all the earth's rivers for the past 40,000 years!

During prehistoric times, an era of fire was followed by an era of water. At first there was ocean everywhere. Then, during the Silurian period, the tops of mountains gradually appeared above the waves, islands emerged, disappeared beneath temporary floods, rose again, were fused to form continents, and finally the earth's geography settled into what we have today. Solid matter had wrested from liquid matter some 37,657,000 square miles, hence 12,916,000,000 hectares.

The outlines of the continents allow the seas to be divided into five major parts: the frozen Arctic and Antarctic oceans, the Indian Ocean, the Atlantic Ocean, and the Pacific Ocean.

The Pacific Ocean extends north to south between the two polar circles and east to west between America and Asia over an expanse of 145° of longitude. It's the most tranquil of the seas; its currents are wide and slow–moving, its tides moderate, its rainfall abundant. And this was the ocean that I was first destined to cross under these strangest of auspices.

"If you don't mind, professor," Captain Nemo told me, "we'll determine our exact position and fix the starting point of our voyage. It's fifteen minutes before noon. I'm going to rise to the surface of the water."

The captain pressed an electric bell three times. The pumps began to expel water from the ballast tanks; on the pressure gauge, a needle marked the decreasing pressures that indicated the Nautilus's upward progress; then the needle stopped.

"Here we are," the Captain said.

I made my way to the central companionway, which led to the platform. I climbed its metal steps, passed through the open hatches, and arrived topside on the Nautilus.

The platform emerged only eighty centimeters above the waves. The Nautilus's bow and stern boasted that spindle–shaped outline that had caused the ship to be compared appropriately to a long cigar. I noted the slight overlap of its sheet–iron plates, which resembled the scales covering the bodies of our big land reptiles. So I had a perfectly natural explanation for why, despite the best spyglasses, this boat had always been mistaken for a marine animal.

Near the middle of the platform, the skiff was half set in the ship's hull, making a slight bulge. Fore and aft stood two cupolas of moderate height, their sides slanting and partly inset with heavy biconvex glass, one reserved for the helmsman steering the Nautilus, the other for the brilliance of the powerful electric beacon lighting his way.

The sea was magnificent, the skies clear. This long aquatic vehicle could barely feel the broad undulations of the ocean. A mild breeze out of the east rippled the surface of the water. Free of all mist, the horizon was ideal for taking sights.

There was nothing to be seen. Not a reef, not an islet. No more Abraham Lincoln. A deserted immenseness.

Raising his sextant, Captain Nemo took the altitude of the sun, which would give him his latitude. He waited for a few minutes until the orb touched the rim of the horizon. While he was taking his sights, he didn't move a muscle, and the instrument couldn't have been steadier in hands made out of marble.

"Noon," he said. "Professor, whenever you're ready. . . ."

I took one last look at the sea, a little yellowish near the landing places of Japan, and I went below again to the main lounge.

There the captain fixed his position and used a chronometer to calculate his longitude, which he double–checked against his previous observations of hour angles. Then he told me:

"Professor Aronnax, we're in longitude 137° 15' west—"

"West of which meridian?" I asked quickly, hoping the captain's reply might give me a clue to his nationality.

"Sir," he answered me, "I have chronometers variously set to the meridians of Paris, Greenwich, and Washington, D.C. But in your honor, I'll use the one for Paris."

This reply told me nothing. I bowed, and the commander went on:

"We're in longitude 137° 15' west of the meridian of Paris, and latitude 30° 7' north, in other words, about 300 miles from the shores of Japan. At noon on this day of November 8, we hereby begin our voyage of exploration under the waters."

"May God be with us!" I replied.

"And now, professor," the captain added, "I'll leave you to your intellectual pursuits. I've set our course east–northeast at a depth of fifty meters. Here are some large–scale charts on which you'll be able to follow that course. The lounge is at your disposal, and with your permission, I'll take my leave."

Captain Nemo bowed. I was left to myself, lost in my thoughts. They all centered on the Nautilus's commander. Would I ever learn the nationality of this eccentric man who had boasted of having none? His sworn hate for humanity, a hate that perhaps was bent on some dreadful revenge—what had provoked it? Was he one of those unappreciated scholars, one of those geniuses "embittered by the world," as Conseil expressed it, a latter–day Galileo, or maybe one of those men of science, like America's Commander Maury, whose careers were ruined by political revolutions? I couldn't say yet. As for me, whom fate had just brought aboard his vessel, whose life he had held in the balance: he had received me coolly but hospitably. Only, he never took the hand I extended to him. He never extended his own.

For an entire hour I was deep in these musings, trying to probe this mystery that fascinated me so. Then my eyes focused on a huge world map displayed on the table, and I put my finger on the very spot where our just–determined longitude and latitude intersected.

Like the continents, the sea has its rivers. These are exclusive currents that can be identified by their temperature and color, the most remarkable being the one called the Gulf Stream. Science has defined the global paths of five chief currents: one in the north Atlantic, a second in the south Atlantic, a third in the north Pacific, a fourth in the south Pacific, and a fifth in the southern Indian Ocean. Also it's likely that a sixth current used to exist in the northern Indian Ocean, when the Caspian and Aral Seas joined up with certain large Asian lakes to form a single uniform expanse of water.

Now then, at the spot indicated on the world map, one of these seagoing rivers was rolling by, the Kuroshio of the Japanese, the Black Current: heated by perpendicular rays from the tropical sun, it leaves the Bay of Bengal, crosses the Strait of Malacca, goes up the shores of Asia, and curves into the north Pacific as far as the Aleutian Islands, carrying along trunks of camphor trees and other local items, the pure indigo of its warm waters sharply contrasting with the ocean's waves. It was this current the Nautilus was about to cross. I watched it on the map with my eyes, I saw it lose itself in the immenseness of the Pacific, and I felt myself swept along with it, when Ned Land and Conseil appeared in the lounge doorway.

My two gallant companions stood petrified at the sight of the wonders on display.

"Where are we?" the Canadian exclaimed. "In the Quebec Museum?"

"Begging master's pardon," Conseil answered, "but this seems more like the Sommerard artifacts exhibition!"

"My friends," I replied, signaling them to enter, "you're in neither Canada nor France, but securely aboard the Nautilus, fifty meters below sea level."

"If master says so, then so be it," Conseil answered. "But in all honesty, this lounge is enough to astonish even someone Flemish like myself."

"Indulge your astonishment, my friend, and have a look, because there's plenty of work here for a classifier of your talents."

Conseil needed no encouraging. Bending over the glass cases, the gallant lad was already muttering choice words from the naturalist's vocabulary: class Gastropoda, family Buccinoidea, genus Cowry, species Cypraea madagascariensis, etc.

Meanwhile Ned Land, less dedicated to conchology, questioned me about my interview with Captain Nemo. Had I discovered who he was, where he came from, where he was heading, how deep he was taking us? In short, a thousand questions I had no time to answer.

I told him everything I knew—or, rather, everything I didn't know—and I asked him what he had seen or heard on his part.

"Haven't seen or heard a thing!" the Canadian replied. "I haven't even spotted the crew of this boat. By any chance, could they be electric too?"

"Electric?"

"Oh ye gods, I'm half tempted to believe it! But back to you, Professor Aronnax," Ned Land said, still hanging on to his ideas. "Can't you tell me how many men are on board? Ten, twenty, fifty, a hundred?"

"I'm unable to answer you, Mr. Land. And trust me on this: for the time being, get rid of these notions of taking over the Nautilus or escaping from it. This boat is a masterpiece of modern technology, and I'd be sorry to have missed it! Many people would welcome the circumstances that have been handed us, just to walk in the midst of these wonders. So keep calm, and let's see what's happening around us."

"See!" the harpooner exclaimed. "There's nothing to see, nothing we'll ever see from this sheet–iron prison! We're simply running around blindfolded—"

Ned Land was just pronouncing these last words when we were suddenly plunged into darkness, utter darkness. The ceiling lights went out so quickly, my eyes literally ached, just as if we had experienced the opposite sensation of going from the deepest gloom to the brightest sunlight.

We stood stock–still, not knowing what surprise was waiting for us, whether pleasant or unpleasant. But a sliding sound became audible. You could tell that some panels were shifting over the Nautilus's sides.

"It's the beginning of the end!" Ned Land said.

". . . order Hydromedusa," Conseil muttered.

Suddenly, through two oblong openings, daylight appeared on both sides of the lounge. The liquid masses came into view, brightly lit by the ship's electric outpourings. We were separated from the sea by two panes of glass. Initially I shuddered at the thought that these fragile partitions could break; but strong copper bands secured them, giving them nearly infinite resistance.

The sea was clearly visible for a one–mile radius around the Nautilus. What a sight! What pen could describe it? Who could portray the effects of this light through these translucent sheets of water, the subtlety of its progressive shadings into the ocean's upper and lower strata?

The transparency of salt water has long been recognized. Its clarity is believed to exceed that of spring water. The mineral and organic substances it holds in suspension actually increase its translucency. In certain parts of the Caribbean Sea, you can see the sandy bottom with startling distinctness as deep as 145 meters down, and the penetrating power of the sun's rays seems to give out only at a depth of 300 meters. But in this fluid setting traveled by the Nautilus, our electric glow was being generated in the very heart of the waves. It was no longer illuminated water, it was liquid light.

If we accept the hypotheses of the microbiologist Ehrenberg—who believes that these underwater depths are lit up by phosphorescent organisms—nature has certainly saved one of her most prodigious sights for residents of the sea, and I could judge for myself from the thousandfold play of the light. On both sides I had windows opening over these unexplored depths. The darkness in the lounge enhanced the brightness outside, and we stared as if this clear glass were the window of an immense aquarium.

The Nautilus seemed to be standing still. This was due to the lack of landmarks. But streaks of water, parted by the ship's spur, sometimes threaded before our eyes with extraordinary speed.

In wonderment, we leaned on our elbows before these show windows, and our stunned silence remained unbroken until Conseil said:

"You wanted to see something, Ned my friend; well, now you have something to see!"

"How unusual!" the Canadian put in, setting aside his tantrums and getaway schemes while submitting to this irresistible allure. "A man would go an even greater distance just to stare at such a sight!"

"Ah!" I exclaimed. "I see our captain's way of life! He's found himself a separate world that saves its most astonishing wonders just for him!"

"But where are the fish?" the Canadian ventured to observe. "I don't see any fish!"

"Why would you care, Ned my friend?" Conseil replied. "Since you have no knowledge of them."

"Me? A fisherman!" Ned Land exclaimed.

And on this subject a dispute arose between the two friends, since both were knowledgeable about fish, but from totally different standpoints.

Everyone knows that fish make up the fourth and last class in the vertebrate branch. They have been quite aptly defined as:

"cold–blooded vertebrates with a double circulatory system, breathing through gills, and designed to live in water."

They consist of two distinct series: the series of bony fish, in other words, those whose spines have vertebrae made of bone; and cartilaginous fish, in other words, those whose spines have vertebrae made of cartilage.

Possibly the Canadian was familiar with this distinction, but Conseil knew far more about it; and since he and Ned were now fast friends, he just had to show off. So he told the harpooner:

"Ned my friend, you're a slayer of fish, a highly skilled fisherman. You've caught a large number of these fascinating animals. But I'll bet you don't know how they're classified."

"Sure I do," the harpooner replied in all seriousness. "They're classified into fish we eat and fish we don't eat!"

"Spoken like a true glutton," Conseil replied. "But tell me, are you familiar with the differences between bony fish and cartilaginous fish?"

"Just maybe, Conseil."

"And how about the subdivisions of these two large classes?"

"I haven't the foggiest notion," the Canadian replied.

"All right, listen and learn, Ned my friend! Bony fish are subdivided into six orders. Primo, the acanthopterygians, whose upper jaw is fully formed and free–moving, and whose gills take the shape of a comb. This order consists of fifteen families, in other words, three–quarters of all known fish. Example: the common perch."

"Pretty fair eating," Ned Land replied.

"Secundo," Conseil went on, "the abdominals, whose pelvic fins hang under the abdomen to the rear of the pectorals but aren't attached to the shoulder bone, an order that's divided into five families and makes up the great majority of freshwater fish. Examples: carp, pike."

"Ugh!" the Canadian put in with distinct scorn. "You can keep the freshwater fish!"

"Tertio," Conseil said, "the subbrachians, whose pelvic fins are attached under the pectorals and hang directly from the shoulder bone. This order contains four families. Examples: flatfish such as sole, turbot, dab, plaice, brill, etc."

"Excellent, really excellent!" the harpooner exclaimed, interested in fish only from an edible viewpoint.

"Quarto," Conseil went on, unabashed, "the apods, with long bodies that lack pelvic fins and are covered by a heavy, often glutinous skin, an order consisting of only one family. Examples: common eels and electric eels."

"So–so, just so–so!" Ned Land replied.

"Quinto," Conseil said, "the lophobranchians, which have fully formed, free–moving jaws but whose gills consist of little tufts arranged in pairs along their gill arches. This order includes only one family. Examples: seahorses and dragonfish."

"Bad, very bad!" the harpooner replied.

"Sexto and last," Conseil said, "the plectognaths, whose maxillary bone is firmly attached to the side of the intermaxillary that forms the jaw, and whose palate arch is locked to the skull by sutures that render the jaw immovable, an order lacking true pelvic fins and which consists of two families. Examples: puffers and moonfish."

"They're an insult to a frying pan!" the Canadian exclaimed.

"Are you grasping all this, Ned my friend?" asked the scholarly Conseil.

"Not a lick of it, Conseil my friend," the harpooner replied. "But keep going, because you fill me with fascination."

"As for cartilaginous fish," Conseil went on unflappably, "they consist of only three orders."

"Good news," Ned put in.

"Primo, the cyclostomes, whose jaws are fused into a flexible ring and whose gill openings are simply a large number of holes, an order consisting of only one family. Example: the lamprey."

"An acquired taste," Ned Land replied.

"Secundo, the selacians, with gills resembling those of the cyclostomes but whose lower jaw is free–moving. This order, which is the most important in the class, consists of two families. Examples: the ray and the shark."

"What!" Ned Land exclaimed. "Rays and man–eaters in the same order? Well, Conseil my friend, on behalf of the rays, I wouldn't advise you to put them in the same fish tank!"

"Tertio," Conseil replied, "The sturionians, whose gill opening is the usual single slit adorned with a gill cover, an order consisting of four genera. Example: the sturgeon."

"Ah, Conseil my friend, you saved the best for last, in my opinion anyhow! And that's all of 'em?"

"Yes, my gallant Ned," Conseil replied. "And note well, even when one has grasped all this, one still knows next to nothing, because these families are subdivided into genera, subgenera, species, varieties—"

"All right, Conseil my friend," the harpooner said, leaning toward the glass panel, "here come a couple of your varieties now!"

"Yes! Fish!" Conseil exclaimed. "One would think he was in front of an aquarium!"

"No," I replied, "because an aquarium is nothing more than a cage, and these fish are as free as birds in the air!"

"Well, Conseil my friend, identify them! Start naming them!" Ned Land exclaimed.

"Me?" Conseil replied. "I'm unable to! That's my employer's bailiwick!"

And in truth, although the fine lad was a classifying maniac, he was no naturalist, and I doubt that he could tell a bonito from a tuna. In short, he was the exact opposite of the Canadian, who knew nothing about classification but could instantly put a name to any fish.

"A triggerfish," I said.

"It's a Chinese triggerfish," Ned Land replied.

"Genus Balistes, family Scleroderma, order Plectognatha," Conseil muttered.

Assuredly, Ned and Conseil in combination added up to one outstanding naturalist.

The Canadian was not mistaken. Cavorting around the Nautilus was a school of triggerfish with flat bodies, grainy skins, armed with stings on their dorsal fins, and with four prickly rows of quills quivering on both sides of their tails. Nothing could have been more wonderful than the skin covering them: white underneath, gray above, with spots of gold sparkling in the dark eddies of the waves. Around them, rays were undulating like sheets flapping in the wind, and among these I spotted, much to my glee, a Chinese ray, yellowish on its topside, a dainty pink on its belly, and armed with three stings behind its eyes; a rare species whose very existence was still doubted in Lacépède's day, since that pioneering classifier of fish had seen one only in a portfolio of Japanese drawings.

For two hours a whole aquatic army escorted the Nautilus. In the midst of their leaping and cavorting, while they competed with each other in beauty, radiance, and speed, I could distinguish some green wrasse, bewhiskered mullet marked with pairs of black lines, white gobies from the genus Eleotris with curved caudal fins and violet spots on the back, wonderful Japanese mackerel from the genus Scomber with blue bodies and silver heads, glittering azure goldfish whose name by itself gives their full description, several varieties of porgy or gilthead (some banded gilthead with fins variously blue and yellow, some with horizontal heraldic bars and enhanced by a black strip around their caudal area, some with color zones and elegantly corseted in their six waistbands), trumpetfish with flutelike beaks that looked like genuine seafaring woodcocks and were sometimes a meter long, Japanese salamanders, serpentine moray eels from the genus Echidna that were six feet long with sharp little eyes and a huge mouth bristling with teeth; etc.

Our wonderment stayed at an all–time fever pitch. Our exclamations were endless. Ned identified the fish, Conseil classified them, and as for me, I was in ecstasy over the verve of their movements and the beauty of their forms. Never before had I been given the chance to glimpse these animals alive and at large in their native element.

Given such a complete collection from the seas of Japan and China, I won't mention every variety that passed before our dazzled eyes. More numerous than birds in the air, these fish raced right up to us, no doubt attracted by the brilliant glow of our electric beacon.

Suddenly daylight appeared in the lounge. The sheet–iron panels slid shut. The magical vision disappeared. But for a good while I kept dreaming away, until the moment my eyes focused on the instruments hanging on the wall. The compass still showed our heading as east–northeast, the pressure gauge indicated a pressure of five atmospheres (corresponding to a depth of fifty meters), and the electric log gave our speed as fifteen miles per hour.

I waited for Captain Nemo. But he didn't appear. The clock marked the hour of five.

Ned Land and Conseil returned to their cabin. As for me, I repaired to my stateroom. There I found dinner ready for me. It consisted of turtle soup made from the daintiest hawksbill, a red mullet with white, slightly flaky flesh, whose liver, when separately prepared, makes delicious eating, plus loin of imperial angelfish, whose flavor struck me as even better than salmon.

I spent the evening in reading, writing, and thinking. Then drowsiness overtook me, I stretched out on my eelgrass mattress, and I fell into a deep slumber, while the Nautilus glided through the swiftly flowing Black Current.

An Invitation in Writing

THE NEXT DAY, November 9, I woke up only after a long, twelve–hour slumber. Conseil, a creature of habit, came to ask "how master's night went," and to offer his services. He had left his Canadian friend sleeping like a man who had never done anything else.

I let the gallant lad babble as he pleased, without giving him much in the way of a reply. I was concerned about Captain Nemo's absence during our session the previous afternoon, and I hoped to see him again today.

Soon I had put on my clothes, which were woven from strands of seashell tissue. More than once their composition provoked comments from Conseil. I informed him that they were made from the smooth, silken filaments with which the fan mussel, a type of seashell quite abundant along Mediterranean beaches, attaches itself to rocks. In olden times, fine fabrics, stockings, and gloves were made from such filaments, because they were both very soft and very warm. So the Nautilus's crew could dress themselves at little cost, without needing a thing from cotton growers, sheep, or silkworms on shore.

As soon as I was dressed, I made my way to the main lounge. It was deserted.

I dove into studying the conchological treasures amassed inside the glass cases. I also investigated the huge plant albums that were filled with the rarest marine herbs, which, although they were pressed and dried, still kept their wonderful colors. Among these valuable water plants, I noted various seaweed: some Cladostephus verticillatus, peacock's tails, fig–leafed caulerpa, grain–bearing beauty bushes, delicate rosetangle tinted scarlet, sea colander arranged into fan shapes, mermaid's cups that looked like the caps of squat mushrooms and for years had been classified among the zoophytes; in short, a complete series of algae.

The entire day passed without my being honored by a visit from Captain Nemo. The panels in the lounge didn't open. Perhaps they didn't want us to get tired of these beautiful things.

The Nautilus kept to an east–northeasterly heading, a speed of twelve miles per hour, and a depth between fifty and sixty meters.

Next day, November 10: the same neglect, the same solitude. I didn't see a soul from the crew. Ned and Conseil spent the better part of the day with me. They were astonished at the captain's inexplicable absence. Was this eccentric man ill? Did he want to change his plans concerning us?

But after all, as Conseil noted, we enjoyed complete freedom, we were daintily and abundantly fed. Our host had kept to the terms of his agreement. We couldn't complain, and moreover the very uniqueness of our situation had such generous rewards in store for us, we had no grounds for criticism.

That day I started my diary of these adventures, which has enabled me to narrate them with the most scrupulous accuracy; and one odd detail: I wrote it on paper manufactured from marine eelgrass.

Early in the morning on November 11, fresh air poured through the Nautilus's interior, informing me that we had returned to the surface of the ocean to renew our oxygen supply. I headed for the central companionway and climbed onto the platform.

It was six o'clock. I found the weather overcast, the sea gray but calm. Hardly a billow. I hoped to encounter Captain Nemo there—would he come? I saw only the helmsman imprisoned in his glass–windowed pilothouse. Seated on the ledge furnished by the hull of the skiff, I inhaled the sea's salty aroma with great pleasure.

Little by little, the mists were dispersed under the action of the sun's rays. The radiant orb cleared the eastern horizon. Under its gaze, the sea caught on fire like a trail of gunpowder. Scattered on high, the clouds were colored in bright, wonderfully shaded hues, and numerous "ladyfingers" warned of daylong winds.

But what were mere winds to this Nautilus, which no storms could intimidate!

So I was marveling at this delightful sunrise, so life–giving and cheerful, when I heard someone climbing onto the platform.

I was prepared to greet Captain Nemo, but it was his chief officer who appeared—whom I had already met during our first visit with the captain. He advanced over the platform, not seeming to notice my presence. A powerful spyglass to his eye, he scrutinized every point of the horizon with the utmost care. Then, his examination over, he approached the hatch and pronounced a phrase whose exact wording follows below. I remember it because, every morning, it was repeated under the same circumstances. It ran like this:

"Nautron respoc lorni virch."

What it meant I was unable to say.

These words pronounced, the chief officer went below again. I thought the Nautilus was about to resume its underwater navigating. So I went down the hatch and back through the gangways to my stateroom.

Five days passed in this way with no change in our situation. Every morning I climbed onto the platform. The same phrase was pronounced by the same individual. Captain Nemo did not appear.

I was pursuing the policy that we had seen the last of him, when on November 16, while reentering my stateroom with Ned and Conseil, I found a note addressed to me on the table.

I opened it impatiently. It was written in a script that was clear and neat but a bit "Old English" in style, its characters reminding me of German calligraphy.

The note was worded as follows:

Professor Aronnax

Aboard the Nautilus

November 16, 1867

Captain Nemo invites Professor Aronnax on a hunting trip that will take place tomorrow morning in his Crespo Island forests. He hopes nothing will prevent the professor from attending, and he looks forward with pleasure to the professor's companions joining him.

CAPTAIN NEMO,

Commander of the Nautilus.

"A hunting trip!" Ned exclaimed.

"And in his forests on Crespo Island!" Conseil added.

"But does this mean the old boy goes ashore?" Ned Land went on.

"That seems to be the gist of it," I said, rereading the letter.

"Well, we've got to accept!" the Canadian answered. "Once we're on solid ground, we'll figure out a course of action. Besides, it wouldn't pain me to eat a couple slices of fresh venison!"

Without trying to reconcile the contradictions between Captain Nemo's professed horror of continents or islands and his invitation to go hunting in a forest, I was content to reply:

"First let's look into this Crespo Island."

I consulted the world map; and in latitude 32° 40' north and longitude 167° 50' west, I found an islet that had been discovered in 1801 by Captain Crespo, which old Spanish charts called Rocca de la Plata, in other words, "Silver Rock." So we were about 1,800 miles from our starting point, and by a slight change of heading, the Nautilus was bringing us back toward the southeast.

I showed my companions this small, stray rock in the middle of the north Pacific.

"If Captain Nemo does sometimes go ashore," I told them, "at least he only picks desert islands!"

Ned Land shook his head without replying; then he and Conseil left me. After supper was served me by the mute and emotionless steward, I fell asleep; but not without some anxieties.

When I woke up the next day, November 17, I sensed that the Nautilus was completely motionless. I dressed hurriedly and entered the main lounge.

Captain Nemo was there waiting for me. He stood up, bowed, and asked if it suited me to come along.

Since he made no allusion to his absence the past eight days, I also refrained from mentioning it, and I simply answered that my companions and I were ready to go with him.

"Only, sir," I added, "I'll take the liberty of addressing a question to you."

"Address away, Professor Aronnax, and if I'm able to answer, I will."

"Well then, Captain, how is it that you've severed all ties with the shore, yet you own forests on Crespo Island?"

"Professor," the captain answered me, "these forests of mine don't bask in the heat and light of the sun. They aren't frequented by lions, tigers, panthers, or other quadrupeds. They're known only to me. They grow only for me. These forests aren't on land, they're actual underwater forests."

"Underwater forests!" I exclaimed.

"Yes, professor."

"And you're offering to take me to them?"

"Precisely."

"On foot?"

"Without getting your feet wet."

"While hunting?"

"While hunting."

"Rifles in hand?"

"Rifles in hand."

I stared at the Nautilus's commander with an air anything but flattering to the man.

"Assuredly," I said to myself, "he's contracted some mental illness. He's had a fit that's lasted eight days and isn't over even yet. What a shame! I liked him better eccentric than insane!"

These thoughts were clearly readable on my face; but Captain Nemo remained content with inviting me to follow him, and I did so like a man resigned to the worst.

We arrived at the dining room, where we found breakfast served.

"Professor Aronnax," the captain told me, "I beg you to share my breakfast without formality. We can chat while we eat. Because, although I promised you a stroll in my forests, I made no pledge to arrange for your encountering a restaurant there. Accordingly, eat your breakfast like a man who'll probably eat dinner only when it's extremely late."

I did justice to this meal. It was made up of various fish and some slices of sea cucumber, that praiseworthy zoophyte, all garnished with such highly appetizing seaweed as the Porphyra laciniata and the Laurencia primafetida. Our beverage consisted of clear water to which, following the captain's example, I added some drops of a fermented liquor extracted by the Kamchatka process from the seaweed known by name as Rhodymenia palmata.

At first Captain Nemo ate without pronouncing a single word. Then he told me:

"Professor, when I proposed that you go hunting in my Crespo forests, you thought I was contradicting myself. When I informed you that it was an issue of underwater forests, you thought I'd gone insane. Professor, you must never make snap judgments about your fellow man."

"But, Captain, believe me—"

"Kindly listen to me, and you'll see if you have grounds for accusing me of insanity or self–contradiction."

"I'm all attention."

"Professor, you know as well as I do that a man can live underwater so long as he carries with him his own supply of breathable air. For underwater work projects, the workman wears a waterproof suit with his head imprisoned in a metal capsule, while he receives air from above by means of force pumps and flow regulators."

"That's the standard equipment for a diving suit," I said.

"Correct, but under such conditions the man has no freedom. He's attached to a pump that sends him air through an india–rubber hose; it's an actual chain that fetters him to the shore, and if we were to be bound in this way to the Nautilus, we couldn't go far either."

"Then how do you break free?" I asked.

"We use the Rouquayrol–Denayrouze device, invented by two of your fellow countrymen but refined by me for my own special uses, thereby enabling you to risk these new physiological conditions without suffering any organic disorders. It consists of a tank built from heavy sheet iron in which I store air under a pressure of fifty atmospheres. This tank is fastened to the back by means of straps, like a soldier's knapsack. Its top part forms a box where the air is regulated by a bellows mechanism and can be released only at its proper tension. In the Rouquayrol device that has been in general use, two india–rubber hoses leave this box and feed to a kind of tent that imprisons the operator's nose and mouth; one hose is for the entrance of air to be inhaled, the other for the exit of air to be exhaled, and the tongue closes off the former or the latter depending on the breather's needs. But in my case, since I face considerable pressures at the bottom of the sea, I needed to enclose my head in a copper sphere, like those found on standard diving suits, and the two hoses for inhalation and exhalation now feed to that sphere."

"That's perfect, Captain Nemo, but the air you carry must be quickly depleted; and once it contains no more than 15% oxygen, it becomes unfit for breathing."

"Surely, but as I told you, Professor Aronnax, the Nautilus's pumps enable me to store air under considerable pressure, and given this circumstance, the tank on my diving equipment can supply breathable air for nine or ten hours."

"I've no more objections to raise," I replied. "I'll only ask you, Captain: how can you light your way at the bottom of the ocean?"

"With the Ruhmkorff device, Professor Aronnax. If the first is carried on the back, the second is fastened to the belt. It consists of a Bunsen battery that I activate not with potassium dichromate but with sodium. An induction coil gathers the electricity generated and directs it to a specially designed lantern. In this lantern one finds a glass spiral that contains only a residue of carbon dioxide gas. When the device is operating, this gas becomes luminous and gives off a continuous whitish light. Thus provided for, I breathe and I see."

"Captain Nemo, to my every objection you give such crushing answers, I'm afraid to entertain a single doubt. However, though I have no choice but to accept both the Rouquayrol and Ruhmkorff devices, I'd like to register some reservations about the rifle with which you'll equip me."

"But it isn't a rifle that uses gunpowder," the captain replied.

"Then it's an air gun?"

"Surely. How can I make gunpowder on my ship when I have no saltpeter, sulfur, or charcoal?"

"Even so," I replied, "to fire underwater in a medium that's 855 times denser than air, you'd have to overcome considerable resistance."

"That doesn't necessarily follow. There are certain Fulton–style guns perfected by the Englishmen Philippe–Coles and Burley, the Frenchman Furcy, and the Italian Landi; they're equipped with a special system of airtight fastenings and can fire in underwater conditions. But I repeat: having no gunpowder, I've replaced it with air at high pressure, which is abundantly supplied me by the Nautilus's pumps."

"But this air must be swiftly depleted."

"Well, in a pinch can't my Rouquayrol tank supply me with more? All I have to do is draw it from an ad hoc spigot. Besides, Professor Aronnax, you'll see for yourself that during these underwater hunting trips, we make no great expenditure of either air or bullets."

"But it seems to me that in this semidarkness, amid this liquid that's so dense in comparison to the atmosphere, a gunshot couldn't carry far and would prove fatal only with difficulty!"

"On the contrary, sir, with this rifle every shot is fatal; and as soon as the animal is hit, no matter how lightly, it falls as if struck by lightning."

"Why?"

"Because this rifle doesn't shoot ordinary bullets but little glass capsules invented by the Austrian chemist Leniebroek, and I have a considerable supply of them. These glass capsules are covered with a strip of steel and weighted with a lead base; they're genuine little Leyden jars charged with high–voltage electricity. They go off at the slightest impact, and the animal, no matter how strong, drops dead. I might add that these capsules are no bigger than number 4 shot, and the chamber of any ordinary rifle could hold ten of them."

"I'll quit debating," I replied, getting up from the table. "And all that's left is for me to shoulder my rifle. So where you go, I'll go."

Captain Nemo led me to the Nautilus's stern, and passing by Ned and Conseil's cabin, I summoned my two companions, who instantly followed us.

Then we arrived at a cell located within easy access of the engine room; in this cell we were to get dressed for our stroll.

Strolling the Plains

THIS CELL, properly speaking, was the Nautilus's arsenal and wardrobe. Hanging from its walls, a dozen diving outfits were waiting for anybody who wanted to take a stroll.

After seeing these, Ned Land exhibited an obvious distaste for the idea of putting one on.

"But my gallant Ned," I told him, "the forests of Crespo Island are simply underwater forests!"

"Oh great!" put in the disappointed harpooner, watching his dreams of fresh meat fade away. "And you, Professor Aronnax, are you going to stick yourself inside these clothes?"

"It has to be, Mr. Ned."

"Have it your way, sir," the harpooner replied, shrugging his shoulders. "But speaking for myself, I'll never get into those things unless they force me!"

"No one will force you, Mr. Land," Captain Nemo said.

"And is Conseil going to risk it?" Ned asked.

"Where master goes, I go," Conseil replied.

At the captain's summons, two crewmen came to help us put on these heavy, waterproof clothes, made from seamless india rubber and expressly designed to bear considerable pressures. They were like suits of armor that were both yielding and resistant, you might say. These clothes consisted of jacket and pants. The pants ended in bulky footwear adorned with heavy lead soles. The fabric of the jacket was reinforced with copper mail that shielded the chest, protected it from the water's pressure, and allowed the lungs to function freely; the sleeves ended in supple gloves that didn't impede hand movements.

These perfected diving suits, it was easy to see, were a far cry from such misshapen costumes as the cork breastplates, leather jumpers, seagoing tunics, barrel helmets, etc., invented and acclaimed in the 18th century.

Conseil and I were soon dressed in these diving suits, as were Captain Nemo and one of his companions—a herculean type who must have been prodigiously strong. All that remained was to encase one's head in its metal sphere. But before proceeding with this operation, I asked the captain for permission to examine the rifles set aside for us.

One of the Nautilus's men presented me with a streamlined rifle whose butt was boilerplate steel, hollow inside, and of fairly large dimensions. This served as a tank for the compressed air, which a trigger–operated valve could release into the metal chamber. In a groove where the butt was heaviest, a cartridge clip held some twenty electric bullets that, by means of a spring, automatically took their places in the barrel of the rifle. As soon as one shot had been fired, another was ready to go off.

"Captain Nemo," I said, "this is an ideal, easy–to–use weapon. I ask only to put it to the test. But how will we reach the bottom of the sea?"

"Right now, professor, the Nautilus is aground in ten meters of water, and we've only to depart."

"But how will we set out?"

"You'll see."

Captain Nemo inserted his cranium into its spherical headgear. Conseil and I did the same, but not without hearing the Canadian toss us a sarcastic "happy hunting." On top, the suit ended in a collar of threaded copper onto which the metal helmet was screwed. Three holes, protected by heavy glass, allowed us to see in any direction with simply a turn of the head inside the sphere. Placed on our backs, the Rouquayrol device went into operation as soon as it was in position, and for my part, I could breathe with ease.

The Ruhmkorff lamp hanging from my belt, my rifle in hand, I was ready to go forth. But in all honesty, while imprisoned in these heavy clothes and nailed to the deck by my lead soles, it was impossible for me to take a single step.

But this circumstance had been foreseen, because I felt myself propelled into a little room adjoining the wardrobe. Towed in the same way, my companions went with me. I heard a door with watertight seals close after us, and we were surrounded by profound darkness.

After some minutes a sharp hissing reached my ears. I felt a distinct sensation of cold rising from my feet to my chest. Apparently a stopcock inside the boat was letting in water from outside, which overran us and soon filled up the room. Contrived in the Nautilus's side, a second door then opened. We were lit by a subdued light. An instant later our feet were treading the bottom of the sea.

And now, how can I convey the impressions left on me by this stroll under the waters. Words are powerless to describe such wonders! When even the painter's brush can't depict the effects unique to the liquid element, how can the writer's pen hope to reproduce them?

Captain Nemo walked in front, and his companion followed us a few steps to the rear. Conseil and I stayed next to each other, as if daydreaming that through our metal carapaces, a little polite conversation might still be possible! Already I no longer felt the bulkiness of my clothes, footwear, and air tank, nor the weight of the heavy sphere inside which my head was rattling like an almond in its shell. Once immersed in water, all these objects lost a part of their weight equal to the weight of the liquid they displaced, and thanks to this law of physics discovered by Archimedes, I did just fine. I was no longer an inert mass, and I had, comparatively speaking, great freedom of movement.

Lighting up the seafloor even thirty feet beneath the surface of the ocean, the sun astonished me with its power. The solar rays easily crossed this aqueous mass and dispersed its dark colors. I could easily distinguish objects 100 meters away. Farther on, the bottom was tinted with fine shades of ultramarine; then, off in the distance, it turned blue and faded in the midst of a hazy darkness. Truly, this water surrounding me was just a kind of air, denser than the atmosphere on land but almost as transparent. Above me I could see the calm surface of the ocean.

We were walking on sand that was fine–grained and smooth, not wrinkled like beach sand, which preserves the impressions left by the waves. This dazzling carpet was a real mirror, throwing back the sun's rays with startling intensity. The outcome: an immense vista of reflections that penetrated every liquid molecule. Will anyone believe me if I assert that at this thirty–foot depth, I could see as if it was broad daylight?

For a quarter of an hour, I trod this blazing sand, which was strewn with tiny crumbs of seashell. Looming like a long reef, the Nautilus's hull disappeared little by little, but when night fell in the midst of the waters, the ship's beacon would surely facilitate our return on board, since its rays carried with perfect distinctness. This effect is difficult to understand for anyone who has never seen light beams so sharply defined on shore. There the dust that saturates the air gives such rays the appearance of a luminous fog; but above water as well as underwater, shafts of electric light are transmitted with incomparable clarity.

Meanwhile we went ever onward, and these vast plains of sand seemed endless. My hands parted liquid curtains that closed again behind me, and my footprints faded swiftly under the water's pressure.

Soon, scarcely blurred by their distance from us, the forms of some objects took shape before my eyes. I recognized the lower slopes of some magnificent rocks carpeted by the finest zoophyte specimens, and right off, I was struck by an effect unique to this medium.

By then it was ten o'clock in the morning. The sun's rays hit the surface of the waves at a fairly oblique angle, decomposing by refraction as though passing through a prism; and when this light came in contact with flowers, rocks, buds, seashells, and polyps, the edges of these objects were shaded with all seven hues of the solar spectrum. This riot of rainbow tints was a wonder, a feast for the eyes: a genuine kaleidoscope of red, green, yellow, orange, violet, indigo, and blue; in short, the whole palette of a color–happy painter! If only I had been able to share with Conseil the intense sensations rising in my brain, competing with him in exclamations of wonderment! If only I had known, like Captain Nemo and his companion, how to exchange thoughts by means of prearranged signals! So, for lack of anything better, I talked to myself: I declaimed inside this copper box that topped my head, spending more air on empty words than was perhaps advisable.

Conseil, like me, had stopped before this splendid sight. Obviously, in the presence of these zoophyte and mollusk specimens, the fine lad was classifying his head off. Polyps and echinoderms abounded on the seafloor: various isis coral, cornularian coral living in isolation, tufts of virginal genus Oculina formerly known by the name "white coral," prickly fungus coral in the shape of mushrooms, sea anemone holding on by their muscular disks, providing a literal flowerbed adorned by jellyfish from the genus Porpita wearing collars of azure tentacles, and starfish that spangled the sand, including veinlike feather stars from the genus Asterophyton that were like fine lace embroidered by the hands of water nymphs, their festoons swaying to the faint undulations caused by our walking. It filled me with real chagrin to crush underfoot the gleaming mollusk samples that littered the seafloor by the thousands: concentric comb shells, hammer shells, coquina (seashells that actually hop around), top–shell snails, red helmet shells, angel–wing conchs, sea hares, and so many other exhibits from this inexhaustible ocean. But we had to keep walking, and we went forward while overhead there scudded schools of Portuguese men–of–war that let their ultramarine tentacles drift in their wakes, medusas whose milky white or dainty pink parasols were festooned with azure tassels and shaded us from the sun's rays, plus jellyfish of the species Pelagia panopyra that, in the dark, would have strewn our path with phosphorescent glimmers!

All these wonders I glimpsed in the space of a quarter of a mile, barely pausing, following Captain Nemo whose gestures kept beckoning me onward. Soon the nature of the seafloor changed. The plains of sand were followed by a bed of that viscous slime Americans call "ooze," which is composed exclusively of seashells rich in limestone or silica. Then we crossed a prairie of algae, open–sea plants that the waters hadn't yet torn loose, whose vegetation grew in wild profusion. Soft to the foot, these densely textured lawns would have rivaled the most luxuriant carpets woven by the hand of man. But while this greenery was sprawling under our steps, it didn't neglect us overhead. The surface of the water was crisscrossed by a floating arbor of marine plants belonging to that superabundant algae family that numbers more than 2,000 known species. I saw long ribbons of fucus drifting above me, some globular, others tubular: Laurencia, Cladostephus with the slenderest foliage, Rhodymenia palmata resembling the fan shapes of cactus. I observed that green–colored plants kept closer to the surface of the sea, while reds occupied a medium depth, which left blacks and browns in charge of designing gardens and flowerbeds in the ocean's lower strata.

These algae are a genuine prodigy of creation, one of the wonders of world flora. This family produces both the biggest and smallest vegetables in the world. Because, just as 40,000 near–invisible buds have been counted in one five–square–millimeter space, so also have fucus plants been gathered that were over 500 meters long!

We had been gone from the Nautilus for about an hour and a half. It was almost noon. I spotted this fact in the perpendicularity of the sun's rays, which were no longer refracted. The magic of these solar colors disappeared little by little, with emerald and sapphire shades vanishing from our surroundings altogether. We walked with steady steps that rang on the seafloor with astonishing intensity. The tiniest sounds were transmitted with a speed to which the ear is unaccustomed on shore. In fact, water is a better conductor of sound than air, and under the waves noises carry four times as fast.

Just then the seafloor began to slope sharply downward. The light took on a uniform hue. We reached a depth of 100 meters, by which point we were undergoing a pressure of ten atmospheres. But my diving clothes were built along such lines that I never suffered from this pressure. I felt only a certain tightness in the joints of my fingers, and even this discomfort soon disappeared. As for the exhaustion bound to accompany a two–hour stroll in such unfamiliar trappings—it was nil. Helped by the water, my movements were executed with startling ease.

Arriving at this 300–foot depth, I still detected the sun's rays, but just barely. Their intense brilliance had been followed by a reddish twilight, a midpoint between day and night. But we could see well enough to find our way, and it still wasn't necessary to activate the Ruhmkorff device.

Just then Captain Nemo stopped. He waited until I joined him, then he pointed a finger at some dark masses outlined in the shadows a short distance away.

"It's the forest of Crespo Island," I thought; and I was not mistaken.

An Underwater Forest

WE HAD FINALLY arrived on the outskirts of this forest, surely one of the finest in Captain Nemo's immense domains. He regarded it as his own and had laid the same claim to it that, in the first days of the world, the first men had to their forests on land. Besides, who else could dispute his ownership of this underwater property? What other, bolder pioneer would come, ax in hand, to clear away its dark underbrush?

This forest was made up of big treelike plants, and when we entered beneath their huge arches, my eyes were instantly struck by the unique arrangement of their branches—an arrangement that I had never before encountered.

None of the weeds carpeting the seafloor, none of the branches bristling from the shrubbery, crept, or leaned, or stretched on a horizontal plane. They all rose right up toward the surface of the ocean. Every filament or ribbon, no matter how thin, stood ramrod straight. Fucus plants and creepers were growing in stiff perpendicular lines, governed by the density of the element that generated them. After I parted them with my hands, these otherwise motionless plants would shoot right back to their original positions. It was the regime of verticality.

I soon grew accustomed to this bizarre arrangement, likewise to the comparative darkness surrounding us. The seafloor in this forest was strewn with sharp chunks of stone that were hard to avoid. Here the range of underwater flora seemed pretty comprehensive to me, as well as more abundant than it might have been in the arctic or tropical zones, where such exhibits are less common. But for a few minutes I kept accidentally confusing the two kingdoms, mistaking zoophytes for water plants, animals for vegetables. And who hasn't made the same blunder? Flora and fauna are so closely associated in the underwater world!

I observed that all these exhibits from the vegetable kingdom were attached to the seafloor by only the most makeshift methods. They had no roots and didn't care which solid objects secured them, sand, shells, husks, or pebbles; they didn't ask their hosts for sustenance, just a point of purchase. These plants are entirely self–propagating, and the principle of their existence lies in the water that sustains and nourishes them. In place of leaves, most of them sprouted blades of unpredictable shape, which were confined to a narrow gamut of colors consisting only of pink, crimson, green, olive, tan, and brown. There I saw again, but not yet pressed and dried like the Nautilus's specimens, some peacock's tails spread open like fans to stir up a cooling breeze, scarlet rosetangle, sea tangle stretching out their young and edible shoots, twisting strings of kelp from the genus Nereocystis that bloomed to a height of fifteen meters, bouquets of mermaid's cups whose stems grew wider at the top, and a number of other open–sea plants, all without flowers. "It's an odd anomaly in this bizarre element!" as one witty naturalist puts it. "The animal kingdom blossoms, and the vegetable kingdom doesn't!"

These various types of shrubbery were as big as trees in the temperate zones; in the damp shade between them, there were clustered actual bushes of moving flowers, hedges of zoophytes in which there grew stony coral striped with twisting furrows, yellowish sea anemone from the genus Caryophylia with translucent tentacles, plus anemone with grassy tufts from the genus Zoantharia; and to complete the illusion, minnows flitted from branch to branch like a swarm of hummingbirds, while there rose underfoot, like a covey of snipe, yellow fish from the genus Lepisocanthus with bristling jaws and sharp scales, flying gurnards, and pinecone fish.

Near one o'clock, Captain Nemo gave the signal to halt. Speaking for myself, I was glad to oblige, and we stretched out beneath an arbor of winged kelp, whose long thin tendrils stood up like arrows.

This short break was a delight. It lacked only the charm of conversation. But it was impossible to speak, impossible to reply. I simply nudged my big copper headpiece against Conseil's headpiece. I saw a happy gleam in the gallant lad's eyes, and to communicate his pleasure, he jiggled around inside his carapace in the world's silliest way.

After four hours of strolling, I was quite astonished not to feel any intense hunger. What kept my stomach in such a good mood I'm unable to say. But, in exchange, I experienced that irresistible desire for sleep that comes over every diver. Accordingly, my eyes soon closed behind their heavy glass windows and I fell into an uncontrollable doze, which until then I had been able to fight off only through the movements of our walking. Captain Nemo and his muscular companion were already stretched out in this clear crystal, setting us a fine naptime example.

. How long I was sunk in this torpor I cannot estimate; but when I awoke, it seemed as if the sun were settling toward the horizon. Captain Nemo was already up, and I had started to stretch my limbs, when an unexpected apparition brought me sharply to my feet.

A few paces away, a monstrous, meter–high sea spider was staring at me with beady eyes, poised to spring at me. Although my diving suit was heavy enough to protect me from this animal's bites, I couldn't keep back a shudder of horror. Just then Conseil woke up, together with the Nautilus's sailor. Captain Nemo alerted his companion to this hideous crustacean, which a swing of the rifle butt quickly brought down, and I watched the monster's horrible legs writhing in dreadful convulsions.

This encounter reminded me that other, more daunting animals must be lurking in these dark reaches, and my diving suit might not be adequate protection against their attacks. Such thoughts hadn't previously crossed my mind, and I was determined to keep on my guard. Meanwhile I had assumed this rest period would be the turning point in our stroll, but I was mistaken; and instead of heading back to the Nautilus, Captain Nemo continued his daring excursion.

The seafloor kept sinking, and its significantly steeper slope took us to greater depths. It must have been nearly three o'clock when we reached a narrow valley gouged between high, vertical walls and located 150 meters down. Thanks to the perfection of our equipment, we had thus gone ninety meters below the limit that nature had, until then, set on man's underwater excursions.

I say 150 meters, although I had no instruments for estimating this distance. But I knew that the sun's rays, even in the clearest seas, could reach no deeper. So at precisely this point the darkness became profound. Not a single object was visible past ten paces. Consequently, I had begun to grope my way when suddenly I saw the glow of an intense white light. Captain Nemo had just activated his electric device. His companion did likewise. Conseil and I followed suit. By turning a switch, I established contact between the induction coil and the glass spiral, and the sea, lit up by our four lanterns, was illuminated for a radius of twenty–five meters.

Captain Nemo continued to plummet into the dark depths of this forest, whose shrubbery grew ever more sparse. I observed that vegetable life was disappearing more quickly than animal life. The open–sea plants had already left behind the increasingly arid seafloor, where a prodigious number of animals were still swarming: zoophytes, articulates, mollusks, and fish.

While we were walking, I thought the lights of our Ruhmkorff devices would automatically attract some inhabitants of these dark strata. But if they did approach us, at least they kept at a distance regrettable from the hunter's standpoint. Several times I saw Captain Nemo stop and take aim with his rifle; then, after sighting down its barrel for a few seconds, he would straighten up and resume his walk.

Finally, at around four o'clock, this marvelous excursion came to an end. A wall of superb rocks stood before us, imposing in its sheer mass: a pile of gigantic stone blocks, an enormous granite cliffside pitted with dark caves but not offering a single gradient we could climb up. This was the underpinning of Crespo Island. This was land.

The captain stopped suddenly. A gesture from him brought us to a halt, and however much I wanted to clear this wall, I had to stop. Here ended the domains of Captain Nemo. He had no desire to pass beyond them. Farther on lay a part of the globe he would no longer tread underfoot.

Our return journey began. Captain Nemo resumed the lead in our little band, always heading forward without hesitation. I noted that we didn't follow the same path in returning to the Nautilus. This new route, very steep and hence very arduous, quickly took us close to the surface of the sea. But this return to the upper strata wasn't so sudden that decompression took place too quickly, which could have led to serious organic disorders and given us those internal injuries so fatal to divers. With great promptness, the light reappeared and grew stronger; and the refraction of the sun, already low on the horizon, again ringed the edges of various objects with the entire color spectrum.

At a depth of ten meters, we walked amid a swarm of small fish from every species, more numerous than birds in the air, more agile too; but no aquatic game worthy of a gunshot had yet been offered to our eyes.

Just then I saw the captain's weapon spring to his shoulder and track a moving object through the bushes. A shot went off, I heard a faint hissing, and an animal dropped a few paces away, literally struck by lightning.

It was a magnificent sea otter from the genus Enhydra, the only exclusively marine quadruped. One and a half meters long, this otter had to be worth a good high price. Its coat, chestnut brown above and silver below, would have made one of those wonderful fur pieces so much in demand in the Russian and Chinese markets; the fineness and luster of its pelt guaranteed that it would go for at least F2,000. I was full of wonderment at this unusual mammal, with its circular head adorned by short ears, its round eyes, its white whiskers like those on a cat, its webbed and clawed feet, its bushy tail. Hunted and trapped by fishermen, this valuable carnivore has become extremely rare, and it takes refuge chiefly in the northernmost parts of the Pacific, where in all likelihood its species will soon be facing extinction.

Captain Nemo's companion picked up the animal, loaded it on his shoulder, and we took to the trail again.

For an hour plains of sand unrolled before our steps. Often the seafloor rose to within two meters of the surface of the water. I could then see our images clearly mirrored on the underside of the waves, but reflected upside down: above us there appeared an identical band that duplicated our every movement and gesture; in short, a perfect likeness of the quartet near which it walked, but with heads down and feet in the air.

Another unusual effect. Heavy clouds passed above us, forming and fading swiftly. But after thinking it over, I realized that these so–called clouds were caused simply by the changing densities of the long ground swells, and I even spotted the foaming "white caps" that their breaking crests were proliferating over the surface of the water. Lastly, I couldn't help seeing the actual shadows of large birds passing over our heads, swiftly skimming the surface of the sea.

On this occasion I witnessed one of the finest gunshots ever to thrill the marrow of a hunter. A large bird with a wide wingspan, quite clearly visible, approached and hovered over us. When it was just a few meters above the waves, Captain Nemo's companion took aim and fired. The animal dropped, electrocuted, and its descent brought it within reach of our adroit hunter, who promptly took possession of it. It was an albatross of the finest species, a wonderful specimen of these open–sea fowl.

This incident did not interrupt our walk. For two hours we were sometimes led over plains of sand, sometimes over prairies of seaweed that were quite arduous to cross. In all honesty, I was dead tired by the time I spotted a hazy glow half a mile away, cutting through the darkness of the waters. It was the Nautilus's beacon. Within twenty minutes we would be on board, and there I could breathe easy again—because my tank's current air supply seemed to be quite low in oxygen. But I was reckoning without an encounter that slightly delayed our arrival.

I was lagging behind some twenty paces when I saw Captain Nemo suddenly come back toward me. With his powerful hands he sent me buckling to the ground, while his companion did the same to Conseil. At first I didn't know what to make of this sudden assault, but I was reassured to observe the captain lying motionless beside me.

I was stretched out on the seafloor directly beneath some bushes of algae, when I raised my head and spied two enormous masses hurtling by, throwing off phosphorescent glimmers.

My blood turned cold in my veins! I saw that we were under threat from a fearsome pair of sharks. They were blue sharks, dreadful man–eaters with enormous tails, dull, glassy stares, and phosphorescent matter oozing from holes around their snouts. They were like monstrous fireflies that could thoroughly pulverize a man in their iron jaws! I don't know if Conseil was busy with their classification, but as for me, I looked at their silver bellies, their fearsome mouths bristling with teeth, from a viewpoint less than scientific—more as a victim than as a professor of natural history.

Luckily these voracious animals have poor eyesight. They went by without noticing us, grazing us with their brownish fins; and miraculously, we escaped a danger greater than encountering a tiger deep in the jungle.

Half an hour later, guided by its electric trail, we reached the Nautilus. The outside door had been left open, and Captain Nemo closed it after we reentered the first cell. Then he pressed a button. I heard pumps operating within the ship, I felt the water lowering around me, and in a few moments the cell was completely empty. The inside door opened, and we passed into the wardrobe.

There our diving suits were removed, not without difficulty; and utterly exhausted, faint from lack of food and rest, I repaired to my stateroom, full of wonder at this startling excursion on the bottom of the sea.

Four Thousand Leagues Under the Pacific

BY THE NEXT MORNING, November 18, I was fully recovered from my exhaustion of the day before, and I climbed onto the platform just as the Nautilus's chief officer was pronouncing his daily phrase. It then occurred to me that these words either referred to the state of the sea, or that they meant: "There's nothing in sight."

And in truth, the ocean was deserted. Not a sail on the horizon. The tips of Crespo Island had disappeared during the night. The sea, absorbing every color of the prism except its blue rays, reflected the latter in every direction and sported a wonderful indigo tint. The undulating waves regularly took on the appearance of watered silk with wide stripes.

I was marveling at this magnificent ocean view when Captain Nemo appeared. He didn't seem to notice my presence and began a series of astronomical observations. Then, his operations finished, he went and leaned his elbows on the beacon housing, his eyes straying over the surface of the ocean.

Meanwhile some twenty of the Nautilus's sailors—all energetic, well–built fellows—climbed onto the platform. They had come to pull up the nets left in our wake during the night. These seamen obviously belonged to different nationalities, although indications of European physical traits could be seen in them all. If I'm not mistaken, I recognized some Irishmen, some Frenchmen, a few Slavs, and a native of either Greece or Crete. Even so, these men were frugal of speech and used among themselves only that bizarre dialect whose origin I couldn't even guess. So I had to give up any notions of questioning them.

The nets were hauled on board. They were a breed of trawl resembling those used off the Normandy coast, huge pouches held half open by a floating pole and a chain laced through the lower meshes. Trailing in this way from these iron glove makers, the resulting receptacles scoured the ocean floor and collected every marine exhibit in their path. That day they gathered up some unusual specimens from these fish–filled waterways: anglerfish whose comical movements qualify them for the epithet "clowns," black Commerson anglers equipped with their antennas, undulating triggerfish encircled by little red bands, bloated puffers whose venom is extremely insidious, some olive–hued lampreys, snipefish covered with silver scales, cutlass fish whose electrocuting power equals that of the electric eel and the electric ray, scaly featherbacks with brown crosswise bands, greenish codfish, several varieties of goby, etc.; finally, some fish of larger proportions: a one–meter jack with a prominent head, several fine bonito from the genus Scomber decked out in the colors blue and silver, and three magnificent tuna whose high speeds couldn't save them from our trawl.

I estimate that this cast of the net brought in more than 1,000 pounds of fish. It was a fine catch but not surprising. In essence, these nets stayed in our wake for several hours, incarcerating an entire aquatic world in prisons made of thread. So we were never lacking in provisions of the highest quality, which the Nautilus's speed and the allure of its electric light could continually replenish.

These various exhibits from the sea were immediately lowered down the hatch in the direction of the storage lockers, some to be eaten fresh, others to be preserved.

After its fishing was finished and its air supply renewed, I thought the Nautilus would resume its underwater excursion, and I was getting ready to return to my stateroom, when Captain Nemo turned to me and said without further preamble:

"Look at this ocean, professor! Doesn't it have the actual gift of life? Doesn't it experience both anger and affection? Last evening it went to sleep just as we did, and there it is, waking up after a peaceful night!"

No hellos or good mornings for this gent! You would have thought this eccentric individual was simply continuing a conversation we'd already started!

"See!" he went on. "It's waking up under the sun's caresses! It's going to relive its daily existence! What a fascinating field of study lies in watching the play of its organism. It owns a pulse and arteries, it has spasms, and I side with the scholarly Commander Maury, who discovered that it has a circulation as real as the circulation of blood in animals."

I'm sure that Captain Nemo expected no replies from me, and it seemed pointless to pitch in with "Ah yes," "Exactly," or "How right you are!" Rather, he was simply talking to himself, with long pauses between sentences. He was meditating out loud.

"Yes," he said, "the ocean owns a genuine circulation, and to start it going, the Creator of All Things has only to increase its heat, salt, and microscopic animal life. In essence, heat creates the different densities that lead to currents and countercurrents. Evaporation, which is nil in the High Arctic regions and very active in equatorial zones, brings about a constant interchange of tropical and polar waters. What's more, I've detected those falling and rising currents that make up the ocean's true breathing. I've seen a molecule of salt water heat up at the surface, sink into the depths, reach maximum density at $-2°$ centigrade, then cool off, grow lighter, and rise again. At the poles you'll see the consequences of this phenomenon, and through this law of farseeing nature, you'll understand why water can freeze only at the surface!"

As the captain was finishing his sentence, I said to myself: "The pole! Is this brazen individual claiming he'll take us even to that location?"

Meanwhile the captain fell silent and stared at the element he had studied so thoroughly and unceasingly. Then, going on:

"Salts," he said, "fill the sea in considerable quantities, professor, and if you removed all its dissolved saline content, you'd create a mass measuring 4,500,000 cubic leagues, which if it were spread all over the globe, would form a layer more than ten meters high. And don't think that the presence of these salts is due merely to some whim of nature. No. They make ocean water less open to evaporation and prevent winds from carrying off excessive amounts of steam, which, when condensing, would submerge the temperate zones. Salts play a leading role, the role of stabilizer for the general ecology of the globe!"

Captain Nemo stopped, straightened up, took a few steps along the platform, and returned to me:

"As for those billions of tiny animals," he went on, "those infusoria that live by the millions in one droplet of water, 800,000 of which are needed to weigh one milligram, their role is no less important. They absorb the marine salts, they assimilate the solid elements in the water, and since they create coral and madrepores, they're the true builders of limestone continents! And so, after they've finished depriving our water drop of its mineral nutrients, the droplet gets lighter, rises to the surface, there absorbs more salts left behind through evaporation, gets heavier, sinks again, and brings those tiny animals new elements to absorb. The outcome: a double current, rising and falling, constant movement, constant life! More intense than on land, more abundant, more infinite, such life blooms in every part of this ocean, an element fatal to man, they say, but vital to myriads of animals—and to me!"

When Captain Nemo spoke in this way, he was transfigured, and he filled me with extraordinary excitement.

"There," he added, "out there lies true existence! And I can imagine the founding of nautical towns, clusters of underwater households that, like the Nautilus, would return to the surface of the sea to breathe each morning, free towns if ever there were, independent cities! Then again, who knows whether some tyrant . . ."

Captain Nemo finished his sentence with a vehement gesture. Then, addressing me directly, as if to drive away an ugly thought:

"Professor Aronnax," he asked me, "do you know the depth of the ocean floor?"

"At least, Captain, I know what the major soundings tell us."

"Could you quote them to me, so I can double–check them as the need arises?"

"Here," I replied, "are a few of them that stick in my memory. If I'm not mistaken, an average depth of 8,200 meters was found in the north Atlantic, and 2,500 meters in the Mediterranean. The most remarkable soundings were taken in the south Atlantic near the 35th parallel, and they gave 12,000 meters, 14,091 meters, and 15,149 meters. All in all, it's estimated that if the sea bottom were made level, its average depth would be about seven kilometers."

"Well, professor," Captain Nemo replied, "we'll show you better than that, I hope. As for the average depth of this part of the Pacific, I'll inform you that it's a mere 4,000 meters."

This said, Captain Nemo headed to the hatch and disappeared down the ladder. I followed him and went back to the main lounge. The propeller was instantly set in motion, and the log gave our speed as twenty miles per hour.

Over the ensuing days and weeks, Captain Nemo was very frugal with his visits. I saw him only at rare intervals. His chief officer regularly fixed the positions I found reported on the chart, and in such a way that I could exactly plot the Nautilus's course.

Conseil and Land spent the long hours with me. Conseil had told his friend about the wonders of our undersea stroll, and the Canadian was sorry he hadn't gone along. But I hoped an opportunity would arise for a visit to the forests of Oceania.

Almost every day the panels in the lounge were open for some hours, and our eyes never tired of probing the mysteries of the underwater world.

The Nautilus's general heading was southeast, and it stayed at a depth between 100 and 150 meters. However, from Lord–knows–what whim, one day it did a diagonal dive by means of its slanting fins, reaching strata located 2,000 meters underwater. The thermometer indicated a temperature of 4.25° centigrade, which at this depth seemed to be a temperature common to all latitudes.

On November 26, at three o'clock in the morning, the Nautilus cleared the Tropic of Cancer at longitude 172°. On the 27th it passed in sight of the Hawaiian Islands, where the famous Captain Cook met his death on February 14, 1779. By then we had fared 4,860 leagues from our starting point. When I arrived on the platform that morning, I saw the Island of Hawaii two miles to leeward, the largest of the seven islands making up this group. I could clearly distinguish the tilled soil on its outskirts, the various mountain chains running parallel with its coastline, and its volcanoes, crowned by Mauna Kea, whose elevation is 5,000 meters above sea level. Among other specimens from these waterways, our nets brought up some peacock–tailed flabellarian coral, polyps flattened into stylish shapes and unique to this part of the ocean.

The Nautilus kept to its southeasterly heading. On December 1 it cut the equator at longitude 142°, and on the 4th of the same month, after a quick crossing marked by no incident, we raised the Marquesas Islands. Three miles off, in latitude 8° 57' south and longitude 139° 32' west, I spotted Martin Point on Nuku Hiva, chief member of this island group that belongs to France. I could make out only its wooded mountains on the horizon, because Captain Nemo hated to hug shore. There our nets brought up some fine fish samples: dolphinfish with azure fins, gold tails, and flesh that's unrivaled in the entire world, wrasse from the genus Hologymnosus that were nearly denuded of scales but exquisite in flavor, knifejaws with bony beaks, yellowish albacore that were as tasty as bonito, all fish worth classifying in the ship's pantry.

After leaving these delightful islands to the protection of the French flag, the Nautilus covered about 2,000 miles from December 4 to the 11th. Its navigating was marked by an encounter with an immense school of squid, unusual mollusks that are near neighbors of the cuttlefish. French fishermen give them the name "cuckoldfish," and they belong to the class Cephalopoda, family Dibranchiata, consisting of themselves together with cuttlefish and argonauts. The naturalists of antiquity made a special study of them, and these animals furnished many ribald figures of speech for soapbox orators in the Greek marketplace, as well as excellent dishes for the tables of rich citizens, if we're to believe Athenæus, a Greek physician predating Galen.

It was during the night of December 9–10 that the Nautilus encountered this army of distinctly nocturnal mollusks. They numbered in the millions. They were migrating from the temperate zones toward zones still warmer, following the itineraries of herring and sardines. We stared at them through our thick glass windows: they swam backward with tremendous speed, moving by means of their locomotive tubes, chasing fish and mollusks, eating the little ones, eaten by the big ones, and tossing in indescribable confusion the ten feet that nature has rooted in their heads like a hairpiece of pneumatic snakes. Despite its speed, the Nautilus navigated for several hours in the midst of this school of animals, and its nets brought up an incalculable number, among which I recognized all nine species that Professor Orbigny has classified as native to the Pacific Ocean.

During this crossing, the sea continually lavished us with the most marvelous sights. Its variety was infinite. It changed its setting and decor for the mere pleasure of our eyes, and we were called upon not simply to contemplate the works of our Creator in the midst of the liquid element, but also to probe the ocean's most daunting mysteries.

During the day of December 11, I was busy reading in the main lounge. Ned Land and Conseil were observing the luminous waters through the gaping panels. The Nautilus was motionless. Its ballast tanks full, it was sitting at a depth of 1,000 meters in a comparatively unpopulated region of the ocean where only larger fish put in occasional appearances.

Just then I was studying a delightful book by Jean Macé, The Servants of the Stomach, and savoring its ingenious teachings, when Conseil interrupted my reading.

"Would master kindly come here for an instant?" he said to me in an odd voice.

"What is it, Conseil?"

"It's something that master should see."

I stood up, went, leaned on my elbows before the window, and I saw it.

In the broad electric daylight, an enormous black mass, quite motionless, hung suspended in the midst of the waters. I observed it carefully, trying to find out the nature of this gigantic cetacean. Then a sudden thought crossed my mind.

"A ship!" I exclaimed.

"Yes," the Canadian replied, "a disabled craft that's sinking straight down!"

Ned Land was not mistaken. We were in the presence of a ship whose severed shrouds still hung from their clasps. Its hull looked in good condition, and it must have gone under only a few hours before. The stumps of three masts, chopped off two feet above the deck, indicated a flooding ship that had been forced to sacrifice its masting. But it had heeled sideways, filling completely, and it was listing to port even yet. A sorry sight, this carcass lost under the waves, but sorrier still was the sight on its deck, where, lashed with ropes to prevent their being washed overboard, some human corpses still lay! I counted four of them—four men, one still standing at the helm—then a woman, halfway out of a skylight on the afterdeck, holding a child in her arms. This woman was young. Under the brilliant lighting of the Nautilus's rays, I could make out her features, which the water hadn't yet decomposed. With a supreme effort, she had lifted her child above her head, and the poor little creature's arms were still twined around its mother's neck! The postures of the four seamen seemed ghastly to me, twisted from convulsive movements, as if making a last effort to break loose from the ropes that bound them to their ship. And the helmsman, standing alone, calmer, his face smooth and serious, his grizzled hair plastered to his brow, his hands clutching the wheel, seemed even yet to be guiding his wrecked three–master through the ocean depths!

What a scene! We stood dumbstruck, hearts pounding, before this shipwreck caught in the act, as if it had been photographed in its final moments, so to speak! And already I could see enormous sharks moving in, eyes ablaze, drawn by the lure of human flesh!

Meanwhile, turning, the Nautilus made a circle around the sinking ship, and for an instant I could read the board on its stern:

The Florida
Sunderland, England

Vanikoro

THIS DREADFUL SIGHT was the first of a whole series of maritime catastrophes that the Nautilus would encounter on its run. When it plied more heavily traveled seas, we often saw wrecked hulls rotting in midwater, and farther down, cannons, shells, anchors, chains, and a thousand other iron objects rusting away.

Meanwhile, continuously swept along by the Nautilus, where we lived in near isolation, we raised the Tuamotu Islands on December 11, that old "dangerous group" associated with the French global navigator Commander Bougainville; it stretches from Ducie Island to Lazareff Island over an area of 500 leagues from the east–southeast to the west–northwest, between latitude 13° 30' and 23° 50' south, and between longitude 125° 30' and 151° 30' west. This island group covers a surface area of 370 square leagues, and it's made up of some sixty subgroups, among which we noted the Gambier group, which is a French protectorate. These islands are coral formations. Thanks to the work of polyps, a slow but steady upheaval will someday connect these islands to each other. Later on, this new island will be fused to its neighboring island groups, and a fifth continent will stretch from New Zealand and New Caledonia as far as the Marquesas Islands.

The day I expounded this theory to Captain Nemo, he answered me coldly:

"The earth doesn't need new continents, but new men!"

Sailors' luck led the Nautilus straight to Reao Island, one of the most unusual in this group, which was discovered in 1822 by Captain Bell aboard the Minerva. So I was able to study the madreporic process that has created the islands in this ocean.

Madrepores, which one must guard against confusing with precious coral, clothe their tissue in a limestone crust, and their variations in structure have led my famous mentor Professor Milne–Edwards to classify them into five divisions. The tiny microscopic animals that secrete this polypary live by the billions in the depths of their cells. Their limestone deposits build up into rocks, reefs, islets, islands. In some places, they form atolls, a circular ring surrounding a lagoon or small inner lake that gaps place in contact with the sea. Elsewhere, they take the shape of barrier reefs, such as those that exist along the coasts of New Caledonia and several of the Tuamotu Islands. In still other localities, such as Réunion Island and the island of Mauritius, they build fringing reefs, high, straight walls next to which the ocean's depth is considerable.

While cruising along only a few cable lengths from the underpinning of Reao Island, I marveled at the gigantic piece of work accomplished by these microscopic laborers. These walls were the express achievements of madrepores known by the names fire coral, finger coral, star coral, and stony coral. These polyps grow exclusively in the agitated strata at the surface of the sea, and so it's in the upper reaches that they begin these substructures, which sink little by little together with the secreted rubble binding them. This, at least, is the theory of Mr. Charles Darwin, who thus explains the formation of atolls—a theory superior, in my view, to the one that says these madreporic edifices sit on the summits of mountains or volcanoes submerged a few feet below sea level.

I could observe these strange walls quite closely: our sounding lines indicated that they dropped perpendicularly for more than 300 meters, and our electric beams made the bright limestone positively sparkle.

In reply to a question Conseil asked me about the growth rate of these colossal barriers, I thoroughly amazed him by saying that scientists put it at an eighth of an inch per biennium.

"Therefore," he said to me, "to build these walls, it took . . . ?"

"192,000 years, my gallant Conseil, which significantly extends the biblical Days of Creation. What's more, the formation of coal—in other words, the petrification of forests swallowed by floods—and the cooling of basaltic rocks likewise call for a much longer period of time. I might add that those 'days' in the Bible must represent whole epochs and not literally the lapse of time between two sunrises, because according to the Bible itself, the sun doesn't date from the first day of Creation."

When the Nautilus returned to the surface of the ocean, I could take in Reao Island over its whole flat, wooded expanse. Obviously its madreporic rocks had been made fertile by tornadoes and thunderstorms. One day, carried off by a hurricane from neighboring shores, some seed fell onto these limestone beds, mixing with decomposed particles of fish and marine plants to form vegetable humus. Propelled by the waves, a coconut arrived on this new coast. Its germ took root. Its tree grew tall, catching steam off the water. A brook was born. Little by little, vegetation spread. Tiny animals—worms, insects—rode ashore on tree trunks snatched from islands to windward. Turtles came to lay their eggs. Birds nested in the young trees. In this way animal life developed, and drawn by the greenery and fertile soil, man appeared. And that's how these islands were formed, the immense achievement of microscopic animals.

Near evening Reao Island melted into the distance, and the Nautilus noticeably changed course. After touching the Tropic of Capricorn at longitude 135°, it headed west–northwest, going back up the whole intertropical zone. Although the summer sun lavished its rays on us, we never suffered from the heat, because thirty or forty meters underwater, the temperature didn't go over 10° to 12° centigrade.

By December 15 we had left the alluring Society Islands in the west, likewise elegant Tahiti, queen of the Pacific. In the morning I spotted this island's lofty summits a few miles to leeward. Its waters supplied excellent fish for the tables on board: mackerel, bonito, albacore, and a few varieties of that sea serpent named the moray eel.

The Nautilus had cleared 8,100 miles. We logged 9,720 miles when we passed between the Tonga Islands, where crews from the Argo, Port–au–Prince, and Duke of Portland had perished, and the island group of Samoa, scene of the slaying of Captain de Langle, friend of that long–lost navigator, the Count de La Pérouse. Then we raised the Fiji Islands, where savages slaughtered sailors from the Union, as well as Captain Bureau, commander of the Darling Josephine out of Nantes, France.

Extending over an expanse of 100 leagues north to south, and over 90 leagues east to west, this island group lies between latitude 2° and 6° south, and between longitude 174° and 179° west. It consists of a number of islands, islets, and reefs, among which we noted the islands of Viti Levu, Vanua Levu, and Kadavu.

It was the Dutch navigator Tasman who discovered this group in 1643, the same year the Italian physicist Torricelli invented the barometer and King Louis XIV ascended the French throne. I'll let the reader decide which of these deeds was more beneficial to humanity. Coming later, Captain Cook in 1774, Rear Admiral d'Entrecasteaux in 1793, and finally Captain Dumont d'Urville in 1827, untangled the whole chaotic geography of this island group. The Nautilus drew near Wailea Bay, an unlucky place for England's Captain Dillon, who was the first to shed light on the longstanding mystery surrounding the disappearance of ships under the Count de La Pérouse.

This bay, repeatedly dredged, furnished a huge supply of excellent oysters. As the Roman playwright Seneca recommended, we opened them right at our table, then stuffed ourselves. These mollusks belonged to the species known by name as Ostrea lamellosa, whose members are quite common off Corsica. This Wailea oysterbank must have been extensive, and for certain, if they hadn't been controlled by numerous natural checks, these clusters of shellfish would have ended up jam–packing the bay, since as many as 2,000,000 eggs have been counted in a single individual.

And if Mr. Ned Land did not repent of his gluttony at our oyster fest, it's because oysters are the only dish that never causes indigestion. In fact, it takes no less than sixteen dozen of these headless mollusks to supply the 315 grams that satisfy one man's minimum daily requirement for nitrogen.

On December 25 the Nautilus navigated amid the island group of the New Hebrides, which the Portuguese seafarer Queirós discovered in 1606, which Commander Bougainville explored in 1768, and to which Captain Cook gave its current name in 1773. This group is chiefly made up of nine large islands and forms a 120–league strip from the north–northwest to the south–southeast, lying between latitude 2° and 15° south, and between longitude 164° and 168°. At the moment of our noon sights, we passed fairly close to the island of Aurou, which looked to me like a mass of green woods crowned by a peak of great height.

That day it was yuletide, and it struck me that Ned Land badly missed celebrating "Christmas," that genuine family holiday where Protestants are such zealots.

I hadn't seen Captain Nemo for over a week, when, on the morning of the 27th, he entered the main lounge, as usual acting as if he'd been gone for just five minutes. I was busy tracing the Nautilus's course on the world map. The captain approached, placed a finger over a position on the chart, and pronounced just one word:

"Vanikoro."

This name was magic! It was the name of those islets where vessels under the Count de La Pérouse had miscarried. I straightened suddenly.

"The Nautilus is bringing us to Vanikoro?" I asked.

"Yes, professor," the captain replied.

"And I'll be able to visit those famous islands where the Compass and the Astrolabe came to grief?"

"If you like, professor."

"When will we reach Vanikoro?"

"We already have, professor."

Followed by Captain Nemo, I climbed onto the platform, and from there my eyes eagerly scanned the horizon.

In the northeast there emerged two volcanic islands of unequal size, surrounded by a coral reef whose circuit measured forty miles. We were facing the island of Vanikoro proper, to which Captain Dumont d'Urville had given the name "Island of the Search"; we lay right in front of the little harbor of Vana, located in latitude 16° 4' south and longitude 164° 32' east. Its shores seemed covered with greenery from its beaches to its summits inland, crowned by Mt. Kapogo, which is 476 fathoms high.

After clearing the outer belt of rocks via a narrow passageway, the Nautilus lay inside the breakers where the sea had a depth of thirty to forty fathoms. Under the green shade of some tropical evergreens, I spotted a few savages who looked extremely startled at our approach. In this long, blackish object advancing flush with the water, didn't they see some fearsome cetacean that they were obliged to view with distrust?

Just then Captain Nemo asked me what I knew about the shipwreck of the Count de La Pérouse.

"What everybody knows, captain," I answered him.

"And could you kindly tell me what everybody knows?" he asked me in a gently ironic tone.

"Very easily."

I related to him what the final deeds of Captain Dumont d'Urville had brought to light, deeds described here in this heavily condensed summary of the whole matter.

In 1785 the Count de La Pérouse and his subordinate, Captain de Langle, were sent by King Louis XVI of France on a voyage to circumnavigate the globe. They boarded two sloops of war, the Compass and the Astrolabe, which were never seen again.

In 1791, justly concerned about the fate of these two sloops of war, the French government fitted out two large cargo boats, the Search and the Hope, which left Brest on September 28 under orders from Rear Admiral Bruni d'Entrecasteaux. Two months later, testimony from a certain Commander Bowen, aboard the Albemarle, alleged that rubble from shipwrecked vessels had been seen on the coast of New Georgia. But d'Entrecasteaux was unaware of this news—which seemed a bit dubious anyhow—and headed toward the Admiralty Islands, which had been named in a report by one Captain Hunter as the site of the Count de La Pérouse's shipwreck.

They looked in vain. The Hope and the Search passed right by Vanikoro without stopping there; and overall, this voyage was plagued by misfortune, ultimately costing the lives of Rear Admiral d'Entrecasteaux, two of his subordinate officers, and several seamen from his crew.

It was an old hand at the Pacific, the English adventurer Captain Peter Dillon, who was the first to pick up the trail left by castaways from the wrecked vessels. On May 15, 1824, his ship, the St. Patrick, passed by Tikopia Island, one of the New Hebrides. There a native boatman pulled alongside in a dugout canoe and sold Dillon a silver sword hilt bearing the imprint of characters engraved with a cutting tool known as a burin. Furthermore, this native boatman claimed that during a stay in Vanikoro six years earlier, he had seen two Europeans belonging to ships that had run aground on the island's reefs many years before.

Dillon guessed that the ships at issue were those under the Count de La Pérouse, ships whose disappearance had shaken the entire world. He tried to reach Vanikoro, where, according to the native boatman, a good deal of rubble from the shipwreck could still be found, but winds and currents prevented his doing so.

Dillon returned to Calcutta. There he was able to interest the Asiatic Society and the East India Company in his discovery. A ship named after the Search was placed at his disposal, and he departed on January 23, 1827, accompanied by a French deputy.

This new Search, after putting in at several stops over the Pacific, dropped anchor before Vanikoro on July 7, 1827, in the same harbor of Vana where the Nautilus was currently floating.

There Dillon collected many relics of the shipwreck: iron utensils, anchors, eyelets from pulleys, swivel guns, an eighteen–pound shell, the remains of some astronomical instruments, a piece of sternrail, and a bronze bell bearing the inscription "Made by Bazin," the foundry mark at Brest Arsenal around 1785. There could no longer be any doubt.

Finishing his investigations, Dillon stayed at the site of the casualty until the month of October. Then he left Vanikoro, headed toward New Zealand, dropped anchor at Calcutta on April 7, 1828, and returned to France, where he received a very cordial welcome from King Charles X.

But just then the renowned French explorer Captain Dumont d'Urville, unaware of Dillon's activities, had already set sail to search elsewhere for the site of the shipwreck. In essence, a whaling vessel had reported that some medals and a Cross of St. Louis had been found in the hands of savages in the Louisiade Islands and New Caledonia.

So Captain Dumont d'Urville had put to sea in command of a vessel named after the Astrolabe, and just two months after Dillon had left Vanikoro, Dumont d'Urville dropped anchor before Hobart. There he heard about Dillon's findings, and he further learned that a certain James Hobbs, chief officer on the Union out of Calcutta, had put to shore on an island located in latitude 8° 18' south and longitude 156° 30' east, and had noted the natives of those waterways making use of iron bars and red fabrics.

Pretty perplexed, Dumont d'Urville didn't know if he should give credence to these reports, which had been carried in some of the less reliable newspapers; nevertheless, he decided to start on Dillon's trail.

On February 10, 1828, the new Astrolabe hove before Tikopia Island, took on a guide and interpreter in the person of a deserter who had settled there, plied a course toward Vanikoro, raised it on February 12, sailed along its reefs until the 14th, and only on the 20th dropped anchor inside its barrier in the harbor of Vana.

On the 23rd, several officers circled the island and brought back some rubble of little importance. The natives, adopting a system of denial and evasion, refused to guide them to the site of the casualty. This rather shady conduct aroused the suspicion that the natives had mistreated the castaways; and in truth, the natives seemed afraid that Dumont d'Urville had come to avenge the Count de La Pérouse and his unfortunate companions.

But on the 26th, appeased with gifts and seeing that they didn't need to fear any reprisals, the natives led the chief officer, Mr. Jacquinot, to the site of the shipwreck.

At this location, in three or four fathoms of water between the Paeu and Vana reefs, there lay some anchors, cannons, and ingots of iron and lead, all caked with limestone concretions. A launch and whaleboat from the new Astrolabe were steered to this locality, and after going to exhausting lengths, their crews managed to dredge up an anchor weighing 1,800 pounds, a cast–iron eight–pounder cannon, a lead ingot, and two copper swivel guns.

Questioning the natives, Captain Dumont d'Urville also learned that after La Pérouse's two ships had miscarried on the island's reefs, the count had built a smaller craft, only to go off and miscarry a second time. Where? Nobody knew.

The commander of the new Astrolabe then had a monument erected under a tuft of mangrove, in memory of the famous navigator and his companions. It was a simple quadrangular pyramid, set on a coral base, with no ironwork to tempt the natives' avarice.

Then Dumont d'Urville tried to depart; but his crews were run down from the fevers raging on these unsanitary shores, and quite ill himself, he was unable to weigh anchor until March 17.

Meanwhile, fearing that Dumont d'Urville wasn't abreast of Dillon's activities, the French government sent a sloop of war to Vanikoro, the Bayonnaise under Commander Legoarant de Tromelin, who had been stationed on the American west coast. Dropping anchor before Vanikoro a few months after the new Astrolabe's departure, the Bayonnaise didn't find any additional evidence but verified that the savages hadn't disturbed the memorial honoring the Count de La Pérouse.

This is the substance of the account I gave Captain Nemo.

"So," he said to me, "the castaways built a third ship on Vanikoro Island, and to this day, nobody knows where it went and perished?"

"Nobody knows."

Captain Nemo didn't reply but signaled me to follow him to the main lounge. The Nautilus sank a few meters beneath the waves, and the panels opened.

I rushed to the window and saw crusts of coral: fungus coral, siphonula coral, alcyon coral, sea anemone from the genus Caryophylia, plus myriads of charming fish including greenfish, damselfish, sweepers, snappers, and squirrelfish;

underneath this coral covering I detected some rubble the old dredges hadn't been able to tear free—iron stirrups, anchors, cannons, shells, tackle from a capstan, a stempost, all objects hailing from the wrecked ships and now carpeted in moving flowers.

And as I stared at this desolate wreckage, Captain Nemo told me in a solemn voice:

"Commander La Pérouse set out on December 7, 1785, with his ships, the Compass and the Astrolabe. He dropped anchor first at Botany Bay, visited the Tonga Islands and New Caledonia, headed toward the Santa Cruz Islands, and put in at Nomuka, one of the islands in the Ha'apai group. Then his ships arrived at the unknown reefs of Vanikoro. Traveling in the lead, the Compass ran afoul of breakers on the southerly coast. The Astrolabe went to its rescue and also ran aground. The first ship was destroyed almost immediately. The second, stranded to leeward, held up for some days. The natives gave the castaways a fair enough welcome. The latter took up residence on the island and built a smaller craft with rubble from the two large ones. A few seamen stayed voluntarily in Vanikoro. The others, weak and ailing, set sail with the Count de La Pérouse. They headed to the Solomon Islands, and they perished with all hands on the westerly coast of the chief island in that group, between Cape Deception and Cape Satisfaction!"

"And how do you know all this?" I exclaimed.

"Here's what I found at the very site of that final shipwreck!"

Captain Nemo showed me a tin box, stamped with the coat of arms of France and all corroded by salt water. He opened it and I saw a bundle of papers, yellowed but still legible.

They were the actual military orders given by France's Minister of the Navy to Commander La Pérouse, with notes along the margin in the handwriting of King Louis XVI!

"Ah, what a splendid death for a seaman!" Captain Nemo then said. "A coral grave is a tranquil grave, and may Heaven grant that my companions and I rest in no other!"

The Torres Strait

DURING THE NIGHT of December 27–28, the Nautilus left the waterways of Vanikoro behind with extraordinary speed. Its heading was southwesterly, and in three days it had cleared the 750 leagues that separated La Pérouse's islands from the southeastern tip of Papua.

On January 1, 1868, bright and early, Conseil joined me on the platform.

"Will master," the gallant lad said to me, "allow me to wish him a happy new year?"

"Good heavens, Conseil, it's just like old times in my office at the Botanical Gardens in Paris! I accept your kind wishes and I thank you for them. Only, I'd like to know what you mean by a 'happy year' under the circumstances in which we're placed. Is it a year that will bring our imprisonment to an end, or a year that will see this strange voyage continue?"

"Ye gods," Conseil replied, "I hardly know what to tell master. We're certainly seeing some unusual things, and for two months we've had no time for boredom. The latest wonder is always the most astonishing, and if this progression keeps up, I can't imagine what its climax will be. In my opinion, we'll never again have such an opportunity."

"Never, Conseil."

"Besides, Mr. Nemo really lives up to his Latin name, since he couldn't be less in the way if he didn't exist."

"True enough, Conseil."

"Therefore, with all due respect to master, I think a 'happy year' would be a year that lets us see everything—"

"Everything, Conseil? No year could be that long. But what does Ned Land think about all this?"

"Ned Land's thoughts are exactly the opposite of mine," Conseil replied. "He has a practical mind and a demanding stomach. He's tired of staring at fish and eating them day in and day out. This shortage of wine, bread, and meat isn't suitable for an upstanding Anglo–Saxon, a man accustomed to beefsteak and unfazed by regular doses of brandy or gin!"

"For my part, Conseil, that doesn't bother me in the least, and I've adjusted very nicely to the diet on board."

"So have I," Conseil replied. "Accordingly, I think as much about staying as Mr. Land about making his escape. Thus, if this new year isn't a happy one for me, it will be for him, and vice versa. No matter what happens, one of us will be pleased. So, in conclusion, I wish master to have whatever his heart desires."

"Thank you, Conseil. Only I must ask you to postpone the question of new year's gifts, and temporarily accept a hearty handshake in their place. That's all I have on me."

"Master has never been more generous," Conseil replied.

And with that, the gallant lad went away.

By January 2 we had fared 11,340 miles, hence 5,250 leagues, from our starting point in the seas of Japan. Before the Nautilus's spur there stretched the dangerous waterways of the Coral Sea, off the northeast coast of Australia. Our boat cruised along a few miles away from that daunting shoal where Captain Cook's ships wellnigh miscarried on June 10, 1770. The craft that Cook was aboard charged into some coral rock, and if his vessel didn't go down, it was thanks to the circumstance that a piece of coral broke off in the collision and plugged the very hole it had made in the hull.

I would have been deeply interested in visiting this long, 360–league reef, against which the ever–surging sea broke with the fearsome intensity of thunderclaps. But just then the Nautilus's slanting fins took us to great depths, and I could see nothing of those high coral walls. I had to rest content with the various specimens of fish brought up by our nets. Among others I noted some long–finned albacore, a species in the genus Scomber, as big as tuna, bluish on the flanks, and streaked with crosswise stripes that disappear when the animal dies. These fish followed us in schools and supplied our table with very dainty flesh. We also caught a large number of yellow–green gilthead, half a decimeter long and tasting like dorado, plus some flying gurnards, authentic underwater swallows that, on dark nights, alternately streak air and water with their phosphorescent glimmers. Among mollusks and zoophytes, I found in our trawl's meshes various species of alcyonarian coral, sea urchins, hammer shells, spurred–star shells, wentletrap snails, horn shells, glass snails. The local flora was represented by fine floating algae: sea tangle, and kelp from the genus Macrocystis, saturated with the mucilage their pores perspire, from which I selected a wonderful Nemastoma geliniaroidea, classifying it with the natural curiosities in the museum.

On January 4, two days after crossing the Coral Sea, we raised the coast of Papua. On this occasion Captain Nemo told me that he intended to reach the Indian Ocean via the Torres Strait. This was the extent of his remarks. Ned saw with pleasure that this course would bring us, once again, closer to European seas.

The Torres Strait is regarded as no less dangerous for its bristling reefs than for the savage inhabitants of its coasts. It separates Queensland from the huge island of Papua, also called New Guinea.

Papua is 400 leagues long by 130 leagues wide, with a surface area of 40,000 geographic leagues. It's located between latitude 0° 19' and 10° 2' south, and between longitude 128° 23' and 146° 15'. At noon, while the chief officer was taking the sun's altitude, I spotted the summits of the Arfak Mountains, rising in terraces and ending in sharp peaks.

Discovered in 1511 by the Portuguese Francisco Serrano, these shores were successively visited by Don Jorge de Meneses in 1526, by Juan de Grijalva in 1527, by the Spanish general Alvaro de Saavedra in 1528, by Inigo Ortiz in 1545, by the Dutchman Schouten in 1616, by Nicolas Sruick in 1753, by Tasman, Dampier, Fumel, Carteret, Edwards, Bougainville, Cook, McClure, and Thomas Forrest, by Rear Admiral d'Entrecasteaux in 1792, by Louis–Isidore Duperrey in 1823, and by Captain Dumont d'Urville in 1827. "It's the heartland of the blacks who occupy all Malaysia," Mr. de Rienzi has said; and I hadn't the foggiest inkling that sailors' luck was about to bring me face to face with these daunting Andaman aborigines.

So the Nautilus hove before the entrance to the world's most dangerous strait, a passageway that even the boldest navigators hesitated to clear: the strait that Luis Vaez de Torres faced on returning from the South Seas in Melanesia, the strait in which sloops of war under Captain Dumont d'Urville ran aground in 1840 and nearly miscarried with all hands. And even the Nautilus, rising superior to every danger in the sea, was about to become intimate with its coral reefs.

The Torres Strait is about thirty–four leagues wide, but it's obstructed by an incalculable number of islands, islets, breakers, and rocks that make it nearly impossible to navigate. Consequently, Captain Nemo took every desired precaution in crossing it. Floating flush with the water, the Nautilus moved ahead at a moderate pace. Like a cetacean's tail, its propeller churned the waves slowly.

Taking advantage of this situation, my two companions and I found seats on the ever–deserted platform. In front of us stood the pilothouse, and unless I'm extremely mistaken, Captain Nemo must have been inside, steering his Nautilus himself.

Under my eyes I had the excellent charts of the Torres Strait that had been surveyed and drawn up by the hydrographic engineer Vincendon Dumoulin and Sublieutenant (now Admiral) Coupvent–Desbois, who were part of Dumont d'Urville's general staff during his final voyage to circumnavigate the globe. These, along with the efforts of Captain King, are the best charts for untangling the snarl of this narrow passageway, and I consulted them with scrupulous care.

Around the Nautilus the sea was boiling furiously. A stream of waves, bearing from southeast to northwest at a speed of two and a half miles per hour, broke over heads of coral emerging here and there.

"That's one rough sea!" Ned Land told me.

"Abominable indeed," I replied, "and hardly suitable for a craft like the Nautilus."

"That damned captain," the Canadian went on, "must really be sure of his course, because if these clumps of coral so much as brush us, they'll rip our hull into a thousand pieces!"

The situation was indeed dangerous, but as if by magic, the Nautilus seemed to glide right down the middle of these rampaging reefs. It didn't follow the exact course of the Zealous and the new Astrolabe, which had proved so ill–fated for Captain Dumont d'Urville. It went more to the north, hugged the Murray Islands, and returned to the southwest near Cumberland Passage. I thought it was about to charge wholeheartedly into this opening, but it went up to the northwest, through a large number of little–known islands and islets, and steered toward Tound Island and the Bad Channel.

I was already wondering if Captain Nemo, rash to the point of sheer insanity, wanted his ship to tackle the narrows where Dumont d'Urville's two sloops of war had gone aground, when he changed direction a second time and cut straight to the west, heading toward Gueboroa Island.

By then it was three o'clock in the afternoon. The current was slacking off, it was almost full tide. The Nautilus drew near this island, which I can see to this day with its remarkable fringe of screw pines. We hugged it from less than two miles out.

A sudden jolt threw me down. The Nautilus had just struck a reef, and it remained motionless, listing slightly to port.

When I stood up, I saw Captain Nemo and his chief officer on the platform. They were examining the ship's circumstances, exchanging a few words in their incomprehensible dialect.

Here is what those circumstances entailed. Two miles to starboard lay Gueboroa Island, its coastline curving north to west like an immense arm. To the south and east, heads of coral were already on display, left uncovered by the ebbing waters. We had run aground at full tide and in one of those seas whose tides are moderate, an inconvenient state of affairs for floating the Nautilus off. However, the ship hadn't suffered in any way, so solidly joined was its hull. But although it could neither sink nor split open, it was in serious danger of being permanently attached to these reefs, and that would have been the finish of Captain Nemo's submersible.

I was mulling this over when the captain approached, cool and calm, forever in control of himself, looking neither alarmed nor annoyed.

"An accident?" I said to him.

"No, an incident," he answered me.

"But an incident," I replied, "that may oblige you to become a resident again of these shores you avoid!"

Captain Nemo gave me an odd look and gestured no. Which told me pretty clearly that nothing would ever force him to set foot on a land mass again. Then he said:

"No, Professor Aronnax, the Nautilus isn't consigned to perdition. It will still carry you through the midst of the ocean's wonders. Our voyage is just beginning, and I've no desire to deprive myself so soon of the pleasure of your company."

"Even so, Captain Nemo," I went on, ignoring his ironic turn of phrase, "the Nautilus has run aground at a moment when the sea is full. Now then, the tides aren't strong in the Pacific, and if you can't unballast the Nautilus, which seems impossible to me, I don't see how it will float off."

"You're right, professor, the Pacific tides aren't strong," Captain Nemo replied. "But in the Torres Strait, one still finds a meter–and–a–half difference in level between high and low seas. Today is January 4, and in five days the moon will be full. Now then, I'll be quite astonished if that good–natured satellite doesn't sufficiently raise these masses of water and do me a favor for which I'll be forever grateful."

This said, Captain Nemo went below again to the Nautilus's interior, followed by his chief officer. As for our craft, it no longer stirred, staying as motionless as if these coral polyps had already walled it in with their indestructible cement.

"Well, sir?" Ned Land said to me, coming up after the captain's departure.

"Well, Ned my friend, we'll serenely wait for the tide on the 9th, because it seems the moon will have the good nature to float us away!"

"As simple as that?"

"As simple as that."

"So our captain isn't going to drop his anchors, put his engines on the chains, and do anything to haul us off?"

"Since the tide will be sufficient," Conseil replied simply.

The Canadian stared at Conseil, then he shrugged his shoulders. The seaman in him was talking now.

"Sir," he answered, "you can trust me when I say this hunk of iron will never navigate again, on the seas or under them. It's only fit to be sold for its weight. So I think it's time we gave Captain Nemo the slip."

"Ned my friend," I replied, "unlike you, I haven't given up on our valiant Nautilus, and in four days we'll know where we stand on these Pacific tides. Besides, an escape attempt might be timely if we were in sight of the coasts of England or Provence, but in the waterways of Papua it's another story. And we'll always have that as a last resort if the Nautilus doesn't right itself, which I'd regard as a real calamity."

"But couldn't we at least get the lay of the land?" Ned went on. "Here's an island. On this island there are trees. Under those trees land animals loaded with cutlets and roast beef, which I'd be happy to sink my teeth into."

"In this instance our friend Ned is right," Conseil said, "and I side with his views. Couldn't master persuade his friend Captain Nemo to send the three of us ashore, if only so our feet don't lose the knack of treading on the solid parts of our planet?"

"I can ask him," I replied, "but he'll refuse."

"Let master take the risk," Conseil said, "and we'll know where we stand on the captain's affability."

Much to my surprise, Captain Nemo gave me the permission I asked for, and he did so with grace and alacrity, not even exacting my promise to return on board. But fleeing across the New Guinea territories would be extremely dangerous, and I wouldn't have advised Ned Land to try it. Better to be prisoners aboard the Nautilus than to fall into the hands of Papuan natives.

The skiff was put at our disposal for the next morning. I hardly needed to ask whether Captain Nemo would be coming along. I likewise assumed that no crewmen would be assigned to us, that Ned Land would be in sole charge of piloting the longboat. Besides, the shore lay no more than two miles off, and it would be child's play for the Canadian to guide that nimble skiff through those rows of reefs so ill–fated for big ships.

The next day, January 5, after its deck paneling was opened, the skiff was wrenched from its socket and launched to sea from the top of the platform. Two men were sufficient for this operation. The oars were inside the longboat and we had only to take our seats.

At eight o'clock, armed with rifles and axes, we pulled clear of the Nautilus. The sea was fairly calm. A mild breeze blew from shore. In place by the oars, Conseil and I rowed vigorously, and Ned steered us into the narrow lanes between the breakers. The skiff handled easily and sped swiftly.

Ned Land couldn't conceal his glee. He was a prisoner escaping from prison and never dreaming he would need to reenter it.

"Meat!" he kept repeating. "Now we'll eat red meat! Actual game! A real mess call, by thunder! I'm not saying fish aren't good for you, but we mustn't overdo 'em, and a slice of fresh venison grilled over live coals will be a nice change from our standard fare."

"You glutton," Conseil replied, "you're making my mouth water!"

"It remains to be seen," I said, "whether these forests do contain game, and if the types of game aren't of such size that they can hunt the hunter."

"Fine, Professor Aronnax!" replied the Canadian, whose teeth seemed to be as honed as the edge of an ax. "But if there's no other quadruped on this island, I'll eat tiger—tiger sirloin."

"Our friend Ned grows disturbing," Conseil replied.

"Whatever it is," Ned Land went on, "any animal having four feet without feathers, or two feet with feathers, will be greeted by my very own one–gun salute."

"Oh good!" I replied. "The reckless Mr. Land is at it again!"

"Don't worry, Professor Aronnax, just keep rowing!" the Canadian replied. "I only need twenty–five minutes to serve you one of my own special creations."

By 8:30 the Nautilus's skiff had just run gently aground on a sandy strand, after successfully clearing the ring of coral that surrounds Gueboroa Island.

Some Days Ashore

STEPPING ASHORE had an exhilarating effect on me. Ned Land tested the soil with his foot, as if he were laying claim to it. Yet it had been only two months since we had become, as Captain Nemo expressed it, "passengers on the Nautilus," in other words, the literal prisoners of its commander.

In a few minutes we were a gunshot away from the coast. The soil was almost entirely madreporic, but certain dry stream beds were strewn with granite rubble, proving that this island was of primordial origin. The entire horizon was hidden behind a curtain of wonderful forests. Enormous trees, sometimes as high as 200 feet, were linked to each other by garlands of tropical creepers, genuine natural hammocks that swayed in a mild breeze. There were mimosas, banyan trees, beefwood, teakwood, hibiscus, screw pines, palm trees, all mingling in wild profusion; and beneath the shade of their green canopies, at the feet of their gigantic trunks, there grew orchids, leguminous plants, and ferns.

Meanwhile, ignoring all these fine specimens of Papuan flora, the Canadian passed up the decorative in favor of the functional. He spotted a coconut palm, beat down some of its fruit, broke them open, and we drank their milk and ate their meat with a pleasure that was a protest against our standard fare on the Nautilus.

"Excellent!" Ned Land said.

"Exquisite!" Conseil replied.

"And I don't think," the Canadian said, "that your Nemo would object to us stashing a cargo of coconuts aboard his vessel?"

"I imagine not," I replied, "but he won't want to sample them."

"Too bad for him!" Conseil said.

"And plenty good for us!" Ned Land shot back. "There'll be more left over!"

"A word of caution, Mr. Land," I told the harpooner, who was about to ravage another coconut palm. "Coconuts are admirable things, but before we stuff the skiff with them, it would be wise to find out whether this island offers other substances just as useful. Some fresh vegetables would be well received in the Nautilus's pantry."

"Master is right," Conseil replied, "and I propose that we set aside three places in our longboat: one for fruit, another for vegetables, and a third for venison, of which I still haven't glimpsed the tiniest specimen."

"Don't give up so easily, Conseil," the Canadian replied.

"So let's continue our excursion," I went on, "but keep a sharp lookout. This island seems uninhabited, but it still might harbor certain individuals who aren't so finicky about the sort of game they eat!"

"Hee hee!" Ned put in, with a meaningful movement of his jaws.

"Ned! Oh horrors!" Conseil exclaimed.

"Ye gods," the Canadian shot back, "I'm starting to appreciate the charms of cannibalism!"

"Ned, Ned! Don't say that!" Conseil answered. "You a cannibal? Why, I'll no longer be safe next to you, I who share your cabin! Does this mean I'll wake up half devoured one fine day?"

"I'm awfully fond of you, Conseil my friend, but not enough to eat you when there's better food around."

"Then I daren't delay," Conseil replied. "The hunt is on! We absolutely must bag some game to placate this man–eater, or one of these mornings master won't find enough pieces of his manservant to serve him."

While exchanging this chitchat, we entered beneath the dark canopies of the forest, and for two hours we explored it in every direction.

We couldn't have been luckier in our search for edible vegetation, and some of the most useful produce in the tropical zones supplied us with a valuable foodstuff missing on board.

I mean the breadfruit tree, which is quite abundant on Gueboroa Island, and there I chiefly noted the seedless variety that in Malaysia is called "rima."

This tree is distinguished from other trees by a straight trunk forty feet high. To the naturalist's eye, its gracefully rounded crown, formed of big multilobed leaves, was enough to denote the artocarpus that has been so successfully transplanted to the Mascarene Islands east of

Madagascar. From its mass of greenery, huge globular fruit stood out, a decimeter wide and furnished on the outside with creases that assumed a hexangular pattern. It's a handy plant that nature gives to regions lacking in wheat; without needing to be cultivated, it bears fruit eight months out of the year.

Ned Land was on familiar terms with this fruit. He had already eaten it on his many voyages and knew how to cook its edible substance. So the very sight of it aroused his appetite, and he couldn't control himself.

"Sir," he told me, "I'll die if I don't sample a little breadfruit pasta!"

"Sample some, Ned my friend, sample all you like. We're here to conduct experiments, let's conduct them."

"It won't take a minute," the Canadian replied.

Equipped with a magnifying glass, he lit a fire of deadwood that was soon crackling merrily. Meanwhile Conseil and I selected the finest artocarpus fruit. Some still weren't ripe enough, and their thick skins covered white, slightly fibrous pulps. But a great many others were yellowish and gelatinous, just begging to be picked.

This fruit contained no pits. Conseil brought a dozen of them to Ned Land, who cut them into thick slices and placed them over a fire of live coals, all the while repeating:

"You'll see, sir, how tasty this bread is!"

"Especially since we've gone without baked goods for so long," Conseil said.

"It's more than just bread," the Canadian added. "It's a dainty pastry. You've never eaten any, sir?"

"No, Ned."

"All right, get ready for something downright delectable! If you don't come back for seconds, I'm no longer the King of Harpooners!"

After a few minutes, the parts of the fruit exposed to the fire were completely toasted. On the inside there appeared some white pasta, a sort of soft bread center whose flavor reminded me of artichoke.

This bread was excellent, I must admit, and I ate it with great pleasure.

"Unfortunately," I said, "this pasta won't stay fresh, so it seems pointless to make a supply for on board."

"By thunder, sir!" Ned Land exclaimed. "There you go, talking like a naturalist, but meantime I'll be acting like a baker! Conseil, harvest some of this fruit to take with us when we go back."

"And how will you prepare it?" I asked the Canadian.

"I'll make a fermented batter from its pulp that'll keep indefinitely without spoiling. When I want some, I'll just cook it in the galley on board—it'll have a slightly tart flavor, but you'll find it excellent."

"So, Mr. Ned, I see that this bread is all we need—"

"Not quite, professor," the Canadian replied. "We need some fruit to go with it, or at least some vegetables."

"Then let's look for fruit and vegetables."

When our breadfruit harvesting was done, we took to the trail to complete this "dry–land dinner."

We didn't search in vain, and near noontime we had an ample supply of bananas. This delicious produce from the Torrid Zones ripens all year round, and Malaysians, who give them the name "pisang," eat them without bothering to cook them. In addition to bananas, we gathered some enormous jackfruit with a very tangy flavor, some tasty mangoes, and some pineapples of unbelievable size. But this foraging took up a good deal of our time, which, even so, we had no cause to regret.

Conseil kept Ned under observation. The harpooner walked in the lead, and during his stroll through this forest, he gathered with sure hands some excellent fruit that should have completed his provisions.

"So," Conseil asked, "you have everything you need, Ned my friend?"

"Humph!" the Canadian put in.

"What! You're complaining?"

"All this vegetation doesn't make a meal," Ned replied. "Just side dishes, dessert. But where's the soup course? Where's the roast?"

"Right," I said. "Ned promised us cutlets, which seems highly questionable to me."

"Sir," the Canadian replied, "our hunting not only isn't over, it hasn't even started. Patience! We're sure to end up bumping into some animal with either feathers or fur, if not in this locality, then in another."

"And if not today, then tomorrow, because we mustn't wander too far off," Conseil added. "That's why I propose that we return to the skiff."

"What! Already!" Ned exclaimed.

"We ought to be back before nightfall," I said.

"But what hour is it, then?" the Canadian asked.

"Two o'clock at least," Conseil replied.

"How time flies on solid ground!" exclaimed Mr. Ned Land with a sigh of regret.

"Off we go!" Conseil replied.

So we returned through the forest, and we completed our harvest by making a clean sweep of some palm cabbages that had to be picked from the crowns of their trees, some small beans that I recognized as the "abrou" of the Malaysians, and some high–quality yams.

We were overloaded when we arrived at the skiff. However, Ned Land still found these provisions inadequate. But fortune smiled on him. Just as we were boarding, he spotted several trees twenty–five to thirty feet high, belonging to the palm species. As valuable as the actocarpus, these trees are justly ranked among the most useful produce in Malaysia.

They were sago palms, vegetation that grows without being cultivated; like mulberry trees, they reproduce by means of shoots and seeds.

Ned Land knew how to handle these trees. Taking his ax and wielding it with great vigor, he soon stretched out on the ground two or three sago palms, whose maturity was revealed by the white dust sprinkled over their palm fronds.

I watched him more as a naturalist than as a man in hunger. He began by removing from each trunk an inch–thick strip of bark that covered a network of long, hopelessly tangled fibers that were puttied with a sort of gummy flour. This flour was the starch–like sago, an edible substance chiefly consumed by the Melanesian peoples.

For the time being, Ned Land was content to chop these trunks into pieces, as if he were making firewood; later he would extract the flour by sifting it through cloth to separate it from its fibrous ligaments, let it dry out in the sun, and leave it to harden inside molds.

Finally, at five o'clock in the afternoon, laden with all our treasures, we left the island beach and half an hour later pulled alongside the Nautilus. Nobody appeared on our arrival. The enormous sheet–iron cylinder seemed deserted. Our provisions loaded on board, I went below to my stateroom. There I found my supper ready. I ate and then fell asleep.

The next day, January 6: nothing new on board. Not a sound inside, not a sign of life. The skiff stayed alongside in the same place we had left it. We decided to return to Gueboroa Island. Ned Land hoped for better luck in his hunting than on the day before, and he wanted to visit a different part of the forest.

By sunrise we were off. Carried by an inbound current, the longboat reached the island in a matter of moments.

We disembarked, and thinking it best to abide by the Canadian's instincts, we followed Ned Land, whose long legs threatened to outpace us.

Ned Land went westward up the coast; then, fording some stream beds, he reached open plains that were bordered by wonderful forests. Some kingfishers lurked along the watercourses, but they didn't let us approach. Their cautious behavior proved to me that these winged creatures knew where they stood on bipeds of our species, and I concluded that if this island wasn't inhabited, at least human beings paid it frequent visits.

After crossing a pretty lush prairie, we arrived on the outskirts of a small wood, enlivened by the singing and soaring of a large number of birds.

"Still, they're merely birds," Conseil said.

"But some are edible," the harpooner replied.

"Wrong, Ned my friend," Conseil answered, "because I see only ordinary parrots here."

"Conseil my friend," Ned replied in all seriousness, "parrots are like pheasant to people with nothing else on their plates."

"And I might add," I said, "that when these birds are properly cooked, they're at least worth a stab of the fork."

Indeed, under the dense foliage of this wood, a whole host of parrots fluttered from branch to branch, needing only the proper upbringing to speak human dialects. At present they were cackling in chorus with parakeets of every color, with solemn cockatoos that seemed to be pondering some philosophical problem, while bright red lories passed by like pieces of bunting borne on the breeze, in the midst of kalao parrots raucously on the wing, Papuan lories painted the subtlest shades of azure, and a whole variety of delightful winged creatures, none terribly edible.

However, one bird unique to these shores, which never passes beyond the boundaries of the Aru and Papuan Islands, was missing from this collection. But I was given a chance to marvel at it soon enough.

After crossing through a moderately dense thicket, we again found some plains obstructed by bushes. There I saw some magnificent birds soaring aloft, the arrangement of their long feathers causing them to head into the wind. Their undulating flight, the grace of their aerial curves, and the play of their colors allured and delighted the eye. I had no trouble identifying them.

"Birds of paradise!" I exclaimed.

"Order Passeriforma, division Clystomora," Conseil replied.

"Partridge family?" Ned Land asked.

"I doubt it, Mr. Land. Nevertheless, I'm counting on your dexterity to catch me one of these delightful representatives of tropical nature!"

"I'll give it a try, professor, though I'm handier with a harpoon than a rifle."

Malaysians, who do a booming business in these birds with the Chinese, have various methods for catching them that we couldn't use. Sometimes they set snares on the tops of the tall trees that the bird of paradise prefers to inhabit. At other times they capture it with a tenacious glue that paralyzes its movements. They will even go so far as to poison the springs where these fowl habitually drink. But in our case, all we could do was fire at them on the wing, which left us little chance of getting one. And in truth, we used up a good part of our ammunition in vain.

Near eleven o'clock in the morning, we cleared the lower slopes of the mountains that form the island's center, and we still hadn't bagged a thing. Hunger spurred us on. The hunters had counted on consuming the proceeds of their hunting, and they had miscalculated. Luckily, and much to his surprise, Conseil pulled off a right–and–left shot and insured our breakfast. He brought down a white pigeon and a ringdove, which were briskly plucked, hung from a spit, and roasted over a blazing fire of deadwood. While these fascinating animals were cooking, Ned prepared some bread from the artocarpus. Then the pigeon and ringdove were devoured to the bones and declared excellent. Nutmeg, on which these birds habitually gorge themselves, sweetens their flesh and makes it delicious eating.

"They taste like chicken stuffed with truffles," Conseil said.

"All right, Ned," I asked the Canadian, "now what do you need?"

"Game with four paws, Professor Aronnax," Ned Land replied. "All these pigeons are only appetizers, snacks. So till I've bagged an animal with cutlets, I won't be happy!"

"Nor I, Ned, until I've caught a bird of paradise."

"Then let's keep hunting," Conseil replied, "but while heading back to the sea. We've arrived at the foothills of these mountains, and I think we'll do better if we return to the forest regions."

It was good advice and we took it. After an hour's walk we reached a genuine sago palm forest. A few harmless snakes fled underfoot. Birds of paradise stole off at our approach, and I was in real despair of catching one when Conseil, walking in the lead, stooped suddenly, gave a triumphant shout, and came back to me, carrying a magnificent bird of paradise.

"Oh bravo, Conseil!" I exclaimed.

"Master is too kind," Conseil replied.

"Not at all, my boy. That was a stroke of genius, catching one of these live birds with your bare hands!"

"If master will examine it closely, he'll see that I deserve no great praise."

"And why not, Conseil?"

"Because this bird is as drunk as a lord."

"Drunk?"

"Yes, master, drunk from the nutmegs it was devouring under that nutmeg tree where I caught it. See, Ned my friend, see the monstrous results of intemperance!"

"Damnation!" the Canadian shot back. "Considering the amount of gin I've had these past two months, you've got nothing to complain about!"

Meanwhile I was examining this unusual bird. Conseil was not mistaken. Tipsy from that potent juice, our bird of paradise had been reduced to helplessness. It was unable to fly. It was barely able to walk. But this didn't alarm me, and I just let it sleep off its nutmeg.

This bird belonged to the finest of the eight species credited to Papua and its neighboring islands. It was a "great emerald," one of the rarest birds of paradise. It measured three decimeters long. Its head was comparatively small, and its eyes, placed near the opening of its beak, were also small. But it offered a wonderful mixture of hues: a yellow beak, brown feet and claws, hazel wings with purple tips, pale yellow head and scruff of the neck, emerald throat, the belly and chest maroon to brown. Two strands, made of a horn substance covered with down, rose over its tail, which was lengthened by long, very light feathers of wonderful fineness, and they completed the costume of this marvelous bird that the islanders have poetically named "the sun bird."

How I wished I could take this superb bird of paradise back to Paris, to make a gift of it to the zoo at the Botanical Gardens, which doesn't own a single live specimen.

"So it must be a rarity or something?" the Canadian asked, in the tone of a hunter who, from the viewpoint of his art, gives the game a pretty low rating.

"A great rarity, my gallant comrade, and above all very hard to capture alive. And even after they're dead, there's still a major market for these birds. So the natives have figured out how to create fake ones, like people create fake pearls or diamonds."

"What!" Conseil exclaimed. "They make counterfeit birds of paradise?"

"Yes, Conseil."

"And is master familiar with how the islanders go about it?"

"Perfectly familiar. During the easterly monsoon season, birds of paradise lose the magnificent feathers around their tails that naturalists call 'below–the–wing' feathers. These feathers are gathered by the fowl forgers and skillfully fitted onto some poor previously mutilated parakeet. Then they paint over the suture, varnish the bird, and ship the fruits of their unique labors to museums and collectors in Europe."

"Good enough!" Ned Land put in. "If it isn't the right bird, it's still the right feathers, and so long as the merchandise isn't meant to be eaten, I see no great harm!"

But if my desires were fulfilled by the capture of this bird of paradise, those of our Canadian huntsman remained unsatisfied. Luckily, near two o'clock Ned Land brought down a magnificent wild pig of the type the natives call "bari–outang." This animal came in the nick of time for us to bag some real quadruped meat, and it was warmly welcomed. Ned Land proved himself quite gloriously with his gunshot. Hit by an electric bullet, the pig dropped dead on the spot.

The Canadian properly skinned and cleaned it, after removing half a dozen cutlets destined to serve as the grilled meat course of our evening meal. Then the hunt was on again, and once more would be marked by the exploits of Ned and Conseil.

In essence, beating the bushes, the two friends flushed a herd of kangaroos that fled by bounding away on their elastic paws. But these animals didn't flee so swiftly that our electric capsules couldn't catch up with them.

"Oh, professor!" shouted Ned Land, whose hunting fever had gone to his brain. "What excellent game, especially in a stew! What a supply for the Nautilus! Two, three, five down! And just think how we'll devour all this meat ourselves, while those numbskulls on board won't get a shred!"

In his uncontrollable glee, I think the Canadian might have slaughtered the whole horde, if he hadn't been so busy talking! But he was content with a dozen of these fascinating marsupials, which make up the first order of aplacental mammals, as Conseil just had to tell us.

These animals were small in stature. They were a species of those "rabbit kangaroos" that usually dwell in the hollows of trees and are tremendously fast; but although of moderate dimensions, they at least furnish a meat that's highly prized.

We were thoroughly satisfied with the results of our hunting. A gleeful Ned proposed that we return the next day to this magic island, which he planned to depopulate of its every edible quadruped. But he was reckoning without events.

By six o'clock in the evening, we were back on the beach. The skiff was aground in its usual place. The Nautilus, looking like a long reef, emerged from the waves two miles offshore.

Without further ado, Ned Land got down to the important business of dinner. He came wonderfully to terms with its entire cooking. Grilling over the coals, those cutlets from the "bari–outang" soon gave off a succulent aroma that perfumed the air.

But I catch myself following in the Canadian's footsteps. Look at me—in ecstasy over freshly grilled pork! Please grant me a pardon as I've already granted one to Mr. Land, and on the same grounds!

In short, dinner was excellent. Two ringdoves rounded out this extraordinary menu. Sago pasta, bread from the artocarpus, mangoes, half a dozen pineapples, and the fermented liquor from certain coconuts heightened our glee. I suspect that my two fine companions weren't quite as clearheaded as one could wish.

"What if we don't return to the Nautilus this evening?" Conseil said.

"What if we never return to it?" Ned Land added.

Just then a stone whizzed toward us, landed at our feet, and cut short the harpooner's proposition.

The Lightning Bolts of Captain Nemo

WITHOUT STANDING UP, we stared in the direction of the forest, my hand stopping halfway to my mouth, Ned Land's completing its assignment.

"Stones don't fall from the sky," Conseil said, "or else they deserve to be called meteorites."

A second well–polished stone removed a tasty ringdove leg from Conseil's hand, giving still greater relevance to his observation.

We all three stood up, rifles to our shoulders, ready to answer any attack.

"Apes maybe?" Ned Land exclaimed.

"Nearly," Conseil replied. "Savages."

"Head for the skiff!" I said, moving toward the sea.

Indeed, it was essential to beat a retreat because some twenty natives, armed with bows and slings, appeared barely a hundred paces off, on the outskirts of a thicket that masked the horizon to our right.

The skiff was aground ten fathoms away from us.

The savages approached without running, but they favored us with a show of the greatest hostility. It was raining stones and arrows.

Ned Land was unwilling to leave his provisions behind, and despite the impending danger, he clutched his pig on one side, his kangaroos on the other, and scampered off with respectable speed.

In two minutes we were on the strand. Loading provisions and weapons into the skiff, pushing it to sea, and positioning its two oars were the work of an instant. We hadn't gone two cable lengths when a hundred savages, howling and gesticulating, entered the water up to their waists. I looked to see if their appearance might draw some of the Nautilus's men onto the platform. But no. Lying well out, that enormous machine still seemed completely deserted.

Twenty minutes later we boarded ship. The hatches were open. After mooring the skiff, we reentered the Nautilus's interior.

I went below to the lounge, from which some chords were wafting. Captain Nemo was there, leaning over the organ, deep in a musical trance.

"Captain!" I said to him.

He didn't hear me.

"Captain!" I went on, touching him with my hand.

He trembled, and turning around:

"Ah, it's you, professor!" he said to me. "Well, did you have a happy hunt? Was your herb gathering a success?"

"Yes, captain," I replied, "but unfortunately we've brought back a horde of bipeds whose proximity worries me."

"What sort of bipeds?"

"Savages."

"Savages!" Captain Nemo replied in an ironic tone. "You set foot on one of the shores of this globe, professor, and you're surprised to find savages there? Where aren't there savages? And besides, are they any worse than men elsewhere, these people you call savages?"

"But Captain—"

"Speaking for myself, sir, I've encountered them everywhere."

"Well then," I replied, "if you don't want to welcome them aboard the Nautilus, you'd better take some precautions!"

"Easy, professor, no cause for alarm."

"But there are a large number of these natives."

"What's your count?"

"At least a hundred."

"Professor Aronnax," replied Captain Nemo, whose fingers took their places again on the organ keys, "if every islander in Papua were to gather on that beach, the Nautilus would still have nothing to fear from their attacks!"

The captain's fingers then ran over the instrument's keyboard, and I noticed that he touched only its black keys, which gave his melodies a basically Scottish color. Soon he had forgotten my presence and was lost in a reverie that I no longer tried to dispel.

I climbed onto the platform. Night had already fallen, because in this low latitude the sun sets quickly, without any twilight. I could see Gueboroa Island only dimly. But numerous fires had been kindled on the beach, attesting that the natives had no thoughts of leaving it.

For several hours I was left to myself, sometimes musing on the islanders—but no longer fearing them because the captain's unflappable confidence had won me over—and sometimes forgetting them to marvel at the splendors of this tropical night. My memories took wing toward France, in the wake of those zodiacal stars due to twinkle over it in a few hours. The moon shone in the midst of the constellations at their zenith. I then remembered that this loyal, good-natured satellite would return to this same place the day after tomorrow, to raise the tide and tear the Nautilus from its coral bed. Near midnight, seeing that all was quiet over the darkened waves as well as under the waterside trees, I repaired to my cabin and fell into a peaceful sleep.

The night passed without mishap. No doubt the Papuans had been frightened off by the mere sight of this monster aground in the bay, because our hatches stayed open, offering easy access to the Nautilus's interior.

At six o'clock in the morning, January 8, I climbed onto the platform. The morning shadows were lifting. The island was soon on view through the dissolving mists, first its beaches, then its summits.

The islanders were still there, in greater numbers than on the day before, perhaps 500 or 600 of them. Taking advantage of the low tide, some of them had moved forward over the heads of coral to within two cable lengths of the Nautilus. I could easily distinguish them. They obviously were true Papuans, men of fine stock, athletic in build, forehead high and broad, nose large but not flat, teeth white. Their woolly, red–tinted hair was in sharp contrast to their bodies, which were black and glistening like those of Nubians. Beneath their pierced, distended earlobes there dangled strings of beads made from bone. Generally these savages were naked. I noted some women among them, dressed from hip to knee in grass skirts held up by belts made of vegetation. Some of the chieftains adorned their necks with crescents and with necklaces made from beads of red and white glass. Armed with bows, arrows, and shields, nearly all of them carried from their shoulders a sort of net, which held those polished stones their slings hurl with such dexterity.

One of these chieftains came fairly close to the Nautilus, examining it with care. He must have been a "mado" of high rank, because he paraded in a mat of banana leaves that had ragged edges and was accented with bright colors.

I could easily have picked off this islander, he stood at such close range; but I thought it best to wait for an actual show of hostility. Between Europeans and savages, it's acceptable for Europeans to shoot back but not to attack first.

During this whole time of low tide, the islanders lurked near the Nautilus, but they weren't boisterous. I often heard them repeat the word "assai," and from their gestures I understood they were inviting me to go ashore, an invitation I felt obliged to decline.

So the skiff didn't leave shipside that day, much to the displeasure of Mr. Land who couldn't complete his provisions. The adroit Canadian spent his time preparing the meat and flour products he had brought from Gueboroa Island. As for the savages, they went back to shore near eleven o'clock in the morning, when the heads of coral began to disappear under the waves of the rising tide. But I saw their numbers swell considerably on the beach. It was likely that they had come from neighboring islands or from the mainland of Papua proper. However, I didn't see one local dugout canoe.

Having nothing better to do, I decided to dredge these beautiful, clear waters, which exhibited a profusion of shells, zoophytes, and open–sea plants. Besides, it was the last day the Nautilus would spend in these waterways, if, tomorrow, it still floated off to the open sea as Captain Nemo had promised.

So I summoned Conseil, who brought me a small, light dragnet similar to those used in oyster fishing.

"What about these savages?" Conseil asked me. "With all due respect to master, they don't strike me as very wicked!"

"They're cannibals even so, my boy."

"A person can be both a cannibal and a decent man," Conseil replied, "just as a person can be both gluttonous and honorable. The one doesn't exclude the other."

"Fine, Conseil! And I agree that there are honorable cannibals who decently devour their prisoners. However, I'm opposed to being devoured, even in all decency, so I'll keep on my guard, especially since the Nautilus's commander seems to be taking no precautions. And now let's get to work!"

For two hours our fishing proceeded energetically but without bringing up any rarities. Our dragnet was filled with Midas abalone, harp shells, obelisk snails, and especially the finest hammer shells I had seen to that day. We also gathered in a few sea cucumbers, some pearl oysters, and a dozen small turtles that we saved for the ship's pantry.

But just when I least expected it, I laid my hands on a wonder, a natural deformity I'd have to call it, something very seldom encountered. Conseil had just made a cast of the dragnet, and his gear had come back up loaded with a variety of fairly ordinary seashells, when suddenly he saw me plunge my arms swiftly into the net, pull out a shelled animal, and give a conchological yell, in other words, the most piercing yell a human throat can produce.

"Eh? What happened to master?" Conseil asked, very startled. "Did master get bitten?"

"No, my boy, but I'd gladly have sacrificed a finger for such a find!"

"What find?"

"This shell," I said, displaying the subject of my triumph.

"But that's simply an olive shell of the 'tent olive' species, genus Oliva, order Pectinibranchia, class Gastropoda, branch Mollusca—"

"Yes, yes, Conseil! But instead of coiling from right to left, this olive shell rolls from left to right!"

"It can't be!" Conseil exclaimed.

"Yes, my boy, it's a left–handed shell!"

"A left–handed shell!" Conseil repeated, his heart pounding.

"Look at its spiral!"

"Oh, master can trust me on this," Conseil said, taking the valuable shell in trembling hands, "but never have I felt such excitement!"

And there was good reason to be excited! In fact, as naturalists have ventured to observe, "dextrality" is a well–known law of nature. In their rotational and orbital movements, stars and their satellites go from right to left. Man uses his right hand more often than his left, and consequently his various instruments and equipment (staircases, locks, watch springs, etc.) are designed to be used in a right–to–left manner. Now then, nature has generally obeyed this law in coiling her shells. They're right–handed with only rare exceptions, and when by chance a shell's spiral is left–handed, collectors will pay its weight in gold for it.

So Conseil and I were deep in the contemplation of our treasure, and I was solemnly promising myself to enrich the Paris Museum with it, when an ill–timed stone, hurled by one of the islanders, whizzed over and shattered the valuable object in Conseil's hands.

I gave a yell of despair! Conseil pounced on his rifle and aimed at a savage swinging a sling just ten meters away from him. I tried to stop him, but his shot went off and shattered a bracelet of amulets dangling from the islander's arm.

"Conseil!" I shouted. "Conseil!"

"Eh? What? Didn't master see that this man–eater initiated the attack?"

"A shell isn't worth a human life!" I told him.

"Oh, the rascal!" Conseil exclaimed. "I'd rather he cracked my shoulder!"

Conseil was in dead earnest, but I didn't subscribe to his views. However, the situation had changed in only a short time and we hadn't noticed. Now some twenty dugout canoes were surrounding the Nautilus. Hollowed from tree trunks, these dugouts were long, narrow, and well designed for speed, keeping their balance by means of two bamboo poles that floated on the surface of the water. They were maneuvered by skillful, half–naked paddlers, and I viewed their advance with definite alarm.

It was obvious these Papuans had already entered into relations with Europeans and knew their ships. But this long, iron cylinder lying in the bay, with no masts or funnels—what were they to make of it? Nothing good, because at first they kept it at a respectful distance. However, seeing that it stayed motionless, they regained confidence little by little and tried to become more familiar with it. Now then, it was precisely this familiarity that we needed to prevent. Since our weapons made no sound when they went off, they would have only a moderate effect on these islanders, who reputedly respect nothing but noisy mechanisms. Without thunderclaps, lightning bolts would be much less frightening, although the danger lies in the flash, not the noise.

Just then the dugout canoes drew nearer to the Nautilus, and a cloud of arrows burst over us.

"Fire and brimstone, it's hailing!" Conseil said. "And poisoned hail perhaps!"

"We've got to alert Captain Nemo," I said, reentering the hatch.

I went below to the lounge. I found no one there. I ventured a knock at the door opening into the captain's stateroom.

The word "Enter!" answered me. I did so and found Captain Nemo busy with calculations in which there was no shortage of X and other algebraic signs.

"Am I disturbing you?" I said out of politeness.

"Correct, Professor Aronnax," the captain answered me. "But I imagine you have pressing reasons for looking me up?"

"Very pressing. Native dugout canoes are surrounding us, and in a few minutes we're sure to be assaulted by several hundred savages."

"Ah!" Captain Nemo put in serenely. "They've come in their dugouts?"

"Yes, sir."

"Well, sir, closing the hatches should do the trick."

"Precisely, and that's what I came to tell you—"

"Nothing easier," Captain Nemo said.

And he pressed an electric button, transmitting an order to the crew's quarters.

"There, sir, all under control!" he told me after a few moments. "The skiff is in place and the hatches are closed. I don't imagine you're worried that these gentlemen will stave in walls that shells from your frigate couldn't breach?"

"No, Captain, but one danger still remains."

"What's that, sir?"

"Tomorrow at about this time, we'll need to reopen the hatches to renew the Nautilus's air."

"No argument, sir, since our craft breathes in the manner favored by cetaceans."

"But if these Papuans are occupying the platform at that moment, I don't see how you can prevent them from entering."

"Then, sir, you assume they'll board the ship?"

"I'm certain of it."

"Well, sir, let them come aboard. I see no reason to prevent them. Deep down they're just poor devils, these Papuans, and I don't want my visit to Gueboroa Island to cost the life of a single one of these unfortunate people!"

On this note I was about to withdraw; but Captain Nemo detained me and invited me to take a seat next to him. He questioned me with interest on our excursions ashore and on our hunting, but seemed not to understand the Canadian's passionate craving for red meat. Then our conversation skimmed various subjects, and without being more forthcoming, Captain Nemo proved more affable.

Among other things, we came to talk of the Nautilus's circumstances, aground in the same strait where Captain Dumont d'Urville had nearly miscarried. Then, pertinent to this:

"He was one of your great seamen," the captain told me, "one of your shrewdest navigators, that d'Urville! He was the Frenchman's Captain Cook. A man wise but unlucky! Braving the ice banks of the South Pole, the coral of Oceania, the cannibals of the Pacific, only to perish wretchedly in a train wreck! If that energetic man was able to think about his life in its last seconds, imagine what his final thoughts must have been!"

As he spoke, Captain Nemo seemed deeply moved, an emotion I felt was to his credit.

Then, chart in hand, we returned to the deeds of the French navigator: his voyages to circumnavigate the globe, his double attempt at the South Pole, which led to his discovery of the Adélie Coast and the Louis–Philippe Peninsula, finally his hydrographic surveys of the chief islands in Oceania.

"What your d'Urville did on the surface of the sea," Captain Nemo told me, "I've done in the ocean's interior, but more easily, more completely than he. Constantly tossed about by hurricanes, the Zealous and the new Astrolabe couldn't compare with the Nautilus, a quiet work room truly at rest in the midst of the waters!"

"Even so, Captain," I said, "there is one major similarity between Dumont d'Urville's sloops of war and the Nautilus."

"What's that, sir?"

"Like them, the Nautilus has run aground!"

"The Nautilus is not aground, sir," Captain Nemo replied icily. "The Nautilus was built to rest on the ocean floor, and I don't need to undertake the arduous labors, the maneuvers d'Urville had to attempt in order to float off his sloops of war. The Zealous and the new Astrolabe wellnigh perished, but my Nautilus is in no danger. Tomorrow, on the day stated and at the hour stated, the tide will peacefully lift it off, and it will resume its navigating through the seas."

"Captain," I said, "I don't doubt—"

"Tomorrow," Captain Nemo added, standing up, "tomorrow at 2:40 in the afternoon, the Nautilus will float off and exit the Torres Strait undamaged."

Pronouncing these words in an extremely sharp tone, Captain Nemo gave me a curt bow. This was my dismissal, and I reentered my stateroom.

There I found Conseil, who wanted to know the upshot of my interview with the captain.

"My boy," I replied, "when I expressed the belief that these Papuan natives were a threat to his Nautilus, the captain answered me with great irony. So I've just one thing to say to you: have faith in him and sleep in peace."

"Master has no need for my services?"

"No, my friend. What's Ned Land up to?"

"Begging master's indulgence," Conseil replied, "but our friend Ned is concocting a kangaroo pie that will be the eighth wonder!"

I was left to myself; I went to bed but slept pretty poorly. I kept hearing noises from the savages, who were stamping on the platform and letting out deafening yells. The night passed in this way, without the crew ever emerging from their usual inertia. They were no more disturbed by the presence of these man–eaters than soldiers in an armored fortress are troubled by ants running over the armor plate.

I got up at six o'clock in the morning. The hatches weren't open. So the air inside hadn't been renewed; but the air tanks were kept full for any eventuality and would function appropriately to shoot a few cubic meters of oxygen into the Nautilus's thin atmosphere.

I worked in my stateroom until noon without seeing Captain Nemo even for an instant. Nobody on board seemed to be making any preparations for departure.

I still waited for a while, then I made my way to the main lounge. Its timepiece marked 2:30. In ten minutes the tide would reach its maximum elevation, and if Captain Nemo hadn't made a rash promise, the Nautilus would immediately break free. If not, many months might pass before it could leave its coral bed.

But some preliminary vibrations could soon be felt over the boat's hull. I heard its plating grind against the limestone roughness of that coral base.

At 2:35 Captain Nemo appeared in the lounge.

"We're about to depart," he said.

"Ah!" I put in.

"I've given orders to open the hatches."

"What about the Papuans?"

"What about them?" Captain Nemo replied, with a light shrug of his shoulders.

"Won't they come inside the Nautilus?"

"How will they manage that?"

"By jumping down the hatches you're about to open."

"Professor Aronnax," Captain Nemo replied serenely, "the Nautilus's hatches aren't to be entered in that fashion even when they're open."

I gaped at the captain.

"You don't understand?" he said to me.

"Not in the least."

"Well, come along and you'll see!"

I headed to the central companionway. There, very puzzled, Ned Land and Conseil watched the crewmen opening the hatches, while a frightful clamor and furious shouts resounded outside.

The hatch lids fell back onto the outer plating. Twenty horrible faces appeared. But when the first islander laid hands on the companionway railing, he was flung backward by some invisible power, lord knows what! He ran off, howling in terror and wildly prancing around.

Ten of his companions followed him. All ten met the same fate.

Conseil was in ecstasy. Carried away by his violent instincts, Ned Land leaped up the companionway. But as soon as his hands seized the railing, he was thrown backward in his turn.

"Damnation!" he exclaimed. "I've been struck by a lightning bolt!"

These words explained everything to me. It wasn't just a railing that led to the platform, it was a metal cable fully charged with the ship's electricity. Anyone who touched it got a fearsome shock—and such a shock would have been fatal if Captain Nemo had thrown the full current from his equipment into this conducting cable! It could honestly be said that he had stretched between himself and his assailants a network of electricity no one could clear with impunity.

Meanwhile, crazed with terror, the unhinged Papuans beat a retreat. As for us, half laughing, we massaged and comforted poor Ned Land, who was swearing like one possessed.

But just then, lifted off by the tide's final undulations, the Nautilus left its coral bed at exactly that fortieth minute pinpointed by the captain. Its propeller churned the waves with lazy majesty. Gathering speed little by little, the ship navigated on the surface of the ocean, and safe and sound, it left behind the dangerous narrows of the Torres Strait.

"Aegri Somnia"

THE FOLLOWING DAY, January 10, the Nautilus resumed its travels in midwater but at a remarkable speed that I estimated to be at least thirty–five miles per hour. The propeller was going so fast I could neither follow nor count its revolutions.

I thought about how this marvelous electric force not only gave motion, heat, and light to the Nautilus but even protected it against outside attack, transforming it into a sacred ark no profane hand could touch without being blasted; my wonderment was boundless, and it went from the submersible itself to the engineer who had created it.

We were traveling due west and on January 11 we doubled Cape Wessel, located in longitude 135° and latitude 10° north, the western tip of the Gulf of Carpentaria. Reefs were still numerous but more widely scattered and were fixed on the chart with the greatest accuracy. The Nautilus easily avoided the Money breakers to port and the Victoria reefs to starboard, positioned at longitude 130° on the tenth parallel, which we went along rigorously.

On January 13, arriving in the Timor Sea, Captain Nemo raised the island of that name at longitude 122°. This island, whose surface area measures 1,625 square leagues, is governed by rajahs. These aristocrats deem themselves the sons of crocodiles, in other words, descendants with the most exalted origins to which a human being can lay claim. Accordingly, their scaly ancestors infest the island's rivers and are the subjects of special veneration. They are sheltered, nurtured, flattered, pampered, and offered a ritual diet of nubile maidens; and woe to the foreigner who lifts a finger against these sacred saurians.

But the Nautilus wanted nothing to do with these nasty animals. Timor Island was visible for barely an instant at noon while the chief officer determined his position. I also caught only a glimpse of little Roti Island, part of this same group, whose women have a well–established reputation for beauty in the Malaysian marketplace.

After our position fix, the Nautilus's latitude bearings were modulated to the southwest. Our prow pointed to the Indian Ocean. Where would Captain Nemo's fancies take us? Would he head up to the shores of Asia? Would he pull nearer to the beaches of Europe? Unlikely choices for a man who avoided populated areas! So would he go down south? Would he double the Cape of Good Hope, then Cape Horn, and push on to the Antarctic pole? Finally, would he return to the seas of the Pacific, where his Nautilus could navigate freely and easily? Time would tell.

After cruising along the Cartier, Hibernia, Seringapatam, and Scott reefs, the solid element's last exertions against the liquid element, we were beyond all sight of shore by January 14. The Nautilus slowed down in an odd manner, and very unpredictable in its ways, it sometimes swam in the midst of the waters, sometimes drifted on their surface.

During this phase of our voyage, Captain Nemo conducted interesting experiments on the different temperatures in various strata of the sea. Under ordinary conditions, such readings are obtained using some pretty complicated instruments whose findings are dubious to say the least, whether they're thermometric sounding lines, whose glass often shatters under the water's pressure, or those devices based on the varying resistance of metals to electric currents. The results so obtained can't be adequately double–checked. By contrast, Captain Nemo would seek the sea's temperature by going himself into its depths, and when he placed his thermometer in contact with the various layers of liquid, he found the sought–for degree immediately and with certainty.

And so, by loading up its ballast tanks, or by sinking obliquely with its slanting fins, the Nautilus successively reached depths of 3,000, 4,000, 5,000, 7,000, 9,000, and 10,000 meters, and the ultimate conclusion from these experiments was that, in all latitudes, the sea had a permanent temperature of 4.5° centigrade at a depth of 1,000 meters.

I watched these experiments with the most intense fascination. Captain Nemo brought a real passion to them. I often wondered why he took these observations. Were they for the benefit of his fellow man? It was unlikely, because sooner or later his work would perish with him in some unknown sea! Unless he intended the results of his experiments for me. But that meant this strange voyage of mine would come to an end, and no such end was in sight.

Be that as it may, Captain Nemo also introduced me to the different data he had obtained on the relative densities of the water in our globe's chief seas. From this news I derived some personal enlightenment having nothing to do with science.

It happened the morning of January 15. The captain, with whom I was strolling on the platform, asked me if I knew how salt water differs in density from sea to sea. I said no, adding that there was a lack of rigorous scientific observations on this subject.

"I've taken such observations," he told me, "and I can vouch for their reliability."

"Fine," I replied, "but the Nautilus lives in a separate world, and the secrets of its scientists don't make their way ashore."

"You're right, professor," he told me after a few moments of silence. "This is a separate world. It's as alien to the earth as the planets accompanying our globe around the sun, and we'll never become familiar with the work of scientists on Saturn or Jupiter. But since fate has linked our two lives, I can reveal the results of my observations to you."

"I'm all attention, Captain."

"You're aware, Professor, that salt water is denser than fresh water, but this density isn't uniform. In essence, if I represent the density of fresh water by 1.000, then I find 1.028 for the waters of the Atlantic, 1.026 for the waters of the Pacific, 1.030 for the waters of the Mediterranean—"

Aha, I thought, so he ventures into the Mediterranean?

"—1.018 for the waters of the Ionian Sea, and 1.029 for the waters of the Adriatic."

Assuredly, the Nautilus didn't avoid the heavily traveled seas of Europe, and from this insight I concluded that the ship would take us back—perhaps very soon—to more civilized shores. I expected Ned Land to greet this news with unfeigned satisfaction.

For several days our work hours were spent in all sorts of experiments, on the degree of salinity in waters of different depths, or on their electric properties, coloration, and transparency, and in every instance Captain Nemo displayed an ingenuity equaled only by his graciousness toward me. Then I saw no more of him for some days and again lived on board in seclusion.

On January 16 the Nautilus seemed to have fallen asleep just a few meters beneath the surface of the water. Its electric equipment had been turned off, and the motionless propeller let it ride with the waves. I assumed that the crew were busy with interior repairs, required by the engine's strenuous mechanical action.

My companions and I then witnessed an unusual sight. The panels in the lounge were open, and since the Nautilus's beacon was off, a hazy darkness reigned in the midst of the waters. Covered with heavy clouds, the stormy sky gave only the faintest light to the ocean's upper strata.

I was observing the state of the sea under these conditions, and even the largest fish were nothing more than ill–defined shadows, when the Nautilus was suddenly transferred into broad daylight. At first I thought the beacon had gone back on and was casting its electric light into the liquid mass. I was mistaken, and after a hasty examination I discovered my error.

The Nautilus had drifted into the midst of some phosphorescent strata, which, in this darkness, came off as positively dazzling. This effect was caused by myriads of tiny, luminous animals whose brightness increased when they glided over the metal hull of our submersible. In the midst of these luminous sheets of water, I then glimpsed flashes of light, like those seen inside a blazing furnace from streams of molten lead or from masses of metal brought to a white heat—flashes so intense that certain areas of the light became shadows by comparison, in a fiery setting from which every shadow should seemingly have been banished. No, this was no longer the calm emission of our usual lighting! This light throbbed with unprecedented vigor and activity! You sensed that it was alive!

In essence, it was a cluster of countless open–sea infusoria, of noctiluca an eighth of an inch wide, actual globules of transparent jelly equipped with a threadlike tentacle, up to 25,000 of which have been counted in thirty cubic centimeters of water. And the power of their light was increased by those glimmers unique to medusas, starfish, common jellyfish, angel–wing clams, and other phosphorescent zoophytes, which were saturated with grease from organic matter decomposed by the sea, and perhaps with mucus secreted by fish.

For several hours the Nautilus drifted in this brilliant tide, and our wonderment grew when we saw huge marine animals cavorting in it, like the fire–dwelling salamanders of myth. In the midst of these flames that didn't burn, I could see swift, elegant porpoises, the tireless pranksters of the seas, and sailfish three meters long, those shrewd heralds of hurricanes, whose fearsome broadswords sometimes banged against the lounge window. Then smaller fish appeared: miscellaneous triggerfish, leather jacks, unicornfish, and a hundred others that left stripes on this luminous atmosphere in their course.

Some magic lay behind this dazzling sight! Perhaps some atmospheric condition had intensified this phenomenon? Perhaps a storm had been unleashed on the surface of the waves? But only a few meters down, the Nautilus felt no tempest's fury, and the ship rocked peacefully in the midst of the calm waters.

And so it went, some new wonder constantly delighting us. Conseil observed and classified his zoophytes, articulates, mollusks, and fish. The days passed quickly, and I no longer kept track of them. Ned, as usual, kept looking for changes of pace from our standard fare. Like actual snails, we were at home in our shell, and I can vouch that it's easy to turn into a full–fledged snail.

So this way of living began to seem simple and natural to us, and we no longer envisioned a different lifestyle on the surface of the planet earth, when something happened to remind us of our strange circumstances.

On January 18 the Nautilus lay in longitude 105° and latitude 15° south. The weather was threatening, the sea rough and billowy. The wind was blowing a strong gust from the east. The barometer, which had been falling for some days, forecast an approaching struggle of the elements.

I had climbed onto the platform just as the chief officer was taking his readings of hour angles. Out of habit I waited for him to pronounce his daily phrase. But that day it was replaced by a different phrase, just as incomprehensible. Almost at once I saw Captain Nemo appear, lift his spyglass, and inspect the horizon.

For some minutes the captain stood motionless, rooted to the spot contained within the field of his lens. Then he lowered his spyglass and exchanged about ten words with his chief officer. The latter seemed to be in the grip of an excitement he tried in vain to control. More in command of himself, Captain Nemo remained cool. Furthermore, he seemed to be raising certain objections that his chief officer kept answering with flat assurances. At least that's what I gathered from their differences in tone and gesture.

As for me, I stared industriously in the direction under observation but without spotting a thing. Sky and water merged into a perfectly clean horizon line.

Meanwhile Captain Nemo strolled from one end of the platform to the other, not glancing at me, perhaps not even seeing me. His step was firm but less regular than usual. Sometimes he would stop, cross his arms over his chest, and observe the sea. What could he be looking for over that immense expanse? By then the Nautilus lay hundreds of miles from the nearest coast!

The chief officer kept lifting his spyglass and stubbornly examining the horizon, walking up and down, stamping his foot, in his nervous agitation a sharp contrast to his superior.

But this mystery would inevitably be cleared up, and soon, because Captain Nemo gave orders to increase speed; at once the engine stepped up its drive power, setting the propeller in swifter rotation.

Just then the chief officer drew the captain's attention anew. The latter interrupted his strolling and aimed his spyglass at the point indicated. He observed it a good while. As for me, deeply puzzled, I went below to the lounge and brought back an excellent long–range telescope I habitually used. Leaning my elbows on the beacon housing, which jutted from the stern of the platform, I got set to scour that whole stretch of sky and sea.

But no sooner had I peered into the eyepiece than the instrument was snatched from my hands.

I spun around. Captain Nemo was standing before me, but I almost didn't recognize him. His facial features were transfigured. Gleaming with dark fire, his eyes had shrunk beneath his frowning brow. His teeth were half bared. His rigid body, clenched fists, and head drawn between his shoulders, all attested to a fierce hate breathing from every pore. He didn't move. My spyglass fell from his hand and rolled at his feet.

Had I accidentally caused these symptoms of anger? Did this incomprehensible individual think I had detected some secret forbidden to guests on the Nautilus?

No! I wasn't the subject of his hate because he wasn't even looking at me; his eyes stayed stubbornly focused on that inscrutable point of the horizon.

Finally Captain Nemo regained his self–control. His facial appearance, so profoundly changed, now resumed its usual calm. He addressed a few words to his chief officer in their strange language, then he turned to me:

"Professor Aronnax," he told me in a tone of some urgency, "I ask that you now honor one of the binding agreements between us."

"Which one, Captain?"

"You and your companions must be placed in confinement until I see fit to set you free."

"You're in command," I answered, gaping at him. "But may I address a question to you?"

"You may not, sir."

After that, I stopped objecting and started obeying, since resistance was useless.

I went below to the cabin occupied by Ned Land and Conseil, and I informed them of the captain's decision. I'll let the reader decide how this news was received by the Canadian. In any case, there was no time for explanations. Four crewmen were waiting at the door, and they led us to the cell where we had spent our first night aboard the Nautilus.

Ned Land tried to lodge a complaint, but the only answer he got was a door shut in his face.

"Will master tell me what this means?" Conseil asked me.

I told my companions what had happened. They were as astonished as I was, but no wiser.

Then I sank into deep speculation, and Captain Nemo's strange facial seizure kept haunting me. I was incapable of connecting two ideas in logical order, and I had strayed into the most absurd hypotheses, when I was snapped out of my mental struggles by these words from Ned Land:

"Well, look here! Lunch is served!"

Indeed, the table had been laid. Apparently Captain Nemo had given this order at the same time he commanded the Nautilus to pick up speed.

"Will master allow me to make him a recommendation?" Conseil asked me.

"Yes, my boy," I replied.

"Well, master needs to eat his lunch! It's prudent, because we have no idea what the future holds."

"You're right, Conseil."

"Unfortunately," Ned Land said, "they've only given us the standard menu."

"Ned my friend," Conseil answered, "what would you say if they'd given us no lunch at all?"

This dose of sanity cut the harpooner's complaints clean off.

We sat down at the table. Our meal proceeded pretty much in silence. I ate very little. Conseil, everlastingly prudent, "force–fed" himself; and despite the menu, Ned Land didn't waste a bite. Then, lunch over, each of us propped himself in a corner.

Just then the luminous globe lighting our cell went out, leaving us in profound darkness. Ned Land soon dozed off, and to my astonishment, Conseil also fell into a heavy slumber. I was wondering what could have caused this urgent need for sleep, when I felt a dense torpor saturate my brain. I tried to keep my eyes open, but they closed in spite of me. I was in the grip of anguished hallucinations. Obviously some sleep–inducing substance had been laced into the food we'd just eaten! So imprisonment wasn't enough to conceal Captain Nemo's plans from us—sleep was needed as well!

Then I heard the hatches close. The sea's undulations, which had been creating a gentle rocking motion, now ceased. Had the Nautilus left the surface of the ocean? Was it reentering the motionless strata deep in the sea?

I tried to fight off this drowsiness. It was impossible. My breathing grew weaker. I felt a mortal chill freeze my dull, nearly paralyzed limbs. Like little domes of lead, my lids fell over my eyes. I couldn't raise them. A morbid sleep, full of hallucinations, seized my whole being. Then the visions disappeared and left me in utter oblivion.

The Coral Realm

THE NEXT DAY I woke up with my head unusually clear. Much to my surprise, I was in my stateroom. No doubt my companions had been put back in their cabin without noticing it any more than I had. Like me, they would have no idea what took place during the night, and to unravel this mystery I could count only on some future happenstance.

I then considered leaving my stateroom. Was I free or still a prisoner? Perfectly free. I opened my door, headed down the gangways, and climbed the central companionway. Hatches that had been closed the day before were now open. I arrived on the platform.

Ned Land and Conseil were there waiting for me. I questioned them. They knew nothing. Lost in a heavy sleep of which they had no memory, they were quite startled to be back in their cabin.

As for the Nautilus, it seemed as tranquil and mysterious as ever. It was cruising on the surface of the waves at a moderate speed. Nothing seemed to have changed on board.

Ned Land observed the sea with his penetrating eyes. It was deserted. The Canadian sighted nothing new on the horizon, neither sail nor shore. A breeze was blowing noisily from the west, and disheveled by the wind, long billows made the submersible roll very noticeably.

After renewing its air, the Nautilus stayed at an average depth of fifteen meters, enabling it to return quickly to the surface of the waves. And, contrary to custom, it executed such a maneuver several times during that day of January 19. The chief officer would then climb onto the platform, and his usual phrase would ring through the ship's interior.

As for Captain Nemo, he didn't appear. Of the other men on board, I saw only my emotionless steward, who served me with his usual mute efficiency.

Near two o'clock I was busy organizing my notes in the lounge, when the captain opened the door and appeared. I bowed to him. He gave me an almost imperceptible bow in return, without saying a word to me. I resumed my work, hoping he might give me some explanation of the previous afternoon's events. He did nothing of the sort. I stared at him. His face looked exhausted; his reddened eyes hadn't been refreshed by sleep; his facial features expressed profound sadness, real chagrin. He walked up and down, sat and stood, picked up a book at random, discarded it immediately, consulted his instruments without taking his customary notes, and seemed unable to rest easy for an instant.

Finally he came over to me and said:

"Are you a physician, Professor Aronnax?"

This inquiry was so unexpected that I stared at him a good while without replying.

"Are you a physician?" he repeated. "Several of your scientific colleagues took their degrees in medicine, such as Gratiolet, Moquin–Tandon, and others."

"That's right," I said, "I am a doctor, I used to be on call at the hospitals. I was in practice for several years before joining the museum."

"Excellent, sir."

My reply obviously pleased Captain Nemo. But not knowing what he was driving at, I waited for further questions, ready to reply as circumstances dictated.

"Professor Aronnax," the captain said to me, "would you consent to give your medical attentions to one of my men?"

"Someone is sick?"

"Yes."

"I'm ready to go with you."

"Come."

I admit that my heart was pounding. Lord knows why, but I saw a definite connection between this sick crewman and yesterday's happenings, and the mystery of those events concerned me at least as much as the man's sickness.

Captain Nemo led me to the Nautilus's stern and invited me into a cabin located next to the sailors' quarters.

On a bed there lay a man some forty years old, with strongly molded features, the very image of an Anglo–Saxon.

I bent over him. Not only was he sick, he was wounded. Swathed in blood–soaked linen, his head was resting on a folded pillow. I undid the linen bandages, while the wounded man gazed with great staring eyes and let me proceed without making a single complaint.

It was a horrible wound. The cranium had been smashed open by some blunt instrument, leaving the naked brains exposed, and the cerebral matter had suffered deep abrasions. Blood clots had formed in this dissolving mass, taking on the color of wine dregs. Both contusion and concussion of the brain had occurred. The sick man's breathing was labored, and muscle spasms quivered in his face. Cerebral inflammation was complete and had brought on a paralysis of movement and sensation.

I took the wounded man's pulse. It was intermittent. The body's extremities were already growing cold, and I saw that death was approaching without any possibility of my holding it in check. After dressing the poor man's wound, I redid the linen bandages around his head, and I turned to Captain Nemo.

"How did he get this wound?" I asked him.

"That's not important," the captain replied evasively. "The Nautilus suffered a collision that cracked one of the engine levers, and it struck this man. My chief officer was standing beside him. This man leaped forward to intercept the blow. A brother lays down his life for his brother, a friend for his friend, what could be simpler? That's the law for everyone on board the Nautilus. But what's your diagnosis of his condition?"

I hesitated to speak my mind.

"You may talk freely," the captain told me. "This man doesn't understand French."

I took a last look at the wounded man, then I replied:

"This man will be dead in two hours."

"Nothing can save him?"

"Nothing."

Captain Nemo clenched his fists, and tears slid from his eyes, which I had thought incapable of weeping.

For a few moments more I observed the dying man, whose life was ebbing little by little. He grew still more pale under the electric light that bathed his deathbed. I looked at his intelligent head, furrowed with premature wrinkles that misfortune, perhaps misery, had etched long before. I was hoping to detect the secret of his life in the last words that might escape from his lips!

"You may go, Professor Aronnax," Captain Nemo told me.

I left the captain in the dying man's cabin and I repaired to my stateroom, very moved by this scene. All day long I was aquiver with gruesome forebodings. That night I slept poorly, and between my fitful dreams, I thought I heard a distant moaning, like a funeral dirge. Was it a prayer for the dead, murmured in that language I couldn't understand?

The next morning I climbed on deck. Captain Nemo was already there. As soon as he saw me, he came over.

"Professor," he said to me, "would it be convenient for you to make an underwater excursion today?"

"With my companions?" I asked.

"If they're agreeable."

"We're yours to command, Captain."

"Then kindly put on your diving suits."

As for the dead or dying man, he hadn't come into the picture. I rejoined Ned Land and Conseil. I informed them of Captain Nemo's proposition. Conseil was eager to accept, and this time the Canadian proved perfectly amenable to going with us.

It was eight o'clock in the morning. By 8:30 we were suited up for this new stroll and equipped with our two devices for lighting and breathing. The double door opened, and accompanied by Captain Nemo with a dozen crewmen following, we set foot on the firm seafloor where the Nautilus was resting, ten meters down.

A gentle slope gravitated to an uneven bottom whose depth was about fifteen fathoms. This bottom was completely different from the one I had visited during my first excursion under the waters of the Pacific Ocean. Here I saw no fine–grained sand, no underwater prairies, not one open–sea forest. I immediately recognized the wondrous region in which Captain Nemo did the honors that day. It was the coral realm.

In the zoophyte branch, class Alcyonaria, one finds the order Gorgonaria, which contains three groups: sea fans, isidian polyps, and coral polyps. It's in this last that precious coral belongs, an unusual substance that, at different times, has been classified in the mineral, vegetable, and animal kingdoms. Medicine to the ancients, jewelry to the moderns, it wasn't decisively placed in the animal kingdom until 1694, by Peysonnel of Marseilles.

A coral is a unit of tiny animals assembled over a polypary that's brittle and stony in nature. These polyps have a unique generating mechanism that reproduces them via the budding process, and they have an individual existence while also participating in a communal life. Hence they embody a sort of natural socialism. I was familiar with the latest research on this bizarre zoophyte—which turns to stone while taking on a tree form, as some naturalists have very aptly observed—and nothing could have been more fascinating to me than to visit one of these petrified forests that nature has planted on the bottom of the sea.

We turned on our Ruhmkorff devices and went along a coral shoal in the process of forming, which, given time, will someday close off this whole part of the Indian Ocean. Our path was bordered by hopelessly tangled bushes, formed from snarls of shrubs all covered with little star–shaped, white–streaked flowers. Only, contrary to plants on shore, these tree forms become attached to rocks on the seafloor by heading from top to bottom.

Our lights produced a thousand delightful effects while playing over these brightly colored boughs. I fancied I saw these cylindrical, membrane–filled tubes trembling beneath the water's undulations. I was tempted to gather their fresh petals, which were adorned with delicate tentacles, some newly in bloom, others barely opened, while nimble fish with fluttering fins brushed past them like flocks of birds. But if my hands came near the moving flowers of these sensitive, lively creatures, an alarm would instantly sound throughout the colony. The white petals retracted into their red sheaths, the flowers vanished before my eyes, and the bush changed into a chunk of stony nipples.

Sheer chance had placed me in the presence of the most valuable specimens of this zoophyte. This coral was the equal of those fished up from the Mediterranean off the Barbary Coast or the shores of France and Italy. With its bright colors, it lived up to those poetic names of blood flower and blood foam that the industry confers on its finest exhibits. Coral sells for as much as ₣500 per kilogram, and in this locality the liquid strata hid enough to make the fortunes of a whole host of coral fishermen. This valuable substance often merges with other polyparies, forming compact, hopelessly tangled units known as "macciota," and I noted some wonderful pink samples of this coral.

But as the bushes shrank, the tree forms magnified. Actual petrified thickets and long alcoves from some fantastic school of architecture kept opening up before our steps. Captain Nemo entered beneath a dark gallery whose gentle slope took us to a depth of 100 meters. The light from our glass coils produced magical effects at times, lingering on the wrinkled roughness of some natural arch, or some overhang suspended like a chandelier, which our lamps flecked with fiery sparks. Amid these shrubs of precious coral, I observed other polyps no less unusual: melita coral, rainbow coral with jointed outgrowths, then a few tufts of genus Corallina, some green and others red, actually a type of seaweed encrusted with limestone salts, which, after long disputes, naturalists have finally placed in the vegetable kingdom. But as one intellectual has remarked, "Here, perhaps, is the actual point where life rises humbly out of slumbering stone, but without breaking away from its crude starting point."

Finally, after two hours of walking, we reached a depth of about 300 meters, in other words, the lowermost limit at which coral can begin to form. But here it was no longer some isolated bush or a modest grove of low timber. It was an immense forest, huge mineral vegetation, enormous petrified trees linked by garlands of elegant hydras from the genus Plumularia, those tropical creepers of the sea, all decked out in shades and gleams. We passed freely under their lofty boughs, lost up in the shadows of the waves, while at our feet organ–pipe coral, stony coral, star coral, fungus coral, and sea anemone from the genus Caryophylia formed a carpet of flowers all strewn with dazzling gems.

What an indescribable sight! Oh, if only we could share our feelings! Why were we imprisoned behind these masks of metal and glass! Why were we forbidden to talk with each other! At least let us lead the lives of the fish that populate this liquid element, or better yet, the lives of amphibians, which can spend long hours either at sea or on shore, traveling through their double domain as their whims dictate!

Meanwhile Captain Nemo had called a halt. My companions and I stopped walking, and turning around, I saw the crewmen form a semicircle around their leader. Looking with greater care, I observed that four of them were carrying on their shoulders an object that was oblong in shape.

At this locality we stood in the center of a huge clearing surrounded by the tall tree forms of this underwater forest. Our lamps cast a sort of brilliant twilight over the area, making inordinately long shadows on the seafloor. Past the boundaries of the clearing, the darkness deepened again, relieved only by little sparkles given off by the sharp crests of coral.

Ned Land and Conseil stood next to me. We stared, and it dawned on me that I was about to witness a strange scene. Observing the seafloor, I saw that it swelled at certain points from low bulges that were encrusted with limestone deposits and arranged with a symmetry that betrayed the hand of man.

In the middle of the clearing, on a pedestal of roughly piled rocks, there stood a cross of coral, extending long arms you would have thought were made of petrified blood.

At a signal from Captain Nemo, one of his men stepped forward and, a few feet from this cross, detached a mattock from his belt and began to dig a hole.

I finally understood! This clearing was a cemetery, this hole a grave, that oblong object the body of the man who must have died during the night! Captain Nemo and his men had come to bury their companion in this communal resting place on the inaccessible ocean floor!

No! My mind was reeling as never before! Never had ideas of such impact raced through my brain! I didn't want to see what my eyes saw!

Meanwhile the grave digging went slowly. Fish fled here and there as their retreat was disturbed. I heard the pick ringing on the limestone soil, its iron tip sometimes giving off sparks when it hit a stray piece of flint on the sea bottom. The hole grew longer, wider, and soon was deep enough to receive the body.

Then the pallbearers approached. Wrapped in white fabric made from filaments of the fan mussel, the body was lowered into its watery grave. Captain Nemo, arms crossed over his chest, knelt in a posture of prayer, as did all the friends of him who had loved them. . . . My two companions and I bowed reverently.

The grave was then covered over with the rubble dug from the seafloor, and it formed a low mound.

When this was done, Captain Nemo and his men stood up; then they all approached the grave, sank again on bended knee, and extended their hands in a sign of final farewell. . . .

Then the funeral party went back up the path to the Nautilus, returning beneath the arches of the forest, through the thickets, along the coral bushes, going steadily higher.

Finally the ship's rays appeared. Their luminous trail guided us to the Nautilus. By one o'clock we had returned.

After changing clothes, I climbed onto the platform, and in the grip of dreadfully obsessive thoughts, I sat next to the beacon.

Captain Nemo rejoined me. I stood up and said to him:

"So, as I predicted, that man died during the night?"

"Yes, Professor Aronnax," Captain Nemo replied.

"And now he rests beside his companions in that coral cemetery?"

"Yes, forgotten by the world but not by us! We dig the graves, then entrust the polyps with sealing away our dead for eternity!"

And with a sudden gesture, the captain hid his face in his clenched fists, vainly trying to hold back a sob. Then he added:

"There lies our peaceful cemetery, hundreds of feet beneath the surface of the waves!"

"At least, captain, your dead can sleep serenely there, out of the reach of sharks!"

"Yes, sir," Captain Nemo replied solemnly, "of sharks and men!"

Second Part

The Indian Ocean

NOW WE BEGIN the second part of this voyage under the seas. The first ended in that moving scene at the coral cemetery, which left a profound impression on my mind. And so Captain Nemo would live out his life entirely in the heart of this immense sea, and even his grave lay ready in its impenetrable depths. There the last sleep of the Nautilus's occupants, friends bound together in death as in life, would be disturbed by no monster of the deep! "No man either!" the captain had added.

Always that same fierce, implacable defiance of human society!

As for me, I was no longer content with the hypotheses that satisfied Conseil. That fine lad persisted in seeing the Nautilus's commander as merely one of those unappreciated scientists who repay humanity's indifference with contempt. For Conseil, the captain was still a misunderstood genius who, tired of the world's deceptions, had been driven to take refuge in this inaccessible environment where he was free to follow his instincts. But to my mind, this hypothesis explained only one side of Captain Nemo.

In fact, the mystery of that last afternoon when we were locked in prison and put to sleep, the captain's violent precaution of snatching from my grasp a spyglass poised to scour the horizon, and the fatal wound given that man during some unexplained collision suffered by the Nautilus, all led me down a plain trail. No! Captain Nemo wasn't content simply to avoid humanity! His fearsome submersible served not only his quest for freedom, but also, perhaps, it was used in Lord–knows–what schemes of dreadful revenge.

Right now, nothing is clear to me, I still glimpse only glimmers in the dark, and I must limit my pen, as it were, to taking dictation from events.

But nothing binds us to Captain Nemo. He believes that escaping from the Nautilus is impossible. We are not even constrained by our word of honor. No promises fetter us. We're simply captives, prisoners masquerading under the name "guests" for the sake of everyday courtesy. Even so, Ned Land hasn't given up all hope of recovering his freedom. He's sure to take advantage of the first chance that comes his way. No doubt I will do likewise. And yet I will feel some regret at making off with the Nautilus's secrets, so generously unveiled for us by Captain Nemo! Because, ultimately, should we detest or admire this man? Is he the persecutor or the persecuted? And in all honesty, before I leave him forever, I want to finish this underwater tour of the world, whose first stages have been so magnificent. I want to observe the full series of these wonders gathered under the seas of our globe. I want to see what no man has seen yet, even if I must pay for this insatiable curiosity with my life! What are my discoveries to date? Nothing, relatively speaking—since so far we've covered only 6,000 leagues across the Pacific!

Nevertheless, I'm well aware that the Nautilus is drawing near to populated shores, and if some chance for salvation becomes available to us, it would be sheer cruelty to sacrifice my companions to my passion for the unknown. I must go with them, perhaps even guide them. But will this opportunity ever arise? The human being, robbed of his free will, craves such an opportunity; but the scientist, forever inquisitive, dreads it.

That day, January 21, 1868, the chief officer went at noon to take the sun's altitude. I climbed onto the platform, lit a cigar, and watched him at work. It seemed obvious to me that this man didn't understand French, because I made several remarks in a loud voice that were bound to provoke him to some involuntary show of interest had he understood them; but he remained mute and emotionless.

While he took his sights with his sextant, one of the Nautilus's sailors—that muscular man who had gone with us to Crespo Island during our first underwater excursion—came up to clean the glass panes of the beacon. I then examined the fittings of this mechanism, whose power was increased a hundredfold by biconvex lenses that were designed like those in a lighthouse and kept its rays productively focused. This electric lamp was so constructed as to yield its maximum illuminating power. In essence, its light was generated in a vacuum, insuring both its steadiness and intensity. Such a vacuum also reduced wear on the graphite points between which the luminous arc expanded. This was an important savings for Captain Nemo, who couldn't easily renew them. But under these conditions, wear and tear were almost nonexistent.

When the Nautilus was ready to resume its underwater travels, I went below again to the lounge. The hatches closed once more, and our course was set due west.

We then plowed the waves of the Indian Ocean, vast liquid plains with an area of 550,000,000 hectares, whose waters are so transparent it makes you dizzy to lean over their surface. There the Nautilus generally drifted at a depth between 100 and 200 meters. It behaved in this way for some days. To anyone without my grand passion for the sea, these hours would surely have seemed long and monotonous; but my daily strolls on the platform where I was revived by the life–giving ocean air, the sights in the rich waters beyond the lounge windows, the books to be read in the library, and the composition of my memoirs, took up all my time and left me without a moment of weariness or boredom.

All in all, we enjoyed a highly satisfactory state of health. The diet on board agreed with us perfectly, and for my part, I could easily have gone without those changes of pace that Ned Land, in a spirit of protest, kept taxing his ingenuity to supply us. What's more, in this constant temperature we didn't even have to worry about catching colds. Besides, the ship had a good stock of the madrepore Dendrophylia, known in Provence by the name sea fennel, and a poultice made from the dissolved flesh of its polyps will furnish an excellent cough medicine.

For some days we saw a large number of aquatic birds with webbed feet, known as gulls or sea mews. Some were skillfully slain, and when cooked in a certain fashion, they make a very acceptable platter of water game. Among the great wind riders—carried over long distances from every shore and resting on the waves from their exhausting flights—I spotted some magnificent albatross, birds belonging to the Longipennes (long–winged) family, whose discordant calls sound like the braying of an ass. The Totipalmes (fully webbed) family was represented by swift frigate birds, nimbly catching fish at the surface, and by numerous tropic birds of the genus Phaeton, among others the red–tailed tropic bird, the size of a pigeon, its white plumage shaded with pink tints that contrasted with its dark–hued wings.

The Nautilus's nets hauled up several types of sea turtle from the hawksbill genus with arching backs whose scales are highly prized. Diving easily, these reptiles can remain a good while underwater by closing the fleshy valves located at the external openings of their nasal passages. When they were captured, some hawksbills were still asleep inside their carapaces, a refuge from other marine animals. The flesh of these turtles was nothing memorable, but their eggs made an excellent feast.

As for fish, they always filled us with wonderment when, staring through the open panels, we could unveil the secrets of their aquatic lives. I noted several species I hadn't previously been able to observe.

I'll mention chiefly some trunkfish unique to the Red Sea, the sea of the East Indies, and that part of the ocean washing the coasts of equinoctial America. Like turtles, armadillos, sea urchins, and crustaceans, these fish are protected by armor plate that's neither chalky nor stony but actual bone. Sometimes this armor takes the shape of a solid triangle, sometimes that of a solid quadrangle. Among the triangular type, I noticed some half a decimeter long, with brown tails, yellow fins, and wholesome, exquisitely tasty flesh; I even recommend that they be acclimatized to fresh water, a change, incidentally, that a number of saltwater fish can make with ease. I'll also mention some quadrangular trunkfish topped by four large protuberances along the back; trunkfish sprinkled with white spots on the underside of the body, which make good house pets like certain birds; boxfish armed with stings formed by extensions of their bony crusts, and whose odd grunting has earned them the nickname "sea pigs"; then some trunkfish known as dromedaries, with tough, leathery flesh and big conical humps.

From the daily notes kept by Mr. Conseil, I also retrieve certain fish from the genus Tetradon unique to these seas: southern puffers with red backs and white chests distinguished by three lengthwise rows of filaments, and jugfish, seven inches long, decked out in the brightest colors. Then, as specimens of other genera, blowfish resembling a dark brown egg, furrowed with white bands, and lacking tails; globefish, genuine porcupines of the sea, armed with stings and able to inflate themselves until they look like a pin cushion bristling with needles; seahorses common to every ocean; flying dragonfish with long snouts and highly distended pectoral fins shaped like wings, which enable them, if not to fly, at least to spring into the air; spatula–shaped paddlefish whose tails are covered with many scaly rings; snipefish with long jaws, excellent animals twenty–five centimeters long and gleaming with the most cheerful colors; bluish gray dragonets with wrinkled heads; myriads of leaping blennies with black stripes and long pectoral fins, gliding over the surface of the water with prodigious speed; delicious sailfish that can hoist their fins in a favorable current like so many unfurled sails; splendid nurseryfish on which nature has lavished yellow, azure, silver, and gold; yellow mackerel with wings made of filaments; bullheads forever spattered with mud, which make distinct hissing sounds; sea robins whose livers are thought to be poisonous; ladyfish that can flutter their eyelids; finally, archerfish with long, tubular snouts, real oceangoing flycatchers, armed with a rifle unforeseen by either Remington or Chassepot: it slays insects by shooting them with a simple drop of water.

From the eighty–ninth fish genus in Lacépède's system of classification, belonging to his second subclass of bony fish (characterized by gill covers and a bronchial membrane), I noted some scorpionfish whose heads are adorned with stings and which have only one dorsal fin; these animals are covered with small scales, or have none at all, depending on the subgenus to which they belong. The second subgenus gave us some Didactylus specimens three to four decimeters long, streaked with yellow, their heads having a phantasmagoric appearance. As for the first subgenus, it furnished several specimens of that bizarre fish aptly nicknamed "toadfish," whose big head is sometimes gouged with deep cavities, sometimes swollen with protuberances; bristling with stings and strewn with nodules, it sports hideously irregular horns; its body and tail are adorned with callosities; its stings can inflict dangerous injuries; it's repulsive and horrible.

From January 21 to the 23rd, the Nautilus traveled at the rate of 250 leagues in twenty–four hours, hence 540 miles at twenty–two miles per hour. If, during our trip, we were able to identify these different varieties of fish, it's because they were attracted by our electric light and tried to follow alongside; but most of them were outdistanced by our speed and soon fell behind; temporarily, however, a few managed to keep pace in the Nautilus's waters.

On the morning of the 24th, in latitude 12° 5' south and longitude 94° 33', we raised Keeling Island, a madreporic upheaving planted with magnificent coconut trees, which had been visited by Mr. Darwin and Captain Fitzroy. The Nautilus cruised along a short distance off the shore of this desert island. Our dragnets brought up many specimens of polyps and echinoderms plus some unusual shells from the branch Mollusca. Captain Nemo's treasures were enhanced by some valuable exhibits from the delphinula snail species, to which I joined some pointed star coral, a sort of parasitic polypary that often attaches itself to seashells.

Soon Keeling Island disappeared below the horizon, and our course was set to the northwest, toward the tip of the Indian peninsula.

"Civilization!" Ned Land told me that day. "Much better than those Papuan Islands where we ran into more savages than venison! On this Indian shore, professor, there are roads and railways, English, French, and Hindu villages. We wouldn't go five miles without bumping into a fellow countryman. Come on now, isn't it time for our sudden departure from Captain Nemo?"

"No, no, Ned," I replied in a very firm tone. "Let's ride it out, as you seafaring fellows say. The Nautilus is approaching populated areas. It's going back toward Europe, let it take us there. After we arrive in home waters, we can do as we see fit. Besides, I don't imagine Captain Nemo will let us go hunting on the coasts of Malabar or Coromandel as he did in the forests of New Guinea."

"Well, sir, can't we manage without his permission?"

I didn't answer the Canadian. I wanted no arguments. Deep down, I was determined to fully exploit the good fortune that had put me on board the Nautilus.

After leaving Keeling Island, our pace got generally slower. It also got more unpredictable, often taking us to great depths. Several times we used our slanting fins, which internal levers could set at an oblique angle to our waterline. Thus we went as deep as two or three kilometers down but without ever verifying the lowest depths of this sea near India, which soundings of 13,000 meters have been unable to reach. As for the temperature in these lower strata, the thermometer always and invariably indicated 4° centigrade. I merely observed that in the upper layers, the water was always colder over shallows than in the open sea.

On January 25, the ocean being completely deserted, the Nautilus spent the day on the surface, churning the waves with its powerful propeller and making them spurt to great heights. Under these conditions, who wouldn't have mistaken it for a gigantic cetacean? I spent three–quarters of the day on the platform. I stared at the sea. Nothing on the horizon, except near four o'clock in the afternoon a long steamer to the west, running on our opposite tack. Its masting was visible for an instant, but it couldn't have seen the Nautilus because we were lying too low in the water. I imagine that steamboat belonged to the Peninsular & Oriental line, which provides service from the island of Ceylon to Sidney, also calling at King George Sound and Melbourne.

At five o'clock in the afternoon, just before that brief twilight that links day with night in tropical zones, Conseil and I marveled at an unusual sight.

It was a delightful animal whose discovery, according to the ancients, is a sign of good luck. Aristotle, Athenaeus, Pliny, and Oppian studied its habits and lavished on its behalf all the scientific poetry of Greece and Italy. They called it "nautilus" and "pompilius." But modern science has not endorsed these designations, and this mollusk is now known by the name argonaut.

Anyone consulting Conseil would soon learn from the gallant lad that the branch Mollusca is divided into five classes; that the first class features the Cephalopoda (whose members are sometimes naked, sometimes covered with a shell), which consists of two families, the Dibranchiata and the Tetrabranchiata, which are distinguished by their number of gills; that the family Dibranchiata includes three genera, the argonaut, the squid, and the cuttlefish, and that the family Tetrabranchiata contains only one genus, the nautilus. After this catalog, if some recalcitrant listener confuses the argonaut, which is acetabuliferous (in other words, a bearer of suction tubes), with the nautilus, which is tentaculiferous (a bearer of tentacles), it will be simply unforgivable.

Now, it was a school of argonauts then voyaging on the surface of the ocean. We could count several hundred of them. They belonged to that species of argonaut covered with protuberances and exclusive to the seas near India.

These graceful mollusks were swimming backward by means of their locomotive tubes, sucking water into these tubes and then expelling it. Six of their eight tentacles were long, thin, and floated on the water, while the other two were rounded into palms and spread to the wind like light sails. I could see perfectly their undulating, spiral-shaped shells, which Cuvier aptly compared to an elegant cockleboat. It's an actual boat indeed. It transports the animal that secretes it without the animal sticking to it.

"The argonaut is free to leave its shell," I told Conseil, "but it never does."

"Not unlike Captain Nemo," Conseil replied sagely. "Which is why he should have christened his ship the Argonaut."

For about an hour the Nautilus cruised in the midst of this school of mollusks. Then, lord knows why, they were gripped with a sudden fear. As if at a signal, every sail was abruptly lowered; arms folded, bodies contracted, shells turned over by changing their center of gravity, and the whole flotilla disappeared under the waves. It was instantaneous, and no squadron of ships ever maneuvered with greater togetherness.

Just then night fell suddenly, and the waves barely surged in the breeze, spreading placidly around the Nautilus's side plates.

The next day, January 26, we cut the equator on the 82nd meridian and we reentered the northern hemisphere.

During that day a fearsome school of sharks provided us with an escort. Dreadful animals that teem in these seas and make them extremely dangerous. There were Port Jackson sharks with a brown back, a whitish belly, and eleven rows of teeth, bigeye sharks with necks marked by a large black spot encircled in white and resembling an eye, and Isabella sharks whose rounded snouts were strewn with dark speckles. Often these powerful animals rushed at the lounge window with a violence less than comforting. By this point Ned Land had lost all self–control. He wanted to rise to the surface of the waves and harpoon the monsters, especially certain smooth–hound sharks whose mouths were paved with teeth arranged like a mosaic, and some big five–meter tiger sharks that insisted on personally provoking him. But the Nautilus soon picked up speed and easily left astern the fastest of these man–eaters.

On January 27, at the entrance to the huge Bay of Bengal, we repeatedly encountered a gruesome sight: human corpses floating on the surface of the waves! Carried by the Ganges to the high seas, these were deceased Indian villagers who hadn't been fully devoured by vultures, the only morticians in these parts. But there was no shortage of sharks to assist them with their undertaking chores.

Near seven o'clock in the evening, the Nautilus lay half submerged, navigating in the midst of milky white waves. As far as the eye could see, the ocean seemed lactified. Was it an effect of the moon's rays? No, because the new moon was barely two days old and was still lost below the horizon in the sun's rays. The entire sky, although lit up by stellar radiation, seemed pitch–black in comparison with the whiteness of these waters.

Conseil couldn't believe his eyes, and he questioned me about the causes of this odd phenomenon. Luckily I was in a position to answer him.

"That's called a milk sea," I told him, "a vast expanse of white waves often seen along the coasts of Amboina and in these waterways."

"But," Conseil asked, "could master tell me the cause of this effect, because I presume this water hasn't really changed into milk!"

"No, my boy, and this whiteness that amazes you is merely due to the presence of myriads of tiny creatures called infusoria, a sort of diminutive glowworm that's colorless and gelatinous in appearance, as thick as a strand of hair, and no longer than one–fifth of a millimeter. Some of these tiny creatures stick together over an area of several leagues."

"Several leagues!" Conseil exclaimed.

"Yes, my boy, and don't even try to compute the number of these infusoria. You won't pull it off, because if I'm not mistaken, certain navigators have cruised through milk seas for more than forty miles."

I'm not sure that Conseil heeded my recommendation, because he seemed to be deep in thought, no doubt trying to calculate how many one–fifths of a millimeter are found in forty square miles. As for me, I continued to observe this phenomenon. For several hours the Nautilus's spur sliced through these whitish waves, and I watched it glide noiselessly over this soapy water, as if it were cruising through those foaming eddies that a bay's currents and countercurrents sometimes leave between each other.

Near midnight the sea suddenly resumed its usual hue, but behind us all the way to the horizon, the skies kept mirroring the whiteness of those waves and for a good while seemed imbued with the hazy glow of an aurora borealis.

A New Proposition from Captain Nemo

ON JANUARY 28, in latitude 9° 4' north, when the Nautilus returned at noon to the surface of the sea, it lay in sight of land some eight miles to the west. Right off, I observed a cluster of mountains about 2,000 feet high, whose shapes were very whimsically sculpted. After our position fix, I reentered the lounge, and when our bearings were reported on the chart, I saw that we were off the island of Ceylon, that pearl dangling from the lower lobe of the Indian peninsula.

I went looking in the library for a book about this island, one of the most fertile in the world. Sure enough, I found a volume entitled Ceylon and the Singhalese by H. C. Sirr, Esq. Reentering the lounge, I first noted the bearings of Ceylon, on which antiquity lavished so many different names. It was located between latitude 5° 55' and 9° 49' north, and between longitude 79° 42' and 82° 4' east of the meridian of Greenwich; its length is 275 miles; its maximum width, 150 miles; its circumference, 900 miles; its surface area, 24,448 square miles, in other words, a little smaller than that of Ireland.

Just then Captain Nemo and his chief officer appeared.

The captain glanced at the chart. Then, turning to me:

"The island of Ceylon," he said, "is famous for its pearl fisheries. Would you be interested, Professor Aronnax, in visiting one of those fisheries?"

"Certainly, Captain."

"Fine. It's easily done. Only, when we see the fisheries, we'll see no fishermen. The annual harvest hasn't yet begun. No matter. I'll give orders to make for the Gulf of Mannar, and we'll arrive there late tonight."

The captain said a few words to his chief officer who went out immediately. Soon the Nautilus reentered its liquid element, and the pressure gauge indicated that it was staying at a depth of thirty feet.

With the chart under my eyes, I looked for the Gulf of Mannar. I found it by the 9th parallel off the northwestern shores of Ceylon. It was formed by the long curve of little Mannar Island. To reach it we had to go all the way up Ceylon's west coast.

"Professor," Captain Nemo then told me, "there are pearl fisheries in the Bay of Bengal, the seas of the East Indies, the seas of China and Japan, plus those seas south of the United States, the Gulf of Panama and the Gulf of California; but it's off Ceylon that such fishing reaps its richest rewards. No doubt we'll be arriving a little early. Fishermen gather in the Gulf of Mannar only during the month of March, and for thirty days some 300 boats concentrate on the lucrative harvest of these treasures from the sea. Each boat is manned by ten oarsmen and ten fishermen. The latter divide into two groups, dive in rotation, and descend to a depth of twelve meters with the help of a heavy stone clutched between their feet and attached by a rope to their boat."

"You mean," I said, "that such primitive methods are still all that they use?"

"All," Captain Nemo answered me, "although these fisheries belong to the most industrialized people in the world, the English, to whom the Treaty of Amiens granted them in 1802."

"Yet it strikes me that diving suits like yours could perform yeoman service in such work."

"Yes, since those poor fishermen can't stay long underwater. On his voyage to Ceylon, the Englishman Percival made much of a Kaffir who stayed under five minutes without coming up to the surface, but I find that hard to believe. I know that some divers can last up to fifty–seven seconds, and highly skillful ones to eighty–seven; but such men are rare, and when the poor fellows climb back on board, the water coming out of their noses and ears is tinted with blood. I believe the average time underwater that these fishermen can tolerate is thirty seconds, during which they hastily stuff their little nets with all the pearl oysters they can tear loose. But these fishermen generally don't live to advanced age: their vision weakens, ulcers break out on their eyes, sores form on their bodies, and some are even stricken with apoplexy on the ocean floor."

"Yes," I said, "it's a sad occupation, and one that exists only to gratify the whims of fashion. But tell me, Captain, how many oysters can a boat fish up in a workday?"

"About 40,000 to 50,000. It's even said that in 1814, when the English government went fishing on its own behalf, its divers worked just twenty days and brought up 76,000,000 oysters."

"At least," I asked, "the fishermen are well paid, aren't they?"

"Hardly, professor. In Panama they make just $1.00 per week. In most places they earn only a penny for each oyster that has a pearl, and they bring up so many that have none!"

"Only one penny to those poor people who make their employers rich! That's atrocious!"

"On that note, professor," Captain Nemo told me, "you and your companions will visit the Mannar oysterbank, and if by chance some eager fisherman arrives early, well, we can watch him at work."

"That suits me, captain."

"By the way, Professor Aronnax, you aren't afraid of sharks, are you?"

"Sharks?" I exclaimed.

This struck me as a pretty needless question, to say the least.

"Well?" Captain Nemo went on.

"I admit, Captain, I'm not yet on very familiar terms with that genus of fish."

"We're used to them, the rest of us," Captain Nemo answered. "And in time you will be too. Anyhow, we'll be armed, and on our way we might hunt a man–eater or two. It's a fascinating sport. So, professor, I'll see you tomorrow, bright and early."

This said in a carefree tone, Captain Nemo left the lounge.

If you're invited to hunt bears in the Swiss mountains, you might say: "Oh good, I get to go bear hunting tomorrow!" If you're invited to hunt lions on the Atlas plains or tigers in the jungles of India, you might say: "Ha! Now's my chance to hunt lions and tigers!" But if you're invited to hunt sharks in their native element, you might want to think it over before accepting.

As for me, I passed a hand over my brow, where beads of cold sweat were busy forming.

"Let's think this over," I said to myself, "and let's take our time. Hunting otters in underwater forests, as we did in the forests of Crespo Island, is an acceptable activity. But to roam the bottom of the sea when you're almost certain to meet man–eaters in the neighborhood, that's another story! I know that in certain countries, particularly the Andaman Islands, Negroes don't hesitate to attack sharks, dagger in one hand and noose in the other; but I also know that many who face those fearsome animals don't come back alive. Besides, I'm not a Negro, and even if I were a Negro, in this instance I don't think a little hesitation on my part would be out of place."

And there I was, fantasizing about sharks, envisioning huge jaws armed with multiple rows of teeth and capable of cutting a man in half. I could already feel a definite pain around my pelvic girdle. And how I resented the offhand manner in which the captain had extended his deplorable invitation! You would have thought it was an issue of going into the woods on some harmless fox hunt!

"Thank heavens!" I said to myself. "Conseil will never want to come along, and that'll be my excuse for not going with the captain."

As for Ned Land, I admit I felt less confident of his wisdom. Danger, however great, held a perennial attraction for his aggressive nature.

I went back to reading Sirr's book, but I leafed through it mechanically. Between the lines I kept seeing fearsome, wide–open jaws.

Just then Conseil and the Canadian entered with a calm, even gleeful air. Little did they know what was waiting for them.

"Ye gods, sir!" Ned Land told me. "Your Captain Nemo—the devil take him—has just made us a very pleasant proposition!"

"Oh!" I said "You know about—"

"With all due respect to master," Conseil replied, "the Nautilus's commander has invited us, together with master, for a visit tomorrow to Ceylon's magnificent pearl fisheries. He did so in the most cordial terms and conducted himself like a true gentleman."

"He didn't tell you anything else?"

"Nothing, sir," the Canadian replied. "He said you'd already discussed this little stroll."

"Indeed," I said. "But didn't he give you any details on—"

"Not a one, Mr. Naturalist. You will be going with us, right?"

"Me? Why yes, certainly, of course! I can see that you like the idea, Mr. Land."

"Yes! It will be a really unusual experience!"

"And possibly dangerous!" I added in an insinuating tone.

"Dangerous?" Ned Land replied. "A simple trip to an oysterbank?"

Assuredly, Captain Nemo hadn't seen fit to plant the idea of sharks in the minds of my companions. For my part, I stared at them with anxious eyes, as if they were already missing a limb or two. Should I alert them? Yes, surely, but I hardly knew how to go about it.

"Would master," Conseil said to me, "give us some background on pearl fishing?"

"On the fishing itself?" I asked. "Or on the occupational hazards that—"

"On the fishing," the Canadian replied. "Before we tackle the terrain, it helps to be familiar with it."

"All right, sit down, my friends, and I'll teach you everything I myself have just been taught by the Englishman H. C. Sirr!"

Ned and Conseil took seats on a couch, and right off the Canadian said to me: "Sir, just what is a pearl exactly?"

"My gallant Ned," I replied, "for poets a pearl is a tear from the sea; for Orientals it's a drop of solidified dew; for the ladies it's a jewel they can wear on their fingers, necks, and ears that's oblong in shape, glassy in luster, and formed from mother–of–pearl; for chemists it's a mixture of calcium phosphate and calcium carbonate with a little gelatin protein; and finally, for naturalists it's a simple festering secretion from the organ that produces mother–of–pearl in certain bivalves."

"Branch Mollusca," Conseil said, "class Acephala, order Testacea."

"Correct, my scholarly Conseil. Now then, those Testacea capable of producing pearls include rainbow abalone, turbo snails, giant clams, and saltwater scallops—briefly, all those that secrete mother–of–pearl, in other words, that blue, azure, violet, or white substance lining the insides of their valves."

"Are mussels included too?" the Canadian asked.

"Yes! The mussels of certain streams in Scotland, Wales, Ireland, Saxony, Bohemia, and France."

"Good!" the Canadian replied. "From now on we'll pay closer attention to 'em."

"But," I went on, "for secreting pearls, the ideal mollusk is the pearl oyster Meleagrina margaritifera, that valuable shellfish. Pearls result simply from mother–of–pearl solidifying into a globular shape. Either they stick to the oyster's shell, or they become embedded in the creature's folds. On the valves a pearl sticks fast; on the flesh it lies loose. But its nucleus is always some small, hard object, say a sterile egg or a grain of sand, around which the mother–of–pearl is deposited in thin, concentric layers over several years in succession."

"Can one find several pearls in the same oyster?" Conseil asked.

"Yes, my boy. There are some shellfish that turn into real jewel coffers. They even mention one oyster, about which I remain dubious, that supposedly contained at least 150 sharks."

"150 sharks!" Ned Land yelped.

"Did I say sharks?" I exclaimed hastily. "I meant 150 pearls. Sharks wouldn't make sense."

"Indeed," Conseil said. "But will master now tell us how one goes about extracting these pearls?"

"One proceeds in several ways, and often when pearls stick to the valves, fishermen even pull them loose with pliers. But usually the shellfish are spread out on mats made from the esparto grass that covers the beaches. Thus they die in the open air, and by the end of ten days they've rotted sufficiently. Next they're immersed in huge tanks of salt water, then they're opened up and washed. At this point the sorters begin their twofold task. First they remove the layers of mother–of–pearl, which are known in the industry by the names legitimate silver, bastard white, or bastard black, and these are shipped out in cases weighing 125 to 150 kilograms. Then they remove the oyster's meaty tissue, boil it, and finally strain it, in order to extract even the smallest pearls."

"Do the prices of these pearls differ depending on their size?" Conseil asked.

"Not only on their size," I replied, "but also according to their shape, their water—in other words, their color—and their orient—in other words, that dappled, shimmering glow that makes them so delightful to the eye. The finest pearls are called virgin pearls, or paragons; they form in isolation within the mollusk's tissue. They're white, often opaque but sometimes of opalescent transparency, and usually spherical or pear–shaped. The spherical ones are made into bracelets; the pear–shaped ones into earrings, and since they're the most valuable, they're priced individually. The other pearls that stick to the oyster's shell are more erratically shaped and are priced by weight. Finally, classed in the lowest order, the smallest pearls are known by the name seed pearls; they're priced by the measuring cup and are used mainly in the creation of embroidery for church vestments."

"But it must be a long, hard job, sorting out these pearls by size," the Canadian said.

"No, my friend. That task is performed with eleven strainers, or sieves, that are pierced with different numbers of holes. Those pearls staying in the strainers with twenty to eighty holes are in the first order. Those not slipping through the sieves pierced with 100 to 800 holes are in the second order. Finally, those pearls for which one uses strainers pierced with 900 to 1,000 holes make up the seed pearls."

"How ingenious," Conseil said, "to reduce dividing and classifying pearls to a mechanical operation. And could master tell us the profits brought in by harvesting these banks of pearl oysters?"

"According to Sirr's book," I replied, "these Ceylon fisheries are farmed annually for a total profit of 3,000,000 man–eaters."

"Francs!" Conseil rebuked.

"Yes, francs! ₣3,000,000!" I went on. "But I don't think these fisheries bring in the returns they once did. Similarly, the Central American fisheries used to make an annual profit of ₣4,000,000 during the reign of King Charles V, but now they bring in only two–thirds of that amount. All in all, it's estimated that ₣9,000,000 is the current yearly return for the whole pearl–harvesting industry."

"But," Conseil asked, "haven't certain famous pearls been quoted at extremely high prices?"

"Yes, my boy. They say Julius Caesar gave Servilia a pearl worth ₣120,000 in our currency."

"I've even heard stories," the Canadian said, "about some lady in ancient times who drank pearls in vinegar."

"Cleopatra," Conseil shot back.

"It must have tasted pretty bad," Ned Land added.

"Abominable, Ned my friend," Conseil replied. "But when a little glass of vinegar is worth ₣1,500,000, its taste is a small price to pay."

"I'm sorry I didn't marry the gal," the Canadian said, throwing up his hands with an air of discouragement.

"Ned Land married to Cleopatra?" Conseil exclaimed.

"But I was all set to tie the knot, Conseil," the Canadian replied in all seriousness, "and it wasn't my fault the whole business fell through. I even bought a pearl necklace for my fiancée, Kate Tender, but she married somebody else instead. Well, that necklace cost me only $1.50, but you can absolutely trust me on this, professor, its pearls were so big, they wouldn't have gone through that strainer with twenty holes."

"My gallant Ned," I replied, laughing, "those were artificial pearls, ordinary glass beads whose insides were coated with Essence of Orient."

"Wow!" the Canadian replied. "That Essence of Orient must sell for quite a large sum."

"As little as zero! It comes from the scales of a European carp, it's nothing more than a silver substance that collects in the water and is preserved in ammonia. It's worthless."

"Maybe that's why Kate Tender married somebody else," replied Mr. Land philosophically.

"But," I said, "getting back to pearls of great value, I don't think any sovereign ever possessed one superior to the pearl owned by Captain Nemo."

"This one?" Conseil said, pointing to a magnificent jewel in its glass case.

"Exactly. And I'm certainly not far off when I estimate its value at 2,000,000 . . . uh . . ."

"Francs!" Conseil said quickly.

"Yes," I said, "₣2,000,000, and no doubt all it cost our captain was the effort to pick it up."

"Ha!" Ned Land exclaimed. "During our stroll tomorrow, who says we won't run into one just like it?"

"Bah!" Conseil put in.

"And why not?"

"What good would a pearl worth millions do us here on the Nautilus?"

"Here, no," Ned Land said. "But elsewhere. . . ."

"Oh! Elsewhere!" Conseil put in, shaking his head.

"In fact," I said, "Mr. Land is right. And if we ever brought back to Europe or America a pearl worth millions, it would make the story of our adventures more authentic—and much more rewarding."

"That's how I see it," the Canadian said.

"But," said Conseil, who perpetually returned to the didactic side of things, "is this pearl fishing ever dangerous?"

"No," I replied quickly, "especially if one takes certain precautions."

"What risks would you run in a job like that?" Ned Land said. "Swallowing a few gulps of salt water?"

"Whatever you say, Ned." Then, trying to imitate Captain Nemo's carefree tone, I asked, "By the way, gallant Ned, are you afraid of sharks?"

"Me?" the Canadian replied. "I'm a professional harpooner! It's my job to make a mockery of them!"

"It isn't an issue," I said, "of fishing for them with a swivel hook, hoisting them onto the deck of a ship, chopping off the tail with a sweep of the ax, opening the belly, ripping out the heart, and tossing it into the sea."

"So it's an issue of . . . ?"

"Yes, precisely."

"In the water?"

"In the water."

"Ye gods, just give me a good harpoon! You see, sir, these sharks are badly designed. They have to roll their bellies over to snap you up, and in the meantime . . ."

Ned Land had a way of pronouncing the word "snap" that sent chills down the spine.

"Well, how about you, Conseil? What are your feelings about these man–eaters?"

"Me?" Conseil said. "I'm afraid I must be frank with master."

Good for you, I thought.

"If master faces these sharks," Conseil said, "I think his loyal manservant should face them with him!"

A Pearl Worth Ten Million

NIGHT FELL. I went to bed. I slept pretty poorly. Man–eaters played a major role in my dreams. And I found it more or less appropriate that the French word for shark, requin, has its linguistic roots in the word requiem.

The next day at four o'clock in the morning, I was awakened by the steward whom Captain Nemo had placed expressly at my service. I got up quickly, dressed, and went into the lounge.

Captain Nemo was waiting for me.

"Professor Aronnax," he said to me, "are you ready to start?"

"I'm ready."

"Kindly follow me."

"What about my companions, Captain?"

"They've been alerted and are waiting for us."

"Aren't we going to put on our diving suits?" I asked.

"Not yet. I haven't let the Nautilus pull too near the coast, and we're fairly well out from the Mannar oysterbank. But I have the skiff ready, and it will take us to the exact spot where we'll disembark, which will save us a pretty long trek. It's carrying our diving equipment, and we'll suit up just before we begin our underwater exploring."

Captain Nemo took me to the central companionway whose steps led to the platform. Ned and Conseil were there, enraptured with the "pleasure trip" getting under way. Oars in position, five of the Nautilus's sailors were waiting for us aboard the skiff, which was moored alongside. The night was still dark. Layers of clouds cloaked the sky and left only a few stars in view. My eyes flew to the side where land lay, but I saw only a blurred line covering three–quarters of the horizon from southwest to northwest. Going up Ceylon's west coast during the night, the Nautilus lay west of the bay, or rather that gulf formed by the mainland and Mannar Island. Under these dark waters there stretched the bank of shellfish, an inexhaustible field of pearls more than twenty miles long.

Captain Nemo, Conseil, Ned Land, and I found seats in the stern of the skiff. The longboat's coxswain took the tiller; his four companions leaned into their oars; the moorings were cast off and we pulled clear.

The skiff headed southward. The oarsmen took their time. I watched their strokes vigorously catch the water, and they always waited ten seconds before rowing again, following the practice used in most navies. While the longboat coasted, drops of liquid flicked from the oars and hit the dark troughs of the waves, pitter–pattering like splashes of molten lead. Coming from well out, a mild swell made the skiff roll gently, and a few cresting billows lapped at its bow.

We were silent. What was Captain Nemo thinking? Perhaps that this approaching shore was too close for comfort, contrary to the Canadian's views in which it still seemed too far away. As for Conseil, he had come along out of simple curiosity.

Near 5:30 the first glimmers of light on the horizon defined the upper lines of the coast with greater distinctness. Fairly flat to the east, it swelled a little toward the south. Five miles still separated it from us, and its beach merged with the misty waters. Between us and the shore, the sea was deserted. Not a boat, not a diver. Profound solitude reigned over this gathering place of pearl fishermen. As Captain Nemo had commented, we were arriving in these waterways a month too soon.

At six o'clock the day broke suddenly, with that speed unique to tropical regions, which experience no real dawn or dusk. The sun's rays pierced the cloud curtain gathered on the easterly horizon, and the radiant orb rose swiftly.

I could clearly see the shore, which featured a few sparse trees here and there.

The skiff advanced toward Mannar Island, which curved to the south. Captain Nemo stood up from his thwart and studied the sea.

At his signal the anchor was lowered, but its chain barely ran because the bottom lay no more than a meter down, and this locality was one of the shallowest spots near the bank of shellfish. Instantly the skiff wheeled around under the ebb tide's outbound thrust.

"Here we are, Professor Aronnax," Captain Nemo then said. "You observe this confined bay? A month from now in this very place, the numerous fishing boats of the harvesters will gather, and these are the waters their divers will ransack so daringly. This bay is felicitously laid out for their type of fishing. It's sheltered from the strongest winds, and the sea is never very turbulent here, highly favorable conditions for diving work. Now let's put on our underwater suits, and we'll begin our stroll."

I didn't reply, and while staring at these suspicious waves, I began to put on my heavy aquatic clothes, helped by the longboat's sailors. Captain Nemo and my two companions suited up as well. None of the Nautilus's men were to go with us on this new excursion.

Soon we were imprisoned up to the neck in india–rubber clothing, and straps fastened the air devices onto our backs. As for the Ruhmkorff device, it didn't seem to be in the picture. Before inserting my head into its copper capsule, I commented on this to the captain.

"Our lighting equipment would be useless to us," the captain answered me. "We won't be going very deep, and the sun's rays will be sufficient to light our way. Besides, it's unwise to carry electric lanterns under these waves. Their brightness might unexpectedly attract certain dangerous occupants of these waterways."

As Captain Nemo pronounced these words, I turned to Conseil and Ned Land. But my two friends had already encased their craniums in their metal headgear, and they could neither hear nor reply.

I had one question left to address to Captain Nemo.

"What about our weapons?" I asked him. "Our rifles?"

"Rifles! What for? Don't your mountaineers attack bears dagger in hand? And isn't steel surer than lead? Here's a sturdy blade. Slip it under your belt and let's be off."

I stared at my companions. They were armed in the same fashion, and Ned Land was also brandishing an enormous harpoon he had stowed in the skiff before leaving the Nautilus.

Then, following the captain's example, I let myself be crowned with my heavy copper sphere, and our air tanks immediately went into action.

An instant later, the longboat's sailors helped us overboard one after the other, and we set foot on level sand in a meter and a half of water. Captain Nemo gave us a hand signal. We followed him down a gentle slope and disappeared under the waves.

There the obsessive fears in my brain left me. I became surprisingly calm again. The ease with which I could move increased my confidence, and the many strange sights captivated my imagination.

The sun was already sending sufficient light under these waves. The tiniest objects remained visible. After ten minutes of walking, we were in five meters of water, and the terrain had become almost flat.

Like a covey of snipe over a marsh, there rose underfoot schools of unusual fish from the genus Monopterus, whose members have no fin but their tail. I recognized the Javanese eel, a genuine eight–decimeter serpent with a bluish gray belly, which, without the gold lines over its flanks, could easily be confused with the conger eel. From the butterfish genus, whose oval bodies are very flat, I observed several adorned in brilliant colors and sporting a dorsal fin like a sickle, edible fish that, when dried and marinated, make an excellent dish known by the name "karawade"; then some sea poachers, fish belonging to the genus Aspidophoroides, whose bodies are covered with scaly armor divided into eight lengthwise sections.

Meanwhile, as the sun got progressively higher, it lit up the watery mass more and more. The seafloor changed little by little. Its fine–grained sand was followed by a genuine causeway of smooth crags covered by a carpet of mollusks and zoophytes. Among other specimens in these two branches, I noted some windowpane oysters with thin valves of unequal size, a type of ostracod unique to the Red Sea and the Indian Ocean, then orange–hued lucina with circular shells, awl–shaped auger shells, some of those Persian murex snails that supply the Nautilus with such wonderful dye, spiky periwinkles fifteen centimeters long that rose under the waves like hands ready to grab you, turban snails with shells made of horn and bristling all over with spines, lamp shells, edible duck clams that feed the Hindu marketplace, subtly luminous jellyfish of the species Pelagia panopyra, and finally some wonderful Oculina flabelliforma, magnificent sea fans that fashion one of the most luxuriant tree forms in this ocean.

In the midst of this moving vegetation, under arbors of water plants, there raced legions of clumsy articulates, in particular some fanged frog crabs whose carapaces form a slightly rounded triangle, robber crabs exclusive to these waterways, and horrible parthenope crabs whose appearance was repulsive to the eye. One animal no less hideous, which I encountered several times, was the enormous crab that Mr. Darwin observed, to which nature has given the instinct and requisite strength to eat coconuts; it scrambles up trees on the beach and sends the coconuts tumbling; they fracture in their fall and are opened by its powerful pincers. Here, under these clear waves, this crab raced around with matchless agility, while green turtles from the species frequenting the Malabar coast moved sluggishly among the crumbling rocks.

Near seven o'clock we finally surveyed the bank of shellfish, where pearl oysters reproduce by the millions. These valuable mollusks stick to rocks, where they're strongly attached by a mass of brown filaments that forbids their moving about. In this respect oysters are inferior even to mussels, to whom nature has not denied all talent for locomotion.

The shellfish Meleagrina, that womb for pearls whose valves are nearly equal in size, has the shape of a round shell with thick walls and a very rough exterior. Some of these shells were furrowed with flaky, greenish bands that radiated down from the top. These were the young oysters. The others had rugged black surfaces, measured up to fifteen centimeters in width, and were ten or more years old.

Captain Nemo pointed to this prodigious heap of shellfish, and I saw that these mines were genuinely inexhaustible, since nature's creative powers are greater than man's destructive instincts. True to those instincts, Ned Land greedily stuffed the finest of these mollusks into a net he carried at his side.

But we couldn't stop. We had to follow the captain, who headed down trails seemingly known only to himself. The seafloor rose noticeably, and when I lifted my arms, sometimes they would pass above the surface of the sea. Then the level of the oysterbank would lower unpredictably. Often we went around tall, pointed rocks rising like pyramids. In their dark crevices huge crustaceans, aiming their long legs like heavy artillery, watched us with unblinking eyes, while underfoot there crept millipedes, bloodworms, aricia worms, and annelid worms, whose antennas and tubular tentacles were incredibly long.

Just then a huge cave opened up in our path, hollowed from a picturesque pile of rocks whose smooth heights were completely hung with underwater flora. At first this cave looked pitch–black to me. Inside, the sun's rays seemed to diminish by degrees. Their hazy transparency was nothing more than drowned light.

Captain Nemo went in. We followed him. My eyes soon grew accustomed to this comparative gloom. I distinguished the unpredictably contoured springings of a vault, supported by natural pillars firmly based on a granite foundation, like the weighty columns of Tuscan architecture. Why had our incomprehensible guide taken us into the depths of this underwater crypt? I would soon find out.

After going down a fairly steep slope, our feet trod the floor of a sort of circular pit. There Captain Nemo stopped, and his hand indicated an object that I hadn't yet noticed.

It was an oyster of extraordinary dimensions, a titanic giant clam, a holy–water font that could have held a whole lake, a basin more than two meters wide, hence even bigger than the one adorning the Nautilus's lounge.

I approached this phenomenal mollusk. Its mass of filaments attached it to a table of granite, and there it grew by itself in the midst of the cave's calm waters. I estimated the weight of this giant clam at 300 kilograms. Hence such an oyster held fifteen kilos of meat, and you'd need the stomach of King Gargantua to eat a couple dozen.

Captain Nemo was obviously familiar with this bivalve's existence. This wasn't the first time he'd paid it a visit, and I thought his sole reason for leading us to this locality was to show us a natural curiosity. I was mistaken. Captain Nemo had an explicit personal interest in checking on the current condition of this giant clam.

The mollusk's two valves were partly open. The captain approached and stuck his dagger vertically between the shells to discourage any ideas about closing; then with his hands he raised the fringed, membrane–filled tunic that made up the animal's mantle.

There, between its leaflike folds, I saw a loose pearl as big as a coconut. Its globular shape, perfect clarity, and wonderful orient made it a jewel of incalculable value. Carried away by curiosity, I stretched out my hand to take it, weigh it, fondle it! But the captain stopped me, signaled no, removed his dagger in one swift motion, and let the two valves snap shut.

I then understood Captain Nemo's intent. By leaving the pearl buried beneath the giant clam's mantle, he allowed it to grow imperceptibly. With each passing year the mollusk's secretions added new concentric layers. The captain alone was familiar with the cave where this wonderful fruit of nature was "ripening"; he alone reared it, so to speak, in order to transfer it one day to his dearly beloved museum. Perhaps, following the examples of oyster farmers in China and India, he had even predetermined the creation of this pearl by sticking under the mollusk's folds some piece of glass or metal that was gradually covered with mother–of–pearl. In any case, comparing this pearl to others I already knew about, and to those shimmering in the captain's collection, I estimated that it was worth at least ℉10,000,000. It was a superb natural curiosity rather than a luxurious piece of jewelry, because I don't know of any female ear that could handle it.

Our visit to this opulent giant clam came to an end. Captain Nemo left the cave, and we climbed back up the bank of shellfish in the midst of these clear waters not yet disturbed by divers at work.

We walked by ourselves, genuine loiterers stopping or straying as our fancies dictated. For my part, I was no longer worried about those dangers my imagination had so ridiculously exaggerated. The shallows drew noticeably closer to the surface of the sea, and soon, walking in only a meter of water, my head passed well above the level of the ocean. Conseil rejoined me, and gluing his huge copper capsule to mine, his eyes gave me a friendly greeting. But this lofty plateau measured only a few fathoms, and soon we reentered Our Element. I think I've now earned the right to dub it that.

Ten minutes later, Captain Nemo stopped suddenly. I thought he'd called a halt so that we could turn and start back. No. With a gesture he ordered us to crouch beside him at the foot of a wide crevice. His hand motioned toward a spot within the liquid mass, and I looked carefully.

Five meters away a shadow appeared and dropped to the seafloor. The alarming idea of sharks crossed my mind. But I was mistaken, and once again we didn't have to deal with monsters of the deep.

It was a man, a living man, a black Indian fisherman, a poor devil who no doubt had come to gather what he could before harvest time. I saw the bottom of his dinghy, moored a few feet above his head. He would dive and go back up in quick succession. A stone cut in the shape of a sugar loaf, which he gripped between his feet while a rope connected it to his boat, served to lower him more quickly to the ocean floor. This was the extent of his equipment. Arriving on the seafloor at a depth of about five meters, he fell to his knees and stuffed his sack with shellfish gathered at random. Then he went back up, emptied his sack, pulled up his stone, and started all over again, the whole process lasting only thirty seconds.

This diver didn't see us. A shadow cast by our crag hid us from his view. And besides, how could this poor Indian ever have guessed that human beings, creatures like himself, were near him under the waters, eavesdropping on his movements, not missing a single detail of his fishing!

So he went up and down several times. He gathered only about ten shellfish per dive, because he had to tear them from the banks where each clung with its tough mass of filaments. And how many of these oysters for which he risked his life would have no pearl in them!

I observed him with great care. His movements were systematically executed, and for half an hour no danger seemed to threaten him. So I had gotten used to the sight of this fascinating fishing when all at once, just as the Indian was kneeling on the seafloor, I saw him make a frightened gesture, stand, and gather himself to spring back to the surface of the waves.

I understood his fear. A gigantic shadow appeared above the poor diver. It was a shark of huge size, moving in diagonally, eyes ablaze, jaws wide open!

I was speechless with horror, unable to make a single movement.

With one vigorous stroke of its fins, the voracious animal shot toward the Indian, who jumped aside and avoided the shark's bite but not the thrashing of its tail, because that tail struck him across the chest and stretched him out on the seafloor.

This scene lasted barely a few seconds. The shark returned, rolled over on its back, and was getting ready to cut the Indian in half, when Captain Nemo, who was stationed beside me, suddenly stood up. Then he strode right toward the monster, dagger in hand, ready to fight it at close quarters.

Just as it was about to snap up the poor fisherman, the man–eater saw its new adversary, repositioned itself on its belly, and headed swiftly toward him.

I can see Captain Nemo's bearing to this day. Bracing himself, he waited for the fearsome man–eater with wonderful composure, and when the latter rushed at him, the captain leaped aside with prodigious quickness, avoided a collision, and sank his dagger into its belly. But that wasn't the end of the story. A dreadful battle was joined.

The shark bellowed, so to speak. Blood was pouring into the waves from its wounds. The sea was dyed red, and through this opaque liquid I could see nothing else.

Nothing else until the moment when, through a rift in the clouds, I saw the daring captain clinging to one of the animal's fins, fighting the monster at close quarters, belaboring his enemy's belly with stabs of the dagger yet unable to deliver the deciding thrust, in other words, a direct hit to the heart. In its struggles the man–eater churned the watery mass so furiously, its eddies threatened to knock me over.

I wanted to run to the captain's rescue. But I was transfixed with horror, unable to move.

I stared, wild–eyed. I saw the fight enter a new phase. The captain fell to the seafloor, toppled by the enormous mass weighing him down. Then the shark's jaws opened astoundingly wide, like a pair of industrial shears, and that would have been the finish of Captain Nemo had not Ned Land, quick as thought, rushed forward with his harpoon and driven its dreadful point into the shark's underside.

The waves were saturated with masses of blood. The waters shook with the movements of the man–eater, which thrashed about with indescribable fury. Ned Land hadn't missed his target. This was the monster's death rattle. Pierced to the heart, it was struggling with dreadful spasms whose aftershocks knocked Conseil off his feet.

Meanwhile Ned Land pulled the captain clear. Uninjured, the latter stood up, went right to the Indian, quickly cut the rope binding the man to his stone, took the fellow in his arms, and with a vigorous kick of the heel, rose to the surface of the sea.

The three of us followed him, and a few moments later, miraculously safe, we reached the fisherman's longboat.

Captain Nemo's first concern was to revive this unfortunate man. I wasn't sure he would succeed. I hoped so, since the poor devil hadn't been under very long. But that stroke from the shark's tail could have been his deathblow.

Fortunately, after vigorous massaging by Conseil and the captain, I saw the nearly drowned man regain consciousness little by little. He opened his eyes. How startled he must have felt, how frightened even, at seeing four huge, copper craniums leaning over him!

And above all, what must he have thought when Captain Nemo pulled a bag of pearls from a pocket in his diving suit and placed it in the fisherman's hands? This magnificent benefaction from the Man of the Waters to the poor Indian from Ceylon was accepted by the latter with trembling hands. His bewildered eyes indicated that he didn't know to what superhuman creatures he owed both his life and his fortune.

At the captain's signal we returned to the bank of shellfish, and retracing our steps, we walked for half an hour until we encountered the anchor connecting the seafloor with the Nautilus's skiff.

Back on board, the sailors helped divest us of our heavy copper carapaces. Captain Nemo's first words were spoken to the Canadian.

"Thank you, Mr. Land," he told him.

"Tit for tat, Captain," Ned Land replied. "I owed it to you."

The ghost of a smile glided across the captain's lips, and that was all.

"To the Nautilus," he said.

The longboat flew over the waves. A few minutes later we encountered the shark's corpse again, floating.

From the black markings on the tips of its fins, I recognized the dreadful Squalus melanopterus from the seas of the East Indies, a variety in the species of sharks proper. It was more than twenty–five feet long; its enormous mouth occupied a third of its body. It was an adult, as could be seen from the six rows of teeth forming an isosceles triangle in its upper jaw.

Conseil looked at it with purely scientific fascination, and I'm sure he placed it, not without good reason, in the class of cartilaginous fish, order Chondropterygia with fixed gills, family Selacia, genus Squalus.

While I was contemplating this inert mass, suddenly a dozen of these voracious melanoptera appeared around our longboat; but, paying no attention to us, they pounced on the corpse and quarreled over every scrap of it.

By 8:30 we were back on board the Nautilus.

There I fell to thinking about the incidents that marked our excursion over the Mannar oysterbank. Two impressions inevitably stood out. One concerned Captain Nemo's matchless bravery, the other his devotion to a human being, a representative of that race from which he had fled beneath the seas. In spite of everything, this strange man hadn't yet succeeded in completely stifling his heart.

When I shared these impressions with him, he answered me in a tone touched with emotion:

"That Indian, professor, lives in the land of the oppressed, and I am to this day, and will be until my last breath, a native of that same land!"

The Red Sea

DURING THE DAY of January 29, the island of Ceylon disappeared below the horizon, and at a speed of twenty miles per hour, the Nautilus glided into the labyrinthine channels that separate the Maldive and Laccadive Islands. It likewise hugged Kiltan Island, a shore of madreporic origin discovered by Vasco da Gama in 1499 and one of nineteen chief islands in the island group of the Laccadives, located between latitude 10° and 14° 30' north, and between longitude 50° 72' and 69° east.

By then we had fared 16,220 miles, or 7,500 leagues, from our starting point in the seas of Japan.

The next day, January 30, when the Nautilus rose to the surface of the ocean, there was no more land in sight. Setting its course to the north–northwest, the ship headed toward the Gulf of Oman, carved out between Arabia and the Indian peninsula and providing access to the Persian Gulf.

This was obviously a blind alley with no possible outlet. So where was Captain Nemo taking us? I was unable to say. Which didn't satisfy the Canadian, who that day asked me where we were going.

"We're going, Mr. Ned, where the Captain's fancy takes us."

"His fancy," the Canadian replied, "won't take us very far. The Persian Gulf has no outlet, and if we enter those waters, it won't be long before we return in our tracks."

"All right, we'll return, Mr. Land, and after the Persian Gulf, if the Nautilus wants to visit the Red Sea, the Strait of Bab el Mandeb is still there to let us in!"

"I don't have to tell you, sir," Ned Land replied, "that the Red Sea is just as landlocked as the gulf, since the Isthmus of Suez hasn't been cut all the way through yet; and even if it was, a boat as secretive as ours wouldn't risk a canal intersected with locks. So the Red Sea won't be our way back to Europe either."

"But I didn't say we'd return to Europe."

"What do you figure, then?"

"I figure that after visiting these unusual waterways of Arabia and Egypt, the Nautilus will go back down to the Indian Ocean, perhaps through Mozambique Channel, perhaps off the Mascarene Islands, and then make for the Cape of Good Hope."

"And once we're at the Cape of Good Hope?" the Canadian asked with typical persistence.

"Well then, we'll enter that Atlantic Ocean with which we aren't yet familiar. What's wrong, Ned my friend? Are you tired of this voyage under the seas? Are you bored with the constantly changing sight of these underwater wonders? Speaking for myself, I'll be extremely distressed to see the end of a voyage so few men will ever have a chance to make."

"But don't you realize, Professor Aronnax," the Canadian replied, "that soon we'll have been imprisoned for three whole months aboard this Nautilus?"

"No, Ned, I didn't realize it, I don't want to realize it, and I don't keep track of every day and every hour."

"But when will it be over?"

"In its appointed time. Meanwhile there's nothing we can do about it, and our discussions are futile. My gallant Ned, if you come and tell me, 'A chance to escape is available to us,' then I'll discuss it with you. But that isn't the case, and in all honesty, I don't think Captain Nemo ever ventures into European seas."

This short dialogue reveals that in my mania for the Nautilus, I was turning into the spitting image of its commander.

As for Ned Land, he ended our talk in his best speechifying style: "That's all fine and dandy. But in my humble opinion, a life in jail is a life without joy."

For four days until February 3, the Nautilus inspected the Gulf of Oman at various speeds and depths. It seemed to be traveling at random, as if hesitating over which course to follow, but it never crossed the Tropic of Cancer.

After leaving this gulf we raised Muscat for an instant, the most important town in the country of Oman. I marveled at its strange appearance in the midst of the black rocks surrounding it, against which the white of its houses and forts stood out sharply. I spotted the rounded domes of its mosques, the elegant tips of its minarets, and its fresh, leafy terraces. But it was only a fleeting vision, and the Nautilus soon sank beneath the dark waves of these waterways.

Then our ship went along at a distance of six miles from the Arabic coasts of Mahra and Hadhramaut, their undulating lines of mountains relieved by a few ancient ruins. On February 5 we finally put into the Gulf of Aden, a genuine funnel stuck into the neck of Bab el Mandeb and bottling these Indian waters in the Red Sea.

On February 6 the Nautilus cruised in sight of the city of Aden, perched on a promontory connected to the continent by a narrow isthmus, a sort of inaccessible Gibraltar whose fortifications the English rebuilt after capturing it in 1839. I glimpsed the octagonal minarets of this town, which used to be one of the wealthiest, busiest commercial centers along this coast, as the Arab historian Idrisi tells it.

I was convinced that when Captain Nemo reached this point, he would back out again; but I was mistaken, and much to my surprise, he did nothing of the sort.

The next day, February 7, we entered the Strait of Bab el Mandeb, whose name means "Gate of Tears" in the Arabic language. Twenty miles wide, it's only fifty–two kilometers long, and with the Nautilus launched at full speed, clearing it was the work of barely an hour. But I didn't see a thing, not even Perim Island where the British government built fortifications to strengthen Aden's position. There were many English and French steamers plowing this narrow passageway, liners going from Suez to Bombay, Calcutta, Melbourne, Réunion Island, and Mauritius; far too much traffic for the Nautilus to make an appearance on the surface. So it wisely stayed in midwater.

Finally, at noon, we were plowing the waves of the Red Sea.

The Red Sea: that great lake so famous in biblical traditions, seldom replenished by rains, fed by no important rivers, continually drained by a high rate of evaporation, its water level dropping a meter and a half every year! If it were fully landlocked like a lake, this odd gulf might dry up completely; on this score it's inferior to its neighbors, the Caspian Sea and the Dead Sea, whose levels lower only to the point where their evaporation exactly equals the amounts of water they take to their hearts.

This Red Sea is 2,600 kilometers long with an average width of 240. In the days of the Ptolemies and the Roman emperors, it was a great commercial artery for the world, and when its isthmus has been cut through, it will completely regain that bygone importance that the Suez railways have already brought back in part.

I would not even attempt to understand the whim that induced Captain Nemo to take us into this gulf. But I wholeheartedly approved of the Nautilus's entering it. It adopted a medium pace, sometimes staying on the surface, sometimes diving to avoid some ship, and so I could observe both the inside and topside of this highly unusual sea.

On February 8, as early as the first hours of daylight, Mocha appeared before us: a town now in ruins, whose walls would collapse at the mere sound of a cannon, and which shelters a few leafy date trees here and there. This once–important city used to contain six public marketplaces plus twenty–six mosques, and its walls, protected by fourteen forts, fashioned a three–kilometer girdle around it.

Then the Nautilus drew near the beaches of Africa, where the sea is considerably deeper. There, through the open panels and in a midwater of crystal clarity, our ship enabled us to study wonderful bushes of shining coral and huge chunks of rock wrapped in splendid green furs of algae and fucus. What an indescribable sight, and what a variety of settings and scenery where these reefs and volcanic islands leveled off by the Libyan coast! But soon the Nautilus hugged the eastern shore where these tree forms appeared in all their glory. This was off the coast of Tihama, and there such zoophyte displays not only flourished below sea level but they also fashioned picturesque networks that unreeled as high as ten fathoms above it; the latter were more whimsical but less colorful than the former, which kept their bloom thanks to the moist vitality of the waters.

How many delightful hours I spent in this way at the lounge window! How many new specimens of underwater flora and fauna I marveled at beneath the light of our electric beacon! Mushroom–shaped fungus coral, some slate–colored sea anemone including the species Thalassianthus aster among others, organ–pipe coral arranged like flutes and just begging for a puff from the god Pan, shells unique to this sea that dwell in madreporic cavities and whose bases are twisted into squat spirals, and finally a thousand samples of a polypary I hadn't observed until then: the common sponge.

First division in the polyp group, the class Spongiaria has been created by scientists precisely for this unusual exhibit whose usefulness is beyond dispute. The sponge is definitely not a plant, as some naturalists still believe, but an animal of the lowest order, a polypary inferior even to coral. Its animal nature isn't in doubt, and we can't accept even the views of the ancients, who regarded it as halfway between plant and animal. But I must say that naturalists are not in agreement on the structural mode of sponges. For some it's a polypary, and for others, such as Professor Milne–Edwards, it's a single, solitary individual.

The class Spongiaria contains about 300 species that are encountered in a large number of seas and even in certain streams, where they've been given the name freshwater sponges. But their waters of choice are the Red Sea and the Mediterranean near the Greek Islands or the coast of Syria. These waters witness the reproduction and growth of soft, delicate bath sponges whose prices run as high as Fr150 apiece: the yellow sponge from Syria, the horn sponge from Barbary, etc. But since I had no hope of studying these zoophytes in the seaports of the Levant, from which we were separated by the insuperable Isthmus of Suez, I had to be content with observing them in the waters of the Red Sea.

So I called Conseil to my side, while at an average depth of eight to nine meters, the Nautilus slowly skimmed every beautiful rock on the easterly coast.

There sponges grew in every shape, globular, stalklike, leaflike, fingerlike. With reasonable accuracy, they lived up to their nicknames of basket sponges, chalice sponges, distaff sponges, elkhorn sponges, lion's paws, peacock's tails, and Neptune's gloves—designations bestowed on them by fishermen, more poetically inclined than scientists. A gelatinous, semifluid substance coated the fibrous tissue of these sponges, and from this tissue there escaped a steady trickle of water that, after carrying sustenance to each cell, was being expelled by a contracting movement. This jellylike substance disappears when the polyp dies, emitting ammonia as it rots. Finally nothing remains but the fibers, either gelatinous or made of horn, that constitute your household sponge, which takes on a russet hue and is used for various tasks depending on its degree of elasticity, permeability, or resistance to saturation.

These polyparies were sticking to rocks, shells of mollusks, and even the stalks of water plants. They adorned the smallest crevices, some sprawling, others standing or hanging like coral outgrowths. I told Conseil that sponges are fished up in two ways, either by dragnet or by hand. The latter method calls for the services of a diver, but it's preferable because it spares the polypary's tissue, leaving it with a much higher market value.

Other zoophytes swarming near the sponges consisted chiefly of a very elegant species of jellyfish; mollusks were represented by varieties of squid that, according to Professor Orbigny, are unique to the Red Sea; and reptiles by virgata turtles belonging to the genus Chelonia, which furnished our table with a dainty but wholesome dish.

As for fish, they were numerous and often remarkable. Here are the ones that the Nautilus's nets most frequently hauled on board: rays, including spotted rays that were oval in shape and brick red in color, their bodies strewn with erratic blue speckles and identifiable by their jagged double stings, silver–backed skates,

common stingrays with stippled tails, butterfly rays that looked like huge
two–meter cloaks flapping at middepth, toothless guitarfish that were a type of
cartilaginous fish closer to the shark, trunkfish known as dromedaries that were
one and a half feet long and had humps ending in backward–curving stings,
serpentine moray eels with silver tails and bluish backs plus brown pectorals
trimmed in gray piping, a species of butterfish called the fiatola decked out in thin
gold stripes and the three colors of the French flag, Montague blennies four
decimeters long, superb jacks handsomely embellished by seven black crosswise
streaks with blue and yellow fins plus gold and silver scales, snooks, standard
mullet with yellow heads, parrotfish, wrasse, triggerfish, gobies, etc., plus a
thousand other fish common to the oceans we had already crossed.

On February 9 the Nautilus cruised in the widest part of the Red Sea,
measuring 190 miles straight across from Suakin on the west coast to Qunfidha
on the east coast.

At noon that day after our position fix, Captain Nemo climbed onto the
platform, where I happened to be. I vowed not to let him go below again without
at least sounding him out on his future plans. As soon as he saw me, he came
over, graciously offered me a cigar, and said to me:

"Well, professor, are you pleased with this Red Sea? Have you seen enough of
its hidden wonders, its fish and zoophytes, its gardens of sponges and forests of
coral? Have you glimpsed the towns built on its shores?"

"Yes, Captain Nemo," I replied, "and the Nautilus is wonderfully suited to this
whole survey. Ah, it's a clever boat!"

"Yes, sir, clever, daring, and invulnerable! It fears neither the Red Sea's
dreadful storms nor its currents and reefs."

"Indeed," I said, "this sea is mentioned as one of the worst, and in the days of
the ancients, if I'm not mistaken, it had an abominable reputation."

"Thoroughly abominable, Professor Aronnax. The Greek and Latin historians
can find nothing to say in its favor, and the Greek geographer Strabo adds that it's
especially rough during the rainy season and the period of summer prevailing
winds. The Arab Idrisi, referring to it by the name Gulf of Colzoum, relates that
ships perished in large numbers on its sandbanks and that no one risked
navigating it by night. This, he claims, is a sea subject to fearful hurricanes, strewn
with inhospitable islands, and 'with nothing good to offer,' either on its surface or
in its depths. As a matter of fact, the same views can also be found in Arrian,
Agatharchides, and Artemidorus."

"One can easily see," I answered, "that those historians didn't navigate aboard
the Nautilus."

"Indeed," the captain replied with a smile, "and in this respect, the moderns
aren't much farther along than the ancients. It took many centuries to discover

the mechanical power of steam! Who knows whether we'll see a second Nautilus within the next 100 years! Progress is slow, Professor Aronnax."

"It's true," I replied. "Your ship is a century ahead of its time, perhaps several centuries. It would be most unfortunate if such a secret were to die with its inventor!"

Captain Nemo did not reply. After some minutes of silence:

"We were discussing," he said, "the views of ancient historians on the dangers of navigating this Red Sea?"

"True," I replied. "But weren't their fears exaggerated?"

"Yes and no, Professor Aronnax," answered Captain Nemo, who seemed to know "his Red Sea" by heart. "To a modern ship, well rigged, solidly constructed, and in control of its course thanks to obedient steam, some conditions are no longer hazardous that offered all sorts of dangers to the vessels of the ancients. Picture those early navigators venturing forth in sailboats built from planks lashed together with palm–tree ropes, caulked with powdered resin, and coated with dogfish grease. They didn't even have instruments for taking their bearings, they went by guesswork in the midst of currents they barely knew. Under such conditions, shipwrecks had to be numerous. But nowadays steamers providing service between Suez and the South Seas have nothing to fear from the fury of this gulf, despite the contrary winds of its monsoons. Their captains and passengers no longer prepare for departure with sacrifices to placate the gods, and after returning, they don't traipse in wreaths and gold ribbons to say thanks at the local temple."

"Agreed," I said. "And steam seems to have killed off all gratitude in seamen's hearts. But since you seem to have made a special study of this sea, Captain, can you tell me how it got its name?"

"Many explanations exist on the subject, Professor Aronnax. Would you like to hear the views of one chronicler in the 14th century?"

"Gladly."

"This fanciful fellow claims the sea was given its name after the crossing of the Israelites, when the Pharaoh perished in those waves that came together again at Moses' command:

To mark that miraculous sequel, the sea turned a red without equal.

Thus no other course would do but to name it for its hue."

"An artistic explanation, Captain Nemo," I replied, "but I'm unable to rest content with it. So I'll ask you for your own personal views."

"Here they come. To my thinking, Professor Aronnax, this 'Red Sea' designation must be regarded as a translation of the Hebrew word Edrom, and if the ancients gave it that name, it was because of the unique color of its waters."

"Until now, however, I've seen only clear waves, without any unique hue."

"Surely, but as we move ahead to the far end of this gulf, you'll note its odd appearance. I recall seeing the bay of El Tur completely red, like a lake of blood."

"And you attribute this color to the presence of microscopic algae?"

"Yes. It's a purplish, mucilaginous substance produced by those tiny buds known by the name trichodesmia, 40,000 of which are needed to occupy the space of one square millimeter. Perhaps you'll encounter them when we reach El Tur."

"Hence, Captain Nemo, this isn't the first time you've gone through the Red Sea aboard the Nautilus?"

"No, sir."

"Then, since you've already mentioned the crossing of the Israelites and the catastrophe that befell the Egyptians, I would ask if you've ever discovered any traces under the waters of that great historic event?"

"No, professor, and for an excellent reason."

"What's that?"

"It's because that same locality where Moses crossed with all his people is now so clogged with sand, camels can barely get their legs wet. You can understand that my Nautilus wouldn't have enough water for itself."

"And that locality is . . . ?" I asked.

"That locality lies a little above Suez in a sound that used to form a deep estuary when the Red Sea stretched as far as the Bitter Lakes. Now, whether or not their crossing was literally miraculous, the Israelites did cross there in returning to the Promised Land, and the Pharaoh's army did perish at precisely that locality. So I think that excavating those sands would bring to light a great many weapons and tools of Egyptian origin."

"Obviously," I replied. "And for the sake of archaeology, let's hope that sooner or later such excavations do take place, once new towns are settled on the isthmus after the Suez Canal has been cut through—a canal, by the way, of little use to a ship such as the Nautilus!"

"Surely, but of great use to the world at large," Captain Nemo said. "The ancients well understood the usefulness to commerce of connecting the Red Sea with the Mediterranean, but they never dreamed of cutting a canal between the two, and instead they picked the Nile as their link. If we can trust tradition, it was probably Egypt's King Sesostris who started digging the canal needed to join the Nile with the Red Sea. What's certain is that in 615 B.C. King Necho II was hard at work on a canal that was fed by Nile water and ran through the Egyptian plains opposite Arabia. This canal could be traveled in four days, and it was so wide, two triple-tiered galleys could pass through it abreast. Its construction was continued by Darius the Great, son of Hystaspes, and probably completed by King Ptolemy II. Strabo saw it used for shipping; but the weakness of its slope between its starting point, near Bubastis, and the Red Sea left it navigable only a few months out of the year. This canal served commerce until the century of Rome's Antonine emperors; it was then abandoned and covered with sand, subsequently reinstated by Arabia's Caliph Omar I, and finally filled in for good in 761 or 762 A.D. by Caliph Al–Mansur, in an effort to prevent supplies from reaching Mohammed ibn Abdullah, who had rebelled against him. During his Egyptian campaign, your General Napoleon Bonaparte discovered traces of this old canal in the Suez desert, and when the tide caught him by surprise, he wellnigh perished just a few hours before rejoining his regiment at Hadjaroth, the very place where Moses had pitched camp 3,300 years before him."

"Well, Captain, what the ancients hesitated to undertake, Mr. de Lesseps is now finishing up; his joining of these two seas will shorten the route from Cadiz to the East Indies by 9,000 kilometers, and he'll soon change Africa into an immense island."

"Yes, Professor Aronnax, and you have every right to be proud of your fellow countryman. Such a man brings a nation more honor than the greatest commanders! Like so many others, he began with difficulties and setbacks, but he triumphed because he has the volunteer spirit. And it's sad to think that this deed, which should have been an international deed, which would have insured that any administration went down in history, will succeed only through the efforts of one man. So all hail to Mr. de Lesseps!"

"Yes, all hail to that great French citizen," I replied, quite startled by how emphatically Captain Nemo had just spoken.

"Unfortunately," he went on, "I can't take you through that Suez Canal, but the day after tomorrow, you'll be able to see the long jetties of Port Said when we're in the Mediterranean."

"In the Mediterranean!" I exclaimed.

"Yes, professor. Does that amaze you?"

"What amazes me is thinking we'll be there the day after tomorrow."

"Oh really?"

"Yes, captain, although since I've been aboard your vessel, I should have formed the habit of not being amazed by anything!"

"But what is it that startles you?"

"The thought of how hideously fast the Nautilus will need to go, if it's to double the Cape of Good Hope, circle around Africa, and lie in the open Mediterranean by the day after tomorrow."

"And who says it will circle Africa, professor? What's this talk about doubling the Cape of Good Hope?"

"But unless the Nautilus navigates on dry land and crosses over the isthmus—"

"Or under it, Professor Aronnax."

"Under it?"

"Surely," Captain Nemo replied serenely. "Under that tongue of land, nature long ago made what man today is making on its surface."

"What! There's a passageway?"

"Yes, an underground passageway that I've named the Arabian Tunnel. It starts below Suez and leads to the Bay of Pelusium."

"But isn't that isthmus only composed of quicksand?"

"To a certain depth. But at merely fifty meters, one encounters a firm foundation of rock."

"And it's by luck that you discovered this passageway?" I asked, more and more startled.

"Luck plus logic, professor, and logic even more than luck."

"Captain, I hear you, but I can't believe my ears."

"Oh, sir! The old saying still holds good: Aures habent et non audient! Not only does this passageway exist, but I've taken advantage of it on several occasions. Without it, I wouldn't have ventured today into such a blind alley as the Red Sea."

"Is it indiscreet to ask how you discovered this tunnel?"

"Sir," the captain answered me, "there can be no secrets between men who will never leave each other."

I ignored this innuendo and waited for Captain Nemo's explanation.

"Professor," he told me, "the simple logic of the naturalist led me to discover this passageway, and I alone am familiar with it. I'd noted that in the Red Sea and the Mediterranean there exist a number of absolutely identical species of fish: eels, butterfish, greenfish, bass, jewelfish, flying fish. Certain of this fact, I wondered if there weren't a connection between the two seas. If there were, its underground current had to go from the Red Sea to the Mediterranean simply because of their difference in level. So I caught a large number of fish in the vicinity of Suez. I slipped copper rings around their tails and tossed them back into the sea. A few months later off the coast of Syria, I recaptured a few specimens of my fish, adorned with their telltale rings. So this proved to me that some connection existed between the two seas. I searched for it with my Nautilus, I discovered it, I ventured into it; and soon, professor, you also will have cleared my Arabic tunnel!"

Arabian Tunnel

THE SAME DAY, I reported to Conseil and Ned Land that part of the foregoing conversation directly concerning them. When I told them we would be lying in Mediterranean waters within two days, Conseil clapped his hands, but the Canadian shrugged his shoulders.

"An underwater tunnel!" he exclaimed. "A connection between two seas! Who ever heard of such malarkey!"

"Ned my friend," Conseil replied, "had you ever heard of the Nautilus? No, yet here it is! So don't shrug your shoulders so blithely, and don't discount something with the feeble excuse that you've never heard of it."

"We'll soon see!" Ned Land shot back, shaking his head. "After all, I'd like nothing better than to believe in your captain's little passageway, and may Heaven grant it really does take us to the Mediterranean."

The same evening, at latitude 21° 30' north, the Nautilus was afloat on the surface of the sea and drawing nearer to the Arab coast. I spotted Jidda, an important financial center for Egypt, Syria, Turkey, and the East Indies. I could distinguish with reasonable clarity the overall effect of its buildings, the ships made fast along its wharves, and those bigger vessels whose draft of water required them to drop anchor at the port's offshore mooring. The sun, fairly low on the horizon, struck full force on the houses in this town, accenting their whiteness. Outside the city limits, some wood or reed huts indicated the quarter where the bedouins lived.

Soon Jidda faded into the shadows of evening, and the Nautilus went back beneath the mildly phosphorescent waters.

The next day, February 10, several ships appeared, running on our opposite tack. The Nautilus resumed its underwater navigating; but at the moment of our noon sights, the sea was deserted and the ship rose again to its waterline.

With Ned and Conseil, I went to sit on the platform. The coast to the east looked like a slightly blurred mass in a damp fog.

Leaning against the sides of the skiff, we were chatting of one thing and another, when Ned Land stretched his hand toward a point in the water, saying to me:

"See anything out there, professor?"

"No, Ned," I replied, "but you know I don't have your eyes."

"Take a good look," Ned went on. "There, ahead to starboard, almost level with the beacon! Don't you see a mass that seems to be moving around?"

"Right," I said after observing carefully, "I can make out something like a long, blackish object on the surface of the water."

"A second Nautilus?" Conseil said.

"No," the Canadian replied, "unless I'm badly mistaken, that's some marine animal."

"Are there whales in the Red Sea?" Conseil asked.

"Yes, my boy," I replied, "they're sometimes found here."

"That's no whale," continued Ned Land, whose eyes never strayed from the object they had sighted. "We're old chums, whales and I, and I couldn't mistake their little ways."

"Let's wait and see," Conseil said. "The Nautilus is heading that direction, and we'll soon know what we're in for."

In fact, that blackish object was soon only a mile away from us. It looked like a huge reef stranded in midocean. What was it? I still couldn't make up my mind.

"Oh, it's moving off! It's diving!" Ned Land exclaimed. "Damnation! What can that animal be? It doesn't have a forked tail like baleen whales or sperm whales, and its fins look like sawed–off limbs."

"But in that case—" I put in.

"Good lord," the Canadian went on, "it's rolled over on its back, and it's raising its breasts in the air!"

"It's a siren!" Conseil exclaimed. "With all due respect to master, it's an actual mermaid!"

That word "siren" put me back on track, and I realized that the animal belonged to the order Sirenia: marine creatures that legends have turned into mermaids, half woman, half fish.

"No," I told Conseil, "that's no mermaid, it's an unusual creature of which only a few specimens are left in the Red Sea. That's a dugong."

"Order Sirenia, group Pisciforma, subclass Monodelphia, class Mammalia, branch Vertebrata," Conseil replied.

And when Conseil has spoken, there's nothing else to be said.

Meanwhile Ned Land kept staring. His eyes were gleaming with desire at the sight of that animal. His hands were ready to hurl a harpoon. You would have thought he was waiting for the right moment to jump overboard and attack the creature in its own element.

"Oh, sir," he told me in a voice trembling with excitement, "I've never killed anything like that!"

His whole being was concentrated in this last word.

Just then Captain Nemo appeared on the platform. He spotted the dugong. He understood the Canadian's frame of mind and addressed him directly:

"If you held a harpoon, Mr. Land, wouldn't your hands be itching to put it to work?"

"Positively, sir."

"And just for one day, would it displease you to return to your fisherman's trade and add this cetacean to the list of those you've already hunted down?"

"It wouldn't displease me one bit."

"All right, you can try your luck!"

"Thank you, sir," Ned Land replied, his eyes ablaze.

"Only," the captain went on, "I urge you to aim carefully at this animal, in your own personal interest."

"Is the dugong dangerous to attack?" I asked, despite the Canadian's shrug of the shoulders.

"Yes, sometimes," the captain replied. "These animals have been known to turn on their assailants and capsize their longboats. But with Mr. Land that danger isn't to be feared. His eye is sharp, his arm is sure. If I recommend that he aim carefully at this dugong, it's because the animal is justly regarded as fine game, and I know Mr. Land doesn't despise a choice morsel."

"Aha!" the Canadian put in. "This beast offers the added luxury of being good to eat?"

"Yes, Mr. Land. Its flesh is actual red meat, highly prized, and set aside throughout Malaysia for the tables of aristocrats. Accordingly, this excellent animal has been hunted so bloodthirstily that, like its manatee relatives, it has become more and more scarce."

"In that case, Captain," Conseil said in all seriousness, "on the offchance that this creature might be the last of its line, wouldn't it be advisable to spare its life, in the interests of science?"

"Maybe," the Canadian answered, "it would be better to hunt it down, in the interests of mealtime."

"Then proceed, Mr. Land," Captain Nemo replied.

Just then, as mute and emotionless as ever, seven crewmen climbed onto the platform. One carried a harpoon and line similar to those used in whale fishing. Its deck paneling opened, the skiff was wrenched from its socket and launched to sea. Six rowers sat on the thwarts, and the coxswain took the tiller. Ned, Conseil, and I found seats in the stern.

"Aren't you coming, Captain?" I asked.

"No, sir, but I wish you happy hunting."

The skiff pulled clear, and carried off by its six oars, it headed swiftly toward the dugong, which by then was floating two miles from the Nautilus.

Arriving within a few cable lengths of the cetacean, our longboat slowed down, and the sculls dipped noiselessly into the tranquil waters. Harpoon in hand, Ned Land went to take his stand in the skiff's bow. Harpoons used for hunting whales are usually attached to a very long rope that pays out quickly when the wounded animal drags it with him. But this rope measured no more than about ten fathoms, and its end had simply been fastened to a small barrel that, while floating, would indicate the dugong's movements beneath the waters.

I stood up and could clearly observe the Canadian's adversary. This dugong—which also boasts the name halicore—closely resembled a manatee. Its oblong body ended in a very long caudal fin and its lateral fins in actual fingers. It differs from the manatee in that its upper jaw is armed with two long, pointed teeth that form diverging tusks on either side.

This dugong that Ned Land was preparing to attack was of colossal dimensions, easily exceeding seven meters in length. It didn't stir and seemed to be sleeping on the surface of the waves, a circumstance that should have made it easier to capture.

The skiff approached cautiously to within three fathoms of the animal. The oars hung suspended above their rowlocks. I was crouching. His body leaning slightly back, Ned Land brandished his harpoon with expert hands.

Suddenly a hissing sound was audible, and the dugong disappeared. Although the harpoon had been forcefully hurled, it apparently had hit only water.

"Damnation!" exclaimed the furious Canadian. "I missed it!"

"No," I said, "the animal's wounded, there's its blood; but your weapon didn't stick in its body."

"My harpoon! Get my harpoon!" Ned Land exclaimed.

The sailors went back to their sculling, and the coxswain steered the longboat toward the floating barrel. We fished up the harpoon, and the skiff started off in pursuit of the animal.

The latter returned from time to time to breathe at the surface of the sea. Its wound hadn't weakened it because it went with tremendous speed. Driven by energetic arms, the longboat flew on its trail. Several times we got within a few fathoms of it, and the Canadian hovered in readiness to strike; but then the dugong would steal away with a sudden dive, and it proved impossible to overtake the beast.

I'll let you assess the degree of anger consuming our impatient Ned Land. He hurled at the hapless animal the most potent swearwords in the English language. For my part, I was simply distressed to see this dugong outwit our every scheme.

We chased it unflaggingly for a full hour, and I'd begun to think it would prove too difficult to capture, when the animal got the untimely idea of taking revenge on us, a notion it would soon have cause to regret. It wheeled on the skiff, to assault us in its turn.

This maneuver did not escape the Canadian.

"Watch out!" he said.

The coxswain pronounced a few words in his bizarre language, and no doubt he alerted his men to keep on their guard.

Arriving within twenty feet of the skiff, the dugong stopped, sharply sniffing the air with its huge nostrils, pierced not at the tip of its muzzle but on its topside. Then it gathered itself and sprang at us.

The skiff couldn't avoid the collision. Half overturned, it shipped a ton or two of water that we had to bail out. But thanks to our skillful coxswain, we were fouled on the bias rather than broadside, so we didn't capsize. Clinging to the stempost, Ned Land thrust his harpoon again and again into the gigantic animal, which imbedded its teeth in our gunwale and lifted the longboat out of the water as a lion would lift a deer. We were thrown on top of each other, and I have no idea how the venture would have ended had not the Canadian, still thirsting for the beast's blood, finally pierced it to the heart.

I heard its teeth grind on sheet iron, and the dugong disappeared, taking our harpoon along with it. But the barrel soon popped up on the surface, and a few moments later the animal's body appeared and rolled over on its back. Our skiff rejoined it, took it in tow, and headed to the Nautilus.

It took pulleys of great strength to hoist this dugong onto the platform. The beast weighed 5,000 kilograms. It was carved up in sight of the Canadian, who remained to watch every detail of the operation. At dinner the same day, my steward served me some slices of this flesh, skillfully dressed by the ship's cook. I found it excellent, even better than veal if not beef.

The next morning, February 11, the Nautilus's pantry was enriched by more dainty game. A covey of terns alighted on the Nautilus. They were a species of Sterna nilotica unique to Egypt: beak black, head gray and stippled, eyes surrounded by white dots, back, wings, and tail grayish, belly and throat white, feet red. Also caught were a couple dozen Nile duck, superior–tasting wildfowl whose neck and crown of the head are white speckled with black.

By then the Nautilus had reduced speed. It moved ahead at a saunter, so to speak. I observed that the Red Sea's water was becoming less salty the closer we got to Suez.

Near five o'clock in the afternoon, we sighted Cape Ras Mohammed to the north. This cape forms the tip of Arabia Petraea, which lies between the Gulf of Suez and the Gulf of Aqaba.

The Nautilus entered the Strait of Jubal, which leads to the Gulf of Suez. I could clearly make out a high mountain crowning Ras Mohammed between the two gulfs. It was Mt. Horeb, that biblical Mt. Sinai on whose summit Moses met God face to face, that summit the mind's eye always pictures as wreathed in lightning.

At six o'clock, sometimes afloat and sometimes submerged, the Nautilus passed well out from El Tur, which sat at the far end of a bay whose waters seemed to be dyed red, as Captain Nemo had already mentioned. Then night fell in the midst of a heavy silence occasionally broken by the calls of pelicans and nocturnal birds, by the sound of surf chafing against rocks, or by the distant moan of a steamer churning the waves of the gulf with noisy blades.

From eight to nine o'clock, the Nautilus stayed a few meters beneath the waters. According to my calculations, we had to be quite close to Suez. Through the panels in the lounge, I spotted rocky bottoms brightly lit by our electric rays. It seemed to me that the strait was getting narrower and narrower.

At 9:15 when our boat returned to the surface, I climbed onto the platform. I was quite impatient to clear Captain Nemo's tunnel, couldn't sit still, and wanted to breathe the fresh night air.

Soon, in the shadows, I spotted a pale signal light glimmering a mile away, half discolored by mist.

"A floating lighthouse," said someone next to me.

I turned and discovered the captain.

"That's the floating signal light of Suez," he went on. "It won't be long before we reach the entrance to the tunnel."

"It can't be very easy to enter it."

"No, sir. Accordingly, I'm in the habit of staying in the pilothouse and directing maneuvers myself. And now if you'll kindly go below, Professor Aronnax, the Nautilus is about to sink beneath the waves, and it will only return to the surface after we've cleared the Arabian Tunnel."

I followed Captain Nemo. The hatch closed, the ballast tanks filled with water, and the submersible sank some ten meters down.

Just as I was about to repair to my stateroom, the captain stopped me.

"Professor," he said to me, "would you like to go with me to the wheelhouse?"

"I was afraid to ask," I replied.

"Come along, then. This way, you'll learn the full story about this combination underwater and underground navigating."

Captain Nemo led me to the central companionway. In midstair he opened a door, went along the upper gangways, and arrived at the wheelhouse, which, as you know, stands at one end of the platform.

It was a cabin measuring six feet square and closely resembling those occupied by the helmsmen of steamboats on the Mississippi or Hudson rivers. In the center stood an upright wheel geared to rudder cables running to the Nautilus's stern. Set in the cabin's walls were four deadlights, windows of biconvex glass that enabled the man at the helm to see in every direction.

The cabin was dark; but my eyes soon grew accustomed to its darkness and I saw the pilot, a muscular man whose hands rested on the pegs of the wheel. Outside, the sea was brightly lit by the beacon shining behind the cabin at the other end of the platform.

"Now," Captain Nemo said, "let's look for our passageway."

Electric wires linked the pilothouse with the engine room, and from this cabin the captain could simultaneously signal heading and speed to his Nautilus. He pressed a metal button and at once the propeller slowed down significantly.

I stared in silence at the high, sheer wall we were skirting just then, the firm base of the sandy mountains on the coast. For an hour we went along it in this fashion, staying only a few meters away. Captain Nemo never took his eyes off the two concentric circles of the compass hanging in the cabin. At a mere gesture from him, the helmsman would instantly change the Nautilus's heading.

Standing by the port deadlight, I spotted magnificent coral substructures, zoophytes, algae, and crustaceans with enormous quivering claws that stretched forth from crevices in the rock.

At 10:15 Captain Nemo himself took the helm. Dark and deep, a wide gallery opened ahead of us. The Nautilus was brazenly swallowed up. Strange rumblings were audible along our sides. It was the water of the Red Sea, hurled toward the Mediterranean by the tunnel's slope. Our engines tried to offer resistance by churning the waves with propeller in reverse, but the Nautilus went with the torrent, as swift as an arrow.

Along the narrow walls of this passageway, I saw only brilliant streaks, hard lines, fiery furrows, all scrawled by our speeding electric light. With my hand I tried to curb the pounding of my heart.

At 10:35 Captain Nemo left the steering wheel and turned to me:

"The Mediterranean," he told me.

In less than twenty minutes, swept along by the torrent, the Nautilus had just cleared the Isthmus of Suez.

The Greek Islands

AT SUNRISE the next morning, February 12, the Nautilus rose to the surface of the waves.

I rushed onto the platform. The hazy silhouette of Pelusium was outlined three miles to the south. A torrent had carried us from one sea to the other. But although that tunnel was easy to descend, going back up must have been impossible.

Near seven o'clock Ned and Conseil joined me. Those two inseparable companions had slept serenely, utterly unaware of the Nautilus's feat.

"Well, Mr. Naturalist," the Canadian asked in a gently mocking tone, "and how about that Mediterranean?"

"We're floating on its surface, Ned my friend."

"What!" Conseil put in. "Last night . . . ?"

"Yes, last night, in a matter of minutes, we cleared that insuperable isthmus."

"I don't believe a word of it," the Canadian replied.

"And you're in the wrong, Mr. Land," I went on. "That flat coastline curving southward is the coast of Egypt."

"Tell it to the marines, sir," answered the stubborn Canadian.

"But if Master says so," Conseil told him, "then so be it."

"What's more, Ned," I said, "Captain Nemo himself did the honors in his tunnel, and I stood beside him in the pilothouse while he steered the Nautilus through that narrow passageway."

"You hear, Ned?" Conseil said.

"And you, Ned, who have such good eyes," I added, "you can spot the jetties of Port Said stretching out to sea."

The Canadian looked carefully.

"Correct," he said. "You're right, Professor, and your captain's a superman. We're in the Mediterranean. Fine. So now let's have a chat about our little doings, if you please, but in such a way that nobody overhears."

I could easily see what the Canadian was driving at. In any event, I thought it best to let him have his chat, and we all three went to sit next to the beacon, where we were less exposed to the damp spray from the billows.

"Now, Ned, we're all ears," I said. "What have you to tell us?"

"What I've got to tell you is very simple," the Canadian replied. "We're in Europe, and before Captain Nemo's whims take us deep into the polar seas or back to Oceania, I say we should leave this Nautilus."

I confess that such discussions with the Canadian always baffled me. I didn't want to restrict my companions' freedom in any way, and yet I had no desire to leave Captain Nemo. Thanks to him and his submersible, I was finishing my undersea research by the day, and I was rewriting my book on the great ocean depths in the midst of its very element. Would I ever again have such an opportunity to observe the ocean's wonders? Absolutely not! So I couldn't entertain this idea of leaving the Nautilus before completing our course of inquiry.

"Ned my friend," I said, "answer me honestly. Are you bored with this ship? Are you sorry that fate has cast you into Captain Nemo's hands?"

The Canadian paused for a short while before replying. Then, crossing his arms:

"Honestly," he said, "I'm not sorry about this voyage under the seas. I'll be glad to have done it, but in order to have done it, it has to finish. That's my feeling."

"It will finish, Ned."

"Where and when?"

"Where? I don't know. When? I can't say. Or, rather, I suppose it will be over when these seas have nothing more to teach us. Everything that begins in this world must inevitably come to an end."

"I think as Master does," Conseil replied, "and it's extremely possible that after crossing every sea on the globe, Captain Nemo will bid the three of us a fond farewell."

"Bid us a fond farewell?" the Canadian exclaimed. "You mean beat us to a fare–thee–well!"

"Let's not exaggerate, Mr. Land," I went on. "We have nothing to fear from the captain, but neither do I share Conseil's views. We're privy to the Nautilus's secrets, and I don't expect that its commander, just to set us free, will meekly stand by while we spread those secrets all over the world."

"But in that case what do you expect?" the Canadian asked.

"That we'll encounter advantageous conditions for escaping just as readily in six months as now."

"Great Scott!" Ned Land put in. "And where, if you please, will we be in six months, Mr. Naturalist?"

"Perhaps here, perhaps in China. You know how quickly the Nautilus moves. It crosses oceans like swallows cross the air or express trains continents. It doesn't fear heavily traveled seas. Who can say it won't hug the coasts of France, England, or America, where an escape attempt could be carried out just as effectively as here."

"Professor Aronnax," the Canadian replied, "your arguments are rotten to the core. You talk way off in the future: 'We'll be here, we'll be there!' Me, I'm talking about right now: we are here, and we must take advantage of it!"

I was hard pressed by Ned Land's common sense, and I felt myself losing ground. I no longer knew what arguments to put forward on my behalf.

"Sir," Ned went on, "let's suppose that by some impossibility, Captain Nemo offered your freedom to you this very day. Would you accept?"

"I don't know," I replied.

"And suppose he adds that this offer he's making you today won't ever be repeated, then would you accept?"

I did not reply.

"And what thinks our friend Conseil?" Ned Land asked.

"Your friend Conseil," the fine lad replied serenely, "has nothing to say for himself. He's a completely disinterested party on this question. Like his master, like his comrade Ned, he's a bachelor. Neither wife, parents, nor children are waiting for him back home. He's in Master's employ, he thinks like Master, he speaks like Master, and much to his regret, he can't be counted on to form a majority. Only two persons face each other here: Master on one side, Ned Land on the other. That said, your friend Conseil is listening, and he's ready to keep score."

I couldn't help smiling as Conseil wiped himself out of existence. Deep down, the Canadian must have been overjoyed at not having to contend with him.

"Then, sir," Ned Land said, "since Conseil is no more, we'll have this discussion between just the two of us. I've talked, you've listened. What's your reply?"

It was obvious that the matter had to be settled, and evasions were distasteful to me.

"Ned my friend," I said, "here's my reply. You have right on your side and my arguments can't stand up to yours. It will never do to count on Captain Nemo's benevolence. The most ordinary good sense would forbid him to set us free. On the other hand, good sense decrees that we take advantage of our first opportunity to leave the Nautilus."

"Fine, Professor Aronnax, that's wisely said."

"But one proviso," I said, "just one. The opportunity must be the real thing. Our first attempt to escape must succeed, because if it misfires, we won't get a second chance, and Captain Nemo will never forgive us."

"That's also well put," the Canadian replied. "But your proviso applies to any escape attempt, whether it happens in two years or two days. So this is still the question: if a promising opportunity comes up, we have to grab it."

"Agreed. And now, Ned, will you tell me what you mean by a promising opportunity?"

"One that leads the Nautilus on a cloudy night within a short distance of some European coast."

"And you'll try to get away by swimming?"

"Yes, if we're close enough to shore and the ship's afloat on the surface. No, if we're well out and the ship's navigating under the waters."

"And in that event?"

"In that event I'll try to get hold of the skiff. I know how to handle it. We'll stick ourselves inside, undo the bolts, and rise to the surface, without the helmsman in the bow seeing a thing."

"Fine, Ned. Stay on the lookout for such an opportunity, but don't forget, one slipup will finish us."

"I won't forget, sir."

"And now, Ned, would you like to know my overall thinking on your plan?"

"Gladly, Professor Aronnax."

"Well then, I think—and I don't mean 'I hope'—that your promising opportunity won't ever arise."

"Why not?"

"Because Captain Nemo recognizes that we haven't given up all hope of recovering our freedom, and he'll keep on his guard, above all in seas within sight of the coasts of Europe."

"I'm of Master's opinion," Conseil said.

"We'll soon see," Ned Land replied, shaking his head with a determined expression.

"And now, Ned Land," I added, "let's leave it at that. Not another word on any of this. The day you're ready, alert us and we're with you. I turn it all over to you."

That's how we ended this conversation, which later was to have such serious consequences. At first, I must say, events seemed to confirm my forecasts, much to the Canadian's despair. Did Captain Nemo view us with distrust in these heavily traveled seas, or did he simply want to hide from the sight of those ships of every nation that plowed the Mediterranean? I have no idea, but usually he stayed in midwater and well out from any coast. Either the Nautilus surfaced only enough to let its pilothouse emerge, or it slipped away to the lower depths, although, between the Greek Islands and Asia Minor, we didn't find bottom even at 2,000 meters down.

Accordingly, I became aware of the isle of Karpathos, one of the Sporades Islands, only when Captain Nemo placed his finger over a spot on the world map and quoted me this verse from Virgil:

Est in Carpathio Neptuni gurgite vates

Caeruleus Proteus . . .

It was indeed that bygone abode of Proteus, the old shepherd of King Neptune's flocks: an island located between Rhodes and Crete, which Greeks now call Karpathos, Italians Scarpanto. Through the lounge window I could see only its granite bedrock.

The next day, February 14, I decided to spend a few hours studying the fish of this island group; but for whatever reason, the panels remained hermetically sealed. After determining the Nautilus's heading, I noted that it was proceeding toward the ancient island of Crete, also called Candia. At the time I had shipped aboard the Abraham Lincoln, this whole island was in rebellion against its tyrannical rulers, the Ottoman Empire of Turkey. But since then I had absolutely no idea what happened to this revolution, and Captain Nemo, deprived of all contact with the shore, was hardly the man to keep me informed.

So I didn't allude to this event when, that evening, I chanced to be alone with the captain in the lounge. Besides, he seemed silent and preoccupied. Then, contrary to custom, he ordered that both panels in the lounge be opened, and going from the one to the other, he carefully observed the watery mass. For what purpose? I hadn't a guess, and for my part, I spent my time studying the fish that passed before my eyes.

Among others I noted that sand goby mentioned by Aristotle and commonly known by the name sea loach, which is encountered exclusively in the salty waters next to the Nile Delta. Near them some semiphosphorescent red porgy rolled by, a variety of gilthead that the Egyptians ranked among their sacred animals, lauding them in religious ceremonies when their arrival in the river's waters announced the fertile flood season. I also noticed some wrasse known as the tapiro, three decimeters long, bony fish with transparent scales whose bluish gray color is mixed with red spots; they're enthusiastic eaters of marine vegetables, which gives them an exquisite flavor; hence these tapiro were much in demand by the epicures of ancient Rome, and their entrails were dressed with brains of peacock, tongue of flamingo, and testes of moray to make that divine platter that so enraptured the Roman emperor Vitellius.

Another resident of these seas caught my attention and revived all my memories of antiquity. This was the remora, which travels attached to the bellies of sharks; as the ancients tell it, when these little fish cling to the undersides of a ship, they can bring it to a halt, and by so impeding Mark Antony's vessel during the Battle of Actium, one of them facilitated the victory of Augustus Caesar. From such slender threads hang the destinies of nations! I also observed some wonderful snappers belonging to the order Lutianida, sacred fish for the Greeks, who claimed they could drive off sea monsters from the waters they frequent; their Greek name anthias means "flower," and they live up to it in the play of their colors and in those fleeting reflections that turn their dorsal fins into watered silk; their hues are confined to a gamut of reds, from the pallor of pink to the glow of ruby. I couldn't take my eyes off these marine wonders, when I was suddenly jolted by an unexpected apparition.

In the midst of the waters, a man appeared, a diver carrying a little leather bag at his belt. It was no corpse lost in the waves. It was a living man, swimming vigorously, sometimes disappearing to breathe at the surface, then instantly diving again.

I turned to Captain Nemo, and in an agitated voice:

"A man! A castaway!" I exclaimed. "We must rescue him at all cost!"

The captain didn't reply but went to lean against the window.

The man drew near, and gluing his face to the panel, he stared at us.

To my deep astonishment, Captain Nemo gave him a signal. The diver answered with his hand, immediately swam up to the surface of the sea, and didn't reappear.

"Don't be alarmed," the captain told me. "That's Nicolas from Cape Matapan, nicknamed 'Il Pesce.' He's well known throughout the Cyclades Islands. A bold diver! Water is his true element, and he lives in the sea more than on shore, going constantly from one island to another, even to Crete."

"You know him, captain?"

"Why not, Professor Aronnax?"

This said, Captain Nemo went to a cabinet standing near the lounge's left panel. Next to this cabinet I saw a chest bound with hoops of iron, its lid bearing a copper plaque that displayed the Nautilus's monogram with its motto Mobilis in Mobili.

Just then, ignoring my presence, the captain opened this cabinet, a sort of safe that contained a large number of ingots.

They were gold ingots. And they represented an enormous sum of money. Where had this precious metal come from? How had the captain amassed this gold, and what was he about to do with it?

I didn't pronounce a word. I gaped. Captain Nemo took out the ingots one by one and arranged them methodically inside the chest, filling it to the top. At which point I estimate that it held more than 1,000 kilograms of gold, in other words, close to ₣5,000,000.

After securely fastening the chest, Captain Nemo wrote an address on its lid in characters that must have been modern Greek.

Captain Nemo   191

This done, the captain pressed a button whose wiring was in communication with the crew's quarters. Four men appeared and, not without difficulty, pushed the chest out of the lounge. Then I heard them hoist it up the iron companionway by means of pulleys.

Just then Captain Nemo turned to me:

"You were saying, Professor?" he asked me.

"I wasn't saying a thing, Captain."

"Then, sir, with your permission, I'll bid you good evening."

And with that, Captain Nemo left the lounge.

I reentered my stateroom, very puzzled, as you can imagine. I tried in vain to fall asleep. I kept searching for a relationship between the appearance of the diver and that chest filled with gold. Soon, from certain rolling and pitching movements, I sensed that the Nautilus had left the lower strata and was back on the surface of the water.

Then I heard the sound of footsteps on the platform. I realized that the skiff was being detached and launched to sea. For an instant it bumped the Nautilus's side, then all sounds ceased.

Two hours later, the same noises, the same comings and goings, were repeated. Hoisted on board, the longboat was readjusted into its socket, and the Nautilus plunged back beneath the waves.

So those millions had been delivered to their address. At what spot on the continent? Who was the recipient of Captain Nemo's gold?

The next day I related the night's events to Conseil and the Canadian, events that had aroused my curiosity to a fever pitch. My companions were as startled as I was.

"But where does he get those millions?" Ned Land asked.

To this no reply was possible. After breakfast I made my way to the lounge and went about my work. I wrote up my notes until five o'clock in the afternoon. Just then—was it due to some personal indisposition?—I felt extremely hot and had to take off my jacket made of fan mussel fabric. A perplexing circumstance because we weren't in the low latitudes, and besides, once the Nautilus was submerged, it shouldn't be subject to any rise in temperature. I looked at the pressure gauge. It marked a depth of sixty feet, a depth beyond the reach of atmospheric heat.

I kept on working, but the temperature rose to the point of becoming unbearable.

"Could there be a fire on board?" I wondered.

I was about to leave the lounge when Captain Nemo entered. He approached the thermometer, consulted it, and turned to me:

"42° centigrade," he said.

"I've detected as much, Captain," I replied, "and if it gets even slightly hotter, we won't be able to stand it."

"Oh, professor, it won't get any hotter unless we want it to!"

"You mean you can control this heat?"

"No, but I can back away from the fireplace producing it."

"So it's outside?"

"Surely. We're cruising in a current of boiling water."

"It can't be!" I exclaimed.

"Look."

The panels had opened, and I could see a completely white sea around the Nautilus. Steaming sulfurous fumes uncoiled in the midst of waves bubbling like water in a boiler. I leaned my hand against one of the windows, but the heat was so great, I had to snatch it back.

"Where are we?" I asked.

"Near the island of Santorini, professor," the captain answered me, "and right in the channel that separates the volcanic islets of Nea Kameni and Palea Kameni. I wanted to offer you the unusual sight of an underwater eruption."

"I thought," I said, "that the formation of such new islands had come to an end."

"Nothing ever comes to an end in these volcanic waterways," Captain Nemo replied, "and thanks to its underground fires, our globe is continuously under construction in these regions. According to the Latin historians Cassiodorus and Pliny, by the year 19 of the Christian era, a new island, the divine Thera, had already appeared in the very place these islets have more recently formed. Then Thera sank under the waves, only to rise and sink once more in the year 69 A.D. From that day to this, such plutonic construction work has been in abeyance. But on February 3, 1866, a new islet named George Island emerged in the midst of sulfurous steam near Nea Kameni and was fused to it on the 6th of the same month. Seven days later, on February 13, the islet of Aphroessa appeared, leaving a ten–meter channel between itself and Nea Kameni. I was in these seas when that phenomenon occurred and I was able to observe its every phase. The islet of Aphroessa was circular in shape, measuring 300 feet in diameter and thirty feet in height. It was made of black, glassy lava mixed with bits of feldspar. Finally, on March 10, a smaller islet called Reka appeared next to Nea Kameni, and since then, these three islets have fused to form one single, selfsame island."

"What about this channel we're in right now?" I asked.

"Here it is," Captain Nemo replied, showing me a chart of the Greek Islands. "You observe that I've entered the new islets in their place."

"But will this channel fill up one day?"

"Very likely, Professor Aronnax, because since 1866 eight little lava islets have surged up in front of the port of St. Nicolas on Palea Kameni. So it's obvious that

Nea and Palea will join in days to come. In the middle of the Pacific, tiny infusoria build continents, but here they're built by volcanic phenomena. Look, sir! Look at the construction work going on under these waves."

I returned to the window. The Nautilus was no longer moving. The heat had become unbearable. From the white it had recently been, the sea was turning red, a coloration caused by the presence of iron salts. Although the lounge was hermetically sealed, it was filling with an intolerable stink of sulfur, and I could see scarlet flames of such brightness, they overpowered our electric light.

I was swimming in perspiration, I was stifling, I was about to be cooked. Yes, I felt myself cooking in actual fact!

"We can't stay any longer in this boiling water," I told the captain.

"No, it wouldn't be advisable," replied Nemo the Emotionless.

He gave an order. The Nautilus tacked about and retreated from this furnace it couldn't brave with impunity. A quarter of an hour later, we were breathing fresh air on the surface of the waves.

It then occurred to me that if Ned had chosen these waterways for our escape attempt, we wouldn't have come out alive from this sea of fire.

The next day, February 16, we left this basin, which tallies depths of 3,000 meters between Rhodes and Alexandria, and passing well out from Cerigo Island after doubling Cape Matapan, the Nautilus left the Greek Islands behind.

The Mediterranean in Forty–Eight Hours

THE MEDITERRANEAN, your ideal blue sea: to Greeks simply "the sea," to Hebrews "the great sea," to Romans mare nostrum. Bordered by orange trees, aloes, cactus, and maritime pine trees, perfumed with the scent of myrtle, framed by rugged mountains, saturated with clean, transparent air but continuously under construction by fires in the earth, this sea is a genuine battlefield where Neptune and Pluto still struggle for world domination. Here on these beaches and waters, says the French historian Michelet, a man is revived by one of the most invigorating climates in the world.

But as beautiful as it was, I could get only a quick look at this basin whose surface area comprises 2,000,000 square kilometers. Even Captain Nemo's personal insights were denied me, because that mystifying individual didn't appear one single time during our high–speed crossing. I estimate that the Nautilus covered a track of some 600 leagues under the waves of this sea, and this voyage was accomplished in just twenty–four hours times two. Departing from the waterways of Greece on the morning of February 16, we cleared the Strait of Gibraltar by sunrise on the 18th.

It was obvious to me that this Mediterranean, pinned in the middle of those shores he wanted to avoid, gave Captain Nemo no pleasure. Its waves and breezes brought back too many memories, if not too many regrets. Here he no longer had the ease of movement and freedom of maneuver that the oceans allowed him, and his Nautilus felt cramped so close to the coasts of both Africa and Europe.

Accordingly, our speed was twenty–five miles (that is, twelve four–kilometer leagues) per hour. Needless to say, Ned Land had to give up his escape plans, much to his distress. Swept along at the rate of twelve to thirteen meters per second, he could hardly make use of the skiff. Leaving the Nautilus under these conditions would have been like jumping off a train racing at this speed, a rash move if there ever was one. Moreover, to renew our air supply, the submersible rose to the surface of the waves only at night, and relying solely on compass and log, it steered by dead reckoning.

Inside the Mediterranean, then, I could catch no more of its fast–passing scenery than a traveler might see from an express train; in other words, I could view only the distant horizons because the foregrounds flashed by like lightning. But Conseil and I were able to observe those Mediterranean fish whose powerful fins kept pace for a while in the Nautilus's waters. We stayed on watch before the lounge windows, and our notes enable me to reconstruct, in a few words, the ichthyology of this sea.

Among the various fish inhabiting it, some I viewed, others I glimpsed, and the rest I missed completely because of the Nautilus's speed. Kindly allow me to sort them out using this whimsical system of classification. It will at least convey the quickness of my observations.

In the midst of the watery mass, brightly lit by our electric beams, there snaked past those one–meter lampreys that are common to nearly every clime. A type of ray from the genus Oxyrhynchus, five feet wide, had a white belly with a spotted, ash–gray back and was carried along by the currents like a huge, wide–open shawl. Other rays passed by so quickly I couldn't tell if they deserved that name "eagle ray" coined by the ancient Greeks, or those designations of "rat ray," "bat ray," and "toad ray" that modern fishermen have inflicted on them. Dogfish known as topes, twelve feet long and especially feared by divers, were racing with each other. Looking like big bluish shadows, thresher sharks went by, eight feet long and gifted with an extremely acute sense of smell. Dorados from the genus Sparus, some measuring up to thirteen decimeters, appeared in silver and azure costumes encircled with ribbons, which contrasted with the dark color of their fins; fish sacred to the goddess Venus, their eyes set in brows of gold; a valuable species that patronizes all waters fresh or salt, equally at home in rivers, lakes, and oceans, living in every clime, tolerating any temperature, their line dating back to prehistoric times on this earth yet preserving all its beauty from those far–off days. Magnificent sturgeons, nine to ten meters long and extremely fast, banged their powerful tails against the glass of our panels, showing bluish backs with small brown spots; they resemble sharks, without equaling their strength, and are encountered in every sea; in the spring they delight in swimming up the great rivers, fighting the currents of the Volga, Danube, Po, Rhine, Loire, and Oder, while feeding on herring, mackerel, salmon, and codfish; although they belong to the class of cartilaginous fish, they rate as a delicacy; they're eaten fresh, dried, marinated, or salt–preserved, and in olden times they were borne in triumph to the table of the Roman epicure Lucullus.

But whenever the Nautilus drew near the surface, those denizens of the Mediterranean I could observe most productively belonged to the sixty–third genus of bony fish. These were tuna from the genus Scomber, blue–black on top, silver on the belly armor, their dorsal stripes giving off a golden gleam. They are said to follow ships in search of refreshing shade from the hot tropical sun, and they did just that with the Nautilus, as they had once done with the vessels of the Count de La Pérouse. For long hours they competed in speed with our submersible. I couldn't stop marveling at these animals so perfectly cut out for racing, their heads small, their bodies sleek, spindle–shaped, and in some cases over three meters long, their pectoral fins gifted with remarkable strength, their caudal fins forked. Like certain flocks of birds, whose speed they equal, these tuna swim in triangle formation, which prompted the ancients to say they'd boned up on geometry and military strategy. And yet they can't escape the Provençal fishermen, who prize them as highly as did the ancient inhabitants of Turkey and Italy; and these valuable animals, as oblivious as if they were deaf and blind, leap right into the Marseilles tuna nets and perish by the thousands.

Just for the record, I'll mention those Mediterranean fish that Conseil and I barely glimpsed. There were whitish eels of the species Gymnotus fasciatus that passed like elusive wisps of steam, conger eels three to four meters long that were tricked out in green, blue, and yellow, three–foot hake with a liver that makes a dainty morsel, wormfish drifting like thin seaweed, sea robins that poets call lyrefish and seamen pipers and whose snouts have two jagged triangular plates shaped like old Homer's lyre, swallowfish swimming as fast as the bird they're named after, redheaded groupers whose dorsal fins are trimmed with filaments, some shad (spotted with black, gray, brown, blue, yellow, and green) that actually respond to tinkling handbells, splendid diamond–shaped turbot that were like aquatic pheasants with yellowish fins stippled in brown and the left topside mostly marbled in brown and yellow, finally schools of wonderful red mullet, real oceanic birds of paradise that ancient Romans bought for as much as 10,000 sesterces apiece, and which they killed at the table, so they could heartlessly watch it change color from cinnabar red when alive to pallid white when dead.

And as for other fish common to the Atlantic and Mediterranean, I was unable to observe miralets, triggerfish, puffers, seahorses, jewelfish, trumpetfish, blennies, gray mullet, wrasse, smelt, flying fish, anchovies, sea bream, porgies, garfish, or any of the chief representatives of the order Pleuronecta, such as sole, flounder, plaice, dab, and brill, simply because of the dizzying speed with which the Nautilus hustled through these opulent waters.

As for marine mammals, on passing by the mouth of the Adriatic Sea, I thought I recognized two or three sperm whales equipped with the single dorsal fin denoting the genus Physeter, some pilot whales from the genus Globicephalus exclusive to the Mediterranean, the forepart of the head striped with small distinct lines, and also a dozen seals with white bellies and black coats, known by the name monk seals and just as solemn as if they were three–meter Dominicans.

For his part, Conseil thought he spotted a turtle six feet wide and adorned with three protruding ridges that ran lengthwise. I was sorry to miss this reptile, because from Conseil's description, I believe I recognized the leatherback turtle, a pretty rare species. For my part, I noted only some loggerhead turtles with long carapaces.

As for zoophytes, for a few moments I was able to marvel at a wonderful, orange–hued hydra from the genus Galeolaria that clung to the glass of our port panel; it consisted of a long, lean filament that spread out into countless branches and ended in the most delicate lace ever spun by the followers of Arachne. Unfortunately I couldn't fish up this wonderful specimen, and surely no other Mediterranean zoophytes would have been offered to my gaze, if, on the evening of the 16th, the Nautilus hadn't slowed down in an odd fashion. This was the situation.

By then we were passing between Sicily and the coast of Tunisia. In the cramped space between Cape Bon and the Strait of Messina, the sea bottom rises almost all at once. It forms an actual ridge with only seventeen meters of water remaining above it, while the depth on either side is 170 meters. Consequently, the Nautilus had to maneuver with caution so as not to bump into this underwater barrier.

I showed Conseil the position of this long reef on our chart of the Mediterranean.

"But with all due respect to Master," Conseil ventured to observe, "it's like an actual isthmus connecting Europe to Africa."

"Yes, my boy," I replied, "it cuts across the whole Strait of Sicily, and Smith's soundings prove that in the past, these two continents were genuinely connected between Cape Boeo and Cape Farina."

"I can easily believe it," Conseil said.

"I might add," I went on, "that there's a similar barrier between Gibraltar and Ceuta, and in prehistoric times it closed off the Mediterranean completely."

"Gracious!" Conseil put in. "Suppose one day some volcanic upheaval raises these two barriers back above the waves!"

"That's most unlikely, Conseil."

"If Master will allow me to finish, I mean that if this phenomenon occurs, it might prove distressing to Mr. de Lesseps, who has gone to such pains to cut through his isthmus!"

"Agreed, but I repeat, Conseil: such a phenomenon won't occur. The intensity of these underground forces continues to diminish. Volcanoes were quite numerous in the world's early days, but they're going extinct one by one; the heat inside the earth is growing weaker, the temperature in the globe's lower strata is cooling appreciably every century, and to our globe's detriment, because its heat is its life."

"But the sun—"

"The sun isn't enough, Conseil. Can it restore heat to a corpse?"

"Not that I've heard."

"Well, my friend, someday the earth will be just such a cold corpse. Like the moon, which long ago lost its vital heat, our globe will become lifeless and unlivable."

"In how many centuries?" Conseil asked.

"In hundreds of thousands of years, my boy."

"Then we have ample time to finish our voyage," Conseil replied, "if Ned Land doesn't mess things up!"

Thus reassured, Conseil went back to studying the shallows that the Nautilus was skimming at moderate speed.

On the rocky, volcanic seafloor, there bloomed quite a collection of moving flora: sponges, sea cucumbers, jellyfish called sea gooseberries that were adorned with reddish tendrils and gave off a subtle phosphorescence, members of the genus Beroe that are commonly known by the name melon jellyfish and are bathed in the shimmer of the whole solar spectrum, free–swimming crinoids one meter wide that reddened the waters with their crimson hue, treelike basket stars of the greatest beauty, sea fans from the genus Pavonacea with long stems, numerous edible sea urchins of various species, plus green sea anemones with a grayish trunk and a brown disk lost beneath the olive–colored tresses of their tentacles.

Conseil kept especially busy observing mollusks and articulates, and although his catalog is a little dry, I wouldn't want to wrong the gallant lad by leaving out his personal observations.

From the branch Mollusca, he mentions numerous comb–shaped scallops, hooflike spiny oysters piled on top of each other, triangular coquina, three–pronged glass snails with yellow fins and transparent shells, orange snails from the genus Pleurobranchus that looked like eggs spotted or speckled with greenish dots, members of the genus Aplysia also known by the name sea hares, other sea hares from the genus Dolabella, plump paper–bubble shells, umbrella shells exclusive to the Mediterranean, abalone whose shell produces a mother–of–pearl much in demand, pilgrim scallops, saddle shells that diners in the French province of Languedoc are said to like better than oysters, some of those cockleshells so dear to the citizens of Marseilles, fat white venus shells that are among the clams so abundant off the coasts of North America and eaten in such quantities by New Yorkers, variously colored comb shells with gill covers, burrowing date mussels with a peppery flavor I relish, furrowed heart cockles whose shells have riblike ridges on their arching summits, triton shells pocked with scarlet bumps, carniaira snails with backward–curving tips that make them resemble flimsy gondolas, crowned ferola snails, atlanta snails with spiral shells, gray nudibranchs from the genus Tethys that were spotted with white and covered by fringed mantles, nudibranchs from the suborder Eolidea that looked like small slugs, sea butterflies crawling on their backs, seashells from the genus Auricula including the oval–shaped Auricula myosotis, tan wentletrap snails, common periwinkles, violet snails, cineraira snails, rock borers, ear shells, cabochon snails, pandora shells, etc.

As for the articulates, in his notes Conseil has very appropriately divided them into six classes, three of which belong to the marine world. These classes are the Crustacea, Cirripedia, and Annelida.

Crustaceans are subdivided into nine orders, and the first of these consists of the decapods, in other words, animals whose head and thorax are usually fused, whose cheek–and–mouth mechanism is made up of several pairs of appendages, and whose thorax has four, five, or six pairs of walking legs. Conseil used the methods of our mentor Professor Milne–Edwards, who puts the decapods in three divisions: Brachyura, Macrura, and Anomura. These names may look a tad fierce, but they're accurate and appropriate. Among the Brachyura, Conseil mentions some amanthia crabs whose fronts were armed with two big diverging tips, those inachus scorpions that—lord knows why—symbolized wisdom to the ancient Greeks, spider crabs of the massena and spinimane varieties that had probably gone astray in these shallows because they usually live in the lower depths, xanthid crabs, pilumna crabs, rhomboid crabs, granular box crabs (easy on the digestion, as Conseil ventured to observe), toothless masked crabs, ebalia crabs, cymopolia crabs, woolly–handed crabs, etc. Among the Macrura (which are subdivided into five families: hardshells, burrowers, crayfish, prawns, and ghost crabs) Conseil mentions some common spiny lobsters whose females supply a meat highly prized, slipper lobsters or common shrimp, waterside gebia shrimp, and all sorts of edible species, but he says nothing of the crayfish subdivision that includes the true lobster, because spiny lobsters are the only type in the Mediterranean. Finally, among the Anomura, he saw common drocina crabs dwelling inside whatever abandoned seashells they could take over, homola crabs with spiny fronts, hermit crabs, hairy porcelain crabs, etc.

There Conseil's work came to a halt. He didn't have time to finish off the class Crustacea through an examination of its stomatopods, amphipods, homopods, isopods, trilobites, branchiopods, ostracods, and entomostraceans. And in order to complete his study of marine articulates, he needed to mention the class Cirripedia, which contains water fleas and carp lice, plus the class Annelida, which he would have divided without fail into tubifex worms and dorsibranchian worms. But having gone past the shallows of the Strait of Sicily, the Nautilus resumed its usual deep–water speed. From then on, no more mollusks, no more zoophytes, no more articulates. Just a few large fish sweeping by like shadows.

During the night of February 16–17, we entered the second Mediterranean basin, whose maximum depth we found at 3,000 meters. The Nautilus, driven downward by its propeller and slanting fins, descended to the lowest strata of this sea.

There, in place of natural wonders, the watery mass offered some thrilling and dreadful scenes to my eyes. In essence, we were then crossing that part of the whole Mediterranean so fertile in casualties. From the coast of Algiers to the beaches of Provence, how many ships have wrecked, how many vessels have vanished! Compared to the vast liquid plains of the Pacific, the Mediterranean is a mere lake, but it's an unpredictable lake with fickle waves, today kindly and affectionate to those frail single–masters drifting between a double ultramarine of sky and water, tomorrow bad–tempered and turbulent, agitated by the winds, demolishing the strongest ships beneath sudden waves that smash down with a headlong wallop.

So, in our swift cruise through these deep strata, how many vessels I saw lying on the seafloor, some already caked with coral, others clad only in a layer of rust, plus anchors, cannons, shells, iron fittings, propeller blades, parts of engines, cracked cylinders, staved–in boilers, then hulls floating in midwater, here upright, there overturned.

Some of these wrecked ships had perished in collisions, others from hitting granite reefs. I saw a few that had sunk straight down, their masting still upright, their rigging stiffened by the water. They looked like they were at anchor by some immense, open, offshore mooring where they were waiting for their departure time. When the Nautilus passed between them, covering them with sheets of electricity, they seemed ready to salute us with their colors and send us their serial numbers! But no, nothing but silence and death filled this field of catastrophes!

I observed that these Mediterranean depths became more and more cluttered with such gruesome wreckage as the Nautilus drew nearer to the Strait of Gibraltar. By then the shores of Africa and Europe were converging, and in this narrow space collisions were commonplace. There I saw numerous iron undersides, the phantasmagoric ruins of steamers, some lying down, others rearing up like fearsome animals. One of these boats made a dreadful first impression:

sides torn open, funnel bent, paddle wheels stripped to the mountings, rudder separated from the sternpost and still hanging from an iron chain, the board on its stern eaten away by marine salts! How many lives were dashed in this shipwreck! How many victims were swept under the waves! Had some sailor on board lived to tell the story of this dreadful disaster, or do the waves still keep this casualty a secret? It occurred to me, lord knows why, that this boat buried under the sea might have been the Atlas, lost with all hands some twenty years ago and never heard from again! Oh, what a gruesome tale these Mediterranean depths could tell, this huge boneyard where so much wealth has been lost, where so many victims have met their deaths!

Meanwhile, briskly unconcerned, the Nautilus ran at full propeller through the midst of these ruins. On February 18, near three o'clock in the morning, it hove before the entrance to the Strait of Gibraltar.

There are two currents here: an upper current, long known to exist, that carries the ocean's waters into the Mediterranean basin; then a lower countercurrent, the only present–day proof of its existence being logic. In essence, the Mediterranean receives a continual influx of water not only from the Atlantic but from rivers emptying into it; since local evaporation isn't enough to restore the balance, the total amount of added water should make this sea's level higher every year. Yet this isn't the case, and we're naturally forced to believe in the existence of some lower current that carries the Mediterranean's surplus through the Strait of Gibraltar and into the Atlantic basin.

And so it turned out. The Nautilus took full advantage of this countercurrent. It advanced swiftly through this narrow passageway. For an instant I could glimpse the wonderful ruins of the Temple of Hercules, buried undersea, as Pliny and Avianus have mentioned, together with the flat island they stand on; and a few minutes later, we were floating on the waves of the Atlantic.

The Bay of Vigo

THE ATLANTIC! A vast expanse of water whose surface area is 25,000,000 square miles, with a length of 9,000 miles and an average width of 2,700. A major sea nearly unknown to the ancients, except perhaps the Carthaginians, those Dutchmen of antiquity who went along the west coasts of Europe and Africa on their commercial junkets! An ocean whose parallel winding shores form an immense perimeter fed by the world's greatest rivers: the St. Lawrence, Mississippi, Amazon, Plata, Orinoco, Niger, Senegal, Elbe, Loire, and Rhine, which bring it waters from the most civilized countries as well as the most undeveloped areas! A magnificent plain of waves plowed continuously by ships of every nation, shaded by every flag in the world, and ending in those two dreadful headlands so feared by navigators, Cape Horn and the Cape of Tempests! The Nautilus broke these waters with the edge of its spur after doing nearly 10,000 leagues in three and a half months, a track longer than a great circle of the earth. Where were we heading now, and what did the future have in store for us?

Emerging from the Strait of Gibraltar, the Nautilus took to the high seas. It returned to the surface of the waves, so our daily strolls on the platform were restored to us.

I climbed onto it instantly, Ned Land and Conseil along with me. Twelve miles away, Cape St. Vincent was hazily visible, the southwestern tip of the Hispanic peninsula. The wind was blowing a pretty strong gust from the south. The sea was swelling and surging. Its waves made the Nautilus roll and jerk violently. It was nearly impossible to stand up on the platform, which was continuously buffeted by this enormously heavy sea. After inhaling a few breaths of air, we went below once more.

I repaired to my stateroom. Conseil returned to his cabin; but the Canadian, looking rather worried, followed me. Our quick trip through the Mediterranean hadn't allowed him to put his plans into execution, and he could barely conceal his disappointment.

After the door to my stateroom was closed, he sat and stared at me silently.

"Ned my friend," I told him, "I know how you feel, but you mustn't blame yourself. Given the way the Nautilus was navigating, it would have been sheer insanity to think of escaping!"

Ned Land didn't reply. His pursed lips and frowning brow indicated that he was in the grip of his monomania.

"Look here," I went on, "as yet there's no cause for despair. We're going up the coast of Portugal. France and England aren't far off, and there we'll easily find refuge. Oh, I grant you, if the Nautilus had emerged from the Strait of Gibraltar and made for that cape in the south, if it were taking us toward those regions that have no continents, then I'd share your alarm. But we now know that Captain Nemo doesn't avoid the seas of civilization, and in a few days I think we can safely take action."

Ned Land stared at me still more intently and finally unpursed his lips:

"We'll do it this evening," he said.

I straightened suddenly. I admit that I was less than ready for this announcement. I wanted to reply to the Canadian, but words failed me.

"We agreed to wait for the right circumstances," Ned Land went on. "Now we've got those circumstances. This evening we'll be just a few miles off the coast of Spain. It'll be cloudy tonight. The wind's blowing toward shore. You gave me your promise, Professor Aronnax, and I'm counting on you."

Since I didn't say anything, the Canadian stood up and approached me:

"We'll do it this evening at nine o'clock," he said. "I've alerted Conseil. By that time Captain Nemo will be locked in his room and probably in bed. Neither the mechanics or the crewmen will be able to see us. Conseil and I will go to the central companionway. As for you, Professor Aronnax, you'll stay in the library two steps away and wait for my signal. The oars, mast, and sail are in the skiff. I've even managed to stow some provisions inside. I've gotten hold of a monkey wrench to unscrew the nuts bolting the skiff to the Nautilus's hull. So everything's ready. I'll see you this evening."

"The sea is rough," I said.

"Admitted," the Canadian replied, "but we've got to risk it. Freedom is worth paying for. Besides, the longboat's solidly built, and a few miles with the wind behind us is no big deal. By tomorrow, who knows if this ship won't be 100 leagues out to sea? If circumstances are in our favor, between ten and eleven this evening we'll be landing on some piece of solid ground, or we'll be dead. So we're in God's hands, and I'll see you this evening!"

This said, the Canadian withdrew, leaving me close to dumbfounded. I had imagined that if it came to this, I would have time to think about it, to talk it over. My stubborn companion hadn't granted me this courtesy. But after all, what would I have said to him? Ned Land was right a hundred times over. These were near–ideal circumstances, and he was taking full advantage of them. In my selfish personal interests, could I go back on my word and be responsible for ruining the future lives of my companions? Tomorrow, might not Captain Nemo take us far away from any shore?

Just then a fairly loud hissing told me that the ballast tanks were filling, and the Nautilus sank beneath the waves of the Atlantic.

I stayed in my stateroom. I wanted to avoid the captain, to hide from his eyes the agitation overwhelming me. What an agonizing day I spent, torn between my desire to regain my free will and my regret at abandoning this marvelous Nautilus, leaving my underwater research incomplete! How could I relinquish this ocean—"my own Atlantic," as I liked to call it—without observing its lower strata, without wresting from it the kinds of secrets that had been revealed to me by the seas of the East Indies and the Pacific! I was putting down my novel half read, I was waking up as my dream neared its climax! How painfully the hours passed, as I sometimes envisioned myself safe on shore with my companions, or, despite my better judgment, as I sometimes wished that some unforeseen circumstances would prevent Ned Land from carrying out his plans.

Twice I went to the lounge. I wanted to consult the compass. I wanted to see if the Nautilus's heading was actually taking us closer to the coast or spiriting us farther away. But no. The Nautilus was still in Portuguese waters. Heading north, it was cruising along the ocean's beaches.

So I had to resign myself to my fate and get ready to escape. My baggage wasn't heavy. My notes, nothing more.

As for Captain Nemo, I wondered what he would make of our escaping, what concern or perhaps what distress it might cause him, and what he would do in the twofold event of our attempt either failing or being found out! Certainly I had no complaints to register with him, on the contrary. Never was hospitality more wholehearted than his. Yet in leaving him I couldn't be accused of ingratitude. No solemn promises bound us to him. In order to keep us captive, he had counted only on the force of circumstances and not on our word of honor. But his avowed intention to imprison us forever on his ship justified our every effort.

I hadn't seen the captain since our visit to the island of Santorini. Would fate bring me into his presence before our departure? I both desired and dreaded it. I listened for footsteps in the stateroom adjoining mine. Not a sound reached my ear. His stateroom had to be deserted.

Then I began to wonder if this eccentric individual was even on board. Since that night when the skiff had left the Nautilus on some mysterious mission, my ideas about him had subtly changed. In spite of everything, I thought that Captain Nemo must have kept up some type of relationship with the shore. Did he himself never leave the Nautilus? Whole weeks had often gone by without my encountering him. What was he doing all the while? During all those times I'd thought he was convalescing in the grip of some misanthropic fit, was he instead far away from the ship, involved in some secret activity whose nature still eluded me?

All these ideas and a thousand others assaulted me at the same time. In these strange circumstances the scope for conjecture was unlimited. I felt an unbearable queasiness. This day of waiting seemed endless. The hours struck too slowly to keep up with my impatience.

As usual, dinner was served me in my stateroom. Full of anxiety, I ate little. I left the table at seven o'clock. 120 minutes—I was keeping track of them—still separated me from the moment I was to rejoin Ned Land. My agitation increased. My pulse was throbbing violently. I couldn't stand still. I walked up and down, hoping to calm my troubled mind with movement. The possibility of perishing in our reckless undertaking was the least of my worries; my heart was pounding at the thought that our plans might be discovered before we had left the Nautilus, at the thought of being hauled in front of Captain Nemo and finding him angered, or worse, saddened by my deserting him.

I wanted to see the lounge one last time. I went down the gangways and arrived at the museum where I had spent so many pleasant and productive hours. I stared at all its wealth, all its treasures, like a man on the eve of his eternal exile, a man departing to return no more. For so many days now, these natural wonders and artistic masterworks had been central to my life, and I was about to leave them behind forever. I wanted to plunge my eyes through the lounge window and into these Atlantic waters; but the panels were hermetically sealed, and a mantle of sheet iron separated me from this ocean with which I was still unfamiliar.

Crossing through the lounge, I arrived at the door, contrived in one of the canted corners, that opened into the captain's stateroom. Much to my astonishment, this door was ajar. I instinctively recoiled. If Captain Nemo was in his stateroom, he might see me. But, not hearing any sounds, I approached. The stateroom was deserted. I pushed the door open. I took a few steps inside. Still the same austere, monastic appearance.

Just then my eye was caught by some etchings hanging on the wall, which I hadn't noticed during my first visit. They were portraits of great men of history who had spent their lives in perpetual devotion to a great human ideal: Thaddeus Kosciusko, the hero whose dying words had been Finis Poloniae; Markos Botzaris, for modern Greece the reincarnation of Sparta's King Leonidas; Daniel O'Connell, Ireland's defender; George Washington, founder of the American Union; Daniele Manin, the Italian patriot; Abraham Lincoln, dead from the bullet of a believer in slavery; and finally, that martyr for the redemption of the black race, John Brown, hanging from his gallows as Victor Hugo's pencil has so terrifyingly depicted.

What was the bond between these heroic souls and the soul of Captain Nemo? From this collection of portraits could I finally unravel the mystery of his existence? Was he a fighter for oppressed peoples, a liberator of enslaved races? Had he figured in the recent political or social upheavals of this century? Was he a hero of that dreadful civil war in America, a war lamentable yet forever glorious . . . ?

Suddenly the clock struck eight. The first stroke of its hammer on the chime snapped me out of my musings. I shuddered as if some invisible eye had plunged into my innermost thoughts, and I rushed outside the stateroom.

There my eyes fell on the compass. Our heading was still northerly. The log indicated a moderate speed, the pressure gauge a depth of about sixty feet. So circumstances were in favor of the Canadian's plans.

I stayed in my stateroom. I dressed warmly: fishing boots, otter cap, coat of fan–mussel fabric lined with sealskin. I was ready. I was waiting. Only the propeller's vibrations disturbed the deep silence reigning on board. I cocked an ear and listened. Would a sudden outburst of voices tell me that Ned Land's escape plans had just been detected? A ghastly uneasiness stole through me. I tried in vain to recover my composure.

A few minutes before nine o'clock, I glued my ear to the captain's door. Not a sound. I left my stateroom and returned to the lounge, which was deserted and plunged in near darkness.

I opened the door leading to the library. The same inadequate light, the same solitude. I went to man my post near the door opening into the well of the central companionway. I waited for Ned Land's signal.

At this point the propeller's vibrations slowed down appreciably, then they died out altogether. Why was the Nautilus stopping? Whether this layover would help or hinder Ned Land's schemes I couldn't have said.

The silence was further disturbed only by the pounding of my heart.

Suddenly I felt a mild jolt. I realized the Nautilus had come to rest on the ocean floor. My alarm increased. The Canadian's signal hadn't reached me. I longed to rejoin Ned Land and urge him to postpone his attempt. I sensed that we were no longer navigating under normal conditions.

Just then the door to the main lounge opened and Captain Nemo appeared. He saw me, and without further preamble:

"Ah, Professor," he said in an affable tone, "I've been looking for you. Do you know your Spanish history?"

Even if he knew it by heart, a man in my disturbed, befuddled condition couldn't have quoted a syllable of his own country's history.

"Well?" Captain Nemo went on. "Did you hear my question? Do you know the history of Spain?"

"Very little of it," I replied.

"The most learned men," the captain said, "still have much to learn. Have a seat," he added, "and I'll tell you about an unusual episode in this body of history."

The captain stretched out on a couch, and I mechanically took a seat near him, but half in the shadows.

"Professor," he said, "listen carefully. This piece of history concerns you in one definite respect, because it will answer a question you've no doubt been unable to resolve."

"I'm listening, Captain," I said, not knowing what my partner in this dialogue was driving at, and wondering if this incident related to our escape plans.

"Professor," Captain Nemo went on, "if you're amenable, we'll go back in time to 1702. You're aware of the fact that in those days your King Louis XIV thought an imperial gesture would suffice to humble the Pyrenees in the dust, so he inflicted his grandson, the Duke of Anjou, on the Spaniards. Reigning more or less poorly under the name King Philip V, this aristocrat had to deal with mighty opponents abroad.

"In essence, the year before, the royal houses of Holland, Austria, and England had signed a treaty of alliance at The Hague, aiming to wrest the Spanish crown from King Philip V and to place it on the head of an archduke whom they prematurely dubbed King Charles III.

"Spain had to withstand these allies. But the country had practically no army or navy. Yet it wasn't short of money, provided that its galleons, laden with gold and silver from America, could enter its ports. Now then, late in 1702 Spain was expecting a rich convoy, which France ventured to escort with a fleet of twenty–three vessels under the command of Admiral de Chateau–Renault, because by that time the allied navies were roving the Atlantic.

"This convoy was supposed to put into Cadiz, but after learning that the English fleet lay across those waterways, the admiral decided to make for a French port.

"The Spanish commanders in the convoy objected to this decision. They wanted to be taken to a Spanish port, if not to Cadiz, then to the Bay of Vigo, located on Spain's northwest coast and not blockaded.

"Admiral de Chateau–Renault was so indecisive as to obey this directive, and the galleons entered the Bay of Vigo.

"Unfortunately this bay forms an open, offshore mooring that's impossible to defend. So it was essential to hurry and empty the galleons before the allied fleets arrived, and there would have been ample time for this unloading, if a wretched question of trade agreements hadn't suddenly come up.

"Are you clear on the chain of events?" Captain Nemo asked me.

"Perfectly clear," I said, not yet knowing why I was being given this history lesson.

"Then I'll continue. Here's what came to pass. The tradesmen of Cadiz had negotiated a charter whereby they were to receive all merchandise coming from the West Indies. Now then, unloading the ingots from those galleons at the port of Vigo would have been a violation of their rights. So they lodged a complaint in Madrid, and they obtained an order from the indecisive King Philip V: without unloading, the convoy would stay in custody at the offshore mooring of Vigo until the enemy fleets had retreated.

"Now then, just as this decision was being handed down, English vessels arrived in the Bay of Vigo on October 22, 1702. Despite his inferior forces, Admiral de Chateau–Renault fought courageously. But when he saw that the convoy's wealth was about to fall into enemy hands, he burned and scuttled the galleons, which went to the bottom with their immense treasures."

Captain Nemo stopped. I admit it: I still couldn't see how this piece of history concerned me.

"Well?" I asked him.

"Well, Professor Aronnax," Captain Nemo answered me, "we're actually in that Bay of Vigo, and all that's left is for you to probe the mysteries of the place."

The captain stood up and invited me to follow him. I'd had time to collect myself. I did so. The lounge was dark, but the sea's waves sparkled through the transparent windows. I stared.

Around the Nautilus for a half–mile radius, the waters seemed saturated with electric light. The sandy bottom was clear and bright. Dressed in diving suits, crewmen were busy clearing away half–rotted barrels and disemboweled trunks in the midst of the dingy hulks of ships. Out of these trunks and kegs spilled ingots of gold and silver, cascades of jewels, pieces of eight. The sand was heaped with them. Then, laden with these valuable spoils, the men returned to the Nautilus, dropped off their burdens inside, and went to resume this inexhaustible fishing for silver and gold.

I understood. This was the setting of that battle on October 22, 1702. Here, in this very place, those galleons carrying treasure to the Spanish government had gone to the bottom. Here, whenever he needed, Captain Nemo came to withdraw these millions to ballast his Nautilus. It was for him, for him alone, that America had yielded up its precious metals. He was the direct, sole heir to these treasures wrested from the Incas and those peoples conquered by Hernando Cortez!

"Did you know, professor," he asked me with a smile, "that the sea contained such wealth?"

"I know it's estimated," I replied, "that there are 2,000,000 metric tons of silver held in suspension in seawater."

"Surely, but in extracting that silver, your expenses would outweigh your profits. Here, by contrast, I have only to pick up what other men have lost, and not only in this Bay of Vigo but at a thousand other sites where ships have gone down, whose positions are marked on my underwater chart. Do you understand now that I'm rich to the tune of billions?"

"I understand, Captain. Nevertheless, allow me to inform you that by harvesting this very Bay of Vigo, you're simply forestalling the efforts of a rival organization."

"What organization?"

"A company chartered by the Spanish government to search for these sunken galleons. The company's investors were lured by the bait of enormous gains, because this scuttled treasure is estimated to be worth ₣500,000,000."

"It was 500,000,000 francs," Captain Nemo replied, "but no more!"

"Right," I said. "Hence a timely warning to those investors would be an act of charity. Yet who knows if it would be well received? Usually what gamblers regret the most isn't the loss of their money so much as the loss of their insane hopes. But ultimately I feel less sorry for them than for the thousands of unfortunate people who would have benefited from a fair distribution of this wealth, whereas now it will be of no help to them!"

No sooner had I voiced this regret than I felt it must have wounded Captain Nemo.

"No help!" he replied with growing animation. "Sir, what makes you assume this wealth goes to waste when I'm the one amassing it? Do you think I toil to gather this treasure out of selfishness? Who says I don't put it to good use? Do you think I'm unaware of the suffering beings and oppressed races living on this earth, poor people to comfort, victims to avenge? Don't you understand . . . ?"

Captain Nemo stopped on these last words, perhaps sorry that he had said too much. But I had guessed. Whatever motives had driven him to seek independence under the seas, he remained a human being before all else! His heart still throbbed for suffering humanity, and his immense philanthropy went out both to downtrodden races and to individuals!

And now I knew where Captain Nemo had delivered those millions, when the Nautilus navigated the waters where Crete was in rebellion against the Ottoman Empire!

A Lost Continent

THE NEXT MORNING, February 19, I beheld the Canadian entering my stateroom. I was expecting this visit. He wore an expression of great disappointment.

"Well, sir?" he said to me.

"Well, Ned, the fates were against us yesterday."

"Yes! That damned captain had to call a halt just as we were going to escape from his boat."

"Yes, Ned, he had business with his bankers."

"His bankers?"

"Or rather his bank vaults. By which I mean this ocean, where his wealth is safer than in any national treasury."

I then related the evening's incidents to the Canadian, secretly hoping he would come around to the idea of not deserting the captain; but my narrative had no result other than Ned's voicing deep regret that he hadn't strolled across the Vigo battlefield on his own behalf.

"Anyhow," he said, "it's not over yet! My first harpoon missed, that's all! We'll succeed the next time, and as soon as this evening, if need be . . ."

"What's the Nautilus's heading?" I asked.

"I've no idea," Ned replied.

"All right, at noon we'll find out what our position is!"

The Canadian returned to Conseil's side. As soon as I was dressed, I went into the lounge. The compass wasn't encouraging. The Nautilus's course was south–southwest. We were turning our backs on Europe.

I could hardly wait until our position was reported on the chart. Near 11:30 the ballast tanks emptied, and the submersible rose to the surface of the ocean. I leaped onto the platform. Ned Land was already there.

No more shore in sight. Nothing but the immenseness of the sea. A few sails were on the horizon, no doubt ships going as far as Cape São Roque to find favorable winds for doubling the Cape of Good Hope. The sky was overcast. A squall was on the way.

Furious, Ned tried to see through the mists on the horizon. He still hoped that behind all that fog there lay those shores he longed for.

At noon the sun made a momentary appearance. Taking advantage of this rift in the clouds, the chief officer took the orb's altitude. Then the sea grew turbulent, we went below again, and the hatch closed once more.

When I consulted the chart an hour later, I saw that the Nautilus's position was marked at longitude 16° 17' and latitude 33° 22', a good 150 leagues from the nearest coast. It wouldn't do to even dream of escaping, and I'll let the reader decide how promptly the Canadian threw a tantrum when I ventured to tell him our situation.

As for me, I wasn't exactly grief–stricken. I felt as if a heavy weight had been lifted from me, and I was able to resume my regular tasks in a state of comparative calm.

Near eleven o'clock in the evening, I received a most unexpected visit from Captain Nemo. He asked me very graciously if I felt exhausted from our vigil the night before. I said no.

"Then, Professor Aronnax, I propose an unusual excursion."

"Propose away, Captain."

"So far you've visited the ocean depths only by day and under sunlight. Would you like to see these depths on a dark night?"

"Very much."

"I warn you, this will be an exhausting stroll. We'll need to walk long hours and scale a mountain. The roads aren't terribly well kept up."

"Everything you say, Captain, just increases my curiosity. I'm ready to go with you."

"Then come along, professor, and we'll go put on our diving suits."

Arriving at the wardrobe, I saw that neither my companions nor any crewmen would be coming with us on this excursion. Captain Nemo hadn't even suggested my fetching Ned or Conseil.

In a few moments we had put on our equipment. Air tanks, abundantly charged, were placed on our backs, but the electric lamps were not in readiness. I commented on this to the captain.

"They'll be useless to us," he replied.

I thought I hadn't heard him right, but I couldn't repeat my comment because the captain's head had already disappeared into its metal covering. I finished harnessing myself, I felt an alpenstock being placed in my hand, and a few minutes later, after the usual procedures, we set foot on the floor of the Atlantic, 300 meters down.

Midnight was approaching. The waters were profoundly dark, but Captain Nemo pointed to a reddish spot in the distance, a sort of wide glow shimmering about two miles from the Nautilus. What this fire was, what substances fed it, how and why it kept burning in the liquid mass, I couldn't say. Anyhow it lit our way, although hazily, but I soon grew accustomed to this unique gloom, and in these circumstances I understood the uselessness of the Ruhmkorff device.

Side by side, Captain Nemo and I walked directly toward this conspicuous flame. The level seafloor rose imperceptibly. We took long strides, helped by our alpenstocks; but in general our progress was slow, because our feet kept sinking into a kind of slimy mud mixed with seaweed and assorted flat stones.

As we moved forward, I heard a kind of pitter–patter above my head. Sometimes this noise increased and became a continuous crackle. I soon realized the cause. It was a heavy rainfall rattling on the surface of the waves. Instinctively I worried that I might get soaked! By water in the midst of water! I couldn't help smiling at this outlandish notion. But to tell the truth, wearing these heavy diving suits, you no longer feel the liquid element, you simply think you're in the midst of air a little denser than air on land, that's all.

After half an hour of walking, the seafloor grew rocky. Jellyfish, microscopic crustaceans, and sea–pen coral lit it faintly with their phosphorescent glimmers. I glimpsed piles of stones covered by a couple million zoophytes and tangles of algae. My feet often slipped on this viscous seaweed carpet, and without my alpenstock I would have fallen more than once. When I turned around, I could still see the Nautilus's whitish beacon, which was starting to grow pale in the distance.

Those piles of stones just mentioned were laid out on the ocean floor with a distinct but inexplicable symmetry. I spotted gigantic furrows trailing off into the distant darkness, their length incalculable. There also were other peculiarities I couldn't make sense of. It seemed to me that my heavy lead soles were crushing a litter of bones that made a dry crackling noise. So what were these vast plains we were now crossing? I wanted to ask the captain, but I still didn't grasp that sign language that allowed him to chat with his companions when they went with him on his underwater excursions.

Meanwhile the reddish light guiding us had expanded and inflamed the horizon. The presence of this furnace under the waters had me extremely puzzled. Was it some sort of electrical discharge? Was I approaching some natural phenomenon still unknown to scientists on shore? Or, rather (and this thought did cross my mind), had the hand of man intervened in that blaze? Had human beings fanned those flames? In these deep strata would I meet up with more of Captain Nemo's companions, friends he was about to visit who led lives as strange as his own? Would I find a whole colony of exiles down here, men tired of the world's woes, men who had sought and found independence in the ocean's lower depths? All these insane, inadmissible ideas dogged me, and in this frame of mind, continually excited by the series of wonders passing before my eyes, I wouldn't have been surprised to find on this sea bottom one of those underwater towns Captain Nemo dreamed about!

Our path was getting brighter and brighter. The red glow had turned white and was radiating from a mountain peak about 800 feet high. But what I saw was simply a reflection produced by the crystal waters of these strata. The furnace that was the source of this inexplicable light occupied the far side of the mountain.

In the midst of the stone mazes furrowing this Atlantic seafloor, Captain Nemo moved forward without hesitation. He knew this dark path. No doubt he had often traveled it and was incapable of losing his way. I followed him with unshakeable confidence. He seemed like some Spirit of the Sea, and as he walked ahead of me, I marveled at his tall figure, which stood out in black against the glowing background of the horizon.

It was one o'clock in the morning. We arrived at the mountain's lower gradients. But in grappling with them, we had to venture up difficult trails through a huge thicket.

Yes, a thicket of dead trees! Trees without leaves, without sap, turned to stone by the action of the waters, and crowned here and there by gigantic pines. It was like a still–erect coalfield, its roots clutching broken soil, its boughs clearly outlined against the ceiling of the waters like thin, black, paper cutouts. Picture a forest clinging to the sides of a peak in the Harz Mountains, but a submerged forest. The trails were cluttered with algae and fucus plants, hosts of crustaceans swarming among them. I plunged on, scaling rocks, straddling fallen tree trunks, snapping marine creepers that swayed from one tree to another, startling the fish that flitted from branch to branch. Carried away, I didn't feel exhausted any more. I followed a guide who was immune to exhaustion.

What a sight! How can I describe it! How can I portray these woods and rocks in this liquid setting, their lower parts dark and sullen, their upper parts tinted red in this light whose intensity was doubled by the reflecting power of the waters! We scaled rocks that crumbled behind us, collapsing in enormous sections with the hollow rumble of an avalanche. To our right and left there were carved gloomy galleries where the eye lost its way. Huge glades opened up, seemingly cleared by the hand of man, and I sometimes wondered whether some residents of these underwater regions would suddenly appear before me.

But Captain Nemo kept climbing. I didn't want to fall behind. I followed him boldly. My alpenstock was a great help. One wrong step would have been disastrous on the narrow paths cut into the sides of these chasms, but I walked along with a firm tread and without the slightest feeling of dizziness. Sometimes

I leaped over a crevasse whose depth would have made me recoil had I been in the midst of glaciers on shore; sometimes I ventured out on a wobbling tree trunk fallen across a gorge, without looking down, having eyes only for marveling at the wild scenery of this region. There, leaning on erratically cut foundations, monumental rocks seemed to defy the laws of balance. From between their stony knees, trees sprang up like jets under fearsome pressure, supporting other trees that supported them in turn. Next, natural towers with wide, steeply carved battlements leaned at angles that, on dry land, the laws of gravity would never have authorized.

And I too could feel the difference created by the water's powerful density—despite my heavy clothing, copper headpiece, and metal soles, I climbed the most impossibly steep gradients with all the nimbleness, I swear it, of a chamois or a Pyrenees mountain goat!

As for my account of this excursion under the waters, I'm well aware that it sounds incredible! I'm the chronicler of deeds seemingly impossible and yet incontestably real. This was no fantasy. This was what I saw and felt!

Two hours after leaving the Nautilus, we had cleared the timberline, and 100 feet above our heads stood the mountain peak, forming a dark silhouette against the brilliant glare that came from its far slope. Petrified shrubs rambled here and there in sprawling zigzags. Fish rose in a body at our feet like birds startled in tall grass. The rocky mass was gouged with impenetrable crevices, deep caves, unfathomable holes at whose far ends I could hear fearsome things moving around. My blood would curdle as I watched some enormous antenna bar my path, or saw some frightful pincer snap shut in the shadow of some cavity! A thousand specks of light glittered in the midst of the gloom. They were the eyes of gigantic crustaceans crouching in their lairs, giant lobsters rearing up like spear carriers and moving their claws with a scrap–iron clanking, titanic crabs aiming their bodies like cannons on their carriages, and hideous devilfish intertwining their tentacles like bushes of writhing snakes.

What was this astounding world that I didn't yet know? In what order did these articulates belong, these creatures for which the rocks provided a second carapace? Where had nature learned the secret of their vegetating existence, and for how many centuries had they lived in the ocean's lower strata?

But I couldn't linger. Captain Nemo, on familiar terms with these dreadful animals, no longer minded them. We arrived at a preliminary plateau where still other surprises were waiting for me. There picturesque ruins took shape, betraying the hand of man, not our Creator. They were huge stacks of stones in which you could distinguish the indistinct forms of palaces and temples, now arrayed in hosts of blossoming zoophytes, and over it all, not ivy but a heavy mantle of algae and fucus plants.

But what part of the globe could this be, this land swallowed by cataclysms? Who had set up these rocks and stones like the dolmens of prehistoric times? Where was I, where had Captain Nemo's fancies taken me?

I wanted to ask him. Unable to, I stopped him. I seized his arm. But he shook his head, pointed to the mountain's topmost peak, and seemed to tell me:

"Come on! Come with me! Come higher!"

I followed him with one last burst of energy, and in a few minutes I had scaled the peak, which crowned the whole rocky mass by some ten meters.

I looked back down the side we had just cleared. There the mountain rose only 700 to 800 feet above the plains; but on its far slope it crowned the receding bottom of this part of the Atlantic by a height twice that. My eyes scanned the distance and took in a vast area lit by intense flashes of light. In essence, this mountain was a volcano. Fifty feet below its peak, amid a shower of stones and slag, a wide crater vomited torrents of lava that were dispersed in fiery cascades into the heart of the liquid mass. So situated, this volcano was an immense torch that lit up the lower plains all the way to the horizon.

As I said, this underwater crater spewed lava, but not flames. Flames need oxygen from the air and are unable to spread underwater; but a lava flow, which contains in itself the principle of its incandescence, can rise to a white heat, overpower the liquid element, and turn it into steam on contact. Swift currents swept away all this diffuse gas, and torrents of lava slid to the foot of the mountain, like the disgorgings of a Mt. Vesuvius over the city limits of a second Torre del Greco.

In fact, there beneath my eyes was a town in ruins, demolished, overwhelmed, laid low, its roofs caved in, its temples pulled down, its arches dislocated, its columns stretching over the earth; in these ruins you could still detect the solid proportions of a sort of Tuscan architecture; farther off, the remains of a gigantic aqueduct; here, the caked heights of an acropolis along with the fluid forms of a Parthenon; there, the remnants of a wharf, as if some bygone port had long ago harbored merchant vessels and triple–tiered war galleys on the shores of some lost ocean; still farther off, long rows of collapsing walls, deserted thoroughfares, a whole Pompeii buried under the waters, which Captain Nemo had resurrected before my eyes!

Where was I? Where was I? I had to find out at all cost, I wanted to speak, I wanted to rip off the copper sphere imprisoning my head.

But Captain Nemo came over and stopped me with a gesture. Then, picking up a piece of chalky stone, he advanced to a black basaltic rock and scrawled this one word:

ATLANTIS

What lightning flashed through my mind! Atlantis, that ancient land of Meropis mentioned by the historian Theopompus; Plato's Atlantis; the continent whose very existence has been denied by such philosophers and scientists as Origen, Porphyry, Iamblichus, d'Anville, Malte–Brun, and Humboldt, who entered its disappearance in the ledger of myths and folk tales; the country whose reality has nevertheless been accepted by such other thinkers as Posidonius, Pliny, Ammianus Marcellinus, Tertullian, Engel, Scherer, Tournefort, Buffon, and d'Avezac; I had this land right under my eyes, furnishing its own unimpeachable evidence of the catastrophe that had overtaken it! So this was the submerged region that had existed outside Europe, Asia, and Libya, beyond the Pillars of Hercules, home of those powerful Atlantean people against whom ancient Greece had waged its earliest wars!

The writer whose narratives record the lofty deeds of those heroic times is Plato himself. His dialogues Timæus and Critias were drafted with the poet and legislator Solon as their inspiration, as it were.

One day Solon was conversing with some elderly wise men in the Egyptian capital of Sais, a town already 8,000 years of age, as documented by the annals engraved on the sacred walls of its temples. One of these elders related the history of another town 1,000 years older still. This original city of Athens, ninety centuries old, had been invaded and partly destroyed by the Atlanteans. These Atlanteans, he said, resided on an immense continent greater than Africa and Asia combined, taking in an area that lay between latitude 12° and 40° north. Their dominion extended even to Egypt. They tried to enforce their rule as far as Greece, but they had to retreat before the indomitable resistance of the Hellenic people. Centuries passed. A cataclysm occurred—floods, earthquakes. A single night and day were enough to obliterate this Atlantis, whose highest peaks (Madeira, the Azores, the Canaries, the Cape Verde Islands) still emerge above the waves.

These were the historical memories that Captain Nemo's scrawl sent rushing through my mind. Thus, led by the strangest of fates, I was treading underfoot one of the mountains of that continent! My hands were touching ruins many thousands of years old, contemporary with prehistoric times! I was walking in the very place where contemporaries of early man had walked! My heavy soles were crushing the skeletons of animals from the age of fable, animals that used to take cover in the shade of these trees now turned to stone!

Oh, why was I so short of time! I would have gone down the steep slopes of this mountain, crossed this entire immense continent, which surely connects Africa with America, and visited its great prehistoric cities. Under my eyes there perhaps lay the warlike town of Makhimos or the pious village of Eusebes, whose gigantic inhabitants lived for whole centuries and had the strength to raise blocks of stone that still withstood the action of the waters. One day perhaps, some volcanic phenomenon will bring these sunken ruins back to the surface of the waves! Numerous underwater volcanoes have been sighted in this part of the ocean, and many ships have felt terrific tremors when passing over these turbulent depths. A few have heard hollow noises that announced some struggle of the elements far below, others have hauled in volcanic ash hurled above the waves. As far as the equator this whole seafloor is still under construction by plutonic forces. And in some remote epoch, built up by volcanic disgorgings and successive layers of lava, who knows whether the peaks of these fire–belching mountains may reappear above the surface of the Atlantic!

As I mused in this way, trying to establish in my memory every detail of this impressive landscape, Captain Nemo was leaning his elbows on a moss–covered monument, motionless as if petrified in some mute trance. Was he dreaming of those lost generations, asking them for the secret of human destiny? Was it here that this strange man came to revive himself, basking in historical memories, reliving that bygone life, he who had no desire for our modern one? I would have given anything to know his thoughts, to share them, understand them!

We stayed in this place an entire hour, contemplating its vast plains in the lava's glow, which sometimes took on a startling intensity. Inner boilings sent quick shivers running through the mountain's crust. Noises from deep underneath, clearly transmitted by the liquid medium, reverberated with majestic amplitude.

Just then the moon appeared for an instant through the watery mass, casting a few pale rays over this submerged continent. It was only a fleeting glimmer, but its effect was indescribable. The captain stood up and took one last look at these immense plains; then his hand signaled me to follow him.

We went swiftly down the mountain. Once past the petrified forest, I could see the Nautilus's beacon twinkling like a star. The captain walked straight toward it, and we were back on board just as the first glimmers of dawn were whitening the surface of the ocean.

The Underwater Coalfields

THE NEXT DAY, February 20, I overslept. I was so exhausted from the night before, I didn't get up until eleven o'clock. I dressed quickly. I hurried to find out the Nautilus's heading. The instruments indicated that it was running southward at a speed of twenty miles per hour and a depth of 100 meters.

Conseil entered. I described our nocturnal excursion to him, and since the panels were open, he could still catch a glimpse of this submerged continent.

In fact, the Nautilus was skimming only ten meters over the soil of these Atlantis plains. The ship scudded along like an air balloon borne by the wind over some prairie on land; but it would be more accurate to say that we sat in the lounge as if we were riding in a coach on an express train. As for the foregrounds passing before our eyes, they were fantastically carved rocks, forests of trees that had crossed over from the vegetable kingdom into the mineral kingdom, their motionless silhouettes sprawling beneath the waves. There also were stony masses buried beneath carpets of axidia and sea anemone, bristling with long, vertical water plants, then strangely contoured blocks of lava that testified to all the fury of those plutonic developments.

While this bizarre scenery was glittering under our electric beams, I told Conseil the story of the Atlanteans, who had inspired the old French scientist Jean Bailly to write so many entertaining—albeit utterly fictitious—pages. I told the lad about the wars of these heroic people. I discussed the question of Atlantis with the fervor of a man who no longer had any doubts. But Conseil was so distracted he barely heard me, and his lack of interest in any commentary on this historical topic was soon explained.

In essence, numerous fish had caught his eye, and when fish pass by, Conseil vanishes into his world of classifying and leaves real life behind. In which case I could only tag along and resume our ichthyological research.

Even so, these Atlantic fish were not noticeably different from those we had observed earlier. There were rays of gigantic size, five meters long and with muscles so powerful they could leap above the waves, sharks of various species including a fifteen–foot glaucous shark with sharp triangular teeth and so transparent it was almost invisible amid the waters, brown lantern sharks, prism–shaped humantin sharks armored with protuberant hides, sturgeons resembling their relatives in the Mediterranean, trumpet–snouted pipefish a foot and a half long, yellowish brown with small gray fins and no teeth or tongue, unreeling like slim, supple snakes.

Among bony fish, Conseil noticed some blackish marlin three meters long with a sharp sword jutting from the upper jaw, bright–colored weevers known in Aristotle's day as sea dragons and whose dorsal stingers make them quite dangerous to pick up, then dolphinfish with brown backs striped in blue and edged in gold, handsome dorados, moonlike opahs that look like azure disks but which the sun's rays turn into spots of silver, finally eight–meter swordfish from the genus Xiphias, swimming in schools, sporting yellowish sickle–shaped fins and six–foot broadswords, stalwart animals, plant eaters rather than fish eaters, obeying the tiniest signals from their females like henpecked husbands.

But while observing these different specimens of marine fauna, I didn't stop examining the long plains of Atlantis. Sometimes an unpredictable irregularity in the seafloor would force the Nautilus to slow down, and then it would glide into the narrow channels between the hills with a cetacean's dexterity. If the labyrinth became hopelessly tangled, the submersible would rise above it like an airship, and after clearing the obstacle, it would resume its speedy course just a few meters above the ocean floor. It was an enjoyable and impressive way of navigating that did indeed recall the maneuvers of an airship ride, with the major difference that the Nautilus faithfully obeyed the hands of its helmsman.

The terrain consisted mostly of thick slime mixed with petrified branches, but it changed little by little near four o'clock in the afternoon; it grew rockier and seemed to be strewn with pudding stones and a basaltic gravel called "tuff," together with bits of lava and sulfurous obsidian. I expected these long plains to change into mountain regions, and in fact, as the Nautilus was executing certain turns, I noticed that the southerly horizon was blocked by a high wall that seemed to close off every exit. Its summit obviously poked above the level of the ocean. It had to be a continent or at least an island, either one of the Canaries or one of the Cape Verde Islands. Our bearings hadn't been marked on the chart—perhaps deliberately—and I had no idea what our position was. In any case this wall seemed to signal the end of Atlantis, of which, all in all, we had crossed only a small part.

Nightfall didn't interrupt my observations. I was left to myself. Conseil had repaired to his cabin. The Nautilus slowed down, hovering above the muddled masses on the seafloor, sometimes grazing them as if wanting to come to rest, sometimes rising unpredictably to the surface of the waves. Then I glimpsed a few bright constellations through the crystal waters, specifically five or six of those zodiacal stars trailing from the tail end of Orion.

I would have stayed longer at my window, marveling at these beauties of sea and sky, but the panels closed. Just then the Nautilus had arrived at the perpendicular face of that high wall. How the ship would maneuver I hadn't a guess. I repaired to my stateroom. The Nautilus did not stir. I fell asleep with the firm intention of waking up in just a few hours.

But it was eight o'clock the next day when I returned to the lounge. I stared at the pressure gauge. It told me that the Nautilus was afloat on the surface of the ocean. Furthermore, I heard the sound of footsteps on the platform. Yet there were no rolling movements to indicate the presence of waves undulating above me.

I climbed as far as the hatch. It was open. But instead of the broad daylight I was expecting, I found that I was surrounded by total darkness. Where were we? Had I been mistaken? Was it still night? No! Not one star was twinkling, and nighttime is never so utterly black.

I wasn't sure what to think, when a voice said to me:

"Is that you, Professor?"

"Ah, Captain Nemo!" I replied. "Where are we?"

"Underground, Professor."

"Underground!" I exclaimed. "And the Nautilus is still floating?"

"It always floats."

"But I don't understand!"

"Wait a little while. Our beacon is about to go on, and if you want some light on the subject, you'll be satisfied."

I set foot on the platform and waited. The darkness was so profound I couldn't see even Captain Nemo. However, looking at the zenith directly overhead, I thought I caught sight of a feeble glimmer, a sort of twilight filtering through a circular hole. Just then the beacon suddenly went on, and its intense brightness made that hazy light vanish.

This stream of electricity dazzled my eyes, and after momentarily shutting them, I looked around. The Nautilus was stationary. It was floating next to an embankment shaped like a wharf. As for the water now buoying the ship, it was a lake completely encircled by an inner wall about two miles in diameter, hence six miles around. Its level—as indicated by the pressure gauge—would be the same as the outside level, because some connection had to exist between this lake and the sea. Slanting inward over their base, these high walls converged to form a vault shaped like an immense upside–down funnel that measured 500 or 600 meters in height. At its summit there gaped the circular opening through which I had detected that faint glimmer, obviously daylight.

Before more carefully examining the interior features of this enormous cavern, and before deciding if it was the work of nature or humankind, I went over to Captain Nemo.

"Where are we?" I said.

"In the very heart of an extinct volcano," the captain answered me, "a volcano whose interior was invaded by the sea after some convulsion in the earth. While you were sleeping, professor, the Nautilus entered this lagoon through a natural channel that opens ten meters below the surface of the ocean. This is our home port, secure, convenient, secret, and sheltered against winds from any direction! Along the coasts of your continents or islands, show me any offshore mooring that can equal this safe refuge for withstanding the fury of hurricanes."

"Indeed," I replied, "here you're in perfect safety, Captain Nemo. Who could reach you in the heart of a volcano? But don't I see an opening at its summit?"

"Yes, its crater, a crater formerly filled with lava, steam, and flames, but which now lets in this life–giving air we're breathing."

"But which volcanic mountain is this?" I asked.

"It's one of the many islets with which this sea is strewn. For ships a mere reef, for us an immense cavern. I discovered it by chance, and chance served me well."

"But couldn't someone enter through the mouth of its crater?"

"No more than I could exit through it. You can climb about 100 feet up the inner base of this mountain, but then the walls overhang, they lean too far in to be scaled."

"I can see, Captain, that nature is your obedient servant, any time or any place. You're safe on this lake, and nobody else can visit its waters. But what's the purpose of this refuge? The Nautilus doesn't need a harbor."

"No, professor, but it needs electricity to run, batteries to generate its electricity, sodium to feed its batteries, coal to make its sodium, and coalfields from which to dig its coal. Now then, right at this spot the sea covers entire forests that sank underwater in prehistoric times; today, turned to stone, transformed into carbon fuel, they offer me inexhaustible coal mines."

"So, Captain, your men practice the trade of miners here?"

"Precisely. These mines extend under the waves like the coalfields at Newcastle. Here, dressed in diving suits, pick and mattock in hand, my men go out and dig this carbon fuel for which I don't need a single mine on land. When I burn this combustible to produce sodium, the smoke escaping from the mountain's crater gives it the appearance of a still-active volcano."

"And will we see your companions at work?"

"No, at least not this time, because I'm eager to continue our underwater tour of the world. Accordingly, I'll rest content with drawing on my reserve stock of sodium. We'll stay here long enough to load it on board, in other words, a single workday, then we'll resume our voyage. So, Professor Aronnax, if you'd like to explore this cavern and circle its lagoon, seize the day."

I thanked the captain and went to look for my two companions, who hadn't yet left their cabin. I invited them to follow me, not telling them where we were.

They climbed onto the platform. Conseil, whom nothing could startle, saw it as a perfectly natural thing to fall asleep under the waves and wake up under a mountain. But Ned Land had no idea in his head other than to see if this cavern offered some way out.

After breakfast near ten o'clock, we went down onto the embankment.

"So here we are, back on shore," Conseil said.

"I'd hardly call this shore," the Canadian replied. "And besides, we aren't on it but under it."

A sandy beach unfolded before us, measuring 500 feet at its widest point between the waters of the lake and the foot of the mountain's walls. Via this strand you could easily circle the lake. But the base of these high walls consisted of broken soil over which there lay picturesque piles of volcanic blocks and enormous pumice stones. All these crumbling masses were covered with an enamel polished by the action of underground fires, and they glistened under the stream of electric light from our beacon. Stirred up by our footsteps, the mica-rich dust on this beach flew into the air like a cloud of sparks.

The ground rose appreciably as it moved away from the sand flats by the waves, and we soon arrived at some long, winding gradients, genuinely steep paths that allowed us to climb little by little; but we had to tread cautiously in the midst of pudding stones that weren't cemented together, and our feet kept skidding on glassy trachyte, made of feldspar and quartz crystals.

The volcanic nature of this enormous pit was apparent all around us. I ventured to comment on it to my companions.

"Can you picture," I asked them, "what this funnel must have been like when it was filled with boiling lava, and the level of that incandescent liquid rose right to the mountain's mouth, like cast iron up the insides of a furnace?"

"I can picture it perfectly," Conseil replied. "But will Master tell me why this huge smelter suspended operations, and how it is that an oven was replaced by the tranquil waters of a lake?"

"In all likelihood, Conseil, because some convulsion created an opening below the surface of the ocean, the opening that serves as a passageway for the Nautilus. Then the waters of the Atlantic rushed inside the mountain. There ensued a dreadful struggle between the elements of fire and water, a struggle ending in King Neptune's favor. But many centuries have passed since then, and this submerged volcano has changed into a peaceful cavern."

"That's fine," Ned Land answered. "I accept the explanation, but in our personal interests, I'm sorry this opening the professor mentions wasn't made above sea level."

"But Ned my friend," Conseil answered, "if it weren't an underwater passageway, the Nautilus couldn't enter it!"

"And I might add, Mr. Land," I said, "that the waters wouldn't have rushed under the mountain, and the volcano would still be a volcano. So you have nothing to be sorry about."

Our climb continued. The gradients got steeper and narrower. Sometimes they were cut across by deep pits that had to be cleared. Masses of overhanging rock had to be gotten around. You slid on your knees, you crept on your belly. But helped by the Canadian's strength and Conseil's dexterity, we overcame every obstacle.

At an elevation of about thirty meters, the nature of the terrain changed without becoming any easier. Pudding stones and trachyte gave way to black basaltic rock: here, lying in slabs all swollen with blisters; there, shaped like actual prisms and arranged into a series of columns that supported the springings of this immense vault, a wonderful sample of natural architecture. Then, among this basaltic rock, there snaked long, hardened lava flows inlaid with veins of bituminous coal and in places covered by wide carpets of sulfur. The sunshine coming through the crater had grown stronger, shedding a hazy light over all the volcanic waste forever buried in the heart of this extinct mountain.

But when we had ascended to an elevation of about 250 feet, we were stopped by insurmountable obstacles. The converging inside walls changed into overhangs, and our climb into a circular stroll. At this topmost level the vegetable kingdom began to challenge the mineral kingdom. Shrubs, and even a few trees, emerged from crevices in the walls. I recognized some spurges that let their caustic, purgative sap trickle out. There were heliotropes, very remiss at living up to their sun–worshipping reputations since no sunlight ever reached them; their clusters of flowers drooped sadly, their colors and scents were faded. Here and there chrysanthemums sprouted timidly at the feet of aloes with long, sad, sickly leaves. But between these lava flows I spotted little violets that still gave off a subtle fragrance, and I confess that I inhaled it with delight. The soul of a flower is its scent, and those splendid water plants, flowers of the sea, have no souls!

We had arrived at the foot of a sturdy clump of dragon trees, which were splitting the rocks with exertions of their muscular roots, when Ned Land exclaimed:

"Oh, sir, a hive!"

"A hive?" I answered, with a gesture of utter disbelief.

"Yes, a hive," the Canadian repeated, "with bees buzzing around!"

I went closer and was forced to recognize the obvious. At the mouth of a hole cut in the trunk of a dragon tree, there swarmed thousands of these ingenious insects so common to all the Canary Islands, where their output is especially prized.

Naturally enough, the Canadian wanted to lay in a supply of honey, and it would have been ill–mannered of me to say no. He mixed sulfur with some dry leaves, set them on fire with a spark from his tinderbox, and proceeded to smoke the bees out. Little by little the buzzing died down and the disemboweled hive yielded several pounds of sweet honey. Ned Land stuffed his haversack with it.

"When I've mixed this honey with our breadfruit batter," he told us, "I'll be ready to serve you a delectable piece of cake."

"But of course," Conseil put in, "it will be gingerbread!"

"I'm all for gingerbread," I said, "but let's resume this fascinating stroll."

At certain turns in the trail we were going along, the lake appeared in its full expanse. The ship's beacon lit up that whole placid surface, which experienced neither ripples nor undulations. The Nautilus lay perfectly still. On its platform and on the embankment, crewmen were bustling around, black shadows that stood out clearly in the midst of the luminous air.

Just then we went around the highest ridge of these rocky foothills that supported the vault. Then I saw that bees weren't the animal kingdom's only representatives inside this volcano. Here and in the shadows, birds of prey soared and whirled, flying away from nests perched on tips of rock. There were sparrow hawks with white bellies, and screeching kestrels. With all the speed their stiltlike legs could muster, fine fat bustards scampered over the slopes. I'll let the reader decide whether the Canadian's appetite was aroused by the sight of this tasty game, and whether he regretted having no rifle in his hands. He tried to make stones do the work of bullets, and after several fruitless attempts, he managed to wound one of these magnificent bustards. To say he risked his life twenty times in order to capture this bird is simply the unadulterated truth; but he fared so well, the animal went into his sack to join the honeycombs.

By then we were forced to go back down to the beach because the ridge had become impossible. Above us, the yawning crater looked like the wide mouth of a well. From where we stood, the sky was pretty easy to see, and I watched clouds race by, disheveled by the west wind, letting tatters of mist trail over the mountain's summit. Proof positive that those clouds kept at a moderate altitude, because this volcano didn't rise more than 1,800 feet above the level of the ocean.

Half an hour after the Canadian's latest exploits, we were back on the inner beach. There the local flora was represented by a wide carpet of samphire, a small umbelliferous plant that keeps quite nicely, which also boasts the names glasswort, saxifrage, and sea fennel. Conseil picked a couple bunches. As for the local fauna, it included thousands of crustaceans of every type: lobsters, hermit crabs, prawns, mysid shrimps, daddy longlegs, rock crabs, and a prodigious number of seashells, such as cowries, murex snails, and limpets.

In this locality there gaped the mouth of a magnificent cave. My companions and I took great pleasure in stretching out on its fine–grained sand. Fire had polished the sparkling enamel of its inner walls, sprinkled all over with mica–rich dust. Ned Land tapped these walls and tried to probe their thickness. I couldn't help smiling. Our conversation then turned to his everlasting escape plans, and without going too far, I felt I could offer him this hope: Captain Nemo had gone down south only to replenish his sodium supplies. So I hoped he would now hug the coasts of Europe and America, which would allow the Canadian to try again with a greater chance of success.

We were stretched out in this delightful cave for an hour. Our conversation, lively at the outset, then languished. A definite drowsiness overcame us. Since I saw no good reason to resist the call of sleep, I fell into a heavy doze. I dreamed—one doesn't choose his dreams—that my life had been reduced to the vegetating existence of a simple mollusk. It seemed to me that this cave made up my double–valved shell. . . .

Suddenly Conseil's voice startled me awake.

"Get up! Get up!" shouted the fine lad.

"What is it?" I asked, in a sitting position.

"The water's coming up to us!"

I got back on my feet. Like a torrent the sea was rushing into our retreat, and since we definitely were not mollusks, we had to clear out.

In a few seconds we were safe on top of the cave.

"What happened?" Conseil asked. "Some new phenomenon?"

"Not quite, my friends!" I replied. "It was the tide, merely the tide, which wellnigh caught us by surprise just as it did Sir Walter Scott's hero! The ocean outside is rising, and by a perfectly natural law of balance, the level of this lake is also rising. We've gotten off with a mild dunking. Let's go change clothes on the Nautilus."

Three–quarters of an hour later, we had completed our circular stroll and were back on board. Just then the crewmen finished loading the sodium supplies, and the Nautilus could have departed immediately.

But Captain Nemo gave no orders. Would he wait for nightfall and exit through his underwater passageway in secrecy? Perhaps.

Be that as it may, by the next day the Nautilus had left its home port and was navigating well out from any shore, a few meters beneath the waves of the Atlantic.

The Sargasso Sea

THE Nautilus didn't change direction. For the time being, then, we had to set aside any hope of returning to European seas. Captain Nemo kept his prow pointing south. Where was he taking us? I was afraid to guess.

That day the Nautilus crossed an odd part of the Atlantic Ocean. No one is unaware of the existence of that great warm–water current known by name as the Gulf Stream. After emerging from channels off Florida, it heads toward Spitzbergen. But before entering the Gulf of Mexico near latitude 44° north, this current divides into two arms; its chief arm makes for the shores of Ireland and Norway while the second flexes southward at the level of the Azores; then it hits the coast of Africa, sweeps in a long oval, and returns to the Caribbean Sea.

Now then, this second arm—more accurately, a collar—forms a ring of warm water around a section of cool, tranquil, motionless ocean called the Sargasso Sea. This is an actual lake in the open Atlantic, and the great current's waters take at least three years to circle it.

Properly speaking, the Sargasso Sea covers every submerged part of Atlantis. Certain authors have even held that the many weeds strewn over this sea were torn loose from the prairies of that ancient continent. But it's more likely that these grasses, algae, and fucus plants were carried off from the beaches of Europe and America, then taken as far as this zone by the Gulf Stream. This is one of the reasons why Christopher Columbus assumed the existence of a New World. When the ships of that bold investigator arrived in the Sargasso Sea, they had great difficulty navigating in the midst of these weeds, which, much to their crews' dismay, slowed them down to a halt; and they wasted three long weeks crossing this sector.

Such was the region our Nautilus was visiting just then: a genuine prairie, a tightly woven carpet of algae, gulfweed, and bladder wrack so dense and compact a craft's stempost couldn't tear through it without difficulty. Accordingly, not wanting to entangle his propeller in this weed–choked mass, Captain Nemo stayed at a depth some meters below the surface of the waves.

The name Sargasso comes from the Spanish word sargazo, meaning gulfweed. This gulfweed, the swimming gulfweed or berry carrier, is the chief substance making up this immense shoal. And here's why these water plants collect in this placid Atlantic basin, according to the expert on the subject, Commander Maury, author of The Physical Geography of the Sea.

The explanation he gives seems to entail a set of conditions that everybody knows: "Now," Maury says, "if bits of cork or chaff, or any floating substance, be put into a basin, and a circular motion be given to the water, all the light substances will be found crowding together near the center of the pool, where there is the least motion. Just such a basin is the Atlantic Ocean to the Gulf Stream, and the Sargasso Sea is the center of the whirl."

I share Maury's view, and I was able to study the phenomenon in this exclusive setting where ships rarely go. Above us, huddled among the brown weeds, there floated objects originating from all over: tree trunks ripped from the Rocky Mountains or the Andes and sent floating down the Amazon or the Mississippi, numerous pieces of wreckage, remnants of keels or undersides, bulwarks staved in and so weighed down with seashells and barnacles, they couldn't rise to the surface of the ocean. And the passing years will someday bear out Maury's other view that by collecting in this way over the centuries, these substances will be turned to stone by the action of the waters and will then form inexhaustible coalfields. Valuable reserves prepared by farseeing nature for that time when man will have exhausted his mines on the continents.

In the midst of this hopelessly tangled fabric of weeds and fucus plants, I noted some delightful pink–colored, star–shaped alcyon coral, sea anemone trailing the long tresses of their tentacles, some green, red, and blue jellyfish, and especially those big rhizostome jellyfish that Cuvier described, whose bluish parasols are trimmed with violet festoons.

We spent the whole day of February 22 in the Sargasso Sea, where fish that dote on marine plants and crustaceans find plenty to eat. The next day the ocean resumed its usual appearance.

From this moment on, for nineteen days from February 23 to March 12, the Nautilus stayed in the middle of the Atlantic, hustling us along at a constant speed of 100 leagues every twenty–four hours. It was obvious that Captain Nemo wanted to carry out his underwater program, and I had no doubt that he intended, after doubling Cape Horn, to return to the Pacific South Seas.

So Ned Land had good reason to worry. In these wide seas empty of islands, it was no longer feasible to jump ship. Nor did we have any way to counter Captain Nemo's whims. We had no choice but to acquiesce; but if we couldn't attain our end through force or cunning, I liked to think we might achieve it through persuasion. Once this voyage was over, might not Captain Nemo consent to set us free in return for our promise never to reveal his existence? Our word of honor, which we sincerely would have kept. However, this delicate question would have to be negotiated with the captain. But how would he receive our demands for freedom? At the very outset and in no uncertain terms, hadn't he declared that the secret of his life required that we be permanently imprisoned on board the Nautilus? Wouldn't he see my four–month silence as a tacit acceptance of this situation? Would my returning to this subject arouse suspicions that could jeopardize our escape plans, if we had promising circumstances for trying again later on? I weighed all these considerations, turned them over in my mind, submitted them to Conseil, but he was as baffled as I was. In short, although I'm not easily discouraged, I realized that my chances of ever seeing my fellow men again were shrinking by the day, especially at a time when Captain Nemo was recklessly racing toward the south Atlantic!

During those nineteen days just mentioned, no unique incidents distinguished our voyage. I saw little of the captain. He was at work. In the library I often found books he had left open, especially books on natural history. He had thumbed through my work on the great ocean depths, and the margins were covered with his notes, which sometimes contradicted my theories and formulations. But the captain remained content with this method of refining my work, and he rarely discussed it with me. Sometimes I heard melancholy sounds reverberating from the organ, which he played very expressively, but only at night in the midst of the most secretive darkness, while the Nautilus slumbered in the wilderness of the ocean.

During this part of our voyage, we navigated on the surface of the waves for entire days. The sea was nearly deserted. A few sailing ships, laden for the East Indies, were heading toward the Cape of Good Hope. One day we were chased by the longboats of a whaling vessel, which undoubtedly viewed us as some enormous baleen whale of great value. But Captain Nemo didn't want these gallant gentlemen wasting their time and energy, so he ended the hunt by diving beneath the waters. This incident seemed to fascinate Ned Land intensely. I'm sure the Canadian was sorry that these fishermen couldn't harpoon our sheet–iron cetacean and mortally wound it.

During this period the fish Conseil and I observed differed little from those we had already studied in other latitudes. Chief among them were specimens of that dreadful cartilaginous genus that's divided into three subgenera numbering at least thirty–two species: striped sharks five meters long, the head squat and wider than the body, the caudal fin curved, the back with seven big, black, parallel lines running lengthwise; then perlon sharks, ash gray, pierced with seven gill openings, furnished with a single dorsal fin placed almost exactly in the middle of the body.

Some big dogfish also passed by, a voracious species of shark if there ever was one. With some justice, fishermen's yarns aren't to be trusted, but here's what a few of them relate. Inside the corpse of one of these animals there were found a buffalo head and a whole calf; in another, two tuna and a sailor in uniform; in yet another, a soldier with his saber; in another, finally, a horse with its rider. In candor, none of these sounds like divinely inspired truth. But the fact remains that not a single dogfish let itself get caught in the Nautilus's nets, so I can't vouch for their voracity.

Schools of elegant, playful dolphin swam alongside for entire days. They went in groups of five or six, hunting in packs like wolves over the countryside; moreover, they're just as voracious as dogfish, if I can believe a certain Copenhagen professor who says that from one dolphin's stomach, he removed thirteen porpoises and fifteen seals. True, it was a killer whale, belonging to the biggest known species, whose length sometimes exceeds twenty–four feet. The family Delphinia numbers ten genera, and the dolphins I saw were akin to the genus Delphinorhynchus, remarkable for an extremely narrow muzzle four times as long as the cranium. Measuring three meters, their bodies were black on top, underneath a pinkish white strewn with small, very scattered spots.

From these seas I'll also mention some unusual specimens of croakers, fish from the order Acanthopterygia, family Scienidea. Some authors—more artistic than scientific—claim that these fish are melodious singers, that their voices in unison put on concerts unmatched by human choristers. I don't say nay, but to my regret these croakers didn't serenade us as we passed.

Finally, to conclude, Conseil classified a large number of flying fish. Nothing could have made a more unusual sight than the marvelous timing with which dolphins hunt these fish. Whatever the range of its flight, however evasive its trajectory (even up and over the Nautilus), the hapless flying fish always found a dolphin to welcome it with open mouth. These were either flying gurnards or kitelike sea robins, whose lips glowed in the dark, at night scrawling fiery streaks in the air before plunging into the murky waters like so many shooting stars.

Our navigating continued under these conditions until March 13. That day the Nautilus was put to work in some depth–sounding experiments that fascinated me deeply.

By then we had fared nearly 13,000 leagues from our starting point in the Pacific high seas. Our position fix placed us in latitude 45° 37' south and longitude 37° 53' west. These were the same waterways where Captain Denham, aboard the Herald, payed out 14,000 meters of sounding line without finding bottom. It was here too that Lieutenant Parker, aboard the American frigate Congress, was unable to reach the underwater soil at 15,149 meters.

Captain Nemo decided to take his Nautilus down to the lowest depths in order to double–check these different soundings. I got ready to record the results of this experiment. The panels in the lounge opened, and maneuvers began for reaching those strata so prodigiously far removed.

It was apparently considered out of the question to dive by filling the ballast tanks. Perhaps they wouldn't sufficiently increase the Nautilus's specific gravity. Moreover, in order to come back up, it would be necessary to expel the excess water, and our pumps might not have been strong enough to overcome the outside pressure.

Captain Nemo decided to make for the ocean floor by submerging on an appropriately gradual diagonal with the help of his side fins, which were set at a 45° angle to the Nautilus's waterline. Then the propeller was brought to its maximum speed, and its four blades churned the waves with indescribable violence.

Under this powerful thrust the Nautilus's hull quivered like a resonating chord, and the ship sank steadily under the waters. Stationed in the lounge, the captain and I watched the needle swerving swiftly over the pressure gauge. Soon we had gone below the livable zone where most fish reside. Some of these animals can thrive only at the surface of seas or rivers, but a minority can dwell at fairly great depths. Among the latter I observed a species of dogfish called the cow shark that's equipped with six respiratory slits, the telescope fish with its enormous eyes, the armored gurnard with gray thoracic fins plus black pectoral fins and a breastplate protected by pale red slabs of bone, then finally the grenadier, living at a depth of 1,200 meters, by that point tolerating a pressure of 120 atmospheres.

I asked Captain Nemo if he had observed any fish at more considerable depths.

"Fish? Rarely!" he answered me. "But given the current state of marine science, who are we to presume, what do we really know of these depths?"

"Just this, Captain. In going toward the ocean's lower strata, we know that vegetable life disappears more quickly than animal life. We know that moving creatures can still be encountered where water plants no longer grow. We know that oysters and pilgrim scallops live in 2,000 meters of water, and that Admiral McClintock, England's hero of the polar seas, pulled in a live sea star from a depth of 2,500 meters. We know that the crew of the Royal Navy's Bulldog fished up a starfish from 2,620 fathoms, hence from a depth of more than one vertical league. Would you still say, Captain Nemo, that we really know nothing?"

"No, Professor," the captain replied, "I wouldn't be so discourteous. Yet I'll ask you to explain how these creatures can live at such depths?"

"I explain it on two grounds," I replied. "In the first place, because vertical currents, which are caused by differences in the water's salinity and density, can produce enough motion to sustain the rudimentary lifestyles of sea lilies and starfish."

"True," the captain put in.

"In the second place, because oxygen is the basis of life, and we know that the amount of oxygen dissolved in salt water increases rather than decreases with depth, that the pressure in these lower strata helps to concentrate their oxygen content."

"Oho! We know that, do we?" Captain Nemo replied in a tone of mild surprise. "Well, Professor, we have good reason to know it because it's the truth. I might add, in fact, that the air bladders of fish contain more nitrogen than oxygen when these animals are caught at the surface of the water, and conversely, more oxygen than nitrogen when they're pulled up from the lower depths. Which bears out your formulation. But let's continue our observations."

My eyes flew back to the pressure gauge. The instrument indicated a depth of 6,000 meters. Our submergence had been going on for an hour. The Nautilus slid downward on its slanting fins, still sinking. These deserted waters were wonderfully clear, with a transparency impossible to convey. An hour later we were at 13,000 meters—about three and a quarter vertical leagues—and the ocean floor was nowhere in sight.

However, at 14,000 meters I saw blackish peaks rising in the midst of the waters. But these summits could have belonged to mountains as high or even higher than the Himalayas or Mt. Blanc, and the extent of these depths remained incalculable.

Despite the powerful pressures it was undergoing, the Nautilus sank still deeper. I could feel its sheet–iron plates trembling down to their riveted joins; metal bars arched; bulkheads groaned; the lounge windows seemed to be warping inward under the water's pressure. And this whole sturdy mechanism would surely have given way, if, as its captain had said, it weren't capable of resisting like a solid block.

While grazing these rocky slopes lost under the waters, I still spotted some seashells, tube worms, lively annelid worms from the genus Spirorbis, and certain starfish specimens.

But soon these last representatives of animal life vanished, and three vertical leagues down, the Nautilus passed below the limits of underwater existence just as an air balloon rises above the breathable zones in the sky. We reached a depth of 16,000 meters—four vertical leagues—and by then the Nautilus's plating was tolerating a pressure of 1,600 atmospheres, in other words, 1,600 kilograms per each square centimeter on its surface!

"What an experience!" I exclaimed. "Traveling these deep regions where no man has ever ventured before! Look, captain! Look at these magnificent rocks, these uninhabited caves, these last global haunts where life is no longer possible!

What unheard–of scenery, and why are we reduced to preserving it only as a memory?"

"Would you like," Captain Nemo asked me, "to bring back more than just a memory?"

"What do you mean?"

"I mean that nothing could be easier than taking a photograph of this underwater region!"

Before I had time to express the surprise this new proposition caused me, a camera was carried into the lounge at Captain Nemo's request. The liquid setting, electrically lit, unfolded with perfect clarity through the wide–open panels. No shadows, no blurs, thanks to our artificial light. Not even sunshine could have been better for our purposes. With the thrust of its propeller curbed by the slant of its fins, the Nautilus stood still. The camera was aimed at the scenery on the ocean floor, and in a few seconds we had a perfect negative.

I attach a print of the positive. In it you can view these primordial rocks that have never seen the light of day, this nether granite that forms the powerful foundation of our globe, the deep caves cut into the stony mass, the outlines of incomparable distinctness whose far edges stand out in black as if from the brush of certain Flemish painters. In the distance is a mountainous horizon, a wondrously undulating line that makes up the background of this landscape. The general effect of these smooth rocks is indescribable: black, polished, without moss or other blemish, carved into strange shapes, sitting firmly on a carpet of sand that sparkled beneath our streams of electric light.

Meanwhile, his photographic operations over, Captain Nemo told me:

"Let's go back up, professor. We mustn't push our luck and expose the Nautilus too long to these pressures."

"Let's go back up!" I replied.

"Hold on tight."

Before I had time to realize why the captain made this recommendation, I was hurled to the carpet.

Its fins set vertically, its propeller thrown in gear at the captain's signal, the Nautilus rose with lightning speed, shooting upward like an air balloon into the sky. Vibrating resonantly, it knifed through the watery mass. Not a single detail was visible. In four minutes it had cleared the four vertical leagues separating it from the surface of the ocean, and after emerging like a flying fish, it fell back into the sea, making the waves leap to prodigious heights.

Sperm Whales and Baleen Whales

DURING THE NIGHT of March 13–14, the Nautilus resumed its southward heading. Once it was abreast of Cape Horn, I thought it would strike west of the cape, make for Pacific seas, and complete its tour of the world. It did nothing of the sort and kept moving toward the southernmost regions. So where was it bound? The pole? That was insanity. I was beginning to think that the captain's recklessness more than justified Ned Land's worst fears.

For a good while the Canadian had said nothing more to me about his escape plans. He had become less sociable, almost sullen. I could see how heavily this protracted imprisonment was weighing on him. I could feel the anger building in him. Whenever he encountered the captain, his eyes would flicker with dark fire, and I was in constant dread that his natural vehemence would cause him to do something rash.

That day, March 14, he and Conseil managed to find me in my stateroom. I asked them the purpose of their visit.

"To put a simple question to you, sir," the Canadian answered me.

"Go on, Ned."

"How many men do you think are on board the Nautilus?"

"I'm unable to say, my friend."

"It seems to me," Ned Land went on, "that it wouldn't take much of a crew to run a ship like this one."

"Correct," I replied. "Under existing conditions some ten men at the most should be enough to operate it."

"All right," the Canadian said, "then why should there be any more than that?"

"Why?" I answered.

I stared at Ned Land, whose motives were easy to guess.

"Because," I said, "if I can trust my hunches, if I truly understand the captain's way of life, his Nautilus isn't simply a ship. It's meant to be a refuge for people like its commander, people who have severed all ties with the shore."

"Perhaps," Conseil said, "but in a nutshell, the Nautilus can hold only a certain number of men, so couldn't Master estimate their maximum?"

"How, Conseil?"

"By calculating it. Master is familiar with the ship's capacity, hence the amount of air it contains; on the other hand, Master knows how much air each man consumes in the act of breathing, and he can compare this data with the fact that the Nautilus must rise to the surface every twenty–four hours . . ."

Conseil didn't finish his sentence, but I could easily see what he was driving at.

"I follow you," I said. "But while they're simple to do, such calculations can give only a very uncertain figure."

"No problem," the Canadian went on insistently.

"Then here's how to calculate it," I replied. "In one hour each man consumes the oxygen contained in 100 liters of air, hence during twenty–four hours the oxygen contained in 2,400 liters. Therefore, we must look for the multiple of 2,400 liters of air that gives us the amount found in the Nautilus."

"Precisely," Conseil said.

"Now then," I went on, "the Nautilus's capacity is 1,500 metric tons, and that of a ton is 1,000 liters, so the Nautilus holds 1,500,000 liters of air, which, divided by 2,400 . . ."

I did a quick pencil calculation.

". . . gives us the quotient of 625. Which is tantamount to saying that the air contained in the Nautilus would be exactly enough for 625 men over twenty–four hours."

"625!" Ned repeated.

"But rest assured," I added, "that between passengers, seamen, or officers, we don't total one–tenth of that figure."

"Which is still too many for three men!" Conseil muttered.

"So, my poor Ned, I can only counsel patience."

"And," Conseil replied, "even more than patience, resignation."

Conseil had said the true word.

"Even so," he went on, "Captain Nemo can't go south forever! He'll surely have to stop, if only at the Ice Bank, and he'll return to the seas of civilization! Then it will be time to resume Ned Land's plans."

The Canadian shook his head, passed his hand over his brow, made no reply, and left us.

"With Master's permission, I'll make an observation to him," Conseil then told me. "Our poor Ned broods about all the things he can't have. He's haunted by his former life. He seems to miss everything that's denied us. He's obsessed by his old memories and it's breaking his heart. We must understand him. What does he have to occupy him here? Nothing. He isn't a scientist like Master, and he doesn't share our enthusiasm for the sea's wonders. He would risk anything just to enter a tavern in his own country!"

To be sure, the monotony of life on board must have seemed unbearable to the Canadian, who was accustomed to freedom and activity. It was a rare event that could excite him. That day, however, a development occurred that reminded him of his happy years as a harpooner.

Near eleven o'clock in the morning, while on the surface of the ocean, the Nautilus fell in with a herd of baleen whales. This encounter didn't surprise me, because I knew these animals were being hunted so relentlessly that they took refuge in the ocean basins of the high latitudes.

In the maritime world and in the realm of geographic exploration, whales have played a major role. This is the animal that first dragged the Basques in its wake, then Asturian Spaniards, Englishmen, and Dutchmen, emboldening them against the ocean's perils, and leading them to the ends of the earth. Baleen whales like to frequent the southernmost and northernmost seas. Old legends even claim that these cetaceans led fishermen to within a mere seven leagues of the North Pole.

Although this feat is fictitious, it will someday come true, because it's likely that by hunting whales in the Arctic or Antarctic regions, man will finally reach this unknown spot on the globe.

We were seated on the platform next to a tranquil sea. The month of March, since it's the equivalent of October in these latitudes, was giving us some fine autumn days. It was the Canadian—on this topic he was never mistaken—who sighted a baleen whale on the eastern horizon. If you looked carefully, you could see its blackish back alternately rise and fall above the waves, five miles from the Nautilus.

"Wow!" Ned Land exclaimed. "If I were on board a whaler, there's an encounter that would be great fun! That's one big animal! Look how high its blowholes are spouting all that air and steam! Damnation! Why am I chained to this hunk of sheet iron!"

"Why, Ned!" I replied. "You still aren't over your old fishing urges?"

"How could a whale fisherman forget his old trade, sir? Who could ever get tired of such exciting hunting?"

"You've never fished these seas, Ned?"

"Never, sir. Just the northernmost seas, equally in the Bering Strait and the Davis Strait."

"So the southern right whale is still unknown to you. Until now it's the bowhead whale you've hunted, and it won't risk going past the warm waters of the equator."

"Oh, professor, what are you feeding me?" the Canadian answered in a tolerably skeptical tone.

"I'm feeding you the facts."

"By thunder! In '65, just two and a half years ago, I to whom you speak, I myself stepped onto the carcass of a whale near Greenland, and its flank still carried the marked harpoon of a whaling ship from the Bering Sea. Now I ask you, after it had been wounded west of America, how could this animal be killed in the east, unless it had cleared the equator and doubled Cape Horn or the Cape of Good Hope?"

"I agree with our friend Ned," Conseil said, "and I'm waiting to hear how Master will reply to him."

"Master will reply, my friends, that baleen whales are localized, according to species, within certain seas that they never leave. And if one of these animals went from the Bering Strait to the Davis Strait, it's quite simply because there's some passageway from the one sea to the other, either along the coasts of Canada or Siberia."

"You expect us to fall for that?" the Canadian asked, tipping me a wink.

"If Master says so," Conseil replied.

"Which means," the Canadian went on, "since I've never fished these waterways, I don't know the whales that frequent them?"

"That's what I've been telling you, Ned."

"All the more reason to get to know them," Conseil answered.

"Look! Look!" the Canadian exclaimed, his voice full of excitement. "It's approaching! It's coming toward us! It's thumbing its nose at me! It knows I can't do a blessed thing to it!"

Ned stamped his foot. Brandishing an imaginary harpoon, his hands positively trembled.

"These cetaceans," he asked, "are they as big as the ones in the northernmost seas?"

"Pretty nearly, Ned."

"Because I've seen big baleen whales, sir, whales measuring up to 100 feet long! I've even heard that those rorqual whales off the Aleutian Islands sometimes get over 150 feet."

"That strikes me as exaggerated," I replied. "Those animals are only members of the genus Balaenoptera furnished with dorsal fins, and like sperm whales, they're generally smaller than the bowhead whale."

"Oh!" exclaimed the Canadian, whose eyes hadn't left the ocean. "It's getting closer, it's coming into the Nautilus's waters!"

Then, going on with his conversation:

"You talk about sperm whales," he said, "as if they were little beasts! But there are stories of gigantic sperm whales. They're shrewd cetaceans. I hear that some will cover themselves with algae and fucus plants. People mistake them for islets. They pitch camp on top, make themselves at home, light a fire—"

"Build houses," Conseil said.

"Yes, funny man," Ned Land replied. "Then one fine day the animal dives and drags all its occupants down into the depths."

"Like in the voyages of Sinbad the Sailor," I answered, laughing. "Oh, Mr. Land, you're addicted to tall tales! What sperm whales you're handing us! I hope you don't really believe in them!"

"Mr. Naturalist," the Canadian replied in all seriousness, "when it comes to whales, you can believe anything! (Look at that one move! Look at it stealing away!) People claim these animals can circle around the world in just fifteen days."

"I don't say nay."

"But what you undoubtedly don't know, Professor Aronnax, is that at the beginning of the world, whales traveled even quicker."

"Oh really, Ned! And why so?"

"Because in those days their tails moved side to side, like those on fish, in other words, their tails were straight up, thrashing the water from left to right, right to left. But spotting that they swam too fast, our Creator twisted their tails, and ever since they've been thrashing the waves up and down, at the expense of their speed."

"Fine, Ned," I said, then resurrected one of the Canadian's expressions. "You expect us to fall for that?"

"Not too terribly," Ned Land replied, "and no more than if I told you there are whales that are 300 feet long and weigh 1,000,000 pounds."

"That's indeed considerable," I said. "But you must admit that certain cetaceans do grow to significant size, since they're said to supply as much as 120 metric tons of oil."

"That I've seen," the Canadian said.

"I can easily believe it, Ned, just as I can believe that certain baleen whales equal 100 elephants in bulk. Imagine the impact of such a mass if it were launched at full speed!"

"Is it true," Conseil asked, "that they can sink ships?"

"Ships? I doubt it," I replied. "However, they say that in 1820, right in these southern seas, a baleen whale rushed at the Essex and pushed it backward at a speed of four meters per second. Its stern was flooded, and the Essex went down fast."

Ned looked at me with a bantering expression.

"Speaking for myself," he said, "I once got walloped by a whale's tail—in my longboat, needless to say. My companions and I were launched to an altitude of six meters. But next to the Professor's whale, mine was just a baby."

"Do these animals live a long time?" Conseil asked.

"A thousand years," the Canadian replied without hesitation.

"And how, Ned," I asked, "do you know that's so?"

"Because people say so."

"And why do people say so?"

"Because people know so."

"No, Ned! People don't know so, they suppose so, and here's the logic with which they back up their beliefs. When fishermen first hunted whales 400 years ago, these animals grew to bigger sizes than they do today. Reasonably enough, it's assumed that today's whales are smaller because they haven't had time to reach their full growth. That's why the Count de Buffon's encyclopedia says that cetaceans can live, and even must live, for a thousand years. You understand?"

Ned Land didn't understand. He no longer even heard me. That baleen whale kept coming closer. His eyes devoured it.

"Oh!" he exclaimed. "It's not just one whale, it's ten, twenty, a whole gam! And I can't do a thing! I'm tied hand and foot!"

"But Ned my friend," Conseil said, "why not ask Captain Nemo for permission to hunt—"

Before Conseil could finish his sentence, Ned Land scooted down the hatch and ran to look for the captain. A few moments later, the two of them reappeared on the platform.

Captain Nemo observed the herd of cetaceans cavorting on the waters a mile from the Nautilus.

"They're southern right whales," he said. "There goes the fortune of a whole whaling fleet."

"Well, sir," the Canadian asked, "couldn't I hunt them, just so I don't forget my old harpooning trade?"

"Hunt them? What for?" Captain Nemo replied. "Simply to destroy them? We have no use for whale oil on this ship."

"But, sir," the Canadian went on, "in the Red Sea you authorized us to chase a dugong!"

"There it was an issue of obtaining fresh meat for my crew. Here it would be killing for the sake of killing. I'm well aware that's a privilege reserved for mankind, but I don't allow such murderous pastimes. When your peers, Mr. Land, destroy decent, harmless creatures like the southern right whale or the bowhead whale, they commit a reprehensible offense. Thus they've already depopulated all of Baffin Bay, and they'll wipe out a whole class of useful animals. So leave these poor cetaceans alone. They have quite enough natural enemies, such as sperm whales, swordfish, and sawfish, without you meddling with them."

I'll let the reader decide what faces the Canadian made during this lecture on hunting ethics. Furnishing such arguments to a professional harpooner was a waste of words. Ned Land stared at Captain Nemo and obviously missed his meaning. But the captain was right. Thanks to the mindless, barbaric bloodthirstiness of fishermen, the last baleen whale will someday disappear from the ocean.

Ned Land whistled "Yankee Doodle" between his teeth, stuffed his hands in his pockets, and turned his back on us.

Meanwhile Captain Nemo studied the herd of cetaceans, then addressed me:

"I was right to claim that baleen whales have enough natural enemies without counting man. These specimens will soon have to deal with mighty opponents. Eight miles to leeward, Professor Aronnax, can you see those blackish specks moving about?"

"Yes, Captain," I replied.

"Those are sperm whales, dreadful animals that I've sometimes encountered in herds of 200 or 300! As for them, they're cruel, destructive beasts, and they deserve to be exterminated."

The Canadian turned swiftly at these last words.

"Well, Captain," I said, "on behalf of the baleen whales, there's still time—"

"It's pointless to run any risks, professor. The Nautilus will suffice to disperse these sperm whales. It's armed with a steel spur quite equal to Mr. Land's harpoon, I imagine."

The Canadian didn't even bother shrugging his shoulders. Attacking cetaceans with thrusts from a spur! Who ever heard of such malarkey!

"Wait and see, Professor Aronnax," Captain Nemo said. "We'll show you a style of hunting with which you aren't yet familiar. We'll take no pity on these ferocious cetaceans. They're merely mouth and teeth!"

Mouth and teeth! There's no better way to describe the long–skulled sperm whale, whose length sometimes exceeds twenty–five meters. The enormous head of this cetacean occupies about a third of its body. Better armed than a baleen whale, whose upper jaw is adorned solely with whalebone, the sperm whale is equipped with twenty–five huge teeth that are twenty centimeters high, have cylindrical, conical summits, and weigh two pounds each. In the top part of this enormous head, inside big cavities separated by cartilage, you'll find 300 to 400 kilograms of that valuable oil called "spermaceti." The sperm whale is an awkward animal, more tadpole than fish, as Professor Frédol has noted. It's poorly constructed, being "defective," so to speak, over the whole left side of its frame, with good eyesight only in its right eye.

Meanwhile that monstrous herd kept coming closer. It had seen the baleen whales and was preparing to attack. You could tell in advance that the sperm whales would be victorious, not only because they were better built for fighting than their harmless adversaries, but also because they could stay longer underwater before returning to breathe at the surface.

There was just time to run to the rescue of the baleen whales. The Nautilus proceeded to midwater. Conseil, Ned, and I sat in front of the lounge windows. Captain Nemo made his way to the helmsman's side to operate his submersible as an engine of destruction. Soon I felt the beats of our propeller getting faster, and we picked up speed.

The battle between sperm whales and baleen whales had already begun when the Nautilus arrived. It maneuvered to cut into the herd of long–skulled predators. At first the latter showed little concern at the sight of this new monster meddling in the battle. But they soon had to sidestep its thrusts.

What a struggle! Ned Land quickly grew enthusiastic and even ended up applauding. Brandished in its captain's hands, the Nautilus was simply a fearsome harpoon. He hurled it at those fleshy masses and ran them clean through, leaving behind two squirming animal halves. As for those daunting strokes of the tail hitting our sides, the ship never felt them. No more than the collisions it caused. One sperm whale exterminated, it ran at another, tacked on the spot so as not to miss its prey, went ahead or astern, obeyed its rudder, dived when the cetacean sank to deeper strata, rose with it when it returned to the surface, struck it head–on or slantwise, hacked at it or tore it, and from every direction and at any speed, skewered it with its dreadful spur.

What bloodshed! What a hubbub on the surface of the waves! What sharp hisses and snorts unique to these frightened animals! Their tails churned the normally peaceful strata into actual billows.

This Homeric slaughter dragged on for an hour, and the long–skulled predators couldn't get away. Several times ten or twelve of them teamed up, trying to crush the Nautilus with their sheer mass. Through the windows you could see their enormous mouths paved with teeth, their fearsome eyes. Losing all self–control, Ned Land hurled threats and insults at them. You could feel them clinging to the submersible like hounds atop a wild boar in the underbrush. But by forcing the pace of its propeller, the Nautilus carried them off, dragged them under, or brought them back to the upper level of the waters, untroubled by their enormous weight or their powerful grip.

Finally this mass of sperm whales thinned out. The waves grew tranquil again. I felt us rising to the surface of the ocean. The hatch opened and we rushed onto the platform.

The sea was covered with mutilated corpses. A fearsome explosion couldn't have slashed, torn, or shredded these fleshy masses with greater violence. We were floating in the midst of gigantic bodies, bluish on the back, whitish on the belly, and all deformed by enormous protuberances. A few frightened sperm whales were fleeing toward the horizon. The waves were dyed red over an area of several miles, and the Nautilus was floating in the middle of a sea of blood.

Captain Nemo rejoined us.

"Well, Mr. Land?" he said.

"Well, sir," replied the Canadian, whose enthusiasm had subsided, "it's a dreadful sight for sure. But I'm a hunter not a butcher, and this is plain butchery."

"It was a slaughter of destructive animals," the captain replied, "and the Nautilus is no butcher knife."

"I prefer my harpoon," the Canadian answered.

"To each his own," the captain replied, staring intently at Ned Land.

I was in dread the latter would give way to some violent outburst that might have had deplorable consequences. But his anger was diverted by the sight of a baleen whale that the Nautilus had pulled alongside of just then.

This animal had been unable to escape the teeth of those sperm whales. I recognized the southern right whale, its head squat, its body dark all over. Anatomically, it's distinguished from the white whale and the black right whale by the fusion of its seven cervical vertebrae, and it numbers two more ribs than its relatives. Floating on its side, its belly riddled with bites, the poor cetacean was dead. Still hanging from the tip of its mutilated fin was a little baby whale that it had been unable to rescue from the slaughter. Its open mouth let water flow through its whalebone like a murmuring surf.

Captain Nemo guided the Nautilus next to the animal's corpse. Two of his men climbed onto the whale's flank, and to my astonishment, I saw them draw from its udders all the milk they held, in other words, enough to fill two or three casks.

The captain offered me a cup of this still–warm milk. I couldn't help showing my distaste for such a beverage. He assured me that this milk was excellent, no different from cow's milk.

I sampled it and agreed. So this milk was a worthwhile reserve ration for us, because in the form of salt butter or cheese, it would provide a pleasant change of pace from our standard fare.

From that day on, I noted with some uneasiness that Ned Land's attitudes toward Captain Nemo grew worse and worse, and I decided to keep a close watch on the Canadian's movements and activities.

The Ice Bank

THE Nautilus resumed its unruffled southbound heading. It went along the 50th meridian with considerable speed. Would it go to the pole? I didn't think so, because every previous attempt to reach this spot on the globe had failed. Besides, the season was already quite advanced, since March 13 on Antarctic shores corresponds with September 13 in the northernmost regions, which marks the beginning of the equinoctial period.

On March 14 at latitude 55°, I spotted floating ice, plain pale bits of rubble twenty to twenty–five feet long, which formed reefs over which the sea burst into foam. The Nautilus stayed on the surface of the ocean. Having fished in the Arctic seas, Ned Land was already familiar with the sight of icebergs. Conseil and I were marveling at them for the first time.

In the sky toward the southern horizon, there stretched a dazzling white band. English whalers have given this the name "ice blink." No matter how heavy the clouds may be, they can't obscure this phenomenon. It announces the presence of a pack, or shoal, of ice.

Indeed, larger blocks of ice soon appeared, their brilliance varying at the whim of the mists. Some of these masses displayed green veins, as if scrawled with undulating lines of copper sulfate. Others looked like enormous amethysts, letting the light penetrate their insides. The latter reflected the sun's rays from the thousand facets of their crystals. The former, tinted with a bright limestone sheen, would have supplied enough building material to make a whole marble town.

The farther down south we went, the more these floating islands grew in numbers and prominence. Polar birds nested on them by the thousands. These were petrels, cape pigeons, or puffins, and their calls were deafening. Mistaking the Nautilus for the corpse of a whale, some of them alighted on it and prodded its resonant sheet iron with pecks of their beaks.

During this navigating in the midst of the ice, Captain Nemo often stayed on the platform. He observed these deserted waterways carefully. I saw his calm eyes sometimes perk up. In these polar seas forbidden to man, did he feel right at home, the lord of these unreachable regions? Perhaps. But he didn't say. He stood still, reviving only when his pilot's instincts took over. Then, steering his Nautilus with consummate dexterity, he skillfully dodged the masses of ice, some of which measured several miles in length, their heights varying from seventy to eighty meters. Often the horizon seemed completely closed off. Abreast of latitude 60°, every passageway had disappeared. Searching with care, Captain Nemo soon found a narrow opening into which he brazenly slipped, well aware, however, that it would close behind him.

Guided by his skillful hands, the Nautilus passed by all these different masses of ice, which are classified by size and shape with a precision that enraptured Conseil: "icebergs," or mountains; "ice fields," or smooth, limitless tracts; "drift ice," or floating floes; "packs," or broken tracts, called "patches" when they're circular and "streams" when they form long strips.

The temperature was fairly low. Exposed to the outside air, the thermometer marked –2° to –3° centigrade. But we were warmly dressed in furs, for which seals and aquatic bears had paid the price. Evenly heated by all its electric equipment, the Nautilus's interior defied the most intense cold. Moreover, to find a bearable temperature, the ship had only to sink just a few meters beneath the waves.

Two months earlier we would have enjoyed perpetual daylight in this latitude; but night already fell for three or four hours, and later it would cast six months of shadow over these circumpolar regions.

On March 15 we passed beyond the latitude of the South Shetland and South Orkney Islands. The captain told me that many tribes of seals used to inhabit these shores; but English and American whalers, in a frenzy of destruction, slaughtered all the adults, including pregnant females, and where life and activity once existed, those fishermen left behind only silence and death.

Going along the 55th meridian, the Nautilus cut the Antarctic Circle on March 16 near eight o'clock in the morning. Ice completely surrounded us and closed off the horizon. Nevertheless, Captain Nemo went from passageway to passageway, always proceeding south.

"But where's he going?" I asked.

"Straight ahead," Conseil replied. "Ultimately, when he can't go any farther, he'll stop."

"I wouldn't bet on it!" I replied.

And in all honesty, I confess that this venturesome excursion was far from displeasing to me. I can't express the intensity of my amazement at the beauties of these new regions. The ice struck superb poses. Here, its general effect suggested an oriental town with countless minarets and mosques. There, a city in ruins, flung to the ground by convulsions in the earth. These views were varied continuously by the sun's oblique rays, or were completely swallowed up by gray mists in the middle of blizzards. Then explosions, cave–ins, and great iceberg somersaults would occur all around us, altering the scenery like the changing landscape in a diorama.

If the Nautilus was submerged during these losses of balance, we heard the resulting noises spread under the waters with frightful intensity, and the collapse of these masses created daunting eddies down to the ocean's lower strata. The Nautilus then rolled and pitched like a ship left to the fury of the elements.

Often, no longer seeing any way out, I thought we were imprisoned for good, but Captain Nemo, guided by his instincts, discovered new passageways from the tiniest indications. He was never wrong when he observed slender threads of bluish water streaking through these ice fields. Accordingly, I was sure that he had already risked his Nautilus in the midst of the Antarctic seas.

However, during the day of March 16, these tracts of ice completely barred our path. It wasn't the Ice Bank as yet, just huge ice fields cemented together by the cold. This obstacle couldn't stop Captain Nemo, and he launched his ship against the ice fields with hideous violence. The Nautilus went into these brittle masses like a wedge, splitting them with dreadful cracklings. It was an old–fashioned battering ram propelled with infinite power. Hurled aloft, ice rubble fell back around us like hail. Through brute force alone, the submersible carved out a channel for itself. Carried away by its momentum, the ship sometimes mounted on top of these tracts of ice and crushed them with its weight, or at other times, when cooped up beneath the ice fields, it split them with simple pitching movements, creating wide punctures.

Violent squalls assaulted us during the daytime. Thanks to certain heavy mists, we couldn't see from one end of the platform to the other. The wind shifted abruptly to every point on the compass. The snow was piling up in such packed layers, it had to be chipped loose with blows from picks. Even in a temperature of merely –5° centigrade, every outside part of the Nautilus was covered with ice. A ship's rigging would have been unusable, because all its tackle would have jammed in the grooves of the pulleys. Only a craft without sails, driven by an electric motor that needed no coal, could face such high latitudes.

Under these conditions the barometer generally stayed quite low. It fell as far as 73.5 centimeters. Our compass indications no longer offered any guarantees. The deranged needles would mark contradictory directions as we approached the southern magnetic pole, which doesn't coincide with the South Pole proper. In fact, according to the astronomer Hansteen, this magnetic pole is located fairly close to latitude 70° and longitude 130°, or abiding by the observations of

Louis–Isidore Duperrey, in longitude 135° and latitude 70° 30'. Hence we had to transport compasses to different parts of the ship, take many readings, and strike an average. Often we could chart our course only by guesswork, a less than satisfactory method in the midst of these winding passageways whose landmarks change continuously.

At last on March 18, after twenty futile assaults, the Nautilus was decisively held in check. No longer was it an ice stream, patch, or field—it was an endless, immovable barrier formed by ice mountains fused to each other.

"The Ice Bank!" the Canadian told me.

For Ned Land, as well as for every navigator before us, I knew that this was the great insurmountable obstacle. When the sun appeared for an instant near noon, Captain Nemo took a reasonably accurate sight that gave our position as longitude 51° 30' and latitude 67° 39' south. This was a position already well along in these Antarctic regions.

As for the liquid surface of the sea, there was no longer any semblance of it before our eyes. Before the Nautilus's spur there lay vast broken plains, a tangle of confused chunks with all the helter–skelter unpredictability typical of a river's surface a short while before its ice breakup; but in this case the proportions were gigantic. Here and there stood sharp peaks, lean spires that rose as high as 200 feet; farther off, a succession of steeply cut cliffs sporting a grayish tint, huge mirrors that reflected the sparse rays of a sun half drowned in mist. Beyond, a stark silence reigned in this desolate natural setting, a silence barely broken by the flapping wings of petrels or puffins. By this point everything was frozen, even sound.

So the Nautilus had to halt in its venturesome course among these tracts of ice.

"Sir," Ned Land told me that day, "if your captain goes any farther . . ."

"Yes?"

"He'll be a superman."

"How so, Ned?"

"Because nobody can clear the Ice Bank. Your captain's a powerful man, but damnation, he isn't more powerful than nature. If she draws a boundary line, there you stop, like it or not!"

"Correct, Ned Land, but I still want to know what's behind this Ice Bank! Behold my greatest source of irritation—a wall!"

"Master is right," Conseil said. "Walls were invented simply to frustrate scientists. All walls should be banned."

"Fine!" the Canadian put in. "But we already know what's behind this Ice Bank."

"What?" I asked.

"Ice, ice, and more ice."

"You may be sure of that, Ned," I answered, "but I'm not. That's why I want to see for myself."

"Well, Professor," the Canadian replied, "you can just drop that idea! You've made it to the Ice Bank, which is already far enough, but you won't get any farther, neither your Captain Nemo or his Nautilus. And whether he wants to or not, we'll head north again, in other words, to the land of sensible people."

I had to agree that Ned Land was right, and until ships are built to navigate over tracts of ice, they'll have to stop at the Ice Bank.

Indeed, despite its efforts, despite the powerful methods it used to split this ice, the Nautilus was reduced to immobility. Ordinarily, when someone can't go any farther, he still has the option of returning in his tracks. But here it was just as impossible to turn back as to go forward, because every passageway had closed behind us, and if our submersible remained even slightly stationary, it would be frozen in without delay. Which is exactly what happened near two o'clock in the afternoon, and fresh ice kept forming over the ship's sides with astonishing speed. I had to admit that Captain Nemo's leadership had been most injudicious.

Just then I was on the platform. Observing the situation for some while, the captain said to me:

"Well, Professor! What think you?"

"I think we're trapped, Captain."

"Trapped! What do you mean?"

"I mean we can't go forward, backward, or sideways. I think that's the standard definition of 'trapped,' at least in the civilized world."

"So, Professor Aronnax, you think the Nautilus won't be able to float clear?"

"Only with the greatest difficulty, Captain, since the season is already too advanced for you to depend on an ice breakup."

"Oh, Professor," Captain Nemo replied in an ironic tone, "you never change! You see only impediments and obstacles! I promise you, not only will the Nautilus float clear, it will go farther still!"

"Farther south?" I asked, gaping at the captain.

"Yes, sir, it will go to the pole."

"To the pole!" I exclaimed, unable to keep back a movement of disbelief.

"Yes," the captain replied coolly, "the Antarctic pole, that unknown spot crossed by every meridian on the globe. As you know, I do whatever I like with my Nautilus."

Yes, I did know that! I knew this man was daring to the point of being foolhardy. But to overcome all the obstacles around the South Pole—even more unattainable than the North Pole, which still hadn't been reached by the boldest navigators—wasn't this an absolutely insane undertaking, one that could occur only in the brain of a madman?

It then dawned on me to ask Captain Nemo if he had already discovered this pole, which no human being had ever trod underfoot.

"No, sir," he answered me, "but we'll discover it together. Where others have failed, I'll succeed. Never before has my Nautilus cruised so far into these southernmost seas, but I repeat: it will go farther still."

"I'd like to believe you, Captain," I went on in a tone of some sarcasm. "Oh I do believe you! Let's forge ahead! There are no obstacles for us! Let's shatter this Ice Bank! Let's blow it up, and if it still resists, let's put wings on the Nautilus and fly over it!"

"Over it, Professor?" Captain Nemo replied serenely. "No, not over it, but under it."

"Under it!" I exclaimed.

A sudden insight into Captain Nemo's plans had just flashed through my mind. I understood. The marvelous talents of his Nautilus would be put to work once again in this superhuman undertaking!

"I can see we're starting to understand each other, Professor," Captain Nemo told me with a half smile. "You already glimpse the potential—myself, I'd say the success—of this attempt. Maneuvers that aren't feasible for an ordinary ship are easy for the Nautilus. If a continent emerges at the pole, we'll stop at that continent. But on the other hand, if open sea washes the pole, we'll go to that very place!"

"Right," I said, carried away by the captain's logic. "Even though the surface of the sea has solidified into ice, its lower strata are still open, thanks to that divine justice that puts the maximum density of salt water one degree above its freezing point. And if I'm not mistaken, the submerged part of this Ice Bank is in a four–to–one ratio to its emerging part."

"Very nearly, Professor. For each foot of iceberg above the sea, there are three more below. Now then, since these ice mountains don't exceed a height of 100 meters, they sink only to a depth of 300 meters. And what are 300 meters to the Nautilus?"

"A mere nothing, sir."

"We could even go to greater depths and find that temperature layer common to all ocean water, and there we'd brave with impunity the –30° or –40° cold on the surface."

"True, sir, very true," I replied with growing excitement.

"Our sole difficulty," Captain Nemo went on, "lies in our staying submerged for several days without renewing our air supply."

"That's all?" I answered. "The Nautilus has huge air tanks; we'll fill them up and they'll supply all the oxygen we need."

"Good thinking, Professor Aronnax," the captain replied with a smile. "But since I don't want to be accused of foolhardiness, I'm giving you all my objections in advance."

"You have more?"

"Just one. If a sea exists at the South Pole, it's possible this sea may be completely frozen over, so we couldn't come up to the surface!"

"My dear sir, have you forgotten that the Nautilus is armed with a fearsome spur? Couldn't it be launched diagonally against those tracts of ice, which would break open from the impact?"

"Ah, Professor, you're full of ideas today!"

"Besides, Captain," I added with still greater enthusiasm, "why wouldn't we find open sea at the South Pole just as at the North Pole? The cold–temperature poles and the geographical poles don't coincide in either the northern or southern hemispheres, and until proof to the contrary, we can assume these two spots on the earth feature either a continent or an ice–free ocean."

"I think as you do, Professor Aronnax," Captain Nemo replied. "I'll only point out that after raising so many objections against my plan, you're now crushing me under arguments in its favor."

Captain Nemo was right. I was outdoing him in daring! It was I who was sweeping him to the pole. I was leading the way, I was out in front . . . but no, you silly fool! Captain Nemo already knew the pros and cons of this question, and it amused him to see you flying off into impossible fantasies!

Nevertheless, he didn't waste an instant. At his signal, the chief officer appeared. The two men held a quick exchange in their incomprehensible language, and either the chief officer had been alerted previously or he found the plan feasible, because he showed no surprise.

But as unemotional as he was, he couldn't have been more impeccably emotionless than Conseil when I told the fine lad our intention of pushing on to the South Pole. He greeted my announcement with the usual "As Master wishes," and I had to be content with that. As for Ned Land, no human shoulders ever executed a higher shrug than the pair belonging to our Canadian.

"Honestly, sir," he told me. "You and your Captain Nemo, I pity you both!"

"But we will go to the pole, Mr. Land."

"Maybe, but you won't come back!"

And Ned Land reentered his cabin, "to keep from doing something desperate," he said as he left me.

Meanwhile preparations for this daring attempt were getting under way. The Nautilus's powerful pumps forced air down into the tanks and stored it under high pressure. Near four o'clock Captain Nemo informed me that the platform hatches were about to be closed. I took a last look at the dense Ice Bank we were going to conquer. The weather was fair, the skies reasonably clear, the cold quite brisk, namely –12° centigrade; but after the wind had lulled, this temperature didn't seem too unbearable.

Equipped with picks, some ten men climbed onto the Nautilus's sides and cracked loose the ice around the ship's lower plating, which was soon set free. This operation was swiftly executed because the fresh ice was still thin. We all reentered the interior. The main ballast tanks were filled with the water that hadn't yet congealed at our line of flotation. The Nautilus submerged without delay.

I took a seat in the lounge with Conseil. Through the open window we stared at the lower strata of this southernmost ocean. The thermometer rose again. The needle on the pressure gauge swerved over its dial.

About 300 meters down, just as Captain Nemo had predicted, we cruised beneath the undulating surface of the Ice Bank. But the Nautilus sank deeper still. It reached a depth of 800 meters. At the surface this water gave a temperature of –12° centigrade, but now it gave no more than –10°. Two degrees had already been gained. Thanks to its heating equipment, the Nautilus's temperature, needless to say, stayed at a much higher degree. Every maneuver was accomplished with extraordinary precision.

"With all due respect to Master," Conseil told me, "we'll pass it by."

"I fully expect to!" I replied in a tone of deep conviction.

Now in open water, the Nautilus took a direct course to the pole without veering from the 52nd meridian. From 67° 30' to 90°, twenty–two and a half° of latitude were left to cross, in other words, slightly more than 500 leagues. The Nautilus adopted an average speed of twenty–six miles per hour, the speed of an express train. If it kept up this pace, forty hours would do it for reaching the pole.

For part of the night, the novelty of our circumstances kept Conseil and me at the lounge window. The sea was lit by our beacon's electric rays. But the depths were deserted. Fish didn't linger in these imprisoned waters. Here they found merely a passageway for going from the Antarctic Ocean to open sea at the pole. Our progress was swift. You could feel it in the vibrations of the long steel hull.

Near two o'clock in the morning, I went to snatch a few hours of sleep. Conseil did likewise. I didn't encounter Captain Nemo while going down the gangways. I assumed that he was keeping to the pilothouse.

The next day, March 19, at five o'clock in the morning, I was back at my post in the lounge. The electric log indicated that the Nautilus had reduced speed. By then it was rising to the surface, but cautiously, while slowly emptying its ballast tanks.

My heart was pounding. Would we emerge into the open and find the polar air again?

No. A jolt told me that the Nautilus had bumped the underbelly of the Ice Bank, still quite thick to judge from the hollowness of the accompanying noise.

Indeed, we had "struck bottom," to use nautical terminology, but in the opposite direction and at a depth of 3,000 feet. That gave us 4,000 feet of ice overhead, of which 1,000 feet emerged above water. So the Ice Bank was higher here than we had found it on the outskirts. A circumstance less than encouraging.

Several times that day, the Nautilus repeated the same experiment and always it bumped against this surface that formed a ceiling above it. At certain moments the ship encountered ice at a depth of 900 meters, denoting a thickness of 1,200 meters, of which 300 meters rose above the level of the ocean. This height had tripled since the moment the Nautilus had dived beneath the waves.

I meticulously noted these different depths, obtaining the underwater profile of this upside–down mountain chain that stretched beneath the sea.

By evening there was still no improvement in our situation. The ice stayed between 400 and 500 meters deep. It was obviously shrinking, but what a barrier still lay between us and the surface of the ocean!

By then it was eight o'clock. The air inside the Nautilus should have been renewed four hours earlier, following daily practice on board. But I didn't suffer very much, although Captain Nemo hadn't yet made demands on the supplementary oxygen in his air tanks.

That night my sleep was fitful. Hope and fear besieged me by turns. I got up several times. The Nautilus continued groping. Near three o'clock in the morning, I observed that we encountered the Ice Bank's underbelly at a depth of only fifty meters. So only 150 feet separated us from the surface of the water. Little by little the Ice Bank was turning into an ice field again. The mountains were changing back into plains.

My eyes didn't leave the pressure gauge. We kept rising on a diagonal, going along this shiny surface that sparkled beneath our electric rays. Above and below, the Ice Bank was subsiding in long gradients. Mile after mile it was growing thinner.

Finally, at six o'clock in the morning on that memorable day of March 19, the lounge door opened. Captain Nemo appeared.

"Open sea!" he told me.

The South Pole

I RUSHED UP onto the platform. Yes, open sea! Barely a few sparse floes, some moving icebergs; a sea stretching into the distance; hosts of birds in the air and myriads of fish under the waters, which varied from intense blue to olive green depending on the depth. The thermometer marked 3° centigrade. It was as if a comparative springtime had been locked up behind that Ice Bank, whose distant masses were outlined on the northern horizon.

"Are we at the pole?" I asked the captain, my heart pounding.

"I've no idea," he answered me. "At noon we'll fix our position."

"But will the sun show through this mist?" I said, staring at the grayish sky.

"No matter how faintly it shines, it will be enough for me," the captain replied.

To the south, ten miles from the Nautilus, a solitary islet rose to a height of 200 meters. We proceeded toward it, but cautiously, because this sea could have been strewn with reefs.

In an hour we had reached the islet. Two hours later we had completed a full circle around it. It measured four to five miles in circumference. A narrow channel separated it from a considerable shore, perhaps a continent whose limits we couldn't see. The existence of this shore seemed to bear out Commander Maury's hypotheses. In essence, this ingenious American has noted that between the South Pole and the 60th parallel, the sea is covered with floating ice of dimensions much greater than any found in the north Atlantic. From this fact he drew the conclusion that the Antarctic Circle must contain considerable shores, since icebergs can't form on the high seas but only along coastlines. According to his calculations, this frozen mass enclosing the southernmost pole forms a vast ice cap whose width must reach 4,000 kilometers.

Meanwhile, to avoid running aground, the Nautilus halted three cable lengths from a strand crowned by superb piles of rocks. The skiff was launched to sea. Two crewmen carrying instruments, the captain, Conseil, and I were on board. It was ten o'clock in the morning. I hadn't seen Ned Land. No doubt, in the presence of the South Pole, the Canadian hated having to eat his words.

A few strokes of the oar brought the skiff to the sand, where it ran aground. Just as Conseil was about to jump ashore, I held him back.

"Sir," I told Captain Nemo, "to you belongs the honor of first setting foot on this shore."

"Yes, sir," the captain replied, "and if I have no hesitation in treading this polar soil, it's because no human being until now has left a footprint here."

So saying, he leaped lightly onto the sand. His heart must have been throbbing with intense excitement. He scaled an overhanging rock that ended in a small promontory and there, mute and motionless, with crossed arms and blazing eyes, he seemed to be laying claim to these southernmost regions. After spending five minutes in this trance, he turned to us.

"Whenever you're ready, sir," he called to me.

I got out, Conseil at my heels, leaving the two men in the skiff.

Over an extensive area, the soil consisted of that igneous gravel called "tuff," reddish in color as if made from crushed bricks. The ground was covered with slag, lava flows, and pumice stones. Its volcanic origin was unmistakable. In certain localities thin smoke holes gave off a sulfurous odor, showing that the inner fires still kept their wide-ranging power. Nevertheless, when I scaled a high escarpment, I could see no volcanoes within a radius of several miles. In these

Antarctic districts, as is well known, Sir James Clark Ross had found the craters of Mt. Erebus and Mt. Terror in fully active condition on the 167th meridian at latitude 77° 32'.

The vegetation on this desolate continent struck me as quite limited. A few lichens of the species Usnea melanoxanthra sprawled over the black rocks. The whole meager flora of this region consisted of certain microscopic buds, rudimentary diatoms made up of a type of cell positioned between two quartz–rich shells, plus long purple and crimson fucus plants, buoyed by small air bladders and washed up on the coast by the surf.

The beach was strewn with mollusks: small mussels, limpets, smooth heart–shaped cockles, and especially some sea butterflies with oblong, membrane–filled bodies whose heads are formed from two rounded lobes. I also saw myriads of those northernmost sea butterflies three centimeters long, which a baleen whale can swallow by the thousands in one gulp. The open waters at the shoreline were alive with these delightful pteropods, true butterflies of the sea.

Among other zoophytes present in these shallows, there were a few coral tree forms that, according to Sir James Clark Ross, live in these Antarctic seas at depths as great as 1,000 meters; then small alcyon coral belonging to the species Procellaria pelagica, also a large number of starfish unique to these climes, plus some feather stars spangling the sand.

But it was in the air that life was superabundant. There various species of birds flew and fluttered by the thousands, deafening us with their calls. Crowding the rocks, other fowl watched without fear as we passed and pressed familiarly against our feet. These were auks, as agile and supple in water, where they are sometimes mistaken for fast bonito, as they are clumsy and heavy on land. They uttered outlandish calls and participated in numerous public assemblies that featured much noise but little action.

Among other fowl I noted some sheathbills from the wading–bird family, the size of pigeons, white in color, the beak short and conical, the eyes framed by red circles. Conseil laid in a supply of them, because when they're properly cooked, these winged creatures make a pleasant dish. In the air there passed sooty albatross with four–meter wingspans, birds aptly dubbed "vultures of the ocean," also gigantic petrels including several with arching wings, enthusiastic eaters of seal that are known as quebrantahuesos, and cape pigeons, a sort of small duck, the tops of their bodies black and white—in short, a whole series of petrels, some whitish with wings trimmed in brown, others blue and exclusive to these Antarctic seas, the former "so oily," I told Conseil, "that inhabitants of the Faroe Islands simply fit the bird with a wick, then light it up."

"With that minor addition," Conseil replied, "these fowl would make perfect lamps! After this, we should insist that nature equip them with wicks in advance!"

Half a mile farther on, the ground was completely riddled with penguin nests, egg–laying burrows from which numerous birds emerged. Later Captain Nemo had hundreds of them hunted because their black flesh is highly edible. They brayed like donkeys. The size of a goose with slate–colored bodies, white undersides, and lemon–colored neck bands, these animals let themselves be stoned to death without making any effort to get away.

Meanwhile the mists didn't clear, and by eleven o'clock the sun still hadn't made an appearance. Its absence disturbed me. Without it, no sights were possible. Then how could we tell whether we had reached the pole?

When I rejoined Captain Nemo, I found him leaning silently against a piece of rock and staring at the sky. He seemed impatient, baffled. But what could we do? This daring and powerful man couldn't control the sun as he did the sea.

Noon arrived without the orb of day appearing for a single instant. You couldn't even find its hiding place behind the curtain of mist. And soon this mist began to condense into snow.

"Until tomorrow," the captain said simply; and we went back to the Nautilus, amid flurries in the air.

During our absence the nets had been spread, and I observed with fascination the fish just hauled on board. The Antarctic seas serve as a refuge for an extremely large number of migratory fish that flee from storms in the subpolar zones, in truth only to slide down the gullets of porpoises and seals. I noted some one–decimeter southern bullhead, a species of whitish cartilaginous fish overrun with bluish gray stripes and armed with stings, then some Antarctic rabbitfish three feet long, the body very slender, the skin a smooth silver white, the head rounded, the topside furnished with three fins, the snout ending in a trunk that curved back toward the mouth. I sampled its flesh but found it tasteless, despite Conseil's views, which were largely approving.

The blizzard lasted until the next day. It was impossible to stay on the platform. From the lounge, where I was writing up the incidents of this excursion to the polar continent, I could hear the calls of petrel and albatross cavorting in the midst of the turmoil. The Nautilus didn't stay idle, and cruising along the coast, it advanced some ten miles farther south amid the half light left by the sun as it skimmed the edge of the horizon.

The next day, March 20, it stopped snowing. The cold was a little more brisk. The thermometer marked –2° centigrade. The mist had cleared, and on that day I hoped our noon sights could be accomplished.

Since Captain Nemo hadn't yet appeared, only Conseil and I were taken ashore by the skiff. The soil's nature was still the same: volcanic. Traces of lava, slag, and basaltic rock were everywhere, but I couldn't find the crater that had vomited them up. There as yonder, myriads of birds enlivened this part of the polar continent. But they had to share their dominion with huge herds of marine mammals that looked at us with gentle eyes. These were seals of various species, some stretched out on the ground, others lying on drifting ice floes, several leaving or reentering the sea. Having never dealt with man, they didn't run off at our approach, and I counted enough of them thereabouts to provision a couple hundred ships.

"Ye gods," Conseil said, "it's fortunate that Ned Land didn't come with us!"

"Why so, Conseil?"

"Because that madcap hunter would kill every animal here."

"Every animal may be overstating it, but in truth I doubt we could keep our Canadian friend from harpooning some of these magnificent cetaceans. Which would be an affront to Captain Nemo, since he hates to slay harmless beasts needlessly."

"He's right."

"Certainly, Conseil. But tell me, haven't you finished classifying these superb specimens of marine fauna?"

"Master is well aware," Conseil replied, "that I'm not seasoned in practical application. When master has told me these animals' names . . ."

"They're seals and walruses."

"Two genera," our scholarly Conseil hastened to say, "that belong to the family Pinnipedia, order Carnivora, group Unguiculata, subclass Monodelphia, class Mammalia, branch Vertebrata."

"Very nice, Conseil," I replied, "but these two genera of seals and walruses are each divided into species, and if I'm not mistaken, we now have a chance to actually look at them. Let's."

It was eight o'clock in the morning. We had four hours to ourselves before the sun could be productively observed. I guided our steps toward a huge bay that made a crescent–shaped incision in the granite cliffs along the beach.

There, all about us, I swear that the shores and ice floes were crowded with marine mammals as far as the eye could see, and I involuntarily looked around for old Proteus, that mythological shepherd who guarded King Neptune's immense flocks. To be specific, these were seals. They formed distinct male–and–female groups, the father watching over his family, the mother suckling her little ones, the stronger youngsters emancipated a few paces away. When these mammals wanted to relocate, they moved in little jumps made by contracting their bodies, clumsily helped by their imperfectly developed flippers, which, as with their manatee relatives, form actual forearms. In the water, their ideal element, I must say these animals swim wonderfully thanks to their flexible backbones, narrow pelvises, close–cropped hair, and webbed feet. Resting on shore, they assumed extremely graceful positions. Consequently, their gentle features, their sensitive expressions equal to those of the loveliest women, their soft, limpid eyes, their

charming poses, led the ancients to glorify them by metamorphosing the males
into sea gods and the females into mermaids.

I drew Conseil's attention to the considerable growth of the cerebral lobes
found in these intelligent cetaceans. No mammal except man has more abundant
cerebral matter. Accordingly, seals are quite capable of being educated; they make
good pets, and together with certain other naturalists, I think these animals can
be properly trained to perform yeoman service as hunting dogs for fishermen.

Most of these seals were sleeping on the rocks or the sand. Among those
properly termed seals—which have no external ears, unlike sea lions whose ears
protrude—I observed several varieties of the species stenorhynchus, three meters
long, with white hair, bulldog heads, and armed with ten teeth in each jaw: four
incisors in both the upper and lower, plus two big canines shaped like the
fleur-de-lis. Among them slithered some sea elephants, a type of seal with a short,
flexible trunk; these are the giants of the species, with a circumference of twenty
feet and a length of ten meters. They didn't move as we approached.

"Are these animals dangerous?" Conseil asked me.

"Only if they're attacked," I replied. "But when these giant seals defend their
little ones, their fury is dreadful, and it isn't rare for them to smash a fisherman's
longboat to bits."

"They're within their rights," Conseil answered.

"I don't say nay."

Two miles farther on, we were stopped by a promontory that screened the bay
from southerly winds. It dropped straight down to the sea, and surf foamed against
it. From beyond this ridge there came fearsome bellows, such as a herd of cattle
might produce.

"Gracious," Conseil put in, "a choir of bulls?"

"No," I said, "a choir of walruses."

"Are they fighting with each other?"

"Either fighting or playing."

"With all due respect to Master, this we must see."

"Then see it we must, Conseil."

And there we were, climbing these blackish rocks amid sudden landslides and
over stones slippery with ice. More than once I took a tumble at the expense of
my backside. Conseil, more cautious or more stable, barely faltered and would
help me up, saying:

"If Master's legs would kindly adopt a wider stance, Master will keep his
balance."

Arriving at the topmost ridge of this promontory, I could see vast white plains
covered with walruses. These animals were playing among themselves. They were
howling not in anger but in glee.

Walruses resemble seals in the shape of their bodies and the arrangement of their limbs. But their lower jaws lack canines and incisors, and as for their upper canines, they consist of two tusks eighty centimeters long with a circumference of thirty–three centimeters at the socket. Made of solid ivory, without striations, harder than elephant tusks, and less prone to yellowing, these teeth are in great demand. Accordingly, walruses are the victims of a mindless hunting that soon will destroy them all, since their hunters indiscriminately slaughter pregnant females and youngsters, and over 4,000 individuals are destroyed annually.

Passing near these unusual animals, I could examine them at my leisure since they didn't stir. Their hides were rough and heavy, a tan color leaning toward a reddish brown; their coats were short and less than abundant. Some were four meters long. More tranquil and less fearful than their northern relatives, they posted no sentinels on guard duty at the approaches to their campsite.

After examining this community of walruses, I decided to return in my tracks. It was eleven o'clock, and if Captain Nemo found conditions favorable for taking his sights, I wanted to be present at the operation. But I held no hopes that the sun would make an appearance that day. It was hidden from our eyes by clouds squeezed together on the horizon. Apparently the jealous orb didn't want to reveal this inaccessible spot on the globe to any human being.

Yet I decided to return to the Nautilus. We went along a steep, narrow path that ran over the cliff's summit. By 11:30 we had arrived at our landing place. The beached skiff had brought the captain ashore. I spotted him standing on a chunk of basalt. His instruments were beside him. His eyes were focused on the northern horizon, along which the sun was sweeping in its extended arc.

I found a place near him and waited without speaking. Noon arrived, and just as on the day before, the sun didn't put in an appearance.

It was sheer bad luck. Our noon sights were still lacking. If we couldn't obtain them tomorrow, we would finally have to give up any hope of fixing our position.

In essence, it was precisely March 20. Tomorrow, the 21st, was the day of the equinox; the sun would disappear below the horizon for six months not counting refraction, and after its disappearance the long polar night would begin. Following the September equinox, the sun had emerged above the northerly horizon, rising in long spirals until December 21. At that time, the summer solstice of these southernmost districts, the sun had started back down, and tomorrow it would cast its last rays.

I shared my thoughts and fears with Captain Nemo.

"You're right, Professor Aronnax," he told me. "If I can't take the sun's altitude tomorrow, I won't be able to try again for another six months. But precisely because sailors' luck has led me into these seas on March 21, it will be easy to get our bearings if the noonday sun does appear before our eyes."

"Why easy, Captain?"

"Because when the orb of day sweeps in such long spirals, it's difficult to measure its exact altitude above the horizon, and our instruments are open to committing serious errors."

"Then what can you do?"

"I use only my chronometer," Captain Nemo answered me. "At noon tomorrow, March 21, if, after accounting for refraction, the sun's disk is cut exactly in half by the northern horizon, that will mean I'm at the South Pole."

"Right," I said. "Nevertheless, it isn't mathematically exact proof, because the equinox needn't fall precisely at noon."

"No doubt, sir, but the error will be under 100 meters, and that's close enough for us. Until tomorrow then."

Captain Nemo went back on board. Conseil and I stayed behind until five o'clock, surveying the beach, observing and studying. The only unusual object I picked up was an auk's egg of remarkable size, for which a collector would have paid more than F1,000. Its cream–colored tint, plus the streaks and markings that decorated it like so many hieroglyphics, made it a rare trinket. I placed it in Conseil's hands, and holding it like precious porcelain from China, that cautious, sure–footed lad got it back to the Nautilus in one piece.

There I put this rare egg inside one of the glass cases in the museum. I ate supper, feasting with appetite on an excellent piece of seal liver whose flavor reminded me of pork. Then I went to bed; but not without praying, like a good Hindu, for the favors of the radiant orb.

The next day, March 21, bright and early at five o'clock in the morning, I climbed onto the platform. I found Captain Nemo there.

"The weather is clearing a bit," he told me. "I have high hopes. After breakfast we'll make our way ashore and choose an observation post."

This issue settled, I went to find Ned Land. I wanted to take him with me. The obstinate Canadian refused, and I could clearly see that his tight–lipped mood and his bad temper were growing by the day. Under the circumstances I ultimately wasn't sorry that he refused. In truth, there were too many seals ashore, and it would never do to expose this impulsive fisherman to such temptations.

Breakfast over, I made my way ashore. The Nautilus had gone a few more miles during the night. It lay well out, a good league from the coast, which was crowned by a sharp peak 400 to 500 meters high. In addition to me, the skiff carried Captain Nemo, two crewmen, and the instruments—in other words, a chronometer, a spyglass, and a barometer.

During our crossing I saw numerous baleen whales belonging to the three species unique to these southernmost seas: the bowhead whale (or "right whale," according to the English), which has no dorsal fin; the humpback whale from the genus Balaenoptera (in other words, "winged whales"), beasts with wrinkled bellies and huge whitish fins that, genus name regardless, do not yet form wings;

and the finback whale, yellowish brown, the swiftest of all cetaceans. This powerful animal is audible from far away when it sends up towering spouts of air and steam that resemble swirls of smoke. Herds of these different mammals were playing about in the tranquil waters, and I could easily see that this Antarctic polar basin now served as a refuge for those cetaceans too relentlessly pursued by hunters.

I also noted long, whitish strings of salps, a type of mollusk found in clusters, and some jellyfish of large size that swayed in the eddies of the billows.

By nine o'clock we had pulled up to shore. The sky was growing brighter. Clouds were fleeing to the south. Mists were rising from the cold surface of the water. Captain Nemo headed toward the peak, which he no doubt planned to make his observatory. It was an arduous climb over sharp lava and pumice stones in the midst of air often reeking with sulfurous fumes from the smoke holes. For a man out of practice at treading land, the captain scaled the steepest slopes with a supple agility I couldn't equal, and which would have been envied by hunters of Pyrenees mountain goats.

It took us two hours to reach the summit of this half–crystal, half–basalt peak. From there our eyes scanned a vast sea, which scrawled its boundary line firmly against the background of the northern sky. At our feet: dazzling tracts of white. Over our heads: a pale azure, clear of mists. North of us: the sun's disk, like a ball of fire already cut into by the edge of the horizon. From the heart of the waters: jets of liquid rising like hundreds of magnificent bouquets. Far off, like a sleeping cetacean: the Nautilus. Behind us to the south and east: an immense shore, a chaotic heap of rocks and ice whose limits we couldn't see.

Arriving at the summit of this peak, Captain Nemo carefully determined its elevation by means of his barometer, since he had to take this factor into account in his noon sights.

At 11:45 the sun, by then seen only by refraction, looked like a golden disk, dispersing its last rays over this deserted continent and down to these seas not yet plowed by the ships of man.

Captain Nemo had brought a spyglass with a reticular eyepiece, which corrected the sun's refraction by means of a mirror, and he used it to observe the orb sinking little by little along a very extended diagonal that reached below the horizon. I held the chronometer. My heart was pounding mightily. If the lower half of the sun's disk disappeared just as the chronometer said noon, we were right at the pole.

"Noon!" I called.

"The South Pole!" Captain Nemo replied in a solemn voice, handing me the spyglass, which showed the orb of day cut into two exactly equal parts by the horizon.

I stared at the last rays wreathing this peak, while shadows were gradually climbing its gradients.

Just then, resting his hand on my shoulder, Captain Nemo said to me:

"In 1600, sir, the Dutchman Gheritk was swept by storms and currents, reaching latitude 64° south and discovering the South Shetland Islands. On January 17, 1773, the famous Captain Cook went along the 38th meridian, arriving at latitude 67° 30'; and on January 30, 1774, along the 109th meridian, he reached latitude 71° 15'. In 1819 the Russian Bellinghausen lay on the 69th parallel, and in 1821 on the 66th at longitude 111° west. In 1820 the Englishman Bransfield stopped at 65°. That same year the American Morrel, whose reports are dubious, went along the 42nd meridian, finding open sea at latitude 70° 14'. In 1825 the Englishman Powell was unable to get beyond 62°. That same year a humble seal fisherman, the Englishman Weddell, went as far as latitude 72° 14' on the 35th meridian, and as far as 74° 15' on the 36th. In 1829 the Englishman Forster, commander of the Chanticleer, laid claim to the Antarctic continent in latitude 63° 26' and longitude 66° 26'. On February 1, 1831, the Englishman Biscoe discovered Enderby Land at latitude 68° 50', Adelaide Land at latitude 67° on February 5, 1832, and Graham Land at latitude 64° 45' on February 21. In 1838 the Frenchman Dumont d'Urville stopped at the Ice Bank in latitude 62° 57', sighting the Louis–Philippe Peninsula; on January 21 two years later, at a new southerly position of 66° 30', he named the Adélie Coast and eight days later, the Clarie Coast at 64° 40'. In 1838 the American Wilkes advanced as far as the 69th parallel on the 100th meridian. In 1839 the Englishman Balleny discovered the Sabrina Coast at the edge of the polar circle. Lastly, on January 12, 1842, with his ships, the Erebus and the Terror, the Englishman Sir James Clark Ross found Victoria Land in latitude 70° 56' and longitude 171° 7' east; on the 23rd of that same month, he reached the 74th parallel, a position denoting the Farthest South attained until then; on the 27th he lay at 76° 8'; on the 28th at 77° 32'; on February 2 at 78° 4'; and late in 1842 he returned to 71° but couldn't get beyond it. Well now! In 1868, on this 21st day of March, I myself, Captain Nemo, have reached the South Pole at 90°, and I hereby claim this entire part of the globe, equal to one–sixth of the known continents."

"In the name of which sovereign, Captain?"

"In my own name, sir!"

So saying, Captain Nemo unfurled a black flag bearing a gold "N" on its quartered bunting. Then, turning toward the orb of day, whose last rays were licking at the sea's horizon:

"Farewell, O sun!" he called. "Disappear, O radiant orb! Retire beneath this open sea, and let six months of night spread their shadows over my new domains!"

Accident or Incident?

THE NEXT DAY, March 22, at six o'clock in the morning, preparations for departure began. The last gleams of twilight were melting into night. The cold was brisk. The constellations were glittering with startling intensity. The wonderful Southern Cross, polar star of the Antarctic regions, twinkled at its zenith.

The thermometer marked −12° centigrade, and a fresh breeze left a sharp nip in the air. Ice floes were increasing over the open water. The sea was starting to congeal everywhere. Numerous blackish patches were spreading over its surface, announcing the imminent formation of fresh ice. Obviously this southernmost basin froze over during its six–month winter and became utterly inaccessible. What happened to the whales during this period? No doubt they went beneath the Ice Bank to find more feasible seas. As for seals and walruses, they were accustomed to living in the harshest climates and stayed on in these icy waterways. These animals know by instinct how to gouge holes in the ice fields and keep them continually open; they go to these holes to breathe. Once the birds have migrated northward to escape the cold, these marine mammals remain as sole lords of the polar continent.

Meanwhile the ballast tanks filled with water and the Nautilus sank slowly. At a depth of 1,000 feet, it stopped. Its propeller churned the waves and it headed due north at a speed of fifteen miles per hour. Near the afternoon it was already cruising under the immense frozen carapace of the Ice Bank.

As a precaution, the panels in the lounge stayed closed, because the Nautilus's hull could run afoul of some submerged block of ice. So I spent the day putting my notes into final form. My mind was completely wrapped up in my memories of the pole. We had reached that inaccessible spot without facing exhaustion or danger, as if our seagoing passenger carriage had glided there on railroad tracks. And now we had actually started our return journey. Did it still have comparable surprises in store for me? I felt sure it did, so inexhaustible is this series of underwater wonders! As it was, in the five and a half months since fate had brought us on board, we had cleared 14,000 leagues, and over this track longer than the earth's equator, so many fascinating or frightening incidents had beguiled our voyage: that hunting trip in the Crespo forests, our running aground in the Torres Strait, the coral cemetery, the pearl fisheries of Ceylon, the Arabic tunnel, the fires of Santorini, those millions in the Bay of Vigo, Atlantis, the South Pole! During the night all these memories crossed over from one dream to the next, not giving my brain a moment's rest.

At three o'clock in the morning, I was awakened by a violent collision. I sat up in bed, listening in the darkness, and then was suddenly hurled into the middle of my stateroom. Apparently the Nautilus had gone aground, then heeled over sharply.

Leaning against the walls, I dragged myself down the gangways to the lounge, whose ceiling lights were on. The furniture had been knocked over. Fortunately the glass cases were solidly secured at the base and had stood fast. Since we were no longer vertical, the starboard pictures were glued to the tapestries, while those to port had their lower edges hanging a foot away from the wall. So the Nautilus was lying on its starboard side, completely stationary to boot.

In its interior I heard the sound of footsteps and muffled voices. But Captain Nemo didn't appear. Just as I was about to leave the lounge, Ned Land and Conseil entered.

"What happened?" I instantly said to them.

"I came to ask Master that," Conseil replied.

"Damnation!" the Canadian exclaimed. "I know full well what happened! The Nautilus has gone aground, and judging from the way it's listing, I don't think it'll pull through like that first time in the Torres Strait."

"But," I asked, "are we at least back on the surface of the sea?"

"We have no idea," Conseil replied.

"It's easy to find out," I answered.

I consulted the pressure gauge. Much to my surprise, it indicated a depth of 360 meters.

"What's the meaning of this?" I exclaimed.

"We must confer with Captain Nemo," Conseil said.

"But where do we find him?" Ned Land asked.

"Follow me," I told my two companions.

We left the lounge. Nobody in the library. Nobody by the central companionway or the crew's quarters. I assumed that Captain Nemo was stationed in the pilothouse. Best to wait. The three of us returned to the lounge.

I'll skip over the Canadian's complaints. He had good grounds for an outburst. I didn't answer him back, letting him blow off all the steam he wanted.

We had been left to ourselves for twenty minutes, trying to detect the tiniest noises inside the Nautilus, when Captain Nemo entered. He didn't seem to see us. His facial features, usually so emotionless, revealed a certain uneasiness. He studied the compass and pressure gauge in silence, then went and put his finger on the world map at a spot in the sector depicting the southernmost seas.

I hesitated to interrupt him. But some moments later, when he turned to me, I threw back at him a phrase he had used in the Torres Strait:

"An incident, Captain?"

"No, sir," he replied, "this time an accident."

"Serious?"

"Perhaps."

"Is there any immediate danger?"

"No."

"The Nautilus has run aground?"

"Yes."

"And this accident came about . . . ?"

"Through nature's unpredictability not man's incapacity. No errors were committed in our maneuvers. Nevertheless, we can't prevent a loss of balance from taking its toll. One may defy human laws, but no one can withstand the laws of nature."

Captain Nemo had picked an odd time to philosophize. All in all, this reply told me nothing.

"May I learn, sir," I asked him, "what caused this accident?"

"An enormous block of ice, an entire mountain, has toppled over," he answered me. "When an iceberg is eroded at the base by warmer waters or by repeated collisions, its center of gravity rises. Then it somersaults, it turns completely upside down. That's what happened here. When it overturned, one of these blocks hit the Nautilus as it was cruising under the waters. Sliding under our hull, this block then raised us with irresistible power, lifting us into less congested strata where we now lie on our side."

"But can't we float the Nautilus clear by emptying its ballast tanks, to regain our balance?"

"That, sir, is being done right now. You can hear the pumps working. Look at the needle on the pressure gauge. It indicates that the Nautilus is rising, but this block of ice is rising with us, and until some obstacle halts its upward movement, our position won't change."

Indeed, the Nautilus kept the same heel to starboard. No doubt it would straighten up once the block came to a halt. But before that happened, who knew if we might not hit the underbelly of the Ice Bank and be hideously squeezed between two frozen surfaces?

I mused on all the consequences of this situation. Captain Nemo didn't stop studying the pressure gauge. Since the toppling of this iceberg, the Nautilus had risen about 150 feet, but it still stayed at the same angle to the perpendicular.

Suddenly a slight movement could be felt over the hull. Obviously the Nautilus was straightening a bit. Objects hanging in the lounge were visibly returning to their normal positions. The walls were approaching the vertical. Nobody said a word. Hearts pounding, we could see and feel the ship righting itself. The floor was becoming horizontal beneath our feet. Ten minutes went by.

"Finally, we're upright!" I exclaimed.

"Yes," Captain Nemo said, heading to the lounge door.

"But will we float off?" I asked him.

"Certainly," he replied, "since the ballast tanks aren't yet empty, and when they are, the Nautilus must rise to the surface of the sea."

The captain went out, and soon I saw that at his orders, the Nautilus had halted its upward movement. In fact, it soon would have hit the underbelly of the Ice Bank, but it had stopped in time and was floating in midwater.

"That was a close call!" Conseil then said.

"Yes. We could have been crushed between these masses of ice, or at least imprisoned between them. And then, with no way to renew our air supply. . . . Yes, that was a close call!"

"If it's over with!" Ned Land muttered.

I was unwilling to get into a pointless argument with the Canadian and didn't reply. Moreover, the panels opened just then, and the outside light burst through the uncovered windows.

We were fully afloat, as I have said; but on both sides of the Nautilus, about ten meters away, there rose dazzling walls of ice. There also were walls above and below. Above, because the Ice Bank's underbelly spread over us like an immense ceiling. Below, because the somersaulting block, shifting little by little, had found points of purchase on both side walls and had gotten jammed between them. The Nautilus was imprisoned in a genuine tunnel of ice about twenty meters wide and filled with quiet water. So the ship could easily exit by going either ahead or astern, sinking a few hundred meters deeper, and then taking an open passageway beneath the Ice Bank.

The ceiling lights were off, yet the lounge was still brightly lit. This was due to the reflecting power of the walls of ice, which threw the beams of our beacon right back at us. Words cannot describe the effects produced by our galvanic rays on these huge, whimsically sculpted blocks, whose every angle, ridge, and facet gave off a different glow depending on the nature of the veins running inside the ice. It was a dazzling mine of gems, in particular sapphires and emeralds, whose jets of blue and green crisscrossed. Here and there, opaline hues of infinite subtlety raced among sparks of light that were like so many fiery diamonds, their brilliance more than any eye could stand. The power of our beacon was increased a hundredfold, like a lamp shining through the biconvex lenses of a world–class lighthouse.

"How beautiful!" Conseil exclaimed.

"Yes," I said, "it's a wonderful sight! Isn't it, Ned?"

"Oh damnation, yes!" Ned Land shot back. "It's superb! I'm furious that I have to admit it. Nobody has ever seen the like. But this sight could cost us dearly. And in all honesty, I think we're looking at things God never intended for human eyes."

Ned was right. It was too beautiful. All at once a yell from Conseil made me turn around.

"What is it?" I asked.

"Master must close his eyes! Master mustn't look!"

With that, Conseil clapped his hands over his eyes.

"But what's wrong, my boy?"

"I've been dazzled, struck blind!"

Involuntarily my eyes flew to the window, but I couldn't stand the fire devouring it.

I realized what had happened. The Nautilus had just started off at great speed. All the tranquil glimmers of the ice walls had then changed into blazing streaks. The sparkles from these myriads of diamonds were merging with each other. Swept along by its propeller, the Nautilus was traveling through a sheath of flashing light.

Then the panels in the lounge closed. We kept our hands over our eyes, which were utterly saturated with those concentric gleams that swirl before the retina when sunlight strikes it too intensely. It took some time to calm our troubled vision.

Finally we lowered our hands.

"Ye gods, I never would have believed it," Conseil said.

"And I still don't believe it!" the Canadian shot back.

"When we return to shore, jaded from all these natural wonders," Conseil added, "think how we'll look down on those pitiful land masses, those puny works of man! No, the civilized world won't be good enough for us!"

Such words from the lips of this emotionless Flemish boy showed that our enthusiasm was near the boiling point. But the Canadian didn't fail to throw his dram of cold water over us.

"The civilized world!" he said, shaking his head. "Don't worry, Conseil my friend, we're never going back to that world!"

By this point it was five o'clock in the morning. Just then there was a collision in the Nautilus's bow. I realized that its spur had just bumped a block of ice. It must have been a faulty maneuver because this underwater tunnel was obstructed by such blocks and didn't make for easy navigating. So I had assumed that Captain Nemo, in adjusting his course, would go around each obstacle or would hug the walls and follow the windings of the tunnel. In either case our forward motion wouldn't receive an absolute check. Nevertheless, contrary to my expectations, the Nautilus definitely began to move backward.

"We're going astern?" Conseil said.

"Yes," I replied. "Apparently the tunnel has no way out at this end."

"And so . . . ?"

"So," I said, "our maneuvers are quite simple. We'll return in our tracks and go out the southern opening. That's all."

As I spoke, I tried to sound more confident than I really felt. Meanwhile the Nautilus accelerated its backward movement, and running with propeller in reverse, it swept us along at great speed.

"This'll mean a delay," Ned said.

"What are a few hours more or less, so long as we get out."

"Yes," Ned Land repeated, "so long as we get out!"

I strolled for a little while from the lounge into the library. My companions kept their seats and didn't move. Soon I threw myself down on a couch and picked up a book, which my eyes skimmed mechanically.

A quarter of an hour later, Conseil approached me, saying:

"Is it deeply fascinating, this volume Master is reading?"

"Tremendously fascinating," I replied.

"I believe it. Master is reading his own book!"

"My own book?"

Indeed, my hands were holding my own work on the great ocean depths. I hadn't even suspected. I closed the book and resumed my strolling. Ned and Conseil stood up to leave.

"Stay here, my friends," I said, stopping them. "Let's stay together until we're out of this blind alley."

"As Master wishes," Conseil replied.

The hours passed. I often studied the instruments hanging on the lounge wall. The pressure gauge indicated that the Nautilus stayed at a constant depth of 300 meters, the compass that it kept heading south, the log that it was traveling at a speed of twenty miles per hour, an excessive speed in such a cramped area. But Captain Nemo knew that by this point there was no such thing as too fast, since minutes were now worth centuries.

At 8:25 a second collision took place. This time astern. I grew pale. My companions came over. I clutched Conseil's hand. Our eyes questioned each other, and more directly than if our thoughts had been translated into words.

Just then the captain entered the lounge. I went to him.

"Our path is barred to the south?" I asked him.

"Yes, sir. When it overturned, that iceberg closed off every exit."

"We're boxed in?"

"Yes."

Shortage of Air

CONSEQUENTLY, above, below, and around the Nautilus, there were impenetrable frozen walls. We were the Ice Bank's prisoners! The Canadian banged a table with his fearsome fist. Conseil kept still. I stared at the captain. His face had resumed its usual emotionlessness. He crossed his arms. He pondered. The Nautilus did not stir.

The captain then broke into speech:

"Gentlemen," he said in a calm voice, "there are two ways of dying under the conditions in which we're placed."

This inexplicable individual acted like a mathematics professor working out a problem for his pupils.

"The first way," he went on, "is death by crushing. The second is death by asphyxiation. I don't mention the possibility of death by starvation because the Nautilus's provisions will certainly last longer than we will. Therefore, let's concentrate on our chances of being crushed or asphyxiated."

"As for asphyxiation, Captain," I replied, "that isn't a cause for alarm, because the air tanks are full."

"True," Captain Nemo went on, "but they'll supply air for only two days. Now then, we've been buried beneath the waters for thirty–six hours, and the Nautilus's heavy atmosphere already needs renewing. In another forty–eight hours, our reserve air will be used up."

"Well then, Captain, let's free ourselves within forty–eight hours!"

"We'll try to at least, by cutting through one of these walls surrounding us."

"Which one?" I asked.

"Borings will tell us that. I'm going to ground the Nautilus on the lower shelf, then my men will put on their diving suits and attack the thinnest of these ice walls."

"Can the panels in the lounge be left open?"

"Without ill effect. We're no longer in motion."

Captain Nemo went out. Hissing sounds soon told me that water was being admitted into the ballast tanks. The Nautilus slowly settled and rested on the icy bottom at a depth of 350 meters, the depth at which the lower shelf of ice lay submerged.

"My friends," I said, "we're in a serious predicament, but I'm counting on your courage and energy."

"Sir," the Canadian replied, "this is no time to bore you with my complaints. I'm ready to do anything I can for the common good."

"Excellent, Ned," I said, extending my hand to the Canadian.

"I might add," he went on, "that I'm as handy with a pick as a harpoon. If I can be helpful to the captain, he can use me any way he wants."

"He won't turn down your assistance. Come along, Ned."

I led the Canadian to the room where the Nautilus's men were putting on their diving suits. I informed the captain of Ned's proposition, which was promptly accepted. The Canadian got into his underwater costume and was ready as soon as his fellow workers. Each of them carried on his back a Rouquayrol device that the air tanks had supplied with a generous allowance of fresh oxygen. A considerable but necessary drain on the Nautilus's reserves. As for the Ruhmkorff lamps, they were unnecessary in the midst of these brilliant waters saturated with our electric rays.

After Ned was dressed, I reentered the lounge, whose windows had been uncovered; stationed next to Conseil, I examined the strata surrounding and supporting the Nautilus.

Some moments later, we saw a dozen crewmen set foot on the shelf of ice, among them Ned Land, easily recognized by his tall figure. Captain Nemo was with them.

Before digging into the ice, the captain had to obtain borings, to insure working in the best direction. Long bores were driven into the side walls; but after fifteen meters, the instruments were still impeded by the thickness of those walls. It was futile to attack the ceiling since that surface was the Ice Bank itself, more than 400 meters high. Captain Nemo then bored into the lower surface. There we were separated from the sea by a ten–meter barrier. That's how thick the iceberg was. From this point on, it was an issue of cutting out a piece equal in surface area to the Nautilus's waterline. This meant detaching about 6,500 cubic meters, to dig a hole through which the ship could descend below this tract of ice.

Work began immediately and was carried on with tireless tenacity. Instead of digging all around the Nautilus, which would have entailed even greater difficulties, Captain Nemo had an immense trench outlined on the ice, eight meters from our port quarter. Then his men simultaneously staked it off at several points around its circumference. Soon their picks were vigorously attacking this compact matter, and huge chunks were loosened from its mass. These chunks weighed less than the water, and by an unusual effect of specific gravity, each chunk took wing, as it were, to the roof of the tunnel, which thickened above by as much as it diminished below. But this hardly mattered so long as the lower surface kept growing thinner.

After two hours of energetic work, Ned Land reentered, exhausted. He and his companions were replaced by new workmen, including Conseil and me. The Nautilus's chief officer supervised us.

The water struck me as unusually cold, but I warmed up promptly while wielding my pick. My movements were quite free, although they were executed under a pressure of thirty atmospheres.

After two hours of work, reentering to snatch some food and rest, I found a noticeable difference between the clean elastic fluid supplied me by the Rouquayrol device and the Nautilus's atmosphere, which was already charged with carbon dioxide. The air hadn't been renewed in forty–eight hours, and its life–giving qualities were considerably weakened. Meanwhile, after twelve hours had gone by, we had removed from the outlined surface area a slice of ice only one meter thick, hence about 600 cubic meters. Assuming the same work would be accomplished every twelve hours, it would still take five nights and four days to see the undertaking through to completion.

"Five nights and four days!" I told my companions. "And we have oxygen in the air tanks for only two days."

"Without taking into account," Ned answered, "that once we're out of this damned prison, we'll still be cooped up beneath the Ice Bank, without any possible contact with the open air!"

An apt remark. For who could predict the minimum time we would need to free ourselves? Before the Nautilus could return to the surface of the waves, couldn't we all die of asphyxiation? Were this ship and everyone on board doomed to perish in this tomb of ice? It was a dreadful state of affairs. But we faced it head–on, each one of us determined to do his duty to the end.

During the night, in line with my forecasts, a new one–meter slice was removed from this immense socket. But in the morning, wearing my diving suit, I was crossing through the liquid mass in a temperature of –6° to –7° centigrade, when I noted that little by little the side walls were closing in on each other. The liquid strata farthest from the trench, not warmed by the movements of workmen and tools, were showing a tendency to solidify. In the face of this imminent new danger, what would happen to our chances for salvation, and how could we prevent this liquid medium from solidifying, then cracking the Nautilus's hull like glass?

I didn't tell my two companions about this new danger. There was no point in dampening the energy they were putting into our arduous rescue work. But when I returned on board, I mentioned this serious complication to Captain Nemo.

"I know," he told me in that calm tone the most dreadful outlook couldn't change. "It's one more danger, but I don't know any way of warding it off. Our sole chance for salvation is to work faster than the water solidifies. We've got to get there first, that's all."

Get there first! By then I should have been used to this type of talk!

For several hours that day, I wielded my pick doggedly. The work kept me going. Besides, working meant leaving the Nautilus, which meant breathing the clean oxygen drawn from the air tanks and supplied by our equipment, which meant leaving the thin, foul air behind.

Near evening one more meter had been dug from the trench. When I returned on board, I was wellnigh asphyxiated by the carbon dioxide saturating the air. Oh, if only we had the chemical methods that would enable us to drive out this noxious gas! There was no lack of oxygen. All this water contained a considerable amount, and after it was decomposed by our powerful batteries, this life–giving elastic fluid could have been restored to us. I had thought it all out, but to no avail because the carbon dioxide produced by our breathing permeated every part of the ship. To absorb it, we would need to fill containers with potassium hydroxide and shake them continually. But this substance was missing on board and nothing else could replace it.

That evening Captain Nemo was forced to open the spigots of his air tanks and shoot a few spouts of fresh oxygen through the Nautilus's interior. Without this precaution we wouldn't have awakened the following morning.

The next day, March 26, I returned to my miner's trade, working to remove the fifth meter. The Ice Bank's side walls and underbelly had visibly thickened. Obviously they would come together before the Nautilus could break free. For an instant I was gripped by despair. My pick nearly slipped from my hands. What was the point of this digging if I was to die smothered and crushed by this water turning to stone, a torture undreamed of by even the wildest savages! I felt like I was lying in the jaws of a fearsome monster, jaws irresistibly closing.

Supervising our work, working himself, Captain Nemo passed near me just then. I touched him with my hand and pointed to the walls of our prison. The starboard wall had moved forward to a point less than four meters from the Nautilus's hull.

The captain understood and gave me a signal to follow him. We returned on board. My diving suit removed, I went with him to the lounge.

"Professor Aronnax," he told me, "this calls for heroic measures, or we'll be sealed up in this solidified water as if it were cement."

"Yes!" I said. "But what can we do?"

"Oh," he exclaimed, "if only my Nautilus were strong enough to stand that much pressure without being crushed!"

"Well?" I asked, not catching the captain's meaning.

"Don't you understand," he went on, "that the congealing of this water could come to our rescue? Don't you see that by solidifying, it could burst these tracts of ice imprisoning us, just as its freezing can burst the hardest stones? Aren't you aware that this force could be the instrument of our salvation rather than our destruction?"

"Yes, Captain, maybe so. But whatever resistance to crushing the Nautilus may have, it still couldn't stand such dreadful pressures, and it would be squashed as flat as a piece of sheet iron."

"I know it, sir. So we can't rely on nature to rescue us, only our own efforts. We must counteract this solidification. We must hold it in check. Not only are the side walls closing in, but there aren't ten feet of water ahead or astern of the Nautilus. All around us, this freeze is gaining fast."

"How long," I asked, "will the oxygen in the air tanks enable us to breathe on board?"

The captain looked me straight in the eye.

"After tomorrow," he said, "the air tanks will be empty!"

I broke out in a cold sweat. But why should I have been startled by this reply? On March 22 the Nautilus had dived under the open waters at the pole. It was now the 26th. We had lived off the ship's stores for five days! And all remaining breathable air had to be saved for the workmen. Even today as I write these lines, my sensations are so intense that an involuntary terror sweeps over me, and my lungs still seem short of air!

Meanwhile, motionless and silent, Captain Nemo stood lost in thought. An idea visibly crossed his mind. But he seemed to brush it aside. He told himself no. At last these words escaped his lips:

"Boiling water!" he muttered.

"Boiling water?" I exclaimed.

"Yes, sir. We're shut up in a relatively confined area. If the Nautilus's pumps continually injected streams of boiling water into this space, wouldn't that raise its temperature and delay its freezing?"

"It's worth trying!" I said resolutely.

"So let's try it, Professor."

By then the thermometer gave –7° centigrade outside. Captain Nemo led me to the galley where a huge distilling mechanism was at work, supplying drinking water via evaporation. The mechanism was loaded with water, and the full electric heat of our batteries was thrown into coils awash in liquid. In a few minutes the water reached 100° centigrade. It was sent to the pumps while new water replaced it in the process. The heat generated by our batteries was so intense that after simply going through the mechanism, water drawn cold from the sea arrived boiling hot at the body of the pump.

The steaming water was injected into the icy water outside, and after three hours had passed, the thermometer gave the exterior temperature as –6° centigrade. That was one degree gained. Two hours later the thermometer gave only –4°.

After I monitored the operation's progress, double–checking it with many inspections, I told the captain, "It's working."

"I think so," he answered me. "We've escaped being crushed. Now we have only asphyxiation to fear."

During the night the water temperature rose to –1° centigrade. The injections couldn't get it to go a single degree higher. But since salt water freezes only at –2°, I was finally assured that there was no danger of it solidifying.

By the next day, March 27, six meters of ice had been torn from the socket. Only four meters were left to be removed. That still meant forty–eight hours of work. The air couldn't be renewed in the Nautilus's interior. Accordingly, that day it kept getting worse.

An unbearable heaviness weighed me down. Near three o'clock in the afternoon, this agonizing sensation affected me to an intense degree. Yawns dislocated my jaws. My lungs were gasping in their quest for that enkindling elastic fluid required for breathing, now growing scarcer and scarcer. My mind was in a daze. I lay outstretched, strength gone, nearly unconscious. My gallant

Conseil felt the same symptoms, suffered the same sufferings, yet never left my side. He held my hand, he kept encouraging me, and I even heard him mutter: "Oh, if only I didn't have to breathe, to leave more air for Master!" It brought tears to my eyes to hear him say these words.

Since conditions inside were universally unbearable, how eagerly, how happily, we put on our diving suits to take our turns working! Picks rang out on that bed of ice. Arms grew weary, hands were rubbed raw, but who cared about exhaustion, what difference were wounds? Life–sustaining air reached our lungs! We could breathe! We could breathe!

And yet nobody prolonged his underwater work beyond the time allotted him. His shift over, each man surrendered to a gasping companion the air tank that would revive him. Captain Nemo set the example and was foremost in submitting to this strict discipline. When his time was up, he yielded his equipment to another and reentered the foul air on board, always calm, unflinching, and uncomplaining.

That day the usual work was accomplished with even greater energy. Over the whole surface area, only two meters were left to be removed. Only two meters separated us from the open sea. But the ship's air tanks were nearly empty. The little air that remained had to be saved for the workmen. Not an atom for the Nautilus!

When I returned on board, I felt half suffocated. What a night! I'm unable to depict it. Such sufferings are indescribable. The next day I was short–winded. Headaches and staggering fits of dizziness made me reel like a drunk. My companions were experiencing the same symptoms. Some crewmen were at their last gasp.

That day, the sixth of our imprisonment, Captain Nemo concluded that picks and mattocks were too slow to deal with the ice layer still separating us from open water—and he decided to crush this layer. The man had kept his energy and composure. He had subdued physical pain with moral strength. He could still think, plan, and act.

At his orders the craft was eased off, in other words, it was raised from its icy bed by a change in its specific gravity. When it was afloat, the crew towed it, leading it right above the immense trench outlined to match the ship's waterline. Next the ballast tanks filled with water, the boat sank, and was fitted into its socket.

Just then the whole crew returned on board, and the double outside door was closed. By this point the Nautilus was resting on a bed of ice only one meter thick and drilled by bores in a thousand places.

The stopcocks of the ballast tanks were then opened wide, and 100 cubic meters of water rushed in, increasing the Nautilus's weight by 100,000 kilograms.

We waited, we listened, we forgot our sufferings, we hoped once more. We had staked our salvation on this one last gamble.

Despite the buzzing in my head, I soon could hear vibrations under the Nautilus's hull. We tilted. The ice cracked with an odd ripping sound, like paper tearing, and the Nautilus began settling downward.

"We're going through!" Conseil muttered in my ear.

I couldn't answer him. I clutched his hand. I squeezed it in an involuntary convulsion.

All at once, carried away by its frightful excess load, the Nautilus sank into the waters like a cannonball, in other words, dropping as if in a vacuum!

Our full electric power was then put on the pumps, which instantly began to expel water from the ballast tanks. After a few minutes we had checked our fall. The pressure gauge soon indicated an ascending movement. Brought to full speed, the propeller made the sheet–iron hull tremble down to its rivets, and we sped northward.

But how long would it take to navigate under the Ice Bank to the open sea? Another day? I would be dead first!

Half lying on a couch in the library, I was suffocating. My face was purple, my lips blue, my faculties in abeyance. I could no longer see or hear. I had lost all sense of time. My muscles had no power to contract.

I'm unable to estimate the hours that passed in this way. But I was aware that my death throes had begun. I realized that I was about to die . . .

Suddenly I regained consciousness. A few whiffs of air had entered my lungs. Had we risen to the surface of the waves? Had we cleared the Ice Bank?

No! Ned and Conseil, my two gallant friends, were sacrificing themselves to save me. A few atoms of air were still left in the depths of one Rouquayrol device. Instead of breathing it themselves, they had saved it for me, and while they were suffocating, they poured life into me drop by drop! I tried to push the device away. They held my hands, and for a few moments I could breathe luxuriously.

My eyes flew toward the clock. It was eleven in the morning. It had to be March 28. The Nautilus was traveling at the frightful speed of forty miles per hour. It was writhing in the waters.

Where was Captain Nemo? Had he perished? Had his companions died with him?

Just then the pressure gauge indicated we were no more than twenty feet from the surface. Separating us from the open air was a mere tract of ice. Could we break through it?

Perhaps! In any event the Nautilus was going to try. In fact, I could feel it assuming an oblique position, lowering its stern and raising its spur. The admission of additional water was enough to shift its balance. Then, driven by its powerful propeller, it attacked this ice field from below like a fearsome battering ram. It split the barrier little by little, backing up, then putting on full speed against the punctured tract of ice; and finally, carried away by its supreme momentum, it lunged through and onto this frozen surface, crushing the ice beneath its weight.

The hatches were opened—or torn off, if you prefer—and waves of clean air were admitted into every part of the Nautilus.

From Cape Horn to the Amazon

HOW I GOT ONTO the platform I'm unable to say. Perhaps the Canadian transferred me there. But I could breathe, I could inhale the life–giving sea air. Next to me my two companions were getting tipsy on the fresh oxygen particles. Poor souls who have suffered from long starvation mustn't pounce heedlessly on the first food given them. We, on the other hand, didn't have to practice such moderation: we could suck the atoms from the air by the lungful, and it was the breeze, the breeze itself, that poured into us this luxurious intoxication!

"Ahhh!" Conseil was putting in. "What fine oxygen! Let Master have no fears about breathing. There's enough for everyone."

As for Ned Land, he didn't say a word, but his wide–open jaws would have scared off a shark. And what powerful inhalations! The Canadian "drew" like a furnace going full blast.

Our strength returned promptly, and when I looked around, I saw that we were alone on the platform. No crewmen. Not even Captain Nemo. Those strange seamen on the Nautilus were content with the oxygen circulating inside. Not one of them had come up to enjoy the open air.

The first words I pronounced were words of appreciation and gratitude to my two companions. Ned and Conseil had kept me alive during the final hours of our long death throes. But no expression of thanks could repay them fully for such devotion.

"Good lord, Professor," Ned Land answered me, "don't mention it! What did we do that's so praiseworthy? Not a thing. It was a question of simple arithmetic. Your life is worth more than ours. So we had to save it."

"No, Ned," I replied, "it isn't worth more. Nobody could be better than a kind and generous man like yourself!"

"All right, all right!" the Canadian repeated in embarrassment.

"And you, my gallant Conseil, you suffered a great deal."

"Not too much, to be candid with Master. I was lacking a few throatfuls of air, but I would have gotten by. Besides, when I saw Master fainting, it left me without the slightest desire to breathe. It took my breath away, in a manner of . . . "

Confounded by this lapse into banality, Conseil left his sentence hanging.

"My friends," I replied, very moved, "we're bound to each other forever, and I'm deeply indebted to you—"

"Which I'll take advantage of," the Canadian shot back.

"Eh?" Conseil put in.

"Yes," Ned Land went on. "You can repay your debt by coming with me when I leave this infernal Nautilus."

"By the way," Conseil said, "are we going in a favorable direction?"

"Yes," I replied, "because we're going in the direction of the sun, and here the sun is due north."

"Sure," Ned Land went on, "but it remains to be seen whether we'll make for the Atlantic or the Pacific, in other words, whether we'll end up in well–traveled or deserted seas."

I had no reply to this, and I feared that Captain Nemo wouldn't take us homeward but rather into that huge ocean washing the shores of both Asia and America. In this way he would complete his underwater tour of the world, going back to those seas where the Nautilus enjoyed the greatest freedom. But if we returned to the Pacific, far from every populated shore, what would happen to Ned Land's plans?

We would soon settle this important point. The Nautilus traveled swiftly. Soon we had cleared the Antarctic Circle plus the promontory of Cape Horn. We were abreast of the tip of South America by March 31 at seven o'clock in the evening.

By then all our past sufferings were forgotten. The memory of that imprisonment under the ice faded from our minds. We had thoughts only of the future. Captain Nemo no longer appeared, neither in the lounge nor on the platform. The positions reported each day on the world map were put there by the chief officer, and they enabled me to determine the Nautilus's exact heading. Now then, that evening it became obvious, much to my satisfaction, that we were returning north by the Atlantic route.

I shared the results of my observations with the Canadian and Conseil.

"That's good news," the Canadian replied, "but where's the Nautilus going?"

"I'm unable to say, Ned."

"After the South Pole, does our captain want to tackle the North Pole, then go back to the Pacific by the notorious Northwest Passage?"

"I wouldn't double dare him," Conseil replied.

"Oh well," the Canadian said, "we'll give him the slip long before then."

"In any event," Conseil added, "he's a superman, that Captain Nemo, and we'll never regret having known him."

"Especially once we've left him," Ned Land shot back.

The next day, April 1, when the Nautilus rose to the surface of the waves a few minutes before noon, we raised land to the west. It was Tierra del Fuego, the Land of Fire, a name given it by early navigators after they saw numerous curls of smoke rising from the natives' huts. This Land of Fire forms a huge cluster of islands over thirty leagues long and eighty leagues wide, extending between latitude 53° and 56° south, and between longitude 67° 50' and 77° 15' west. Its coastline looked flat, but high mountains rose in the distance. I even thought I glimpsed Mt. Sarmiento, whose elevation is 2,070 meters above sea level: a pyramid–shaped block of shale with a very sharp summit, which, depending on whether it's clear or veiled in vapor, "predicts fair weather or foul," as Ned Land told me.

"A first–class barometer, my friend."

"Yes, sir, a natural barometer that didn't let me down when I navigated the narrows of the Strait of Magellan."

Just then its peak appeared before us, standing out distinctly against the background of the skies. This forecast fair weather. And so it proved.

Going back under the waters, the Nautilus drew near the coast, cruising along it for only a few miles. Through the lounge windows I could see long creepers and gigantic fucus plants, bulb–bearing seaweed of which the open sea at the pole had revealed a few specimens; with their smooth, viscous filaments, they measured as much as 300 meters long; genuine cables more than an inch thick and very tough, they're often used as mooring lines for ships. Another weed, known by the name velp and boasting four–foot leaves, was crammed into the coral concretions and carpeted the ocean floor. It served as both nest and nourishment for myriads of crustaceans and mollusks, for crabs and cuttlefish. Here seals and otters could indulge in a sumptuous meal, mixing meat from fish with vegetables from the sea, like the English with their Irish stews.

The Nautilus passed over these lush, luxuriant depths with tremendous speed. Near evening it approached the Falkland Islands, whose rugged summits I recognized the next day. The sea was of moderate depth. So not without good reason, I assumed that these two islands, plus the many islets surrounding them, used to be part of the Magellan coastline. The Falkland Islands were probably discovered by the famous navigator John Davis, who gave them the name Davis Southern Islands. Later Sir Richard Hawkins called them the Maidenland, after the Blessed Virgin. Subsequently, at the beginning of the 18th century, they were named the Malouines by fishermen from Saint–Malo in Brittany, then finally dubbed the Falklands by the English, to whom they belong today.

In these waterways our nets brought up fine samples of algae, in particular certain fucus plants whose roots were laden with the world's best mussels. Geese and duck alighted by the dozens on the platform and soon took their places in the ship's pantry. As for fish, I specifically observed some bony fish belonging to the goby genus, especially some gudgeon two decimeters long, sprinkled with whitish and yellow spots.

I likewise marveled at the numerous medusas, including the most beautiful of their breed, the compass jellyfish, unique to the Falkland seas. Some of these jellyfish were shaped like very smooth, semispheric parasols with russet stripes and fringes of twelve neat festoons. Others looked like upside–down baskets from which wide leaves and long red twigs were gracefully trailing. They swam with quiverings of their four leaflike arms, letting the opulent tresses of their tentacles dangle in the drift. I wanted to preserve a few specimens of these delicate zoophytes, but they were merely clouds, shadows, illusions, melting and evaporating outside their native element.

When the last tips of the Falkland Islands had disappeared below the horizon, the Nautilus submerged to a depth between twenty and twenty–five meters and went along the South American coast. Captain Nemo didn't put in an appearance.

We didn't leave these Patagonian waterways until April 3, sometimes cruising under the ocean, sometimes on its surface. The Nautilus passed the wide estuary formed by the mouth of the Rio de la Plata, and on April 4 we lay abreast of Uruguay, albeit fifty miles out. Keeping to its northerly heading, it followed the long windings of South America. By then we had fared 16,000 leagues since coming on board in the seas of Japan.

Near eleven o'clock in the morning, we cut the Tropic of Capricorn on the 37th meridian, passing well out from Cape Frio. Much to Ned Land's displeasure, Captain Nemo had no liking for the neighborhood of Brazil's populous shores, because he shot by with dizzying speed. Not even the swiftest fish or birds could keep up with us, and the natural curiosities in these seas completely eluded our observation.

This speed was maintained for several days, and on the evening of April 9, we raised South America's easternmost tip, Cape São Roque. But then the Nautilus veered away again and went looking for the lowest depths of an underwater valley gouged between this cape and Sierra Leone on the coast of Africa. Abreast of the West Indies, this valley forks into two arms, and to the north it ends in an enormous depression 9,000 meters deep. From this locality to the Lesser Antilles, the ocean's geologic profile features a steeply cut cliff six kilometers high, and abreast of the Cape Verde Islands, there's another wall just as imposing; together these two barricades confine the whole submerged continent of Atlantis. The floor of this immense valley is made picturesque by mountains that furnish these underwater depths with scenic views. This description is based mostly on certain hand–drawn charts kept in the Nautilus's library, charts obviously rendered by Captain Nemo himself from his own personal observations.

For two days we visited these deep and deserted waters by means of our slanting fins. The Nautilus would do long, diagonal dives that took us to every level. But on April 11 it rose suddenly, and the shore reappeared at the mouth of the Amazon River, a huge estuary whose outflow is so considerable, it desalts the sea over an area of several leagues.

We cut the Equator. Twenty miles to the west lay Guiana, French territory where we could easily have taken refuge. But the wind was blowing a strong gust, and the furious billows would not allow us to face them in a mere skiff. No doubt Ned Land understood this because he said nothing to me. For my part, I made no allusion to his escape plans because I didn't want to push him into an attempt that was certain to misfire.

I was readily compensated for this delay by fascinating research. During those two days of April 11–12, the Nautilus didn't leave the surface of the sea, and its trawl brought up a simply miraculous catch of zoophytes, fish, and reptiles.

Some zoophytes were dredged up by the chain of our trawl. Most were lovely sea anemone belonging to the family Actinidia, including among other species, the Phyctalis protexta, native to this part of the ocean: a small cylindrical trunk adorned with vertical lines, mottled with red spots, and crowned by a wondrous blossoming of tentacles. As for mollusks, they consisted of exhibits I had already observed: turret snails, olive shells of the "tent olive" species with neatly intersecting lines and russet spots standing out sharply against a flesh–colored background, fanciful spider conchs that looked like petrified scorpions, transparent glass snails, argonauts, some highly edible cuttlefish, and certain species of squid that the naturalists of antiquity classified with the flying fish, which are used chiefly as bait for catching cod.

As for the fish in these waterways, I noted various species that I hadn't yet had the opportunity to study. Among cartilaginous fish: some brook lamprey, a type of eel fifteen inches long, head greenish, fins violet, back bluish gray, belly a silvery brown strewn with bright spots, iris of the eye encircled in gold, unusual animals that the Amazon's current must have swept out to sea because their natural habitat is fresh water; sting rays, the snout pointed, the tail long, slender, and armed with an extensive jagged sting; small one–meter sharks with gray and whitish hides, their teeth arranged in several backward–curving rows, fish commonly known by the name carpet shark; batfish, a sort of reddish isosceles triangle half a meter long, whose pectoral fins are attached by fleshy extensions that make these fish look like bats, although an appendage made of horn, located near the nostrils, earns them the nickname of sea unicorns; lastly, a couple species of triggerfish, the cucuyo whose stippled flanks glitter with a sparkling gold color, and the bright purple leatherjacket whose hues glisten like a pigeon's throat.

I'll finish up this catalog, a little dry but quite accurate, with the series of bony fish I observed: eels belonging to the genus Apteronotus whose snow–white snout is very blunt, the body painted a handsome black and armed with a very long, slender, fleshy whip; long sardines from the genus Odontognathus, like three–decimeter pike, shining with a bright silver glow; Guaranian mackerel furnished with two anal fins; black–tinted rudderfish that you catch by using torches, fish measuring two meters and boasting white, firm, plump meat that, when fresh, tastes like eel, when dried, like smoked salmon; semired wrasse sporting scales only at the bases of their dorsal and anal fins; grunts on which gold and silver mingle their luster with that of ruby and topaz; yellow–tailed gilthead whose flesh is extremely dainty and whose phosphorescent properties give them away in the midst of the waters; porgies tinted orange, with slender tongues; croakers with gold caudal fins; black surgeonfish; four–eyed fish from Surinam, etc.

This "et cetera" won't keep me from mentioning one more fish that Conseil, with good reason, will long remember.

One of our nets had hauled up a type of very flat ray that weighed some twenty kilograms; with its tail cut off, it would have formed a perfect disk. It was white underneath and reddish on top, with big round spots of deep blue encircled in black, its hide quite smooth and ending in a double–lobed fin. Laid out on the platform, it kept struggling with convulsive movements, trying to turn over, making such efforts that its final lunge was about to flip it into the sea. But Conseil, being very possessive of his fish, rushed at it, and before I could stop him, he seized it with both hands.

Instantly there he was, thrown on his back, legs in the air, his body half paralyzed, and yelling:

"Oh, sir, sir! Will you help me!"

For once in his life, the poor lad didn't address me "in the third person."

The Canadian and I sat him up; we massaged his contracted arms, and when he regained his five senses, that eternal classifier mumbled in a broken voice:

"Class of cartilaginous fish, order Chondropterygia with fixed gills, suborder Selacia, family Rajiiforma, genus electric ray."

"Yes, my friend," I answered, "it was an electric ray that put you in this deplorable state."

"Oh, Master can trust me on this," Conseil shot back. "I'll be revenged on that animal!"

"How?"

"I'll eat it."

Which he did that same evening, but strictly as retaliation. Because, frankly, it tasted like leather.

Poor Conseil had assaulted an electric ray of the most dangerous species, the cumana. Living in a conducting medium such as water, this bizarre animal can electrocute other fish from several meters away, so great is the power of its electric organ, an organ whose two chief surfaces measure at least twenty–seven square feet.

During the course of the next day, April 12, the Nautilus drew near the coast of Dutch Guiana, by the mouth of the Maroni River. There several groups of sea cows were living in family units. These were manatees, which belong to the order

Sirenia, like the dugong and Steller's sea cow. Harmless and unaggressive, these fine animals were six to seven meters long and must have weighed at least 4,000 kilograms each. I told Ned Land and Conseil that farseeing nature had given these mammals a major role to play. In essence, manatees, like seals, are designed to graze the underwater prairies, destroying the clusters of weeds that obstruct the mouths of tropical rivers.

"And do you know," I added, "what happened since man has almost completely wiped out these beneficial races? Rotting weeds have poisoned the air, and this poisoned air causes the yellow fever that devastates these wonderful countries. This toxic vegetation has increased beneath the seas of the Torrid Zone, so the disease spreads unchecked from the mouth of the Rio de la Plata to Florida!"

And if Professor Toussenel is correct, this plague is nothing compared to the scourge that will strike our descendants once the seas are depopulated of whales and seals. By then, crowded with jellyfish, squid, and other devilfish, the oceans will have become huge centers of infection, because their waves will no longer possess "these huge stomachs that God has entrusted with scouring the surface of the sea."

Meanwhile, without scorning these theories, the Nautilus's crew captured half a dozen manatees. In essence, it was an issue of stocking the larder with excellent red meat, even better than beef or veal. Their hunting was not a fascinating sport. The manatees let themselves be struck down without offering any resistance. Several thousand kilos of meat were hauled below, to be dried and stored.

The same day an odd fishing practice further increased the Nautilus's stores, so full of game were these seas. Our trawl brought up in its meshes a number of fish whose heads were topped by little oval slabs with fleshy edges. These were suckerfish from the third family of the subbrachian Malacopterygia. These flat disks on their heads consist of crosswise plates of movable cartilage, between which the animals can create a vacuum, enabling them to stick to objects like suction cups.

The remoras I had observed in the Mediterranean were related to this species. But the creature at issue here was an Echeneis osteochara, unique to this sea. Right after catching them, our seamen dropped them in buckets of water.

Its fishing finished, the Nautilus drew nearer to the coast. In this locality a number of sea turtles were sleeping on the surface of the waves. It would have been difficult to capture these valuable reptiles, because they wake up at the slightest sound, and their solid carapaces are harpoon–proof. But our suckerfish would effect their capture with extraordinary certainty and precision. In truth, this animal is a living fishhook, promising wealth and happiness to the greenest fisherman in the business.

The Nautilus's men attached to each fish's tail a ring that was big enough not to hamper its movements, and to this ring a long rope whose other end was moored on board.

Thrown into the sea, the suckerfish immediately began to play their roles, going and fastening themselves onto the breastplates of the turtles. Their tenacity was so great, they would rip apart rather than let go. They were hauled in, still sticking to the turtles that came aboard with them.

In this way we caught several loggerheads, reptiles a meter wide and weighing 200 kilos. They're extremely valuable because of their carapaces, which are covered with big slabs of horn, thin, brown, transparent, with white and yellow markings. Besides, they were excellent from an edible viewpoint, with an exquisite flavor comparable to the green turtle.

This fishing ended our stay in the waterways of the Amazon, and that evening the Nautilus took to the high seas once more.

The Devilfish

FOR SOME DAYS the Nautilus kept veering away from the American coast. It obviously didn't want to frequent the waves of the Gulf of Mexico or the Caribbean Sea. Yet there was no shortage of water under its keel, since the average depth of these seas is 1,800 meters; but these waterways, strewn with islands and plowed by steamers, probably didn't agree with Captain Nemo.

On April 16 we raised Martinique and Guadalupe from a distance of about thirty miles. For one instant I could see their lofty peaks.

The Canadian was quite disheartened, having counted on putting his plans into execution in the gulf, either by reaching shore or by pulling alongside one of the many boats plying a coastal trade from one island to another. An escape attempt would have been quite feasible, assuming Ned Land managed to seize the skiff without the captain's knowledge. But in midocean it was unthinkable.

The Canadian, Conseil, and I had a pretty long conversation on this subject. For six months we had been prisoners aboard the Nautilus. We had fared 17,000 leagues, and as Ned Land put it, there was no end in sight. So he made me a proposition I hadn't anticipated. We were to ask Captain Nemo this question straight out: did the captain mean to keep us on board his vessel permanently?

This measure was distasteful to me. To my mind it would lead nowhere. We could hope for nothing from the Nautilus's commander but could depend only on ourselves. Besides, for some time now the man had been gloomier, more withdrawn, less sociable. He seemed to be avoiding me. I encountered him only at rare intervals. He used to take pleasure in explaining the underwater wonders to me; now he left me to my research and no longer entered the lounge.

What changes had come over him? From what cause? I had no reason to blame myself. Was our presence on board perhaps a burden to him? Even so, I cherished no hopes that the man would set us free.

So I begged Ned to let me think about it before taking action. If this measure proved fruitless, it could arouse the captain's suspicions, make our circumstances even more arduous, and jeopardize the Canadian's plans. I might add that I could hardly use our state of health as an argument. Except for that grueling ordeal under the Ice Bank at the South Pole, we had never felt better, neither Ned, Conseil, nor I. The nutritious food, life–giving air, regular routine, and uniform temperature kept illness at bay; and for a man who didn't miss his past existence on land, for a Captain Nemo who was at home here, who went where he wished, who took paths mysterious to others if not himself in attaining his ends, I could understand such a life. But we ourselves hadn't severed all ties with humanity. For my part, I didn't want my new and unusual research to be buried with my bones. I had now earned the right to pen the definitive book on the sea, and sooner or later I wanted that book to see the light of day.

There once more, through the panels opening into these Caribbean waters ten meters below the surface of the waves, I found so many fascinating exhibits to describe in my daily notes! Among other zoophytes there were Portuguese men–of–war known by the name Physalia pelagica, like big, oblong bladders with a pearly sheen, spreading their membranes to the wind, letting their blue tentacles drift like silken threads; to the eye delightful jellyfish, to the touch actual nettles that ooze a corrosive liquid. Among the articulates there were annelid worms one and a half meters long, furnished with a pink proboscis, equipped with 1,700 organs of locomotion, snaking through the waters, and as they went, throwing off every gleam in the solar spectrum. From the fish branch there were manta rays, enormous cartilaginous fish ten feet long and weighing 600 pounds, their pectoral fin triangular, their midback slightly arched, their eyes attached to the edges of the face at the front of the head; they floated like wreckage from a ship, sometimes fastening onto our windows like opaque shutters. There were American triggerfish for which nature has ground only black and white pigments, feather–shaped gobies that were long and plump with yellow fins and jutting jaws, sixteen–decimeter mackerel with short, sharp teeth, covered with small scales, and related to the albacore species. Next came swarms of red mullet corseted in gold stripes from head to tail, their shining fins all aquiver, genuine masterpieces of jewelry, formerly sacred to the goddess Diana, much in demand by rich Romans, and about which the old saying goes: "He who catches them doesn't eat them!" Finally, adorned with emerald ribbons and dressed in velvet and silk, golden angelfish passed before our eyes like courtiers in the paintings of Veronese; spurred gilthead stole by with their swift thoracic fins; thread herring fifteen inches long were wrapped in their phosphorescent glimmers; gray mullet thrashed

278   **Jules Verne**

the sea with their big fleshy tails; red salmon seemed to mow the waves with their slicing pectorals; and silver moonfish, worthy of their name, rose on the horizon of the waters like the whitish reflections of many moons.

How many other marvelous new specimens I still could have observed if, little by little, the Nautilus hadn't settled to the lower strata! Its slanting fins drew it to depths of 2,000 and 3,500 meters. There animal life was represented by nothing more than sea lilies, starfish, delightful crinoids with bell–shaped heads like little chalices on straight stems, top–shell snails, blood–red tooth shells, and fissurella snails, a large species of coastal mollusk.

By April 20 we had risen to an average level of 1,500 meters. The nearest land was the island group of the Bahamas, scattered like a batch of cobblestones over the surface of the water. There high underwater cliffs reared up, straight walls made of craggy chunks arranged like big stone foundations, among which there gaped black caves so deep our electric rays couldn't light them to the far ends.

These rocks were hung with huge weeds, immense sea tangle, gigantic fucus—a genuine trellis of water plants fit for a world of giants.

In discussing these colossal plants, Conseil, Ned, and I were naturally led into mentioning the sea's gigantic animals. The former were obviously meant to feed the latter. However, through the windows of our almost motionless Nautilus, I could see nothing among these long filaments other than the chief articulates of the division Brachyura: long–legged spider crabs, violet crabs, and sponge crabs unique to the waters of the Caribbean.

It was about eleven o'clock when Ned Land drew my attention to a fearsome commotion out in this huge seaweed.

"Well," I said, "these are real devilfish caverns, and I wouldn't be surprised to see some of those monsters hereabouts."

"What!" Conseil put in. "Squid, ordinary squid from the class Cephalopoda?"

"No," I said, "devilfish of large dimensions. But friend Land is no doubt mistaken, because I don't see a thing."

"That's regrettable," Conseil answered. "I'd like to come face to face with one of those devilfish I've heard so much about, which can drag ships down into the depths. Those beasts go by the name of krake—"

"Fake is more like it," the Canadian replied sarcastically.

"Krakens!" Conseil shot back, finishing his word without wincing at his companion's witticism.

"Nobody will ever make me believe," Ned Land said, "that such animals exist."

"Why not?" Conseil replied. "We sincerely believed in Master's narwhale."

"We were wrong, Conseil."

"No doubt, but there are others with no doubts who believe to this day!"

"Probably, Conseil. But as for me, I'm bound and determined not to accept the existence of any such monster till I've dissected it with my own two hands."

"Yet," Conseil asked me, "doesn't Master believe in gigantic devilfish?"

"Yikes! Who in Hades ever believed in them?" the Canadian exclaimed.

"Many people, Ned my friend," I said.

"No fishermen. Scientists maybe!"

"Pardon me, Ned. Fishermen and scientists!"

"Why, I to whom you speak," Conseil said with the world's straightest face, "I recall perfectly seeing a large boat dragged under the waves by the arms of a cephalopod."

"You saw that?" the Canadian asked.

"Yes, Ned."

"With your own two eyes?"

"With my own two eyes."

"Where, may I ask?"

"In Saint–Malo," Conseil returned unflappably.

"In the harbor?" Ned Land said sarcastically.

"No, in a church," Conseil replied.

"In a church!" the Canadian exclaimed.

"Yes, Ned my friend. It had a picture that portrayed the devilfish in question."

"Oh good!" Ned Land exclaimed with a burst of laughter. "Mr. Conseil put one over on me!"

"Actually he's right," I said. "I've heard about that picture. But the subject it portrays is taken from a legend, and you know how to rate legends in matters of natural history! Besides, when it's an issue of monsters, the human imagination always tends to run wild. People not only claimed these devilfish could drag ships under, but a certain Olaus Magnus tells of a cephalopod a mile long that looked more like an island than an animal. There's also the story of how the Bishop of Trondheim set up an altar one day on an immense rock. After he finished saying mass, this rock started moving and went back into the sea. The rock was a devilfish."

"And that's everything we know?" the Canadian asked.

"No," I replied, "another bishop, Pontoppidan of Bergen, also tells of a devilfish so large a whole cavalry regiment could maneuver on it."

"They sure did go on, those oldtime bishops!" Ned Land said.

"Finally, the naturalists of antiquity mention some monsters with mouths as big as a gulf, which were too huge to get through the Strait of Gibraltar."

"Good work, men!" the Canadian put in.

"But in all these stories, is there any truth?" Conseil asked.

"None at all, my friends, at least in those that go beyond the bounds of credibility and fly off into fable or legend. Yet for the imaginings of these storytellers there had to be, if not a cause, at least an excuse. It can't be denied that some species of squid and other devilfish are quite large, though still smaller than cetaceans. Aristotle put the dimensions of one squid at five cubits, or 3.1 meters. Our fishermen frequently see specimens over 1.8 meters long. The museums in Trieste and Montpellier have preserved some devilfish carcasses measuring two meters. Besides, according to the calculations of naturalists, one of these animals only six feet long would have tentacles as long as twenty–seven. Which is enough to make a fearsome monster."

"Does anybody fish for 'em nowadays?" the Canadian asked.

"If they don't fish for them, sailors at least sight them. A friend of mine, Captain Paul Bos of Le Havre, has often sworn to me that he encountered one of these monsters of colossal size in the seas of the East Indies. But the most astonishing event, which proves that these gigantic animals undeniably exist, took place a few years ago in 1861."

"What event was that?" Ned Land asked.

"Just this. In 1861, to the northeast of Tenerife and fairly near the latitude where we are right now, the crew of the gunboat Alecto spotted a monstrous squid swimming in their waters. Commander Bouguer approached the animal and attacked it with blows from harpoons and blasts from rifles, but without much success because bullets and harpoons crossed its soft flesh as if it were semiliquid jelly. After several fruitless attempts, the crew managed to slip a noose around the mollusk's body. This noose slid as far as the caudal fins and came to a halt. Then they tried to haul the monster on board, but its weight was so considerable that when they tugged on the rope, the animal parted company with its tail; and deprived of this adornment, it disappeared beneath the waters."

"Finally, an actual event," Ned Land said.

"An indisputable event, my gallant Ned. Accordingly, people have proposed naming this devilfish Bouguer's Squid."

"And how long was it?" the Canadian asked.

"Didn't it measure about six meters?" said Conseil, who was stationed at the window and examining anew the crevices in the cliff.

"Precisely," I replied.

"Wasn't its head," Conseil went on, "crowned by eight tentacles that quivered in the water like a nest of snakes?"

"Precisely."

"Weren't its eyes prominently placed and considerably enlarged?"

"Yes, Conseil."

"And wasn't its mouth a real parrot's beak but of fearsome size?"

"Correct, Conseil."

"Well, with all due respect to Master," Conseil replied serenely, "if this isn't Bouguer's Squid, it's at least one of his close relatives!"

I stared at Conseil. Ned Land rushed to the window.

"What an awful animal!" he exclaimed.

I stared in my turn and couldn't keep back a movement of revulsion. Before my eyes there quivered a horrible monster worthy of a place among the most farfetched teratological legends.

It was a squid of colossal dimensions, fully eight meters long. It was traveling backward with tremendous speed in the same direction as the Nautilus. It gazed with enormous, staring eyes that were tinted sea green. Its eight arms (or more accurately, feet) were rooted in its head, which has earned these animals the name cephalopod; its arms stretched a distance twice the length of its body and were writhing like the serpentine hair of the Furies. You could plainly see its 250 suckers, arranged over the inner sides of its tentacles and shaped like semispheric capsules. Sometimes these suckers fastened onto the lounge window by creating vacuums against it. The monster's mouth—a beak made of horn and shaped like that of a parrot—opened and closed vertically. Its tongue, also of horn substance and armed with several rows of sharp teeth, would flicker out from between these genuine shears. What a freak of nature! A bird's beak on a mollusk! Its body was spindle–shaped and swollen in the middle, a fleshy mass that must have weighed 20,000 to 25,000 kilograms. Its unstable color would change with tremendous speed as the animal grew irritated, passing successively from bluish gray to reddish brown.

What was irritating this mollusk? No doubt the presence of the Nautilus, even more fearsome than itself, and which it couldn't grip with its mandibles or the suckers on its arms. And yet what monsters these devilfish are, what vitality our Creator has given them, what vigor in their movements, thanks to their owning a triple heart!

Sheer chance had placed us in the presence of this squid, and I didn't want to lose this opportunity to meticulously study such a cephalopod specimen. I overcame the horror that its appearance inspired in me, picked up a pencil, and began to sketch it.

"Perhaps this is the same as the Alecto's," Conseil said.

"Can't be," the Canadian replied, "because this one's complete while the other one lost its tail!"

"That doesn't necessarily follow," I said. "The arms and tails of these animals grow back through regeneration, and in seven years the tail on Bouguer's Squid has surely had time to sprout again."

"Anyhow," Ned shot back, "if it isn't this fellow, maybe it's one of those!"

Indeed, other devilfish had appeared at the starboard window. I counted seven of them. They provided the Nautilus with an escort, and I could hear their beaks gnashing on the sheet–iron hull. We couldn't have asked for a more devoted following.

I continued sketching. These monsters kept pace in our waters with such precision, they seemed to be standing still, and I could have traced their outlines in miniature on the window. But we were moving at a moderate speed.

All at once the Nautilus stopped. A jolt made it tremble through its entire framework.

"Did we strike bottom?" I asked.

"In any event we're already clear," the Canadian replied, "because we're afloat."

The Nautilus was certainly afloat, but it was no longer in motion. The blades of its propeller weren't churning the waves. A minute passed. Followed by his chief officer, Captain Nemo entered the lounge.

I hadn't seen him for a good while. He looked gloomy to me. Without speaking to us, without even seeing us perhaps, he went to the panel, stared at the devilfish, and said a few words to his chief officer.

The latter went out. Soon the panels closed. The ceiling lit up.

I went over to the captain.

"An unusual assortment of devilfish," I told him, as carefree as a collector in front of an aquarium.

"Correct, Mr. Naturalist," he answered me, "and we're going to fight them at close quarters."

I gaped at the captain. I thought my hearing had gone bad.

"At close quarters?" I repeated.

"Yes, sir. Our propeller is jammed. I think the horn–covered mandibles of one of these squid are entangled in the blades. That's why we aren't moving."

"And what are you going to do?"

"Rise to the surface and slaughter the vermin."

"A difficult undertaking."

"Correct. Our electric bullets are ineffective against such soft flesh, where they don't meet enough resistance to go off. But we'll attack the beasts with axes."

"And harpoons, sir," the Canadian said, "if you don't turn down my help."

"I accept it, Mr. Land."

"We'll go with you," I said. And we followed Captain Nemo, heading to the central companionway.

There some ten men were standing by for the assault, armed with boarding axes. Conseil and I picked up two more axes. Ned Land seized a harpoon.

By then the Nautilus had returned to the surface of the waves. Stationed on the top steps, one of the seamen undid the bolts of the hatch. But he had scarcely unscrewed the nuts when the hatch flew up with tremendous violence, obviously pulled open by the suckers on a devilfish's arm.

Instantly one of those long arms glided like a snake into the opening, and twenty others were quivering above. With a sweep of the ax, Captain Nemo chopped off this fearsome tentacle, which slid writhing down the steps.

Just as we were crowding each other to reach the platform, two more arms lashed the air, swooped on the seaman stationed in front of Captain Nemo, and carried the fellow away with irresistible violence.

Captain Nemo gave a shout and leaped outside. We rushed after him.

What a scene! Seized by the tentacle and glued to its suckers, the unfortunate man was swinging in the air at the mercy of this enormous appendage. He gasped, he choked, he yelled: "Help! Help!" These words, pronounced in French, left me deeply stunned! So I had a fellow countryman on board, perhaps several! I'll hear his harrowing plea the rest of my life!

The poor fellow was done for. Who could tear him from such a powerful grip? Even so, Captain Nemo rushed at the devilfish and with a sweep of the ax hewed one more of its arms. His chief officer struggled furiously with other monsters crawling up the Nautilus's sides. The crew battled with flailing axes. The Canadian, Conseil, and I sank our weapons into these fleshy masses. An intense, musky odor filled the air. It was horrible.

For an instant I thought the poor man entwined by the devilfish might be torn loose from its powerful suction. Seven arms out of eight had been chopped off. Brandishing its victim like a feather, one lone tentacle was writhing in the air. But just as Captain Nemo and his chief officer rushed at it, the animal shot off a spout of blackish liquid, secreted by a pouch located in its abdomen. It blinded us. When this cloud had dispersed, the squid was gone, and so was my poor fellow countryman!

What rage then drove us against these monsters! We lost all self–control. Ten or twelve devilfish had overrun the Nautilus's platform and sides. We piled helter–skelter into the thick of these sawed–off snakes, which darted over the platform amid waves of blood and sepia ink. It seemed as if these viscous tentacles grew back like the many heads of Hydra. At every thrust Ned Land's harpoon would plunge into a squid's sea–green eye and burst it. But my daring companion was suddenly toppled by the tentacles of a monster he could not avoid.

Oh, my heart nearly exploded with excitement and horror! The squid's fearsome beak was wide open over Ned Land. The poor man was about to be cut in half. I ran to his rescue. But Captain Nemo got there first. His ax disappeared between the two enormous mandibles, and the Canadian, miraculously saved, stood and plunged his harpoon all the way into the devilfish's triple heart.

"Tit for tat," Captain Nemo told the Canadian. "I owed it to myself!"

Ned bowed without answering him.

This struggle had lasted a quarter of an hour. Defeated, mutilated, battered to death, the monsters finally yielded to us and disappeared beneath the waves.

Red with blood, motionless by the beacon, Captain Nemo stared at the sea that had swallowed one of his companions, and large tears streamed from his eyes.

The Gulf Stream

THIS DREADFUL SCENE on April 20 none of us will ever be able to forget. I wrote it up in a state of intense excitement. Later I reviewed my narrative. I read it to Conseil and the Canadian. They found it accurate in detail but deficient in impact. To convey such sights, it would take the pen of our most famous poet, Victor Hugo, author of The Toilers of the Sea.

As I said, Captain Nemo wept while staring at the waves. His grief was immense. This was the second companion he had lost since we had come aboard. And what a way to die! Smashed, strangled, crushed by the fearsome arms of a devilfish, ground between its iron mandibles, this friend would never rest with his companions in the placid waters of their coral cemetery!

As for me, what had harrowed my heart in the thick of this struggle was the despairing yell given by this unfortunate man. Forgetting his regulation language, this poor Frenchman had reverted to speaking his own mother tongue to fling out one supreme plea! Among the Nautilus's crew, allied body and soul with Captain Nemo and likewise fleeing from human contact, I had found a fellow countryman! Was he the only representative of France in this mysterious alliance, obviously made up of individuals from different nationalities? This was just one more of those insoluble problems that kept welling up in my mind!

Captain Nemo reentered his stateroom, and I saw no more of him for a good while. But how sad, despairing, and irresolute he must have felt, to judge from this ship whose soul he was, which reflected his every mood! The Nautilus no longer kept to a fixed heading. It drifted back and forth, riding with the waves like a corpse. Its propeller had been disentangled but was barely put to use. It was navigating at random. It couldn't tear itself away from the setting of this last struggle, from this sea that had devoured one of its own!

Ten days went by in this way. It was only on May 1 that the Nautilus openly resumed its northbound course, after raising the Bahamas at the mouth of Old Bahama Channel. We then went with the current of the sea's greatest river, which has its own banks, fish, and temperature. I mean the Gulf Stream.

It is indeed a river that runs independently through the middle of the Atlantic, its waters never mixing with the ocean's waters. It's a salty river, saltier than the sea surrounding it. Its average depth is 3,000 feet, its average width sixty miles. In certain localities its current moves at a speed of four kilometers per hour. The unchanging volume of its waters is greater than that of all the world's rivers combined.

As discovered by Commander Maury, the true source of the Gulf Stream, its starting point, if you prefer, is located in the Bay of Biscay. There its waters, still weak in temperature and color, begin to form. It goes down south, skirts equatorial Africa, warms its waves in the rays of the Torrid Zone, crosses the Atlantic, reaches Cape São Roque on the coast of Brazil, and forks into two branches, one going to the Caribbean Sea for further saturation with heat particles. Then, entrusted with restoring the balance between hot and cold temperatures and with mixing tropical and northern waters, the Gulf Stream begins to play its stabilizing role. Attaining a white heat in the Gulf of Mexico, it heads north up the American coast, advances as far as Newfoundland, swerves away under the thrust of a cold current from the Davis Strait, and resumes its ocean course by going along a great circle of the earth on a rhumb line; it then divides into two arms near the 43rd parallel; one, helped by the northeast trade winds, returns to the Bay of Biscay and the Azores; the other washes the shores of Ireland and Norway with lukewarm water, goes beyond Spitzbergen, where its temperature falls to 4° centigrade, and fashions the open sea at the pole.

It was on this oceanic river that the Nautilus was then navigating. Leaving Old Bahama Channel, which is fourteen leagues wide by 350 meters deep, the Gulf Stream moves at the rate of eight kilometers per hour. Its speed steadily decreases as it advances northward, and we must pray that this steadiness continues, because, as experts agree, if its speed and direction were to change, the climates of Europe would undergo disturbances whose consequences are incalculable.

Near noon I was on the platform with Conseil. I shared with him the relevant details on the Gulf Stream. When my explanation was over, I invited him to dip his hands into its current.

Conseil did so, and he was quite astonished to experience no sensation of either hot or cold.

"That comes," I told him, "from the water temperature of the Gulf Stream, which, as it leaves the Gulf of Mexico, is barely different from your blood temperature. This Gulf Stream is a huge heat generator that enables the coasts of Europe to be decked in eternal greenery. And if Commander Maury is correct, were one to harness the full warmth of this current, it would supply enough heat to keep molten a river of iron solder as big as the Amazon or the Missouri."

Just then the Gulf Stream's speed was 2.25 meters per second. So distinct is its current from the surrounding sea, its confined waters stand out against the ocean and operate on a different level from the colder waters. Murky as well, and very rich in saline material, their pure indigo contrasts with the green waves surrounding them. Moreover, their line of demarcation is so clear that abreast of the Carolinas, the Nautilus's spur cut the waves of the Gulf Stream while its propeller was still churning those belonging to the ocean.

This current swept along with it a whole host of moving creatures. Argonauts, so common in the Mediterranean, voyaged here in schools of large numbers. Among cartilaginous fish, the most remarkable were rays whose ultra slender tails made up nearly a third of the body, which was shaped like a huge diamond twenty–five feet long; then little one–meter sharks, the head large, the snout short and rounded, the teeth sharp and arranged in several rows, the body seemingly covered with scales.

Among bony fish, I noted grizzled wrasse unique to these seas, deep–water gilthead whose iris has a fiery gleam, one–meter croakers whose large mouths bristle with small teeth and which let out thin cries, black rudderfish like those I've already discussed, blue dorados accented with gold and silver, rainbow–hued parrotfish that can rival the loveliest tropical birds in coloring, banded blennies with triangular heads, bluish flounder without scales, toadfish covered with a crosswise yellow band in the shape of a □, swarms of little freckled gobies stippled with brown spots, lungfish with silver heads and yellow tails, various specimens of salmon, mullet with slim figures and a softly glowing radiance that Lacépède dedicated to the memory of his wife, and finally the American cavalla, a handsome fish decorated by every honorary order, bedizened with their every ribbon, frequenting the shores of this great nation where ribbons and orders are held in such low esteem.

I might add that during the night, the Gulf Stream's phosphorescent waters rivaled the electric glow of our beacon, especially in the stormy weather that frequently threatened us.

On May 8, while abreast of North Carolina, we were across from Cape Hatteras once more. There the Gulf Stream is seventy–five miles wide and 210 meters deep. The Nautilus continued to wander at random. Seemingly, all supervision had been jettisoned. Under these conditions I admit that we could easily have gotten away. In fact, the populous shores offered ready refuge everywhere. The sea was plowed continuously by the many steamers providing service between the Gulf of Mexico and New York or Boston, and it was crossed night and day by little schooners engaged in coastal trade over various points on the American shore. We could hope to be picked up. So it was a promising opportunity, despite the thirty miles that separated the Nautilus from these Union coasts.

But one distressing circumstance totally thwarted the Canadian's plans. The weather was thoroughly foul. We were approaching waterways where storms are commonplace, the very homeland of tornadoes and cyclones specifically engendered by the Gulf Stream's current. To face a frequently raging sea in a frail skiff was a race to certain disaster. Ned Land conceded this himself. So he champed at the bit, in the grip of an intense homesickness that could be cured only by our escape.

"Sir," he told me that day, "it's got to stop. I want to get to the bottom of this. Your Nemo's veering away from shore and heading up north. But believe you me, I had my fill at the South Pole and I'm not going with him to the North Pole."

"What can we do, Ned, since it isn't feasible to escape right now?"

"I keep coming back to my idea. We've got to talk to the captain. When we were in your own country's seas, you didn't say a word. Now that we're in mine, I intend to speak up. Before a few days are out, I figure the Nautilus will lie abreast of Nova Scotia, and from there to Newfoundland is the mouth of a large gulf, and the St. Lawrence empties into that gulf, and the St. Lawrence is my own river, the river running by Quebec, my hometown—and when I think about all this, my gorge rises and my hair stands on end! Honestly, sir, I'd rather jump overboard! I can't stay here any longer! I'm suffocating!"

The Canadian was obviously at the end of his patience. His vigorous nature couldn't adapt to this protracted imprisonment. His facial appearance was changing by the day. His moods grew gloomier and gloomier. I had a sense of what he was suffering because I also was gripped by homesickness. Nearly seven months had gone by without our having any news from shore. Moreover, Captain Nemo's reclusiveness, his changed disposition, and especially his total silence since the battle with the devilfish all made me see things in a different light. I no longer felt the enthusiasm of our first days on board. You needed to be Flemish like Conseil to accept these circumstances, living in a habitat designed for cetaceans and other denizens of the deep. Truly, if that gallant lad had owned gills instead of lungs, I think he would have made an outstanding fish!

"Well, sir?" Ned Land went on, seeing that I hadn't replied.

"Well, Ned, you want me to ask Captain Nemo what he intends to do with us?"

"Yes, sir."

"Even though he has already made that clear?"

"Yes. I want it settled once and for all. Speak just for me, strictly on my behalf, if you want."

"But I rarely encounter him. He positively avoids me."

"All the more reason you should go look him up."

"I'll confer with him, Ned."

"When?" the Canadian asked insistently.

"When I encounter him."

"Professor Aronnax, would you like me to go find him myself?"

"No, let me do it. Tomorrow—"

"Today," Ned Land said.

"So be it. I'll see him today," I answered the Canadian, who, if he took action himself, would certainly have ruined everything.

I was left to myself. His request granted, I decided to dispose of it immediately. I like things over and done with.

I reentered my stateroom. From there I could hear movements inside Captain Nemo's quarters. I couldn't pass up this chance for an encounter. I knocked on his door. I received no reply. I knocked again, then tried the knob. The door opened.

I entered. The captain was there. He was bending over his worktable and hadn't heard me. Determined not to leave without questioning him, I drew closer. He looked up sharply, with a frowning brow, and said in a pretty stern tone:

"Oh, it's you! What do you want?"

"To speak with you, Captain."

"But I'm busy, sir, I'm at work. I give you the freedom to enjoy your privacy, can't I have the same for myself?"

This reception was less than encouraging. But I was determined to give as good as I got.

"Sir," I said coolly, "I need to speak with you on a matter that simply can't wait."

"Whatever could that be, sir?" he replied sarcastically. "Have you made some discovery that has escaped me? Has the sea yielded up some novel secret to you?"

We were miles apart. But before I could reply, he showed me a manuscript open on the table and told me in a more serious tone:

"Here, Professor Aronnax, is a manuscript written in several languages. It contains a summary of my research under the sea, and God willing, it won't perish with me. Signed with my name, complete with my life story, this manuscript will be enclosed in a small, unsinkable contrivance. The last surviving man on the Nautilus will throw this contrivance into the sea, and it will go wherever the waves carry it."

The man's name! His life story written by himself! So the secret of his existence might someday be unveiled? But just then I saw this announcement only as a lead-in to my topic.

"Captain," I replied, "I'm all praise for this idea you're putting into effect. The fruits of your research must not be lost. But the methods you're using strike me as primitive. Who knows where the winds will take that contrivance, into whose hands it may fall? Can't you find something better? Can't you or one of your men—"

"Never, sir," the captain said, swiftly interrupting me.

"But my companions and I would be willing to safeguard this manuscript, and if you give us back our freedom—"

"Your freedom!" Captain Nemo put in, standing up.

"Yes, sir, and that's the subject on which I wanted to confer with you. For seven months we've been aboard your vessel, and I ask you today, in the name of my companions as well as myself, if you intend to keep us here forever."

"Professor Aronnax," Captain Nemo said, "I'll answer you today just as I did seven months ago: whomever boards the Nautilus must never leave it."

"What you're inflicting on us is outright slavery!"

"Call it anything you like."

"But every slave has the right to recover his freedom! By any worthwhile, available means!"

"Who has denied you that right?" Captain Nemo replied. "Did I ever try to bind you with your word of honor?"

The captain stared at me, crossing his arms.

"Sir," I told him, "to take up this subject a second time would be distasteful to both of us. So let's finish what we've started. I repeat: it isn't just for myself that I raise this issue. To me, research is a relief, a potent diversion, an enticement, a passion that can make me forget everything else. Like you, I'm a man neglected and unknown, living in the faint hope that someday I can pass on to future generations the fruits of my labors—figuratively speaking, by means of some contrivance left to the luck of winds and waves. In short, I can admire you and comfortably go with you while playing a role I only partly understand; but I still catch glimpses of other aspects of your life that are surrounded by involvements and secrets that, alone on board, my companions and I can't share. And even when our hearts could beat with yours, moved by some of your griefs or stirred by your deeds of courage and genius, we've had to stifle even the slightest token of that sympathy that arises at the sight of something fine and good, whether it comes from friend or enemy. All right then! It's this feeling of being alien to your deepest concerns that makes our situation unacceptable, impossible, even impossible for me but especially for Ned Land. Every man, by virtue of his very humanity, deserves fair treatment. Have you considered how a love of freedom and hatred of slavery could lead to plans of vengeance in a temperament like the Canadian's, what he might think, attempt, endeavor . . . ?"

I fell silent. Captain Nemo stood up.

"Ned Land can think, attempt, or endeavor anything he wants, what difference is it to me? I didn't go looking for him! I don't keep him on board for my pleasure! As for you, Professor Aronnax, you're a man able to understand anything, even silence. I have nothing more to say to you. Let this first time you've come to discuss this subject also be the last, because a second time I won't even listen."

I withdrew. From that day forward our position was very strained. I reported this conversation to my two companions.

"Now we know," Ned said, "that we can't expect a thing from this man. The Nautilus is nearing Long Island. We'll escape, no matter what the weather."

But the skies became more and more threatening. There were conspicuous signs of a hurricane on the way. The atmosphere was turning white and milky. Slender sheaves of cirrus clouds were followed on the horizon by layers of nimbocumulus. Other low clouds fled swiftly. The sea grew towering, inflated by long swells. Every bird had disappeared except a few petrels, friends of the storms. The barometer fell significantly, indicating a tremendous tension in the surrounding haze. The mixture in our stormglass decomposed under the influence of the electricity charging the air. A struggle of the elements was approaching.

The storm burst during the daytime of May 13, just as the Nautilus was cruising abreast of Long Island, a few miles from the narrows to Upper New York Bay. I'm able to describe this struggle of the elements because Captain Nemo didn't flee into the ocean depths; instead, from some inexplicable whim, he decided to brave it out on the surface.

The wind was blowing from the southwest, initially a stiff breeze, in other words, with a speed of fifteen meters per second, which built to twenty–five meters near three o'clock in the afternoon. This is the figure for major storms.

Unshaken by these squalls, Captain Nemo stationed himself on the platform. He was lashed around the waist to withstand the monstrous breakers foaming over the deck. I hoisted and attached myself to the same place, dividing my wonderment between the storm and this incomparable man who faced it head–on.

The raging sea was swept with huge tattered clouds drenched by the waves. I saw no more of the small intervening billows that form in the troughs of the big crests. Just long, soot–colored undulations with crests so compact they didn't foam. They kept growing taller. They were spurring each other on. The Nautilus, sometimes lying on its side, sometimes standing on end like a mast, rolled and pitched frightfully.

Near five o'clock a torrential rain fell, but it lulled neither wind nor sea. The hurricane was unleashed at a speed of forty–five meters per second, hence almost forty leagues per hour. Under these conditions houses topple, roof tiles puncture doors, iron railings snap in two, and twenty–four–pounder cannons relocate. And yet in the midst of this turmoil, the Nautilus lived up to that saying of an expert engineer: "A well–constructed hull can defy any sea!" This submersible was no resisting rock that waves could demolish; it was a steel spindle, obediently in motion, without rigging or masting, and able to brave their fury with impunity.

Meanwhile I was carefully examining these unleashed breakers. They measured up to fifteen meters in height over a length of 150 to 175 meters, and the speed of their propagation (half that of the wind) was fifteen meters per second. Their volume and power increased with the depth of the waters. I then understood the role played by these waves, which trap air in their flanks and release it in the depths of the sea where its oxygen brings life. Their utmost pressure—it has been calculated—can build to 3,000 kilograms on every square foot of surface they strike. It was such waves in the Hebrides that repositioned a stone block weighing 84,000 pounds. It was their relatives in the tidal wave on December 23, 1854, that toppled part of the Japanese city of Tokyo, then went that same day at 700 kilometers per hour to break on the beaches of America.

After nightfall the storm grew in intensity. As in the 1860 cyclone on Réunion Island, the barometer fell to 710 millimeters. At the close of day, I saw a big ship passing on the horizon, struggling painfully. It lay to at half steam in an effort to hold steady on the waves. It must have been a steamer on one of those lines out of New York to Liverpool or Le Havre. It soon vanished into the shadows.

At ten o'clock in the evening, the skies caught on fire. The air was streaked with violent flashes of lightning. I couldn't stand this brightness, but Captain Nemo stared straight at it, as if to inhale the spirit of the storm. A dreadful noise filled the air, a complicated noise made up of the roar of crashing breakers, the howl of the wind, claps of thunder. The wind shifted to every point of the horizon, and the cyclone left the east to return there after passing through north, west, and south, moving in the opposite direction of revolving storms in the southern hemisphere.

Oh, that Gulf Stream! It truly lives up to its nickname, the Lord of Storms! All by itself it creates these fearsome cyclones through the difference in temperature between its currents and the superimposed layers of air.

The rain was followed by a downpour of fire. Droplets of water changed into exploding tufts. You would have thought Captain Nemo was courting a death worthy of himself, seeking to be struck by lightning. In one hideous pitching movement, the Nautilus reared its steel spur into the air like a lightning rod, and I saw long sparks shoot down it.

Shattered, at the end of my strength, I slid flat on my belly to the hatch. I opened it and went below to the lounge. By then the storm had reached its maximum intensity. It was impossible to stand upright inside the Nautilus.

Captain Nemo reentered near midnight. I could hear the ballast tanks filling little by little, and the Nautilus sank gently beneath the surface of the waves.

Through the lounge's open windows, I saw large, frightened fish passing like phantoms in the fiery waters. Some were struck by lightning right before my eyes!

The Nautilus kept descending. I thought it would find calm again at fifteen meters down. No. The upper strata were too violently agitated. It needed to sink to fifty meters, searching for a resting place in the bowels of the sea.

But once there, what tranquility we found, what silence, what peace all around us! Who would have known that a dreadful hurricane was then unleashed on the surface of this ocean?

In Latitude 47° 24' and Longitude 17° 28'

IN THE AFTERMATH of this storm, we were thrown back to the east. Away went any hope of escaping to the landing places of New York or the St. Lawrence. In despair, poor Ned went into seclusion like Captain Nemo. Conseil and I no longer left each other.

As I said, the Nautilus veered to the east. To be more accurate, I should have said to the northeast. Sometimes on the surface of the waves, sometimes beneath them, the ship wandered for days amid these mists so feared by navigators. These are caused chiefly by melting ice, which keeps the air extremely damp. How many ships have perished in these waterways as they tried to get directions from the hazy lights on the coast! How many casualties have been caused by these opaque mists! How many collisions have occurred with these reefs, where the breaking surf is covered by the noise of the wind! How many vessels have rammed each other, despite their running lights, despite the warnings given by their bosun's pipes and alarm bells!

So the floor of this sea had the appearance of a battlefield where every ship defeated by the ocean still lay, some already old and encrusted, others newer and reflecting our beacon light on their ironwork and copper undersides. Among these vessels, how many went down with all hands, with their crews and hosts of immigrants, at these trouble spots so prominent in the statistics: Cape Race, St. Paul Island, the Strait of Belle Isle, the St. Lawrence estuary! And in only a few years, how many victims have been furnished to the obituary notices by the Royal Mail, Inman, and Montreal lines; by vessels named the Solway, the Isis, the Paramatta, the Hungarian, the Canadian, the Anglo–Saxon, the Humboldt, and the United States, all run aground; by the Arctic and the Lyonnais, sunk in collisions; by the President, the Pacific, and the City of Glasgow, lost for reasons unknown; in the midst of their gloomy rubble, the Nautilus navigated as if passing the dead in review!

By May 15 we were off the southern tip of the Grand Banks of Newfoundland. These banks are the result of marine sedimentation, an extensive accumulation of organic waste brought either from the equator by the Gulf Stream's current, or from the North Pole by the countercurrent of cold water that skirts the American coast. Here, too, erratically drifting chunks collect from the ice breakup. Here a huge boneyard forms from fish, mollusks, and zoophytes dying over it by the billions.

The sea is of no great depth at the Grand Banks. A few hundred fathoms at best. But to the south there is a deep, suddenly occurring depression, a

3,000–meter pit. Here the Gulf Stream widens. Its waters come to full bloom. It loses its speed and temperature, but it turns into a sea.

Among the fish that the Nautilus startled on its way, I'll mention a one–meter lumpfish, blackish on top with orange on the belly and rare among its brethren in that it practices monogamy, a good–sized eelpout, a type of emerald moray whose flavor is excellent, wolffish with big eyes in a head somewhat resembling a canine's, viviparous blennies whose eggs hatch inside their bodies like those of snakes, bloated gobio (or black gudgeon) measuring two decimeters, grenadiers with long tails and gleaming with a silvery glow, speedy fish venturing far from their High Arctic seas.

Our nets also hauled in a bold, daring, vigorous, and muscular fish armed with prickles on its head and stings on its fins, a real scorpion measuring two to three meters, the ruthless enemy of cod, blennies, and salmon; it was the bullhead of the northerly seas, a fish with red fins and a brown body covered with nodules. The Nautilus's fishermen had some trouble getting a grip on this animal, which, thanks to the formation of its gill covers, can protect its respiratory organs from any parching contact with the air and can live out of water for a good while.

And I'll mention—for the record—some little banded blennies that follow ships into the northernmost seas, sharp–snouted carp exclusive to the north Atlantic, scorpionfish, and lastly the gadoid family, chiefly the cod species, which I detected in their waters of choice over these inexhaustible Grand Banks.

Because Newfoundland is simply an underwater peak, you could call these cod mountain fish. While the Nautilus was clearing a path through their tight ranks, Conseil couldn't refrain from making this comment:

"Mercy, look at these cod!" he said. "Why, I thought cod were flat, like dab or sole!"

"Innocent boy!" I exclaimed. "Cod are flat only at the grocery store, where they're cut open and spread out on display. But in the water they're like mullet, spindle–shaped and perfectly built for speed."

"I can easily believe Master," Conseil replied. "But what crowds of them! What swarms!"

"Bah! My friend, there'd be many more without their enemies, scorpionfish and human beings! Do you know how many eggs have been counted in a single female?"

"I'll go all out," Conseil replied. "500,000."

"11,000,000, my friend."

"11,000,000! I refuse to accept that until I count them myself."

"So count them, Conseil. But it would be less work to believe me. Besides, Frenchmen, Englishmen, Americans, Danes, and Norwegians catch these cod by the thousands. They're eaten in prodigious quantities, and without the astonishing fertility of these fish, the seas would soon be depopulated of them.

Accordingly, in England and America alone, 5,000 ships manned by 75,000 seamen go after cod. Each ship brings back an average catch of 4,400 fish, making 22,000,000. Off the coast of Norway, the total is the same."

"Fine," Conseil replied, "I'll take Master's word for it. I won't count them."

"Count what?"

"Those 11,000,000 eggs. But I'll make one comment."

"What's that?"

"If all their eggs hatched, just four codfish could feed England, America, and Norway."

As we skimmed the depths of the Grand Banks, I could see perfectly those long fishing lines, each armed with 200 hooks, that every boat dangled by the dozens. The lower end of each line dragged the bottom by means of a small grappling iron, and at the surface it was secured to the buoy–rope of a cork float. The Nautilus had to maneuver shrewdly in the midst of this underwater spiderweb.

But the ship didn't stay long in these heavily traveled waterways. It went up to about latitude 42°. This brought it abreast of St. John's in Newfoundland and Heart's Content, where the Atlantic Cable reaches its end point.

Instead of continuing north, the Nautilus took an easterly heading, as if to go along this plateau on which the telegraph cable rests, where multiple soundings have given the contours of the terrain with the utmost accuracy.

It was on May 17, about 500 miles from Heart's Content and 2,800 meters down, that I spotted this cable lying on the seafloor. Conseil, whom I hadn't alerted, mistook it at first for a gigantic sea snake and was gearing up to classify it in his best manner. But I enlightened the fine lad and let him down gently by giving him various details on the laying of this cable.

The first cable was put down during the years 1857–1858; but after transmitting about 400 telegrams, it went dead. In 1863 engineers built a new cable that measured 3,400 kilometers, weighed 4,500 metric tons, and was shipped aboard the Great Eastern. This attempt also failed.

Now then, on May 25 while submerged to a depth of 3,836 meters, the Nautilus lay in precisely the locality where this second cable suffered the rupture that ruined the undertaking. It happened 638 miles from the coast of Ireland. At around two o'clock in the afternoon, all contact with Europe broke off. The electricians on board decided to cut the cable before fishing it up, and by eleven o'clock that evening they had retrieved the damaged part. They repaired the joint and its splice; then the cable was resubmerged. But a few days later it snapped again and couldn't be recovered from the ocean depths.

These Americans refused to give up. The daring Cyrus Field, who had risked his whole fortune to promote this undertaking, called for a new bond issue. It sold out immediately. Another cable was put down under better conditions. Its sheaves of conducting wire were insulated within a gutta–percha covering, which was protected by a padding of textile material enclosed in a metal sheath. The Great Eastern put back to sea on July 13, 1866.

The operation proceeded apace. Yet there was one hitch. As they gradually unrolled this third cable, the electricians observed on several occasions that someone had recently driven nails into it, trying to damage its core. Captain Anderson, his officers, and the engineers put their heads together, then posted a warning that if the culprit were detected, he would be thrown overboard without a trial. After that, these villainous attempts were not repeated.

By July 23 the Great Eastern was lying no farther than 800 kilometers from Newfoundland when it received telegraphed news from Ireland of an armistice signed between Prussia and Austria after the Battle of Sadova. Through the mists on the 27th, it sighted the port of Heart's Content. The undertaking had ended happily, and in its first dispatch, young America addressed old Europe with these wise words so rarely understood: "Glory to God in the highest, and peace on earth to men of good will."

I didn't expect to find this electric cable in mint condition, as it looked on leaving its place of manufacture. The long snake was covered with seashell rubble and bristling with foraminifera; a crust of caked gravel protected it from any mollusks that might bore into it. It rested serenely, sheltered from the sea's motions, under a pressure favorable to the transmission of that electric spark that goes from America to Europe in 32/100 of a second. This cable will no doubt last indefinitely because, as observers note, its gutta–percha casing is improved by a stay in salt water.

Besides, on this well–chosen plateau, the cable never lies at depths that could cause a break. The Nautilus followed it to its lowest reaches, located 4,431 meters down, and even there it rested without any stress or strain. Then we returned to the locality where the 1863 accident had taken place.

There the ocean floor formed a valley 120 kilometers wide, into which you could fit Mt. Blanc without its summit poking above the surface of the waves. This valley is closed off to the east by a sheer wall 2,000 meters high. We arrived there on May 28, and the Nautilus lay no farther than 150 kilometers from Ireland.

Would Captain Nemo head up north and beach us on the British Isles? No. Much to my surprise, he went back down south and returned to European seas. As we swung around the Emerald Isle, I spotted Cape Clear for an instant, plus the lighthouse on Fastnet Rock that guides all those thousands of ships setting out from Glasgow or Liverpool.

An important question then popped into my head. Would the Nautilus dare to tackle the English Channel? Ned Land (who promptly reappeared after we hugged shore) never stopped questioning me. What could I answer him? Captain

Nemo remained invisible. After giving the Canadian a glimpse of American shores, was he about to show me the coast of France?

But the Nautilus kept gravitating southward. On May 30, in sight of Land's End, it passed between the lowermost tip of England and the Scilly Islands, which it left behind to starboard.

If it was going to enter the English Channel, it clearly needed to head east. It did not.

All day long on May 31, the Nautilus swept around the sea in a series of circles that had me deeply puzzled. It seemed to be searching for a locality that it had some trouble finding. At noon Captain Nemo himself came to take our bearings. He didn't address a word to me. He looked gloomier than ever. What was filling him with such sadness? Was it our proximity to these European shores? Was he reliving his memories of that country he had left behind? If so, what did he feel? Remorse or regret? For a good while these thoughts occupied my mind, and I had a hunch that fate would soon give away the captain's secrets.

The next day, June 1, the Nautilus kept to the same tack. It was obviously trying to locate some precise spot in the ocean. Just as on the day before, Captain Nemo came to take the altitude of the sun. The sea was smooth, the skies clear. Eight miles to the east, a big steamship was visible on the horizon line. No flag was flapping from the gaff of its fore–and–aft sail, and I couldn't tell its nationality.

A few minutes before the sun passed its zenith, Captain Nemo raised his sextant and took his sights with the utmost precision. The absolute calm of the waves facilitated this operation. The Nautilus lay motionless, neither rolling nor pitching.

I was on the platform just then. After determining our position, the captain pronounced only these words:

"It's right here!"

He went down the hatch. Had he seen that vessel change course and seemingly head toward us? I'm unable to say.

I returned to the lounge. The hatch closed, and I heard water hissing in the ballast tanks. The Nautilus began to sink on a vertical line, because its propeller was in check and no longer furnished any forward motion.

Some minutes later it stopped at a depth of 833 meters and came to rest on the seafloor.

The ceiling lights in the lounge then went out, the panels opened, and through the windows I saw, for a half–mile radius, the sea brightly lit by the beacon's rays.

I looked to port and saw nothing but the immenseness of these tranquil waters.

To starboard, a prominent bulge on the sea bottom caught my attention. You would have thought it was some ruin enshrouded in a crust of whitened seashells, as if under a mantle of snow. Carefully examining this mass, I could identify the swollen outlines of a ship shorn of its masts, which must have sunk bow first. This casualty certainly dated from some far–off time. To be so caked with the limestone of these waters, this wreckage must have spent many a year on the ocean floor.

What ship was this? Why had the Nautilus come to visit its grave? Was it something other than a maritime accident that had dragged this craft under the waters?

I wasn't sure what to think, but next to me I heard Captain Nemo's voice slowly say:

"Originally this ship was christened the Marseillais. It carried seventy–four cannons and was launched in 1762. On August 13, 1778, commanded by La Poype–Vertrieux, it fought valiantly against the Preston. On July 4, 1779, as a member of the squadron under Admiral d'Estaing, it assisted in the capture of the island of Grenada. On September 5, 1781, under the Count de Grasse, it took part in the Battle of Chesapeake Bay. In 1794 the new Republic of France changed the name of this ship. On April 16 of that same year, it joined the squadron at Brest under Rear Admiral Villaret de Joyeuse, who was entrusted with escorting a convoy of wheat coming from America under the command of Admiral Van Stabel. In this second year of the French Revolutionary Calendar, on the 11th and 12th days in the Month of Pasture, this squadron fought an encounter with English vessels. Sir, today is June 1, 1868, or the 13th day in the Month of Pasture. Seventy–four years ago to the day, at this very spot in latitude 47° 24' and longitude 17° 28', this ship sank after a heroic battle; its three masts gone, water in its hold, a third of its crew out of action, it preferred to go to the bottom with its 356 seamen rather than surrender; and with its flag nailed up on the afterdeck, it disappeared beneath the waves to shouts of 'Long live the Republic!'"

"This is the Avenger!" I exclaimed.

"Yes, sir! The Avenger! A splendid name!" Captain Nemo murmured, crossing his arms.

A Mass Execution

THE WAY HE SAID THIS, the unexpectedness of this scene, first the biography of this patriotic ship, then the excitement with which this eccentric individual pronounced these last words—the name Avenger whose significance could not escape me—all this, taken together, had a profound impact on my mind. My eyes never left the captain. Hands outstretched toward the sea, he contemplated the proud wreck with blazing eyes. Perhaps I would never learn who he was, where he came from or where he was heading, but more and more I could see a distinction between the man and the scientist. It was no ordinary misanthropy that kept Captain Nemo and his companions sequestered inside the

Nautilus's plating, but a hate so monstrous or so sublime that the passing years could never weaken it.

Did this hate also hunger for vengeance? Time would soon tell.

Meanwhile the Nautilus rose slowly to the surface of the sea, and I watched the Avenger's murky shape disappearing little by little. Soon a gentle rolling told me that we were afloat in the open air.

Just then a hollow explosion was audible. I looked at the captain. The captain did not stir.

"Captain?" I said.

He didn't reply.

I left him and climbed onto the platform. Conseil and the Canadian were already there.

"What caused that explosion?" I asked.

"A cannon going off," Ned Land replied.

I stared in the direction of the ship I had spotted. It was heading toward the Nautilus, and you could tell it had put on steam. Six miles separated it from us.

"What sort of craft is it, Ned?"

"From its rigging and its low masts," the Canadian replied, "I bet it's a warship. Here's hoping it pulls up and sinks this damned Nautilus!"

"Ned my friend," Conseil replied, "what harm could it do the Nautilus? Will it attack us under the waves? Will it cannonade us at the bottom of the sea?"

"Tell me, Ned," I asked, "can you make out the nationality of that craft?"

Creasing his brow, lowering his lids, and puckering the corners of his eyes, the Canadian focused the full power of his gaze on the ship for a short while.

"No, sir," he replied. "I can't make out what nation it's from. It's flying no flag. But I'll swear it's a warship, because there's a long pennant streaming from the peak of its mainmast."

For a quarter of an hour, we continued to watch the craft bearing down on us. But it was inconceivable to me that it had discovered the Nautilus at such a distance, still less that it knew what this underwater machine really was.

Soon the Canadian announced that the craft was a big battleship, a double–decker ironclad complete with ram. Dark, dense smoke burst from its two funnels. Its furled sails merged with the lines of its yardarms. The gaff of its fore–and–aft sail flew no flag. Its distance still kept us from distinguishing the colors of its pennant, which was fluttering like a thin ribbon.

It was coming on fast. If Captain Nemo let it approach, a chance for salvation might be available to us.

"Sir," Ned Land told me, "if that boat gets within a mile of us, I'm jumping overboard, and I suggest you follow suit."

I didn't reply to the Canadian's proposition but kept watching the ship, which was looming larger on the horizon. Whether it was English, French, American, or Russian, it would surely welcome us aboard if we could just get to it.

"Master may recall," Conseil then said, "that we have some experience with swimming. He can rely on me to tow him to that vessel, if he's agreeable to going with our friend Ned."

Before I could reply, white smoke streamed from the battleship's bow. Then, a few seconds later, the waters splashed astern of the Nautilus, disturbed by the fall of a heavy object. Soon after, an explosion struck my ears.

"What's this? They're firing at us!" I exclaimed.

"Good lads!" the Canadian muttered.

"That means they don't see us as castaways clinging to some wreckage!"

"With all due respect to Master—gracious!" Conseil put in, shaking off the water that had sprayed over him from another shell. "With all due respect to master, they've discovered the narwhale and they're cannonading the same."

"But it must be clear to them," I exclaimed, "that they're dealing with human beings."

"Maybe that's why!" Ned Land replied, staring hard at me.

The full truth dawned on me. Undoubtedly people now knew where they stood on the existence of this so-called monster. Undoubtedly the latter's encounter with the Abraham Lincoln, when the Canadian hit it with his harpoon, had led Commander Farragut to recognize the narwhale as actually an underwater boat, more dangerous than any unearthly cetacean!

Yes, this had to be the case, and undoubtedly they were now chasing this dreadful engine of destruction on every sea!

Dreadful indeed, if, as we could assume, Captain Nemo had been using the Nautilus in works of vengeance! That night in the middle of the Indian Ocean, when he imprisoned us in the cell, hadn't he attacked some ship? That man now buried in the coral cemetery, wasn't he the victim of some collision caused by the Nautilus? Yes, I repeat: this had to be the case. One part of Captain Nemo's secret life had been unveiled. And now, even though his identity was still unknown, at least the nations allied against him knew they were no longer hunting some fairy–tale monster, but a man who had sworn an implacable hate toward them!

This whole fearsome sequence of events appeared in my mind's eye. Instead of encountering friends on this approaching ship, we would find only pitiless enemies.

Meanwhile shells fell around us in increasing numbers. Some, meeting the liquid surface, would ricochet and vanish into the sea at considerable distances. But none of them reached the Nautilus.

By then the ironclad was no more than three miles off. Despite its violent cannonade, Captain Nemo hadn't appeared on the platform. And yet if one of those conical shells had scored a routine hit on the Nautilus's hull, it could have been fatal to him.

The Canadian then told me:

"Sir, we've got to do everything we can to get out of this jam! Let's signal them! Damnation! Maybe they'll realize we're decent people!"

Ned Land pulled out his handkerchief to wave it in the air. But he had barely unfolded it when he was felled by an iron fist, and despite his great strength, he tumbled to the deck.

"Scum!" the captain shouted. "Do you want to be nailed to the Nautilus's spur before it charges that ship?"

Dreadful to hear, Captain Nemo was even more dreadful to see. His face was pale from some spasm of his heart, which must have stopped beating for an instant. His pupils were hideously contracted. His voice was no longer speaking, it was bellowing. Bending from the waist, he shook the Canadian by the shoulders.

Then, dropping Ned and turning to the battleship, whose shells were showering around him:

"O ship of an accursed nation, you know who I am!" he shouted in his powerful voice. "And I don't need your colors to recognize you! Look! I'll show you mine!"

And in the bow of the platform, Captain Nemo unfurled a black flag, like the one he had left planted at the South Pole.

Just then a shell hit the Nautilus's hull obliquely, failed to breach it, ricocheted near the captain, and vanished into the sea.

Captain Nemo shrugged his shoulders. Then, addressing me:

"Go below!" he told me in a curt tone. "You and your companions, go below!"

"Sir," I exclaimed, "are you going to attack this ship?"

"Sir, I'm going to sink it."

"You wouldn't!"

"I will," Captain Nemo replied icily. "You're ill–advised to pass judgment on me, sir. Fate has shown you what you weren't meant to see. The attack has come. Our reply will be dreadful. Get back inside!"

"From what country is that ship?"

"You don't know? Fine, so much the better! At least its nationality will remain a secret to you. Go below!"

The Canadian, Conseil, and I could only obey. Some fifteen of the Nautilus's seamen surrounded their captain and stared with a feeling of implacable hate at the ship bearing down on them. You could feel the same spirit of vengeance enkindling their every soul.

I went below just as another projectile scraped the Nautilus's hull, and I heard the captain exclaim:

"Shoot, you demented vessel! Shower your futile shells! You won't escape the Nautilus's spur! But this isn't the place where you'll perish! I don't want your wreckage mingling with that of the Avenger!"

I repaired to my stateroom. The captain and his chief officer stayed on the platform. The propeller was set in motion. The Nautilus swiftly retreated, putting us outside the range of the vessel's shells. But the chase continued, and Captain Nemo was content to keep his distance.

Near four o'clock in the afternoon, unable to control the impatience and uneasiness devouring me, I went back to the central companionway. The hatch was open. I ventured onto the platform. The captain was still strolling there, his steps agitated. He stared at the ship, which stayed to his leeward five or six miles off. He was circling it like a wild beast, drawing it eastward, letting it chase after him. Yet he didn't attack. Was he, perhaps, still undecided?

I tried to intervene one last time. But I had barely queried Captain Nemo when the latter silenced me:

"I'm the law, I'm the tribunal! I'm the oppressed, and there are my oppressors! Thanks to them, I've witnessed the destruction of everything I loved, cherished, and venerated—homeland, wife, children, father, and mother! There lies everything I hate! Not another word out of you!"

I took a last look at the battleship, which was putting on steam. Then I rejoined Ned and Conseil.

"We'll escape!" I exclaimed.

"Good," Ned put in. "Where's that ship from?"

"I've no idea. But wherever it's from, it will sink before nightfall. In any event, it's better to perish with it than be accomplices in some act of revenge whose merits we can't gauge."

"That's my feeling," Ned Land replied coolly. "Let's wait for nightfall."

Night fell. A profound silence reigned on board. The compass indicated that the Nautilus hadn't changed direction. I could hear the beat of its propeller, churning the waves with steady speed. Staying on the surface of the water, it rolled gently, sometimes to one side, sometimes to the other.

My companions and I had decided to escape as soon as the vessel came close enough for us to be heard—or seen, because the moon would wax full in three days and was shining brightly. Once we were aboard that ship, if we couldn't ward off the blow that threatened it, at least we could do everything that circumstances permitted. Several times I thought the Nautilus was about to attack. But it was content to let its adversary approach, and then it would quickly resume its retreating ways.

Part of the night passed without incident. We kept watch for an opportunity to take action. We talked little, being too keyed up. Ned Land was all for jumping overboard. I forced him to wait. As I saw it, the Nautilus would attack the double–decker on the surface of the waves, and then it would be not only possible but easy to escape.

At three o'clock in the morning, full of uneasiness, I climbed onto the platform. Captain Nemo hadn't left it. He stood in the bow next to his flag, which a mild breeze was unfurling above his head. His eyes never left that vessel. The extraordinary intensity of his gaze seemed to attract it, beguile it, and draw it more surely than if he had it in tow!

The moon then passed its zenith. Jupiter was rising in the east. In the midst of this placid natural setting, sky and ocean competed with each other in tranquility, and the sea offered the orb of night the loveliest mirror ever to reflect its image.

And when I compared this deep calm of the elements with all the fury seething inside the plating of this barely perceptible Nautilus, I shivered all over.

The vessel was two miles off. It drew nearer, always moving toward the phosphorescent glow that signaled the Nautilus's presence. I saw its green and red running lights, plus the white lantern hanging from the large stay of its foremast. Hazy flickerings were reflected on its rigging and indicated that its furnaces were pushed to the limit. Showers of sparks and cinders of flaming coal escaped from its funnels, spangling the air with stars.

I stood there until six o'clock in the morning, Captain Nemo never seeming to notice me. The vessel lay a mile and a half off, and with the first glimmers of daylight, it resumed its cannonade. The time couldn't be far away when the Nautilus would attack its adversary, and my companions and I would leave forever this man I dared not judge.

I was about to go below to alert them, when the chief officer climbed onto the platform. Several seamen were with him. Captain Nemo didn't see them, or didn't want to see them. They carried out certain procedures that, on the Nautilus, you could call "clearing the decks for action." They were quite simple. The manropes that formed a handrail around the platform were lowered. Likewise the pilothouse and the beacon housing were withdrawn into the hull until they lay exactly flush with it. The surface of this long sheet–iron cigar no longer offered a single protrusion that could hamper its maneuvers.

I returned to the lounge. The Nautilus still emerged above the surface. A few morning gleams infiltrated the liquid strata. Beneath the undulations of the billows, the windows were enlivened by the blushing of the rising sun. That dreadful day of June 2 had dawned.

At seven o'clock the log told me that the Nautilus had reduced speed. I realized that it was letting the warship approach. Moreover, the explosions grew more intensely audible. Shells furrowed the water around us, drilling through it with an odd hissing sound.

"My friends," I said, "it's time. Let's shake hands, and may God be with us!"

Ned Land was determined, Conseil calm, I myself nervous and barely in control.

We went into the library. Just as I pushed open the door leading to the well of the central companionway, I heard the hatch close sharply overhead.

The Canadian leaped up the steps, but I stopped him. A well–known hissing told me that water was entering the ship's ballast tanks. Indeed, in a few moments the Nautilus had submerged some meters below the surface of the waves.

I understood this maneuver. It was too late to take action. The Nautilus wasn't going to strike the double–decker where it was clad in impenetrable iron armor, but below its waterline, where the metal carapace no longer protected its planking.

We were prisoners once more, unwilling spectators at the performance of this gruesome drama. But we barely had time to think. Taking refuge in my stateroom, we stared at each other without pronouncing a word. My mind was in a total daze. My mental processes came to a dead stop. I hovered in that painful state that predominates during the period of anticipation before some frightful explosion. I waited, I listened, I lived only through my sense of hearing!

Meanwhile the Nautilus's speed had increased appreciably. So it was gathering momentum. Its entire hull was vibrating.

Suddenly I let out a yell. There had been a collision, but it was comparatively mild. I could feel the penetrating force of the steel spur. I could hear scratchings and scrapings. Carried away with its driving power, the Nautilus had passed through the vessel's mass like a sailmaker's needle through canvas!

I couldn't hold still. Frantic, going insane, I leaped out of my stateroom and rushed into the lounge.

Captain Nemo was there. Mute, gloomy, implacable, he was staring through the port panel.

An enormous mass was sinking beneath the waters, and the Nautilus, missing none of its death throes, was descending into the depths with it. Ten meters away, I could see its gaping hull, into which water was rushing with a sound of thunder, then its double rows of cannons and railings. Its deck was covered with dark, quivering shadows.

The water was rising. Those poor men leaped up into the shrouds, clung to the masts, writhed beneath the waters. It was a human anthill that an invading sea had caught by surprise!

Paralyzed, rigid with anguish, my hair standing on end, my eyes popping out of my head, short of breath, suffocating, speechless, I stared—I too! I was glued to the window by an irresistible allure!

The enormous vessel settled slowly. Following it down, the Nautilus kept watch on its every movement. Suddenly there was an eruption. The air compressed inside the craft sent its decks flying, as if the powder stores had been ignited. The thrust of the waters was so great, the Nautilus swerved away.

The poor ship then sank more swiftly. Its mastheads appeared, laden with victims, then its crosstrees bending under clusters of men, finally the peak of its mainmast. Then the dark mass disappeared, and with it a crew of corpses dragged under by fearsome eddies. . . .

I turned to Captain Nemo. This dreadful executioner, this true archangel of hate, was still staring. When it was all over, Captain Nemo headed to the door of his stateroom, opened it, and entered. I followed him with my eyes.

On the rear paneling, beneath the portraits of his heroes, I saw the portrait of a still–youthful woman with two little children. Captain Nemo stared at them for a few moments, stretched out his arms to them, sank to his knees, and melted into sobs.

The Last Words of Captain Nemo

THE PANELS CLOSED over this frightful view, but the lights didn't go on in the lounge. Inside the Nautilus all was gloom and silence. It left this place of devastation with prodigious speed, 100 feet beneath the waters. Where was it going? North or south? Where would the man flee after this horrible act of revenge?

I reentered my stateroom, where Ned and Conseil were waiting silently. Captain Nemo filled me with insurmountable horror. Whatever he had once suffered at the hands of humanity, he had no right to mete out such punishment. He had made me, if not an accomplice, at least an eyewitness to his vengeance! Even this was intolerable.

At eleven o'clock the electric lights came back on. I went into the lounge. It was deserted. I consulted the various instruments. The Nautilus was fleeing northward at a speed of twenty–five miles per hour, sometimes on the surface of the sea, sometimes thirty feet beneath it.

After our position had been marked on the chart, I saw that we were passing into the mouth of the English Channel, that our heading would take us to the northernmost seas with incomparable speed.

I could barely glimpse the swift passing of longnose sharks, hammerhead sharks, spotted dogfish that frequent these waters, big eagle rays, swarms of seahorse looking like knights on a chessboard, eels quivering like fireworks serpents, armies of crab that fled obliquely by crossing their pincers over their carapaces, finally schools of porpoise that held contests of speed with the Nautilus. But by this point observing, studying, and classifying were out of the question.

By evening we had cleared 200 leagues up the Atlantic. Shadows gathered and gloom overran the sea until the moon came up.

I repaired to my stateroom. I couldn't sleep. I was assaulted by nightmares. That horrible scene of destruction kept repeating in my mind's eye.

From that day forward, who knows where the Nautilus took us in the north Atlantic basin? Always at incalculable speed! Always amid the High Arctic mists! Did it call at the capes of Spitzbergen or the shores of Novaya Zemlya? Did it visit such uncharted seas as the White Sea, the Kara Sea, the Gulf of Ob, the Lyakhov Islands, or those unknown beaches on the Siberian coast? I'm unable to say. I lost track of the passing hours. Time was in abeyance on the ship's clocks. As happens in the polar regions, it seemed that night and day no longer followed their normal sequence. I felt myself being drawn into that strange domain where the overwrought imagination of Edgar Allan Poe was at home. Like his fabled Arthur Gordon Pym, I expected any moment to see that "shrouded human figure, very far larger in its proportions than any dweller among men," thrown across the cataract that protects the outskirts of the pole!

I estimate—but perhaps I'm mistaken—that the Nautilus's haphazard course continued for fifteen or twenty days, and I'm not sure how long this would have gone on without the catastrophe that ended our voyage. As for Captain Nemo, he was no longer in the picture. As for his chief officer, the same applied. Not one crewman was visible for a single instant. The Nautilus cruised beneath the waters almost continuously. When it rose briefly to the surface to renew our air, the hatches opened and closed as if automated. No more positions were reported on the world map. I didn't know where we were.

I'll also mention that the Canadian, at the end of his strength and patience, made no further appearances. Conseil couldn't coax a single word out of him and feared that, in a fit of delirium while under the sway of a ghastly homesickness, Ned would kill himself. So he kept a devoted watch on his friend every instant.

You can appreciate that under these conditions, our situation had become untenable.

One morning—whose date I'm unable to specify—I was slumbering near the first hours of daylight, a painful, sickly slumber. Waking up, I saw Ned Land leaning over me, and I heard him tell me in a low voice:

"We're going to escape!"

I sat up.

"When?" I asked.

"Tonight. There doesn't seem to be any supervision left on the Nautilus. You'd think a total daze was reigning on board. Will you be ready, sir?"

"Yes. Where are we?"

"In sight of land. I saw it through the mists just this morning, twenty miles to the east."

"What land is it?"

"I've no idea, but whatever it is, there we'll take refuge."

"Yes, Ned! We'll escape tonight even if the sea swallows us up!"

"The sea's rough, the wind's blowing hard, but a twenty–mile run in the Nautilus's nimble longboat doesn't scare me. Unknown to the crew, I've stowed some food and flasks of water inside."

"I'm with you."

"What's more," the Canadian added, "if they catch me, I'll defend myself, I'll fight to the death."

"Then we'll die together, Ned my friend."

My mind was made up. The Canadian left me. I went out on the platform, where I could barely stand upright against the jolts of the billows. The skies were threatening, but land lay inside those dense mists, and we had to escape. Not a single day, or even a single hour, could we afford to lose.

I returned to the lounge, dreading yet desiring an encounter with Captain Nemo, wanting yet not wanting to see him. What would I say to him? How could I hide the involuntary horror he inspired in me? No! It was best not to meet him face to face! Best to try and forget him! And yet . . . !

How long that day seemed, the last I would spend aboard the Nautilus! I was left to myself. Ned Land and Conseil avoided speaking to me, afraid they would give themselves away.

At six o'clock I ate supper, but I had no appetite. Despite my revulsion, I forced it down, wanting to keep my strength up.

At 6:30 Ned Land entered my stateroom. He told me:

"We won't see each other again before we go. At ten o'clock the moon won't be up yet. We'll take advantage of the darkness. Come to the skiff. Conseil and I will be inside waiting for you."

The Canadian left without giving me time to answer him.

I wanted to verify the Nautilus's heading. I made my way to the lounge. We were racing north–northeast with frightful speed, fifty meters down.

I took one last look at the natural wonders and artistic treasures amassed in the museum, this unrivaled collection doomed to perish someday in the depths of the seas, together with its curator. I wanted to establish one supreme impression in my mind. I stayed there an hour, basking in the aura of the ceiling lights, passing in review the treasures shining in their glass cases. Then I returned to my stateroom.

There I dressed in sturdy seafaring clothes. I gathered my notes and packed them tenderly about my person. My heart was pounding mightily. I couldn't curb its pulsations. My anxiety and agitation would certainly have given me away if Captain Nemo had seen me.

What was he doing just then? I listened at the door to his stateroom. I heard the sound of footsteps. Captain Nemo was inside. He hadn't gone to bed. With his every movement I imagined he would appear and ask me why I wanted to escape! I felt in a perpetual state of alarm. My imagination magnified this sensation. The feeling became so acute, I wondered whether it wouldn't be better to enter the captain's stateroom, dare him face to face, brave it out with word and deed!

It was an insane idea. Fortunately I controlled myself and stretched out on the bed to soothe my bodily agitation. My nerves calmed a little, but with my brain so aroused, I did a swift review of my whole existence aboard the Nautilus, every pleasant or unpleasant incident that had crossed my path since I went overboard from the Abraham Lincoln: the underwater hunting trip, the Torres Strait, our running aground, the savages of Papua, the coral cemetery, the Suez passageway, the island of Santorini, the Cretan diver, the Bay of Vigo, Atlantis, the Ice Bank, the South Pole, our imprisonment in the ice, the battle with the devilfish, the storm in the Gulf Stream, the Avenger, and that horrible scene of the vessel sinking with its crew . . . ! All these events passed before my eyes like backdrops unrolling upstage in a theater. In this strange setting Captain Nemo then grew fantastically. His features were accentuated, taking on superhuman proportions. He was no longer my equal, he was the Man of the Waters, the Spirit of the Seas.

By then it was 9:30. I held my head in both hands to keep it from bursting. I closed my eyes. I no longer wanted to think. A half hour still to wait! A half hour of nightmares that could drive me insane!

Just then I heard indistinct chords from the organ, melancholy harmonies from some undefinable hymn, actual pleadings from a soul trying to sever its earthly ties. I listened with all my senses at once, barely breathing, immersed like Captain Nemo in this musical trance that was drawing him beyond the bounds of this world.

Then a sudden thought terrified me. Captain Nemo had left his stateroom. He was in the same lounge I had to cross in order to escape. There I would encounter him one last time. He would see me, perhaps speak to me! One gesture from him could obliterate me, a single word shackle me to his vessel!

Even so, ten o'clock was about to strike. It was time to leave my stateroom and rejoin my companions.

I dared not hesitate, even if Captain Nemo stood before me. I opened the door cautiously, but as it swung on its hinges, it seemed to make a frightful noise. This noise existed, perhaps, only in my imagination!

I crept forward through the Nautilus's dark gangways, pausing after each step to curb the pounding of my heart.

I arrived at the corner door of the lounge. I opened it gently. The lounge was plunged in profound darkness. Chords from the organ were reverberating faintly. Captain Nemo was there. He didn't see me. Even in broad daylight I doubt that he would have noticed me, so completely was he immersed in his trance.

I inched over the carpet, avoiding the tiniest bump whose noise might give me away. It took me five minutes to reach the door at the far end, which led into the library.

I was about to open it when a gasp from Captain Nemo nailed me to the spot. I realized that he was standing up. I even got a glimpse of him because some rays of light from the library had filtered into the lounge. He was coming toward me, arms crossed, silent, not walking but gliding like a ghost. His chest was heaving, swelling with sobs. And I heard him murmur these words, the last of his to reach my ears:

"O almighty God! Enough! Enough!"

Was it a vow of repentance that had just escaped from this man's conscience . . . ?

Frantic, I rushed into the library. I climbed the central companionway, and going along the upper gangway, I arrived at the skiff. I went through the opening that had already given access to my two companions.

"Let's go, let's go!" I exclaimed.

"Right away!" the Canadian replied.

First, Ned Land closed and bolted the opening cut into the Nautilus's sheet iron, using the monkey wrench he had with him. After likewise closing the opening in the skiff, the Canadian began to unscrew the nuts still bolting us to the underwater boat.

Suddenly a noise from the ship's interior became audible. Voices were answering each other hurriedly. What was it? Had they spotted our escape? I felt Ned Land sliding a dagger into my hand.

"Yes," I muttered, "we know how to die!"

The Canadian paused in his work. But one word twenty times repeated, one dreadful word, told me the reason for the agitation spreading aboard the Nautilus. We weren't the cause of the crew's concern.

"Maelstrom! Maelstrom!" they were shouting.

The Maelstrom! Could a more frightening name have rung in our ears under more frightening circumstances? Were we lying in the dangerous waterways off the Norwegian coast? Was the Nautilus being dragged into this whirlpool just as the skiff was about to detach from its plating?

As you know, at the turn of the tide, the waters confined between the Faroe and Lofoten Islands rush out with irresistible violence. They form a vortex from which no ship has ever been able to escape. Monstrous waves race together from every point of the horizon. They form a whirlpool aptly called "the ocean's navel," whose attracting power extends a distance of fifteen kilometers. It can suck down not only ships but whales, and even polar bears from the northernmost regions.

This was where the Nautilus had been sent accidentally—or perhaps deliberately—by its captain. It was sweeping around in a spiral whose radius kept growing smaller and smaller. The skiff, still attached to the ship's plating, was likewise carried around at dizzying speed. I could feel us whirling. I was experiencing that accompanying nausea that follows such continuous spinning motions. We were in dread, in the last stages of sheer horror, our blood frozen in our veins, our nerves numb, drenched in cold sweat as if from the throes of dying! And what a noise around our frail skiff! What roars echoing from several miles away! What crashes from the waters breaking against sharp rocks on the seafloor, where the hardest objects are smashed, where tree trunks are worn down and worked into "a shaggy fur," as Norwegians express it!

What a predicament! We were rocking frightfully. The Nautilus defended itself like a human being. Its steel muscles were cracking. Sometimes it stood on end, the three of us along with it!

"We've got to hold on tight," Ned said, "and screw the nuts down again! If we can stay attached to the Nautilus, we can still make it . . . !"

He hadn't finished speaking when a cracking sound occurred. The nuts gave way, and ripped out of its socket, the skiff was hurled like a stone from a sling into the midst of the vortex.

My head struck against an iron timber, and with this violent shock I lost consciousness.

Conclusion

WE COME TO the conclusion of this voyage under the seas. What happened that night, how the skiff escaped from the Maelstrom's fearsome eddies, how Ned Land, Conseil, and I got out of that whirlpool, I'm unable to say. But when I regained consciousness, I was lying in a fisherman's hut on one of the Lofoten Islands. My two companions, safe and sound, were at my bedside clasping my hands. We embraced each other heartily.

Just now we can't even dream of returning to France. Travel between upper Norway and the south is limited. So I have to wait for the arrival of a steamboat that provides bimonthly service from North Cape.

So it is here, among these gallant people who have taken us in, that I'm reviewing my narrative of these adventures. It is accurate. Not a fact has been omitted, not a detail has been exaggerated. It's the faithful record of this inconceivable expedition into an element now beyond human reach, but where progress will someday make great inroads.

Will anyone believe me? I don't know. Ultimately it's unimportant. What I can now assert is that I've earned the right to speak of these seas, beneath which in less than ten months, I've cleared 20,000 leagues in this underwater tour of the world that has shown me so many wonders across the Pacific, the Indian Ocean, the Red Sea, the Mediterranean, the Atlantic, the southernmost and northernmost seas!

But what happened to the Nautilus? Did it withstand the Maelstrom's clutches? Is Captain Nemo alive? Is he still under the ocean pursuing his frightful program of revenge, or did he stop after that latest mass execution? Will the waves someday deliver that manuscript that contains his full life story? Will I finally learn the man's name? Will the nationality of the stricken warship tell us the nationality of Captain Nemo?

I hope so. I likewise hope that his powerful submersible has defeated the sea inside its most dreadful whirlpool, that the Nautilus has survived where so many ships have perished! If this is the case and Captain Nemo still inhabits the ocean—his adopted country—may the hate be appeased in that fierce heart! May the contemplation of so many wonders extinguish the spirit of vengeance in him! May the executioner pass away, and the scientist continue his peaceful exploration of the seas! If his destiny is strange, it's also sublime. Haven't I encompassed it myself? Didn't I lead ten months of this otherworldly existence? Thus to that question asked 6,000 years ago in the Book of Ecclesiastes—"Who can fathom the soundless depths?"—two men out of all humanity have now earned the right to reply. Captain Nemo and I.

The Mysterious Island

Part 1—Dropped from the Clouds

Chapter 1

"Are we rising again?" "No. On the contrary." "Are we descending?" "Worse than that, captain! we are falling!" "For Heaven's sake heave out the ballast!" "There! the last sack is empty!" "Does the balloon rise?" "No!" "I hear a noise like the dashing of waves. The sea is below the car! It cannot be more than 500 feet from us!" "Overboard with every weight! ... everything!"

Such were the loud and startling words which resounded through the air, above the vast watery desert of the Pacific, about four o'clock in the evening of the 23rd of March, 1865.

Few can possibly have forgotten the terrible storm from the northeast, in the middle of the equinox of that year. The tempest raged without intermission from the 18th to the 26th of March. Its ravages were terrible in America, Europe, and Asia, covering a distance of eighteen hundred miles, and extending obliquely to the equator from the thirty-fifth north parallel to the fortieth south parallel. Towns were overthrown, forests uprooted, coasts devastated by the mountains of water which were precipitated on them, vessels cast on the shore, which the published accounts numbered by hundreds, whole districts leveled by waterspouts which destroyed everything they passed over, several thousand people crushed on land or drowned at sea; such were the traces of its fury, left by this devastating tempest. It surpassed in disasters those which so frightfully ravaged Havana and Guadalupe, one on the 25th of October, 1810, the other on the 26th of July, 1825.

But while so many catastrophes were taking place on land and at sea, a drama not less exciting was being enacted in the agitated air.

In fact, a balloon, as a ball might be carried on the summit of a waterspout, had been taken into the circling movement of a column of air and had traversed space at the rate of ninety miles an hour, turning round and round as if seized by some aerial maelstrom.

Beneath the lower point of the balloon swung a car, containing five passengers, scarcely visible in the midst of the thick vapor mingled with spray which hung over the surface of the ocean.

Whence, it may be asked, had come that plaything of the tempest? From what part of the world did it rise? It surely could not have started during the storm. But the storm had raged five days already, and the first symptoms were manifested on the 18th. It cannot be doubted that the balloon came from a great distance, for it could not have traveled less than two thousand miles in twenty-four hours.

At any rate the passengers, destitute of all marks for their guidance, could not have possessed the means of reckoning the route traversed since their departure. It was a remarkable fact that, although in the very midst of the furious tempest, they did not suffer from it. They were thrown about and whirled round and round without feeling the rotation in the slightest degree, or being sensible that they were removed from a horizontal position.

Their eyes could not pierce through the thick mist which had gathered beneath the car. Dark vapor was all around them. Such was the density of the atmosphere that they could not be certain whether it was day or night. No reflection of light, no sound from inhabited land, no roaring of the ocean could have reached them, through the obscurity, while suspended in those elevated zones. Their rapid descent alone had informed them of the dangers which they ran from the waves. However, the balloon, lightened of heavy articles, such as ammunition, arms, and provisions, had risen into the higher layers of the atmosphere, to a height of 4,500 feet. The voyagers, after having discovered that the sea extended beneath them, and thinking the dangers above less dreadful than those below, did not hesitate to throw overboard even their most useful articles, while they endeavored to lose no more of that fluid, the life of their enterprise, which sustained them above the abyss.

The night passed in the midst of alarms which would have been death to less energetic souls. Again the day appeared and with it the tempest began to moderate. From the beginning of that day, the 24th of March, it showed symptoms of abating. At dawn, some of the lighter clouds had risen into the more lofty regions of the air. In a few hours the wind had changed from a hurricane to a fresh breeze, that is to say, the rate of the transit of the atmospheric layers was diminished by half. It was still what sailors call "a close-reefed topsail breeze," but the commotion in the elements had none the less considerably diminished.

Towards eleven o'clock, the lower region of the air was sensibly clearer. The atmosphere threw off that chilly dampness which is felt after the passage of a great meteor. The storm did not seem to have gone farther to the west. It appeared to have exhausted itself. Could it have passed away in electric sheets, as is sometimes the case with regard to the typhoons of the Indian Ocean?

But at the same time, it was also evident that the balloon was again slowly descending with a regular movement. It appeared as if it were, little by little, collapsing, and that its case was lengthening and extending, passing from a spherical to an oval form. Towards midday the balloon was hovering above the sea at a height of only 2,000 feet. It contained 50,000 cubic feet of gas, and, thanks to its capacity, it could maintain itself a long time in the air, although it should reach a great altitude or might be thrown into a horizontal position.

Perceiving their danger, the passengers cast away the last articles which still weighed down the car, the few provisions they had kept, everything, even to their pocket-knives, and one of them, having hoisted himself on to the circles which united the cords of the net, tried to secure more firmly the lower point of the balloon.

It was, however, evident to the voyagers that the gas was failing, and that the balloon could no longer be sustained in the higher regions. They must infallibly perish!

There was not a continent, nor even an island, visible beneath them. The watery expanse did not present a single speck of land, not a solid surface upon which their anchor could hold.

It was the open sea, whose waves were still dashing with tremendous violence! It was the ocean, without any visible limits, even for those whose gaze, from their commanding position, extended over a radius of forty miles. The vast liquid plain, lashed without mercy by the storm, appeared as if covered with herds of furious chargers, whose white and disheveled crests were streaming in the wind. No land was in sight, not a solitary ship could be seen. It was necessary at any cost to arrest their downward course, and to prevent the balloon from being engulfed in the waves. The voyagers directed all their energies to this urgent work. But, notwithstanding their efforts, the balloon still fell, and at the same time shifted with the greatest rapidity, following the direction of the wind, that is to say, from the northeast to the southwest.

Frightful indeed was the situation of these unfortunate men. They were evidently no longer masters of the machine. All their attempts were useless. The case of the balloon collapsed more and more. The gas escaped without any possibility of retaining it. Their descent was visibly accelerated, and soon after midday the car hung within 600 feet of the ocean.

It was impossible to prevent the escape of gas, which rushed through a large rent in the silk. By lightening the car of all the articles which it contained, the passengers had been able to prolong their suspension in the air for a few hours. But the inevitable catastrophe could only be retarded, and if land did not appear before night, voyagers, car, and balloon must to a certainty vanish beneath the waves.

They now resorted to the only remaining expedient. They were truly dauntless men, who knew how to look death in the face. Not a single murmur escaped from their lips. They were determined to struggle to the last minute, to do anything to retard their fall. The car was only a sort of willow basket, unable to float, and there was not the slightest possibility of maintaining it on the surface of the sea.

Two more hours passed and the balloon was scarcely 400 feet above the water.

At that moment a loud voice, the voice of a man whose heart was inaccessible to fear, was heard. To this voice responded others not less determined. "Is everything thrown out?" "No, here are still 2,000 dollars in gold." A heavy bag immediately plunged into the sea. "Does the balloon rise?" "A little, but it will not be long before it falls again." "What still remains to be thrown out?" "Nothing." "Yes! the car!" "Let us catch hold of the net, and into the sea with the car."

This was, in fact, the last and only mode of lightening the balloon. The ropes which held the car were cut, and the balloon, after its fall, mounted 2,000 feet. The five voyagers had hoisted themselves into the net, and clung to the meshes, gazing at the abyss.

The delicate sensibility of balloons is well known. It is sufficient to throw out the lightest article to produce a difference in its vertical position. The apparatus in the air is like a balance of mathematical precision. It can be thus easily understood that when it is lightened of any considerable weight its movement will be impetuous and sudden. So it happened on this occasion. But after being suspended for an instant aloft, the balloon began to redescend, the gas escaping by the rent which it was impossible to repair.

The men had done all that men could do. No human efforts could save them now.

They must trust to the mercy of Him who rules the elements.

At four o'clock the balloon was only 500 feet above the surface of the water.

A loud barking was heard. A dog accompanied the voyagers, and was held pressed close to his master in the meshes of the net.

"Top has seen something," cried one of the men. Then immediately a loud voice shouted,—

"Land! land!" The balloon, which the wind still drove towards the southwest, had since daybreak gone a considerable distance, which might be reckoned by hundreds of miles, and a tolerably high land had, in fact, appeared in that direction. But this land was still thirty miles off. It would not take less than an hour to get to it, and then there was the chance of falling to leeward.

An hour! Might not the balloon before that be emptied of all the fluid it yet retained?

Such was the terrible question! The voyagers could distinctly see that solid spot which they must reach at any cost. They were ignorant of what it was, whether an island or a continent, for they did not know to what part of the world the hurricane had driven them. But they must reach this land, whether inhabited or desolate, whether hospitable or not.

It was evident that the balloon could no longer support itself! Several times already had the crests of the enormous billows licked the bottom of the net, making it still heavier, and the balloon only half rose, like a bird with a wounded wing. Half an hour later the land was not more than a mile off, but the balloon, exhausted, flabby, hanging in great folds, had gas in its upper part alone. The voyagers, clinging to the net, were still too heavy for it, and soon, half plunged into the sea, they were beaten by the furious waves. The balloon-case bulged out again, and the wind, taking it, drove it along like a vessel. Might it not possibly thus reach the land?

But, when only two fathoms off, terrible cries resounded from four pairs of lungs at once. The balloon, which had appeared as if it would never again rise, suddenly made an unexpected bound, after having been struck by a tremendous sea. As if it had been at that instant relieved of a new part of its weight, it mounted to a height of 1,500 feet, and here it met a current of wind, which instead of taking it directly to the coast, carried it in a nearly parallel direction.

At last, two minutes later, it reproached obliquely, and finally fell on a sandy beach, out of the reach of the waves.

The voyagers, aiding each other, managed to disengage themselves from the meshes of the net. The balloon, relieved of their weight, was taken by the wind, and like a wounded bird which revives for an instant, disappeared into space.

But the car had contained five passengers, with a dog, and the balloon only left four on the shore.

The missing person had evidently been swept off by the sea, which had just struck the net, and it was owing to this circumstance that the lightened balloon rose the last time, and then soon after reached the land. Scarcely had the four castaways set foot on firm ground, than they all, thinking of the absent one, simultaneously exclaimed, "Perhaps he will try to swim to land! Let us save him! let us save him!"

Chapter 2

Those whom the hurricane had just thrown on this coast were neither aeronauts by profession nor amateurs. They were prisoners of war whose boldness had induced them to escape in this extraordinary manner.

A hundred times they had almost perished! A hundred times had they almost fallen from their torn balloon into the depths of the ocean. But Heaven had reserved them for a strange destiny, and after having, on the 20th of March, escaped from Richmond, besieged by the troops of General Ulysses Grant, they found themselves seven thousand miles from the capital of Virginia, which was the principal stronghold of the South, during the terrible War of Secession. Their aerial voyage had lasted five days.

The curious circumstances which led to the escape of the prisoners were as follows:

That same year, in the month of February, 1865, in one of the coups de main by which General Grant attempted, though in vain, to possess himself of Richmond, several of his officers fell into the power of the enemy and were detained in the town. One of the most distinguished was Captain Cyrus Harding. He was a native of Massachusetts, a first-class engineer, to whom the government had confided, during the war, the direction of the railways, which were so important at that time. A true Northerner, thin, bony, lean, about forty-five years of age; his close-cut hair and his beard, of which he only kept a thick mustache, were already getting gray. He had one-of those finely-developed heads which appear made to be struck on a medal, piercing eyes, a serious mouth, the physiognomy of a clever man of the military school. He was one of those engineers who began by handling the hammer and pickaxe, like generals who first act as common soldiers. Besides mental power, he also possessed great manual dexterity. His muscles exhibited remarkable proofs of tenacity. A man of action as well as a man of thought, all he did was without effort to one of his vigorous and sanguine temperament. Learned, clear-headed, and practical, he fulfilled in all emergencies those three conditions which united ought to insure human success—activity of mind and body, impetuous wishes, and powerful will. He might have taken for his motto that of William of Orange in the 17th century: "I can undertake and persevere even without hope of success." Cyrus Harding was courage personified. He had been in all the battles of that war. After having begun as a volunteer at Illinois, under Ulysses Grant, he fought at Paducah, Belmont, Pittsburg Landing, at the siege of Corinth, Port Gibson, Black River, Chattanooga, the Wilderness, on the Potomac, everywhere and valiantly, a soldier worthy of the general who said, "I never count my dead!" And hundreds of times Captain Harding had almost been among those who were not counted by the terrible Grant; but in these combats where he never spared himself, fortune favored him till the moment when he was wounded and taken prisoner on the field of battle near Richmond. At the same time and on the same day another important personage fell into the hands of the Southerners. This was no other than Gideon Spilett, a reporter for the New York Herald, who had been ordered to follow the changes of the war in the midst of the Northern armies.

Gideon Spilett was one of that race of indomitable English or American chroniclers, like Stanley and others, who stop at nothing to obtain exact information, and transmit it to their journal in the shortest possible time. The newspapers of the Union, such as the New York Herald, are genuine powers, and their reporters are men to be reckoned with. Gideon Spilett ranked among the first of those reporters: a man of great merit, energetic, prompt and ready for anything, full of ideas, having traveled over the whole world, soldier and artist, enthusiastic in council, resolute in action, caring neither for trouble, fatigue, nor danger, when in pursuit of information, for himself first, and then for his journal, a perfect treasury of knowledge on all sorts of curious subjects, of the unpublished, of the unknown, and of the impossible. He was one of those intrepid observers who write under fire, "reporting" among bullets, and to whom every danger is welcome.

He also had been in all the battles, in the first rank, revolver in one hand, note-book in the other; grape-shot never made his pencil tremble. He did not fatigue the wires with incessant telegrams, like those who speak when they have nothing to say, but each of his notes, short, decisive, and clear, threw light on some important point. Besides, he was not wanting in humor. It was he who, after the affair of the Black River, determined at any cost to keep his place at the wicket of the telegraph office, and after having announced to his journal the result of the battle, telegraphed for two hours the first chapters of the Bible. It cost the New York Herald two thousand dollars, but the New York Herald published the first intelligence.

Gideon Spilett was tall. He was rather more than forty years of age. Light whiskers bordering on red surrounded his face. His eye was steady, lively, rapid in its changes. It was the eye of a man accustomed to take in at a glance all the details of a scene. Well built, he was inured to all climates, like a bar of steel hardened in cold water.

For ten years Gideon Spilett had been the reporter of the New York Herald, which he enriched by his letters and drawings, for he was as skilful in the use of the pencil as of the pen. When he was captured, he was in the act of making a description and sketch of the battle. The last words in his note-book were these: "A Southern rifleman has just taken aim at me, but—" The Southerner notwithstanding missed Gideon Spilett, who, with his usual fortune, came out of this affair without a scratch.

Cyrus Harding and Gideon Spilett, who did not know each other except by reputation, had both been carried to Richmond. The engineer's wounds rapidly healed, and it was during his convalescence that he made acquaintance with the reporter. The two men then learned to appreciate each other. Soon their common aim had but one object, that of escaping, rejoining Grant's army, and fighting together in the ranks of the Federals.

The two Americans had from the first determined to seize every chance; but although they were allowed to wander at liberty in the town, Richmond was so strictly guarded, that escape appeared impossible. In the meanwhile Captain Harding was rejoined by a servant who was devoted to him in life and in death. This intrepid fellow was a Negro born on the engineer's estate, of a slave father and mother, but to whom Cyrus, who was an Abolitionist from conviction and heart, had long since given his freedom. The once slave, though free, would not leave his master. He would have died for him. He was a man of about thirty, vigorous, active, clever, intelligent, gentle, and calm, sometimes naive, always merry, obliging, and honest. His name was Nebuchadnezzar, but he only answered to the familiar abbreviation of Neb.

When Neb heard that his master had been made prisoner, he left Massachusetts without hesitating an instant, arrived before Richmond, and by dint of stratagem and shrewdness, after having risked his life twenty times over, managed to penetrate into the besieged town. The pleasure of Harding on seeing his servant, and the joy of Neb at finding his master, can scarcely be described.

But though Neb had been able to make his way into Richmond, it was quite another thing to get out again, for the Northern prisoners were very strictly watched. Some extraordinary opportunity was needed to make the attempt with any chance of success, and this opportunity not only did not present itself, but was very difficult to find.

Meanwhile Grant continued his energetic operations. The victory of Petersburg had been very dearly bought. His forces, united to those of Butler, had as yet been unsuccessful before Richmond, and nothing gave the prisoners any hope of a speedy deliverance.

The reporter, to whom his tedious captivity did not offer a single incident worthy of note, could stand it no longer. His usually active mind was occupied with one sole thought—how he might get out of Richmond at any cost. Several times had he even made the attempt, but was stopped by some insurmountable obstacle. However, the siege continued; and if the prisoners were anxious to escape and join Grant's army, certain of the besieged were no less anxious to join the Southern forces. Among them was one Jonathan Forster, a determined Southerner. The truth was, that if the prisoners of the Secessionists could not leave the town, neither could the Secessionists themselves while the Northern army invested it. The Governor of Richmond for a long time had been unable to communicate with General Lee, and he very much wished to make known to him the situation of the town, so as to hasten the march of the army to their relief. Thus Jonathan Forster accordingly conceived the idea of rising in a balloon, so as to pass over the besieging lines, and in that way reach the Secessionist camp.

The Governor authorized the attempt. A balloon was manufactured and placed at the disposal of Forster, who was to be accompanied by five other persons. They were furnished with arms in case they might have to defend themselves when they alighted, and provisions in the event of their aerial voyage being prolonged.

The departure of the balloon was fixed for the 18th of March. It should be effected during the night, with a northwest wind of moderate force, and the aeronauts calculated that they would reach General Lee's camp in a few hours.

But this northwest wind was not a simple breeze. From the 18th it was evident that it was changing to a hurricane. The tempest soon became such that Forster's departure was deferred, for it was impossible to risk the balloon and those whom it carried in the midst of the furious elements.

The balloon, inflated on the great square of Richmond, was ready to depart on the first abatement of the wind, and, as may be supposed, the impatience among the besieged to see the storm moderate was very great.

The 18th, the 19th of March passed without any alteration in the weather. There was even great difficulty in keeping the balloon fastened to the ground, as the squalls dashed it furiously about.

The night of the 19th passed, but the next morning the storm blew with redoubled force. The departure of the balloon was impossible.

On that day the engineer, Cyrus Harding, was accosted in one of the streets of Richmond by a person whom he did not in the least know. This was a sailor named Pencroft, a man of about thirty-five or forty years of age, strongly built, very sunburnt, and possessed of a pair of bright sparkling eyes and a remarkably good physiognomy. Pencroft was an American from the North, who had sailed all the ocean over, and who had gone through every possible and almost impossible adventure that a being with two feet and no wings would encounter. It is needless to say that he was a bold, dashing fellow, ready to dare anything and was astonished at nothing. Pencroft at the beginning of the year had gone to Richmond on business, with a young boy of fifteen from New Jersey, son of a former captain, an orphan, whom he loved as if he had been his own child. Not having been able to leave the town before the first operations of the siege, he found himself shut up, to his great disgust; but, not accustomed to succumb to difficulties, he resolved to escape by some means or other. He knew the engineer-officer by reputation; he knew with what impatience that determined man chafed under his restraint. On this day he did not, therefore, hesitate to accost him, saying, without circumlocution, "Have you had enough of Richmond, captain?"

The engineer looked fixedly at the man who spoke, and who added, in a low voice,—

"Captain Harding, will you try to escape?"

"When?" asked the engineer quickly, and it was evident that this question was uttered without consideration, for he had not yet examined the stranger who addressed him. But after having with a penetrating eye observed the open face of the sailor, he was convinced that he had before him an honest man.

"Who are you?" he asked briefly.

Pencroft made himself known.

"Well," replied Harding, "and in what way do you propose to escape?"

"By that lazy balloon which is left there doing nothing, and which looks to me as if it was waiting on purpose for us—"

There was no necessity for the sailor to finish his sentence. The engineer understood him at once. He seized Pencroft by the arm, and dragged him to his house. There the sailor developed his project, which was indeed extremely simple. They risked nothing but their lives in its execution. The hurricane was in all its violence, it is true, but so clever and daring an engineer as Cyrus Harding knew perfectly well how to manage a balloon. Had he himself been as well acquainted with the art of sailing in the air as he was with the navigation of a ship, Pencroft would not have hesitated to set out, of course taking his young friend Herbert with him; for, accustomed to brave the fiercest tempests of the ocean, he was not to be hindered on account of the hurricane.

Captain Harding had listened to the sailor without saying a word, but his eyes shone with satisfaction. Here was the long-sought-for opportunity—he was not a man to let it pass. The plan was feasible, though, it must be confessed, dangerous in the extreme. In the night, in spite of their guards, they might approach the balloon, slip into the car, and then cut the cords which held it. There was no doubt that they might be killed, but on the other hand they might succeed, and without this storm!—Without this storm the balloon would have started already and the looked-for opportunity would not have then presented itself.

"I am not alone!" said Harding at last.

"How many people do you wish to bring with you?" asked the sailor.

"Two; my friend Spilett, and my servant Neb."

"That will be three," replied Pencroft; "and with Herbert and me five. But the balloon will hold six—"

"That will be enough, we will go," answered Harding in a firm voice.

This "we" included Spilett, for the reporter, as his friend well knew, was not a man to draw back, and when the project was communicated to him he approved of it unreservedly. What astonished him was, that so simple an idea had not occurred to him before. As to Neb, he followed his master wherever his master wished to go.

"This evening, then," said Pencroft, "we will all meet out there."

"This evening, at ten o'clock," replied Captain Harding; "and Heaven grant that the storm does not abate before our departure."

Pencroft took leave of the two friends, and returned to his lodging, where young Herbert Brown had remained. The courageous boy knew of the sailor's plan, and it was not without anxiety that he awaited the result of the proposal being made to the engineer. Thus five determined persons were about to abandon themselves to the mercy of the tempestuous elements!

No! the storm did not abate, and neither Jonathan Forster nor his companions dreamed of confronting it in that frail car.

It would be a terrible journey. The engineer only feared one thing; it was that the balloon, held to the ground and dashed about by the wind, would be torn into shreds. For several hours he roamed round the nearly-deserted square, surveying the apparatus. Pencroft did the same on his side, his hands in his pockets, yawning now and then like a man who did not know how to kill the time, but really dreading, like his friend, either the escape or destruction of the balloon. Evening arrived. The night was dark in the extreme. Thick mists passed like clouds close to the ground. Rain fell mingled with snow, it was very cold. A mist hung over Richmond. It seemed as if the violent storm had produced a truce between the besiegers and the besieged, and that the cannon were silenced by the louder detonations of the storm. The streets of the town were deserted. It had not even appeared necessary in that horrible weather to place a guard in the square, in the midst of which plunged the balloon. Everything favored the departure of the prisoners, but what might possibly be the termination of the hazardous voyage they contemplated in the midst of the furious elements?—

"Dirty weather!" exclaimed Pencroft, fixing his hat firmly on his head with a blow of his fist; "but pshaw, we shall succeed all the same!"

At half-past nine, Harding and his companions glided from different directions into the square, which the gas-lamps, extinguished by the wind, had left in total obscurity. Even the enormous balloon, almost beaten to the ground, could not be seen. Independently of the sacks of ballast, to which the cords of the net were fastened, the car was held by a strong cable passed through a ring in the pavement. The five prisoners met by the car. They had not been perceived, and such was the darkness that they could not even see each other.

Without speaking a word, Harding, Spilett, Neb, and Herbert took their places in the car, while Pencroft by the engineer's order detached successively the bags of ballast. It was the work of a few minutes only, and the sailor rejoined his companions.

The balloon was then only held by the cable, and the engineer had nothing to do but to give the word.

At that moment a dog sprang with a bound into the car. It was Top, a favorite of the engineer. The faithful creature, having broken his chain, had followed his master. He, however, fearing that its additional weight might impede their ascent, wished to send away the animal.

"One more will make but little difference, poor beast!" exclaimed Pencroft, heaving out two bags of sand, and as he spoke letting go the cable; the balloon ascending in an oblique direction, disappeared, after having dashed the car against two chimneys, which it threw down as it swept by them.

Then, indeed, the full rage of the hurricane was exhibited to the voyagers. During the night the engineer could not dream of descending, and when day broke, even a glimpse of the earth below was intercepted by fog.

Five days had passed when a partial clearing allowed them to see the wide extending ocean beneath their feet, now lashed into the maddest fury by the gale.

Our readers will recollect what befell these five daring individuals who set out on their hazardous expedition in the balloon on the 20th of March. Five days afterwards four of them were thrown on a desert coast, seven thousand miles from their country! But one of their number was missing, the man who was to be their guide, their leading spirit, the engineer, Captain Harding! The instant they had recovered their feet, they all hurried to the beach in the hopes of rendering him assistance.

Chapter 3

The engineer, the meshes of the net having given way, had been carried off by a wave. His dog also had disappeared. The faithful animal had voluntarily leaped out to help his master. "Forward," cried the reporter; and all four, Spilett, Herbert, Pencroft, and Neb, forgetting their fatigue, began their search. Poor Neb shed bitter tears, giving way to despair at the thought of having lost the only being he loved on earth.

Only two minutes had passed from the time when Cyrus Harding disappeared to the moment when his companions set foot on the ground. They had hopes therefore of arriving in time to save him. "Let us look for him! let us look for him!" cried Neb.

"Yes, Neb," replied Gideon Spilett, "and we will find him too!"

"Living, I trust!"

"Still living!"

"Can he swim?" asked Pencroft.

"Yes," replied Neb, "and besides, Top is there."

The sailor, observing the heavy surf on the shore, shook his head.

The engineer had disappeared to the north of the shore, and nearly half a mile from the place where the castaways had landed. The nearest point of the beach he could reach was thus fully that distance off.

It was then nearly six o'clock. A thick fog made the night very dark. The castaways proceeded toward the north of the land on which chance had thrown them, an unknown region, the geographical situation of which they could not even guess. They were walking upon a sandy soil, mingled with stones, which appeared destitute of any sort of vegetation. The ground, very unequal and rough, was in some places perfectly riddled with holes, making walking extremely painful. From these holes escaped every minute great birds of clumsy flight, which flew in all directions. Others, more active, rose in flocks and passed in clouds over their heads. The sailor thought he recognized gulls and cormorants, whose shrill cries rose above the roaring of the sea.

From time to time the castaways stopped and shouted, then listened for some response from the ocean, for they thought that if the engineer had landed, and they had been near to the place, they would have heard the barking of the dog Top, even should Harding himself have been unable to give any sign of existence. They stopped to listen, but no sound arose above the roaring of the waves and the dashing of the surf. The little band then continued their march forward, searching into every hollow of the shore.

After walking for twenty minutes, the four castaways were suddenly brought to a standstill by the sight of foaming billows close to their feet. The solid ground ended here. They found themselves at the extremity of a sharp point on which the sea broke furiously.

"It is a promontory," said the sailor; "we must retrace our steps, holding towards the right, and we shall thus gain the mainland."

"But if he is there," said Neb, pointing to the ocean, whose waves shone of a snowy white in the darkness. "Well, let us call again," and all uniting their voices, they gave a vigorous shout, but there came no reply. They waited for a lull, then began again; still no reply.

The castaways accordingly returned, following the opposite side of the promontory, over a soil equally sandy and rugged. However, Pencroft observed that the shore was more equal, that the ground rose, and he declared that it was joined by a long slope to a hill, whose massive front he thought that he could see looming indistinctly through the mist. The birds were less numerous on this part of the shore; the sea was also less tumultuous, and they observed that the agitation of the waves was diminished. The noise of the surf was scarcely heard. This side of the promontory evidently formed a semicircular bay, which the sharp point sheltered from the breakers of the open sea. But to follow this direction was to go south, exactly opposite to that part of the coast where Harding might have landed. After a walk of a mile and a half, the shore presented no curve which would permit them to return to the north. This promontory, of which they had turned the point, must be attached to the mainland. The castaways, although their strength was nearly exhausted, still marched courageously forward, hoping every moment to meet with a sudden angle which would set them in the first direction. What was their disappointment, when, after trudging nearly two miles, having reached an elevated point composed of slippery rocks, they found themselves again stopped by the sea.

"We are on an islet," said Pencroft, "and we have surveyed it from one extremity to the other."

The sailor was right; they had been thrown, not on a continent, not even on an island, but on an islet which was not more than two miles in length, with even a less breadth.

Was this barren spot the desolate refuge of sea-birds, strewn with stones and destitute of vegetation, attached to a more important archipelago? It was impossible to say. When the voyagers from their car saw the land through the mist, they had not been able to reconnoiter it sufficiently. However, Pencroft, accustomed with his sailor eyes to piece through the gloom, was almost certain that he could clearly distinguish in the west confused masses which indicated an elevated coast. But they could not in the dark determine whether it was a single island, or connected with others. They could not leave it either, as the sea surrounded them; they must therefore put off till the next day their search for the engineer, from whom, alas! not a single cry had reached them to show that he was still in existence.

"The silence of our friend proves nothing," said the reporter. "Perhaps he has fainted or is wounded, and unable to reply directly, so we will not despair."

The reporter then proposed to light a fire on a point of the islet, which would serve as a signal to the engineer. But they searched in vain for wood or dry brambles; nothing but sand and stones were to be found. The grief of Neb and his companions, who were all strongly attached to the intrepid Harding, can be better pictured than described. It was too evident that they were powerless to help him. They must wait with what patience they could for daylight. Either the engineer had been able to save himself, and had already found a refuge on some point of the coast, or he was lost for ever! The long and painful hours passed by. The cold was intense. The castaways suffered cruelly, but they scarcely perceived it. They did not even think of taking a minute's rest. Forgetting everything but their chief, hoping or wishing to hope on, they continued to walk up and down on this sterile spot, always returning to its northern point, where they could approach nearest to the scene of the catastrophe. They listened, they called, and then uniting their voices, they endeavored to raise even a louder shout than before, which would be transmitted to a great distance. The wind had now fallen almost to a calm, and the noise of the sea began also to subside. One of Neb's shouts even appeared to produce an echo. Herbert directed Pencroft's attention to it, adding, "That proves that there is a coast to the west, at no great distance." The sailor nodded; besides, his eyes could not deceive him. If he had discovered land, however indistinct it might appear, land was sure to be there. But that distant echo was the only response produced by Neb's shouts, while a heavy gloom hung over all the part east of the island.

Meanwhile, the sky was clearing little by little. Towards midnight the stars shone out, and if the engineer had been there with his companions he would have remarked that these stars did not belong to the Northern Hemisphere. The Polar Star was not visible, the constellations were not those which they had been accustomed to see in the United States; the Southern Cross glittered brightly in the sky.

The night passed away. Towards five o'clock in the morning of the 25th of March, the sky began to lighten; the horizon still remained dark, but with daybreak a thick mist rose from the sea, so that the eye could scarcely penetrate beyond twenty feet or so from where they stood. At length the fog gradually unrolled itself in great heavily moving waves.

It was unfortunate, however, that the castaways could distinguish nothing around them. While the gaze of the reporter and Neb were cast upon the ocean, the sailor and Herbert looked eagerly for the coast in the west. But not a speck of land was visible. "Never mind," said Pencroft, "though I do not see the land, I feel it... it is there... there... as sure as the fact that we are no longer at Richmond." But the fog was not long in rising. It was only a fine-weather mist. A hot sun soon penetrated to the surface of the island. About half-past six, three-quarters of an hour after sunrise, the mist became more transparent. It grew thicker above, but cleared away below. Soon the isle appeared as if it had descended from a cloud, then the sea showed itself around them, spreading far away towards the east, but bounded on the west by an abrupt and precipitous coast.

Yes! the land was there. Their safety was at least provisionally insured. The islet and the coast were separated by a channel about half a mile in breadth, through which rushed an extremely rapid current.

However, one of the castaways, following the impulse of his heart, immediately threw himself into the current, without consulting his companions, without saying a single word. It was Neb. He was in haste to be on the other side, and to climb towards the north. It had been impossible to hold him back. Pencroft called him in vain. The reporter prepared to follow him, but Pencroft stopped him. "Do you want to cross the channel?" he asked. "Yes," replied Spilett. "All right!" said the seaman; "wait a bit; Neb is well able to carry help to his master. If we venture into the channel, we risk being carried into the open sea by the current, which is running very strong; but, if I'm not wrong, it is ebbing. See, the tide is going down over the sand. Let us have patience, and at low water it is possible we may find a fordable passage." "You are right," replied the reporter, "we will not separate more than we can help."

During this time Neb was struggling vigorously against the current. He was crossing in an oblique direction. His black shoulders could be seen emerging at each stroke. He was carried down very quickly, but he also made way towards the shore. It took more than half an hour to cross from the islet to the land, and he reached the shore several hundred feet from the place which was opposite to the point from which he had started.

Landing at the foot of a high wall of granite, he shook himself vigorously; and then, setting off running, soon disappeared behind a rocky point, which projected to nearly the height of the northern extremity of the islet.

Neb's companions had watched his daring attempt with painful anxiety, and when he was out of sight, they fixed their attention on the land where their hope of safety lay, while eating some shell-fish with which the sand was strewn. It was a wretched repast, but still it was better than nothing. The opposite coast formed one vast bay, terminating on the south by a very sharp point, which was destitute of all vegetation, and was of a very wild aspect. This point abutted on the shore in a grotesque outline of high granite rocks. Towards the north, on the contrary, the bay widened, and a more rounded coast appeared, trending from the southwest to the northeast, and terminating in a slender cape. The distance between these two extremities, which made the bow of the bay, was about eight miles. Half a mile from the shore rose the islet, which somewhat resembled the carcass of a gigantic whale. Its extreme breadth was not more than a quarter of a mile.

Opposite the islet, the beach consisted first of sand, covered with black stones, which were now appearing little by little above the retreating tide. The second level was separated by a perpendicular granite cliff, terminated at the top by an unequal edge at a height of at least 300 feet. It continued thus for a length of three miles, ending suddenly on the right with a precipice which looked as if cut by the hand of man. On the left, above the promontory, this irregular and jagged cliff descended by a long slope of conglomerated rocks till it mingled with the ground of the southern point. On the upper plateau of the coast not a tree appeared. It was a flat tableland like that above Cape Town at the Cape of Good Hope, but of reduced proportions; at least so it appeared seen from the islet. However, verdure was not wanting to the right beyond the precipice. They could easily distinguish a confused mass of great trees, which extended beyond the limits of their view. This verdure relieved the eye, so long wearied by the continued ranges of granite. Lastly, beyond and above the plateau, in a northwesterly direction and at a distance of at least seven miles, glittered a white summit which reflected the sun's rays. It was that of a lofty mountain, capped with snow.

The question could not at present be decided whether this land formed an island, or whether it belonged to a continent. But on beholding the convulsed masses heaped up on the left, no geologist would have hesitated to give them a volcanic origin, for they were unquestionably the work of subterranean convulsions.

Gideon Spilett, Pencroft, and Herbert attentively examined this land, on which they might perhaps have to live many long years; on which indeed they might even die, should it be out of the usual track of vessels, as was likely to be the case.

"Well," asked Herbert, "what do you say, Pencroft?"

"There is some good and some bad, as in everything," replied the sailor. "We shall see. But now the ebb is evidently making. In three hours we will attempt the passage, and once on the other side, we will try to get out of this scrape, and I hope may find the captain." Pencroft was not wrong in his anticipations. Three hours later at low tide, the greater part of the sand forming the bed of the channel was uncovered. Between the islet and the coast there only remained a narrow channel which would no doubt be easy to cross.

About ten o'clock, Gideon Spilett and his companions stripped themselves of their clothes, which they placed in bundles on their heads, and then ventured into the water, which was not more than five feet deep. Herbert, for whom it was too deep, swam like a fish, and got through capitally. All three arrived without difficulty on the opposite shore. Quickly drying themselves in the sun, they put on their clothes, which they had preserved from contact with the water, and sat down to take counsel together what to do next.

Chapter 4

All at once the reporter sprang up, and telling the sailor that he would rejoin them at that same place, he climbed the cliff in the direction which the Negro Neb had taken a few hours before. Anxiety hastened his steps, for he longed to obtain news of his friend, and he soon disappeared round an angle of the cliff. Herbert wished to accompany him.

"Stop here, my boy," said the sailor; "we have to prepare an encampment, and to try and find rather better grub than these shell-fish. Our friends will want something when they come back. There is work for everybody."

"I am ready," replied Herbert.

"All right," said the sailor; "that will do. We must set about it regularly. We are tired, cold, and hungry; therefore we must have shelter, fire, and food. There is wood in the forest, and eggs in nests; we have only to find a house."

"Very well," returned Herbert, "I will look for a cave among the rocks, and I shall be sure to discover some hole into which we can creep."

"All right," said Pencroft; "go on, my boy."

They both walked to the foot of the enormous wall over the beach, far from which the tide had now retreated; but instead of going towards the north, they went southward. Pencroft had remarked, several hundred feet from the place at which they landed, a narrow cutting, out of which he thought a river or stream might issue. Now, on the one hand it was important to settle themselves in the neighborhood of a good stream of water, and on the other it was possible that the current had thrown Cyrus Harding on the shore there.

The cliff, as has been said, rose to a height of three hundred feet, but the mass was unbroken throughout, and even at its base, scarcely washed by the sea, it did not offer the smallest fissure which would serve as a dwelling. It was a perpendicular wall of very hard granite, which even the waves had not worn away. Towards the summit fluttered myriads of sea-fowl, and especially those of the web-footed species with long, flat, pointed beaks—a clamorous tribe, bold in the presence of man, who probably for the first time thus invaded their domains. Pencroft recognized the skua and other gulls among them, the voracious little sea-mew, which in great numbers nestled in the crevices of the granite. A shot fired among this swarm would have killed a great number, but to fire a shot a gun was needed, and neither Pencroft nor Herbert had one; besides this, gulls and sea-mews are scarcely eatable, and even their eggs have a detestable taste. However, Herbert, who had gone forward a little more to the left, soon came upon rocks covered with sea-weed, which, some hours later, would be hidden by the high tide. On these rocks, in the midst of slippery wrack, abounded bivalve shell-fish, not to be despised by starving people. Herbert called Pencroft, who ran up hastily.

"Here are mussels!" cried the sailor; "these will do instead of eggs!"

"They are not mussels," replied Herbert, who was attentively examining the molluscs attached to the rocks; "they are lithodomes."

"Are they good to eat?" asked Pencroft.

"Perfectly so."

"Then let us eat some lithodomes."

The sailor could rely upon Herbert; the young boy was well up in natural history, and always had had quite a passion for the science. His father had encouraged him in it, by letting him attend the lectures of the best professors in Boston, who were very fond of the intelligent, industrious lad. And his turn for natural history was, more than once in the course of time, of great use, and he was not mistaken in this instance. These lithodomes were oblong shells, suspended in clusters and adhering very tightly to the rocks. They belong to that species of molluscous perforators which excavate holes in the hardest stone; their shell is rounded at both ends, a feature which is not remarked in the common mussel.

Pencroft and Herbert made a good meal of the lithodomes, which were then half opened to the sun. They ate them as oysters, and as they had a strong peppery taste, they were palatable without condiments of any sort.

Their hunger was thus appeased for the time, but not their thirst, which increased after eating these naturally-spiced molluscs. They had then to find fresh water, and it was not likely that it would be wanting in such a capriciously uneven region. Pencroft and Herbert, after having taken the precaution of collecting an ample supply of lithodomes, with which they filled their pockets and handkerchiefs, regained the foot of the cliff.

Two hundred paces farther they arrived at the cutting, through which, as Pencroft had guessed, ran a stream of water, whether fresh or not was to be ascertained. At this place the wall appeared to have been separated by some violent subterranean force. At its base was hollowed out a little creek, the farthest part of which formed a tolerably sharp angle. The watercourse at that part measured one hundred feet in breadth, and its two banks on each side were scarcely twenty feet high. The river became strong almost directly between the two walls of granite, which began to sink above the mouth; it then suddenly turned and disappeared beneath a wood of stunted trees half a mile off.

"Here is the water, and yonder is the wood we require!" said Pencroft. "Well, Herbert, now we only want the house."

The water of the river was limpid. The sailor ascertained that at this time—that is to say, at low tide, when the rising floods did not reach it—it was sweet. This important point established, Herbert looked for some cavity which would serve them as a retreat, but in vain; everywhere the wall appeared smooth, plain, and perpendicular.

However, at the mouth of the watercourse and above the reach of the high tide, the convulsions of nature had formed, not a grotto, but a pile of enormous rocks, such as are often met with in granite countries and which bear the name of "Chimneys."

Pencroft and Herbert penetrated quite far in among the rocks, by sandy passages in which light was not wanting, for it entered through the openings which were left between the blocks, of which some were only sustained by a miracle of equilibrium; but with the light came also air—a regular corridor-gale—and with the wind the sharp cold from the exterior. However, the sailor thought that by stopping-up some of the openings with a mixture of stones and sand, the Chimneys could be rendered habitable. Their geometrical plan represented the typographical sign "&," which signifies "et cetera" abridged, but by isolating the upper mouth of the sign, through which the south and west winds blew so strongly, they could succeed in making the lower part of use.

"Here's our work," said Pencroft, "and if we ever see Captain Harding again, he will know how to make something of this labyrinth."

"We shall see him again, Pencroft," cried Herbert, "and when he returns he must find a tolerable dwelling here. It will be so, if we can make a fireplace in the left passage and keep an opening for the smoke."

"So we can, my boy," replied the sailor, "and these Chimneys will serve our turn. Let us set to work, but first come and get a store of fuel. I think some branches will be very useful in stopping up these openings, through which the wind shrieks like so many fiends."

Herbert and Pencroft left the Chimneys, and, turning the angle, they began to climb the left bank of the river. The current here was quite rapid, and drifted down some dead wood. The rising tide—and it could already be perceived—must drive it back with force to a considerable distance. The sailor then thought that they could utilize this ebb and flow for the transport of heavy objects.

After having walked for a quarter of an hour, the sailor and the boy arrived at the angle which the river made in turning towards the left. From this point its course was pursued through a forest of magnificent trees. These trees still retained their verdure, notwithstanding the advanced season, for they belonged to the family of "coniferae," which is spread over all the regions of the globe, from northern climates to the tropics. The young naturalist recognized especially the "deedara," which are very numerous in the Himalayan zone, and which spread around them a most agreeable odor. Between these beautiful trees sprang up clusters of firs, whose opaque open parasol boughs spread wide around. Among the long grass, Pencroft felt that his feet were crushing dry branches which crackled like fireworks.

"Well, my boy," said he to Herbert, "if I don't know the name of these trees, at any rate I reckon that we may call them 'burning wood,' and just now that's the chief thing we want."

"Let us get a supply," replied Herbert, who immediately set to work.

The collection was easily made. It was not even necessary to lop the trees, for enormous quantities of dead wood were lying at their feet; but if fuel was not wanting, the means of transporting it was not yet found. The wood, being very dry, would burn rapidly; it was therefore necessary to carry to the Chimneys a considerable quantity, and the loads of two men would not be sufficient. Herbert remarked this.

"Well, my boy," replied the sailor, "there must be some way of carrying this wood; there is always a way of doing everything. If we had a cart or a boat, it would be easy enough."

"But we have the river," said Herbert.

"Right," replied Pencroft; "the river will be to us like a road which carries of itself, and rafts have not been invented for nothing."

"Only," observed Herbert, "at this moment our road is going the wrong way, for the tide is rising!"

"We shall be all right if we wait till it ebbs," replied the sailor, "and then we will trust it to carry our fuel to the Chimneys. Let us get the raft ready."

The sailor, followed by Herbert, directed his steps towards the river. They both carried, each in proportion to his strength, a load of wood bound in fagots. They found on the bank also a great quantity of dead branches in the midst of grass, among which the foot of man had probably never before trod. Pencroft began directly to make his raft. In a kind of little bay, created by a point of the shore which broke the current, the sailor and the lad placed some good-sized pieces of wood, which they had fastened together with dry creepers. A raft was thus formed, on which they stacked all they had collected, sufficient, indeed, to have loaded at least twenty men. In an hour the work was finished, and the raft moored to the bank, awaited the turning of the tide.

There were still several hours to be occupied, and with one consent Pencroft and Herbert resolved to gain the upper plateau, so as to have a more extended view of the surrounding country.

Exactly two hundred feet behind the angle formed by the river, the wall, terminated by a fall of rocks, died away in a gentle slope to the edge of the forest. It was a natural staircase. Herbert and the sailor began their ascent; thanks to the vigor of their muscles they reached the summit in a few minutes; and proceeded to the point above the mouth of the river.

On attaining it, their first look was cast upon the ocean which not long before they had traversed in such a terrible condition. They observed, with emotion, all that part to the north of the coast on which the catastrophe had taken place. It was there that Cyrus Harding had disappeared. They looked to see if some portion of their balloon, to which a man might possibly cling, yet existed. Nothing! The sea was but one vast watery desert. As to the coast, it was solitary also. Neither the reporter nor Neb could be anywhere seen. But it was possible that at this time they were both too far away to be perceived.

"Something tells me," cried Herbert, "that a man as energetic as Captain Harding would not let himself be drowned like other people. He must have reached some point of the shore; don't you think so, Pencroft?"

The sailor shook his head sadly. He little expected ever to see Cyrus Harding again; but wishing to leave some hope to Herbert: "Doubtless, doubtless," said he; "our engineer is a man who would get out of a scrape to which any one else would yield."

In the meantime he examined the coast with great attention. Stretched out below them was the sandy shore, bounded on the right of the river's mouth by lines of breakers. The rocks which were visible appeared like amphibious monsters reposing in the surf. Beyond the reef, the sea sparkled beneath the sun's rays. To the south a sharp point closed the horizon, and it could not be seen if the land was prolonged in that direction, or if it ran southeast and southwest, which would have made this coast a very long peninsula. At the northern extremity of the bay the outline of the shore was continued to a great distance in a wider curve. There the shore was low, flat, without cliffs, and with great banks of sand, which the tide left uncovered. Pencroft and Herbert then returned towards the west. Their attention was first arrested by the snow-topped mountain which rose at a distance of six or seven miles. From its first declivities to within two miles of the coast were spread vast masses of wood, relieved by large green patches, caused by the presence of evergreen trees. Then, from the edge of this forest to the shore extended a plain, scattered irregularly with groups of trees. Here and there on the left sparkled through glades the waters of the little river; they could trace its winding course back towards the spurs of the mountain, among which it seemed to spring. At the point where the sailor had left his raft of wood, it began to run between the two high granite walls; but if on the left bank the wall remained clear and abrupt, on the right bank, on the contrary, it sank gradually, the massive sides changed to isolated rocks, the rocks to stones, the stones to shingle running to the extremity of the point.

"Are we on an island?" murmured the sailor.

"At any rate, it seems to be big enough," replied the lad.

"An island, ever so big, is an island all the same!" said Pencroft.

But this important question could not yet be answered. A more perfect survey had to be made to settle the point. As to the land itself, island or continent, it appeared fertile, agreeable in its aspect, and varied in its productions.

"This is satisfactory," observed Pencroft; "and in our misfortune, we must thank Providence for it."

"God be praised!" responded Herbert, whose pious heart was full of gratitude to the Author of all things.

Pencroft and Herbert examined for some time the country on which they had been cast; but it was difficult to guess after so hasty an inspection what the future had in store for them.

They then returned, following the southern crest of the granite platform, bordered by a long fringe of jagged rocks, of the most whimsical shapes. Some hundreds of birds lived there nestled in the holes of the stone; Herbert, jumping over the rocks, startled a whole flock of these winged creatures.

"Oh!" cried he, "those are not gulls nor sea-mews!"

"What are they then?" asked Pencroft.

"Upon my word, one would say they were pigeons!"

"Just so, but these are wild or rock pigeons. I recognize them by the double band of black on the wing, by the white tail, and by their slate-colored plumage. But if the rock-pigeon is good to eat, its eggs must be excellent, and we will soon see how many they may have left in their nests!"

"We will not give them time to hatch, unless it is in the shape of an omelet!" replied Pencroft merrily.

"But what will you make your omelet in?" asked Herbert; "in your hat?"

"Well!" replied the sailor, "I am not quite conjuror enough for that; we must come down to eggs in the shell, my boy, and I will undertake to despatch the hardest!"

Pencroft and Herbert attentively examined the cavities in the granite, and they really found eggs in some of the hollows. A few dozen being collected, were packed in the sailor's handkerchief, and as the time when the tide would be full was approaching, Pencroft and Herbert began to redescend towards the watercourse. When they arrived there, it was an hour after midday. The tide had already turned. They must now avail themselves of the ebb to take the wood to the mouth. Pencroft did not intend to let the raft go away in the current without guidance, neither did he mean to embark on it himself to steer it. But a sailor is never at a loss when there is a question of cables or ropes, and Pencroft rapidly twisted a cord, a few fathoms long, made of dry creepers. This vegetable cable was fastened to the after-part of the raft, and the sailor held it in his hand while Herbert, pushing off the raft with a long pole, kept it in the current. This succeeded capitally. The enormous load of wood drifted down the current. The bank was very equal; there was no fear that the raft would run aground, and before two o'clock they arrived at the river's mouth, a few paces from the Chimneys.

Chapter 5

Pencroft's first care, after unloading the raft, was to render the cave habitable by stopping up all the holes which made it draughty. Sand, stones, twisted branches, wet clay, closed up the galleries open to the south winds. One narrow and winding opening at the side was kept, to lead out the smoke and to make the fire draw. The cave was thus divided into three or four rooms, if such dark dens with which a donkey would scarcely have been contented deserved the name. But they were dry, and there was space to stand upright, at least in the principal room, which occupied the center. The floor was covered with fine sand, and taking all in all they were well pleased with it for want of a better.

"Perhaps," said Herbert, while he and Pencroft were working, "our companions have found a superior place to ours."

"Very likely," replied the seaman; "but, as we don't know, we must work all the same. Better to have two strings to one's bow than no string at all!"

"Oh!" exclaimed Herbert, "how jolly it will be if they were to find Captain Harding and were to bring him back with them!"

"Yes, indeed!" said Pencroft, "that was a man of the right sort."

"Was!" exclaimed Herbert, "do you despair of ever seeing him again?"

"God forbid!" replied the sailor. Their work was soon done, and Pencroft declared himself very well satisfied.

"Now," said he, "our friends can come back when they like. They will find a good enough shelter."

They now had only to make a fireplace and to prepare the supper—an easy task. Large flat stones were placed on the ground at the opening of the narrow passage which had been kept. This, if the smoke did not take the heat out with it, would be enough to maintain an equal temperature inside. Their wood was stowed away in one of the rooms, and the sailor laid in the fireplace some logs and brushwood. The seaman was busy with this, when Herbert asked him if he had any matches.

"Certainly," replied Pencroft, "and I may say happily, for without matches or tinder we should be in a fix."

"Still we might get fire as the savages do," replied Herbert, "by rubbing two bits of dry stick one against the other."

"All right; try, my boy, and let's see if you can do anything besides exercising your arms."

"Well, it's a very simple proceeding, and much used in the islands of the Pacific."

"I don't deny it," replied Pencroft, "but the savages must know how to do it or employ a peculiar wood, for more than once I have tried to get fire in that way, but I could never manage it. I must say I prefer matches. By the bye, where are my matches?"

Pencroft searched in his waistcoat for the box, which was always there, for he was a confirmed smoker. He could not find it; he rummaged the pockets of his trousers, but, to his horror, he could nowhere discover the box.

"Here's a go!" said he, looking at Herbert. "The box must have fallen out of my pocket and got lost! Surely, Herbert, you must have something—a tinder-box—anything that can possibly make fire!"

"No, I haven't, Pencroft."

The sailor rushed out, followed by the boy. On the sand, among the rocks, near the river's bank, they both searched carefully, but in vain. The box was of copper, and therefore would have been easily seen.

"Pencroft," asked Herbert, "didn't you throw it out of the car?"

"I knew better than that," replied the sailor; "but such a small article could easily disappear in the tumbling about we have gone through. I would rather even have lost my pipe! Confound the box! Where can it be?"

"Look here, the tide is going down," said Herbert; "let's run to the place where we landed."

It was scarcely probable that they would find the box, which the waves had rolled about among the pebbles, at high tide, but it was as well to try. Herbert and Pencroft walked rapidly to the point where they had landed the day before, about two hundred feet from the cave. They hunted there, among the shingle, in the clefts of the rocks, but found nothing. If the box had fallen at this place it must have been swept away by the waves. As the sea went down, they searched every little crevice with no result. It was a grave loss in their circumstances, and for the time irreparable. Pencroft could not hide his vexation; he looked very anxious, but said not a word. Herbert tried to console him by observing, that if they had found the matches, they would, very likely, have been wetted by the sea and useless.

"No, my boy," replied the sailor; "they were in a copper box which shut very tightly; and now what are we to do?"

"We shall certainly find some way of making a fire," said Herbert. "Captain Harding or Mr. Spilett will not be without them."

"Yes," replied Pencroft; "but in the meantime we are without fire, and our companions will find but a sorry repast on their return."

"But," said Herbert quickly, "do you think it possible that they have no tinder or matches?"

"I doubt it," replied the sailor, shaking his head, "for neither Neb nor Captain Harding smoke, and I believe that Mr. Spilett would rather keep his note-book than his match-box."

Herbert did not reply. The loss of the box was certainly to be regretted, but the boy was still sure of procuring fire in some way or other. Pencroft, more experienced, did not think so, although he was not a man to trouble himself about a small or great grievance. At any rate, there was only one thing to be done—to await the return of Neb and the reporter; but they must give up the feast of hard eggs which they had meant to prepare, and a meal of raw flesh was not an agreeable prospect either for themselves or for the others.

Before returning to the cave, the sailor and Herbert, in the event of fire being positively unattainable, collected some more shell-fish, and then silently retraced their steps to their dwelling.

Pencroft, his eyes fixed on the ground, still looked for his box. He even climbed up the left bank of the river from its mouth to the angle where the raft had been moored. He returned to the plateau, went over it in every direction, searched among the high grass on the border of the forest, all in vain.

It was five in the evening when he and Herbert re-entered the cave. It is useless to say that the darkest corners of the passages were ransacked before they were obliged to give it up in despair. Towards six o'clock, when the sun was disappearing behind the high lands of the west, Herbert, who was walking up and down on the strand, signalized the return of Neb and Spilett.

They were returning alone!... The boy's heart sank; the sailor had not been deceived in his forebodings; the engineer, Cyrus Harding, had not been found!

The reporter, on his arrival, sat down on a rock, without saying anything. Exhausted with fatigue, dying of hunger, he had not strength to utter a word.

As to Neb, his red eyes showed how he had cried, and the tears which he could not restrain told too clearly that he had lost all hope.

The reporter recounted all that they had done in their attempt to recover Cyrus Harding. He and Neb had surveyed the coast for a distance of eight miles and consequently much beyond the place where the balloon had fallen the last time but one, a fall which was followed by the disappearance of the engineer and the dog Top. The shore was solitary; not a vestige of a mark. Not even a pebble recently displaced; not a trace on the sand; not a human footstep on all that part of the beach. It was clear that that portion of the shore had never been visited by a human being. The sea was as deserted as the land, and it was there, a few hundred feet from the coast, that the engineer must have found a tomb.

As Spilett ended his account, Neb jumped up, exclaiming in a voice which showed how hope struggled within him, "No! he is not dead! he can't be dead! It might happen to any one else, but never to him! He could get out of anything!" Then his strength forsaking him, "Oh! I can do no more!" he murmured.

"Neb," said Herbert, running to him, "we will find him! God will give him back to us! But in the meantime you are hungry, and you must eat something."

So saying, he offered the poor Negro a few handfuls of shell-fish, which was indeed wretched and insufficient food. Neb had not eaten anything for several hours, but he refused them. He could not, would not live without his master.

As to Gideon Spilett, he devoured the shell-fish, then he laid himself down on the sand, at the foot of a rock. He was very weak, but calm. Herbert went up to him, and taking his hand, "Sir," said he, "we have found a shelter which will be better than lying here. Night is advancing. Come and rest! To-morrow we will search farther."

The reporter got up, and guided by the boy went towards the cave. On the way, Pencroft asked him in the most natural tone, if by chance he happened to have a match or two.

The reporter stopped, felt in his pockets, but finding nothing said, "I had some, but I must have thrown them away."

The seaman then put the same question to Neb and received the same answer.

"Confound it!" exclaimed the sailor.

The reporter heard him and seizing his arm, "Have you no matches?" he asked.

"Not one, and no fire in consequence."

"Ah!" cried Neb, "if my master was here, he would know what to do!"

The four castaways remained motionless, looking uneasily at each other. Herbert was the first to break the silence by saying, "Mr. Spilett, you are a smoker and always have matches about you; perhaps you haven't looked well, try again, a single match will be enough!"

The reporter hunted again in the pockets of his trousers, waistcoat, and great-coat, and at last to Pencroft's great joy, no less to his extreme surprise, he felt a tiny piece of wood entangled in the lining of his waistcoat. He seized it with his fingers through the stuff, but he could not get it out. If this was a match and a single one, it was of great importance not to rub off the phosphorus.

"Will you let me try?" said the boy, and very cleverly, without breaking it, he managed to draw out the wretched yet precious little bit of wood which was of such great importance to these poor men. It was unused.

"Hurrah!" cried Pencroft; "it is as good as having a whole cargo!" He took the match, and, followed by his companions, entered the cave.

This small piece of wood, of which so many in an inhabited country are wasted with indifference and are of no value, must here be used with the greatest caution.

The sailor first made sure that it was quite dry; that done, "We must have some paper," said he.

"Here," replied Spilett, after some hesitation tearing a leaf out of his note-book.

Pencroft took the piece of paper which the reporter held out to him, and knelt down before the fireplace. Some handfuls of grass, leaves, and dry moss were placed under the fagots and disposed in such a way that the air could easily circulate, and the dry wood would rapidly catch fire.

Pencroft then twisted the piece of paper into the shape of a cone, as smokers do in a high wind, and poked it in among the moss. Taking a small, rough stone, he wiped it carefully, and with a beating heart, holding his breath, he gently rubbed the match. The first attempt did not produce any effect. Pencroft had not struck hard enough, fearing to rub off the phosphorus.

"No, I can't do it," said he, "my hand trembles, the match has missed fire; I cannot, I will not!" and rising, he told Herbert to take his place.

Certainly the boy had never in all his life been so nervous. Prometheus going to steal the fire from heaven could not have been more anxious. He did not hesitate, however, but struck the match directly.

A little spluttering was heard and a tiny blue flame sprang up, making a choking smoke. Herbert quickly turned the match so as to augment the flame, and then slipped it into the paper cone, which in a few seconds too caught fire, and then the moss.

A minute later the dry wood crackled and a cheerful flame, assisted by the vigorous blowing of the sailor, sprang up in the midst of the darkness.

"At last!" cried Pencroft, getting up; "I was never so nervous before in all my life!"

The flat stones made a capital fireplace. The smoke went quite easily out at the narrow passage, the chimney drew, and an agreeable warmth was not long in being felt.

They must now take great care not to let the fire go out, and always to keep some embers alight. It only needed care and attention, as they had plenty of wood and could renew their store at any time.

Pencroft's first thought was to use the fire by preparing a more nourishing supper than a dish of shell-fish. Two dozen eggs were brought by Herbert. The reporter leaning up in a corner, watched these preparations without saying anything. A threefold thought weighed on his mind. Was Cyrus still alive? If he was alive, where was he? If he had survived from his fall, how was it that he had not found some means of making known his existence? As to Neb, he was roaming about the shore. He was like a body without a soul.

Pencroft knew fifty ways of cooking eggs, but this time he had no choice, and was obliged to content himself with roasting them under the hot cinders. In a few minutes the cooking was done, and the seaman invited the reporter to take his share of the supper. Such was the first repast of the castaways on this unknown coast. The hard eggs were excellent, and as eggs contain everything indispensable to man's nourishment, these poor people thought themselves well off, and were much strengthened by them. Oh! if only one of them had not been missing at this meal! If the five prisoners who escaped from Richmond had been all there, under the piled-up rocks, before this clear, crackling fire on the dry sand, what thanksgiving must they have rendered to Heaven! But the most ingenious, the most learned, he who was their unquestioned chief, Cyrus Harding, was, alas! missing, and his body had not even obtained a burial-place.

Thus passed the 25th of March. Night had come on. Outside could be heard the howling of the wind and the monotonous sound of the surf breaking on the shore. The waves rolled the shingle backwards and forwards with a deafening noise.

The reporter retired into a dark corner after having shortly noted down the occurrences of the day; the first appearance of this new land, the loss of their leader, the exploration of the coast, the incident of the matches, etc.; and then overcome by fatigue, he managed to forget his sorrows in sleep. Herbert went to sleep directly. As to the sailor, he passed the night with one eye on the fire, on which he did not spare fuel. But one of the castaways did not sleep in the cave. The inconsolable, despairing Neb, notwithstanding all that his companions could say to induce him to take some rest, wandered all night long on the shore calling on his master.

Chapter 6

The inventory of the articles possessed by these castaways from the clouds, thrown upon a coast which appeared to be uninhabited, was soon made out. They had nothing, save the clothes which they were wearing at the time of the catastrophe. We must mention, however, a note-book and a watch which Gideon Spilett had kept, doubtless by inadvertence, not a weapon, not a tool, not even a pocket-knife; for while in the car they had thrown out everything to lighten the balloon. The imaginary heroes of Daniel Defoe or of Wyss, as well as Selkirk and Raynal shipwrecked on Juan Fernandez and on the archipelago of the Aucklands, were never in such absolute destitution. Either they had abundant resources from their stranded vessels, in grain, cattle, tools, ammunition, or else some things were thrown up on the coast which supplied them with all the first necessities of life. But here, not any instrument whatever, not a utensil. From nothing they must supply themselves with everything.

And yet, if Cyrus Harding had been with them, if the engineer could have brought his practical science, his inventive mind to bear on their situation, perhaps all hope would not have been lost. Alas! they must hope no longer again to see Cyrus Harding. The castaways could expect nothing but from themselves and from that Providence which never abandons those whose faith is sincere.

But ought they to establish themselves on this part of the coast, without trying to know to what continent it belonged, if it was inhabited, or if they were on the shore of a desert island?

It was an important question, and should be solved with the shortest possible delay. From its answer they would know what measures to take. However, according to Pencroft's advice, it appeared best to wait a few days before commencing an exploration. They must, in fact, prepare some provisions and procure more strengthening food than eggs and molluscs. The explorers, before undertaking new fatigues, must first of all recruit their strength.

The Chimneys offered a retreat sufficient for the present. The fire was lighted, and it was easy to preserve some embers. There were plenty of shell-fish and eggs among the rocks and on the beach. It would be easy to kill a few of the pigeons which were flying by hundreds about the summit of the plateau, either with sticks or stones. Perhaps the trees of the neighboring forest would supply them with eatable fruit. Lastly, the sweet water was there.

It was accordingly settled that for a few days they would remain at the Chimneys so as to prepare themselves for an expedition, either along the shore or into the interior of the country. This plan suited Neb particularly. As obstinate in his ideas as in his presentiments, he was in no haste to abandon this part of the coast, the scene of the catastrophe. He did not, he would not believe in the loss of Cyrus Harding. No, it did not seem to him possible that such a man had ended in this vulgar fashion, carried away by a wave, drowned in the floods, a few hundred feet from a shore. As long as the waves had not cast up the body of the engineer, as long as he, Neb, had not seen with his eyes, touched with his hands the corpse of his master, he would not believe in his death! And this idea rooted itself deeper than ever in his determined heart. An illusion perhaps, but still an illusion to be respected, and one which the sailor did not wish to destroy. As for him, he hoped no longer, but there was no use in arguing with Neb. He was like the dog who will not leave the place where his master is buried, and his grief was such that most probably he would not survive him.

This same morning, the 26th of March, at daybreak, Neb had set out on the shore in a northerly direction, and he had returned to the spot where the sea, no doubt, had closed over the unfortunate Harding.

That day's breakfast was composed solely of pigeon's eggs and lithodomes. Herbert had found some salt deposited by evaporation in the hollows of the rocks, and this mineral was very welcome.

The repast ended, Pencroft asked the reporter if he wished to accompany Herbert and himself to the forest, where they were going to try to hunt. But on consideration, it was thought necessary that someone should remain to keep in the fire, and to be at hand in the highly improbable event of Neb requiring aid. The reporter accordingly remained behind.

"To the chase, Herbert," said the sailor. "We shall find ammunition on our way, and cut our weapons in the forest." But at the moment of starting, Herbert observed, that since they had no tinder, it would perhaps be prudent to replace it by another substance.

"What?" asked Pencroft.

"Burnt linen," replied the boy. "That could in case of need serve for tinder."

The sailor thought it very sensible advice. Only it had the inconvenience of necessitating the sacrifice of a piece of handkerchief. Notwithstanding, the thing was well worth while trying, and a part of Pencroft's large checked handkerchief was soon reduced to the state of a half-burnt rag. This inflammable material was placed in the central chamber at the bottom of a little cavity in the rock, sheltered from all wind and damp.

It was nine o'clock in the morning. The weather was threatening and the breeze blew from the southeast. Herbert and Pencroft turned the angle of the Chimneys, not without having cast a look at the smoke which, just at that place, curled round a point of rock: they ascended the left bank of the river.

Arrived at the forest, Pencroft broke from the first tree two stout branches which he transformed into clubs, the ends of which Herbert rubbed smooth on a rock. Oh! what would they not have given for a knife!

The two hunters now advanced among the long grass, following the bank. From the turning which directed its course to the southwest, the river narrowed gradually and the channel lay between high banks, over which the trees formed a double arch. Pencroft, lest they should lose themselves, resolved to follow the course of the stream, which would always lead them back to the point from which they started. But the bank was not without some obstacles: here, the flexible branches of the trees bent level with the current; there, creepers and thorns which they had to break down with their sticks. Herbert often glided among the broken stumps with the agility of a young cat, and disappeared in the underwood. But Pencroft called him back directly, begging him not to wander away. Meanwhile, the sailor attentively observed the disposition and nature of the surrounding country. On the left bank, the ground, which was flat and marshy, rose imperceptibly towards the interior. It looked there like a network of liquid threads which doubtless reached the river by some underground drain. Sometimes a stream ran through the underwood, which they crossed without difficulty. The opposite shore appeared to be more uneven, and the valley of which the river occupied the bottom was more clearly visible. The hill, covered with trees disposed in terraces, intercepted the view. On the right bank walking would have been difficult, for the declivities fell suddenly, and the trees bending over the water were only sustained by the strength of their roots.

It is needless to add that this forest, as well as the coast already surveyed, was destitute of any sign of human life. Pencroft only saw traces of quadrupeds, fresh footprints of animals, of which he could not recognize the species. In all probability, and such was also Herbert's opinion, some had been left by formidable wild beasts which doubtless would give them some trouble; but nowhere did they observe the mark of an axe on the trees, nor the ashes of a fire, nor the impression of a human foot. On this they might probably congratulate themselves, for on any land in the middle of the Pacific the presence of man was perhaps more to be feared than desired. Herbert and Pencroft speaking little, for the difficulties of the way were great, advanced very slowly, and after walking for an hour they had scarcely gone more than a mile. As yet the hunt had not been successful. However, some birds sang and fluttered in the foliage, and appeared very timid, as if man had inspired them with an instinctive fear. Among others, Herbert described, in a marshy part of the forest, a bird with a long pointed beak, closely resembling the king-fisher, but its plumage was not fine, though of a metallic brilliancy.

"That must be a jacamar," said Herbert, trying to get nearer.

"This will be a good opportunity to taste jacamar," replied the sailor, "if that fellow is in a humor to be roasted!"

Just then, a stone cleverly thrown by the boy, struck the creature on the wing, but the blow did not disable it, and the jacamar ran off and disappeared in an instant.

"How clumsy I am!" cried Herbert.

"No, no, my boy!" replied the sailor. "The blow was well aimed; many a one would have missed it altogether! Come, don't be vexed with yourself. We shall catch it another day!"

As the hunters advanced, the trees were found to be more scattered, many being magnificent, but none bore eatable fruit. Pencroft searched in vain for some of those precious palm-trees which are employed in so many ways in domestic life, and which have been found as far as the fortieth parallel in the Northern Hemisphere, and to the thirty-fifth only in the Southern Hemisphere. But this forest was only composed of coniferae, such as deodaras, already recognized by Herbert, and Douglas pine, similar to those which grow on the northwest coast of America, and splendid firs, measuring a hundred and fifty feet in height.

At this moment a flock of birds, of a small size and pretty plumage, with long glancing tails, dispersed themselves among the branches strewing their feathers, which covered the ground as with fine down. Herbert picked up a few of these feathers, and after having examined them,—

"These are couroucous," said he.

"I should prefer a moor-cock or guinea-fowl," replied Pencroft, "still, if they are good to eat—"

"They are good to eat, and also their flesh is very delicate," replied Herbert. "Besides, if I don't mistake, it is easy to approach and kill them with a stick."

The sailor and the lad, creeping among the grass, arrived at the foot of a tree, whose lower branches were covered with little birds. The couroucous were waiting the passage of insects which served for their nourishment. Their feathery feet could be seen clasping the slender twigs which supported them.

The hunters then rose, and using their sticks like scythes, they mowed down whole rows of these couroucous, who never thought of flying away, and stupidly allowed themselves to be knocked off. A hundred were already heaped on the ground, before the others made up their minds to fly.

"Well," said Pencroft, "here is game, which is quite within the reach of hunters like us. We have only to put out our hands and take it!"

The sailor having strung the couroucou like larks on flexible twigs, they then continued their exploration. The stream here made a bend towards the south, but this detour was probably not prolonged for the river must have its source in the mountain, and be supplied by the melting of the snow which covered the sides of the central cone.

The particular object of their expedition was, as has been said, to procure the greatest possible quantity of game for the inhabitants of the Chimneys. It must be acknowledged that as yet this object had not been attained. So the sailor actively pursued his researches, though he exclaimed, when some animal which he had not even time to recognize fled into the long grass, "If only we had had the dog Top!" But Top had disappeared at the same time as his master, and had probably perished with him.

Towards three o'clock new flocks of birds were seen through certain trees, at whose aromatic berries they were pecking, those of the juniper-tree among others. Suddenly a loud trumpet call resounded through the forest. This strange and sonorous cry was produced by a game bird called grouse in the United States. They soon saw several couples, whose plumage was rich chestnut-brown mottled with dark brown, and tail of the same color. Herbert recognized the males by the two wing-like appendages raised on the neck. Pencroft determined to get hold of at least one of these gallinaceae, which were as large as a fowl, and whose flesh is better than that of a pullet. But it was difficult, for they would not allow themselves to be approached. After several fruitless attempts, which resulted in nothing but scaring the grouse, the sailor said to the lad,—

"Decidedly, since we can't kill them on the wing, we must try to take them with a line."

"Like a fish?" cried Herbert, much surprised at the proposal.

"Like a fish," replied the sailor quite seriously. Pencroft had found among the grass half a dozen grouse nests, each having three or four eggs. He took great care not to touch these nests, to which their proprietors would not fail to return. It was around these that he meant to stretch his lines, not snares, but real fishing-lines. He took Herbert to some distance from the nests, and there prepared his singular apparatus with all the care which a disciple of Izaak Walton would have used. Herbert watched the work with great interest, though rather doubting its success. The lines were made of fine creepers, fastened one to the other, of the length of fifteen or twenty feet. Thick, strong thorns, the points bent back (which were supplied from a dwarf acacia bush) were fastened to the ends of the creepers, by way of hooks. Large red worms, which were crawling on the ground, furnished bait.

This done, Pencroft, passing among the grass and concealing himself skillfully, placed the end of his lines armed with hooks near the grouse nests; then he returned, took the other ends and hid with Herbert behind a large tree. There they both waited patiently; though, it must be said, that Herbert did not reckon much on the success of the inventive Pencroft.

A whole half-hour passed, but then, as the sailor had surmised, several couple of grouse returned to their nests. They walked along, pecking the ground, and not suspecting in any way the presence of the hunters, who, besides, had taken care to place themselves to leeward of the gallinaceae.

The lad felt at this moment highly interested. He held his breath, and Pencroft, his eyes staring, his mouth open, his lips advanced, as if about to taste a piece of grouse, scarcely breathed.

Meanwhile, the birds walked about the hooks, without taking any notice of them. Pencroft then gave little tugs which moved the bait as if the worms had been still alive.

The sailor undoubtedly felt much greater anxiety than does the fisherman, for he does not see his prey coming through the water. The jerks attracted the attention of the gallinaceae, and they attacked the hooks with their beaks. Three voracious grouse swallowed at the same moment bait and hook. Suddenly with a smart jerk, Pencroft "struck" his line, and a flapping of wings showed that the birds were taken.

"Hurrah!" he cried, rushing towards the game, of which he made himself master in an instant.

Herbert clapped his hands. It was the first time that he had ever seen birds taken with a line, but the sailor modestly confessed that it was not his first attempt, and that besides he could not claim the merit of invention.

"And at any rate," added he, "situated as we are, we must hope to hit upon many other contrivances."

The grouse were fastened by their claws, and Pencroft, delighted at not having to appear before their companions with empty hands, and observing that the day had begun to decline, judged it best to return to their dwelling.

The direction was indicated by the river, whose course they had only to follow, and, towards six o'clock, tired enough with their excursion, Herbert and Pencroft arrived at the Chimneys.

Chapter 7

Gideon Spilett was standing motionless on the shore, his arms crossed, gazing over the sea, the horizon of which was lost towards the east in a thick black cloud which was spreading rapidly towards the zenith. The wind was already strong, and increased with the decline of day. The whole sky was of a threatening aspect, and the first symptoms of a violent storm were clearly visible.

Herbert entered the Chimneys, and Pencroft went towards the reporter. The latter, deeply absorbed, did not see him approach.

"We are going to have a dirty night, Mr. Spilett!" said the sailor: "Petrels delight in wind and rain."

The reporter, turning at the moment, saw Pencroft, and his first words were,—

"At what distance from the coast would you say the car was, when the waves carried off our companion?"

The sailor had not expected this question. He reflected an instant and replied,—

"Two cables lengths at the most."

"But what is a cable's length?" asked Gideon Spilett.

"About a hundred and twenty fathoms, or six hundred feet."

"Then," said the reporter, "Cyrus Harding must have disappeared twelve hundred feet at the most from the shore?"

"About that," replied Pencroft.

"And his dog also?"

"Also."

"What astonishes me," rejoined the reporter, "while admitting that our companion has perished, is that Top has also met his death, and that neither the body of the dog nor of his master has been cast on the shore!"

"It is not astonishing, with such a heavy sea," replied the sailor. "Besides, it is possible that currents have carried them farther down the coast."

"Then, it is your opinion that our friend has perished in the waves?" again asked the reporter.

"That is my opinion."

"My own opinion," said Gideon Spilett, "with due deference to your experience, Pencroft, is that in the double fact of the absolute disappearance of Cyrus and Top, living or dead, there is something unaccountable and unlikely."

"I wish I could think like you, Mr. Spilett," replied Pencroft; "unhappily, my mind is made up on this point." Having said this, the sailor returned to the Chimneys. A good fire crackled on the hearth. Herbert had just thrown on an armful of dry wood, and the flame cast a bright light into the darkest parts of the passage.

Pencroft immediately began to prepare the dinner. It appeared best to introduce something solid into the bill of fare, for all needed to get up their strength. The strings of couroucous were kept for the next day, but they plucked a couple of grouse, which were soon spitted on a stick, and roasting before a blazing fire.

At seven in the evening Neb had not returned. The prolonged absence of the Negro made Pencroft very uneasy. It was to be feared that he had met with an accident on this unknown land, or that the unhappy fellow had been driven to some act of despair. But Herbert drew very different conclusions from this absence. According to him, Neb's delay was caused by some new circumstances which had induced him to prolong his search. Also, everything new must be to the advantage of Cyrus Harding. Why had Neb not returned unless hope still detained him? Perhaps he had found some mark, a footstep, a trace which had put him in the right path. Perhaps he was at this moment on a certain track. Perhaps even he was near his master.

Thus the lad reasoned. Thus he spoke. His companions let him talk. The reporter alone approved with a gesture. But what Pencroft thought most probable was, that Neb had pushed his researches on the shore farther than the day before, and that he had not as yet had time to return.

Herbert, however, agitated by vague presentiments, several times manifested an intention to go to meet Neb. But Pencroft assured him that that would be a useless course, that in the darkness and deplorable weather he could not find any traces of Neb, and that it would be much better to wait. If Neb had not made his appearance by the next day, Pencroft would not hesitate to join him in his search.

Gideon Spilett approved of the sailor's opinion that it was best not to divide, and Herbert was obliged to give up his project; but two large tears fell from his eyes.

The reporter could not refrain from embracing the generous boy.

Bad weather now set in. A furious gale from the southeast passed over the coast. The sea roared as it beat over the reef. Heavy rain was dashed by the storm into particles like dust. Ragged masses of vapor drove along the beach, on which the tormented shingles sounded as if poured out in cart-loads, while the sand raised by the wind added as it were mineral dust to that which was liquid, and rendered the united attack insupportable. Between the river's mouth and the end of the cliff, eddies of wind whirled and gusts from this maelstrom lashed the water which ran through the narrow valley. The smoke from the fireplace was also driven back through the opening, filling the passages and rendering them uninhabitable.

Therefore, as the grouse were cooked, Pencroft let the fire die away, and only preserved a few embers buried under the ashes.

At eight o'clock Neb had not appeared, but there was no doubt that the frightful weather alone hindered his return, and that he must have taken refuge in some cave, to await the end of the storm or at least the return of day. As to going to meet him, or attempting to find him, it was impossible.

The game constituted the only dish at supper; the meat was excellent, and Pencroft and Herbert, whose long excursion had rendered them very hungry, devoured it with infinite satisfaction.

Their meal concluded, each retired to the corner in which he had rested the preceding night, and Herbert was not long in going to sleep near the sailor, who had stretched himself beside the fireplace.

Outside, as the night advanced, the tempest also increased in strength, until it was equal to that which had carried the prisoners from Richmond to this land in the Pacific. The tempests which are frequent during the seasons of the equinox, and which are so prolific in catastrophes, are above all terrible over this immense ocean, which opposes no obstacle to their fury. No description can give an idea of the terrific violence of the gale as it beat upon the unprotected coast.

Happily the pile of rocks which formed the Chimneys was solid. It was composed of enormous blocks of granite, a few of which, insecurely balanced, seemed to tremble on their foundations, and Pencroft could feel rapid quiverings under his head as it rested on the rock. But he repeated to himself, and rightly, that there was nothing to fear, and that their retreat would not give way. However he heard the noise of stones torn from the summit of the plateau by the wind, falling down on to the beach. A few even rolled on to the upper part of the Chimneys, or flew off in fragments when they were projected perpendicularly. Twice the sailor rose and intrenched himself at the opening of the passage, so as to take a look in safety at the outside. But there was nothing to be feared from these showers, which were not considerable, and he returned to his couch before the fireplace, where the embers glowed beneath the ashes.

Notwithstanding the fury of the hurricane, the uproar of the tempest, the thunder, and the tumult, Herbert slept profoundly. Sleep at last took possession of Pencroft, whom a seafaring life had habituated to anything. Gideon Spilett alone was kept awake by anxiety. He reproached himself with not having accompanied Neb. It was evident that he had not abandoned all hope. The presentiments which had troubled Herbert did not cease to agitate him also. His thoughts were concentrated on Neb. Why had Neb not returned? He tossed about on his sandy couch, scarcely giving a thought to the struggle of the elements. Now and then, his eyes, heavy with fatigue, closed for an instant, but some sudden thought reopened them almost immediately.

Meanwhile the night advanced, and it was perhaps two hours from morning, when Pencroft, then sound asleep, was vigorously shaken.

"What's the matter?" he cried, rousing himself, and collecting his ideas with the promptitude usual to seamen.

The reporter was leaning over him, and saying,—

"Listen, Pencroft, listen!"

The sailor strained his ears, but could hear no noise beyond those caused by the storm.

"It is the wind," said he.

"No," replied Gideon Spilett, listening again, "I thought I heard—"

"What?"

"The barking of a dog!"

"A dog!" cried Pencroft, springing up.

"Yes—barking—"

"It's not possible!" replied the sailor. "And besides, how, in the roaring of the storm—"

"Stop—listen—" said the reporter.

Pencroft listened more attentively, and really thought he heard, during a lull, distant barking.

"Well!" said the reporter, pressing the sailor's hand.

"Yes—yes!" replied Pencroft.

"It is Top! It is Top!" cried Herbert, who had just awoke; and all three rushed towards the opening of the Chimneys. They had great difficulty in getting out. The wind drove them back. But at last they succeeded, and could only remain standing by leaning against the rocks. They looked about, but could not speak. The darkness was intense. The sea, the sky, the land were all mingled in one black mass. Not a speck of light was visible.

The reporter and his companions remained thus for a few minutes, overwhelmed by the wind, drenched by the rain, blinded by the sand.

Then, in a pause of the tumult, they again heard the barking, which they found must be at some distance.

It could only be Top! But was he alone or accompanied? He was most probably alone, for, if Neb had been with him, he would have made his way more directly towards the Chimneys. The sailor squeezed the reporter's hand, for he could not make himself heard, in a way which signified "Wait!" then he reentered the passage.

An instant after he issued with a lighted fagot, which he threw into the darkness, whistling shrilly.

It appeared as if this signal had been waited for; the barking immediately came nearer, and soon a dog bounded into the passage. Pencroft, Herbert, and Spilett entered after him.

An armful of dry wood was thrown on the embers. The passage was lighted up with a bright flame.

"It is Top!" cried Herbert.

It was indeed Top, a magnificent Anglo-Norman, who derived from these two races crossed the swiftness of foot and the acuteness of smell which are the preeminent qualities of coursing dogs. It was the dog of the engineer, Cyrus Harding. But he was alone! Neither Neb nor his master accompanied him!

How was it that his instinct had guided him straight to the Chimneys, which he did not know? It appeared inexplicable, above all, in the midst of this black night and in such a tempest! But what was still more inexplicable was, that Top was neither tired, nor exhausted, nor even soiled with mud or sand!—Herbert had drawn him towards him, and was patting his head, the dog rubbing his neck against the lad's hands.

"If the dog is found, the master will be found also!" said the reporter.

"God grant it!" responded Herbert. "Let us set off! Top will guide us!"

Pencroft did not make any objection. He felt that Top's arrival contradicted his conjectures. "Come along then!" said he.

Pencroft carefully covered the embers on the hearth. He placed a few pieces of wood among them, so as to keep in the fire until their return. Then, preceded by the dog, who seemed to invite them by short barks to come with him, and followed by the reporter and the boy, he dashed out, after having put up in his handkerchief the remains of the supper.

The storm was then in all its violence, and perhaps at its height. Not a single ray of light from the moon pierced through the clouds. To follow a straight course was difficult. It was best to rely on Top's instinct. They did so. The reporter and Herbert walked behind the dog, and the sailor brought up the rear. It was impossible to exchange a word. The rain was not very heavy, but the wind was terrific.

However, one circumstance favored the seaman and his two companions. The wind being southeast, consequently blew on their backs. The clouds of sand, which otherwise would have been insupportable, from being received behind, did not in consequence impede their progress. In short, they sometimes went faster than they liked, and had some difficulty in keeping their feet; but hope gave them strength, for it was not at random that they made their way along the shore. They had no doubt that Neb had found his master, and that he had sent them the faithful dog. But was the engineer living, or had Neb only sent for his companions that they might render the last duties to the corpse of the unfortunate Harding?

After having passed the precipice, Herbert, the reporter, and Pencroft prudently stepped aside to stop and take breath. The turn of the rocks sheltered them from the wind, and they could breathe after this walk or rather run of a quarter of an hour.

They could now hear and reply to each other, and the lad having pronounced the name of Cyrus Harding, Top gave a few short barks, as much as to say that his master was saved.

"Saved, isn't he?" repeated Herbert; "saved, Top?"

And the dog barked in reply.

They once more set out. The tide began to rise, and urged by the wind it threatened to be unusually high, as it was a spring tide. Great billows thundered against the reef with such violence that they probably passed entirely over the islet, then quite invisible. The mole no longer protected the coast, which was directly exposed to the attacks of the open sea.

As soon as the sailor and his companions left the precipice, the wind struck them again with renewed fury. Though bent under the gale they walked very quickly, following Top, who did not hesitate as to what direction to take.

They ascended towards the north, having on their left an interminable extent of billows, which broke with a deafening noise, and on their right a dark country, the aspect of which it was impossible to guess. But they felt that it was comparatively flat, for the wind passed completely over them, without being driven back as it was when it came in contact with the cliff.

At four o'clock in the morning, they reckoned that they had cleared about five miles. The clouds were slightly raised, and the wind, though less damp, was very sharp and cold. Insufficiently protected by their clothing, Pencroft, Herbert and Spilett suffered cruelly, but not a complaint escaped their lips. They were determined to follow Top, wherever the intelligent animal wished to lead them.

Towards five o'clock day began to break. At the zenith, where the fog was less thick, gray shades bordered the clouds; under an opaque belt, a luminous line clearly traced the horizon. The crests of the billows were tipped with a wild light, and the foam regained its whiteness. At the same time on the left the hilly parts of the coast could be seen, though very indistinctly.

At six o'clock day had broken. The clouds rapidly lifted. The seaman and his companions were then about six miles from the Chimneys. They were following a very flat shore bounded by a reef of rocks, whose heads scarcely emerged from the sea, for they were in deep water. On the left, the country appeared to be one vast extent of sandy downs, bristling with thistles. There was no cliff, and the shore offered no resistance to the ocean but a chain of irregular hillocks. Here and there grew two or three trees, inclined towards the west, their branches projecting in that direction. Quite behind, in the southwest, extended the border of the forest.

At this moment, Top became very excited. He ran forward, then returned, and seemed to entreat them to hasten their steps. The dog then left the beach, and guided by his wonderful instinct, without showing the least hesitation, went straight in among the downs. They followed him. The country appeared an absolute desert. Not a living creature was to be seen.

The downs, the extent of which was large, were composed of hillocks and even of hills, very irregularly distributed. They resembled a Switzerland modeled in sand, and only an amazing instinct could have possibly recognized the way.

Five minutes after having left the beach, the reporter and his two companions arrived at a sort of excavation, hollowed out at the back of a high mound. There Top stopped, and gave a loud, clear bark. Spilett, Herbert, and Pencroft dashed into the cave.

Neb was there, kneeling beside a body extended on a bed of grass.

The body was that of the engineer, Cyrus Harding.

Chapter 8

Neb did not move. Pencroft only uttered one word.

"Living?" he cried.

Neb did not reply. Spilett and the sailor turned pale. Herbert clasped his hands, and remained motionless. The poor Negro, absorbed in his grief, evidently had neither seen his companions nor heard the sailor speak.

The reporter knelt down beside the motionless body, and placed his ear to the engineer's chest, having first torn open his clothes.

A minute—an age!—passed, during which he endeavored to catch the faintest throb of the heart.

Neb had raised himself a little and gazed without seeing. Despair had completely changed his countenance. He could scarcely be recognized, exhausted with fatigue, broken with grief. He believed his master was dead.

Gideon Spilett at last rose, after a long and attentive examination.

"He lives!" said he.

Pencroft knelt in his turn beside the engineer, he also heard a throbbing, and even felt a slight breath on his cheek.

Herbert at a word from the reporter ran out to look for water. He found, a hundred feet off, a limpid stream, which seemed to have been greatly increased by the rains, and which filtered through the sand; but nothing in which to put the water, not even a shell among the downs. The lad was obliged to content himself with dipping his handkerchief in the stream, and with it hastened back to the grotto.

Happily the wet handkerchief was enough for Gideon Spilett, who only wished to wet the engineer's lips. The cold water produced an almost immediate effect. His chest heaved and he seemed to try to speak.

"We will save him!" exclaimed the reporter.

At these words hope revived in Neb's heart. He undressed his master to see if he was wounded, but not so much as a bruise was to be found, either on the head, body, or limbs, which was surprising, as he must have been dashed against the rocks; even the hands were uninjured, and it was difficult to explain how the engineer showed no traces of the efforts which he must have made to get out of reach of the breakers.

But the explanation would come later. When Cyrus was able to speak he would say what had happened. For the present the question was, how to recall him to life, and it appeared likely that rubbing would bring this about; so they set to work with the sailor's jersey.

The engineer, revived by this rude shampooing, moved his arm slightly and began to breathe more regularly. He was sinking from exhaustion, and certainly, had not the reporter and his companions arrived, it would have been all over with Cyrus Harding.

"You thought your master was dead, didn't you?" said the seaman to Neb.

"Yes! quite dead!" replied Neb, "and if Top had not found you, and brought you here, I should have buried my master, and then have lain down on his grave to die!"

It had indeed been a narrow escape for Cyrus Harding!

Neb then recounted what had happened. The day before, after having left the Chimneys at daybreak, he had ascended the coast in a northerly direction, and had reached that part of the shore which he had already visited.

There, without any hope he acknowledged, Neb had searched the beach, among the rocks, on the sand, for the smallest trace to guide him. He examined particularly that part of the beach which was not covered by the high tide, for near the sea the water would have obliterated all marks. Neb did not expect to find his master living. It was for a corpse that he searched, a corpse which he wished to bury with his own hands!

He sought long in vain. This desert coast appeared never to have been visited by a human creature. The shells, those which the sea had not reached, and which might be met with by millions above high-water mark, were untouched. Not a shell was broken.

Neb then resolved to walk along the beach for some miles. It was possible that the waves had carried the body to quite a distant point. When a corpse floats a little distance from a low shore, it rarely happens that the tide does not throw it up, sooner or later. This Neb knew, and he wished to see his master again for the last time.

"I went along the coast for another two miles, carefully examining the beach, both at high and low water, and I had despaired of finding anything, when yesterday, above five in the evening, I saw footprints on the sand."

"Footprints?" exclaimed Pencroft.

"Yes!" replied Neb.

"Did these footprints begin at the water's edge?" asked the reporter.

"No," replied Neb, "only above high-water mark, for the others must have been washed out by the tide."

"Go on, Neb," said Spilett.

"I went half crazy when I saw these footprints. They were very clear and went towards the downs. I followed them for a quarter of a mile, running, but taking care not to destroy them. Five minutes after, as it was getting dark, I heard the barking of a dog. It was Top, and Top brought me here, to my master!"

Neb ended his account by saying what had been his grief at finding the inanimate body, in which he vainly sought for the least sign of life. Now that he had found him dead he longed for him to be alive. All his efforts were useless! Nothing remained to be done but to render the last duties to the one whom he had loved so much! Neb then thought of his companions. They, no doubt, would wish to see the unfortunate man again. Top was there. Could he not rely on the sagacity of the faithful animal? Neb several times pronounced the name of the reporter, the one among his companions whom Top knew best.

Then he pointed to the south, and the dog bounded off in the direction indicated to him.

We have heard how, guided by an instinct which might be looked upon almost as supernatural, Top had found them.

Neb's companions had listened with great attention to this account.

It was unaccountable to them how Cyrus Harding, after the efforts which he must have made to escape from the waves by crossing the rocks, had not received even a scratch. And what could not be explained either was how the engineer had managed to get to this cave in the downs, more than a mile from the shore.

"So, Neb," said the reporter, "it was not you who brought your master to this place."

"No, it was not I," replied the Negro.

"It's very clear that the captain came here by himself," said Pencroft.

"It is clear in reality," observed Spilett, "but it is not credible!"

The explanation of this fact could only be produced from the engineer's own lips, and they must wait for that till speech returned. Rubbing had re-established the circulation of the blood. Cyrus Harding moved his arm again, then his head, and a few incomprehensible words escaped him.

Neb, who was bending over him, spoke, but the engineer did not appear to hear, and his eyes remained closed. Life was only exhibited in him by movement, his senses had not as yet been restored.

Pencroft much regretted not having either fire, or the means of procuring it, for he had, unfortunately, forgotten to bring the burnt linen, which would easily have ignited from the sparks produced by striking together two flints. As to the engineer's pockets, they were entirely empty, except that of his waistcoat, which contained his watch. It was necessary to carry Harding to the Chimneys, and that as soon as possible. This was the opinion of all.

Meanwhile, the care which was lavished on the engineer brought him back to consciousness sooner than they could have expected. The water with which they wetted his lips revived him gradually. Pencroft also thought of mixing with the water some moisture from the titra's flesh which he had brought. Herbert ran to the beach and returned with two large bivalve shells. The sailor concocted something which he introduced between the lips of the engineer, who eagerly drinking it opened his eyes.

Neb and the reporter were leaning over him.

"My master! my master!" cried Neb.

The engineer heard him. He recognized Neb and Spilett, then his other two companions, and his hand slightly pressed theirs.

A few words again escaped him, which showed what thoughts were, even then, troubling his brain. This time he was understood. Undoubtedly they were the same words he had before attempted to utter.

"Island or continent?" he murmured.

"Bother the continent," cried Pencroft hastily; "there is time enough to see about that, captain! we don't care for anything, provided you are living."

The engineer nodded faintly, and then appeased to sleep.

They respected this sleep, and the reporter began immediately to make arrangements for transporting Harding to a more comfortable place. Neb, Herbert, and Pencroft left the cave and directed their steps towards a high mound crowned with a few distorted trees. On the way the sailor could not help repeating,—

"Island or continent! To think of that, when at one's last gasp! What a man!"

Arrived at the summit of the mound, Pencroft and his two companions set to work, with no other tools than their hands, to despoil of its principal branches a rather sickly tree, a sort of marine fir; with these branches they made a litter, on which, covered with grass and leaves, they could carry the engineer.

This occupied them nearly forty minutes, and it was ten o'clock when they returned to Cyrus Harding whom Spilett had not left.

The engineer was just awaking from the sleep, or rather from the drowsiness, in which they had found him. The color was returning to his cheeks, which till now had been as pale as death. He raised himself a little, looked around him, and appeared to ask where he was.

"Can you listen to me without fatigue, Cyrus?" asked the reporter.

"Yes," replied the engineer.

"It's my opinion," said the sailor, "that Captain Harding will be able to listen to you still better, if he will have some more grouse jelly,—for we have grouse, captain," added he, presenting him with a little of this jelly, to which he this time added some of the flesh.

Cyrus Harding ate a little of the grouse, and the rest was divided among his companions, who found it but a meager breakfast, for they were suffering extremely from hunger.

"Well!" said the sailor, "there is plenty of food at the Chimneys, for you must know, captain, that down there, in the south, we have a house, with rooms, beds, and fireplace, and in the pantry, several dozen of birds, which our Herbert calls couroucous. Your litter is ready, and as soon as you feel strong enough we will carry you home."

"Thanks, my friend," replied the engineer; "wait another hour or two, and then we will set out. And now speak, Spilett."

The reporter then told him all that had occurred. He recounted all the events with which Cyrus was unacquainted, the last fall of the balloon, the landing on this unknown land, which appeared a desert (whatever it was, whether island or continent), the discovery of the Chimneys, the search for him, not forgetting of course Neb's devotion, the intelligence exhibited by the faithful Top, as well as many other matters.

"But," asked Harding, in a still feeble voice, "you did not, then, pick me up on the beach?"

"No," replied the reporter.

"And did you not bring me to this cave?"

"No."

"At what distance is this cave from the sea?"

"About a mile," replied Pencroft; "and if you are astonished, captain, we are not less surprised ourselves at seeing you in this place!"

"Indeed," said the engineer, who was recovering gradually, and who took great interest in these details, "indeed it is very singular!"

"But," resumed the sailor, "can you tell us what happened after you were carried off by the sea?"

Cyrus Harding considered. He knew very little. The wave had torn him from the balloon net. He sank at first several fathoms. On returning to the surface, in the half light, he felt a living creature struggling near him. It was Top, who had sprung to his help. He saw nothing of the balloon, which, lightened both of his weight and that of the dog, had darted away like an arrow.

There he was, in the midst of the angry sea, at a distance which could not be less than half a mile from the shore. He attempted to struggle against the billows by swimming vigorously. Top held him up by his clothes; but a strong current seized him and drove him towards the north, and after half an hour of exertion, he sank, dragging Top with him into the depths. From that moment to the moment in which he recovered to find himself in the arms of his friends he remembered nothing.

"However," remarked Pencroft, "you must have been thrown on to the beach, and you must have had strength to walk here, since Neb found your footmarks!"

"Yes... of course," replied the engineer, thoughtfully; "and you found no traces of human beings on this coast?"

"Not a trace," replied the reporter; "besides, if by chance you had met with some deliverer there, just in the nick of time, why should he have abandoned you after having saved you from the waves?"

"You are right, my dear Spilett. Tell me, Neb," added the engineer, turning to his servant, "it was not you who... you can't have had a moment of unconsciousness... during which no, that's absurd.... Do any of the footsteps still remain?" asked Harding.

"Yes, master," replied Neb; "here, at the entrance, at the back of the mound, in a place sheltered from the rain and wind. The storm has destroyed the others."

"Pencroft," said Cyrus Harding, "will you take my shoe and see if it fits exactly to the footprints?"

The sailor did as the engineer requested. While he and Herbert, guided by Neb, went to the place where the footprints were to be found, Cyrus remarked to the reporter,—

"It is a most extraordinary thing!"

"Perfectly inexplicable!" replied Gideon Spilett.

"But do not dwell upon it just now, my dear Spilett, we will talk about it by-and-by."

A moment after the others entered.

There was no doubt about it. The engineer's shoe fitted exactly to the footmarks. It was therefore Cyrus Harding who had left them on the sand.

"Come," said he, "I must have experienced this unconsciousness which I attributed to Neb. I must have walked like a somnambulist, without any knowledge of my steps, and Top must have guided me here, after having dragged me from the waves... Come, Top! Come, old dog!"

The magnificent animal bounded barking to his master, and caresses were lavished on him. It was agreed that there was no other way of accounting for the rescue of Cyrus Harding, and that Top deserved all the honor of the affair.

Towards twelve o'clock, Pencroft having asked the engineer if they could now remove him, Harding, instead of replying, and by an effort which exhibited the most energetic will, got up. But he was obliged to lean on the sailor, or he would have fallen.

"Well done!" cried Pencroft; "bring the captain's litter."

The litter was brought; the transverse branches had been covered with leaves and long grass. Harding was laid on it, and Pencroft, having taken his place at one end and Neb at the other, they started towards the coast. There was a distance of eight miles to be accomplished; but, as they could not go fast, and it would perhaps be necessary to stop frequently, they reckoned that it would take at least six hours to reach the Chimneys. The wind was still strong, but fortunately it did not rain. Although lying down, the engineer, leaning on his elbow, observed the coast, particularly inland. He did not speak, but he gazed; and, no doubt, the appearance of the country, with its inequalities of ground, its forests, its various productions, were impressed on his mind. However, after traveling for two hours, fatigue overcame him, and he slept.

At half-past five the little band arrived at the precipice, and a short time after at the Chimneys.

They stopped, and the litter was placed on the sand; Cyrus Harding was sleeping profoundly, and did not awake.

Pencroft, to his extreme surprise, found that the terrible storm had quite altered the aspect of the place. Important changes had occurred; great blocks of stone lay on the beach, which was also covered with a thick carpet of sea-weed, algae, and wrack. Evidently the sea, passing over the islet, had been carried right up to the foot of the enormous curtain of granite. The soil in front of the cave had been torn away by the violence of the waves. A horrid presentiment flashed across Pencroft's mind. He rushed into the passage, but returned almost immediately, and stood motionless, staring at his companions.... The fire was out; the drowned cinders were nothing but mud; the burnt linen, which was to have served as tinder, had disappeared! The sea had penetrated to the end of the passages, and everything was overthrown and destroyed in the interior of the Chimneys!

Chapter 9

In a few words, Gideon Spilett, Herbert, and Neb were made acquainted with what had happened. This accident, which appeared so very serious to Pencroft, produced different effects on the companions of the honest sailor.

Neb, in his delight at having found his master, did not listen, or rather, did not care to trouble himself with what Pencroft was saying.

Herbert shared in some degree the sailor's feelings.

As to the reporter, he simply replied,—

"Upon my word, Pencroft, it's perfectly indifferent to me!"

"But, I repeat, that we haven't any fire!"

"Pooh!"

"Nor any means of relighting it!"

"Nonsense!"

"But I say, Mr. Spilett—"

"Isn't Cyrus here?" replied the reporter.

"Is not our engineer alive? He will soon find some way of making fire for us!"

"With what?"

"With nothing."

What had Pencroft to say? He could say nothing, for, in the bottom of his heart he shared the confidence which his companions had in Cyrus Harding. The engineer was to them a microcosm, a compound of every science, a possessor of all human knowledge. It was better to be with Cyrus in a desert island, than without him in the most flourishing town in the United States. With him they could want nothing; with him they would never despair. If these brave men had been told that a volcanic eruption would destroy the land, that this land would be engulfed in the depths of the Pacific, they would have imperturbably replied,—

"Cyrus is here!"

While in the palanquin, however, the engineer had again relapsed into unconsciousness, which the jolting to which he had been subjected during his journey had brought on, so that they could not now appeal to his ingenuity. The supper must necessarily be very meager. In fact, all the grouse flesh had been consumed, and there no longer existed any means of cooking more game. Besides, the couroucou which had been reserved had disappeared. They must consider what was to be done.

First of all, Cyrus Harding was carried into the central passage. There they managed to arrange for him a couch of sea-weed which still remained almost dry. The deep sleep which had overpowered him would no doubt be more beneficial to him than any nourishment.

Night had closed in, and the temperature, which had modified when the wind shifted to the northwest, again became extremely cold. Also, the sea having destroyed the partitions which Pencroft had put up in certain places in the passages, the Chimneys, on account of the draughts, had become scarcely habitable. The engineer's condition would, therefore, have been bad enough, if his companions had not carefully covered him with their coats and waistcoats.

Supper, this evening, was of course composed of the inevitable lithodomes, of which Herbert and Neb picked up a plentiful supply on the beach. However, to these molluscs, the lad added some edible sea-weed, which he gathered on high rocks, whose sides were only washed by the sea at the time of high tides. This sea-weed, which belongs to the order of Fucacae, of the genus Sargassum, produces, when dry, a gelatinous matter, rich and nutritious. The reporter and his companions, after having eaten a quantity of lithodomes, sucked the sargassum, of which the taste was very tolerable. It is used in parts of the East very considerably by the natives. "Never mind!" said the sailor, "the captain will help us soon." Meanwhile the cold became very severe, and unhappily they had no means of defending themselves from it.

The sailor, extremely vexed, tried in all sorts of ways to procure fire. Neb helped him in this work. He found some dry moss, and by striking together two pebbles he obtained some sparks, but the moss, not being inflammable enough, did not take fire, for the sparks were really only incandescent, and not at all of the same consistency as those which are emitted from flint when struck in the same manner. The experiment, therefore, did not succeed.

Pencroft, although he had no confidence in the proceeding, then tried rubbing two pieces of dry wood together, as savages do. Certainly, the movement which he and Neb exhibited, if it had been transformed into heat, according to the new theory, would have been enough to heat the boiler of a steamer! It came to nothing. The bits of wood became hot, to be sure, but much less so than the operators themselves.

After working an hour, Pencroft, who was in a complete state of perspiration, threw down the pieces of wood in disgust.

"I can never be made to believe that savages light their fires in this way, let them say what they will," he exclaimed. "I could sooner light my arms by rubbing them against each other!"

The sailor was wrong to despise the proceeding. Savages often kindle wood by means of rapid rubbing. But every sort of wood does not answer for the purpose, and besides, there is "the knack," following the usual expression, and it is probable that Pencroft had not "the knack."

Pencroft's ill humor did not last long. Herbert had taken the bits of wood which he had turned down, and was exerting himself to rub them. The hardy sailor could not restrain a burst of laughter on seeing the efforts of the lad to succeed where he had failed.

"Rub, my boy, rub!" said he.

"I am rubbing," replied Herbert, laughing, "but I don't pretend to do anything else but warm myself instead of shivering, and soon I shall be as hot as you are, my good Pencroft!"

This soon happened. However, they were obliged to give up, for this night at least, the attempt to procure fire. Gideon Spilett repeated, for the twentieth time, that Cyrus Harding would not have been troubled for so small a difficulty. And, in the meantime, he stretched himself in one of the passages on his bed of sand. Herbert, Neb, and Pencroft did the same, while Top slept at his master's feet.

Next day, the 28th of March, when the engineer awoke, about eight in the morning, he saw his companions around him watching his sleep, and, as on the day before, his first words were:—

"Island or continent?" This was his uppermost thought.

"Well!" replied Pencroft, "we don't know anything about it, captain!"

"You don't know yet?"

"But we shall know," rejoined Pencroft, "when you have guided us into the country."

"I think I am able to try it," replied the engineer, who, without much effort, rose and stood upright.

"That's capital!" cried the sailor.

"I feel dreadfully weak," replied Harding. "Give me something to eat, my friends, and it will soon go off. You have fire, haven't you?"

This question was not immediately replied to. But, in a few seconds—

"Alas! we have no fire," said Pencroft, "or rather, captain, we have it no longer!"

And the sailor recounted all that had passed the day before. He amused the engineer by the history of the single match, then his abortive attempt to procure fire in the savages' way.

"We shall consider," replied the engineer, "and if we do not find some substance similar to tinder—"

"Well?" asked the sailor.

"Well, we will make matches.

"Chemicals?"

"Chemicals!"

"It is not more difficult than that," cried the reporter, striking the sailor on the shoulder.

The latter did not think it so simple, but he did not protest. All went out. The weather had become very fine. The sun was rising from the sea's horizon, and touched with golden spangles the prismatic rugosities of the huge precipice.

Having thrown a rapid glance around him, the engineer seated himself on a block of stone. Herbert offered him a few handfuls of shell-fish and sargassum, saying,—

"It is all that we have, Captain Harding."

"Thanks, my boy," replied Harding; "it will do—for this morning at least."

He ate the wretched food with appetite, and washed it down with a little fresh water, drawn from the river in an immense shell.

His companions looked at him without speaking. Then, feeling somewhat refreshed, Cyrus Harding crossed his arms, and said,—

"So, my friends, you do not know yet whether fate has thrown us on an island, or on a continent?"

"No, captain," replied the boy.

"We shall know to-morrow," said the engineer; "till then, there is nothing to be done."

"Yes," replied Pencroft.

"What?"

"Fire," said the sailor, who, also, had a fixed idea.

"We will make it, Pencroft," replied Harding.

"While you were carrying me yesterday, did I not see in the west a mountain which commands the country?"

"Yes," replied Spilett, "a mountain which must be rather high—"

"Well," replied the engineer, "we will climb to the summit to-morrow, and then we shall see if this land is an island or a continent. Till then, I repeat, there is nothing to be done."

"Yes, fire!" said the obstinate sailor again.

"But he will make us a fire!" replied Gideon Spilett, "only have a little patience, Pencroft!"

The seaman looked at Spilett in a way which seemed to say, "If it depended upon you to do it, we wouldn't taste roast meat very soon"; but he was silent.

Meanwhile Captain Harding had made no reply. He appeared to be very little troubled by the question of fire. For a few minutes he remained absorbed in thought; then again speaking,—

"My friends," said he, "our situation is, perhaps, deplorable; but, at any rate, it is very plain. Either we are on a continent, and then, at the expense of greater or less fatigue, we shall reach some inhabited place, or we are on an island. In the latter case, if the island is inhabited, we will try to get out of the scrape with the help of its inhabitants; if it is desert, we will try to get out of the scrape by ourselves."

"Certainly, nothing could be plainer," replied Pencroft.

"But, whether it is an island or a continent," asked Gideon Spilett, "whereabouts do you think, Cyrus, this storm has thrown us?"

"I cannot say exactly," replied the engineer, "but I presume it is some land in the Pacific. In fact, when we left Richmond, the wind was blowing from the northeast, and its very violence greatly proves that it could not have varied. If the direction has been maintained from the northeast to the southwest, we have traversed the States of North Carolina, of South Carolina, of Georgia, the Gulf of Mexico, Mexico, itself, in its narrow part, then a part of the Pacific Ocean. I cannot estimate the distance traversed by the balloon at less than six to seven thousand miles, and, even supposing that the wind had varied half a quarter, it must have brought us either to the archipelago of Mendava, either on the Pomotous, or even, if it had a greater strength than I suppose, to the land of New Zealand. If the last hypothesis is correct, it will be easy enough to get home again. English or Maoris, we shall always find some one to whom we can speak. If, on the contrary, this is the coast of a desert island in some tiny archipelago, perhaps we shall be able to reconnoiter it from the summit of that peak which overlooks the country, and then we shall see how best to establish ourselves here as if we are never to go away."

"Never?" cried the reporter. "You say 'Never,' my dear Cyrus?"

"Better to put things at the worst at first," replied the engineer, "and reserve the best for a surprise."

"Well said," remarked Pencroft. "It is to be hoped, too, that this island, if it be one, is not situated just out of the course of ships; that would be really unlucky!"

"We shall not know what we have to rely on until we have first made the ascent of the mountain," replied the engineer.

"But to-morrow, captain," asked Herbert, "shall you be in a state to bear the fatigue of the ascent?"

"I hope so," replied the engineer, "provided you and Pencroft, my boy, show yourselves quick and clever hunters."

"Captain," said the sailor, "since you are speaking of game, if on my return, I was as certain of roasting it as I am of bringing it back—"

"Bring it back all the same, Pencroft," replied Harding.

It was then agreed that the engineer and the reporter were to pass the day at the Chimneys, so as to examine the shore and the upper plateau. Neb, Herbert, and the sailor were to return to the forest, renew their store of wood, and lay violent hands on every creature, feathered or hairy, which might come within their reach.

They set out accordingly about ten o'clock in the morning, Herbert confident, Neb joyous, Pencroft murmuring aside,—

"If, on my return, I find a fire at the house, I shall believe that the thunder itself came to light it." All three climbed the bank; and arrived at the angle made by the river, the sailor, stopping, said to his two companions,—

"Shall we begin by being hunters or wood-men?"

"Hunters," replied Herbert. "There is Top already in quest."

"We will hunt, then," said the sailor, "and afterwards we can come back and collect our wood."

This agreed to, Herbert, Neb, and Pencroft, after having torn three sticks from the trunk of a young fir, followed Top, who was bounding about among the long grass.

This time, the hunters, instead of following the course of the river, plunged straight into the heart of the forest. There were still the same trees, belonging, for the most part, to the pine family. In certain places, less crowded, growing in clumps, these pines exhibited considerable dimensions, and appeared to indicate, by their development, that the country was situated in a higher latitude than the engineer had supposed. Glades, bristling with stumps worn away by time, were covered with dry wood, which formed an inexhaustible store of fuel. Then, the glade passed, the underwood thickened again, and became almost impenetrable.

It was difficult enough to find the way among the groups of trees, without any beaten track. So the sailor from time to time broke off branches which might be easily recognized. But, perhaps, he was wrong not to follow the watercourse, as he and Herbert had done on their first excursion, for after walking an hour not a creature had shown itself. Top, running under the branches, only roused birds which could not be approached. Even the couroucous were invisible, and it was probable that the sailor would be obliged to return to the marshy part of the forest, in which he had so happily performed his grouse fishing.

"Well, Pencroft," said Neb, in a slightly sarcastic tone, "if this is all the game which you promised to bring back to my master, it won't need a large fire to roast it!"

"Have patience," replied the sailor, "it isn't the game which will be wanting on our return."

"Have you not confidence in Captain Harding?"

"Yes."

"But you don't believe that he will make fire?"

"I shall believe it when the wood is blazing in the fireplace."

"It will blaze, since my master has said so."

"We shall see!"

Meanwhile, the sun had not reached the highest point in its course above the horizon. The exploration, therefore, continued, and was usefully marked by a discovery which Herbert made of a tree whose fruit was edible. This was the stone-pine, which produces an excellent almond, very much esteemed in the temperate regions of America and Europe. These almonds were in a perfect state of maturity, and Herbert described them to his companions, who feasted on them.

"Come," said Pencroft, "sea-weed by way of bread, raw mussels for meat, and almonds for dessert, that's certainly a good dinner for those who have not a single match in their pocket!"

"We mustn't complain," said Herbert.

"I am not complaining, my boy," replied Pencroft, "only I repeat, that meat is a little too much economized in this sort of meal."

"Top has found something!" cried Neb, who ran towards a thicket, in the midst of which the dog had disappeared, barking. With Top's barking were mingled curious gruntings.

The sailor and Herbert had followed Neb. If there was game there this was not the time to discuss how it was to be cooked, but rather, how they were to get hold of it.

The hunters had scarcely entered the bushes when they saw Top engaged in a struggle with an animal which he was holding by the ear. This quadruped was a sort of pig nearly two feet and a half long, of a blackish brown color, lighter below, having hard scanty hair; its toes, then strongly fixed in the ground, seemed to be united by a membrane. Herbert recognized in this animal the capybara, that is to say, one of the largest members of the rodent order.

Meanwhile, the capybara did not struggle against the dog. It stupidly rolled its eyes, deeply buried in a thick bed of fat. Perhaps it saw men for the first time.

However, Neb having tightened his grasp on his stick, was just going to fell the pig, when the latter, tearing itself from Top's teeth, by which it was only held by the tip of its ear, uttered a vigorous grunt, rushed upon Herbert, almost overthrew him, and disappeared in the wood.

"The rascal!" cried Pencroft.

All three directly darted after Top, but at the moment when they joined him the animal had disappeared under the waters of a large pond shaded by venerable pines.

Neb, Herbert, and Pencroft stopped, motionless. Top plunged into the water, but the capybara, hidden at the bottom of the pond, did not appear.

"Let us wait," said the boy, "for he will soon come to the surface to breathe."

"Won't he drown?" asked Neb.

"No," replied Herbert, "since he has webbed feet, and is almost an amphibious animal. But watch him."

Top remained in the water. Pencroft and his two companions went to different parts of the bank, so as to cut off the retreat of the capybara, which the dog was looking for beneath the water.

Herbert was not mistaken. In a few minutes the animal appeared on the surface of the water. Top was upon it in a bound, and kept it from plunging again. An instant later the capybara, dragged to the bank, was killed by a blow from Neb's stick.

"Hurrah!" cried Pencroft, who was always ready with this cry of triumph.

"Give me but a good fire, and this pig shall be gnawed to the bones!"

Pencroft hoisted the capybara on his shoulders, and judging by the height of the sun that it was about two o'clock, he gave the signal to return.

Top's instinct was useful to the hunters, who, thanks to the intelligent animal, were enabled to discover the road by which they had come. Half an hour later they arrived at the river.

Pencroft soon made a raft of wood, as he had done before, though if there was no fire it would be a useless task, and the raft following the current, they returned towards the Chimneys.

But the sailor had not gone fifty paces when he stopped, and again uttering a tremendous hurrah, pointed towards the angle of the cliff,—

"Herbert! Neb! Look!" he shouted.

Smoke was escaping and curling up among the rocks.

Chapter 10

In a few minutes the three hunters were before a crackling fire. The captain and the reporter were there. Pencroft looked from one to the other, his capybara in his hand, without saying a word.

"Well, yes, my brave fellow," cried the reporter.

"Fire, real fire, which will roast this splendid pig perfectly, and we will have a feast presently!"

"But who lighted it?" asked Pencroft.

"The sun!"

Gideon Spilett was quite right in his reply. It was the sun which had furnished the heat which so astonished Pencroft. The sailor could scarcely believe his eyes, and he was so amazed that he did not think of questioning the engineer.

"Had you a burning-glass, sir?" asked Herbert of Harding.

"No, my boy," replied he, "but I made one."

And he showed the apparatus which served for a burning-glass. It was simply two glasses which he had taken from his own and the reporter's watches. Having filled them with water and rendered their edges adhesive by means of a little clay, he thus fabricated a regular burning-glass, which, concentrating the solar rays on some very dry moss, soon caused it to blaze.

The sailor considered the apparatus; then he gazed at the engineer without saying a word, only a look plainly expressed his opinion that if Cyrus Harding was not a magician, he was certainly no ordinary man. At last speech returned to him, and he cried,—

"Note that, Mr. Spilett, note that down on your paper!"

"It is noted," replied the reporter.

Then, Neb helping him, the seaman arranged the spit, and the capybara, properly cleaned, was soon roasting like a suckling-pig before a clear, crackling fire.

The Chimneys had again become more habitable, not only because the passages were warmed by the fire, but because the partitions of wood and mud had been re-established.

It was evident that the engineer and his companions had employed their day well. Cyrus Harding had almost entirely recovered his strength, and had proved it by climbing to the upper plateau. From this point his eye, accustomed to estimate heights and distances, was fixed for a long time on the cone, the summit of which he wished to reach the next day. The mountain, situated about six miles to the northwest, appeared to him to measure 3,500 feet above the level of the sea. Consequently the gaze of an observer posted on its summit would extend over a radius of at least fifty miles. Therefore it was probable that Harding could easily solve the question of "island or continent," to which he attached so much importance.

They supped capitally. The flesh of the capybara was declared excellent. The sargassum and the almonds of the stone-pine completed the repast, during which the engineer spoke little. He was preoccupied with projects for the next day.

Once or twice Pencroft gave forth some ideas upon what it would be best to do; but Cyrus Harding, who was evidently of a methodical mind, only shook his head without uttering a word.

"To-morrow," he repeated, "we shall know what we have to depend upon, and we will act accordingly."

The meal ended, fresh armfuls of wood were thrown on the fire, and the inhabitants of the Chimneys, including the faithful Top, were soon buried in a deep sleep.

No incident disturbed this peaceful night, and the next day, the 29th of March, fresh and active they awoke, ready to undertake the excursion which must determine their fate.

All was ready for the start. The remains of the capybara would be enough to sustain Harding and his companions for at least twenty-four hours.

Besides, they hoped to find more food on the way. As the glasses had been returned to the watches of the engineer and reporter, Pencroft burned a little linen to serve as tinder. As to flint, that would not be wanting in these regions of Plutonic origin. It was half-past seven in the morning when the explorers, armed with sticks, left the Chimneys. Following Pencroft's advice, it appeared best to take the road already traversed through the forest, and to return by another route. It was also the most direct way to reach the mountain. They turned the south angle and followed the left bank of the river, which was abandoned at the point where it formed an elbow towards the southwest. The path, already trodden under the evergreen trees, was found, and at nine o'clock Cyrus Harding and his companions had reached the western border of the forest. The ground, till then, very little undulated, boggy at first, dry and sandy afterwards, had a gentle slope, which ascended from the shore towards the interior of the country. A few very timid animals were seen under the forest-trees. Top quickly started them, but his master soon called him back, for the time had not come to commence hunting; that would be attended to later. The engineer was not a man who would allow himself to be diverted from his fixed idea. It might even have been said that he did not observe the country at all, either in its configuration or in its natural productions, his great aim being to climb the mountain before him, and therefore straight towards it he went. At ten o'clock a halt of a few minutes was made. On leaving the forest, the mountain system of the country appeared before the explorers. The mountain was composed of two cones; the first, truncated at a height of about two thousand five hundred feet, was sustained by buttresses, which appeared to branch out like the talons of an immense claw set on the ground. Between these were narrow valleys, bristling with trees, the last clumps of which rose to the top of the lowest cone. There appeared to be less vegetation on that side of the mountain which was exposed to the northeast, and deep fissures could be seen which, no doubt, were watercourses.

On the first cone rested a second, slightly rounded, and placed a little on one side, like a great round hat cocked over the ear. A Scotchman would have said, "His bonnet was a thocht ajee." It appeared formed of bare earth, here and there pierced by reddish rocks.

They wished to reach the second cone, and proceeding along the ridge of the spurs seemed to be the best way by which to gain it.

"We are on volcanic ground," Cyrus Harding had said, and his companions following him began to ascend by degrees on the back of a spur, which, by a winding and consequently more accessible path, joined the first plateau.

The ground had evidently been convulsed by subterranean force. Here and there stray blocks, numerous debris of basalt and pumice-stone, were met with. In isolated groups rose fir-trees, which, some hundred feet lower, at the bottom of the narrow gorges, formed massive shades almost impenetrable to the sun's rays.

During the first part of the ascent, Herbert remarked on the footprints which indicated the recent passage of large animals.

"Perhaps these beasts will not let us pass by willingly," said Pencroft.

"Well," replied the reporter, who had already hunted the tiger in India, and the lion in Africa, "we shall soon learn how successfully to encounter them. But in the meantime we must be upon our guard!"

They ascended but slowly.

The distance, increased by detours and obstacles which could not be surmounted directly, was long. Sometimes, too, the ground suddenly fell, and they found themselves on the edge of a deep chasm which they had to go round. Thus, in retracing their steps so as to find some practicable path, much time was employed and fatigue undergone for nothing. At twelve o'clock, when the small band of adventurers halted for breakfast at the foot of a large group of firs, near a little stream which fell in cascades, they found themselves still half way from the first plateau, which most probably they would not reach till nightfall. From this point the view of the sea was much extended, but on the right the high promontory prevented their seeing whether there was land beyond it. On the left, the sight extended several miles to the north; but, on the northwest, at the point occupied by the explorers, it was cut short by the ridge of a fantastically-shaped spur, which formed a powerful support of the central cone.

At one o'clock the ascent was continued. They slanted more towards the southwest and again entered among thick bushes. There under the shade of the trees fluttered several couples of gallinaceae belonging to the pheasant species. They were tragopans, ornamented by a pendant skin which hangs over their throats, and by two small, round horns, planted behind the eyes. Among these birds, which were about the size of a fowl, the female was uniformly brown, while the male was gorgeous in his red plumage, decorated with white spots. Gideon Spilett, with a stone cleverly and vigorously thrown, killed one of these tragopans, on which Pencroft, made hungry by the fresh air, had cast greedy eyes.

After leaving the region of bushes, the party, assisted by resting on each other's shoulders, climbed for about a hundred feet up a steep acclivity and reached a level place, with very few trees, where the soil appeared volcanic. It was necessary to ascend by zigzags to make the slope more easy, for it was very steep, and the footing being exceedingly precarious required the greatest caution. Neb and Herbert took the lead, Pencroft the rear, the captain and the reporter between them. The animals which frequented these heights—and there were numerous traces of them—must necessarily belong to those races of sure foot and supple spine, chamois or goat. Several were seen, but this was not the name Pencroft gave them, for all of a sudden—"Sheep!" he shouted.

All stopped about fifty feet from half-a-dozen animals of a large size, with strong horns bent back and flattened towards the point, with a woolly fleece, hidden under long silky hair of a tawny color.

They were not ordinary sheep, but a species usually found in the mountainous regions of the temperate zone, to which Herbert gave the name of the musmon.

"Have they legs and chops?" asked the sailor.

"Yes," replied Herbert.

"Well, then, they are sheep!" said Pencroft.

The animals, motionless among the blocks of basalt, gazed with an astonished eye, as if they saw human bipeds for the first time. Then their fears suddenly aroused, they disappeared, bounding over the rocks.

"Good-bye, till we meet again," cried Pencroft, as he watched them, in such a comical tone that Cyrus Harding, Gideon Spilett, Herbert, and Neb could not help laughing.

The ascent was continued. Here and there were traces of lava. Sulphur springs sometimes stopped their way, and they had to go round them. In some places the sulphur had formed crystals among other substances, such as whitish cinders made of an infinity of little feldspar crystals.

In approaching the first plateau formed by the truncating of the lower cone, the difficulties of the ascent were very great. Towards four o'clock the extreme zone of the trees had been passed. There only remained here and there a few twisted, stunted pines, which must have had a hard life in resisting at this altitude the high winds from the open sea. Happily for the engineer and his companions the weather was beautiful, the atmosphere tranquil; for a high breeze at an elevation of three thousand feet would have hindered their proceedings. The purity of the sky at the zenith was felt through the transparent air. A perfect calm reigned around them. They could not see the sun, then hid by the vast screen of the upper cone, which masked the half-horizon of the west, and whose enormous shadow stretching to the shore increased as the radiant luminary sank in its diurnal course. Vapor—mist rather than clouds—began to appear in the east, and assume all the prismatic colors under the influence of the solar rays.

Five hundred feet only separated the explorers from the plateau, which they wished to reach so as to establish there an encampment for the night, but these five hundred feet were increased to more than two miles by the zigzags which they had to describe. The soil, as it were, slid under their feet.

The slope often presented such an angle that they slipped when the stones worn by the air did not give a sufficient support. Evening came on by degrees, and it was almost night when Cyrus Harding and his companions, much fatigued by an ascent of seven hours, arrived at the plateau of the first cone. It was then necessary to prepare an encampment, and to restore their strength by eating first and sleeping afterwards. This second stage of the mountain rose on a base of rocks, among which it would be easy to find a retreat. Fuel was not abundant. However, a fire could be made by means of the moss and dry brushwood, which covered certain parts of the plateau. While the sailor was preparing his hearth with stones which he put to this use, Neb and Herbert occupied themselves with getting a supply of fuel. They soon returned with a load of brushwood. The steel was struck, the burnt linen caught the sparks of flint, and, under Neb's breath, a crackling fire showed itself in a few minutes under the shelter of the rocks. Their object in lighting a fire was only to enable them to withstand the cold temperature of the night, as it was not employed in cooking the bird, which Neb kept for the next day. The remains of the capybara and some dozens of the stone-pine almonds formed their supper. It was not half-past six when all was finished.

Cyrus Harding then thought of exploring in the half-light the large circular layer which supported the upper cone of the mountain. Before taking any rest, he wished to know if it was possible to get round the base of the cone in the case of its sides being too steep and its summit being inaccessible. This question preoccupied him, for it was possible that from the way the hat inclined, that is to say, towards the north, the plateau was not practicable. Also, if the summit of the mountain could not be reached on one side, and if, on the other, they could not get round the base of the cone, it would be impossible to survey the western part of the country, and their object in making the ascent would in part be altogether unattained.

The engineer, accordingly, regardless of fatigue, leaving Pencroft and Neb to arrange the beds, and Gideon Spilett to note the incidents of the day, began to follow the edge of the plateau, going towards the north. Herbert accompanied him.

The night was beautiful and still, the darkness was not yet deep. Cyrus Harding and the boy walked near each other, without speaking. In some places the plateau opened before them, and they passed without hindrance. In others, obstructed by rocks, there was only a narrow path, in which two persons could not walk abreast. After a walk of twenty minutes, Cyrus Harding and Herbert were obliged to stop. From this point the slope of the two cones became one. No shoulder here separated the two parts of the mountain. The slope, being inclined almost seventy degrees, the path became impracticable.

But if the engineer and the boy were obliged to give up thoughts of following a circular direction, in return an opportunity was given for ascending the cone.

In fact, before them opened a deep hollow. It was the rugged mouth of the crater, by which the eruptive liquid matter had escaped at the periods when the volcano was still in activity. Hardened lava and crusted scoria formed a sort of natural staircase of large steps, which would greatly facilitate the ascent to the summit of the mountain.

Harding took all this in at a glance, and without hesitating, followed by the lad, he entered the enormous chasm in the midst of an increasing obscurity.

There was still a height of a thousand feet to overcome. Would the interior acclivities of the crater be practicable? It would soon be seen. The persevering engineer resolved to continue his ascent until he was stopped. Happily these acclivities wound up the interior of the volcano and favored their ascent.

As to the volcano itself, it could not be doubted that it was completely extinct. No smoke escaped from its sides; not a flame could be seen in the dark hollows; not a roar, not a mutter, no trembling even issued from this black well, which perhaps reached far into the bowels of the earth. The atmosphere inside the crater was filled with no sulphurous vapor. It was more than the sleep of a volcano; it was its complete extinction. Cyrus Harding's attempt would succeed.

Little by little, Herbert and he climbing up the sides of the interior, saw the crater widen above their heads. The radius of this circular portion of the sky, framed by the edge of the cone, increased obviously. At each step, as it were, that the explorers made, fresh stars entered the field of their vision. The magnificent constellations of the southern sky shone resplendently. At the zenith glittered the splendid Antares in the Scorpion, and not far was Alpha Centauri, which is believed to be the nearest star to the terrestrial globe. Then, as the crater widened, appeared Fomalhaut of the Fish, the Southern Triangle, and lastly, nearly at the Antarctic Pole, the glittering Southern Cross, which replaces the Polar Star of the Northern Hemisphere.

It was nearly eight o'clock when Cyrus Harding and Herbert set foot on the highest ridge of the mountain at the summit of the cone.

It was then perfectly dark, and their gaze could not extend over a radius of two miles. Did the sea surround this unknown land, or was it connected in the west with some continent of the Pacific? It could not yet be made out. Towards the west, a cloudy belt, clearly visible at the horizon, increased the gloom, and the eye could not discover if the sky and water were blended together in the same circular line.

But at one point of the horizon a vague light suddenly appeared, which descended slowly in proportion as the cloud mounted to the zenith.

It was the slender crescent moon, already almost disappearing; but its light was sufficient to show clearly the horizontal line, then detached from the cloud, and the engineer could see its reflection trembling for an instant on a liquid surface. Cyrus Harding seized the lad's hand, and in a grave voice,—

"An island!" said he, at the moment when the lunar crescent disappeared beneath the waves.

Chapter 11

Half an hour later Cyrus Harding and Herbert had returned to the encampment. The engineer merely told his companions that the land upon which fate had thrown them was an island, and that the next day they would consult. Then each settled himself as well as he could to sleep, and in that rocky hole, at a height of two thousand five hundred feet above the level of the sea, through a peaceful night, the islanders enjoyed profound repose.

The next day, the 30th of March, after a hasty breakfast, which consisted solely of the roasted tragopan, the engineer wished to climb again to the summit of the volcano, so as more attentively to survey the island upon which he and his companions were imprisoned for life perhaps, should the island be situated at a great distance from any land, or if it was out of the course of vessels which visited the archipelagoes of the Pacific Ocean. This time his companions followed him in the new exploration. They also wished to see the island, on the productions of which they must depend for the supply of all their wants.

It was about seven o'clock in the morning when Cyrus Harding, Herbert, Pencroft, Gideon Spilett, and Neb quitted the encampment. No one appeared to be anxious about their situation. They had faith in themselves, doubtless, but it must be observed that the basis of this faith was not the same with Harding as with his companions. The engineer had confidence, because he felt capable of extorting from this wild country everything necessary for the life of himself and his companions; the latter feared nothing, just because Cyrus Harding was with them. Pencroft especially, since the incident of the relighted fire, would not have despaired for an instant, even if he was on a bare rock, if the engineer was with him on the rock.

"Pshaw," said he, "we left Richmond without permission from the authorities! It will be hard if we don't manage to get away some day or other from a place where certainly no one will detain us!"

Cyrus Harding followed the same road as the evening before. They went round the cone by the plateau which formed the shoulder, to the mouth of the enormous chasm. The weather was magnificent. The sun rose in a pure sky and flooded with his rays all the eastern side of the mountain.

The crater was reached. It was just what the engineer had made it out to be in the dark; that is to say, a vast funnel which extended, widening, to a height of a thousand feet above the plateau. Below the chasm, large thick streaks of lava wound over the sides of the mountain, and thus marked the course of the eruptive matter to the lower valleys which furrowed the northern part of the island.

The interior of the crater, whose inclination did not exceed thirty five to forty degrees, presented no difficulties nor obstacles to the ascent. Traces of very ancient lava were noticed, which probably had overflowed the summit of the cone, before this lateral chasm had opened a new way to it.

As to the volcanic chimney which established a communication between the subterranean layers and the crater, its depth could not be calculated with the eye, for it was lost in obscurity. But there was no doubt as to the complete extinction of the volcano.

Before eight o'clock Harding and his companions were assembled at the summit of the crater, on a conical mound which swelled the northern edge.

"The sea, the sea everywhere!" they cried, as if their lips could not restrain the words which made islanders of them.

The sea, indeed, formed an immense circular sheet of water all around them! Perhaps, on climbing again to the summit of the cone, Cyrus Harding had had a hope of discovering some coast, some island shore, which he had not been able to perceive in the dark the evening before. But nothing appeared on the farthest verge of the horizon, that is to say over a radius of more than fifty miles. No land in sight. Not a sail. Over all this immense space the ocean alone was visible—the island occupied the center of a circumference which appeared to be infinite.

The engineer and his companions, mute and motionless, surveyed for some minutes every point of the ocean, examining it to its most extreme limits. Even Pencroft, who possessed a marvelous power of sight, saw nothing; and certainly if there had been land at the horizon, if it appeared only as an indistinct vapor, the sailor would undoubtedly have found it out, for nature had placed regular telescopes under his eyebrows.

From the ocean their gaze returned to the island which they commanded entirely, and the first question was put by Gideon Spilett in these terms:

"About what size is this island?"

Truly, it did not appear large in the midst of the immense ocean.

Cyrus Harding reflected a few minutes; he attentively observed the perimeter of the island, taking into consideration the height at which he was placed; then,—

"My friends," said he, "I do not think I am mistaken in giving to the shore of the island a circumference of more than a hundred miles."

"And consequently an area?"

"That is difficult to estimate," replied the engineer, "for it is so uneven."

If Cyrus Harding was not mistaken in his calculation, the island had almost the extent of Malta or Zante, in the Mediterranean, but it was at the same time much more irregular and less rich in capes, promontories, points, bays, or creeks. Its strange form caught the eye, and when Gideon Spilett, on the engineer's advice, had drawn the outline, they found that it resembled some fantastic animal, a monstrous leviathan, which lay sleeping on the surface of the Pacific.

This was in fact the exact shape of the island, which it is of consequence to know, and a tolerably correct map of it was immediately drawn by the reporter.

The east part of the shore, where the castaways had landed, formed a wide bay, terminated by a sharp cape, which had been concealed by a high point from Pencroft on his first exploration. At the northeast two other capes closed the bay, and between them ran a narrow gulf, which looked like the half-open jaws of a formidable dog-fish.

From the northeast to the southwest the coast was rounded, like the flattened cranium of an animal, rising again, forming a sort of protuberance which did not give any particular shape to this part of the island, of which the center was occupied by the volcano.

From this point the shore ran pretty regularly north and south, broken at two-thirds of its perimeter by a narrow creek, from which it ended in a long tail, similar to the caudal appendage of a gigantic alligator.

This tail formed a regular peninsula, which stretched more than thirty miles into the sea, reckoning from the cape southeast of the island, already mentioned; it curled round, making an open roadstead, which marked out the lower shore of this strangely-formed land.

At the narrowest part, that is to say between the Chimneys and the creek on the western shore, which corresponded to it in latitude, the island only measured ten miles; but its greatest length, from the jaws at the northeast to the extremity of the tail of the southwest, was not less than thirty miles.

As to the interior of the island, its general aspect was this, very woody throughout the southern part from the mountain to the shore, and arid and sandy in the northern part. Between the volcano and the east coast Cyrus Harding and his companions were surprised to see a lake, bordered with green trees, the existence of which they had not suspected. Seen from this height, the lake appeared to be on the same level as the ocean, but, on reflection, the engineer explained to his companions that the altitude of this little sheet of water must be about three hundred feet, because the plateau, which was its basin, was but a prolongation of the coast.

"Is it a freshwater lake?" asked Pencroft.

"Certainly," replied the engineer, "for it must be fed by the water which flows from the mountain."

"I see a little river which runs into it," said Herbert, pointing out a narrow stream, which evidently took its source somewhere in the west.

"Yes," said Harding; "and since this stream feeds the lake, most probably on the side near the sea there is an outlet by which the surplus water escapes. We shall see that on our return."

This little winding watercourse and the river already mentioned constituted the water-system, at least such as it was displayed to the eyes of the explorers. However, it was possible that under the masses of trees which covered two-thirds of the island, forming an immense forest, other rivers ran towards the sea. It might even be inferred that such was the case, so rich did this region appear in the most magnificent specimens of the flora of the temperate zones. There was no indication of running water in the north, though perhaps there might be stagnant water among the marshes in the northeast; but that was all, in addition to the downs, sand, and aridity which contrasted so strongly with the luxuriant vegetation of the rest of the island.

The volcano did not occupy the central part; it rose, on the contrary, in the northwestern region, and seemed to mark the boundary of the two zones. At the southwest, at the south, and the southeast, the first part of the spurs were hidden under masses of verdure. At the north, on the contrary, one could follow their ramifications, which died away on the sandy plains. It was on this side that, at the time when the mountain was in a state of eruption, the discharge had worn away a passage, and a large heap of lava had spread to the narrow jaw which formed the northeastern gulf.

Cyrus Harding and his companions remained an hour at the top of the mountain. The island was displayed under their eyes, like a plan in relief with different tints, green for the forests, yellow for the sand, blue for the water. They viewed it in its tout-ensemble, nothing remained concealed but the ground hidden by verdure, the hollows of the valleys, and the interior of the volcanic chasms.

One important question remained to be solved, and the answer would have a great effect upon the future of the castaways.

Was the island inhabited?

It was the reporter who put this question, to which after the close examination they had just made, the answer seemed to be in the negative.

Nowhere could the work of a human hand be perceived. Not a group of huts, not a solitary cabin, not a fishery on the shore. No smoke curling in the air betrayed the presence of man. It is true, a distance of nearly thirty miles separated the observers from the extreme points, that is, of the tail which extended to the southwest, and it would have been difficult, even to Pencroft's eyes, to discover a habitation there. Neither could the curtain of verdure, which covered three-quarters of the island, be raised to see if it did not shelter some straggling village. But in general the islanders live on the shores of the narrow spaces which emerge above the waters of the Pacific, and this shore appeared to be an absolute desert.

Until a more complete exploration, it might be admitted that the island was uninhabited. But was it frequented, at least occasionally, by the natives of neighboring islands? It was difficult to reply to this question. No land appeared within a radius of fifty miles. But fifty miles could be easily crossed, either by Malay proas or by the large Polynesian canoes. Everything depended on the position of the island, of its isolation in the Pacific, or of its proximity to archipelagoes. Would Cyrus Harding be able to find out their latitude and longitude without instruments? It would be difficult. Since he was in doubt, it was best to take precautions against a possible descent of neighboring natives.

The exploration of the island was finished, its shape determined, its features made out, its extent calculated, the water and mountain systems ascertained. The disposition of the forests and plains had been marked in a general way on the reporter's plan. They had now only to descend the mountain slopes again, and explore the soil, in the triple point of view, of its mineral, vegetable, and animal resources.

But before giving his companions the signal for departure, Cyrus Harding said to them in a calm, grave voice,—

"Here, my friends, is the small corner of land upon which the hand of the Almighty has thrown us. We are going to live here; a long time, perhaps. Perhaps, too, unexpected help will arrive, if some ship passes by chance. I say by chance, because this is an unimportant island; there is not even a port in which ships could anchor, and it is to be feared that it is situated out of the route usually followed, that is to say, too much to the south for the ships which frequent the archipelagoes of the Pacific, and too much to the north for those which go to Australia by doubling Cape Horn. I wish to hide nothing of our position from you—"

"And you are right, my dear Cyrus," replied the reporter, with animation. "You have to deal with men. They have confidence in you, and you can depend upon them. Is it not so, my friends?"

"I will obey you in everything, captain," said Herbert, seizing the engineer's hand.

"My master always, and everywhere!" cried Neb.

"As for me," said the sailor, "if I ever grumble at work, my name's not Jack Pencroft, and if you like, captain, we will make a little America of this island! We will build towns, we will establish railways, start telegraphs, and one fine day, when it is quite changed, quite put in order and quite civilized, we will go and offer it to the government of the Union. Only, I ask one thing."

"What is that?" said the reporter.

"It is, that we do not consider ourselves castaways, but colonists, who have come here to settle." Harding could not help smiling, and the sailor's idea was adopted. He then thanked his companions, and added, that he would rely on their energy and on the aid of Heaven.

"Well, now let us set off to the Chimneys!" cried Pencroft.

"One minute, my friends," said the engineer. "It seems to me it would be a good thing to give a name to this island, as well as to, the capes, promontories, and watercourses, which we can see.

"Very good," said the reporter. "In the future, that will simplify the instructions which we shall have to give and follow."

"Indeed," said the sailor, "already it is something to be able to say where one is going, and where one has come from. At least, it looks like somewhere."

"The Chimneys, for example," said Herbert.

"Exactly!" replied Pencroft. "That name was the most convenient, and it came to me quite of myself. Shall we keep the name of the Chimneys for our first encampment, captain?"

"Yes, Pencroft, since you have so christened it."

"Good! as for the others, that will be easy," returned the sailor, who was in high spirits. "Let us give them names, as the Robinsons did, whose story Herbert has often read to me; Providence Bay, Whale Point, Cape Disappointment!"

"Or, rather, the names of Captain Harding," said Herbert, "of Mr. Spilett, of Neb!—"

"My name!" cried Neb, showing his sparkling white teeth.

"Why not?" replied Pencroft. "Port Neb, that would do very well! And Cape Gideon—"

"I should prefer borrowing names from our country," said the reporter, "which would remind us of America."

"Yes, for the principal ones," then said Cyrus Harding; "for those of the bays and seas, I admit it willingly. We might give to that vast bay on the east the name of Union Bay, for example; to that large hollow on the south, Washington Bay; to the mountain upon which we are standing, that of Mount Franklin; to that lake which is extended under our eyes, that of Lake Grant; nothing could be better, my friends. These names will recall our country, and those of the great citizens who have honored it; but for the rivers, gulfs, capes, and promontories, which we perceive from the top of this mountain, rather let us choose names which will recall their particular shape. They will impress themselves better on our memory, and at the same time will be more practical. The shape of the island is so strange that we shall not be troubled to imagine what it resembles. As to the streams which we do not know as yet, in different parts of the forest which we shall explore later, the creeks which afterwards will he discovered, we can christen them as we find them. What do you think, my friends?"

The engineer's proposal was unanimously agreed to by his companions. The island was spread out under their eyes like a map, and they had only to give names to all its angles and points. Gideon Spilett would write them down, and the geographical nomenclature of the island would be definitely adopted. First, they named the two bays and the mountain, Union Bay, Washington Bay, and Mount Franklin, as the engineer had suggested.

"Now," said the reporter, "to this peninsula at the southwest of the island, I propose to give the name of Serpentine Peninsula, and that of Reptile-end to the bent tail which terminates it, for it is just like a reptile's tail."

"Adopted," said the engineer.

"Now," said Herbert, pointing to the other extremity of the island, "let us call this gulf which is so singularly like a pair of open jaws, Shark Gulf."

"Capital!" cried Pencroft, "and we can complete the resemblance by naming the two parts of the jaws Mandible Cape."

"But there are two capes," observed the reporter.

"Well," replied Pencroft, "we can have North Mandible Cape and South Mandible Cape."

"They are inscribed," said Spilett.

"There is only the point at the southeastern extremity of the island to be named," said Pencroft.

"That is, the extremity of Union Bay?" asked Herbert.

"Claw Cape," cried Neb directly, who also wished to be godfather to some part of his domain.

In truth, Neb had found an excellent name, for this cape was very like the powerful claw of the fantastic animal which this singularly-shaped island represented.

Pencroft was delighted at the turn things had taken, and their imaginations soon gave to the river which furnished the settlers with drinking water and near which the balloon had thrown them, the name of the Mercy, in true gratitude to Providence. To the islet upon which the castaways had first landed, the name of Safety Island; to the plateau which crowned the high granite precipice above the Chimneys, and from whence the gaze could embrace the whole of the vast bay, the name of Prospect Heights.

Lastly, all the masses of impenetrable wood which covered the Serpentine Peninsula were named the forests of the Far West.

The nomenclature of the visible and known parts of the island was thus finished, and later, they would complete it as they made fresh discoveries.

As to the points of the compass, the engineer had roughly fixed them by the height and position of the sun, which placed Union Bay and Prospect Heights to the east. But the next day, by taking the exact hour of the rising and setting of the sun, and by marking its position between this rising and setting, he reckoned to fix the north of the island exactly, for, in consequence of its situation in the Southern Hemisphere, the sun, at the precise moment of its culmination, passed in the north and not in the south, as, in its apparent movement, it seems to do, to those places situated in the Northern Hemisphere.

Everything was finished, and the settlers had only to descend Mount Franklin to return to the Chimneys, when Pencroft cried out,—

"Well! we are preciously stupid!"

"Why?" asked Gideon Spilett, who had closed his notebook and risen to depart.

"Why! our island! we have forgotten to christen it!"

Herbert was going to propose to give it the engineer's name and all his companions would have applauded him, when Cyrus Harding said simply,—

"Let us give it the name of a great citizen, my friend; of him who now struggles to defend the unity of the American Republic! Let us call it Lincoln Island!"

The engineer's proposal was replied to by three hurrahs.

And that evening, before sleeping, the new colonists talked of their absent country; they spoke of the terrible war which stained it with blood; they could not doubt that the South would soon be subdued, and that the cause of the North, the cause of justice, would triumph, thanks to Grant, thanks to Lincoln!

Now this happened the 30th of March, 1865. They little knew that sixteen days afterwards a frightful crime would be committed in Washington, and that on Good Friday Abraham Lincoln would fall by the hand of a fanatic.

Chapter 12

They now began the descent of the mountain. Climbing down the crater, they went round the cone and reached their encampment of the previous night. Pencroft thought it must be breakfast-time, and the watches of the reporter and engineer were therefore consulted to find out the hour.

That of Gideon Spilett had been preserved from the sea-water, as he had been thrown at once on the sand out of reach of the waves. It was an instrument of excellent quality, a perfect pocket chronometer, which the reporter had not forgotten to wind up carefully every day.

As to the engineer's watch, it, of course, had stopped during the time which he had passed on the downs.

The engineer now wound it up, and ascertaining by the height of the sun that it must be about nine o'clock in the morning, he put his watch at that hour.

"No, my dear Spilett, wait. You have kept the Richmond time, have you not?"

"Yes, Cyrus."

"Consequently, your watch is set by the meridian of that town, which is almost that of Washington?"

"Undoubtedly."

"Very well, keep it thus. Content yourself with winding it up very, exactly, but do not touch the hands. This may be of use to us.

"What will be the good of that?" thought the sailor.

They ate, and so heartily, that the store of game and almonds was totally exhausted. But Pencroft was not at all uneasy, they would supply themselves on the way. Top, whose share had been very much to his taste, would know how to find some fresh game among the brushwood. Moreover, the sailor thought of simply asking the engineer to manufacture some powder and one or two fowling-pieces; he supposed there would be no difficulty in that.

On leaving the plateau, the captain proposed to his companions to return to the Chimneys by a new way. He wished to reconnoiter Lake Grant, so magnificently framed in trees. They therefore followed the crest of one of the spurs, between which the creek that supplied the lake probably had its source. In talking, the settlers already employed the names which they had just chosen, which singularly facilitated the exchange of their ideas. Herbert and Pencroft—the one young and the other very boyish—were enchanted, and while walking, the sailor said,

"Hey, Herbert! how capital it sounds! It will be impossible to lose ourselves, my boy, since, whether we follow the way to Lake Grant, or whether we join the Mercy through the woods of the Far West, we shall be certain to arrive at Prospect Heights, and, consequently, at Union Bay!"

It had been agreed, that without forming a compact band, the settlers should not stray away from each other. It was very certain that the thick forests of the island were inhabited by dangerous animals, and it was prudent to be on their guard. In general, Pencroft, Herbert, and Neb walked first, preceded by Top, who poked his nose into every bush. The reporter and the engineer went together, Gideon Spilett ready to note every incident, the engineer silent for the most part, and only stepping aside to pick up one thing or another, a mineral or vegetable substance, which he put into his pocket, without making any remark.

"What can he be picking up?" muttered Pencroft. "I have looked in vain for anything that's worth the trouble of stooping for."

Towards ten o'clock the little band descended the last declivities of Mount Franklin. As yet the ground was scantily strewn with bushes and trees. They were walking over yellowish calcinated earth, forming a plain of nearly a mile long, which extended to the edge of the wood. Great blocks of that basalt, which, according to Bischof, takes three hundred and fifty millions of years to cool, strewed the plain, very confused in some places. However, there were here no traces of lava, which was spread more particularly over the northern slopes.

Cyrus Harding expected to reach, without incident, the course of the creek, which he supposed flowed under the trees at the border of the plain, when he saw

Herbert running hastily back, while Neb and the sailor were hiding behind the rocks.

"What's the matter, my boy?" asked Spilett.

"Smoke," replied Herbert. "We have seen smoke among the rocks, a hundred paces from us."

"Men in this place?" cried the reporter.

"We must avoid showing ourselves before knowing with whom we have to deal," replied Cyrus Harding. "I trust that there are no natives on this island; I dread them more than anything else. Where is Top?"

"Top is on before."

"And he doesn't bark?"

"No."

"That is strange. However, we must try to call him back."

In a few moments, the engineer, Gideon Spilett, and Herbert had rejoined their two companions, and like them, they kept out of sight behind the heaps of basalt.

From thence they clearly saw smoke of a yellowish color rising in the air.

Top was recalled by a slight whistle from his master, and the latter, signing to his companions to wait for him, glided away among the rocks. The colonists, motionless, anxiously awaited the result of this exploration, when a shout from the engineer made them hasten forward. They soon joined him, and were at once struck with a disagreeable odor which impregnated the atmosphere.

The odor, easily recognized, was enough for the engineer to guess what the smoke was which at first, not without cause, had startled him.

"This fue," said he, "or rather, this smoke is produced by nature alone. There is a sulphur spring there, which will cure all our sore throats."

"Captain!" cried Pencroft. "What a pity that I haven't got a cold!"

The settlers then directed their steps towards the place from which the smoke escaped. They there saw a sulphur spring which flowed abundantly between the rocks, and its waters discharged a strong sulphuric acid odor, after having absorbed the oxygen of the air.

Cyrus Harding, dipping in his hand, felt the water oily to the touch. He tasted it and found it rather sweet. As to its temperature, that he estimated at ninety-five degrees Fahrenheit. Herbert having asked on what he based this calculation,—

"Its quite simple, my boy," said he, "for, in plunging my hand into the water, I felt no sensation either of heat or cold. Therefore it has the same temperature as the human body, which is about ninety-five degrees."

The sulphur spring not being of any actual use to the settlers, they proceeded towards the thick border of the forest, which began some hundred paces off.

There, as they had conjectured, the waters of the stream flowed clear and limpid between high banks of red earth, the color of which betrayed the presence of oxide of iron. From this color, the name of Red Creek was immediately given to the watercourse.

It was only a large stream, deep and clear, formed of the mountain water, which, half river, half torrent, here rippling peacefully over the sand, there falling against the rocks or dashing down in a cascade, ran towards the lake, over a distance of a mile and a half, its breadth varying from thirty to forty feet. Its waters were sweet, and it was supposed that those of the lake were so also. A fortunate circumstance, in the event of their finding on its borders a more suitable dwelling than the Chimneys.

As to the trees, which some hundred feet downwards shaded the banks of the creek, they belonged, for the most part, to the species which abound in the temperate zone of America and Tasmania, and no longer to those coniferae observed in that portion of the island already explored to some miles from Prospect Heights. At this time of the year, the commencement of the month of April, which represents the month of October, in this hemisphere, that is, the beginning of autumn, they were still in full leaf. They consisted principally of casuarinas and eucalypti, some of which next year would yield a sweet manna, similar to the manna of the East. Clumps of Australian cedars rose on the sloping banks, which were also covered with the high grass called "tussac" in New Holland; but the cocoanut, so abundant in the archipelagoes of the Pacific, seemed to be wanting in the island, the latitude, doubtless, being too low.

"What a pity!" said Herbert, "such a useful tree, and which has such beautiful nuts!"

As to the birds, they swarmed among the scanty branches of the eucalypti and casuarinas, which did not hinder the display of their wings. Black, white, or gray cockatoos, paroquets, with plumage of all colors, kingfishers of a sparkling green and crowned with red, blue lories, and various other birds appeared on all sides, as through a prism, fluttering about and producing a deafening clamor. Suddenly, a strange concert of discordant voices resounded in the midst of a thicket. The settlers heard successively the song of birds, the cry of quadrupeds, and a sort of clacking which they might have believed to have escaped from the lips of a native. Neb and Herbert rushed towards the bush, forgetting even the most elementary principles of prudence. Happily, they found there, neither a formidable wild beast nor a dangerous native, but merely half a dozen mocking and singing birds, known as mountain pheasants. A few skillful blows from a stick soon put an end to their concert, and procured excellent food for the evening's dinner.

Herbert also discovered some magnificent pigeons with bronzed wings, some superbly crested, others draped in green, like their congeners at Port-Macquarie; but it was impossible to reach them, or the crows and magpies which flew away in flocks.

A charge of small shot would have made great slaughter among these birds, but the hunters were still limited to sticks and stones, and these primitive weapons proved very insufficient.

Their insufficiency was still more clearly shown when a troop of quadrupeds, jumping, bounding, making leaps of thirty feet, regular flying mammiferae, fled over the thickets, so quickly and at such a height, that one would have thought that they passed from one tree to another like squirrels.

"Kangaroos!" cried Herbert.

"Are they good to eat?" asked Pencroft.

"Stewed," replied the reporter, "their flesh is equal to the best venison!—"

Gideon Spilett had not finished this exciting sentence when the sailor, followed by Neb and Herbert, darted on the kangaroos tracks. Cyrus Harding called them back in vain. But it was in vain too for the hunters to pursue such agile game, which went bounding away like balls. After a chase of five minutes, they lost their breath, and at the same time all sight of the creatures, which disappeared in the wood. Top was not more successful than his masters.

"Captain," said Pencroft, when the engineer and the reporter had rejoined them, "Captain, you see quite well we can't get on unless we make a few guns. Will that be possible?"

"Perhaps," replied the engineer, "but we will begin by first manufacturing some bows and arrows, and I don't doubt that you will become as clever in the use of them as the Australian hunters."

"Bows and arrows!" said Pencroft scornfully. "That's all very well for children!"

"Don't be proud, friend Pencroft," replied the reporter. "Bows and arrows were sufficient for centuries to stain the earth with blood. Powder is but a thing of yesterday, and war is as old as the human race—unhappily."

"Faith, that's true, Mr. Spilett," replied the sailor, "and I always speak too quickly. You must excuse me!"

Meanwhile, Herbert constant to his favorite science, Natural History, reverted to the kangaroos, saying,—

"Besides, we had to deal just now with the species which is most difficult to catch. They were giants with long gray fur; but if I am not mistaken, there exist black and red kangaroos, rock kangaroos, and rat kangaroos, which are more easy to get hold of. It is reckoned that there are about a dozen species."

"Herbert," replied the sailor sententiously, "there is only one species of kangaroos to me, that is 'kangaroo on the spit,' and it's just the one we haven't got this evening!"

They could not help laughing at Master Pencroft's new classification. The honest sailor did not hide his regret at being reduced for dinner to the singing pheasants, but fortune once more showed itself obliging to him.

In fact, Top, who felt that his interest was concerned went and ferreted everywhere with an instinct doubled by a ferocious appetite. It was even probable that if some piece of game did fall into his clutches, none would be left for the hunters, if Top was hunting on his own account; but Neb watched him and he did well.

Towards three o'clock the dog disappeared in the brushwood and gruntings showed that he was engaged in a struggle with some animal. Neb rushed after him, and soon saw Top eagerly devouring a quadruped, which ten seconds later would have been past recognizing in Top's stomach. But fortunately the dog had fallen upon a brood, and besides the victim he was devouring, two other rodents—the animals in question belonged to that order—lay strangled on the turf.

Neb reappeared triumphantly holding one of the rodents in each hand. Their size exceeded that of a rabbit, their hair was yellow, mingled with green spots, and they had the merest rudiments of tails.

The citizens of the Union were at no loss for the right name of these rodents. They were maras, a sort of agouti, a little larger than their congeners of tropical countries, regular American rabbits, with long ears, jaws armed on each side with five molars, which distinguish the agouti.

"Hurrah!" cried Pencroft, "the roast has arrived! and now we can go home."

The walk, interrupted for an instant, was resumed. The limpid waters of the Red Creek flowed under an arch of casuannas, banksias, and gigantic gum-trees. Superb lilacs rose to a height of twenty feet. Other arborescent species, unknown to the young naturalist, bent over the stream, which could be heard murmuring beneath the bowers of verdure.

Meanwhile the stream grew much wider, and Cyrus Harding supposed that they would soon reach its mouth. In fact, on emerging from beneath a thick clump of beautiful trees, it suddenly appeared before their eyes.

The explorers had arrived on the western shore of Lake Grant. The place was well worth looking at. This extent of water, of a circumference of nearly seven miles and an area of two hundred and fifty acres, reposed in a border of diversified trees. Towards the east, through a curtain of verdure, picturesquely raised in some places, sparkled an horizon of sea. The lake was curved at the north, which contrasted with the sharp outline of its lower part. Numerous aquatic birds frequented the shores of this little Ontario, in which the thousand isles of its American namesake were represented by a rock which emerged from its surface, some hundred feet from the southern shore. There lived in harmony several couples of kingfishers perched on a stone, grave, motionless, watching for fish, then darting down, they plunged in with a sharp cry, and reappeared with their prey in their beaks. On the shores and on the islets, strutted wild ducks, pelicans, water-hens, red-beaks, philedons, furnished with a tongue like a brush, and one or two specimens of the splendid menura, the tail of which expands gracefully like a lyre.

As to the water of the lake, it was sweet, limpid, rather dark, and from certain bubblings, and the concentric circles which crossed each other on the surface, it could not be doubted that it abounded in fish.

"This lake is really beautiful!" said Gideon Spilett. "We could live on its borders!"

"We will live there!" replied Harding.

The settlers, wishing to return to the Chimneys by the shortest way, descended towards the angle formed on the south by the junction of the lake's bank. It was not without difficulty that they broke a path through the thickets and brushwood which had never been put aside by the hand of men, and they thus went towards the shore, so as to arrive at the north of Prospect Heights. Two miles were cleared in this direction, and then, after they had passed the last curtain of trees, appeared the plateau, carpeted with thick turf, and beyond that the infinite sea.

To return to the Chimneys, it was enough to cross the plateau obliquely for the space of a mile, and then to descend to the elbow formed by the first detour of the Mercy. But the engineer desired to know how and where the overplus of the water from the lake escaped, and the exploration was prolonged under the trees for a mile and a half towards the north. It was most probable that an overfall existed somewhere, and doubtless through a cleft in the granite. This lake was only, in short, an immense center basin, which was filled by degrees by the creek, and its waters must necessarily pass to the sea by some fall. If it was so, the engineer thought that it might perhaps be possible to utilize this fall and borrow its power, actually lost without profit to any one. They continued then to follow the shores of Lake Grant by climbing the plateau; but, after having gone a mile in this direction, Cyrus Harding had not been able to discover the overfall, which, however, must exist somewhere.

It was then half-past four. In order to prepare for dinner it was necessary that the settlers should return to their dwelling. The little band retraced their steps, therefore, and by the left bank of the Mercy, Cyrus Harding and his companions arrived at the Chimneys.

The fire was lighted, and Neb and Pencroft, on whom the functions of cooks naturally devolved, to the one in his quality of Negro, to the other in that of sailor, quickly prepared some broiled agouti, to which they did great justice.

The repast at length terminated; at the moment when each one was about to give himself up to sleep, Cyrus Harding drew from his pocket little specimens of different sorts of minerals, and just said,—

"My friends, this is iron mineral, this a pyrite, this is clay, this is lime, and this is coal. Nature gives us these things. It is our business to make a right use of them. To-morrow we will commence operations."

Chapter 13

"Well, captain, where are we going to begin?" asked Pencroft next morning of the engineer.

"At the beginning," replied Cyrus Harding.

And in fact, the settlers were compelled to begin "at the very beginning." They did not possess even the tools necessary for making tools, and they were not even in the condition of nature, who, "having time, husbands her strength." They had no time, since they had to provide for the immediate wants of their existence, and though, profiting by acquired experience, they had nothing to invent, still they had everything to make; their iron and their steel were as yet only in the state of minerals, their earthenware in the state of clay, their linen and their clothes in the state of textile material.

It must be said, however, that the settlers were "men" in the complete and higher sense of the word. The engineer Harding could not have been seconded by more intelligent companions, nor with more devotion and zeal. He had tried them. He knew their abilities.

Gideon Spilett, a talented reporter, having learned everything so as to be able to speak of everything, would contribute largely with his head and hands to the colonization of the island. He would not draw back from any task: a determined sportsman, he would make a business of what till then had only been a pleasure to him.

Herbert, a gallant boy, already remarkably well informed in the natural sciences, would render greater service to the common cause.

Neb was devotion personified. Clever, intelligent, indefatigable, robust, with iron health, he knew a little about the work of the forge, and could not fail to be very useful in the colony.

As to Pencroft, he had sailed over every sea, a carpenter in the dockyards in Brooklyn, assistant tailor in the vessels of the state, gardener, cultivator, during his holidays, etc., and like all seamen, fit for anything, he knew how to do everything.

It would have been difficult to unite five men, better fitted to struggle against fate, more certain to triumph over it.

"At the beginning," Cyrus Harding had said. Now this beginning of which the engineer spoke was the construction of an apparatus which would serve to transform the natural substances. The part which heat plays in these transformations is known. Now fuel, wood or coal, was ready for immediate use, an oven must be built to use it.

"What is this oven for?" asked Pencroft.

"To make the pottery which we have need of," replied Harding.

"And of what shall we make the oven?"

"With bricks."

"And the bricks?"

"With clay. Let us start, my friends. To save trouble, we will establish our manufactory at the place of production. Neb will bring provisions, and there will be no lack of fire to cook the food."

"No," replied the reporter; "but if there is a lack of food for want of instruments for the chase?"

"Ah, if we only had a knife!" cried the sailor.

"Well?" asked Cyrus Harding.

"Well! I would soon make a bow and arrows, and then there could be plenty of game in the larder!"

"Yes, a knife, a sharp blade." said the engineer, as if he was speaking to himself.

At this moment his eyes fell upon Top, who was running about on the shore. Suddenly Harding's face became animated.

"Top, here," said he.

The dog came at his master's call. The latter took Top's head between his hands, and unfastening the collar which the animal wore round his neck, he broke it in two, saying,—

"There are two knives, Pencroft!"

Two hurrahs from the sailor was the reply. Top's collar was made of a thin piece of tempered steel. They had only to sharpen it on a piece of sandstone, then to raise the edge on a finer stone. Now sandstone was abundant on the beach, and two hours after the stock of tools in the colony consisted of two sharp blades, which were easily fixed in solid handles.

The production of these their first tools was hailed as a triumph. It was indeed a valuable result of their labor, and a very opportune one. They set out.

Cyrus Harding proposed that they should return to the western shore of the lake, where the day before he had noticed the clayey ground of which he possessed a specimen. They therefore followed the bank of the Mercy, traversed Prospect Heights, and after a walk of five miles or more they reached a glade, situated two hundred feet from Lake Grant.

On the way Herbert had discovered a tree, the branches of which the Indians of South America employ for making their bows. It was the crejimba, of the palm family, which does not bear edible fruit. Long straight branches were cut, the leaves stripped off; it was shaped, stronger in the middle, more slender at the extremities, and nothing remained to be done but to find a plant fit to make the bow-string. This was the "hibiscus heterophyllus," which furnishes fibers of such remarkable tenacity that they have been compared to the tendons of animals. Pencroft thus obtained bows of tolerable strength, for which he only wanted arrows. These were easily made with straight stiff branches, without knots, but the points with which they must be armed, that is to say, a substance to serve in lieu of iron, could not be met with so easily. But Pencroft said, that having done his part of the work, chance would do the rest.

The settlers arrived on the ground which had been discovered the day before. Being composed of the sort of clay which is used for making bricks and tiles, it was very useful for the work in question. There was no great difficulty in it. It was enough to scour the clay with sand, then to mold the bricks and bake them by the heat of a wood fire.

Generally bricks are formed in molds, but the engineer contented himself with making them by hand. All that day and the day following were employed in this work. The clay, soaked in water, was mixed by the feet and hands of the manipulators, and then divided into pieces of equal size. A practiced workman can make, without a machine, about ten thousand bricks in twelve hours; but in their two days work the five brickmakers on Lincoln Island had not made more than three thousand, which were ranged near each other, until the time when their complete desiccation would permit them to be used in building the oven, that is to say, in three or four days.

It was on the 2nd of April that Harding had employed himself in fixing the orientation of the island, or, in other words, the precise spot where the sun rose. The day before he had noted exactly the hour when the sun disappeared beneath the horizon, making allowance for the refraction. This morning he noted, no less exactly, the hour at which it reappeared. Between this setting and rising twelve hours, twenty-four minutes passed. Then, six hours, twelve minutes after its rising, the sun on this day would exactly pass the meridian and the point of the sky which it occupied at this moment would be the north. At the said hour, Cyrus marked this point, and putting in a line with the sun two trees which would serve him for marks, he thus obtained an invariable meridian for his ulterior operations.

The settlers employed the two days before the oven was built in collecting fuel. Branches were cut all round the glade, and they picked up all the fallen wood under the trees. They were also able to hunt with greater success, since Pencroft now possessed some dozen arrows armed with sharp points. It was Top who had famished these points, by bringing in a porcupine, rather inferior eating, but of great value, thanks to the quills with which it bristled. These quills were fixed firmly at the ends of the arrows, the flight of which was made more certain by some cockatoos' feathers. The reporter and Herbert soon became very skilful archers. Game of all sorts in consequence abounded at the Chimneys, capybaras, pigeons, agouties, grouse, etc. The greater part of these animals were killed in the part of the forest on the left bank of the Mercy, to which they gave the name of Jacamar Wood, in remembrance of the bird which Pencroft and Herbert had pursued when on their first exploration.

This game was eaten fresh, but they preserved some capybara hams, by smoking them above a fire of green wood, after having perfumed them with sweet-smelling leaves. However, this food, although very strengthening, was always roast upon roast, and the party would have been delighted to hear some soup bubbling on the hearth, but they must wait till a pot could be made, and, consequently, till the oven was built.

During these excursions, which were not extended far from the brick-field, the hunters could discern the recent passage of animals of a large size, armed with powerful claws, but they could not recognize the species. Cyrus Harding advised them to be very careful, as the forest probably enclosed many dangerous beasts.

And he did right. Indeed, Gideon Spilett and Herbert one day saw an animal which resembled a jaguar. Happily the creature did not attack them, or they might not have escaped without a severe wound. As soon as he could get a regular weapon, that is to say, one of the guns which Pencroft begged for, Gideon Spilett resolved to make desperate war against the ferocious beasts, and exterminate them from the island.

The Chimneys during these few days was not made more comfortable, for the engineer hoped to discover, or build if necessary, a more convenient dwelling. They contented themselves with spreading moss and dry leaves on the sand of the passages, and on these primitive couches the tired workers slept soundly.

They also reckoned the days they had passed on Lincoln Island, and from that time kept a regular account. The 5th of April, which was Wednesday, was twelve days from the time when the wind threw the castaways on this shore.

On the 6th of April, at daybreak, the engineer and his companions were collected in the glade, at the place where they were going to perform the operation of baking the bricks. Naturally this had to be in the open air, and not in a kiln, or rather, the agglomeration of bricks made an enormous kiln, which would bake itself. The fuel, made of well-prepared fagots, was laid on the ground and surrounded with several rows of dried bricks, which soon formed an enormous cube, to the exterior of which they contrived air-holes. The work lasted all day, and it was not till the evening that they set fire to the fagots. No one slept that night, all watching carefully to keep up the fire.

The operation lasted forty-eight hours, and succeeded perfectly. It then became necessary to leave the smoking mass to cool, and during this time Neb and Pencroft, guided by Cyrus Harding, brought, on a hurdle made of interlaced branches, loads of carbonate of lime and common stones, which were very abundant, to the north of the lake. These stones, when decomposed by heat, made a very strong quicklime, greatly increased by slacking, at least as pure as if it had been produced by the calcination of chalk or marble. Mixed with sand the lime made excellent mortar.

The result of these different works was, that, on the 9th of April, the engineer had at his disposal a quantity of prepared lime and some thousands of bricks.

Without losing an instant, therefore, they began the construction of a kiln to bake the pottery, which was indispensable for their domestic use. They succeeded without much difficulty. Five days after, the kiln was supplied with coal, which the engineer had discovered lying open to the sky towards the mouth of the Red Creek, and the first smoke escaped from a chimney twenty feet high. The glade was transformed into a manufactory, and Pencroft was not far wrong in believing that from this kiln would issue all the products of modern industry.

In the meantime what the settlers first manufactured was a common pottery in which to cook their food. The chief material was clay, to which Harding added a little lime and quartz. This paste made regular "pipe-clay," with which they manufactured bowls, cups molded on stones of a proper size, great jars and pots to hold water, etc. The shape of these objects was clumsy and defective, but after they had been baked in a high temperature, the kitchen of the Chimneys was provided with a number of utensils, as precious to the settlers as the most beautifully enameled china. We must mention here that Pencroft, desirous to know if the clay thus prepared was worthy of its name of pipe-clay, made some large pipes, which he thought charming, but for which, alas! he had no tobacco, and that was a great privation to Pencroft. "But tobacco will come, like everything else!" he repeated, in a burst of absolute confidence.

This work lasted till the 15th of April, and the time was well employed. The settlers, having become potters, made nothing but pottery. When it suited Cyrus Harding to change them into smiths, they would become smiths. But the next day being Sunday, and also Easter Sunday, all agreed to sanctify the day by rest. These Americans were religious men, scrupulous observers of the precepts of the Bible, and their situation could not but develop sentiments of confidence towards the Author of all things.

On the evening of the 15th of April they returned to the Chimneys, carrying with them the pottery, the furnace being extinguished until they could put it to a new use. Their return was marked by a fortunate incident; the engineer discovered a substance which replaced tinder. It is known that a spongy, velvety flesh is procured from a certain mushroom of the genus polyporous. Properly prepared, it is extremely inflammable, especially when it has been previously saturated with gunpowder, or boiled in a solution of nitrate or chlorate of potash. But, till then, they had not found any of these polypores or even any of the morels which could replace them. On this day, the engineer, seeing a plant belonging to the wormwood genus, the principal species of which are absinthe, balm-mint, tarragon, etc., gathered several tufts, and, presenting them to the sailor, said,—

"Here, Pencroft, this will please you."

Pencroft looked attentively at the plant, covered with long silky hair, the leaves being clothed with soft down.

"What's that, captain?" asked Pencroft. "Is it tobacco?"

"No," replied Harding, "it is wormwood; Chinese wormwood to the learned, but to us it will be tinder."

When the wormwood was properly dried it provided them with a very inflammable substance, especially afterwards when the engineer had impregnated it with nitrate of potash, of which the island possessed several beds, and which is in truth saltpeter.

The colonists had a good supper that evening. Neb prepared some agouti soup, a smoked capybara ham, to which was added the boiled tubercules of the "caladium macrorhizum," an herbaceous plant of the arum family. They had an excellent taste, and were very nutritious, being something similar to the substance which is sold in England under the name of "Portland sago"; they were also a good substitute for bread, which the settlers in Lincoln Island did not yet possess.

When supper was finished, before sleeping, Harding and his companions went to take the air on the beach. It was eight o'clock in the evening; the night was magnificent. The moon, which had been full five days before, had not yet risen, but the horizon was already silvered by those soft, pale shades which might be called the dawn of the moon. At the southern zenith glittered the circumpolar constellations, and above all the Southern Cross, which some days before the engineer had greeted on the summit of Mount Franklin.

Cyrus Harding gazed for some time at this splendid constellation, which has at its summit and at its base two stars of the first magnitude, at its left arm a star of the second, and at its right arm a star of the third magnitude.

Then, after some minutes thought—

"Herbert," he asked of the lad, "is not this the 15th of April?"

"Yes, captain," replied Herbert.

"Well, if I am not mistaken, to-morrow will be one of the four days in the year in which the real time is identical with average time; that is to say, my boy, that to-morrow, to within some seconds, the sun will pass the meridian just at midday by the clocks. If the weather is fine I think that I shall obtain the longitude of the island with an approximation of some degrees."

"Without instruments, without sextant?" asked Gideon Spilett.

"Yes," replied the engineer. "Also, since the night is clear, I will try, this very evening, to obtain our latitude by calculating the height of the Southern Cross, that is, from the southern pole above the horizon. You understand, my friends, that before undertaking the work of installation in earnest it is not enough to have found out that this land is an island; we must, as nearly as possible, know at what distance it is situated, either from the American continent or Australia, or from the principal archipelagoes of the Pacific."

"In fact," said the reporter, "instead of building a house it would be more important to build a boat, if by chance we are not more than a hundred miles from an inhabited coast."

"That is why," returned Harding, "I am going to try this evening to calculate the latitude of Lincoln Island, and to-morrow, at midday, I will try to calculate the longitude."

If the engineer had possessed a sextant, an apparatus with which the angular distance of objects can be measured with great precision, there would have been no difficulty in the operation. This evening by the height of the pole, the next day by the passing of the sun at the meridian, he would obtain the position of the island. But as they had not one he would have to supply the deficiency.

Harding then entered the Chimneys. By the light of the fire he cut two little flat rulers, which he joined together at one end so as to form a pair of compasses, whose legs could separate or come together. The fastening was fixed with a strong acacia thorn which was found in the wood pile. This instrument finished, the engineer returned to the beach, but as it was necessary to take the height of the pole from above a clear horizon, that is, a sea horizon, and as Claw Cape hid the southern horizon, he was obliged to look for a more suitable station. The best would evidently have been the shore exposed directly to the south; but the Mercy would have to be crossed, and that was a difficulty. Harding resolved, in consequence, to make his observation from Prospect Heights, taking into consideration its height above the level of the sea—a height which he intended to calculate next day by a simple process of elementary geometry.

The settlers, therefore, went to the plateau, ascending the left bank of the Mercy, and placed themselves on the edge which looked northwest and southeast, that is, above the curiously-shaped rocks which bordered the river.

This part of the plateau commanded the heights of the left bank, which sloped away to the extremity of Claw Cape, and to the southern side of the island. No obstacle intercepted their gaze, which swept the horizon in a semi-circle from the cape to Reptile End. To the south the horizon, lighted by the first rays of the moon, was very clearly defined against the sky.

At this moment the Southern Cross presented itself to the observer in an inverted position, the star Alpha marking its base, which is nearer to the southern pole.

This constellation is not situated as near to the antarctic pole as the Polar Star is to the arctic pole. The star Alpha is about twenty-seven degrees from it, but Cyrus Harding knew this and made allowance for it in his calculation. He took care also to observe the moment when it passed the meridian below the pole, which would simplify the operation.

Cyrus Harding pointed one leg of the compasses to the horizon, the other to Alpha, and the space between the two legs gave him the angular distance which separated Alpha from the horizon. In order to fix the angle obtained, he fastened with thorns the two pieces of wood on a third placed transversely, so that their separation should be properly maintained.

That done, there was only the angle to calculate by bringing back the observation to the level of the sea, taking into consideration the depression of the horizon, which would necessitate measuring the height of the cliff. The value of this angle would give the height of Alpha, and consequently that of the pole above the horizon, that is to say, the latitude of the island, since the latitude of a point of the globe is always equal to the height of the pole above the horizon of this point.

The calculations were left for the next day, and at ten o'clock every one was sleeping soundly.

Chapter 14

The next day, the 16th of April, and Easter Sunday, the settlers issued from the Chimneys at daybreak, and proceeded to wash their linen. The engineer intended to manufacture soap as soon as he could procure the necessary materials—soda or potash, fat or oil. The important question of renewing their wardrobe would be treated of in the proper time and place. At any rate their clothes would last at least six months longer, for they were strong, and could resist the wear of manual labor. But all would depend on the situation of the island with regard to inhabited land. This would be settled to-day if the weather permitted.

The sun rising above a clear horizon, announced a magnificent day, one of those beautiful autumn days which are like the last farewells of the warm season.

It was now necessary to complete the observations of the evening before by measuring the height of the cliff above the level of the sea.

"Shall you not need an instrument similar to the one which you used yesterday?" said Herbert to the engineer.

"No, my boy," replied the latter, "we are going to proceed differently, but in as precise a way."

Herbert, wishing to learn everything he could, followed the engineer to the beach. Pencroft, Neb, and the reporter remained behind and occupied themselves in different ways.

Cyrus Harding had provided himself with a straight stick, twelve feet long, which he had measured as exactly as possible by comparing it with his own height, which he knew to a hair. Herbert carried a plumb-line which Harding had given him, that is to say, a simple stone fastened to the end of a flexible fiber. Having reached a spot about twenty feet from the edge of the beach, and nearly five hundred feet from the cliff, which rose perpendicularly, Harding thrust the pole two feet into the sand, and wedging it up carefully, he managed, by means of the plumb-line, to erect it perpendicularly with the plane of the horizon.

That done, he retired the necessary distance, when, lying on the sand, his eye glanced at the same time at the top of the pole and the crest of the cliff. He carefully marked the place with a little stick.

Then addressing Herbert—"Do you know the first principles of geometry?" he asked.

"Slightly, captain," replied Herbert, who did not wish to put himself forward.

"You remember what are the properties of two similar triangles?"

"Yes," replied Herbert; "their homologous sides are proportional."

"Well, my boy, I have just constructed two similar right-angled triangles; the first, the smallest, has for its sides the perpendicular pole, the distance which separates the little stick from the foot of the pole and my visual ray for hypothenuse; the second has for its sides the perpendicular cliff, the height of which we wish to measure, the distance which separates the little stick from the bottom of the cliff, and my visual ray also forms its hypothenuse, which proves to be prolongation of that of the first triangle."

"Ah, captain, I understand!" cried Herbert. "As the distance from the stick to the pole is to the distance from the stick to the base of the cliff, so is the height of the pole to the height of the cliff."

"Just so, Herbert," replied the engineer; "and when we have measured the two first distances, knowing the height of the pole, we shall only have a sum in proportion to do, which will give us the height of the cliff, and will save us the trouble of measuring it directly."

The two horizontal distances were found out by means of the pole, whose length above the sand was exactly ten feet.

The first distance was fifteen feet between the stick and the place where the pole was thrust into the sand.

The second distance between the stick and the bottom of the cliff was five hundred feet.

These measurements finished, Cyrus Harding and the lad returned to the Chimneys.

The engineer then took a flat stone which he had brought back from one of his previous excursions, a sort of slate, on which it was easy to trace figures with a sharp shell. He then proved the following proportions:—

$$15:500::10:x$$
$$500 \times 10 = 5000$$
$$5000 / 15 = 333.3$$

From which it was proved that the granite cliff measured 333 feet in height.

Cyrus Harding then took the instrument which he had made the evening before, the space between its two legs giving the angular distance between the star Alpha and the horizon. He measured, very exactly, the opening of this angle on a circumference which he divided into 360 equal parts. Now, this angle by adding to it the twenty-seven degrees which separated Alpha from the antarctic pole, and by reducing to the level of the sea the height of the cliff on which the observation had been made, was found to be fifty-three degrees. These fifty-three degrees being subtracted from ninety degrees—the distance from the pole to the equator—there remained thirty-seven degrees. Cyrus Harding concluded, therefore, that Lincoln Island was situated on the thirty-seventh degree of the southern latitude, or taking into consideration through the imperfection of the performance, an error of five degrees, that it must be situated between the thirty-fifth and the fortieth parallel.

There was only the longitude to be obtained, and the position of the island would be determined, The engineer hoped to attempt this the same day, at twelve o'clock, at which moment the sun would pass the meridian.

It was decided that Sunday should be spent in a walk, or rather an exploring expedition, to that side of the island between the north of the lake and Shark Gulf, and if there was time they would push their discoveries to the northern side of Cape South Mandible. They would breakfast on the downs, and not return till evening.

At half-past eight the little band was following the edge of the channel. On the other side, on Safety Islet, numerous birds were gravely strutting. They were divers, easily recognized by their cry, which much resembles the braying of a donkey. Pencroft only considered them in an eatable point of view, and learnt with some satisfaction that their flesh, though blackish, is not bad food.

Great amphibious creatures could also be seen crawling on the sand; seals, doubtless, who appeared to have chosen the islet for a place of refuge. It was impossible to think of those animals in an alimentary point of view, for their oily flesh is detestable; however, Cyrus Harding observed them attentively, and without making known his idea, he announced to his companions that very soon they would pay a visit to the islet. The beach was strewn with innumerable shells, some of which would have rejoiced the heart of a conchologist; there were, among others, the phasianella, the terebratual, etc. But what would be of more use, was the discovery, by Neb, at low tide, of a large oysterbed among the rocks, nearly five miles from the Chimneys.

"Neb will not have lost his day," cried Pencroft, looking at the spacious oyster-bed.

"It is really a fortunate discovery," said the reporter, "and as it is said that each oyster produces yearly from fifty to sixty thousand eggs, we shall have an inexhaustible supply there."

"Only I believe that the oyster is not very nourishing," said Herbert.

"No," replied Harding. "The oyster contains very little nitrogen, and if a man lived exclusively on them, he would have to eat not less than fifteen to sixteen dozen a day."

"Capital!" replied Pencroft. "We might swallow dozens and dozens without exhausting the bed. Shall we take some for breakfast?"

And without waiting for a reply to this proposal, knowing that it would be approved of, the sailor and Neb detached a quantity of the molluscs. They put them in a sort of net of hibiscus fiber, which Neb had manufactured, and which already contained food; they then continued to climb the coast between the downs and the sea.

From time to time Harding consulted his watch, so as to be prepared in time for the solar observation, which had to be made exactly at midday.

All that part of the island was very barren as far as the point which closed Union Bay, and which had received the name of Cape South Mandible. Nothing could be seen there but sand and shells, mingled with debris of lava. A few sea-birds frequented this desolate coast, gulls, great albatrosses, as well as wild duck, for which Pencroft had a great fancy. He tried to knock some over with an arrow, but without result, for they seldom perched, and he could not hit them on the wing.

This led the sailor to repeat to the engineer,—

"You see, captain, so long as we have not one or two fowling-pieces, we shall never get anything!"

"Doubtless, Pencroft," replied the reporter, "but it depends on you. Procure us some iron for the barrels, steel for the hammers, saltpeter. coal and sulphur for powder, mercury and nitric acid for the fulminate, and lead for the shot, and the captain will make us first-rate guns."

"Oh!" replied the engineer, "we might, no doubt, find all these substances on the island, but a gun is a delicate instrument, and needs very particular tools. However, we shall see later!"

"Why," cried Pencroft, "were we obliged to throw overboard all the weapons we had with us in the car, all our implements, even our pocket-knives?"

"But if we had not thrown them away, Pencroft, the balloon would have thrown us to the bottom of the sea!" said Herbert.

"What you say is true, my boy," replied the sailor.

Then passing to another idea,—"Think," said he, "how astounded Jonathan Forster and his companions must have been when, next morning, they found the place empty, and the machine flown away!"

"I am utterly indifferent about knowing what they may have thought," said the reporter.

"It was all my idea, that!" said Pencroft, with a satisfied air.

"A splendid idea, Pencroft!" replied Gideon Spilett, laughing, "and which has placed us where we are."

"I would rather be here than in the hands of the Southerners," cried the sailor, "especially since the captain has been kind enough to come and join us again."

"So would I, truly!" replied the reporter. "Besides, what do we want? Nothing."

"If that is not—everything!" replied Pencroft, laughing and shrugging his shoulders. "But, some day or other, we shall find means of going away!"

"Sooner, perhaps, than you imagine, my friends," remarked the engineer, "if Lincoln Island is but a medium distance from an inhabited island, or from a continent. We shall know in an hour. I have not a map of the Pacific, but my memory has preserved a very clear recollection of its southern part. The latitude which I obtained yesterday placed New Zealand to the west of Lincoln Island, and the coast of Chile to the east. But between these two countries, there is a distance of at least six thousand miles. It has, therefore, to be determined what point in this great space the island occupies, and this the longitude will give us presently, with a sufficient approximation, I hope."

"Is not the archipelago of the Pomoutous the nearest point to us in latitude?" asked Herbert.

"Yes," replied the engineer, "but the distance which separates us from it is more than twelve hundred miles."

"And that way?" asked Neb, who followed the conversation with extreme interest, pointing to the south.

"That way, nothing," replied Pencroft.

"Nothing, indeed," added the engineer.

"Well, Cyrus," asked the reporter, "if Lincoln Island is not more than two or three thousand miles from New Zealand or Chile?"

"Well," replied the engineer, "instead of building a house we will build a boat, and Master Pencroft shall be put in command—"

"Well then," cried the sailor, "I am quite ready to be captain—as soon as you can make a craft that's able to keep at sea!"

"We shall do it, if it is necessary," replied Cyrus Harding.

But while these men, who really hesitated at nothing, were talking, the hour approached at which the observation was to be made. What Cyrus Harding was to do to ascertain the passage of the sun at the meridian of the island, without an instrument of any sort, Herbert could not guess.

The observers were then about six miles from the Chimneys, not far from that part of the downs in which the engineer had been found after his enigmatical preservation. They halted at this place and prepared for breakfast, for it was half-past eleven. Herbert went for some fresh water from a stream which ran near, and brought it back in a jug, which Neb had provided.

During these preparations Harding arranged everything for his astronomical observation. He chose a clear place on the shore, which the ebbing tide had left perfectly level. This bed of fine sand was as smooth as ice, not a grain out of place. It was of little importance whether it was horizontal or not, and it did not matter much whether the stick six feet high, which was planted there, rose perpendicularly. On the contrary, the engineer inclined it towards the south, that is to say, in the direction of the coast opposite to the sun, for it must not be forgotten that the settlers in Lincoln Island, as the island was situated in the Southern Hemisphere, saw the radiant planet describe its diurnal arc above the northern, and not above the southern horizon.

Herbert now understood how the engineer was going to proceed to ascertain the culmination of the sun, that is to say its passing the meridian of the island or, in other words, determine due south. It was by means of the shadow cast on the sand by the stick, a way which, for want of an instrument, would give him a suitable approach to the result which he wished to obtain.

In fact, the moment when this shadow would reach its minimum of length would be exactly twelve o'clock, and it would be enough to watch the extremity of the shadow, so as to ascertain the instant when, after having successively diminished, it began to lengthen. By inclining his stick to the side opposite to the sun, Cyrus Harding made the shadow longer, and consequently its modifications would be more easily ascertained. In fact, the longer the needle of a dial is, the more easily can the movement of its point be followed. The shadow of the stick was nothing but the needle of a dial. The moment had come, and Cyrus Harding knelt on the sand, and with little wooden pegs, which he stuck into the sand, he began to mark the successive diminutions of the stick's shadow. His companions, bending over him, watched the operation with extreme interest. The reporter held his chronometer in his hand, ready to tell the hour which it marked when the shadow would be at its shortest. Moreover, as Cyrus Harding was working on the 16th of April, the day on which the true and the average time are identical, the hour given by Gideon Spilett would be the true hour then at Washington, which would simplify the calculation. Meanwhile as the sun slowly advanced, the shadow slowly diminished, and when it appeared to Cyrus Harding that it was beginning to increase, he asked, "What o'clock is it?"

"One minute past five," replied Gideon Spilett directly. They had now only to calculate the operation. Nothing could be easier. It could be seen that there existed, in round numbers, a difference of five hours between the meridian of Washington and that of Lincoln Island, that is to say, it was midday in Lincoln Island when it was already five o'clock in the evening in Washington. Now the sun, in its apparent movement round the earth, traverses one degree in four minutes, or fifteen degrees an hour. Fifteen degrees multiplied by five hours give seventy-five degrees.

Then, since Washington is 77deg 3' 11" as much as to say seventy-seven degrees counted from the meridian of Greenwich which the Americans take for their starting-point for longitudes concurrently with the English—it followed that the island must be situated seventy-seven and seventy-five degrees west of the meridian of Greenwich, that is to say, on the hundred and fifty-second degree of west longitude.

Cyrus Harding announced this result to his companions, and taking into consideration errors of observation, as he had done for the latitude, he believed he could positively affirm that the position of Lincoln Island was between the thirty-fifth and the thirty-seventh parallel, and between the hundred and fiftieth and the hundred and fifty-fifth meridian to the west of the meridian of Greenwich.

The possible fault which he attributed to errors in the observation was, it may be seen, of five degrees on both sides, which, at sixty miles to a degree, would give an error of three hundred miles in latitude and longitude for the exact position.

But this error would not influence the determination which it was necessary to take. It was very evident that Lincoln Island was at such a distance from every country or island that it would be too hazardous to attempt to reach one in a frail boat.

In fact, this calculation placed it at least twelve hundred miles from Tahiti and the islands of the archipelago of the Pomoutous, more than eighteen hundred miles from New Zealand, and more than four thousand five hundred miles from the American coast!

And when Cyrus Harding consulted his memory, he could not remember in any way that such an island occupied, in that part of the Pacific, the situation assigned to Lincoln Island.

Chapter 15

The next day, the 17th of April, the sailor's first words were addressed to Gideon Spilett.

"Well, sir," he asked, "what shall we do to-day?"

"What the captain pleases," replied the reporter.

Till then the engineer's companions had been brickmakers and potters, now they were to become metallurgists.

The day before, after breakfast, they had explored as far as the point of Mandible Cape, seven miles distant from the Chimneys. There, the long series of downs ended, and the soil had a volcanic appearance. There were no longer high cliffs as at Prospect Heights, but a strange and capricious border which surrounded the narrow gulf between the two capes, formed of mineral matter, thrown up by the volcano. Arrived at this point the settlers retraced their steps, and at nightfall entered the Chimneys; but they did not sleep before the question of knowing whether they could think of leaving Lincoln Island or not was definitely settled.

The twelve hundred miles which separated the island from the Pomoutous Island was a considerable distance. A boat could not cross it, especially at the approach of the bad season. Pencroft had expressly declared this. Now, to construct a simple boat even with the necessary tools, was a difficult work, and the colonists not having tools they must begin by making hammers, axes, adzes, saws, augers, planes, etc., which would take some time. It was decided, therefore, that they would winter at Lincoln Island, and that they would look for a more comfortable dwelling than the Chimneys, in which to pass the winter months.

Before anything else could be done it was necessary to make the iron ore, of which the engineer had observed some traces in the northwest part of the island, fit for use by converting it either into iron or into steel.

Metals are not generally found in the ground in a pure state. For the most part they are combined with oxygen or sulphur. Such was the case with the two specimens which Cyrus Harding had brought back, one of magnetic iron, not carbonated, the other a pyrite, also called sulphuret of iron. It was, therefore the first, the oxide of iron, which they must reduce with coal, that is to say, get rid of the oxygen, to obtain it in a pure state. This reduction is made by subjecting the ore with coal to a high temperature, either by the rapid and easy Catalan method, which has the advantage of transforming the ore into iron in a single operation, or by the blast furnace, which first smelts the ore, then changes it into iron, by carrying away the three to four per cent. of coal, which is combined with it.

Now Cyrus Harding wanted iron, and he wished to obtain it as soon as possible. The ore which he had picked up was in itself very pure and rich. It was the oxydulous iron, which is found in confused masses of a deep gray color; it gives a black dust, crystallized in the form of the regular octahedron. Native lodestones consist of this ore, and iron of the first quality is made in Europe from that with which Sweden and Norway are so abundantly supplied. Not far from this vein was the vein of coal already made use of by the settlers. The ingredients for the manufacture being close together would greatly facilitate the treatment of the ore. This is the cause of the wealth of the mines in Great Britain, where the coal aids the manufacture of the metal extracted from the same soil at the same time as itself.

"Then, captain," said Pencroft, "we are going to work iron ore?"

"Yes, my friend," replied the engineer, "and for that—something which will please you—we must begin by having a seal hunt on the islet."

"A seal hunt!" cried the sailor, turning towards Gideon Spilett. "Are seals needed to make iron?"

"Since Cyrus has said so!" replied the reporter.

But the engineer had already left the Chimneys, and Pencroft prepared for the seal hunt, without having received any other explanation.

Cyrus Harding, Herbert, Gideon Spilett, Neb, and the sailor were soon collected on the shore, at a place where the channel left a ford passable at low tide. The hunters could therefore traverse it without getting wet higher than the knee.

Harding then put his foot on the islet for the first, and his companions for the second time.

On their landing some hundreds of penguins looked fearlessly at them. The hunters, armed with sticks, could have killed them easily, but they were not guilty of such useless massacre, as it was important not to frighten the seals, who were lying on the sand several cable lengths off. They also respected certain innocent-looking birds, whose wings were reduced to the state of stumps, spread out like fins, ornamented with feathers of a scaly appearance. The settlers, therefore, prudently advanced towards the north point, walking over ground riddled with little holes, which formed nests for the sea-birds. Towards the extremity of the islet appeared great black heads floating just above the water, having exactly the appearance of rocks in motion.

These were the seals which were to be captured. It was necessary, however, first to allow them to land, for with their close, short hair, and their fusiform conformation, being excellent swimmers, it is difficult to catch them in the sea, while on land their short, webbed feet prevent their having more than a slow, waddling movement.

Pencroft knew the habits of these creatures, and he advised waiting till they were stretched on the sand, when the sun, before long, would send them to sleep. They must then manage to cut off their retreat and knock them on the head.

The hunters, having concealed themselves behind the rocks, waited silently.

An hour passed before the seals came to play on the sand. They could count half a dozen. Pencroft and Herbert then went round the point of the islet, so as to take them in the rear, and cut off their retreat. During this time Cyrus Harding, Spilett, and Neb, crawling behind the rocks, glided towards the future scene of combat.

All at once the tall figure of the sailor appeared. Pencroft shouted. The engineer and his two companions threw themselves between the sea and the seals. Two of the animals soon lay dead on the sand, but the rest regained the sea in safety.

"Here are the seals required, captain!" said the sailor, advancing towards the engineer.

"Capital," replied Harding. "We will make bellows of them!"

"Bellows!" cried Pencroft. "Well! these are lucky seals!"

It was, in fact, a blowing-machine, necessary for the treatment of the ore that the engineer wished to manufacture with the skins of the amphibious creatures.

They were of a medium size, for their length did not exceed six feet. They resembled a dog about the head.

As it was useless to burden themselves with the weight of both the animals, Neb and Pencroft resolved to skin them on the spot, while Cyrus Harding and the reporter continued to explore the islet.

The sailor and the Negro cleverly performed the operation, and three hours afterwards Cyrus Harding had at his disposal two seals' skins, which he intended to use in this state, without subjecting them to any tanning process.

The settlers waited till the tide was again low, and crossing the channel they entered the Chimneys.

The skins had then to be stretched on a frame of wood and sewn by means of fibers so as to preserve the air without allowing too much to escape. Cyrus Harding had nothing but the two steel blades from Top's collar, and yet he was so clever, and his companions aided him with so much intelligence, that three days afterwards the little colony's stock of tools was augmented by a blowing-machine, destined to inject the air into the midst of the ore when it should be subjected to heat—an indispensable condition to the success of the operation.

On the morning of the 20th of April began the "metallic period," as the reporter called it in his notes. The engineer had decided, as has been said, to operate near the veins both of coal and ore. Now, according to his observations, these veins were situated at the foot of the northeast spurs of Mount Franklin, that is to say, a distance of six miles from their home. It was impossible, therefore, to return every day to the Chimneys, and it was agreed that the little colony should camp under a hut of branches, so that the important operation could be followed night and day.

This settled, they set out in the morning. Neb and Pencroft dragged the bellows on a hurdle; also a quantity of vegetables and animals, which they besides could renew on the way.

The road led through Jacamar Wood, which they traversed obliquely from southeast to northwest, and in the thickest part. It was necessary to beat a path, which would in the future form the most direct road to Prospect Heights and Mount Franklin. The trees, belonging to the species already discovered, were magnificent. Herbert found some new ones, among others some which Pencroft called "sham leeks"; for, in spite of their size, they were of the same liliaceous family as the onion, chive, shallot, or asparagus. These trees produce ligneous roots which, when cooked, are excellent; from them, by fermentation, a very agreeable liquor is made. They therefore made a good store of the roots.

The journey through the wood was long; it lasted the whole day, and so allowed plenty of time for examining the flora and fauna. Top, who took special charge of the fauna, ran through the grass and brushwood, putting up all sorts of game. Herbert and Gideon Spilett killed two kangaroos with bows and arrows, and also an animal which strongly resembled both a hedgehog and an ant-eater. It was like the first because it rolled itself into a ball, and bristled with spines, and the second because it had sharp claws, a long slender snout which terminated in a bird's beak, and an extendible tongue, covered with little thorns which served to hold the insects.

"And when it is in the pot," asked Pencroft naturally, "what will it be like?"

"An excellent piece of beef," replied Herbert.

"We will not ask more from it," replied the sailor.

During this excursion they saw several wild boars, which however, did not offer to attack the little band, and it appeared as if they would not meet with any dangerous beasts; when, in a thick part of the wood, the reporter thought he saw, some paces from him, among the lower branches of a tree, an animal which he took for a bear, and which he very tranquilly began to draw. Happily for Gideon Spilett, the animal in question did not belong to the redoubtable family of the plantigrades. It was only a koala, better known under the name of the sloth, being about the size of a large dog, and having stiff hair of a dirty color, the paws armed with strong claws, which enabled it to climb trees and feed on the leaves. Having identified the animal, which they did not disturb, Gideon Spilett erased "bear" from the title of his sketch, putting koala in its place, and the journey was resumed.

At five o'clock in the evening, Cyrus Harding gave the signal to halt. They were now outside the forest, at the beginning of the powerful spurs which supported Mount Franklin towards the west. At a distance of some hundred feet flowed the Red Creek, and consequently plenty of fresh water was within their reach.

The camp was soon organized. In less than an hour, on the edge of the forest, among the trees, a hut of branches interlaced with creepers, and pasted over with clay, offered a tolerable shelter. Their geological researches were put off till the next day. Supper was prepared, a good fire blazed before the hut, the roast turned, and at eight o'clock, while one of the settlers watched to keep up the fire, in case any wild beasts should prowl in the neighborhood, the others slept soundly.

The next day, the 21st of April, Cyrus Harding accompanied by Herbert, went to look for the soil of ancient formation, on which he had already discovered a specimen of ore. They found the vein above ground, near the source of the creek, at the foot of one of the northeastern spurs. This ore, very rich in iron, enclosed in its fusible veinstone, was perfectly suited to the mode of reduction which the engineer intended to employ; that is, the Catalan method, but simplified, as it is used in Corsica. In fact, the Catalan method, properly so called, requires the construction of kilns and crucibles, in which the ore and the coal, placed in alternate layers, are transformed and reduced, But Cyrus Harding intended to economize these constructions, and wished simply to form, with the ore and the coal, a cubic mass, to the center of which he would direct the wind from his bellows. Doubtless, it was the proceeding employed by Tubalcain, and the first metallurgists of the inhabited world. Now that which had succeeded with the grandson of Adam, and which still yielded good results in countries which in ore and fuel, could not but succeed with the settlers in Lincoln Island.

The coal, as well as the ore, was collected without trouble on the surface of the ground. They first broke the ore into little pieces, and cleansed them with the hand from the impurities which soiled their surface. Then coal and ore were arranged in heaps and in successive layers, as the charcoal-burner does with the wood which he wishes to carbonize. In this way, under the influence of the air projected by the blowing-machine, the coal would be transformed into carbonic acid, then into oxide of carbon, its use being to reduce the oxide of iron, that is to say, to rid it of the oxygen.

Thus the engineer proceeded. The bellows of sealskin, furnished at its extremity with a nozzle of clay, which had been previously fabricated in the pottery kiln, was established near the heap of ore. Using the mechanism which consisted of a frame, cords of fiber and counterpoise, he threw into the mass an abundance of air, which by raising the temperature also concurred with the chemical transformation to produce in time pure iron.

The operation was difficult. All the patience, all the ingenuity of the settlers was needed; but at last it succeeded, and the result was a lump of iron, reduced to a spongy state, which it was necessary to shingle and fagot, that is to say, to forge so as to expel from it the liquefied veinstone. These amateur smiths had, of course, no hammer; but they were in no worse a situation than the first metallurgist, and therefore did what, no doubt, he had to do.

A handle was fixed to the first lump, and was used as a hammer to forge the second on a granite anvil, and thus they obtained a coarse but useful metal. At length, after many trials and much fatigue, on the 25th of April several bars of iron were forged, and transformed into tools, crowbars, pincers, pickaxes, spades, etc., which Pencroft and Neb declared to be real jewels. But the metal was not yet in its most serviceable state, that is, of steel. Now steel is a combination of iron and coal, which is extracted, either from the liquid ore, by taking from it the excess of coal, or from the iron by adding to it the coal which was wanting. The first, obtained by the decarburation of the metal, gives natural or puddled steel; the second, produced by the carburation of the iron, gives steel of cementation.

It was the last which Cyrus Harding intended to forge, as he possessed iron in a pure state. He succeeded by heating the metal with powdered coal in a crucible which had previously been manufactured from clay suitable for the purpose.

He then worked this steel, which is malleable both when hot or cold, with the hammer. Neb and Pencroft, cleverly directed, made hatchets, which, heated red-hot, and plunged suddenly into cold water, acquired an excellent temper.

Other instruments, of course roughly fashioned, were also manufactured; blades for planes, axes, hatchets, pieces of steel to be transformed into saws, chisels; then iron for spades, pickaxes, hammers, nails, etc. At last, on the 5th of May, the metallic period ended, the smiths returned to the Chimneys, and new work would soon authorize them to take a fresh title.

Chapter 16

It was the 6th of May, a day which corresponds to the 6th of November in the countries of the Northern Hemisphere. The sky had been obscured for some days, and it was of importance to make preparations for the winter. However, the temperature was not as yet much lower, and a centigrade thermometer, transported to Lincoln Island, would still have marked an average of ten to twelve degrees above zero. This was not surprising, since Lincoln Island, probably situated between the thirty-fifth and fortieth parallel, would be subject, in the Southern Hemisphere, to the same climate as Sicily or Greece in the Northern Hemisphere. But as Greece and Sicily have severe cold, producing snow and ice, so doubtless would Lincoln Island in the severest part of the winter and it was advisable to provide against it.

In any case if cold did not yet threaten them, the rainy season would begin, and on this lonely island, exposed to all the fury of the elements, in mid-ocean, bad weather would be frequent, and probably terrible. The question of a more comfortable dwelling than the Chimneys must therefore be seriously considered and promptly resolved on.

Pencroft, naturally, had some predilection for the retreat which he had discovered, but he well understood that another must be found. The Chimneys had been already visited by the sea, under circumstances which are known, and it would not do to be exposed again to a similar accident.

"Besides," added Cyrus Harding, who this day was talking of these things with his companions, "we have some precautions to take."

"Why? The island is not inhabited," said the reporter.

"That is probable," replied the engineer, "although we have not yet explored the interior; but if no human beings are found, I fear that dangerous animals may abound. It is necessary to guard against a possible attack, so that we shall not be obliged to watch every night, or to keep up a fire. And then, my friends, we must foresee everything. We are here in a part of the Pacific often frequented by Malay pirates—"

"What!" said Herbert, "at such a distance from land?"

"Yes, my boy," replied the engineer. "These pirates are bold sailors as well as formidable enemies, and we must take measures accordingly."

"Well," replied Pencroft, "we will fortify ourselves against savages with two legs as well as against savages with four. But, captain, will it not be best to explore every part of the island before undertaking anything else?"

"That would be best," added Gideon Spilett.

"Who knows if we might not find on the opposite side one of the caverns which we have searched for in vain here?"

"That is true," replied the engineer, "but you forget, my friends, that it will be necessary to establish ourselves in the neighborhood of a watercourse, and that, from the summit of Mount Franklin, we could not see towards the west, either stream or river. Here, on the contrary, we are placed between the Mercy and Lake Grant, an advantage which must not be neglected. And, besides, this side, looking towards the east, is not exposed as the other is to the trade-winds, which in this hemisphere blow from the northwest."

"Then, captain," replied the sailor, "let us build a house on the edge of the lake. Neither bricks nor tools are wanting now. After having been brickmakers, potters, smelters, and smiths, we shall surely know how to be masons!"

"Yes, my friend; but before coming to any decision we must consider the matter thoroughly. A natural dwelling would spare us much work, and would be a surer retreat, for it would be as well defended against enemies from the interior as those from outside."

"That is true, Cyrus," replied the reporter, "but we have already examined all that mass of granite, and there is not a hole, not a cranny!"

"No, not one!" added Pencroft. "Ah, if we were able to dig out a dwelling in that cliff, at a good height, so as to be out of the reach of harm, that would be capital! I can see that on the front which looks seaward, five or six rooms—"

"With windows to light them!" said Herbert, laughing.

"And a staircase to climb up to them!" added Neb.

"You are laughing," cried the sailor, "and why? What is there impossible in what I propose? Haven't we got pickaxes and spades? Won't Captain Harding be able to make powder to blow up the mine? Isn't it true, captain, that you will make powder the very day we want it?"

Cyrus Harding listened to the enthusiastic Pencroft developing his fanciful projects. To attack this mass of granite, even by a mine, was Herculean work, and it was really vexing that nature could not help them at their need. But the engineer did not reply to the sailor except by proposing to examine the cliff more attentively, from the mouth of the river to the angle which terminated it on the north.

They went out, therefore, and the exploration was made with extreme care, over an extent of nearly two miles. But in no place in the bare, straight cliff, could any cavity be found. The nests of the rock pigeons which fluttered at its summit were only, in reality, holes bored at the very top, and on the irregular edge of the granite.

It was a provoking circumstance, and as to attacking this cliff, either with pickaxe or with powder, so as to effect a sufficient excavation, it was not to be thought of. It so happened that, on all this part of the shore, Pencroft had discovered the only habitable shelter, that is to say, the Chimneys, which now had to be abandoned.

The exploration ended, the colonists found themselves at the north angle of the cliff, where it terminated in long slopes which died away on the shore. From this place, to its extreme limit in the west, it only formed a sort of declivity, a thick mass of stones, earth, and sand, bound together by plants, bushes, and grass inclined at an angle of only forty-five degrees. Clumps of trees grew on these slopes, which were also carpeted with thick grass. But the vegetation did not extend far, and a long, sandy plain, which began at the foot of these slopes, reached to the beach.

Cyrus Harding thought, not without reason, that the overplus of the lake must overflow on this side. The excess of water furnished by the Red Creek must also escape by some channel or other. Now the engineer had not yet found this channel on any part of the shore already explored, that is to say, from the mouth of the stream on the west of Prospect Heights.

The engineer now proposed to his companions to climb the slope, and to return to the Chimneys by the heights, while exploring the northern and eastern shores of the lake. The proposal was accepted, and in a few minutes Herbert and Neb were on the upper plateau. Cyrus Harding, Gideon Spilett, and Pencroft followed with more sedate steps.

The beautiful sheet of water glittered through the trees under the rays of the sun. In this direction the country was charming. The eye feasted on the groups of trees. Some old trunks, bent with age, showed black against the verdant grass which covered the ground. Crowds of brilliant cockatoos screamed among the branches, moving prisms, hopping from one bough to another.

The settlers instead of going directly to the north bank of the lake, made a circuit round the edge of the plateau, so as to join the mouth of the creek on its left bank. It was a detour of more than a mile and a half. Walking was easy, for the trees widely spread, left a considerable space between them. The fertile zone evidently stopped at this point, and vegetation would be less vigorous in the part between the course of the Creek and the Mercy.

Cyrus Harding and his companions walked over this new ground with great care. Bows, arrows, and sticks with sharp iron points were their only weapons. However, no wild beast showed itself, and it was probable that these animals frequented rather the thick forests in the south; but the settlers had the disagreeable surprise of seeing Top stop before a snake of great size, measuring from fourteen to fifteen feet in length. Neb killed it by a blow from his stick. Cyrus Harding examined the reptile, and declared it not venomous, for it belonged to that species of diamond serpents which the natives of New South Wales rear. But it was possible that others existed whose bite was mortal such as the deaf vipers with forked tails, which rise up under the feet, or those winged snakes, furnished with two ears, which enable them to proceed with great rapidity. Top, the first moment of surprise over, began a reptile chase with such eagerness, that they feared for his safety. His master called him back directly.

The mouth of the Red Creek, at the place where it entered into the lake, was soon reached. The explorers recognized on the opposite shore the point which they had visited on their descent from Mount Franklin. Cyrus Harding ascertained that the flow of water into it from the creek was considerable. Nature must therefore have provided some place for the escape of the overplus. This doubtless formed a fall, which, if it could be discovered, would be of great use.

The colonists, walking apart, but not straying far from each other, began to skirt the edge of the lake, which was very steep. The water appeared to be full of fish, and Pencroft resolved to make some fishing-rods, so as to try and catch some.

The northeast point was first to be doubled. It might have been supposed that the discharge of water was at this place, for the extremity of the lake was almost on a level with the edge of the plateau. But no signs of this were discovered, and the colonists continued to explore the bank, which, after a slight bend, descended parallel to the shore.

On this side the banks were less woody, but clumps of trees, here and there, added to the picturesqueness of the country. Lake Grant was viewed from thence in all its extent, and no breath disturbed the surface of its waters. Top, in beating the bushes, put up flocks of birds of different kinds, which Gideon Spilett and Herbert saluted with arrows. One was hit by the lad, and fell into some marshy grass. Top rushed forward, and brought a beautiful swimming bird, of a slate color, short beak, very developed frontal plate, and wings edged with white. It was a "coot," the size of a large partridge, belonging to the group of macrodactyls which form the transition between the order of wading birds and that of palmipeds. Sorry game, in truth, and its flavor is far from pleasant. But Top was not so particular in these things as his masters, and it was agreed that the coot should be for his supper.

The settlers were now following the eastern bank of the lake, and they would not be long in reaching the part which they already knew. The engineer was much surprised at not seeing any indication of the discharge of water. The reporter and the sailor talked with him, and he could not conceal his astonishment.

At this moment Top, who had been very quiet till then, gave signs of agitation. The intelligent animal went backwards and forwards on the shore, stopped suddenly, and looked at the water, one paw raised, as if he was pointing at some invisible game; then he barked furiously, and was suddenly silent.

Neither Cyrus Harding nor his companions had at first paid any attention to Top's behavior; but the dog's barking soon became so frequent that the engineer noticed it.

"What is there, Top?" he asked.

The dog bounded towards his master, seeming to be very uneasy, and then rushed again towards the bank. Then, all at once, he plunged into the lake.

"Here, Top!" cried Cyrus Harding, who did not like his dog to venture into the treacherous water.

"What's happening down there?" asked Pencroft, examining the surface of the lake.

"Top smells some amphibious creature," replied Herbert.

"An alligator, perhaps," said the reporter.

"I do not think so," replied Harding. "Alligators are only met with in regions less elevated in latitude."

Meanwhile Top had returned at his master's call, and had regained the shore: but he could not stay quiet; he plunged in among the tall grass, and guided by instinct, he appeared to follow some invisible being which was slipping along under the surface of the water. However the water was calm; not a ripple disturbed its surface. Several times the settlers stopped on the bank, and observed it attentively. Nothing appeared. There was some mystery there.

The engineer was puzzled.

"Let us pursue this exploration to the end," said he.

Half an hour after they had all arrived at the southeast angle of the lake, on Prospect Heights. At this point the examination of the banks of the lake was considered finished, and yet the engineer had not been able to discover how and where the waters were discharged. "There is no doubt this overflow exists," he repeated, "and since it is not visible it must go through the granite cliff at the west!"

"But what importance do you attach to knowing that, my dear Cyrus?" asked Gideon Spilett.

"Considerable importance," replied the engineer; "for if it flows through the cliff there is probably some cavity, which it would be easy to render habitable after turning away the water."

"But is it not possible, captain, that the water flows away at the bottom of the lake," said Herbert, "and that it reaches the sea by some subterranean passage?"

"That might be," replied the engineer, "and should it be so we shall be obliged to build our house ourselves, since nature has not done it for us."

The colonists were about to begin to traverse the plateau to return to the Chimneys, when Top gave new signs of agitation. He barked with fury, and before his master could restrain him, he had plunged a second time into the lake.

All ran towards the bank. The dog was already more than twenty feet off, and Cyrus was calling him back, when an enormous head emerged from the water, which did not appear to be deep in that place.

Herbert recognized directly the species of amphibian to which the tapering head, with large eyes, and adorned with long silky mustaches, belonged.

"A lamantin!" he cried.

It was not a lamantin, but one of that species of the order of cetaceans, which bear the name of the "dugong," for its nostrils were open at the upper part of its snout. The enormous animal rushed on the dog, who tried to escape by returning towards the shore. His master could do nothing to save him, and before Gideon Spilett or Herbert thought of bending their bows, Top, seized by the dugong, had disappeared beneath the water.

Neb, his iron-tipped spear in his hand, wished to go to Top's help, and attack the dangerous animal in its own element.

"No, Neb," said the engineer, restraining his courageous servant.

Meanwhile, a struggle was going on beneath the water, an inexplicable struggle, for in his situation Top could not possibly resist; and judging by the bubbling of the surface it must be also a terrible struggle, and could not but terminate in the death of the dog! But suddenly, in the middle of a foaming circle, Top reappeared. Thrown in the air by some unknown power, he rose ten feet above the surface of the lake, fell again into the midst of the agitated waters, and then soon gained the shore, without any severe wounds, miraculously saved.

Cyrus Harding and his companions could not understand it. What was not less inexplicable was that the struggle still appeared to be going on. Doubtless, the dugong, attacked by some powerful animal, after having released the dog, was fighting on its own account. But it did not last long. The water became red with blood, and the body of the dugong, emerging from the sheet of scarlet which spread around, soon stranded on a little beach at the south angle of the lake. The colonists ran towards it. The dugong was dead. It was an enormous animal, fifteen or sixteen feet long, and must have weighed from three to four thousand pounds. At its neck was a wound, which appeared to have been produced by a sharp blade.

What could the amphibious creature have been, who, by this terrible blow had destroyed the formidable dugong? No one could tell, and much interested in this incident, Harding and his companions returned to the Chimneys.

Chapter 17

The next day, the 7th of May, Harding and Gideon Spilett, leaving Neb to prepare breakfast, climbed Prospect Heights, while Herbert and Pencroft ascended by the river, to renew their store of wood.

The engineer and the reporter soon reached the little beach on which the dugong had been stranded. Already flocks of birds had attacked the mass of flesh, and had to be driven away with stones, for Cyrus wished to keep the fat for the use of the colony. As to the animal's flesh it would furnish excellent food, for in the islands of the Malay Archipelago and elsewhere, it is especially reserved for the table of the native princes. But that was Neb's affair.

At this moment Cyrus Harding had other thoughts. He was much interested in the incident of the day before. He wished to penetrate the mystery of that submarine combat, and to ascertain what monster could have given the dugong so strange a wound. He remained at the edge of the lake, looking, observing; but nothing appeared under the tranquil waters, which sparkled in the first rays of the rising sun.

At the beach, on which lay the body of the dugong, the water was tolerably shallow, but from this point the bottom of the lake sloped gradually, and it was probable that the depth was considerable in the center. The lake might be considered as a large center basin, which was filled by the water from the Red Creek.

"Well, Cyrus," said the reporter, "there seems to be nothing suspicious in this water."

"No, my dear Spilett," replied the engineer, "and I really do not know how to account for the incident of yesterday."

"I acknowledge," returned Spilett, "that the wound given this creature is, at least, very strange, and I cannot explain either how Top was so vigorously cast up out of the water. One could have thought that a powerful arm hurled him up, and that the same arm with a dagger killed the dugong!"

"Yes," replied the engineer, who had become thoughtful; "there is something there that I cannot understand. But do you better understand either, my dear Spilett, in what way I was saved myself—how I was drawn from the waves, and carried to the downs? No! Is it not true? Now, I feel sure that there is some mystery there, which, doubtless, we shall discover some day. Let us observe, but do not dwell on these singular incidents before our companions. Let us keep our remarks to ourselves, and continue our work."

It will be remembered that the engineer had not as yet been able to discover the place where the surplus water escaped, but he knew it must exist somewhere. He was much surprised to see a strong current at this place. By throwing in some bits of wood he found that it set towards the southern angle. He followed the current, and arrived at the south point of the lake.

There was there a sort of depression in the water, as if it was suddenly lost in some fissure in the ground.

Harding listened; placing his ear to the level of the lake, he very distinctly heard the noise of a subterranean fall.

"There," said he, rising, "is the discharge of the water; there, doubtless, by a passage in the granite cliff, it joins the sea, through cavities which we can use to our profit. Well, I can find it!"

The engineer cut a long branch, stripped it of its leaves, and plunging it into the angle between the two banks, he found that there was a large hole one foot only beneath the surface of the water. This hole was the opening so long looked for in vain, and the force of the current was such that the branch was torn from the engineer's hands and disappeared.

"There is no doubt about it now," repeated Harding. "There is the outlet, and I will lay it open to view!"

"How?" asked Gideon Spilett.

"By lowering the level of the water of the lake three feet." "And how will you lower the level?"

"By opening another outlet larger than this."

"At what place, Cyrus?"

"At the part of the bank nearest the coast."

"But it is a mass of granite!" observed Spilett.

"Well," replied Cyrus Harding, "I will blow up the granite, and the water escaping, will subside, so as to lay bare this opening—"

"And make a waterfall, by falling on to the beach," added the reporter.

"A fall that we shall make use of!" replied Cyrus. "Come, come!"

The engineer hurried away his companion, whose confidence in Harding was such that he did not doubt the enterprise would succeed. And yet, how was this granite wall to be opened without powder, and with imperfect instruments? Was not this work upon which the engineer was so bent above their strength?

When Harding and the reporter entered the Chimneys, they found Herbert and Pencroft unloading their raft of wood.

"The woodmen have just finished, captain." said the sailor, laughing, "and when you want masons—"

"Masons,—no, but chemists," replied the engineer.

"Yes," added the reporter, "we are going to blow up the island—"

"Blow up the island?" cried Pencroft.

"Part of it, at least," replied Spilett.

"Listen to me, my friends," said the engineer. And he made known to them the result of his observations.

According to him, a cavity, more or less considerable, must exist in the mass of granite which supported Prospect Heights, and he intended to penetrate into it. To do this, the opening through which the water rushed must first be cleared, and the level lowered by making a larger outlet. Therefore an explosive substance must be manufactured, which would make a deep trench in some other part of the shore. This was what Harding was going to attempt with the minerals which nature placed at his disposal.

It is useless to say with what enthusiasm all, especially Pencroft, received this project. To employ great means, open the granite, create a cascade, that suited the sailor. And he would just as soon be a chemist as a mason or bootmaker, since the engineer wanted chemicals. He would be all that they liked, "even a professor of dancing and deportment," said he to Neb, if that was ever necessary.

Neb and Pencroft were first of all told to extract the grease from the dugong, and to keep the flesh, which was destined for food. Such perfect confidence had they in the engineer, that they set out directly, without even asking a question. A few minutes after them, Cyrus Harding, Herbert, and Gideon Spilett, dragging the hurdle, went towards the vein of coals, where those shistose pyrites abound which are met with in the most recent transition soil, and of which Harding had already found a specimen. All the day being employed in carrying a quantity of these stones to the Chimneys, by evening they had several tons.

The next day, the 8th of May, the engineer began his manipulations. These shistose pyrites being composed principally of coal, flint, alumina, and sulphuret of iron—the latter in excess—it was necessary to separate the sulphuret of iron, and transform it into sulphate as rapidly as possible. The sulphate obtained, the sulphuric acid could then be extracted.

This was the object to be attained. Sulphuric acid is one of the agents the most frequently employed, and the manufacturing importance of a nation can be measured by the consumption which is made of it. This acid would later be of great use to the settlers, in the manufacturing of candles, tanning skins, etc., but this time the engineer reserved it for another use.

Cyrus Harding chose, behind the Chimneys, a site where the ground was perfectly level. On this ground he placed a layer of branches and chopped wood, on which were piled some pieces of shistose pyrites, buttressed one against the other, the whole being covered with a thin layer of pyrites, previously reduced to the size of a nut.

This done, they set fire to the wood, the heat was communicated to the shist, which soon kindled, since it contains coal and sulphur. Then new layers of bruised pyrites were arranged so as to form an immense heap, the exterior of which was covered with earth and grass, several air-holes being left, as if it was a stack of wood which was to be carbonized to make charcoal.

They then left the transformation to complete itself, and it would not take less than ten or twelve days for the sulphuret of iron to be changed to sulphate of iron and the alumina into sulphate of alumina, two equally soluble substances, the others, flint, burnt coal, and cinders, not being so.

While this chemical work was going on, Cyrus Harding proceeded with other operations, which were pursued with more than zeal,—it was eagerness.

Neb and Pencroft had taken away the fat from the dugong, and placed it in large earthen pots. It was then necessary to separate the glycerine from the fat by saponifying it. Now, to obtain this result, it had to be treated either with soda or lime. In fact, one or other of these substances, after having attacked the fat, would form a soap by separating the glycerine, and it was just this glycerine which the engineer wished to obtain. There was no want of lime, only treatment by lime would give calcareous soap, insoluble, and consequently useless, while treatment by soda would furnish, on the contrary, a soluble soap, which could be put to domestic use. Now, a practical man, like Cyrus Harding, would rather try to obtain soda. Was this difficult? No; for marine plants abounded on the shore, glass-wort, ficoides, and all those fucaceae which form wrack. A large quantity of these plants was collected, first dried, then burnt in holes in the open air. The combustion of these plants was kept up for several days, and the result was a compact gray mass, which has been long known under the name of "natural soda."

This obtained, the engineer treated the fat with soda, which gave both a soluble soap and that neutral substance, glycerine.

But this was not all. Cyrus Harding still needed, in view of his future preparation, another substance, nitrate of potash, which is better known under the name of salt niter, or of saltpeter.

Cyrus Harding could have manufactured this substance by treating the carbonate of potash, which would be easily extracted from the cinders of the vegetables, by azotic acid. But this acid was wanting, and he would have been in some difficulty, if nature had not happily furnished the saltpeter, without giving them any other trouble than that of picking it up. Herbert found a vein of it at the foot of Mount Franklin, and they had nothing to do but purify this salt.

These different works lasted a week. They were finished before the transformation of the sulphuret into sulphate of iron had been accomplished. During the following days the settlers had time to construct a furnace of bricks of a particular arrangement, to serve for the distillation of the sulphate or iron when it had been obtained. All this was finished about the 18th of May, nearly at the time when the chemical transformation terminated. Gideon Spilett, Herbert, Neb, and Pencroft, skillfully directed by the engineer, had become most clever workmen. Before all masters, necessity is the one most listened to, and who teaches the best.

When the heap of pyrites had been entirely reduced by fire, the result of the operation, consisting of sulphate of iron, sulphate of alumina, flint, remains of coal, and cinders was placed in a basinful of water. They stirred this mixture, let it settle, then decanted it, and obtained a clear liquid containing in solution sulphate of iron and sulphate of alumina, the other matters remaining solid, since they are insoluble. Lastly, this liquid being partly evaporated, crystals of sulphate of iron were deposited, and the not evaporated liquid, which contained the sulphate of alumina, was thrown away.

Cyrus Harding had now at his disposal a large quantity of these sulphate of iron crystals, from which the sulphuric acid had to be extracted. The making of sulphuric acid is a very expensive manufacture. Considerable works are necessary—a special set of tools, an apparatus of platina, leaden chambers, unassailable by the acid, and in which the transformation is performed, etc. The engineer had none of these at his disposal, but he knew that, in Bohemia especially, sulphuric acid is manufactured by very simple means, which have also the advantage of producing it to a superior degree of concentration. It is thus that the acid known under the name of Nordhausen acid is made.

To obtain sulphuric acid, Cyrus Harding had only one operation to make, to calcine the sulphate of iron crystals in a closed vase, so that the sulphuric acid should distil in vapor, which vapor, by condensation, would produce the acid.

The crystals were placed in pots, and the heat from the furnace would distil the sulphuric acid. The operation was successfully completed, and on the 20th of May, twelve days after commencing it, the engineer was the possessor of the agent which later he hoped to use in so many different ways.

Now, why did he wish for this agent? Simply to produce azotic acid; and that was easy, since saltpeter, attacked by sulphuric acid, gives azotic, or nitric, acid by distillation.

But, after all, how was he going to employ this azotic acid? His companions were still ignorant of this, for he had not informed them of the result at which he aimed.

However, the engineer had nearly accomplished his purpose, and by a last operation he would procure the substance which had given so much trouble.

Taking some azotic acid, he mixed it with glycerine, which had been previously concentrated by evaporation, subjected to the water-bath, and he obtained, without even employing a refrigerant mixture, several pints of an oily yellow mixture.

This last operation Cyrus Harding had made alone, in a retired place, at a distance from the Chimneys, for he feared the danger of an explosion, and when he showed a bottle of this liquid to his friends, he contented himself with saying,—

"Here is nitro-glycerine!"

Jules Verne

It was really this terrible production, of which the explosive power is perhaps tenfold that of ordinary powder, and which has already caused so many accidents. However, since a way has been found to transform it into dynamite, that is to say, to mix with it some solid substance, clay or sugar, porous enough to hold it, the dangerous liquid has been used with some security. But dynamite was not yet known at the time when the settlers worked on Lincoln Island.

"And is it that liquid that is going to blow up our rocks?" said Pencroft incredulously.

"Yes, my friend," replied the engineer, "and this nitro-glycerine will produce so much the more effect, as the granite is extremely hard, and will oppose a greater resistance to the explosion."

"And when shall we see this, captain?"

"To-morrow, as soon as we have dug a hole for the mine, replied the engineer."

The next day, the 21st of May, at daybreak, the miners went to the point which formed the eastern shore of Lake Grant, and was only five hundred feet from the coast. At this place, the plateau inclined downwards from the waters, which were only restrained by their granite case. Therefore, if this case was broken, the water would escape by the opening and form a stream, which, flowing over the inclined surface of the plateau, would rush on to the beach. Consequently, the level of the lake would be greatly lowered, and the opening where the water escaped would be exposed, which was their final aim.

Under the engineer's directions, Pencroft, armed with a pickaxe, which he handled skillfully and vigorously, attacked the granite. The hole was made on the point of the shore, slanting, so that it should meet a much lower level than that of the water of the lake. In this way the explosive force, by scattering the rock, would open a large place for the water to rush out.

The work took some time, for the engineer, wishing to produce a great effect, intended to devote not less than seven quarts of nitro-glycerine to the operation. But Pencroft, relieved by Neb, did so well, that towards four o'clock in the evening, the mine was finished.

Now the question of setting fire to the explosive substance was raised. Generally, nitro-glycerine is ignited by caps of fulminate, which in bursting cause the explosion. A shock is therefore needed to produce the explosion, for, simply lighted, this substance would burn without exploding.

Cyrus Harding could certainly have fabricated a percussion cap. In default of fulminate, he could easily obtain a substance similar to guncotton, since he had azotic acid at his disposal. This substance, pressed in a cartridge, and introduced among the nitro-glycerine, would burst by means of a fuse, and cause the explosion.

But Cyrus Harding knew that nitro-glycerine would explode by a shock. He resolved to employ this means, and try another way, if this did not succeed.

In fact, the blow of a hammer on a few drops of nitro-glycerine, spread out on a hard surface, was enough to create an explosion. But the operator could not be there to give the blow, without becoming a victim to the operation. Harding, therefore, thought of suspending a mass of iron, weighing several pounds, by means of a fiber, to an upright just above the mine. Another long fiber, previously impregnated with sulphur, was attached to the middle of the first, by one end, while the other lay on the ground several feet distant from the mine. The second fiber being set on fire, it would burn till it reached the first. This catching fire in its turn, would break, and the mass of iron would fall on the nitro-glycerine. This apparatus being then arranged, the engineer, after having sent his companions to a distance, filled the hole, so that the nitro-glycerine was on a level with the opening; then he threw a few drops of it on the surface of the rock, above which the mass of iron was already suspended.

This done, Harding lit the end of the sulphured fiber, and leaving the place, he returned with his companions to the Chimneys.

The fiber was intended to burn five and twenty minutes, and, in fact, five and twenty minutes afterwards a most tremendous explosion was heard. The island appeared to tremble to its very foundation. Stones were projected in the air as if by the eruption of a volcano. The shock produced by the displacing of the air was such, that the rocks of the Chimneys shook. The settlers, although they were more than two miles from the mine, were thrown on the ground.

They rose, climbed the plateau, and ran towards the place where the bank of the lake must have been shattered by the explosion.

A cheer escaped them! A large rent was seen in the granite! A rapid stream of water rushed foaming across the plateau and dashed down a height of three hundred feet on to the beach!

Chapter 18

Cyrus Harding's project had succeeded, but, according to his usual habit he showed no satisfaction; with closed lips and a fixed look, he remained motionless. Herbert was in ecstasies, Neb bounded with joy, Pencroft nodded his great head, murmuring these words,—

"Come, our engineer gets on capitally!"

The nitro-glycerine had indeed acted powerfully. The opening which it had made was so large that the volume of water which escaped through this new outlet was at least treble that which before passed through the old one. The result was, that a short time after the operation the level of the lake would be lowered two feet, or more.

The settlers went to the Chimneys to take some pickaxes, iron-tipped spears, string made of fibers, flint and steel; they then returned to the plateau, Top accompanying them.

On the way the sailor could not help saying to the engineer,—

"Don't you think, captain, that by means of that charming liquid you have made, one could blow up the whole of our island?"

"Without any doubt, the island, continents, and the world itself," replied the engineer. "It is only a question of quantity."

"Then could you not use this nitro-glycerine for loading firearms?" asked the sailor.

"No, Pencroft; for it is too explosive a substance. But it would be easy to make some guncotton, or even ordinary powder, as we have azotic acid, saltpeter, sulphur, and coal. Unhappily, it is the guns which we have not got."

"Oh, captain," replied the sailor, "with a little determination—"

Pencroft had erased the word "impossible" from the dictionary of Lincoln Island.

The settlers, having arrived at Prospect Heights, went immediately towards that point of the lake near which was the old opening now uncovered. This outlet had now become practicable, since the water no longer rushed through it, and it would doubtless be easy to explore the interior.

In a few minutes the settlers had reached the lower point of the lake, and a glance showed them that the object had been attained.

In fact, in the side of the lake, and now above the surface of the water, appeared the long-looked-for opening. A narrow ridge, left bare by the retreat of the water, allowed them to approach it. This orifice was nearly twenty feet in width, but scarcely two in height. It was like the mouth of a drain at the edge of the pavement, and therefore did not offer an easy passage to the settlers; but Neb and Pencroft, taking their pickaxes, soon made it of a suitable height.

The engineer then approached, and found that the sides of the opening, in its upper part at least, had not a slope of more than from thirty to thirty-five degrees. It was therefore practicable, and, provided that the declivity did not increase, it would be easy to descend even to the level of the sea. If then, as was probable, some vast cavity existed in the interior of the granite, it might, perhaps, be of great use.

"Well, captain, what are we stopping for?" asked the sailor, impatient to enter the narrow passage. "You see Top has got before us!"

"Very well," replied the engineer. "But we must see our way. Neb, go and cut some resinous branches."

Neb and Herbert ran to the edge of the lake, shaded with pines and other green trees, and soon returned with some branches, which they made into torches. The torches were lighted with flint and steel, and Cyrus Harding leading, the settlers ventured into the dark passage, which the overplus of the lake had formerly filled.

Contrary to what might have been supposed, the diameter of the passage increased as the explorers proceeded, so that they very soon were able to stand upright. The granite, worn by the water for an infinite time, was very slippery, and falls were to be dreaded. But the settlers were all attached to each other by a cord, as is frequently done in ascending mountains. Happily some projections of the granite, forming regular steps, made the descent less perilous. Drops, still hanging from the rocks, shone here and there under the light of the torches, and the explorers guessed that the sides were clothed with innumerable stalactites. The engineer examined this black granite. There was not a stratum, not a break in it. The mass was compact, and of an extremely close grain. The passage dated, then, from the very origin of the island. It was not the water which little by little had hollowed it. Pluto and not Neptune had bored it with his own hand, and on the wall traces of an eruptive work could be distinguished, which all the washing of the water had not been able totally to efface.

The settlers descended very slowly. They could not but feel a certain awe, in this venturing into these unknown depths, for the first time visited by human beings. They did not speak, but they thought; and the thought came to more than one, that some polypus or other gigantic cephalopod might inhabit the interior cavities, which were in communication with the sea. However, Top kept at the head of the little band, and they could rely on the sagacity of the dog, who would not fail to give the alarm if there was any need for it.

After having descended about a hundred feet, following a winding road, Harding who was walking on before, stopped, and his companions came up with him. The place where they had halted was wider, so as to form a cavern of moderate dimensions. Drops of water fell from the vault, but that did not prove that they oozed through the rock. They were simply the last traces left by the torrent which had so long thundered through this cavity, and the air there was pure though slightly damp, but producing no mephitic exhalation.

"Well, my dear Cyrus," said Gideon Spilett, "here is a very secure retreat, well hid in the depths of the rock, but it is, however, uninhabitable."

"Why uninhabitable?" asked the sailor.

"Because it is too small and too dark."

"Couldn't we enlarge it, hollow it out, make openings to let in light and air?" replied Pencroft, who now thought nothing impossible.

"Let us go on with our exploration," said Cyrus Harding. "Perhaps lower down, nature will have spared us this labor."

"We have only gone a third of the way," observed Herbert.

"Nearly a third," replied Harding, "for we have descended a hundred feet from the opening, and it is not impossible that a hundred feet farther down—"

"Where is Top?" asked Neb, interrupting his master.

They searched the cavern, but the dog was not there.

"Most likely he has gone on," said Pencroft.

"Let us join him," replied Harding.

The descent was continued. The engineer carefully observed all the deviations of the passage, and notwithstanding so many detours, he could easily have given an account of its general direction, which went towards the sea.

The settlers had gone some fifty feet farther, when their attention was attracted by distant sounds which came up from the depths. They stopped and listened. These sounds, carried through the passage as through an acoustic tube, came clearly to the ear.

"That is Top barking!" cried Herbert.

"Yes," replied Pencroft, "and our brave dog is barking furiously!"

"We have our iron-tipped spears," said Cyrus Harding. "Keep on your guard, and forward!"

"It is becoming more and more interesting," murmured Gideon Spilett in the sailor's ear, who nodded. Harding and his companions rushed to the help of their dog. Top's barking became more and more perceptible, and it seemed strangely fierce. Was he engaged in a struggle with some animal whose retreat he had disturbed? Without thinking of the danger to which they might be exposed, the explorers were now impelled by an irresistible curiosity, and in a few minutes, sixteen feet lower they rejoined Top.

There the passage ended in a vast and magnificent cavern.

Top was running backwards and forwards, barking furiously. Pencroft and Neb, waving their torches, threw the light into every crevice; and at the same time, Harding, Gideon Spilett, and Herbert, their spears raised, were ready for any emergency which might arise. The enormous cavern was empty. The settlers explored it in every direction. There was nothing there, not an animal, not a human being; and yet Top continued to bark. Neither caresses nor threats could make him be silent.

"There must be a place somewhere, by which the waters of the lake reached the sea," said the engineer.

"Of course," replied Pencroft, "and we must take care not to tumble into a hole."

"Go, Top, go!" cried Harding.

The dog, excited by his master's words, ran towards the extremity of the cavern, and there redoubled his barking.

They followed him, and by the light of the torches, perceived the mouth of a regular well in the granite. It was by this that the water escaped; and this time it was not an oblique and practicable passage, but a perpendicular well, into which it was impossible to venture.

The torches were held over the opening: nothing could be seen. Harding took a lighted branch, and threw it into the abyss. The blazing resin, whose illuminating power increased still more by the rapidity of its fall, lighted up the interior of the well, but yet nothing appeared. The flame then went out with a slight hiss, which showed that it had reached the water, that is to say, the level of the sea.

The engineer, calculating the time employed in its fall, was able to calculate the depth of the well, which was found to be about ninety feet.

The floor of the cavern must thus be situated ninety feet above the level of the sea.

"Here is our dwelling," said Cyrus Harding.

"But it was occupied by some creature," replied Gideon Spilett, whose curiosity was not yet satisfied.

"Well, the creature, amphibious or otherwise, has made off through this opening," replied the engineer, "and has left the place for us."

"Never mind," added the sailor, "I should like very much to be Top just for a quarter of an hour, for he doesn't bark for nothing!"

Cyrus Harding looked at his dog, and those of his companions who were near him might have heard him murmur these words,—

"Yes, I believe that Top knows more than we do about a great many things."

However, the wishes of the settlers were for the most part satisfied. Chance, aided by the marvelous sagacity of their leader, had done them great service. They had now at their disposal a vast cavern, the size of which could not be properly calculated by the feeble light of their torches, but it would certainly be easy to divide it into rooms, by means of brick partitions, or to use it, if not as a house, at least as a spacious apartment. The water which had left it could not return. The place was free.

Two difficulties remained; firstly, the possibility of lighting this excavation in the midst of solid rock; secondly, the necessity of rendering the means of access more easy. It was useless to think of lighting it from above, because of the enormous thickness of the granite which composed the ceiling; but perhaps the outer wall next the sea might be pierced. Cyrus Harding, during the descent, had roughly calculated its obliqueness, and consequently the length of the passage, and was therefore led to believe that the outer wall could not be very thick. If light was thus obtained, so would a means of access, for it would be as easy to pierce a door as windows, and to establish an exterior ladder.

Harding made known his ideas to his companions.

"Then, captain, let us set to work!" replied Pencroft. "I have my pickaxe, and I shall soon make my way through this wall. Where shall I strike?"

"Here," replied the engineer, showing the sturdy sailor a considerable recess in the side, which would much diminish the thickness.

Pencroft attacked the granite, and for half an hour, by the light of the torches, he made the splinters fly around him. Neb relieved him, then Spilett took Neb's place.

This work had lasted two hours, and they began to fear that at this spot the wall would not yield to the pickaxe, when at a last blow given by Gideon Spilett, the instrument, passing through the rock, fell outside.

"Hurrah! hurrah!" cried Pencroft.

The wall only measured there three feet in thickness.

Harding applied his eye to the aperture, which overlooked the ground from a height of eighty feet. Before him was extended the sea-coast, the islet, and beyond the open sea.

Floods of light entered by this hole, inundating the splendid cavern and producing a magic effect! On its left side it did not measure more than thirty feet in height and breadth, but on the right it was enormous, and its vaulted roof rose to a height of more than eighty feet.

In some places granite pillars, irregularly disposed, supported the vaulted roof, as those in the nave of a cathedral, here forming lateral piers, there elliptical arches, adorned with pointed moldings, losing themselves in dark bays, amid the fantastic arches of which glimpses could be caught in the shade, covered with a profusion of projections formed like so many pendants. This cavern was a picturesque mixture of all the styles of Byzantine, Roman, or Gothic architecture ever produced by the hand of man. And yet this was only the work of nature. She alone had hollowed this fairy Aihambra in a mass of granite.

The settlers were overwhelmed with admiration. Where they had only expected to find a narrow cavity, they had found a sort of marvelous palace, and Neb had taken off his hat, as if he had been transported into a temple!

Cries of admiration issued from every mouth. Hurrahs resounded, and the echo was repeated again and again till it died away in the dark naves.

"Ah, my friends!" exclaimed Cyrus Harding, "when we have lighted the interior of this place, and have arranged our rooms and storehouses in the left part, we shall still have this splendid cavern, which we will make our study and our museum!"

"And we will call it?—" asked Herbert.

"Granite House," replied Harding; a name which his companions again saluted with a cheer.

The torches were now almost consumed, and as they were obliged to return by the passage to reach the summit of the plateau, it was decided to put off the work necessary for the arrangement of their new dwelling till the next day.

Before departing, Cyrus Harding leaned once more over the dark well, which descended perpendicularly to the level of the sea. He listened attentively. No noise was heard, not even that of the water, which the undulations of the surge must sometimes agitate in its depths. A flaming branch was again thrown in. The sides of the well were lighted up for an instant, but as at the first time, nothing suspicious was seen.

If some marine monster had been surprised unawares by the retreat of the water, he would by this time have regained the sea by the subterranean passage, before the new opening had been offered to him.

Meanwhile, the engineer was standing motionless, his eyes fixed on the gulf, without uttering a word.

The sailor approached him, and touching his arm, "Captain!" said he.

"What do you want, my friend?" asked the engineer, as if he had returned from the land of dreams.

"The torches will soon go out."

"Forward!" replied Cyrus Harding.

The little band left the cavern and began to ascend through the dark passage. Top closed the rear, still growling every now and then. The ascent was painful enough. The settlers rested a few minutes in the upper grotto, which made a sort of landing-place halfway up the long granite staircase. Then they began to climb again.

Soon fresher air was felt. The drops of water, dried by evaporation, no longer sparkled on the walls. The flaring torches began to grow dim. The one which Neb carried went out, and if they did not wish to find their way in the dark, they must hasten.

This was done, and a little before four o'clock, at the moment when the sailor's torch went out in its turn, Cyrus Harding and his companions passed out of the passage.

Chapter 19

The next day, the 22nd of May, the arrangement of their new dwelling was commenced. In fact, the settlers longed to exchange the insufficient shelter of the Chimneys for this large and healthy retreat, in the midst of solid rock, and sheltered from the water both of the sea and sky. Their former dwelling was not, however, to be entirely abandoned, for the engineer intended to make a manufactory of it for important works. Cyrus Harding's first care was to find out the position of the front of Granite House from the outside. He went to the beach, and as the pickaxe when it escaped from the hands of the reporter must have fallen perpendicularly to the foot of the cliff, the finding it would be sufficient to show the place where the hole had been pierced in the granite.

The pickaxe was easily found, and the hole could be seen in a perpendicular line above the spot where it was stuck in the sand. Some rock pigeons were already flying in and out of the narrow opening; they evidently thought that

Granite House had been discovered on purpose for them. It was the engineer's intention to divide the right portion of the cavern into several rooms, preceded by an entrance passage, and to light it by means of five windows and a door, pierced in the front. Pencroft was much pleased with the five windows, but he could not understand the use of the door, since the passage offered a natural staircase, through which it would always be easy to enter Granite House.

"My friend," replied Harding, "if it is easy for us to reach our dwelling by this passage, it will be equally easy for others besides us. I mean, on the contrary, to block up that opening, to seal it hermetically, and, if it is necessary, to completely hide the entrance by making a dam, and thus causing the water of the lake to rise."

"And how shall we get in?" asked the sailor.

"By an outside ladder," replied Cyrus Harding, "a rope ladder, which, once drawn up, will render access to our dwelling impossible."

"But why so many precautions?" asked Pencroft. "As yet we have seen no dangerous animals. As to our island being inhabited by natives, I don't believe it!"

"Are you quite sure of that, Pencroft?" asked the engineer, looking at the sailor.

"Of course we shall not be quite sure, till we have explored it in every direction," replied Pencroft.

"Yes," said Harding, "for we know only a small portion of it as yet. But at any rate, if we have no enemies in the interior, they may come from the exterior, for parts of the Pacific are very dangerous. We must be provided against every contingency."

Cyrus Harding spoke wisely; and without making any further objection, Pencroft prepared to execute his orders.

The front of Granite House was then to be lighted by five windows and a door, besides a large bay window and some smaller oval ones, which would admit plenty of light to enter into the marvelous nave which was to be their chief room. This facade, situated at a height of eighty feet above the ground, was exposed to the east, and the rising sun saluted it with its first rays. It was found to be just at that part of the cliff which was between the projection at the mouth of the Mercy and a perpendicular line traced above the heap of rocks which formed the Chimneys. Thus the winds from the northeast would only strike it obliquely, for it was protected by the projection. Besides, until the window-frames were made, the engineer meant to close the openings with thick shutters, which would prevent either wind or rain from entering, and which could be concealed in need.

The first work was to make the openings. This would have taken too long with the pickaxe alone, and it is known that Harding was an ingenious man. He had still a quantity of nitro-glycerine at his disposal, and he employed it usefully. By means of this explosive substance the rock was broken open at the very places chosen by the engineer. Then, with the pickaxe and spade, the windows and doors were properly shaped, the jagged edges were smoothed off, and a few days alter the beginning of the work, Granite House was abundantly lighted by the rising sun, whose rays penetrated into its most secret recesses. Following the plan proposed by Cyrus Harding, the space was to be divided into five compartments looking out on the sea; to the right, an entry with a door, which would meet the ladder; then a kitchen, thirty feet long; a dining-room, measuring forty feet; a sleeping-room, of equal size; and lastly, a "Visitor's room," petitioned for by Pencroft, and which was next to the great hall. These rooms, or rather this suite of rooms, would not occupy all the depth of the cave. There would be also a corridor and a storehouse, in which their tools, provisions, and stores would be kept. All the productions of the island, the flora as well as the fauna, were to be there in the best possible state of preservation, and completely sheltered from the damp. There was no want of space, so that each object could be methodically arranged. Besides, the colonists had still at their disposal the little grotto above the great cavern, which was like the garret of the new dwelling.

This plan settled, it had only to be put into execution. The miners became brickmakers again, then the bricks were brought to the foot of Granite House. Till then, Harding and his companions had only entered the cavern by the long passage. This mode of communication obliged them first to climb Prospect Heights, making a detour by the river's bank, and then to descend two hundred feet through the passage, having to climb as far when they wished to return to the plateau. This was a great loss of time, and was also very fatiguing. Cyrus Harding, therefore, resolved to proceed without any further delay to the fabrication of a strong rope ladder, which, once raised, would render Granite House completely inaccessible.

This ladder was manufactured with extreme care, and its uprights, formed of the twisted fibers of a species of cane, had the strength of a thick cable. As to the rounds, they were made of a sort of red cedar, with light, strong branches; and this apparatus was wrought by the masterly hand of Pencroft.

Other ropes were made with vegetable fibers, and a sort of crane with a tackle was fixed at the door. In this way bricks could easily be raised into Granite House. The transport of the materials being thus simplified, the arrangement of the interior could begin immediately. There was no want of lime, and some thousands of bricks were there ready to be used. The framework of the partitions was soon raised, very roughly at first, and in a short time, the cave was divided into rooms and storehouses, according to the plan agreed upon.

These different works progressed rapidly under the direction of the engineer, who himself handled the hammer and the trowel. No labor came amiss to Cyrus Harding, who thus set an example to his intelligent and zealous companions. They worked with confidence, even gaily, Pencroft always having some joke to crack, sometimes carpenter, sometimes rope-maker, sometimes mason, while he

communicated his good humor to all the members of their little world. His faith
in the engineer was complete; nothing could disturb it. He believed him capable
of undertaking anything and succeeding in everything. The question of boots and
clothes—assuredly a serious question,—that of light during the winter months,
utilizing the fertile parts of the island, transforming the wild flora into cultivated
flora, it all appeared easy to him; Cyrus Harding helping, everything would be
done in time. He dreamed of canals facilitating the transport of the riches of the
ground; workings of quarries and mines; machines for every industrial
manufacture; railroads; yes, railroads! of which a network would certainly one day
cover Lincoln Island.

The engineer let Pencroft talk. He did not put down the aspirations of this
brave heart. He knew how communicable confidence is; he even smiled to hear
him speak, and said nothing of the uneasiness for the future which he felt. In fact,
in that part of the Pacific, out of the course of vessels, it was to be feared that no
help would ever come to them. It was on themselves, on themselves alone, that
the settlers must depend, for the distance of Lincoln Island from all other land was
such, that to hazard themselves in a boat, of a necessarily inferior construction,
would be a serious and perilous thing.

"But," as the sailor said, "they quite took the wind out of the sails of the
Robinsons, for whom everything was done by a miracle."

In fact, they were energetic; an energetic man will succeed where an indolent
one would vegetate and inevitably perish.

Herbert distinguished himself in these works. He was intelligent and active;
understanding quickly, he performed well; and Cyrus Harding became more and
more attached to the boy. Herbert had a lively and reverent love for the engineer.
Pencroft saw the close sympathy which existed between the two, but he was not
in the least jealous. Neb was Neb: he was what he would be always, courage, zeal,
devotion, self-denial personified. He had the same faith in his master that
Pencroft had, but he showed it less vehemently. When the sailor was enthusiastic,
Neb always looked as if he would say, "Nothing could be more natural." Pencroft
and he were great friends.

As to Gideon Spilett, he took part in the common work, and was not less
skilful in it than his companions, which always rather astonished the sailor. A
"journalist," clever, not only in understanding, but in performing everything.

The ladder was finally fixed on the 28th of May. There were not less than a
hundred rounds in this perpendicular height of eighty feet. Harding had been
able, fortunately, to divide it in two parts, profiting by an overhanging of the cliff
which made a projection forty feet above the ground. This projection, carefully
leveled by the pickaxe, made a sort of platform, to which they fixed the first
ladder, of which the oscillation was thus diminished one-half, and a rope
permitted it to be raised to the level of Granite House. As to the second ladder,

it was secured both at its lower part, which rested on the projection, and at its upper end, which was fastened to the door. In short the ascent had been made much easier. Besides, Cyrus Harding hoped later to establish an hydraulic apparatus, which would avoid all fatigue and loss of time, for the inhabitants of Granite House.

The settlers soon became habituated to the use of this ladder. They were light and active, and Pencroft, as a sailor, accustomed to run up the masts and shrouds, was able to give them lessons. But it was also necessary to give them to Top. The poor dog, with his four paws, was not formed for this sort of exercise. But Pencroft was such a zealous master, that Top ended by properly performing his ascents, and soon mounted the ladder as readily as his brethren in the circus. It need not be said that the sailor was proud of his pupil. However, more than once Pencroft hoisted him on his back, which Top never complained of.

It must be mentioned here, that during these works, which were actively conducted, for the bad season was approaching, the alimentary question was not neglected. Every day, the reporter and Herbert, who had been voted purveyors to the colony, devoted some hours to the chase. As yet, they only hunted in Jacamar Wood, on the left of the river, because, for want of a bridge or boat, the Mercy had not yet been crossed. All the immense woods, to which the name of the Forests of the Far West had been given, were not explored. They reserved this important excursion for the first fine days of the next spring. But Jacamar Wood was full of game; kangaroos and boars abounded, and the hunters iron-tipped spears and bows and arrows did wonders. Besides, Herbert discovered towards the southwest point of the lagoon a natural warren, a slightly damp meadow, covered with willows and aromatic herbs which scented the air, such as thyme, basil, savory, all the sweet-scented species of the labiated plants, which the rabbits appeared to be particularly fond of.

On the reporter observing that since the table was spread for the rabbits, it was strange that the rabbits themselves should be wanting, the two sportsmen carefully explored the warren. At any rate, it produced an abundance of useful plants, and a naturalist would have had a good opportunity of studying many specimens of the vegetable kingdom. Herbert gathered several shoots of the basil, rosemary, balm, betony, etc., which possess different medicinal properties, some pectoral, astringent, febrifuge, others anti-spasmodic, or anti-rheumatic. When, afterwards, Pencroft asked the use of this collection of herbs,—

"For medicine," replied the lad, "to treat us when we are ill."

"Why should we be ill, since there are no doctors in the island?" asked Pencroft quite seriously.

There was no reply to be made to that, but the lad went on with his collection all the same, and it was well received at Granite House. Besides these medicinal herbs, he added a plant known in North America as "Oswego tea," which made an excellent beverage.

At last, by searching thoroughly, the hunters arrived at the real site of the warren. There the ground was perforated like a sieve.

"Here are the burrows!" cried Herbert.

"Yes," replied the reporter, "so I see."

"But are they inhabited?"

"That is the question."

This was soon answered. Almost immediately, hundreds of little animals, similar to rabbits, fled in every direction, with such rapidity that even Top could not overtake them. Hunters and dog ran in vain; these rodents escaped them easily. But the reporter resolved not to leave the place, until he had captured at least half-a-dozen of the quadrupeds. He wished to stock their larder first, and domesticate those which they might take later. It would not have been difficult to do this, with a few snares stretched at the openings of the burrows. But at this moment they had neither snares, nor anything to make them of. They must, therefore, be satisfied with visiting each hole, and rummaging in it with a stick, hoping by dint of patience to do what could not be done in any other way.

At last, after half an hour, four rodents were taken in their holes. They were similar to their European brethren, and are commonly known by the name of American rabbits.

This produce of the chase was brought back to Granite House, and figured at the evening repast. The tenants of the warren were not at all to be despised, for they were delicious. It was a valuable resource of the colony, and it appeared to be inexhaustible.

On the 31st of May the partitions were finished. The rooms had now only to be furnished, and this would be work for the long winter days. A chimney was established in the first room, which served as a kitchen. The pipe destined to conduct the smoke outside gave some trouble to these amateur bricklayers. It appeared simplest to Harding to make it of brick clay; as creating an outlet for it to the upper plateau was not to be thought of, a hole was pierced in the granite above the window of the kitchen, and the pipe met it like that of an iron stove. Perhaps the winds which blew directly against the facade would make the chimney smoke, but these winds were rare, and besides, Master Neb, the cook, was not so very particular about that.

When these interior arrangements were finished, the engineer occupied himself in blocking up the outlet by the lake, so as to prevent any access by that way. Masses of rock were rolled to the entrance and strongly cemented together. Cyrus Harding did not yet realize his plan of drowning this opening under the waters of the lake, by restoring them to their former level by means of a dam. He contented himself with hiding the obstruction with grass and shrubs, which were planted in the interstices of the rocks, and which next spring would sprout thickly. However, he used the waterfall so as to lead a small stream of fresh water to the new dwelling. A little trench, made below their level, produced this result; and this derivation from a pure and inexhaustible source yielded twenty-five or thirty gallons a day. There would never be any want of water at Granite House. At last all was finished, and it was time, for the bad season was near. Thick shutters closed the windows of the facade, until the engineer had time to make glass.

Gideon Spilett had very artistically arranged on the rocky projections around the windows plants of different kinds, as well as long streaming grass, so that the openings were picturesquely framed in green, which had a pleasing effect.

The inhabitants of this solid, healthy, and secure dwelling, could not but be charmed with their work. The view from the windows extended over a boundless horizon, which was closed by the two Mandible Capes on the north, and Claw Cape on the south. All Union Bay was spread before them. Yes, our brave settlers had reason to be satisfied, and Pencroft was lavish in his praise of what he humorously called, "his apartments on the fifth floor above the ground!"

Chapter 20

The winter season set in with the month of June, which corresponds with the month of December in the Northern Hemisphere. It began with showers and squalls, which succeeded each other without intermission. The tenants of Granite House could appreciate the advantages of a dwelling which sheltered them from the inclement weather. The Chimneys would have been quite insufficient to protect them against the rigor of winter, and it was to be feared that the high tides would make another irruption. Cyrus Harding had taken precautions against this contingency, so as to preserve as much as possible the forge and furnace which were established there.

During the whole of the month of June the time was employed in different occupations, which excluded neither hunting nor fishing, the larder being, therefore, abundantly supplied. Pencroft, so soon as he had leisure, proposed to set some traps, from which he expected great results. He soon made some snares with creepers, by the aid of which the warren henceforth every day furnished its quota of rodents. Neb employed nearly all his time in salting or smoking meat, which insured their always having plenty of provisions. The question of clothes was now seriously discussed, the settlers having no other garments than those they wore when the balloon threw them on the island. These clothes were warm and good; they had taken great care of them as well as of their linen, and they were perfectly whole, but they would soon need to be replaced. Moreover, if the winter was severe, the settlers would suffer greatly from cold.

On this subject the ingenuity of Harding was at fault. They must provide for their most pressing wants, settle their dwelling, and lay in a store of food; thus the cold might come upon them before the question of clothes had been settled. They must therefore make up their minds to pass this first winter without additional clothing. When the fine season came round again, they would regularly hunt those musmons which had been seen on the expedition to Mount Franklin, and the wool once collected, the engineer would know how to make it into strong warm stuff.... How? He would consider.

"Well, we are free to roast ourselves at Granite House!" said Pencroft. "There are heaps of fuel, and no reason for sparing it."

"Besides," added Gideon Spilett, "Lincoln Island is not situated under a very high latitude, and probably the winters here are not severe. Did you not say, Cyrus, that this thirty-fifth parallel corresponded to that of Spain in the other hemisphere?"

"Doubtless," replied the engineer, "but some winters in Spain are very cold! No want of snow and ice; and perhaps Lincoln Island is just as rigourously tried. However, it is an island, and as such, I hope that the temperature will be more moderate."

"Why, captain?" asked Herbert.

"Because the sea, my boy, may be considered as an immense reservoir, in which is stored the heat of the summer. When winter comes, it restores this heat, which insures for the regions near the ocean a medium temperature, less high in summer, but less low in winter."

"We shall prove that," replied Pencroft. "But I don't want to bother myself about whether it will be cold or not. One thing is certain, that is that the days are already short, and the evenings long. Suppose we talk about the question of light."

"Nothing is easier," replied Harding.

"To talk about?" asked the sailor.

"To settle."

"And when shall we begin?"

"To-morrow, by having a seal hunt."

"To make candles?"

"Yes."

Such was the engineer's project; and it was quite feasible, since he had lime and sulphuric acid, while the amphibians of the islet would furnish the fat necessary for the manufacture.

They were now at the 4th of June. It was Whit Sunday and they agreed to observe this feast. All work was suspended, and prayers were offered to Heaven. But these prayers were now thanksgivings. The settlers in Lincoln Island were no longer the miserable castaways thrown on the islet. They asked for nothing more—they gave thanks. The next day, the 5th of June, in rather uncertain weather, they set out for the islet. They had to profit by the low tide to cross the Channel, and it was agreed that they would construct, for this purpose, as well as they could, a boat which would render communication so much easier, and would also permit them to ascend the Mercy, at the time of their grand exploration of the southwest of the island, which was put off till the first fine days.

The seals were numerous, and the hunters, armed with their iron-tipped spears, easily killed half-a-dozen. Neb and Pencroft skinned them, and only brought back to Granite House their fat and skin, this skin being intended for the manufacture of boots.

The result of the hunt was this: nearly three hundred pounds of fat, all to be employed in the fabrication of candles.

The operation was extremely simple, and if it did not yield absolutely perfect results, they were at least very useful. Cyrus Harding would only have had at his disposal sulphuric acid, but by heating this acid with the neutral fatty bodies he could separate the glycerine; then from this new combination, he easily separated the olein, the margarin, and the stearin, by employing boiling water. But to simplify the operation, he preferred to saponify the fat by means of lime. By this he obtained a calcareous soap, easy to decompose by sulphuric acid, which precipitated the lime into the state of sulphate, and liberated the fatty acids.

From these three acids-oleic, margaric, and stearic-the first, being liquid, was driven out by a sufficient pressure. As to the two others, they formed the very substance of which the candles were to be molded.

This operation did not last more than four and twenty hours. The wicks, after several trials, were made of vegetable fibers, and dipped in the liquefied substance, they formed regular stearic candles, molded by the hand, which only wanted whiteness and polish. They would not doubtless have the advantages of the wicks which are impregnated with boracic acid, and which vitrify as they burn and are entirely consumed, but Cyrus Harding having manufactured a beautiful pair of snuffers, these candles would be greatly appreciated during the long evenings in Granite House.

During this month there was no want of work in the interior of their new dwelling. The joiners had plenty to do. They improved their tools, which were very rough, and added others also.

Scissors were made among other things, and the settlers were at last able to cut their hair, and also to shave, or at least trim their beards. Herbert had none, Neb but little, but their companions were bristling in a way which justified the making of the said scissors.

The manufacture of a hand-saw cost infinite trouble, but at last an instrument was obtained which, when vigorously handled, could divide the ligneous fibers of the wood. They then made tables, seats, cupboards, to furnish the principal rooms, and bedsteads, of which all the bedding consisted of grass mattresses. The kitchen, with its shelves, on which rested the cooking utensils, its brick stove, looked very well, and Neb worked away there as earnestly as if he was in a chemist's laboratory.

But the joiners had soon to be replaced by carpenters. In fact, the waterfall created by the explosion rendered the construction of two bridges necessary, one on Prospect Heights, the other on the shore. Now the plateau and the shore were transversely divided by a watercourse, which had to be crossed to reach the northern part of the island. To avoid it the colonists had been obliged to make a considerable detour, by climbing up to the source of the Red Creek. The simplest thing was to establish on the plateau, and on the shore, two bridges from twenty to five and twenty feet in length. All the carpenter's work that was needed was to clear some trees of their branches: this was a business of some days. Directly the bridges were established, Neb and Pencroft profited by them to go to the oyster-bed which had been discovered near the downs. They dragged with them a sort of rough cart, which replaced the former inconvenient hurdle, and brought back some thousands of oysters, which soon increased among the rocks and formed a bed at the mouth of the Mercy. These molluscs were of excellent quality, and the colonists consumed some daily.

It has been seen that Lincoln Island, although its inhabitants had as yet only explored a small portion of it, already contributed to almost all their wants. It was probable that if they hunted into its most secret recesses, in all the wooded part between the Mercy and Reptile Point, they would find new treasures.

The settlers in Lincoln Island had still one privation. There was no want of meat, nor of vegetable products; those ligneous roots which they had found, when subjected to fermentation, gave them an acid drink, which was preferable to cold water; they also made sugar, without canes or beet-roots, by collecting the liquor which distils from the "acer saceharinum," a son of maple-tree, which flourishes in all the temperate zones, and of which the island possessed a great number; they made a very agreeable tea by employing the herbs brought from the warren; lastly, they had an abundance of salt, the only mineral which is used in food... but bread was wanting.

Perhaps in time the settlers could replace this want by some equivalent, it was possible that they might find the sago or the breadfruit tree among the forests of the south, but they had not as yet met with these precious trees. However, Providence came directly to their aid, in an infinitesimal proportion it is true, but Cyrus Harding, with all his intelligence, all his ingenuity, would never have been able to produce that which, by the greatest chance, Herbert one day found in the lining of his waistcoat, which he was occupied in setting to rights.

On this day, as it was raining in torrents, the settlers were assembled in the great hall in Granite House, when the lad cried out all at once,—

"Look here, captain—A grain of corn!"

And he showed his companions a grain—a single grain—which from a hole in his pocket had got into the lining of his waistcoat.

The presence of this grain was explained by the fact that Herbert, when at Richmond, used to feed some pigeons, of which Pencroft had made him a present.

"A grain of corn?" said the engineer quickly.

"Yes, captain; but one, only one!"

"Well, my boy," said Pencroft, laughing, "we're getting on capitally, upon my word! What shall we make with one grain of corn?"

"We will make bread of it," replied Cyrus Harding.

"Bread, cakes, tarts!" replied the sailor. "Come, the bread that this grain of corn will make won't choke us very soon!"

Herbert, not attaching much importance to his discovery, was going to throw away the grain in question; but Harding took it, examined it, found that it was in good condition, and looking the sailor full in the face—"Pencroft," he asked quietly, "do you know how many ears one grain of corn can produce?"

"One, I suppose!" replied the sailor, surprised at the question.

"Ten, Pencroft! And do you know how many grains one ear bears?"

"No, upon my word."

"About eighty!" said Cyrus Harding. "Then, if we plant this grain, at the first crop we shall reap eight hundred grains which at the second will produce six hundred and forty thousand; at the third, five hundred and twelve millions; at the fourth, more than four hundred thousands of millions! There is the proportion."

Harding's companions listened without answering. These numbers astonished them. They were exact, however.

"Yes, my friends," continued the engineer, "such are the arithmetical progressions of prolific nature; and yet what is this multiplication of the grain of corn, of which the ear only bears eight hundred grains, compared to the poppy-plant, which bears thirty-two thousand seeds; to the tobacco-plant, which produces three hundred and sixty thousand? In a few years, without the numerous causes of destruction, which arrests their fecundity, these plants would overrun the earth."

But the engineer had not finished his lecture.

"And now, Pencroft," he continued, "do you know how many bushels four hundred thousand millions of grains would make?"

"No," replied the sailor; "but what I do know is, that I am nothing better than a fool!"

"Well, they would make more than three millions, at a hundred and thirty thousand a bushel, Pencroft."

"Three millions!" cried Pencroft.

"Three millions."

"In four years?"

"In four years," replied Cyrus Harding, "and even in two years, if, as I hope, in this latitude we can obtain two crops a year."

At that, according to his usual custom, Pencroft could not reply otherwise than by a tremendous hurrah.

"So, Herbert," added the engineer, "you have made a discovery of great importance to us. Everything, my friends, everything can serve us in the condition in which we are. Do not forget that, I beg of you."

"No, captain, no, we shan't forget it," replied Pencroft; "and if ever I find one of those tobacco-seeds, which multiply by three hundred and sixty thousand, I assure you I won't throw it away! And now, what must we do?"

"We must plant this grain," replied Herbert.

"Yes," added Gideon Spilett, "and with every possible care, for it bears in itself our future harvests."

"Provided it grows!" cried the sailor.

"It will grow," replied Cyrus Harding.

This was the 20th of June. The time was then propitious for sowing this single precious grain of corn. It was first proposed to plant it in a pot, but upon reflection it was decided to leave it to nature, and confide it to the earth. This was done that very day, and it is needless to add, that every precaution was taken that the experiment might succeed.

The weather having cleared, the settlers climbed the height above Granite House. There, on the plateau, they chose a spot, well sheltered from the wind, and exposed to all the heat of the midday sun. The place was cleared, carefully weeded, and searched for insects and worms; then a bed of good earth, improved with a little lime, was made; it was surrounded by a railing; and the grain was buried in the damp earth.

Did it not seem as if the settlers were laying the first stone of some edifice? It recalled to Pencroft the day on which he lighted his only match, and all the anxiety of the operation. But this time the thing was more serious. In fact, the castaways would have been always able to procure fire, in some mode or other, but no human power could supply another grain of corn, if unfortunately this should be lost!

Chapter 21

From this time Pencroft did not let a single day pass without going to visit what he gravely called his "corn-field." And woe to the insects which dared to venture there! No mercy was shown them.

Towards the end of the month of June, after incessant rain, the weather became decidedly colder, and on the 29th a Fahrenheit thermometer would certainly have announced only twenty degrees above zero, that is considerably below the freezing-point. The next day, the 30th of June, the day which corresponds to the 31st of December in the northern year, was a Friday. Neb remarked that the year finished on a bad day, but Pencroft replied that naturally the next would begin on a good one, which was better.

At any rate it commenced by very severe cold. Ice accumulated at the mouth of the Mercy, and it was not long before the whole expanse of the lake was frozen. The settlers had frequently been obliged to renew their store of wood. Pencroft also had wisely not waited till the river was frozen, but had brought enormous rafts of wood to their destination. The current was an indefatigable moving power, and it was employed in conveying the floating wood to the moment when the frost enchained it. To the fuel which was so abundantly supplied by the forest, they added several cartloads of coal, which had to be brought from the foot of the spurs of Mount Franklin. The powerful heat of the coal was greatly appreciated in the low temperature, which on the 4th of July fell to eight degrees of Fahrenheit, that is, thirteen degrees below zero. A second fireplace had been established in the dining-room, where they all worked together at their different avocations. During this period of cold, Cyrus Harding had great cause to congratulate himself on having brought to Granite House the little stream of water from Lake Grant. Taken below the frozen surface, and conducted through the passage, it preserved its fluidity, and arrived at an interior reservoir which had been hollowed out at the back part of the storeroom, while the overflow ran through the well to the sea.

About this time, the weather being extremely dry, the colonists, clothed as warmly as possible, resolved to devote a day to the exploration of that part of the island between the Mercy and Claw Cape. It was a wide extent of marshy land, and they would probably find good sport, for water-birds ought to swarm there.

They reckoned that it would be about eight or nine miles to go there, and as much to return, so that the whole of the day would be occupied. As an unknown part of the island was about to be explored, the whole colony took part in the expedition. Accordingly, on the 5th of July, at six o'clock in the morning, when day had scarcely broken, Cyrus Harding, Gideon Spilett, Herbert, Neb, and Pencroft, armed with spears, snares, bows and arrows, and provided with provisions, left Granite House, preceded by Top, who bounded before them.

Their shortest way was to cross the Mercy on the ice, which then covered it.

"But," as the engineer justly observed, "that could not take the place of a regular bridge!" So, the construction of a regular bridge was noted in the list of future works.

It was the first time that the settlers had set foot on the right bank of the Mercy, and ventured into the midst of those gigantic and superb coniferae now sprinkled over with snow.

But they had not gone half a mile when from a thicket a whole family of quadrupeds, who had made a home there, disturbed by Top, rushed forth into the open country.

"Ah! I should say those are foxes!" cried Herbert, when he saw the troop rapidly decamping.

They were foxes, but of a very large size, who uttered a sort of barking, at which Top seemed to be very much astonished, for he stopped short in the chase, and gave the swift animals time to disappear.

The dog had reason to be surprised, as he did not know Natural History. But, by their barking, these foxes, with reddish-gray hair, black tails terminating in a white tuft, had betrayed their origin. So Herbert was able, without hesitating, to give them their real name of "Arctic foxes." They are frequently met with in Chile, in the Falkland Islands, and in all parts of America traversed by the thirtieth and fortieth parallels. Herbert much regretted that Top had not been able to catch one of these carnivora.

"Are they good to eat?" asked Pencroft, who only regarded the representatives of the fauna in the island from one special point of view.

"No," replied Herbert; "but zoologists have not yet found out if the eye of these foxes is diurnal or nocturnal, or whether it is correct to class them in the genus dog, properly so called."

Harding could not help smiling on hearing the lad's reflection, which showed a thoughtful mind. As to the sailor, from the moment when he found that the foxes were not classed in the genus eatable, they were nothing to him. However, when a poultry-yard was established at Granite House, he observed that it would be best to take some precautions against a probable visit from these four-legged plunderers, and no one disputed this.

After having turned the point, the settlers saw a long beach washed by the open sea. It was then eight o'clock in the morning. The sky was very clear, as it often is after prolonged cold; but warmed by their walk, neither Harding nor his companions felt the sharpness of the atmosphere too severely. Besides there was no wind, which made it much more bearable. A brilliant sun, but without any calorific action, was just issuing from the ocean. The sea was as tranquil and blue as that of a Mediterranean gulf, when the sky is clear. Claw Cape, bent in the form of a yataghan, tapered away nearly four miles to the southeast. To the left the edge of the marsh was abruptly ended by a little point. Certainly, in this part of Union Bay, which nothing sheltered from the open sea, not even a sandbank, ships beaten by the east winds would have found no shelter. They perceived by the tranquillity of the sea, in which no shallows troubled the waters, by its uniform color, which was stained by no yellow shades, by the absence of even a reef, that the coast was steep and that the ocean there covered a deep abyss. Behind in the west, but at a distance of four miles, rose the first trees of the forests of the Far

West. They might have believed themselves to be on the desolate coast of some island in the Antarctic regions which the ice had invaded. The colonists halted at this place for breakfast. A fire of brushwood and dried seaweed was lighted, and Neb prepared the breakfast of cold meat, to which he added some cups of Oswego tea.

While eating they looked around them. This part of Lincoln Island was very sterile, and contrasted with all the western part. The reporter was thus led to observe that if chance had thrown them at first on the shore, they would have had but a deplorable idea of their future domain.

"I believe that we should not have been able to reach it," replied the engineer, "for the sea is deep, and there is not a rock on which we could have taken refuge. Before Granite House, at least, there were sandbanks, an islet, which multiplied our chances of safety. Here, nothing but the depths!"

"It is singular enough," remarked Spilett, "that this comparatively small island should present such varied ground. This diversity of aspect, logically only belongs to continents of a certain extent. One would really say, that the western part of Lincoln Island, so rich and so fertile, is washed by the warm waters of the Gulf of Mexico, and that its shores to the north and the southeast extend over a sort of Arctic sea."

"You are right, my dear Spilett," replied Cyrus Harding, "I have also observed this. I think the form and also the nature of this island strange. It is a summary of all the aspects which a continent presents, and I should not be surprised if it was a continent formerly."

"What! a continent in the middle of the Pacific?" cried Pencroft.

"Why not?" replied Cyrus Harding. "Why should not Australia, New Ireland, Australasia, united to the archipelagoes of the Pacific, have once formed a sixth part of the world, as important as Europe or Asia, as Africa or the two Americas? To my mind, it is quite possible that all these islands, emerging from this vast ocean, are but the summits of a continent, now submerged, but which was above the waters at a prehistoric period."

"As the Atlantis was formerly," replied Herbert.

"Yes, my boy... if, however, it existed."

"And would Lincoln Island have been a part of that continent?" asked Pencroft.

"It is probable," replied Cyrus Harding, "and that would sufficiently, explain the variety of productions which are seen on its surface."

"And the great number of animals which still inhabit it," added Herbert.

"Yes, my boy," replied the engineer, "and you furnish me with an argument to support my theory. It is certain, after what we have seen, that animals are numerous in this island, and what is more strange, that the species are extremely varied. There is a reason for that, and to me it is that Lincoln Island may have formerly been a part of some vast continent which had gradually sunk below the Pacific."

"Then, some fine day," said Pencroft, who did not appear to be entirely convinced, "the rest of this ancient continent may disappear in its turn, and there will be nothing between America and Asia."

"Yes," replied Harding, "there will be new continents which millions and millions of animalculae are building at this moment."

"And what are these masons?" asked Pencroft.

"Coral insects," replied Cyrus Harding. "By constant work they made the island of Clermont-Tonnerre, and numerous other coral islands in the Pacific Ocean. Forty-seven millions of these insects are needed to weigh a grain, and yet, with the sea-salt they absorb, the solid elements of water which they assimilate, these animalculae produce limestone, and this limestone forms enormous submarine erections, of which the hardness and solidity equal granite. Formerly, at the first periods of creation, nature employing fire, heaved up the land, but now she entrusts to these microscopic creatures the task of replacing this agent, of which the dynamic power in the interior of the globe has evidently diminished—which is proved by the number of volcanoes on the surface of the earth, now actually extinct. And I believe that centuries succeeding to centuries, and insects to insects, this Pacific may one day be changed into a vast continent, which new generations will inhabit and civilize in their turn."

"That will take a long time," said Pencroft.

"Nature has time for it," replied the engineer.

"But what would be the use of new continents?" asked Herbert. "It appears to me that the present extent of habitable countries is sufficient for humanity. Yet nature does nothing uselessly."

"Nothing uselessly, certainly," replied the engineer, "but this is how the necessity of new continents for the future, and exactly on the tropical zone occupied by the coral islands, may be explained. At least to me this explanation appears plausible."

"We are listening, captain," said Herbert.

"This is my idea: philosophers generally admit that some day our globe will end, or rather that animal and vegetable life will no longer be possible, because of the intense cold to which it will be subjected. What they are not agreed upon, is the cause of this cold. Some think that it will arise from the falling of the temperature, which the sun will experience after millions of years; others, from the gradual extinction of the fires in the interior of our globe, which have a greater influence on it than is generally supposed. I hold to this last hypothesis, grounding it on the fact that the moon is really a cold star, which is no longer habitable, although the sun continues to throw on its surface the same amount of heat. If, then, the moon has become cold, it is because the interior fires to which, as do all the stars of the stellar world, it owes its origin, are completely extinct. Lastly, whatever may be the cause, our globe will become cold some day, but this cold will only operate gradually. What will happen, then? The temperate zones, at a more or less distant period, will not be more habitable than the polar regions now are. Then the population of men, as well as the animals, will flow towards the latitudes which are more directly under the solar influence. An immense emigration will take place. Europe, Central Asia, North America, will gradually be abandoned, as well as Australasia and the lower parts of South America. The vegetation will follow the human emigration. The flora will retreat towards the Equator at the same time as the fauna. The central parts of South America and Africa will be the continents chiefly inhabited. The Laplanders and the Samoides will find the climate of the polar regions on the shores of the Mediterranean. Who can say, that at this period, the equatorial regions will not be too small, to contain and nourish terrestrial humanity? Now, may not provident nature, so as to give refuge to all the vegetable and animal emigration, be at present laying the foundation of a new continent under the Equator, and may she not have entrusted these insects with the construction of it? I have often thought of all these things, my friends, and I seriously believe that the aspect of our globe will some day be completely changed; that by the raising of new continents the sea will cover the old, and that, in future ages, a Columbus will go to discover the islands of Chimborazo, of the Himalayas, or of Mont Blanc, remains of a submerged America, Asia, and Europe. Then these new continents will become, in their turn, uninhabitable; heat will die away, as does the heat from a body when the soul has left it; and life will disappear from the globe, if not for ever, at least for a period. Perhaps then, our spheroid will rest—will be left to death—to revive some day under superior conditions! But all that, my friends, is the secret of the Author of all things; and beginning by the work of the insects, I have perhaps let myself be carried too far, in investigating the secrets of the future.

"My dear Cyrus," replied Spilett, "these theories are prophecies to me, and they will be accomplished some day."

"That is the secret of God," said the engineer.

"All that is well and good," then said Pencroft, who had listened with all his might, "but will you tell me, captain, if Lincoln Island has been made by your insects?"

"No," replied Harding; "it is of a purely volcanic origin."

"Then it will disappear some day?"

"That is probable."

"I hope we won't be here then."

"No, don't be uneasy, Pencroft; we shall not be here then, as we have no wish to die here, and hope to get away some time."

"In the meantime," replied Gideon Spilett, "let us establish ourselves here as if forever. There is no use in doing things by halves."

This ended the conversation. Breakfast was finished, the exploration was continued, and the settlers arrived at the border of the marshy region. It was a marsh of which the extent, to the rounded coast which terminated the island at the southeast, was about twenty square miles. The soil was formed of clayey flint-earth, mingled with vegetable matter, such as the remains of rushes, reeds, grass, etc. Here and there beds of grass, thick as a carpet, covered it. In many places icy pools sparkled in the sun. Neither rain nor any river, increased by a sudden swelling, could supply these ponds. They therefore naturally concluded that the marsh was fed by the infiltrations of the soil and it was really so. It was also to be feared that during the heat miasmas would arise, which might produce fevers.

Above the aquatic plants, on the surface of the stagnant water, fluttered numbers of birds. Wild duck, teal, snipe lived there in flocks, and those fearless birds allowed themselves to be easily approached.

One shot from a gun would certainly have brought down some dozen of the birds, they were so close together. The explorers were, however, obliged to content themselves with bows and arrows. The result was less, but the silent arrow had the advantage of not frightening the birds, while the noise of firearms would have dispersed them to all parts of the marsh. The hunters were satisfied, for this time, with a dozen ducks, which had white bodies with a band of cinnamon, a green head, wings black, white, and red, and flattened beak. Herbert called them tadorns. Top helped in the capture of these birds, whose name was given to this marshy part of the island. The settlers had here an abundant reserve of aquatic game. At some future time they meant to explore it more carefully, and it was probable that some of the birds there might be domesticated, or at least brought to the shores of the lake, so that they would be more within their reach.

About five o'clock in the evening Cyrus Harding and his companions retraced their steps to their dwelling by traversing Tadorn's Fens, and crossed the Mercy on the ice-bridge.

At eight in the evening they all entered Granite House.

Chapter 22

This intense cold lasted till the 15th of August, without, however, passing the degree of Fahrenheit already mentioned. When the atmosphere was calm, the low temperature was easily borne, but when the wind blew, the poor settlers, insufficiently clothed, felt it severely. Pencroft regretted that Lincoln Island was not the home of a few families of bears rather than of so many foxes and seals.

"Bears," said he, "are generally very well dressed, and I ask no more than to borrow for the winter the warm cloaks which they have on their backs."

"But," replied Neb, laughing, "perhaps the bears would not consent to give you their cloaks, Pencroft. These beasts are not St. Martins."

"We would make them do it, Neb, we would make them," replied Pencroft, in quite an authoritative tone.

But these formidable carnivora did not exist in the island, or at any rate they had not yet shown themselves.

In the meanwhile, Herbert, Pencroft, and the reporter occupied themselves with making traps on Prospect Heights and at the border of the forest.

According to the sailor, any animal, whatever it was, would be a lawful prize, and the rodents or carnivora which might get into the new snares would be well received at Granite House.

The traps were besides extremely simple; being pits dug in the ground, a platform of branches and grass above, which concealed the opening, and at the bottom some bait, the scent of which would attract animals. It must be mentioned also, that they had not been dug at random, but at certain places where numerous footprints showed that quadrupeds frequented the ground. They were visited every day, and at three different times, during the first days, specimens of those Antarctic foxes which they had already seen on the right bank of the Mercy were found in them.

"Why, there are nothing but foxes in this country!" cried Pencroft, when for the third time he drew one of the animals out of the pit. Looking at it in great disgust, he added, "beasts which are good for nothing!"

"Yes," said Gideon Spilett, "they are good for something!"

"And what is that?"

"To make bait to attract other creatures!"

The reporter was right, and the traps were henceforward baited with the foxes carcasses.

The sailor had also made snares from the long tough fibers of a certain plant, and they were even more successful than the traps. Rarely a day passed without some rabbits from the warren being caught. It was always rabbit, but Neb knew how to vary his sauces and the settlers did not think of complaining.

However, once or twice in the second week of August, the traps supplied the hunters with other animals more useful than foxes, namely, several of those small wild boars which had already been seen to the north of the lake. Pencroft had no need to ask if these beasts were eatable. He could see that by their resemblance to the pig of America and Europe.

"But these are not pigs," said Herbert to him, "I warn you of that, Pencroft."

"My boy," replied the sailor, bending over the trap and drawing out one of these representatives of the family of sus by the little appendage which served it as a tail. "Let me believe that these are pigs."

"Why?"

"Because that pleases me!"

"Are you very fond of pig then, Pencroft?"

"I am very fond of pig," replied the sailor, "particularly of its feet, and if it had eight instead of four, I should like it twice as much!"

As to the animals in question, they were peccaries belonging to one of the four species which are included in the family, and they were also of the species of Tajacu, recognizable by their deep color and the absence of those long teeth with which the mouths of their congeners are armed. These peccaries generally live in herds, and it was probable that they abounded in the woody parts of the island.

At any rate, they were eatable from head to foot, and Pencroft did not ask more from them.

Towards the 15th of August, the state of the atmosphere was suddenly moderated by the wind shifting to the northwest. The temperature rose some degrees, and the accumulated vapor in the air was not long in resolving into snow. All the island was covered with a sheet of white, and showed itself to its inhabitants under a new aspect. The snow fell abundantly for several days, and it soon reached a thickness of two feet.

The wind also blew with great violence, and at the height of Granite House the sea could be heard thundering against the reefs. In some places, the wind, eddying round the corners, formed the snow into tall whirling columns, resembling those waterspouts which turn round on their base, and which vessels attack with a shot from a gun. However, the storm, coming from the northwest, blew across the island, and the position of Granite House preserved it from a direct attack.

But in the midst of this snow-storm, as terrible as if it had been produced in some polar country, neither Cyrus Harding nor his companions could, notwithstanding their wish for it, venture forth, and they remained shut up for five days, from the 20th to the 25th of August. They could hear the tempest raging in Jacamar Wood, which would surely suffer from it. Many of the trees would no doubt be torn up by the roots, but Pencroft consoled himself by thinking that he would not have the trouble of cutting them down.

"The wind is turning woodman, let it alone," he repeated.

Besides, there was no way of stopping it, if they had wished to do so.

How grateful the inhabitants of Granite House then were to Heaven for having prepared for them this solid and immovable retreat! Cyrus Harding had also his legitimate share of thanks, but after all, it was Nature who had hollowed out this vast cavern, and he had only discovered it. There all were in safety, and the tempest could not reach them. If they had constructed a house of bricks and wood on Prospect Heights, it certainly would not have resisted the fury of this storm. As to the Chimneys, it must have been absolutely uninhabitable, for the sea, passing over the islet, would beat furiously against it. But here, in Granite House, in the middle of a solid mass, over which neither the sea nor air had any influence, there was nothing to fear.

During these days of seclusion the settlers did not remain inactive.

There was no want of wood, cut up into planks, in the storeroom, and little by little they completed their furnishing; constructing the most solid of tables and chairs, for material was not spared. Neb and Pencroft were very proud of this rather heavy furniture, which they would not have changed on any account.

Then the carpenters became basket-makers, and they did not succeed badly in this new manufacture. At the point of the lake which projected to the north, they had discovered an osier-bed in which grew a large number of purple osiers. Before the rainy season, Pencroft and Herbert had cut down these useful shrubs, and their branches, well prepared, could now be effectively employed. The first attempts were somewhat crude, but in consequence of the cleverness and intelligence of the workmen, by consulting, and recalling the models which they had seen, and by emulating each other, the possessions of the colony were soon increased by several baskets of different sizes. The storeroom was provided with them, and in special baskets Neb placed his collection of rhizomes, stone-pine almonds, etc.

During the last week of the month of August the weather moderated again. The temperature fell a little, and the tempest abated. The colonists sallied out directly. There was certainly two feet of snow on the shore, but they were able to walk without much difficulty on the hardened surface. Cyrus Harding and his companions climbed Prospect Heights.

What a change! The woods, which they had left green, especially in the part at which the firs predominated, had disappeared under a uniform color. All was white, from the summit of Mount Franklin to the shore, the forests, the plains, the lake, the river. The waters of the Mercy flowed under a roof of ice, which, at each rising and ebbing of the tide, broke up with loud crashes. Numerous birds fluttered over the frozen surface of the lake. Ducks and snipe, teal and guillemots were assembled in thousands. The rocks among which the cascade flowed were bristling with icicles. One might have said that the water escaped by a monstrous gargoyle, shaped with all the imagination of an artist of the Renaissance. As to the damage caused by the storm in the forest, that could not as yet be ascertained; they would have to wait till the snowy covering was dissipated.

Gideon Spilett, Pencroft, and Herbert did not miss this opportunity of going to visit their traps. They did not find them easily, under the snow with which they were covered. They had also to be careful not to fall into one or other of them, which would have been both dangerous and humiliating; to be taken in their own snares! But happily they avoided this unpleasantness, and found their traps perfectly intact. No animal had fallen into them, and yet the footprints in the neighborhood were very numerous, among others, certain very clear marks of claws. Herbert did not hesitate to affirm that some animal of the feline species had passed there, which justified the engineer's opinion that dangerous beasts existed in Lincoln Island. These animals doubtless generally lived in the forests of the Far West, but pressed by hunger, they had ventured as far as Prospect Heights. Perhaps they had smelled out the inhabitants of Granite House. "Now, what are these feline creatures?" asked Pencroft. "They are tigers," replied Herbert. "I thought those beasts were only found in hot countries?"

"On the new continent," replied the lad, "they are found from Mexico to the Pampas of Buenos Aires. Now, as Lincoln Island is nearly under the same latitude as the provinces of La Plata, it is not surprising that tigers are to be met with in it."

"Well, we must look out for them," replied Pencroft.

However, the snow soon disappeared, quickly dissolving under the influence of the rising temperature. Rain fell, and the sheet of white soon vanished. Notwithstanding the bad weather, the settlers renewed their stores of different things, stone-pine almonds, rhizomes, syrup from the maple-tree, for the vegetable part; rabbits from the warren, agouties, and kangaroos for the animal part. This necessitated several excursions into the forest, and they found that a great number of trees had been blown down by the last hurricane. Pencroft and Neb also pushed with the cart as far as the vein of coal, and brought back several tons of fuel. They saw in passing that the pottery kiln had been severely damaged by the wind, at least six feet of it having been blown off.

At the same time as the coal, the store of wood was renewed at Granite House, and they profited by the current of the Mercy having again become free, to float down several rafts. They could see that the cold period was not ended.

A visit was also paid to the Chimneys, and the settlers could not but congratulate themselves on not having been living there during the hurricane. The sea had left unquestionable traces of its ravages. Sweeping over the islet, it had furiously assailed the passages, half filling them with sand, while thick beds of seaweed covered the rocks. While Neb, Herbert, and Pencroft hunted or collected wood, Cyrus Harding and Gideon Spilett busied themselves in putting the Chimneys to rights, and they found the forge and the bellows almost unhurt, protected as they had been from the first by the heaps of sand.

The store of fuel had not been made uselessly. The settlers had not done with the rigorous cold. It is known that, in the Northern Hemisphere, the month of February is principally distinguished by rapid fallings of the temperature. It is the same in the Southern Hemisphere, and the end of the month of August, which is the February of North America, does not escape this climatic law.

About the 25th, after another change from snow to rain, the wind shifted to the southeast, and the cold became, suddenly, very severe. According to the engineer's calculation, the mercurial column of a Fahrenheit thermometer would not have marked less than eight degrees below zero, and this intense cold, rendered still more painful by a sharp gale, lasted for several days. The colonists were again shut up in Granite House, and as it was necessary to hermetically seal all the openings of the facade, only leaving a narrow passage for renewing the air, the consumption of candles was considerable. To economize them, the cavern was often only lighted by the blazing hearths, on which fuel was not spared. Several times, one or other of the settlers descended to the beach in the midst of ice which the waves heaped up at each tide, but they soon climbed up again to Granite House, and it was not without pain and difficulty that their hands could hold to the rounds of the ladder. In consequence of the intense cold, their fingers felt as if burned when they touched the rounds. To occupy the leisure hours, which the tenants of Granite House now had at their disposal, Cyrus Harding undertook an operation which could be performed indoors.

We know that the settlers had no other sugar at their disposal than the liquid substance which they drew from the maple, by making deep incisions in the tree. They contented themselves with collecting this liquor in jars and employing it in this state for different culinary purposes, and the more so, as on growing old, this liquid began to become white and to be of a syrupy consistence.

But there was something better to be made of it, and one day Cyrus Harding announced that they were going to turn into refiners.

"Refiners!" replied Pencroft. "That is rather a warm trade, I think."

"Very warm," answered the engineer.

"Then it will be seasonable!" said the sailor.

This word refining need not awake in the mind thoughts of an elaborate manufactory with apparatus and numerous workmen. No! to crystallize this liquor, only an extremely easy operation is required. Placed on the fire in large earthen pots, it was simply subjected to evaporation, and soon a scum arose to its surface. As soon as this began to thicken, Neb carefully removed it with a wooden spatula; this accelerated the evaporation, and at the same time prevented it from contracting an empyreumatic flavor.

After boiling for several hours on a hot fire, which did as much good to the operators as the substance operated upon, the latter was transformed into a thick syrup. This syrup was poured into clay molds, previously fabricated in the kitchen stove, and to which they had given various shapes. The next day this syrup had become cold, and formed cakes and tablets. This was sugar of rather a reddish color, but nearly transparent and of a delicious taste.

The cold continued to the middle of September, and the prisoners in Granite House began to find their captivity rather tedious. Nearly every day they attempted sorties which they could not prolong. They constantly worked at the improvement of their dwelling. They talked while working. Harding instructed his companions in many things, principally explaining to them the practical applications of science. The colonists had no library at their disposal; but the engineer was a book which was always at hand, always open at the page which one wanted, a book which answered all their questions, and which they often consulted. The time thus passed away pleasantly, these brave men not appearing to have any fears for the future.

However, all were anxious to see, if not the fine season, at least the cessation of the insupportable cold. If only they had been clothed in a way to meet it, how many excursions they would have attempted, either to the downs or to Tadorn's Fens! Game would have been easily approached, and the chase would certainly have been most productive. But Cyrus Harding considered it of importance that no one should injure his health, for he had need of all his hands, and his advice was followed.

But it must be said, that the one who was most impatient of this imprisonment, after Pencroft perhaps, was Top. The faithful dog found Granite House very narrow. He ran backwards and forwards from one room to another, showing in his way how weary he was of being shut up. Harding often remarked that when he approached the dark well which communicated with the sea, and of which the orifice opened at the back of the storeroom, Top uttered singular growlings. He ran round and round this hole, which had been covered with a wooden lid. Sometimes even he tried to put his paws under the lid, as if he wished to raise it. He then yelped in a peculiar way, which showed at once anger and uneasiness.

The engineer observed this maneuver several times.

What could there be in this abyss to make such an impression on the intelligent animal? The well led to the sea, that was certain. Could narrow passages spread from it through the foundations of the island? Did some marine monster come from time to time, to breathe at the bottom of this well? The engineer did not know what to think, and could not refrain from dreaming of many strange improbabilities. Accustomed to go far into the regions of scientific reality, he would not allow himself to be drawn into the regions of the strange and almost of the supernatural; but yet how to explain why Top, one of those sensible dogs who never waste their time in barking at the moon, should persist in trying with scent and hearing to fathom this abyss, if there was nothing there to cause his uneasiness? Top's conduct puzzled Cyrus Harding even more than he cared to acknowledge to himself.

At all events, the engineer only communicated his impressions to Gideon Spilett, for he thought it useless to explain to his companions the suspicions which arose from what perhaps was only Top's fancy.

At last the cold ceased. There had been rain, squalls mingled with snow, hailstorms, gusts of wind, but these inclemencies did not last. The ice melted, the snow disappeared; the shore, the plateau, the banks of the Mercy, the forest, again became practicable. This return of spring delighted the tenants of Granite House, and they soon only passed it in the hours necessary for eating and sleeping.

They hunted much in the second part of September, which led Pencroft to again entreat for the firearms, which he asserted had been promised by Cyrus Harding. The latter, knowing well that without special tools it would be nearly impossible for him to manufacture a gun which would be of any use, still drew back and put off the operation to some future time, observing in his usual dry way, that Herbert and Spilett had become very skilful archers, so that many sorts of excellent animals, agouties, kangaroos, capybaras, pigeons, bustards, wild ducks, snipes, in short, game both with fur and feathers, fell victims to their arrows, and that, consequently, they could wait. But the obstinate sailor would listen to nothing of this, and he would give the engineer no peace till he promised to satisfy his desire. Gideon Spilett, however, supported Pencroft.

"If, which may be doubted," said he, "the island is inhabited by wild beasts, we must think how to fight with and exterminate them. A time may come when this will be our first duty."

But at this period, it was not the question of firearms which occupied Harding, but that of clothes. Those which the settlers wore had passed this winter, but they would not last until next winter. Skins of carnivora or the wool of ruminants must be procured at any price, and since there were plenty of musmons, it was agreed to consult on the means of forming a flock which might be brought up for the use of the colony. An enclosure for the domestic animals, a poultry-yard for the birds, in a word to establish a sort of farm in the island, such were the two important projects for the fine season.

In consequence and in view of these future establishments, it became of much importance that they should penetrate into all the yet unknown parts of Lincoln Island, that is to say, through that thick forest which extended on the right bank of the Mercy, from its mouth to the extremity of the Serpentine Peninsula, as well as on the whole of its western side. But this needed settled weather, and a month must pass before this exploration could be profitably undertaken.

They therefore waited with some impatience, when an incident occurred which increased the desire the settlers had to visit the whole of their domain.

It was the 24th of October. On this day, Pencroft had gone to visit his traps, which he always kept properly baited. In one of them he found three animals which would be very welcome for the larder. They were a female peccary and her two young ones.

Pencroft then returned to Granite House, enchanted with his capture, and, as usual, he made a great show of his game.

"Come, we shall have a grand feast, captain!" he exclaimed. "And you too, Mr. Spilett, you will eat some!"

"I shall be very happy," replied the reporter; "but what is it that I am going to eat?"

"Suckling-pig."

"Oh, indeed, suckling-pig, Pencroft? To hear you, I thought that you were bringing back a young partridge stuffed with truffles!"

"What?" cried Pencroft. "Do you mean to say that you turn up your nose at suckling-pig?"

"No," replied Gideon Spilett, without showing any enthusiasm; "provided one doesn't eat too much."

"That's right, that's right," returned the sailor, who was not pleased whenever he heard his chase made light of. "You like to make objections. Seven months ago, when we landed on the island, you would have been only too glad to have met with such game!"

"Well, well," replied the reporter, "man is never perfect, nor contented."

"Now," said Pencroft, "I hope that Neb will distinguish himself. Look here! These two little peccaries are not more than three months old! They will be as tender as quails! Come along, Neb, come! I will look after the cooking myself."

And the sailor, followed by Neb, entered the kitchen, where they were soon absorbed in their culinary labors.

They were allowed to do it in their own way. Neb, therefore, prepared a magnificent repast—the two little peccaries, kangaroo soup, a smoked ham, stone-pine almonds, Oswego tea; in fact, all the best that they had, but among all the dishes figured in the first rank the savory peccaries.

At five o'clock dinner was served in the dining-room of Granite House. The kangaroo soup was smoking on the table. They found it excellent.

To the soup succeeded the peccaries, which Pencroft insisted on carving himself, and of which he served out monstrous portions to each of the guests.

These suckling-pigs were really delicious, and Pencroft was devouring his share with great gusto, when all at once a cry and an oath escaped him.

"What's the matter?" asked Cyrus Harding.

"The matter? the matter is that I have just broken a tooth!" replied the sailor.

"What, are there pebbles in your peccaries?" said Gideon Spilett.

"I suppose so," replied Pencroft, drawing from his lips the object which had cost him a grinder—!

It was not a pebble—it was a leaden bullet.

Part 2. Abandoned

Chapter 1

It was now exactly seven months since the balloon voyagers had been thrown on Lincoln Island. During that time, notwithstanding the researches they had made, no human being had been discovered. No smoke even had betrayed the presence of man on the surface of the island. No vestiges of his handiwork showed that either at an early or at a late period had man lived there. Not only did it now appear to be uninhabited by any but themselves, but the colonists were compelled to believe that it never had been inhabited. And now, all this scaffolding of reasonings fell before a simple ball of metal, found in the body of an inoffensive rodent! In fact, this bullet must have issued from a firearm, and who but a human being could have used such a weapon?

When Pencroft had placed the bullet on the table, his companions looked at it with intense astonishment. All the consequences likely to result from this incident, notwithstanding its apparent insignificance, immediately took possession of their minds. The sudden apparition of a supernatural being could not have startled them more completely.

Cyrus Harding did not hesitate to give utterance to the suggestions which this fact, at once surprising and unexpected, could not fail to raise in his mind. He took the bullet, turned it over and over, rolled it between his finger and thumb; then, turning to Pencroft, he asked,—

"Are you sure that the peccary wounded by this bullet was not more than three months old?"

"Not more, captain," replied Pencroft. "It was still sucking its mother when I found it in the trap."

"Well," said the engineer, "that proves that within three months a gun-shot was fired in Lincoln Island."

"And that a bullet," added Gideon Spilett, "wounded, though not mortally, this little animal."

"That is unquestionable," said Cyrus Harding, "and these are the deductions which must be drawn from this incident: that the island was inhabited before our arrival, or that men have landed here within three months. Did these men arrive here voluntarily or involuntarily, by disembarking on the shore or by being wrecked? This point can only be cleared up later. As to what they were, Europeans or Malays, enemies or friends of our race, we cannot possibly guess; and if they still inhabit the island, or if they have left it, we know not. But these questions are of too much importance to be allowed to remain long unsettled."

"No! a hundred times no! a thousand times no!" cried the sailor, springing up from the table. "There are no other men than ourselves on Lincoln Island! By my faith! The island isn't large and if it had been inhabited, we should have seen some of the inhabitants long before this!"

"In fact, the contrary would be very astonishing," said Herbert.

"But it would be much more astonishing, I should think," observed the reporter, "if this peccary had been born with a bullet in its inside!"

"At least," said Neb seriously, "if Pencroft has not had—"

"Look here, Neb," burst out Pencroft. "Do you think I could have a bullet in my jaw for five or six months without finding it out? Where could it be hidden?" he asked, opening his mouth to show the two-and-thirty teeth with which it was furnished. "Look well, Neb, and if you find one hollow tooth in this set, I will let you pull out half a dozen!"

"Neb's supposition is certainly inadmissible," replied Harding, who, notwithstanding the gravity of his thoughts, could not restrain a smile. "It is certain that a gun has been fired in the island, within three months at most. But I am inclined to think that the people who landed on this coast were only here a very short time ago, or that they just touched here; for if, when we surveyed the island from the summit of Mount Franklin, it had been inhabited, we should have seen them or we should have been seen ourselves. It is therefore, probable that within only a few weeks castaways have been thrown by a storm on some part of the coast. However that may be, it is of consequence to us to have this point settled."

"I think that we should act with caution," said the reporter.

"Such is my advice," replied Cyrus Harding, "for it is to be feared that Malay pirates have landed on the island!"

"Captain," asked the sailor, "would it not be a good plan, before setting out, to build a canoe in which we could either ascend the river, or, if we liked, coast round the inland? It will not do to be unprovided."

"Your idea is good, Pencroft," replied the engineer, "but we cannot wait for that. It would take at least a month to build a boat."

"Yes, a real boat," replied the sailor; "but we do not want one for a sea voyage, and in five days at the most, I will undertake to construct a canoe fit to navigate the Mercy."

"Five days," cried Neb, "to build a boat?"

"Yes, Neb; a boat in the Indian fashion."

"Of wood?" asked the Negro, looking still unconvinced.

"Of wood," replied Pencroft, "of rather of bark. I repeat, captain, that in five days the work will be finished!"

"In five days, then, be it," replied the engineer.

"But till that time we must be very watchful," said Herbert.

"Very watchful indeed, my friends," replied Harding; "and I beg you to confine your hunting excursions to the neighborhood of Granite House."

The dinner ended less gaily than Pencroft had hoped.

So, then, the island was, or had been, inhabited by others than the settlers. Proved as it was by the incident of the bullet, it was hereafter an unquestionable fact, and such a discovery could not but cause great uneasiness among the colonists.

Cyrus Harding and Gideon Spilett, before sleeping, conversed long about the matter. They asked themselves if by chance this incident might not have some connection with the inexplicable way in which the engineer had been saved, and the other peculiar circumstances which had struck them at different times. However, Cyrus Harding, after having discussed the pros and cons of the question, ended by saying,—

"In short, would you like to know my opinion, my dear Spilett?"

"Yes, Cyrus."

"Well, then, it is this: however minutely we explore the island, we shall find nothing."

The next day Pencroft set to work. He did not mean to build a boat with boards and planking, but simply a flat-bottomed canoe, which would be well suited for navigating the Mercy—above all, for approaching its source, where the water would naturally be shallow. Pieces of bark, fastened one to the other, would form a light boat; and in case of natural obstacles, which would render a portage necessary, it would be easily carried. Pencroft intended to secure the pieces of bark by means of nails, to insure the canoe being water-tight.

It was first necessary to select the trees which would afford a strong and supple bark for the work. Now the last storm had brought down a number of large birch-trees, the bark of which would be perfectly suited for their purpose. Some of these trees lay on the ground, and they had only to be barked, which was the most difficult thing of all, owing to the imperfect tools which the settlers possessed. However, they overcame all difficulties.

While the sailor, seconded by the engineer, thus occupied himself without losing an hour, Gideon Spilett and Herbert were not idle.

They were made purveyors to the colony. The reporter could not but admire the boy, who had acquired great skill in handling the bow and spear. Herbert also showed great courage and much of that presence of mind which may justly be called "the reasoning of bravery." These two companions of the chase, remembering Cyrus Harding's recommendations, did not go beyond a radius of two miles round Granite House; but the borders of the forest furnished a sufficient tribute of agoutis, capybaras, kangaroos, peccaries, etc.; and if the result from the traps was less than during the cold, still the warren yielded its accustomed quota, which might have fed all the colony in Lincoln Island.

Often during these excursions, Herbert talked with Gideon Spilett on the incident of the bullet, and the deductions which the engineer drew from it, and one day—it was the 26th of October—he said—"But, Mr. Spilett, do you not think it very extraordinary that, if any castaways have landed on the island, they have not yet shown themselves near Granite House?"

"Very astonishing if they are still here," replied the reporter, "but not astonishing at all if they are here no longer!"

"So you think that these people have already quitted the island?" returned Herbert.

"It is more than probable, my boy; for if their stay was prolonged, and above all, if they were still here, some accident would have at last betrayed their presence."

"But if they were able to go away," observed the lad, "they could not have been castaways."

"No, Herbert; or, at least, they were what might be called provisional castaways. It is very possible that a storm may have driven them to the island without destroying their vessel, and that, the storm over, they went away again."

"I must acknowledge one thing," said Herbert, "it is that Captain Harding appears rather to fear than desire the presence of human beings on our island."

"In short," responded the reporter, "there are only Malays who frequent these seas, and those fellows are ruffians which it is best to avoid."

"It is not impossible, Mr. Spilett," said Herbert, "that some day or other we may find traces of their landing."

"I do not say no, my boy. A deserted camp, the ashes of a fire, would put us on the track, and this is what we will look for in our next expedition."

The day on which the hunters spoke thus, they were in a part of the forest near the Mercy, remarkable for its beautiful trees. There, among others, rose, to a height of nearly 200 feet above the ground, some of those superb coniferae, to which, in New Zealand, the natives give the name of Kauris.

"I have an idea, Mr. Spilett," said Herbert. "If I were to climb to the top of one of these kauris, I could survey the country for an immense distance round."

"The idea is good," replied the reporter; "but could you climb to the top of those giants?"

"I can at least try," replied Herbert.

The light and active boy then sprang on the first branches, the arrangement of which made the ascent of the kauri easy, and in a few minutes he arrived at the summit, which emerged from the immense plain of verdure.

From this elevated situation his gaze extended over all the southern portion of the island, from Claw Cape on the southeast, to Reptile End on the southwest. To the northwest rose Mount Franklin, which concealed a great part of the horizon.

But Herbert, from the height of his observatory, could examine all the yet unknown portion of the island, which might have given shelter to the strangers whose presence they suspected.

The lad looked attentively. There was nothing in sight on the sea, not a sail, neither on the horizon nor near the island. However, as the bank of trees hid the shore, it was possible that a vessel, especially if deprived of her masts, might lie close to the land and thus be invisible to Herbert.

Neither in the forests of the Far West was anything to be seen. The wood formed an impenetrable screen, measuring several square miles, without a break or an opening. It was impossible even to follow the course of the Mercy, or to ascertain in what part of the mountain it took its source. Perhaps other creeks also ran towards the west, but they could not be seen.

But at last, if all indication of an encampment escaped Herbert's sight could he not even catch a glimpse of smoke, the faintest trace of which would be easily discernible in the pure atmosphere?

For an instant Herbert thought he could perceive a slight smoke in the west, but a more attentive examination showed that he was mistaken. He strained his eyes in every direction, and his sight was excellent. No, decidedly there was nothing there.

Herbert descended to the foot of the kauri, and the two sportsmen returned to Granite House. There Cyrus Harding listened to the lad's account, shook his head and said nothing. It was very evident that no decided opinion could be pronounced on this question until after a complete exploration of the island.

Two days after—the 28th of October—another incident occurred, for which an explanation was again required.

While strolling along the shore about two miles from Granite House, Herbert and Neb were fortunate enough to capture a magnificent specimen of the order of chelonia. It was a turtle of the species Midas, the edible green turtle, so called from the color both of its shell and fat.

Herbert caught sight of this turtle as it was crawling among the rocks to reach the sea.

"Help, Neb, help!" he cried.

Neb ran up.

"What a fine animal!" said Neb; "but how are we to catch it?"

"Nothing is easier, Neb," replied Herbert. "We have only to turn the turtle on its back, and it cannot possibly get away. Take your spear and do as I do."

The reptile, aware of danger, had retired between its carapace and plastron. They no longer saw its head or feet, and it was motionless as a rock.

Herbert and Neb then drove their sticks underneath the animal, and by their united efforts managed without difficulty to turn it on its back. The turtle, which was three feet in length, would have weighed at least four hundred pounds.

"Capital!" cried Neb; "this is something which will rejoice friend Pencroft's heart."

In fact, the heart of friend Pencroft could not fail to be rejoiced, for the flesh of the turtle, which feeds on wrack-grass, is extremely savory. At this moment the creature's head could be seen, which was small, flat, but widened behind by the large temporal fossae hidden under the long roof.

"And now, what shall we do with our prize?" said Neb. "We can't drag it to Granite House!"

"Leave it here, since it cannot turn over," replied Herbert, "and we will come back with the cart to fetch it."

"That is the best plan."

However, for greater precaution, Herbert took the trouble, which Neb deemed superfluous, to wedge up the animal with great stones; after which the two hunters returned to Granite House, following the beach, which the tide had left uncovered. Herbert, wishing to surprise Pencroft, said nothing about the "superb specimen of a chelonian" which they had turned over on the sand; but, two hours later, he and Neb returned with the cart to the place where they had left it. The "superb specimen of a chelonian" was no longer there!

Neb and Herbert stared at each other first; then they stared about them. It was just at this spot that the turtle had been left. The lad even found the stones which he had used, and therefore he was certain of not being mistaken.

"Well!" said Neb, "these beasts can turn themselves over, then?"

"It appears so," replied Herbert, who could not understand it at all, and was gazing at the stones scattered on the sand.

"Well, Pencroft will be disgusted!"

"And Captain Harding will perhaps be very perplexed how to explain this disappearance," thought Herbert.

"Look here," said Neb, who wished to hide his ill-luck, "we won't speak about it."

"On the contrary, Neb, we must speak about it," replied Herbert.

And the two, taking the cart, which there was now no use for, returned to Granite House.

Arrived at the dockyard, where the engineer and the sailor were working together, Herbert recounted what had happened.

"Oh! the stupids!" cried the sailor, "to have let at least fifty meals escape!"

"But, Pencroft," replied Neb, "it wasn't our fault that the beast got away; as I tell you, we had turned it over on its back!"

"Then you didn't turn it over enough!" returned the obstinate sailor.

"Not enough!" cried Herbert.

And he told how he had taken care to wedge up the turtle with stones.

"It is a miracle, then!" replied Pencroft.

"I thought, captain," said Herbert, "that turtles, once placed on their backs, could not regain their feet, especially when they are of a large size?"

"That is true, my boy," replied Cyrus Harding.

"Then how did it manage?"

"At what distance from the sea did you leave this turtle?" asked the engineer, who, having suspended his work, was reflecting on this incident.

"Fifteen feet at the most," replied Herbert.

"And the tide was low at the time?"

"Yes, captain."

"Well," replied the engineer, "what the turtle could not do on the sand it might have been able to do in the water. It turned over when the tide overtook it, and then quietly returned to the deep sea."

"Oh! what stupids we were!" cried Neb.

"That is precisely what I had the honor of telling you before!" returned the sailor.

Cyrus Harding had given this explanation, which, no doubt, was admissible. But was he himself convinced of the accuracy of this explanation? It cannot be said that he was.

Chapter 2

On the 9th of October the bark canoe was entirely finished. Pencroft had kept his promise, and a light boat, the shell of which was joined together by the flexible twigs of the crejimba, had been constructed in five days. A seat in the stern, a second seat in the middle to preserve the equilibrium, a third seat in the bows, rowlocks for the two oars, a scull to steer with, completed the little craft, which was twelve feet long, and did not weigh more than two hundred pounds. The operation of launching it was extremely simple. The canoe was carried to the beach and laid on the sand before Granite House, and the rising tide floated it. Pencroft, who leaped in directly, maneuvered it with the scull and declared it to be just the thing for the purpose to which they wished to put it.

"Hurrah!" cried the sailor, who did not disdain to celebrate thus his own triumph. "With this we could go round—"

"The world?" asked Gideon Spilett.

"No, the island. Some stones for ballast, a mast and a sail, which the captain will make for us some day, and we shall go splendidly! Well, captain—and you, Mr. Spilett; and you, Herbert; and you, Neb—aren't you coming to try our new vessel? Come along! we must see if it will carry all five of us!"

This was certainly a trial which ought to be made. Pencroft soon brought the canoe to the shore by a narrow passage among the rocks, and it was agreed that they should make a trial of the boat that day by following the shore as far as the first point at which the rocks of the south ended.

As they embarked, Neb cried,—

"But your boat leaks rather, Pencroft."

"That's nothing, Neb," replied the sailor; "the wood will get seasoned. In two days there won't be a single leak, and our boat will have no more water in her than there is in the stomach of a drunkard. Jump in!"

They were soon all seated, and Pencroft shoved off. The weather was magnificent, the sea as calm as if its waters were contained within the narrow limits of a lake. Thus the boat could proceed with as much security as if it was ascending the tranquil current of the Mercy.

Neb took one of the oars, Herbert the other, and Pencroft remained in the stern in order to use the scull.

The sailor first crossed the channel, and steered close to the southern point of the islet. A light breeze blew from the south. No roughness was found either in the channel or the green sea. A long swell, which the canoe scarcely felt, as it was heavily laden, rolled regularly over the surface of the water. They pulled out about half a mile distant from the shore, that they might have a good view of Mount Franklin.

Pencroft afterwards returned towards the mouth of the river. The boat then skirted the shore, which, extending to the extreme point, hid all Tadorn's Fens.

This point, of which the distance was increased by the irregularity of the coast, was nearly three miles from the Mercy. The settlers resolved to go to its extremity, and only go beyond it as much as was necessary to take a rapid survey of the coast as far as Claw Cape.

The canoe followed the windings of the shore, avoiding the rocks which fringed it, and which the rising tide began to cover. The cliff gradually sloped away from the mouth of the river to the point. This was formed of granite reeks, capriciously distributed, very different from the cliff at Prospect Heights, and of an extremely wild aspect. It might have been said that an immense cartload of rocks had been emptied out there. There was no vegetation on this sharp promontory, which projected two miles from the forest, and it thus represented a giant's arm stretched out from a leafy sleeve.

The canoe, impelled by the two oars, advanced without difficulty. Gideon Spilett, pencil in one hand and notebook in the other, sketched the coast in bold strokes. Neb, Herbert, and Pencroft chatted, while examining this part of their domain, which was new to them, and, in proportion as the canoe proceeded towards the south, the two Mandible Capes appeared to move, and surround Union Bay more closely.

As to Cyrus Harding, he did not speak; he simply gazed, and by the mistrust which his look expressed, it appeared that he was examining some strange country.

In the meantime, after a voyage of three-quarters of an hour, the canoe reached the extremity of the point, and Pencroft was preparing to return, when Herbert, rising, pointed to a black object, saying,—

"What do I see down there on the beach?"

All eyes turned towards the point indicated.

"Why," said the reporter, "there is something. It looks like part of a wreck half buried in the sand."

"Ah!" cried Pencroft, "I see what it is!"

"What?" asked Neb.

"Barrels, barrels, which perhaps are full," replied the sailor.

"Pull to the shore, Pencroft!" said Cyrus.

A few strokes of the oar brought the canoe into a little creek, and its passengers leaped on shore.

Pencroft was not mistaken. Two barrels were there, half buried in the sand, but still firmly attached to a large chest, which, sustained by them, had floated to the moment when it stranded on the beach.

"There has been a wreck, then, in some part of the island," said Herbert.

"Evidently," replied Spilett.

"But what's in this chest?" cried Pencroft, with very natural impatience. "What's in this chest? It is shut up, and nothing to open it with! Well, perhaps a stone—"

And the sailor, raising a heavy block, was about to break in one of the sides of the chest, when the engineer arrested his hand.

"Pencroft," said he, "can you restrain your impatience for one hour only?"

"But, captain, just think! Perhaps there is everything we want in there!"

"We shall find that out, Pencroft," replied the engineer; "but trust to me, and do not break the chest, which may be useful to us. We must convey it to Granite House, where we can open it easily, and without breaking it. It is quite prepared for a voyage; and since it has floated here, it may just as well float to the mouth of the river."

"You are right, captain, and I was wrong, as usual," replied the sailor.

The engineer's advice was good. In fact, the canoe probably would not have been able to contain the articles possibly enclosed in the chest, which doubtless was heavy, since two empty barrels were required to buoy it up. It was, therefore, much better to tow it to the beach at Granite House.

And now, whence had this chest come? That was the important question. Cyrus Harding and his companions looked attentively around them, and examined the shore for several hundred steps. No other articles or pieces of wreck could be found. Herbert and Neb climbed a high rock to survey the sea, but there was nothing in sight—neither a dismasted vessel nor a ship under sail.

However, there was no doubt that there had been a wreck. Perhaps this incident was connected with that of the bullet? Perhaps strangers had landed on another part of the island? Perhaps they were still there? But the thought which came naturally to the settlers was, that these strangers could not be Malay pirates, for the chest was evidently of American or European make.

All the party returned to the chest, which was of an unusually large size. It was made of oak wood, very carefully closed and covered with a thick hide, which was secured by copper nails. The two great barrels, hermetically sealed, but which sounded hollow and empty, were fastened to its sides by strong ropes, knotted with a skill which Pencroft directly pronounced sailors alone could exhibit. It appeared to be in a perfect state of preservation, which was explained by the fact that it had stranded on a sandy beach, and not among rocks. They had no doubt whatever, on examining it carefully, that it had not been long in the water, and that its arrival on this coast was recent. The water did not appear to have penetrated to the inside, and the articles which it contained were no doubt uninjured.

It was evident that this chest had been thrown overboard from some dismasted vessel driven towards the island, and that, in the hope that it would reach the land, where they might afterwards find it, the passengers had taken the precaution to buoy it up by means of this floating apparatus.

"We will tow this chest to Granite House," said the engineer, "where we can make an inventory of its contents; then, if we discover any of the survivors from the supposed wreck, we can return it to those to whom it belongs. If we find no one—"

"We will keep it for ourselves!" cried Pencroft. "But what in the world can there be in it?"

The sea was already approaching the chest, and the high tide would evidently float it. One of the ropes which fastened the barrels was partly unlashed and used as a cable to unite the floating apparatus with the canoe. Pencroft and Neb then dug away the sand with their oars, so as to facilitate the moving of the chest, towing which the boat soon began to double the point, to which the name of Flotsam Point was given.

The chest was heavy, and the barrels were scarcely sufficient to keep it above water. The sailor also feared every instant that it would get loose and sink to the bottom of the sea. But happily his fears were not realized, and an hour and a half after they set out—all that time had been taken up in going a distance of three miles—the boat touched the beach below Granite House.

Canoe and chest were then hauled up on the sands; and as the tide was then going out, they were soon left high and dry. Neb, hurrying home, brought back some tools with which to open the chest in such a way that it might be injured as little as possible, and they proceeded to its inventory. Pencroft did not try to hide that he was greatly excited.

The sailor began by detaching the two barrels, which, being in good condition, would of course be of use. Then the locks were forced with a cold chisel and hammer, and the lid thrown back. A second casing of zinc lined the interior of the chest, which had been evidently arranged that the articles which it enclosed might under any circumstances be sheltered from damp.

"Oh!" cried Neb, "suppose it's jam!"

"I hope not," replied the reporter.

"If only there was—" said the sailor in a low voice.

"What?" asked Neb, who overheard him.

"Nothing!"

The covering of zinc was torn off and thrown back over the sides of the chest, and by degrees numerous articles of very varied character were produced and strewn about on the sand. At each new object Pencroft uttered fresh hurrahs, Herbert clapped his hands, and Neb danced up and down. There were books which made Herbert wild with joy, and cooking utensils which Neb covered with kisses!

In short, the colonists had reason to be extremely satisfied, for this chest contained tools, weapons, instruments, clothes, books; and this is the exact list of them as stated in Gideon Spilett's note-book: —Tools:—3 knives with several blades, 2 woodmen's axes, 2 carpenter's hatchets, 3 planes, 2 adzes, 1 twibil or mattock, 6 chisels, 2 files, 3 hammers, 3 gimlets, 2 augers, 10 bags of nails and screws, 3 saws of different sizes, 2 boxes of needles.

Weapons:—2 flint-lock guns, 2 for percussion caps, 2 breach-loader carbines, 5 boarding cutlasses, 4 sabers, 2 barrels of powder, each containing twenty-five pounds; 12 boxes of percussion caps.

Instruments:—1 sextant, 1 double opera-glass, 1 telescope, 1 box of mathematical instruments, 1 mariner's compass, 1 Fahrenheit thermometer, 1 aneroid barometer, 1 box containing a photographic apparatus, object-glass, plates, chemicals, etc.

Clothes:—2 dozen shirts of a peculiar material resembling wool, but evidently of a vegetable origin; 3 dozen stockings of the same material.

Utensils:—1 iron pot, 6 copper saucepans, 3 iron dishes, 10 metal plates, 2 kettles, 1 portable stove, 6 table-knives.

Books:—1 Bible, 1 atlas, 1 dictionary of the different Polynesian idioms, 1 dictionary of natural science, in six volumes; 3 reams of white paper, 2 books with blank pages.

"It must be allowed," said the reporter, after the inventory had been made, "that the owner of this chest was a practical man! Tools, weapons, instruments, clothes, utensils, books—nothing is wanting! It might really be said that he expected to be wrecked, and had prepared for it beforehand."

"Nothing is wanting, indeed," murmured Cyrus Harding thoughtfully.

"And for a certainty," added Herbert, "the vessel which carried this chest and its owner was not a Malay pirate!"

"Unless," said Pencroft, "the owner had been taken prisoner by pirates—"

"That is not admissible," replied the reporter. "It is more probable that an American or European vessel has been driven into this quarter, and that her passengers, wishing to save necessaries at least, prepared this chest and threw it overboard."

"Is that your opinion, captain?" asked Herbert.

"Yes, my boy," replied the engineer, "that may have been the case. It is possible that at the moment, or in expectation of a wreck, they collected into this chest different articles of the greatest use in hopes of finding it again on the coast—"

"Even the photographic box!" exclaimed the sailor incredulously.

"As to that apparatus," replied Harding, "I do not quite see the use of it; and a more complete supply of clothes or more abundant ammunition would have been more valuable to us as well as to any other castaways!"

"But isn't there any mark or direction on these instruments, tools, or books, which would tell us something about them?" asked Gideon Spilett.

That might be ascertained. Each article was carefully examined, especially the books, instruments and weapons. Neither the weapons nor the instruments, contrary to the usual custom, bore the name of the maker; they were, besides, in a perfect state, and did not appear to have been used. The same peculiarity marked the tools and utensils; all were new, which proved that the articles had not been taken by chance and thrown into the chest, but, on the contrary, that the choice of things had been well considered and arranged with care. This was also indicated by the second case of metal which had preserved them from damp, and which could not have been soldered in a moment of haste.

As to the dictionaries of natural science and Polynesian idioms, both were English; but they neither bore the name of the publisher nor the date of publication.

The same with the Bible printed in English, in quarto, remarkable from a typographic point of view, and which appeared to have been often used.

The atlas was a magnificent work, comprising maps of every country in the world, and several planispheres arranged upon Mercator's projection, and of which the nomenclature was in French—but which also bore neither date nor name of publisher.

There was nothing, therefore, on these different articles by which they could be traced, and nothing consequently of a nature to show the nationality of the vessel which must have recently passed these shores.

But, wherever the chest might have come from, it was a treasure to the settlers on Lincoln Island. Till then, by making use of the productions of nature, they had created everything for themselves, and, thanks to their intelligence, they had managed without difficulty. But did it not appear as if Providence had wished to reward them by sending them these productions of human industry? Their thanks rose unanimously to Heaven.

However, one of them was not quite satisfied: it was Pencroft. It appeared that the chest did not contain something which he evidently held in great esteem, for in proportion as they approached the bottom of the box, his hurrahs diminished in heartiness, and, the inventory finished, he was heard to mutter these words:—"That's all very fine, but you can see that there is nothing for me in that box!"

This led Neb to say,—

"Why, friend Pencroft, what more do you expect?"

"Half a pound of tobacco," replied Pencroft seriously, "and nothing would have been wanting to complete my happiness!"

No one could help laughing at this speech of the sailor's.

But the result of this discovery of the chest was, that it was now more than ever necessary to explore the island thoroughly. It was therefore agreed that the next morning at break of day, they should set out, by ascending the Mercy so as to reach the western shore. If any castaways had landed on the coast, it was to be feared they were without resources, and it was therefore the more necessary to carry help to them without delay.

During the day the different articles were carried to Granite House, where they were methodically arranged in the great hall. This day—the 29th of October—happened to be a Sunday, and, before going to bed, Herbert asked the engineer if he would not read them something from the Gospel.

"Willingly," replied Cyrus Harding.

He took the sacred volume, and was about to open it, when Pencroft stopped him, saying,—"Captain, I am superstitious. Open at random and read the first verse which, your eye falls upon. We will see if it applies to our situation."

Cyrus Harding smiled at the sailor's idea, and, yielding to his wish, he opened exactly at a place where the leaves were separated by a marker.

Immediately his eyes were attracted by a cross which, made with a pencil, was placed against the eighth verse of the seventh chapter of the Gospel of St. Matthew. He read the verse, which was this:—

"For every one that asketh receiveth; and he that seeketh findeth."

Chapter 3

The next day, the 30th of October, all was ready for the proposed exploring expedition, which recent events had rendered so necessary. In fact, things had so come about that the settlers in Lincoln Island no longer needed help for themselves, but were even able to carry it to others.

It was therefore agreed that they should ascend the Mercy as far as the river was navigable. A great part of the distance would thus be traversed without fatigue, and the explorers could transport their provisions and arms to an advanced point in the west of the island.

It was necessary to think not only of the things which they should take with them, but also of those which they might have by chance to bring back to Granite House. If there had been a wreck on the coast, as was supposed, there would be many things cast up, which would be lawfully their prizes. In the event of this, the cart would have been of more use than the light canoe, but it was heavy and clumsy to drag, and therefore more difficult to use; this led Pencroft to express his regret that the chest had not contained, besides "his halfpound of tobacco," a pair of strong New Jersey horses, which would have been very useful to the colony!

The provisions, which Neb had already packed up, consisted of a store of meat and of several gallons of beer, that is to say enough to sustain them for three days, the time which Harding assigned for the expedition. They hoped besides to supply themselves on the road, and Neb took care not to forget the portable stove.

The only tools the settlers took were the two woodmen's axes, which they could use to cut a path through the thick forests, as also the instruments, the telescope and pocket-compass.

For weapons they selected the two flint-lock guns, which were likely to be more useful to them than the percussion fowling-pieces, the first only requiring flints which could be easily replaced, and the latter needing fulminating caps, a frequent use of which would soon exhaust their limited stock. However, they took also one of the carbines and some cartridges. As to the powder, of which there was about fifty pounds in the barrel, a small supply of it had to be taken, but the engineer hoped to manufacture an explosive substance which would allow them to husband it. To the firearms were added the five cutlasses well sheathed in leather, and, thus supplied, the settlers could venture into the vast forest with some chance of success.

It is useless to add that Pencroft, Herbert, and Neb, thus armed, were at the summit of their happiness, although Cyrus Harding made them promise not to fire a shot unless it was necessary.

At six in the morning the canoe put off from the shore; all had embarked, including Top, and they proceeded to the mouth of the Mercy.

The tide had begun to come up half an hour before. For several hours, therefore, there would be a current, which it was well to profit by, for later the ebb would make it difficult to ascend the river. The tide was already strong, for in three days the moon would be full, and it was enough to keep the boat in the center of the current, where it floated swiftly along between the high banks without its being necessary to increase its speed by the aid of the oars. In a few minutes the explorers arrived at the angle formed by the Mercy and exactly at the place where, seven months before, Pencroft had made his first raft of wood.

After this sudden angle the river widened and flowed under the shade of great evergreen firs.

The aspect of the banks was magnificent. Cyrus Harding and his companions could not but admire the lovely effects so easily produced by nature with water and trees. As they advanced the forest element diminished. On the right bank of the river grew magnificent specimens of the ulmaceae tribe, the precious elm, so valuable to builders, and which withstands well the action of water. Then there were numerous groups belonging to the same family, among others one in particular, the fruit of which produces a very useful oil. Further on, Herbert remarked the lardizabala, a twining shrub which, when bruised in water, furnishes excellent cordage; and two or three ebony trees of a beautiful black, crossed with capricious veins.

From time to time, in certain places where the landing was easy, the canoe was stopped, when Gideon Spilett, Herbert, and Pencroft, their guns in their hands, and preceded by Top, jumped on shore. Without expecting game, some useful plant might be met with, and the young naturalist was delighted with discovering a sort of wild spinach, belonging to the order of chenopodiaceae, and numerous specimens of cruciferae, belonging to the cabbage tribe, which it would certainly be possible to cultivate by transplanting. There were cresses, horseradish, turnips, and lastly, little branching hairy stalks, scarcely more than three feet high, which produced brownish grains.

"Do you know what this plant is?" asked Herbert of the sailor.

"Tobacco!" cried Pencroft, who evidently had never seen his favorite plant except in the bowl of his pipe.

"No, Pencroft," replied Herbert; "this is not tobacco, it is mustard."

"Mustard be hanged!" returned the sailor; "but if by chance you happen to come across a tobacco-plant, my boy, pray don't scorn that!"

"We shall find it some day!" said Gideon Spilett.

"Well!" exclaimed Pencroft, "when that day comes, I do not know what more will be wanting in our island!"

These different plants, which had been carefully rooted up, were carried to the canoe, where Cyrus Harding had remained buried in thought.

The reporter, Herbert, and Pencroft in this manner frequently disembarked, sometimes on the right bank, sometimes on the left bank of the Mercy.

The latter was less abrupt, but the former more wooded. The engineer ascertained by consulting his pocket-compass that the direction of the river from the first turn was obviously southwest and northeast, and nearly straight for a length of about three miles. But it was to be supposed that this direction changed beyond that point, and that the Mercy continued to the north-west, towards the spurs of Mount Franklin, among which the river rose.

During one of these excursions, Gideon Spilett managed to get hold of two couples of living gallinaceae. They were birds with long, thin beaks, lengthened necks, short wings, and without any appearance of a tail. Herbert rightly gave them the name of tinamous, and it was resolved that they should be the first tenants of their future poultry-yard.

But till then the guns had not spoken, and the first report which awoke the echoes of the forest of the Far West was provoked by the appearance of a beautiful bird, resembling the kingfisher.

"I recognize him!" cried Pencroft, and it seemed as if his gun went off by itself.

"What do you recognize?" asked the reporter.

"The bird which escaped us on our first excursion, and from which we gave the name to that part of the forest."

"A jacamar!" cried Herbert.

It was indeed a jacamar, of which the plumage shines with a metallic luster. A shot brought it to the ground, and Top carried it to the canoe. At the same time half a dozen lories were brought down. The lory is of the size of a pigeon, the plumage dashed with green, part of the wings crimson, and its crest bordered with white. To the young boy belonged the honor of this shot, and he was proud enough of it. Lories are better food than the jacamar, the flesh of which is rather tough, but it was difficult to persuade Pencroft that he had not killed the king of eatable birds. It was ten o'clock in the morning when the canoe reached a second angle of the Mercy, nearly five miles from its mouth. Here a halt was made for breakfast under the shade of some splendid trees. The river still measured from sixty to seventy feet in breadth, and its bed from five to six feet in depth. The engineer had observed that it was increased by numerous affluents, but they were unnavigable, being simply little streams. As to the forest, including Jacamar Wood, as well as the forests of the Far West, it extended as far as the eye could reach. In no place, either in the depths of the forests or under the trees on the banks of the Mercy, was the presence of man revealed. The explorers could not discover one suspicious trace. It was evident that the woodman's axe had never touched these trees, that the pioneer's knife had never severed the creepers hanging from one trunk to another in the midst of tangled brushwood and long grass. If castaways had landed on the island, they could not have yet quitted the shore, and it was not in the woods that the survivors of the supposed shipwreck should be sought.

The engineer therefore manifested some impatience to reach the western coast of Lincoln Island, which was at least five miles distant according to his estimation.

The voyage was continued, and as the Mercy appeared to flow not towards the shore, but rather towards Mount Franklin, it was decided that they should use the boat as long as there was enough water under its keel to float it. It was both fatigue spared and time gained, for they would have been obliged to cut a path through the thick wood with their axes. But soon the flow completely failed them, either the tide was going down, and it was about the hour, or it could no longer be felt at this distance from the mouth of the Mercy. They had therefore to make use of the oars. Herbert and Neb each took one, and Pencroft took the scull. The forest soon became less dense, the trees grew further apart and often quite isolated. But the further they were from each other the more magnificent they appeared, profiting, as they did, by the free, pure air which circulated around them.

What splendid specimens of the flora of this latitude! Certainly their presence would have been enough for a botanist to name without hesitation the parallel which traversed Lincoln Island.

"Eucalypti!" cried Herbert.

They were, in fact, those splendid trees, the giants of the extratropical zone, the congeners of the Australian and New Zealand eucalyptus, both situated under the same latitude as Lincoln Island. Some rose to a height of two hundred feet. Their trunks at the base measured twenty feet in circumference, and their bark was covered by a network of farrows containing a red, sweet-smelling gum. Nothing is more wonderful or more singular than those enormous specimens of the order of the myrtaceae, with their leaves placed vertically and not horizontally, so that an edge and not a surface looks upwards, the effect being that the sun's rays penetrate more freely among the trees.

The ground at the foot of the eucalypti was carpeted with grass, and from the bushes escaped flights of little birds, which glittered in the sunlight like winged rubies.

"These are something like trees!" cried Neb; "but are they good for anything?"

"Pooh!" replied Pencroft. "Of course there are vegetable giants as well as human giants, and they are no good, except to show themselves at fairs!"

"I think that you are mistaken, Pencroft," replied Gideon Spilett, "and that the wood of the eucalyptus has begun to be very advantageously employed in cabinet-making."

"And I may add," said Herbert, "that the eucalyptus belongs to a family which comprises many useful members; the guava-tree, from whose fruit guava jelly is made; the clove-tree, which produces the spice; the pomegranate-tree, which bears pomegranates; the Eugeacia Cauliflora, the fruit of which is used in making a tolerable wine; the Ugui myrtle, which contains an excellent alcoholic liquor; the Caryophyllus myrtle, of which the bark forms an esteemed cinnamon; the Eugenia Pimenta, from whence comes Jamaica pepper; the common myrtle, from whose buds and berries spice is sometimes made; the Eucalyptus manifera, which yields a sweet sort of manna; the Guinea Eucalyptus, the sap of which is transformed into beer by fermentation; in short, all those trees known under the name of gum-trees or iron-bark trees in Australia, belong to this family of the myrtaceae, which contains forty-six genera and thirteen hundred species!"

The lad was allowed to run on, and he delivered his little botanical lecture with great animation. Cyrus Harding listened smiling, and Pencroft with an indescribable feeling of pride.

"Very good, Herbert," replied Pencroft, "but I could swear that all those useful specimens you have just told us about are none of them giants like these!"

"That is true, Pencroft."

"That supports what I said," returned the sailor, "namely, that these giants are good for nothing!"

"There you are wrong, Pencroft," said the engineer; "these gigantic eucalypti, which shelter us, are good for something."

"And what is that?"

"To render the countries which they inhabit healthy. Do you know what they are called in Australia and New Zealand?"

"No, captain."

"They are called 'fever trees.'"

"Because they give fevers?"

"No, because they prevent them!"

"Good. I must note that," said the reporter.

"Note it then, my dear Spilett; for it appears proved that the presence of the eucalyptus is enough to neutralize miasmas. This natural antidote has been tried in certain countries in the middle of Europe and the north of Africa where the soil was absolutely unhealthy, and the sanitary condition of the inhabitants has been gradually ameliorated. No more intermittent fevers prevail in the regions now covered with forests of the myrtaceae. This fact is now beyond doubt, and it is a happy circumstance for us settlers in Lincoln Island."

"Ah! what an island! What a blessed island!" cried Pencroft. "I tell you, it wants nothing—unless it is—"

"That will come, Pencroft, that will be found," replied the engineer; "but now we must continue our voyage and push on as far as the river will carry our boat!"

The exploration was therefore continued for another two miles in the midst of country covered with eucalypti, which predominated in the woods of this portion of the island. The space which they occupied extended as far as the eye could reach on each side of the Mercy, which wound along between high green banks. The bed was often obstructed by long weeds, and even by pointed rocks, which rendered the navigation very difficult. The action of the oars was prevented, and Pencroft was obliged to push with a pole. They found also that the water was becoming shallower and shallower, and that the canoe must soon stop. The sun was already sinking towards the horizon, and the trees threw long shadows on the ground. Cyrus Harding, seeing that he could not hope to reach the western coast of the island in one journey, resolved to camp at the place where any further navigation was prevented by want of water. He calculated that they were still five or six miles from the coast, and this distance was too great for them to attempt during the night in the midst of unknown woods.

The boat was pushed on through the forest, which gradually became thicker again, and appeared also to have more inhabitants; for if the eyes of the sailor did not deceive him, he thought he saw bands of monkeys springing among the trees. Sometimes even two or three of these animals stopped at a little distance from the canoe and gazed at the settlers without manifesting any terror, as if, seeing men for the first time, they had not yet learned to fear them. It would have been easy to bring down one of these quadramani with a gunshot, and Pencroft was greatly tempted to fire, but Harding opposed so useless a massacre. This was prudent, for the monkeys, or apes rather, appearing to be very powerful and extremely active, it was useless to provoke an unnecessary aggression, and the creatures might, ignorant of the power of the explorers' firearms, have attacked them. It is true that the sailor considered the monkeys from a purely alimentary point of view, for those animals which are herbivorous make very excellent game; but since they had an abundant supply of provisions, it was a pity to waste their ammunition.

Towards four o'clock, the navigation of the Mercy became exceedingly difficult, for its course was obstructed by aquatic plants and rocks. The banks rose higher and higher, and already they were approaching the spurs of Mount Franklin. The source could not be far off, since it was fed by the water from the southern slopes of the mountain.

"In a quarter of an hour," said the sailor, "we shall be obliged to stop, captain."

"Very well, we will stop, Pencroft, and we will make our encampment for the night."

"At what distance are we from Granite House?" asked Herbert.

"About seven miles," replied the engineer, "taking into calculation, however, the detours of the river, which has carried us to the northwest."

"Shall we go on?" asked the reporter.

"Yes, as long as we can," replied Cyrus Harding. "To-morrow, at break of day, we will leave the canoe, and in two hours I hope we shall cross the distance which separates us from the coast, and then we shall have the whole day in which to explore the shore."

"Go ahead!" replied Pencroft.

But soon the boat grated on the stony bottom of the river, which was now not more than twenty feet in breadth. The trees met like a bower overhead, and caused a half-darkness. They also heard the noise of a waterfall, which showed that a few hundred feet up the river there was a natural barrier.

Presently, after a sudden turn of the river, a cascade appeared through the trees. The canoe again touched the bottom, and in a few minutes it was moored to a trunk near the right bank.

It was nearly five o'clock. The last rays of the sun gleamed through the thick foliage and glanced on the little waterfall, making the spray sparkle with all the colors of the rainbow. Beyond that, the Mercy was lost in the bushwood, where it was fed from some hidden source. The different streams which flowed into it increased it to a regular river further down, but here it was simply a shallow, limpid brook.

It was agreed to camp here, as the place was charming. The colonists disembarked, and a fire was soon lighted under a clump of trees, among the branches of which Cyrus Harding and his companions could, if it was necessary, take refuge for the night.

Supper was quickly devoured, for they were very hungry, and then there was only sleeping to think of. But, as roarings of rather a suspicious nature had been heard during the evening, a good fire was made up for the night, so as to protect the sleepers with its crackling flames. Neb and Pencroft also watched by turns, and did not spare fuel. They thought they saw the dark forms of some wild animals prowling round the camp among the bushes, but the night passed without incident, and the next day, the 31st of October, at five o'clock in the morning, all were on foot, ready for a start.

Chapter 4

It was six o' clock in the morning when the settlers, after a hasty breakfast, set out to reach by the shortest way, the western coast of the island. And how long would it take to do this? Cyrus Harding had said two hours, but of course that depended on the nature of the obstacles they might meet with As it was probable that they would have to cut a path through the grass, shrubs, and creepers, they marched axe in hand, and with guns also ready, wisely taking warning from the cries of the wild beasts heard in the night.

The exact position of the encampment could be determined by the bearing of Mount Franklin, and as the volcano arose in the north at a distance of less than three miles, they had only to go straight towards the southwest to reach the western coast. They set out, having first carefully secured the canoe. Pencroft and Neb carried sufficient provision for the little band for at least two days. It would not thus be necessary to hunt. The engineer advised his companions to refrain from firing, that their presence might not be betrayed to any one near the shore. The first hatchet blows were given among the brushwood in the midst of some mastic-trees, a little above the cascade; and his compass in his hand, Cyrus Harding led the way.

The forest here was composed for the most part of trees which had already been met with near the lake and on Prospect Heights. There were deodars, Douglas firs, casuarinas, gum trees, eucalypti, hibiscus, cedars, and other trees, generally of a moderate size, for their number prevented their growth.

Since their departure, the settlers had descended the slopes which constituted the mountain system of the island, on to a dry soil, but the luxuriant vegetation of which indicated it to be watered either by some subterranean marsh or by some stream. However, Cyrus Harding did not remember having seen, at the time of his excursion to the crater, any other watercourses but the Red Creek and the Mercy.

During the first part of their excursion, they saw numerous troops of monkeys who exhibited great astonishment at the sight of men, whose appearance was so new to them. Gideon Spilett jokingly asked whether these active and merry quadrupeds did not consider him and his companions as degenerate brothers.

And certainly, pedestrians, hindered at each step by bushes, caught by creepers, barred by trunks of trees, did not shine beside those supple animals, who, bounding from branch to branch, were hindered by nothing on their course. The monkeys were numerous, but happily they did not manifest any hostile disposition.

Several pigs, agoutis, kangaroos, and other rodents were seen, also two or three koalas, at which Pencroft longed to have a shot.

"But," said he, "you may jump and play just now; we shall have one or two words to say to you on our way back!"

At half-past nine the way was suddenly found to be barred by an unknown stream, from thirty to forty feet broad, whose rapid current dashed foaming over the numerous rocks which interrupted its course. This creek was deep and clear, but it was absolutely unnavigable.

"We are cut off!" cried Neb.

"No," replied Herbert, "it is only a stream, and we can easily swim over."

"What would be the use of that?" returned Harding. "This creek evidently runs to the sea. Let us remain on this side and follow the bank, and I shall be much astonished if it does not lead us very quickly to the coast. Forward!"

"One minute," said the reporter. "The name of this creek, my friends? Do not let us leave our geography incomplete."

"All right!" said Pencroft.

"Name it, my boy," said the engineer, addressing the lad.

"Will it not be better to wait until we have explored it to its mouth?" answered Herbert.

"Very well," replied Cyrus Harding. "Let us follow it as fast as we can without stopping."

"Still another minute!" said Pencroft.

"What's the matter?" asked the reporter.

"Though hunting is forbidden, fishing is allowed, I suppose," said the sailor.

"We have no time to lose," replied the engineer.

"Oh! five minutes!" replied Pencroft, "I only ask for five minutes to use in the interest of our breakfast!"

And Pencroft, lying down on the bank, plunged his arm into the water, and soon pulled up several dozen of fine crayfish from among the stones.

"These will be good!" cried Neb, going to the sailor's aid.

"As I said, there is everything in this island, except tobacco!" muttered Pencroft with a sigh.

The fishing did not take five minutes, for the crayfish were swarming in the creek. A bag was filled with the crustaceae, whose shells were of a cobalt blue. The settlers then pushed on.

They advanced more rapidly and easily along the bank of the river than in the forest. From time to time they came upon the traces of animals of a large size who had come to quench their thirst at the stream, but none were actually seen, and it was evidently not in this part of the forest that the peccary had received the bullet which had cost Pencroft a grinder.

In the meanwhile, considering the rapid current, Harding was led to suppose that he and his companions were much farther from the western coast than they had at first supposed. In fact, at this hour, the rising tide would have turned back the current of the creek, if its mouth had only been a few miles distant. Now, this effect was not produced, and the water pursued its natural course. The engineer was much astonished at this, and frequently consulted his compass, to assure himself that some turn of the river was not leading them again into the Far West.

However, the creek gradually widened and its waters became less tumultuous. The trees on the right bank were as close together as on the left bank, and it was impossible to distinguish anything beyond them; but these masses of wood were evidently uninhabited, for Top did not bark, and the intelligent animal would not have failed to signal the presence of any stranger in the neighborhood.

At half-past ten, to the great surprise of Cyrus Harding, Herbert, who was a little in front, suddenly stopped and exclaimed,—

"The sea!"

In a few minutes more, the whole western shore of the island lay extended before the eyes of the settlers.

But what a contrast between this and the eastern coast, upon which chance had first thrown them. No granite cliff, no rocks, not even a sandy beach. The forest reached the shore, and the tall trees bending over the water were beaten by the waves. It was not such a shore as is usually formed by nature, either by extending a vast carpet of sand, or by grouping masses of rock, but a beautiful border consisting of the most splendid trees. The bank was raised a little above the level of the sea, and on this luxuriant soil, supported by a granite base, the fine forest trees seemed to be as firmly planted as in the interior of the island.

The colonists were then on the shore of an unimportant little harbor, which would scarcely have contained even two or three fishing-boats. It served as a neck to the new creek, of which the curious thing was that its waters, instead of joining the sea by a gentle slope, fell from a height of more than forty feet, which explained why the rising tide was not felt up the stream. In fact, the tides of the Pacific, even at their maximum elevation, could never reach the level of the river, and, doubtless, millions of years would pass before the water would have worn away the granite and hollowed a practicable mouth.

It was settled that the name of Falls River should be given to this stream. Beyond, towards the north, the forest border was prolonged for a space of nearly two miles; then the trees became scarcer, and beyond that again the picturesque heights described a nearly straight line, which ran north and south. On the contrary, all the part of the shore between Falls River and Reptile End was a mass of wood, magnificent trees, some straight, others bent, so that the long sea-swell bathed their roots. Now, it was this coast, that is, all the Serpentine Peninsula, that was to be explored, for this part of the shore offered a refuge to castaways, which the other wild and barren side must have refused.

The weather was fine and clear, and from a height of a hillock on which Neb and Pencroft had arranged breakfast, a wide view was obtained. There was, however, not a sail in sight; nothing could be seen along the shore as far as the eye could reach. But the engineer would take nothing for granted until he had explored the coast to the very extremity of the Serpentine Peninsula.

Breakfast was soon despatched, and at half-past eleven the captain gave the signal for departure. Instead of proceeding over the summit of a cliff or along a sandy beach, the settlers were obliged to remain under cover of the trees so that they might continue on the shore.

The distance which separated Falls River from Reptile End was about twelve miles. It would have taken the settlers four hours to do this, on a clear ground and without hurrying themselves; but as it was they needed double the time, for what with trees to go round, bushes to cut down, and creepers to chop away, they were impeded at every step, these obstacles greatly lengthening their journey.

There was, however, nothing to show that a shipwreck had taken place recently. It is true that, as Gideon Spilett observed, any remains of it might have drifted out to sea, and they must not take it for granted that because they could find no traces of it, a ship had not been castaway on the coast.

The reporter's argument was just, and besides, the incident of the bullet proved that a shot must have been fired in Lincoln Island within three months.

It was already five o'clock, and there were still two miles between the settlers and the extremity of the Serpentine Peninsula. It was evident that after having reached Reptile End, Harding and his companions would not have time to return before dark to their encampment near the source of the Mercy. It would therefore be necessary to pass the night on the promontory. But they had no lack of provisions, which was lucky, for there were no animals on the shore, though birds, on the contrary, abound—jacamars, couroucous, tragopans, grouse, lories, parrots, cockatoos, pheasants, pigeons, and a hundred others. There was not a tree without a nest, and not a nest which was not full of flapping wings.

Towards seven o'clock the weary explorers arrived at Reptile End. Here the seaside forest ended, and the shore resumed the customary appearance of a coast, with rocks, reefs, and sands. It was possible that something might be found here, but darkness came on, and the further exploration had to be put off to the next day.

Pencroft and Herbert hastened on to find a suitable place for their camp. Among the last trees of the forest of the Far West, the boy found several thick clumps of bamboos.

"Good," said he; "this is a valuable discovery."

"Valuable?" returned Pencroft.

"Certainly," replied Herbert. "I may say, Pencroft, that the bark of the bamboo, cut into flexible laths, is used for making baskets; that this bark, mashed into a paste, is used for the manufacture of Chinese paper; that the stalks furnish, according to their size, canes and pipes and are used for conducting water; that large bamboos make excellent material for building, being light and strong, and being never attacked by insects. I will add that by sawing the bamboo in two at the joint, keeping for the bottom the part of the transverse film which forms the joint, useful cups are obtained, which are much in use among the Chinese. No! you don't care for that. But—"

"But what?"

"But I can tell you, if you are ignorant of it, that in India these bamboos are eaten like asparagus."

"Asparagus thirty feet high!" exclaimed the sailor. "And are they good?"

"Excellent," replied Herbert. "Only it is not the stems of thirty feet high which are eaten, but the young shoots."

"Perfect, my boy, perfect!" replied Pencroft.

"I will also add that the pith of the young stalks, preserved in vinegar, makes a good pickle."

"Better and better, Herbert!"

"And lastly, that the bamboos exude a sweet liquor which can be made into a very agreeable drink."

"Is that all?" asked the sailor.

"That is all!"

"And they don't happen to do for smoking?"

"No, my poor Pencroft."

Herbert and the sailor had not to look long for a place in which to pass the night. The rocks, which must have been violently beaten by the sea under the influence of the winds of the southwest, presented many cavities in which shelter could be found against the night air. But just as they were about to enter one of these caves a loud roaring arrested them.

"Back!" cried Pencroft. "Our guns are only loaded with small shot, and beasts which can roar as loud as that would care no more for it than for grains of salt!" And the sailor, seizing Herbert by the arm, dragged him behind a rock, just as a magnificent animal showed itself at the entrance of the cavern.

It was a jaguar of a size at least equal to its Asiatic congeners, that is to say, it measured five feet from the extremity of its head to the beginning of its tail. The yellow color of its hair was relieved by streaks and regular oblong spots of black, which contrasted with the white of its chest. Herbert recognized it as the ferocious rival of the tiger, as formidable as the puma, which is the rival of the largest wolf!

The jaguar advanced and gazed around him with blazing eyes, his hair bristling as if this was not the first time he had scented men.

At this moment the reporter appeared round a rock, and Herbert, thinking that he had not seen the jaguar, was about to rush towards him, when Gideon Spilett signed to him to remain where he was. This was not his first tiger, and advancing to within ten feet of the animal he remained motionless, his gun to his shoulder, without moving a muscle. The jaguar collected itself for a spring, but at that moment a shot struck it in the eyes, and it fell dead.

Herbert and Pencroft rushed towards the jaguar. Neb and Harding also ran up, and they remained for some instants contemplating the animal as it lay stretched on the ground, thinking that its magnificent skin would be a great ornament to the hall at Granite House.

"Oh, Mr. Spilett, how I admire and envy you!" cried Herbert, in a fit of very natural enthusiasm.

"Well, my boy," replied the reporter, "you could have done the same."

"I! with such coolness!—"

"Imagine to yourself, Herbert, that the jaguar is only a hare, and you would fire as quietly as possible."

"That is," rejoined Pencroft, "that it is not more dangerous than a hare!"

"And now," said Gideon Spilett, "since the jaguar has left its abode, I do not see, my friends, why we should not take possession of it for the night."

"But others may come," said Pencroft.

"It will be enough to light a fire at the entrance of the cavern," said the reporter, "and no wild beasts will dare to cross the threshold."

"Into the jaguar's house, then!" replied the sailor, dragging after him the body of the animal.

While Neb skinned the jaguar, his companions collected an abundant supply of dry wood from the forest, which they heaped up at the cave.

Cyrus Harding, seeing the clump of bamboos, cut a quantity, which he mingled with the other fuel.

This done, they entered the grotto, of which the floor was strewn with bones, the guns were carefully loaded, in case of a sudden attack, they had supper, and then just before they lay down to rest, the heap of wood piled at the entrance was set fire to. Immediately, a regular explosion, or rather a series of reports, broke the silence! The noise was caused by the bamboos, which, as the flames reached them, exploded like fireworks. The noise was enough to terrify even the boldest of wild beasts.

It was not the engineer who had invented this way of causing loud explosions, for, according to Marco Polo, the Tartars have employed it for many centuries to drive away from their encampments the formidable wild beasts of Central Asia.

Chapter 5

Cyrus Harding and his companions slept like innocent marmots in the cave which the jaguar had so politely left at their disposal.

At sunrise all were on the shore at the extremity of the promontory, and their gaze was directed towards the horizon, of which two-thirds of the circumference were visible. For the last time the engineer could ascertain that not a sail nor the wreck of a ship was on the sea, and even with the telescope nothing suspicious could be discovered.

There was nothing either on the shore, at least, in the straight line of three miles which formed the south side of the promontory, for beyond that, rising ground had the rest of the coast, and even from the extremity of the Serpentine Peninsula Claw Cape could not be seen.

The southern coast of the island still remained to be explored. Now should they undertake it immediately, and devote this day to it?

This was not included in their first plan. In fact, when the boat was abandoned at the sources of the Mercy, it had been agreed that after having surveyed the west coast, they should go back to it, and return to Granite House by the Mercy. Harding then thought that the western coast would have offered refuge, either to a ship in distress, or to a vessel in her regular course; but now, as he saw that this coast presented no good anchorage, he wished to seek on the south what they had not been able to find on the west.

Gideon Spilett proposed to continue the exploration, that the question of the supposed wreck might be completely settled, and he asked at what distance Claw Cape might be from the extremity of the peninsula.

"About thirty miles," replied the engineer, "if we take into consideration the curvings of the coast."

"Thirty miles!" returned Spilett. "That would be a long day's march. Nevertheless, I think that we should return to Granite House by the south coast."

"But," observed Herbert, "from Claw Cape to Granite House there must be at least another ten miles.

"Make it forty miles in all," replied the engineer, "and do not hesitate to do it. At least we should survey the unknown shore, and then we shall not have to begin the exploration again."

"Very good," said Pencroft. "But the boat?"

"The boat has remained by itself for one day at the sources of the Mercy," replied Gideon Spilett; "it may just as well stay there two days! As yet, we have had no reason to think that the island is infested by thieves!"

"Yet," said the sailor, "when I remember the history of the turtle, I am far from confident of that."

"The turtle! the turtle!" replied the reporter. "Don't you know that the sea turned it over?"

"Who knows?" murmured the engineer.

"But,—" said Neb.

Neb had evidently something to say, for he opened his mouth to speak and yet said nothing.

"What do you want to say, Neb?" asked the engineer.

"If we return by the shore to Claw Cape," replied Neb, "after having doubled the Cape, we shall be stopped—"

"By the Mercy! of course," replied Herbert, "and we shall have neither bridge nor boat by which to cross."

"But, captain," added Pencroft, "with a few floating trunks we shall have no difficulty in crossing the river."

"Never mind," said Spilett, "it will be useful to construct a bridge if we wish to have an easy access to the Far West!"

"A bridge!" cried Pencroft. "Well, is not the captain the best engineer in his profession? He will make us a bridge when we want one. As to transporting you this evening to the other side of the Mercy, and that without wetting one thread of your clothes, I will take care of that. We have provisions for another day, and besides we can get plenty of game. Forward!"

The reporter's proposal, so strongly seconded by the sailor, received general approbation, for each wished to have their doubts set at rest, and by returning by Claw Cape the exploration would be ended. But there was not an hour to lose, for forty miles was a long march, and they could not hope to reach Granite House before night.

At six o'clock in the morning the little band set out. As a precaution the guns were loaded with ball, and Top, who led the van, received orders to beat about the edge of the forest.

From the extremity of the promontory which formed the tail of the peninsula the coast was rounded for a distance of five miles, which was rapidly passed over, without even the most minute investigations bringing to light the least trace of any old or recent landings; no debris, no mark of an encampment, no cinders of a fire, nor even a footprint!

From the point of the peninsula on which the settlers now were their gaze could extend along the southwest. Twenty-five miles off the coast terminated in the Claw Cape, which loomed dimly through the morning mists, and which, by the phenomenon of the mirage, appeared as if suspended between land and water.

Between the place occupied by the colonists and the other side of the immense bay, the shore was composed, first, of a tract of low land, bordered in the background by trees; then the shore became more irregular, projecting sharp points into the sea, and finally ended in the black rocks which, accumulated in picturesque disorder, formed Claw Cape.

Such was the development of this part of the island, which the settlers took in at a glance, while stopping for an instant.

"If a vessel ran in here," said Pencroft, "she would certainly be lost. Sandbanks and reefs everywhere! Bad quarters!"

"But at least something would be left of the ship," observed the reporter.

"There might be pieces of wood on the rocks, but nothing on the sands," replied the sailor.

"Why?"

"Because the sands are still more dangerous than the rocks, for they swallow up everything that is thrown on them. In a few days the hull of a ship of several hundred tons would disappear entirely in there!"

"So, Pencroft," asked the engineer, "if a ship has been wrecked on these banks, is it not astonishing that there is now no trace of her remaining?"

"No, captain, with the aid of time and tempest. However, it would be surprising, even in this case, that some of the masts or spars should not have been thrown on the beach, out of reach of the waves."

"Let us go on with our search, then," returned Cyrus Harding.

At one o'clock the colonists arrived at the other side of Washington Bay, they having now gone a distance of twenty miles.

They then halted for breakfast.

Here began the irregular coast, covered with lines of rocks and sandbanks. The long sea-swell could be seen breaking over the rocks in the bay, forming a foamy fringe. From this point to Claw Cape the beach was very narrow between the edge of the forest and the reefs.

Walking was now more difficult, on account of the numerous rocks which encumbered the beach. The granite cliff also gradually increased in height, and only the green tops of the trees which crowned it could be seen.

After half an hour's rest, the settlers resumed their journey, and not a spot among the rocks was left unexamined. Pencroft and Neb even rushed into the surf whenever any object attracted their attention. But they found nothing, some curious formations of the rocks having deceived them. They ascertained, however, that eatable shellfish abounded there, but these could not be of any great advantage to them until some easy means of communication had been established between the two banks of the Mercy, and until the means of transport had been perfected.

Nothing therefore which threw any light on the supposed wreck could be found on this shore, yet an object of any importance, such as the hull of a ship, would have been seen directly, or any of her masts and spans would have been washed on shore, just as the chest had been, which was found twenty miles from here. But there was nothing.

Towards three o'clock Harding and his companions arrived at a snug little creek. It formed quite a natural harbor, invisible from the sea, and was entered by a narrow channel.

At the back of this creek some violent convulsion had torn up the rocky border, and a cutting, by a gentle slope, gave access to an upper plateau, which might be situated at least ten miles from Claw Cape, and consequently four miles in a straight line from Prospect Heights. Gideon Spilett proposed to his companions that they should make a halt here. They agreed readily, for their walk had sharpened their appetites; and although it was not their usual dinner-hour, no one refused to strengthen himself with a piece of venison. This luncheon would sustain them until their supper, which they intended to take at Granite House. In a few minutes the settlers, seated under a clump of fine sea-pines, were devouring the provisions which Neb produced from his bag.

This spot was raised from fifty to sixty feet above the level of the sea. The view was very extensive, but beyond the cape it ended in Union Bay. Neither the islet nor Prospect Heights was visible, and could not be from thence, for the rising ground and the curtain of trees closed the northern horizon.

It is useless to add that notwithstanding the wide extent of sea which the explorers could survey, and though the engineer swept the horizon with his glass, no vessel could be found.

The shore was of course examined with the same care from the edge of the water to the cliff, and nothing could be discovered even with the aid of the instrument.

"Well," said Gideon Spilett, "it seems we must make up our minds to console ourselves with thinking that no one will come to dispute with us the possession of Lincoln Island!"

"But the bullet," cried Herbert. "That was not imaginary, I suppose!"

"Hang it, no!" exclaimed Pencroft, thinking of his absent tooth.

"Then what conclusion may be drawn?" asked the reporter.

"This," replied the engineer, "that three months or more ago, a vessel, either voluntarily or not, came here."

"What! then you admit, Cyrus, that she was swallowed up without leaving any trace?" cried the reporter.

"No, my dear Spilett; but you see that if it is certain that a human being set foot on the island, it appears no less certain that he has now left it."

"Then, if I understand you right, captain," said Herbert, "the vessel has left again?"

"Evidently."

"And we have lost an opportunity to get back to our country?" said Neb.

"I fear so."

"Very well, since the opportunity is lost, let us go on; it can't be helped," said Pencroft, who felt home-sickness for Granite House.

But just as they were rising, Top was heard loudly barking; and the dog issued from the wood, holding in his mouth a rag soiled with mud.

Neb seized it. It was a piece of strong cloth!

Top still barked, and by his going and coming, seemed to invite his master to follow him into the forest.

"Now there's something to explain the bullet!" exclaimed Pencroft.

"A castaway!" replied Herbert.

"Wounded, perhaps!" said Neb.

"Or dead!" added the reporter.

All ran after the dog, among the tall pines on the border of the forest. Harding and his companions made ready their firearms, in case of an emergency.

They advanced some way into the wood, but to their great disappointment, they as yet saw no signs of any human being having passed that way. Shrubs and creepers were uninjured, and they had even to cut them away with the axe, as they had done in the deepest recesses of the forest. It was difficult to fancy that any human creature had ever passed there, but yet Top went backward and forward, not like a dog who searches at random, but like a dog being endowed with a mind, who is following up an idea.

In about seven or eight minutes Top stopped in a glade surrounded with tall trees. The settlers gazed around them, but saw nothing, neither under the bushes nor among the trees.

"What is the matter, Top?" said Cyrus Harding.

Top barked louder, bounding about at the foot of a gigantic pine. All at once Pencroft shouted,—" Ho, splendid! capital!"

"What is it?" asked Spilett.

"We have been looking for a wreck at sea or on land!"

"Well?"

"Well; and here we've found one in the air!"

And the sailor pointed to a great white rag, caught in the top of the pine, a fallen scrap of which the dog had brought to them.

"But that is not a wreck!" cried Gideon Spilett.

"I beg your pardon!" returned Pencroft.

"Why? is it—?"

"It is all that remains of our airy boat, of our balloon, which has been caught up aloft there, at the top of that tree!"

Pencroft was not mistaken, and he gave vent to his feelings in a tremendous hurrah, adding,—

"There is good cloth! There is what will furnish us with linen for years. There is what will make us handkerchiefs and shirts! Ha, ha, Mr. Spilett, what do you say to an island where shirts grow on the trees?"

It was certainly a lucky circumstance for the settlers in Lincoln Island that the balloon, after having made its last bound into the air, had fallen on the island and thus given them the opportunity of finding it again, whether they kept the case under its present form, or whether they wished to attempt another escape by it, or whether they usefully employed the several hundred yards of cotton, which was of fine quality. Pencroft's joy was therefore shared by all.

But it was necessary to bring down the remains of the balloon from the tree, to place it in security, and this was no slight task. Neb, Herbert, and the sailor, climbing to the summit of the tree, used all their skill to disengage the now reduced balloon.

The operation lasted two hours, and then not only the case, with its valve, its springs, its brasswork, lay on the ground, but the net, that is to say a considerable quantity of ropes and cordage, and the circle and the anchor. The case, except for the fracture, was in good condition, only the lower portion being torn.

It was a fortune which had fallen from the sky.

"All the same, captain," said the sailor, "if we ever decide to leave the island, it won't be in a balloon, will it? These airboats won't go where we want them to go, and we have had some experience in that way! Look here, we will build a craft of some twenty tons, and then we can make a main-sail, a foresail, and a jib out of that cloth. As to the rest of it, that will help to dress us."

"We shall see, Pencroft," replied Cyrus Harding; "we shall see."

"In the meantime, we must put it in a safe place," said Neb.

They certainly could not think of carrying this load of cloth, ropes, and cordage, to Granite House, for the weight of it was very considerable, and while waiting for a suitable vehicle in which to convey it, it was of importance that this treasure should not be left longer exposed to the mercies of the first storm. The settlers, uniting their efforts, managed to drag it as far as the shore, where they discovered a large rocky cavity, which owing to its position could not be visited either by the wind or rain.

"We needed a locker, and now we have one," said Pencroft; "but as we cannot lock it up, it will be prudent to hide the opening. I don't mean from two-legged thieves, but from those with four paws!"

At six o'clock, all was stowed away, and after having given the creek the very suitable name of "Port Balloon," the settlers pursued their way along Claw Cape. Pencroft and the engineer talked of the different projects which it was agreed to put into execution with the briefest possible delay. It was necessary first of all to throw a bridge over the Mercy, so as to establish an easy communication with the south of the island; then the cart must be taken to bring back the balloon, for the canoe alone could not carry it, then they would build a decked boat, and Pencroft would rig it as a cutter, and they would be able to undertake voyages of circumnavigation round the island, etc.

In the meanwhile night came on, and it was already dark when the settlers reached Flotsam Point, where they had found the precious chest.

The distance between Flotsam Point and Granite House was another four miles, and it was midnight when, after having followed the shore to the mouth of the Mercy, the settlers arrived at the first angle formed by the Mercy.

There the river was eighty feet in breadth, which was awkward to cross, but as Pencroft had taken upon himself to conquer this difficulty, he was compelled to do it. The settlers certainly had reason to be pretty tired. The journey had been long, and the task of getting down the balloon had not rested either their arms or legs. They were anxious to reach Granite House to eat and sleep, and if the bridge had been constructed, in a quarter of an hour they would have been at home.

The night was very dark. Pencroft prepared to keep his promise by constructing a sort of raft, on which to make the passage of the Mercy. He and Neb, armed with axes, chose two trees near the water, and began to attack them at the base.

Cyrus Harding and Spilett, seated on the bank, waited till their companions were ready for their help, while Herbert roamed about, though without going to any distance. All at once, the lad, who had strolled by the river, came running back, and, pointing up the Mercy, exclaimed,—

"What is floating there?"

Pencroft stopped working, and seeing an indistinct object moving through the gloom,—

"A canoe!" cried he.

All approached, and saw to their extreme surprise, a boat floating down the current.

"Boat ahoy!" shouted the sailor, without thinking that perhaps it would be best to keep silence.

No reply. The boat still drifted onward, and it was not more than twelve feet off, when the sailor exclaimed,—

"But it is our own boat! she has broken her moorings, and floated down the current. I must say she has arrived very opportunely."

"Our boat?" murmured the engineer.

Pencroft was right. It was indeed the canoe, of which the rope had undoubtedly broken, and which had come alone from the sources of the Mercy. It was very important to seize it before the rapid current should have swept it away out of the mouth of the river, but Neb and Pencroft cleverly managed this by means of a long pole.

The canoe touched the shore. The engineer leaped in first, and found, on examining the rope, that it had been really worn through by rubbing against the rocks.

"Well," said the reporter to him, in a low voice, "this is a strange thing."

"Strange indeed!" returned Cyrus Harding.

Strange or not, it was very fortunate. Herbert, the reporter, Neb, and Pencroft, embarked in turn. There was no doubt about the rope having been worn through, but the astonishing part of the affair was, that the boat should arrive just at the moment when the settlers were there to seize it on its way, for a quarter of an hour earlier or later it would have been lost in the sea.

If they had been living in the time of genii, this incident would have given them the right to think that the island was haunted by some supernatural being, who used his power in the service of the castaways!

A few strokes of the oar brought the settlers to the mouth of the Mercy. The canoe was hauled up on the beach near the Chimneys, and all proceeded towards the ladder of Granite House.

But at that moment, Top barked angrily, and Neb, who was looking for the first steps, uttered a cry.

There was no longer a ladder!

Chapter 6

Cyrus Harding stood still, without saying a word. His companions searched in the darkness on the wall, in case the wind should have moved the ladder, and on the ground, thinking that it might have fallen down.... But the ladder had quite disappeared. As to ascertaining if a squall had blown it on the landing-place, half way up, that was impossible in the dark.

"If it is a joke," cried Pencroft, "it is a very stupid one! To come home and find no staircase to go up to your room by—that's nothing for weary men to laugh at."

Neb could do nothing but cry out "Oh! oh! oh!"

"I begin to think that very curious things happen in Lincoln Island!" said Pencroft.

"Curious?" replied Gideon Spilett, "not at all, Pencroft, nothing can be more natural. Some one has come during our absence, taken possession of our dwelling and drawn up the ladder."

"Some one," cried the sailor. "But who?"

"Who but the hunter who fired the bullet?" replied the reporter.

"Well, if there is any one up there," replied Pencroft, who began to lose patience, "I will give them a hail, and they must answer."

And in a stentorian voice the sailor gave a prolonged "Halloo!" which was echoed again and again from the cliff and rocks.

The settlers listened and they thought they heard a sort of chuckling laugh, of which they could not guess the origin. But no voice replied to Pencroft, who in vain repeated his vigorous shouts.

There was something indeed in this to astonish the most apathetic of men, and the settlers were not men of that description. In their situation every incident had its importance, and, certainly, during the seven months which they had spent on the island, they had not before met with anything of so surprising a character.

Be that as it may, forgetting their fatigue in the singularity of the event, they remained below Granite House, not knowing what to think, not knowing what to do, questioning each other without any hope of a satisfactory reply, every one starting some supposition each more unlikely than the last. Neb bewailed himself, much disappointed at not being able to get into his kitchen, for the provisions which they had had on their expedition were exhausted, and they had no means of renewing them.

"My friends," at last said Cyrus Harding, "there is only one thing to be done at present; wait for day, and then act according to circumstances. But let us go to the Chimneys. There we shall be under shelter, and if we cannot eat, we can at least sleep."

"But who is it that has played us this cool trick?" again asked Pencroft, unable to make up his mind to retire from the spot.

Whoever it was, the only thing practicable was to do as the engineer proposed, to go to the Chimneys and there wait for day. In the meanwhile Top was ordered to mount guard below the windows of Granite House, and when Top received an order he obeyed it without any questioning. The brave dog therefore remained at the foot of the cliff while his master with his companions sought a refuge among the rocks.

To say that the settlers, notwithstanding their fatigue, slept well on the sandy floor of the Chimneys would not be true. It was not only that they were extremely anxious to find out the cause of what had happened, whether it was the result of an accident which would be discovered at the return of day, or whether on the contrary it was the work of a human being; but they also had very uncomfortable beds. That could not be helped, however, for in some way or other at that moment their dwelling was occupied, and they could not possibly enter it.

Now Granite House was more than their dwelling, it was their warehouse. There were all the stores belonging to the colony, weapons, instruments, tools, ammunition, provisions, etc. To think that all that might be pillaged and that the settlers would have all their work to do over again, fresh weapons and tools to make, was a serious matter. Their uneasiness led one or other of them also to go out every few minutes to see if Top was keeping good watch. Cyrus Harding alone waited with his habitual patience, although his strong mind was exasperated at being confronted with such an inexplicable fact, and he was provoked at himself for allowing a feeling to which he could not give a name, to gain an influence over him. Gideon Spilett shared his feelings in this respect, and the two conversed together in whispers of the inexplicable circumstance which baffled even their intelligence and experience.

"It is a joke," said Pencroft; "it is a trick some one has played us. Well, I don't like such jokes, and the joker had better look out for himself, if he falls into my hands, I can tell him."

As soon as the first gleam of light appeared in the east, the colonists, suitably armed, repaired to the beach under Granite House. The rising sun now shone on the cliff and they could see the windows, the shutters of which were closed, through the curtains of foliage.

All here was in order; but a cry escaped the colonists when they saw that the door, which they had closed on their departure, was now wide open.

Some one had entered Granite House—there could be no more doubt about that.

The upper ladder, which generally hung from the door to the landing, was in its place, but the lower ladder was drawn up and raised to the threshold. It was evident that the intruders had wished to guard themselves against a surprise.

Pencroft hailed again.

No reply.

"The beggars," exclaimed the sailor. "There they are sleeping quietly as if they were in their own house. Hallo there, you pirates, brigands, robbers, sons of John Bull!"

When Pencroft, being a Yankee, treated any one to the epithet of "son of John Bull," he considered he had reached the last limits of insult.

The sun had now completely risen, and the whole facade of Granite House became illuminated by its rays; but in the interior as well as on the exterior all was quiet and calm.

The settlers asked if Granite House was inhabited or not, and yet the position of the ladder was sufficient to show that it was; it was also certain that the inhabitants, whoever they might be, had not been able to escape. But how were they to be got at?

Herbert then thought of fastening a cord to an arrow, and shooting the arrow so that it should pass between the first rounds of the ladder which hung from the threshold. By means of the cord they would then be able to draw down the ladder to the ground, and so re-establish the communication between the beach and Granite House. There was evidently nothing else to be done, and, with a little skill, this method might succeed. Very fortunately bows and arrows had been left at the Chimneys, where they also found a quantity of light hibiscus cord. Pencroft fastened this to a well-feathered arrow. Then Herbert fixing it to his bow, took a careful aim for the lower part of the ladder.

Cyrus Harding, Gideon Spilett, Pencroft, and Neb drew back, so as to see if anything appeared at the windows. The reporter lifted his gun to his shoulder and covered the door.

The bow was bent, the arrow flew, taking the cord with it, and passed between the two last rounds.

The operation had succeeded.

Herbert immediately seized the end of the cord, but, at that moment when he gave it a pull to bring down the ladder, an arm, thrust suddenly out between the wall and the door, grasped it and dragged it inside Granite House.

"The rascals!" shouted the sailor. "If a ball can do anything for you, you shall not have long to wait for it.

"But who was it?" asked Neb.

"Who was it? Didn't you see?"

"No."

"It was a monkey, a sapajou, an orangoutang, a baboon, a gorilla, a sagoin. Our dwelling has been invaded by monkeys, who climbed up the ladder during our absence."

And, at this moment, as if to bear witness to the truth of the sailor's words, two or three quadrumana showed themselves at the windows, from which they had pushed back the shutters, and saluted the real proprietors of the place with a thousand hideous grimaces.

"I knew that it was only a joke," cried Pencroft; "but one of the jokers shall pay the penalty for the rest."

So saying, the sailor, raising his piece, took a rapid aim at one of the monkeys and fired. All disappeared, except one who fell mortally wounded on the beach.

This monkey, which was of a large size, evidently belonged to the first order of the quadrumana. Whether this was a chimpanzee, an orangoutang, or a gorilla, he took rank among the anthropoid apes, who are so called from their resemblance to the human race. However, Herbert declared it to be an orangoutang.

"What a magnificent beast!" cried Neb.

"Magnificent, if you like," replied Pencroft; "but still I do not see how we are to get into our house."

"Herbert is a good marksman," said the reporter, "and his bow is here. He can try again."

"Why, these apes are so cunning," returned Pencroft; "they won't show themselves again at the windows and so we can't kill them; and when I think of the mischief they may do in the rooms and storehouse—"

"Have patience," replied Harding; "these creatures cannot keep us long at bay."

"I shall not be sure of that till I see them down here," replied the sailor. "And now, captain, do you know how many dozens of these fellows are up there?"

It was difficult to reply to Pencroft, and as for the young boy making another attempt, that was not easy; for the lower part of the ladder had been drawn again into the door, and when another pull was given, the line broke and the ladder remained firm. The case was really perplexing. Pencroft stormed. There was a comic side to the situation, but he did not think it funny at all. It was certain that the settlers would end by reinstating themselves in their domicile and driving out the intruders, but when and how? this is what they were not able to say.

Two hours passed, during which the apes took care not to show themselves, but they were still there, and three or four times a nose or a paw was poked out at the door or windows, and was immediately saluted by a gun-shot.

"Let us hide ourselves," at last said the engineer. "Perhaps the apes will think we have gone quite away and will show themselves again. Let Spilett and Herbert conceal themselves behind those rocks and fire on all that may appear."

The engineer's orders were obeyed, and while the reporter and the lad, the best marksmen in the colony, posted themselves in a good position, but out of the monkeys' sight, Neb, Pencroft, and Cyrus climbed the plateau and entered the forest in order to kill some game, for it was now time for breakfast and they had no provisions remaining.

In half an hour the hunters returned with a few rock pigeons, which they roasted as well as they could. Not an ape had appeared. Gideon Spilett and Herbert went to take their share of the breakfast, leaving Top to watch under the windows. They then, having eaten, returned to their post.

Two hours later, their situation was in no degree improved. The quadrumana gave no sign of existence, and it might have been supposed that they had disappeared; but what seemed more probable was that, terrified by the death of one of their companions, and frightened by the noise of the firearms, they had retreated to the back part of the house or probably even into the store-room. And when they thought of the valuables which this storeroom contained, the patience so much recommended by the engineer, fast changed into great irritation, and there certainly was room for it.

"Decidedly it is too bad," said the reporter; "and the worst of it is, there is no way of putting an end to it."

"But we must drive these vagabonds out somehow," cried the sailor. "We could soon get the better of them, even if there are twenty of the rascals; but for that, we must meet them hand to hand. Come now, is there no way of getting at them?"

"Let us try to enter Granite House by the old opening at the lake," replied the engineer.

"Oh!" shouted the sailor, "and I never thought of that."

This was in reality the only way by which to penetrate into Granite House so as to fight with and drive out the intruders. The opening was, it is true, closed up with a wall of cemented stones, which it would be necessary to sacrifice, but that could easily be rebuilt. Fortunately, Cyrus Harding had not as yet effected his project of hiding this opening by raising the waters of the lake, for the operation would then have taken some time.

It was already past twelve o'clock, when the colonists, well armed and provided with picks and spades, left the Chimneys, passed beneath the windows of Granite House, after telling Top to remain at his post, and began to ascend the left bank of the Mercy, so as to reach Prospect Heights.

But they had not made fifty steps in this direction, when they heard the dog barking furiously.

And all rushed down the bank again.

Arrived at the turning, they saw that the situation had changed.

In fact, the apes, seized with a sudden panic, from some unknown cause, were trying to escape. Two or three ran and clambered from one window to another with the agility of acrobats. They were not even trying to replace the ladder, by which it would have been easy to descend; perhaps in their terror they had forgotten this way of escape. The colonists, now being able to take aim without difficulty, fired. Some, wounded or killed, fell back into the rooms, uttering piercing cries. The rest, throwing themselves out, were dashed to pieces in their fall, and in a few minutes, so far as they knew, there was not a living quadrumana in Granite House.

At this moment the ladder was seen to slip over the threshold, then unroll and fall to the ground.

"Hullo!" cried the sailor, "this is queer!"

"Very strange!" murmured the engineer, leaping first up the ladder.

"Take care, captain!" cried Pencroft, "perhaps there are still some of these rascals.

"We shall soon see," replied the engineer, without stopping however.

All his companions followed him, and in a minute they had arrived at the threshold. They searched everywhere. There was no one in the rooms nor in the storehouse, which had been respected by the band of quadrumana.

"Well now, and the ladder," cried the sailor; "who can the gentleman have been who sent us that down?"

But at that moment a cry was heard, and a great orang, who had hidden himself in the passage, rushed into the room, pursued by Neb.

"Ah, the robber!" cried Pencroft.

And hatchet in hand, he was about to cleave the head of the animal, when Cyrus Harding seized his arm, saying,—

"Spare him, Pencroft."

"Pardon this rascal?"

"Yes! it was he who threw us the ladder!"

And the engineer said this in such a peculiar voice that it was difficult to know whether he spoke seriously or not.

Nevertheless, they threw themselves on the orang, who defended himself gallantly, but was soon overpowered and bound.

"There!" said Pencroft. "And what shall we make of him, now we've got him?"

"A servant!" replied Herbert.

The lad was not joking in saying this, for he knew how this intelligent race could be turned to account.

The settlers then approached the ape and gazed at it attentively. He belonged to the family of anthropoid apes, of which the facial angle is not much inferior to that of the Australians and Hottentots. It was an orangoutang, and as such, had neither the ferocity of the gorilla, nor the stupidity of the baboon. It is to this family of the anthropoid apes that so many characteristics belong which prove them to be possessed of an almost human intelligence. Employed in houses, they can wait at table, sweep rooms, brush clothes, clean boots, handle a knife, fork, and spoon properly, and even drink wine... doing everything as well as the best servant that ever walked upon two legs. Buffon possessed one of these apes, who served him for a long time as a faithful and zealous servant.

The one which had been seized in the hall of Granite House was a great fellow, six feet high, with an admirably poportioned frame, a broad chest, head of a moderate size, the facial angle reaching sixty-five degrees, round skull, projecting nose, skin covered with soft glossy hair, in short, a fine specimen of the anthropoids. His eyes, rather smaller than human eyes, sparkled with intelligence; his white teeth glittered under his mustache, and he wore a little curly brown beard.

"A handsome fellow!" said Pencroft; "if we only knew his language, we could talk to him."

"But, master," said Neb, "are you serious? Are we going to take him as a servant?"

"Yes, Neb," replied the engineer, smiling. "But you must not be jealous."

"And I hope he will make an excellent servant," added Herbert. "He appears young, and will be easy to educate, and we shall not be obliged to use force to subdue him, nor draw his teeth, as is sometimes done. He will soon grow fond of his masters if they are kind to him."

"And they will be," replied Pencroft, who had forgotten all his rancor against "the jokers."

Then, approaching the orang,—

"Well, old boy!" he asked, "how are you?"

The orang replied by a little grunt which did not show any anger.

"You wish to join the colony?" again asked the sailor. "You are going to enter the service of Captain Cyrus Harding?"

Another respondent grunt was uttered by the ape.

"And you will be satisfied with no other wages than your food?"

Third affirmative grunt.

"This conversation is slightly monotonous," observed Gideon Spilett.

"So much the better," replied Pencroft; "the best servants are those who talk the least. And then, no wages, do you hear, my boy? We will give you no wages at first, but we will double them afterwards if we are pleased with you."

Thus the colony was increased by a new member. As to his name the sailor begged that in memory of another ape which he had known, he might be called Jupiter, and Jup for short.

And so, without more ceremony, Master Jup was installed in Granite House.

Chapter 7

The settlers in Lincoln Island had now regained their dwelling, without having been obliged to reach it by the old opening, and were therefore spared the trouble of mason's work. It was certainly lucky, that at the moment they were about to set out to do so, the apes had been seized with that terror, no less sudden than inexplicable, which had driven them out of Granite House. Had the animals discovered that they were about to be attacked from another direction? This was the only explanation of their sudden retreat.

During the day the bodies of the apes were carried into the wood, where they were buried; then the settlers busied themselves in repairing the disorder caused by the intruders, disorder but not damage, for although they had turned everything in the rooms topsy-turvy, yet they had broken nothing. Neb relighted his stove, and the stores in the larder furnished a substantial repast, to which all did ample justice.

Jup was not forgotten, and he ate with relish some stonepine almonds and rhizome roots, with which he was abundantly supplied. Pencroft had unfastened his arms, but judged it best to have his legs tied until they were more sure of his submission.

Then, before retiring to rest, Harding and his companions seated round their table, discussed those plans, the execution of which was most pressing. The most important and most urgent was the establishment of a bridge over the Mercy, so as to form a communication with the southern part of the island and Granite House; then the making of an enclosure for the musmons or other woolly animals which they wished to capture.

These two projects would help to solve the difficulty as to their clothing, which was now serious. The bridge would render easy the transport of the balloon case, which would furnish them with linen, and the inhabitants of the enclosure would yield wool which would supply them with winter clothes.

As to the enclosure, it was Cyrus Harding's intention to establish it at the sources of the Red Creek, where the ruminants would find fresh and abundant pasture. The road between Prospect Heights and the sources of the stream was already partly beaten, and with a better cart than the first, the material could be easily conveyed to the spot, especially if they could manage to capture some animals to draw it.

But though there might be no inconvenience in the enclosure being so far from Granite House, it would not be the same with the poultry-yard, to which Neb called the attention of the colonists. It was indeed necessary that the birds should be close within reach of the cook, and no place appeared more favorable for the establishment of the said poultry-yard than that portion of the banks of the lake which was close to the old opening.

Water-birds would prosper there as well as others, and the couple of tinamous taken in their last excursion would be the first to be domesticated.

The next day, the 3rd of November, the new works were begun by the construction of the bridge, and all hands were required for this important task. Saws, hatchets, and hammers were shouldered by the settlers, who, now transformed into carpenters, descended to the shore.

There Pencroft observed,—

"Suppose, that during our absence, Master Jup takes it into his head to draw up the ladder which he so politely returned to us yesterday?"

"Let us tie its lower end down firmly," replied Cyrus Harding.

This was done by means of two stakes securely fixed in the sand. Then the settlers, ascending the left bank of the Mercy, soon arrived at the angle formed by the river.

There they halted, in order to ascertain if the bridge could be thrown across. The place appeared suitable.

In fact, from this spot, to Port Balloon, discovered the day before on the southern coast, there was only a distance of three miles and a half, and from the bridge to the Port, it would be easy to make a good cart-road which would render the communication between Granite House and the south of the island extremely easy.

Cyrus Harding now imparted to his companions a scheme for completely isolating Prospect Heights so as to shelter it from the attacks both of quadrupeds and quadrumana. In this way, Granite House, the Chimneys, the poultry-yard, and all the upper part of the plateau which was to be used for cultivation, would be protected against the depredations of animals. Nothing could be easier than to execute this project, and this is how the engineer intended to set to work.

The plateau was already defended on three sides by water-courses, either artificial or natural. On the northwest, by the shores of Lake Grant, from the entrance of the passage to the breach made in the banks of the lake for the escape of the water.

On the north, from this breach to the sea, by the new water-course which had hollowed out a bed for itself across the plateau and shore, above and below the fall, and it would be enough to dig the bed of this creek a little deeper to make it impracticable for animals, on all the eastern border by the sea itself, from the mouth of the aforesaid creek to the mouth of the Mercy.

Lastly, on the south, from the mouth to the turn of the Mercy where the bridge was to be established.

The western border of the plateau now remained between the turn of the river and the southern angle of the lake, a distance of about a mile, which was open to all comers. But nothing could be easier than to dig a broad deep ditch, which could be filled from the lake, and the overflow of which would throw itself by a rapid fall into the bed of the Mercy. The level of the lake would, no doubt, be somewhat lowered by this fresh discharge of its waters, but Cyrus Harding had ascertained that the volume of water in the Red Creek was considerable enough to allow of the execution of this project.

"So then," added the engineer, "Prospect Heights will become a regular island, being surrounded with water on all sides, and only communicating with the rest of our domain by the bridge which we are about to throw across the Mercy, the two little bridges already established above and below the fall; and, lastly, two other little bridges which must be constructed, one over the canal which I propose to dig, the other across to the left bank of the Mercy. Now, if these bridges can be raised at will, Prospect Heights will be guarded from any surprise."

The bridge was the most urgent work. Trees were selected, cut down, stripped of their branches, and cut into beams, joists, and planks. The end of the bridge which rested on the right bank of the Mercy was to be firm, but the other end on the left bank was to be movable, so that it might be raised by means of a counterpoise, as some canal bridges are managed.

This was certainly a considerable work, and though it was skillfully conducted, it took some time, for the Mercy at this place was eighty feet wide. It was therefore necessary to fix piles in the bed of the river so as to sustain the floor of the bridge and establish a pile-driver to act on the tops of these piles, which would thus form two arches and allow the bridge to support heavy loads.

Happily there was no want of tools with which to shape the wood, nor of iron-work to make it firm, nor of the ingenuity of a man who had a marvelous knowledge of the work, nor lastly, the zeal of his companions, who in seven months had necessarily acquired great skill in the use of their tools; and it must be said that not the least skilful was Gideon Spilett, who in dexterity almost equaled the sailor himself. "Who would ever have expected so much from a newspaper man!" thought Pencroft.

The construction of the Mercy bridge lasted three weeks of regular hard work. They even breakfasted on the scene of their labors, and the weather being magnificent, they only returned to Granite House to sleep.

During this period it may be stated that Master Jup grew more accustomed to his new masters, whose movements he always watched with very inquisitive eyes. However, as a precautionary measure, Pencroft did not as yet allow him complete liberty, rightly wishing to wait until the limits of the plateau should be settled by the projected works. Top and Jup were good friends and played willingly together, but Jup did everything solemnly.

On the 20th of November the bridge was finished. The movable part, balanced by the counterpoise, swung easily, and only a slight effort was needed to rise it; between its hinge and the last cross-bar on which it rested when closed, there existed a space of twenty feet, which was sufficiently wide to prevent any animals from crossing.

The settlers now began to talk of fetching the balloon-case, which they were anxious to place in perfect security; but to bring it, it would be necessary to take a cart to Port Balloon, and consequently, necessary to beat a road through the dense forests of the Far West. This would take some time. Also, Neb and Pencroft having gone to examine into the state of things at Port Balloon, and reported that the stock of cloth would suffer no damage in the grotto where it was stored, it was decided that the work at Prospect Heights should not be discontinued.

"That," observed Pencroft, "will enable us to establish our poultry-yard under better conditions, since we need have no fear of visits from foxes nor the attacks of other beasts."

"Then," added Neb, "we can clear the plateau, and transplant wild plants to it."

"And prepare our second corn-field!" cried the sailor with a triumphant air.

In fact, the first corn-field sown with a single grain had prospered admirably, thanks to Pencroft's care. It had produced the ten ears foretold by the engineer, and each ear containing eighty grains, the colony found itself in possession of eight hundred grains, in six months, which promised a double harvest each year.

These eight hundred grains, except fifty, which were prudently reserved, were to be sown in a new field, but with no less care than was bestowed on the single grain.

The field was prepared, then surrounded with a strong palisade, high and pointed, which quadrupeds would have found difficulty in leaping. As to birds, some scarecrows, due to Pencroft's ingenious brain, were enough to frighten them. The seven hundred and fifty grains deposited in very regular furrows were then left for nature to do the rest.

On the 21st of November, Cyrus Harding began to plan the canal which was to close the plateau on the west, from the south angle of Lake Grant to the angle of the Mercy. There was there two or three feet of vegetable earth, and below that granite. It was therefore necessary to manufacture some more nitro-glycerine, and the nitro-glycerine did its accustomed work. In less than a fortnight a ditch, twelve feet wide and six deep, was dug out in the hard ground of the plateau. A new trench was made by the same means in the rocky border of the lake, forming a small stream, to which they gave the name of Creek Glycerine, and which was thus an affluent of the Mercy. As the engineer had predicted, the level of the lake was lowered, though very slightly. To complete the enclosure the bed of the stream on the beach was considerably enlarged, and the sand supported by means of stakes.

By the end of the first fortnight of December these works were finished, and Prospect Heights—that is to say, a sort of irregular pentagon, having a perimeter of nearly four miles, surrounded by a liquid belt—was completely protected from depredators of every description.

During the month of December, the heat was very great. In spite of it, however, the settlers continued their work, and as they were anxious to possess a poultry-yard they forthwith commenced it.

It is useless to say that since the enclosing of the plateau had been completed, Master Jup had been set at liberty. He did not leave his masters, and evinced no wish to escape. He was a gentle animal, though very powerful and wonderfully active. He was already taught to make himself useful by drawing loads of wood and carting away the stones which were extracted from the bed of Creek Glycerine.

The poultry-yard occupied an area of two hundred square yards, on the southeastern bank of the lake. It was surrounded by a palisade, and in it were constructed various shelters for the birds which were to populate it. These were simply built of branches and divided into compartments, made ready for the expected guests.

The first were the two tinamous, which were not long in having a number of young ones; they had for companions half a dozen ducks, accustomed to the borders of the lake. Some belonged to the Chinese species, of which the wings open like a fan, and which by the brilliancy of their plumage rival the golden pheasants. A few days afterwards, Herbert snared a couple of gallinaceae, with spreading tails composed of long feathers, magnificent alectors, which soon became tame. As to pelicans, kingfishers, water-hens, they came of themselves to the shores of the poultry-yard, and this little community, after some disputes, cooing, screaming, clucking, ended by settling down peacefully, and increased in encouraging proportion for the future use of the colony.

Cyrus Harding, wishing to complete his performance, established a pigeon-house in a corner of the poultry-yard. There he lodged a dozen of those pigeons which frequented the rocks of the plateau. These birds soon became accustomed to returning every evening to their new dwelling, and showed more disposition to domesticate themselves than their congeners, the wood-pigeons.

Lastly, the time had come for turning the balloon-case to use, by cutting it up to make shirts and other articles; for as to keeping it in its present form, and risking themselves in a balloon filled with gas, above a sea of the limits of which they had no idea, it was not to be thought of.

It was necessary to bring the case to Granite House, and the colonists employed themselves in rendering their heavy cart lighter and more manageable. But though they had a vehicle, the moving power was yet to be found.

But did there not exist in the island some animal which might supply the place of the horse, ass, or ox? That was the question.

"Certainly," said Pencroft, "a beast of burden would be very useful to us until the captain has made a steam cart, or even an engine, for some day we shall have a railroad from Granite House to Port Balloon, with a branch line to Mount Franklin!"

One day, the 23rd of December, Neb and Top were heard shouting and barking, each apparently trying to see who could make the most noise. The settlers, who were busy at the Chimneys, ran, fearing some vexatious incident.

What did they see? Two fine animals of a large size that had imprudently ventured on the plateau, when the bridges were open. One would have said they were horses, or at least donkeys, male and female, of a fine shape, dove-colored, the legs and tail white, striped with black on the head and neck. They advanced quietly without showing any uneasiness, and gazed at the men, in whom they could not as yet recognize their future masters.

"These are onagers!" cried Herbert, "animals something between the zebra and the quagga!"

"Why not donkeys?" asked Neb.

"Because they have not long ears, and their shape is more graceful!"

"Donkeys or horses," interrupted Pencroft, "they are 'moving powers,' as the captain would say, and as such must be captured!"

The sailor, without frightening the animals, crept through the grass to the bridge over Creek Glycerine, lowered it, and the onagers were prisoners.

Now, should they seize them with violence and master them by force? No. It was decided that for a few days they should be allowed to roam freely about the plateau, where there was an abundance of grass, and the engineer immediately began to prepare a stable near the poultry-yard, in which the onagers might find food, with a good litter, and shelter during the night.

This done, the movements of the two magnificent creatures were left entirely free, and the settlers avoided even approaching them so as to terrify them. Several times, however, the onagers appeared to wish to leave the plateau, too confined for animals accustomed to the plains and forests. They were then seen following the water-barrier which everywhere presented itself before them, uttering short neighs, then galloping through the grass, and becoming calmer, they would remain entire hours gazing at the woods, from which they were cut off for ever!

In the meantime harness of vegetable fiber had been manufactured, and some days after the capture of the onagers, not only the cart was ready, but a straight road, or rather a cutting, had been made through the forests of the Far West, from the angle of the Mercy to Port Balloon. The cart might then be driven there, and towards the end of December they tried the onagers for the first time.

Pencroft had already coaxed the animals to come and eat out of his hand, and they allowed him to approach without making any difficulty, but once harnessed they reared and could with difficulty be held in. However, it was not long before they submitted to this new service, for the onager, being less refractory than the zebra, is frequently put in harness in the mountainous regions of Southern Africa, and it has even been acclimatized in Europe, under zones of a relative coolness.

On this day all the colony, except Pencroft who walked at the animals' heads, mounted the cart, and set out on the road to Port Balloon.

Of course they were jolted over the somewhat rough road, but the vehicle arrived without any accident, and was soon loaded with the case and rigging of the balloon.

At eight o'clock that evening the cart, after passing over the Mercy bridge, descended the left bank of the river, and stopped on the beach. The onagers being unharnessed, were thence led to their stable, and Pencroft before going to sleep gave vent to his feelings in a deep sigh of satisfaction that awoke all the echoes of Granite House.

Chapter 8

The first week of January was devoted to the manufacture of the linen garments required by the colony. The needles found in the box were used by sturdy if not delicate fingers, and we may be sure that what was sewn was sewn firmly.

There was no lack of thread, thanks to Cyrus Harding's idea of re-employing that which had been already used in the covering of the balloon. This with admirable patience was all unpicked by Gideon Spilett and Herbert, for Pencroft had been obliged to give this work up, as it irritated him beyond measure; but he had no equal in the sewing part of the business. Indeed, everybody knows that sailors have a remarkable aptitude for tailoring.

The cloth of which the balloon-case was made was then cleaned by means of soda and potash, obtained by the incineration of plants, in such a way that the cotton, having got rid of the varnish, resumed its natural softness and elasticity; then, exposed to the action of the atmosphere, it soon became perfectly white. Some dozen shirts and sock—the latter not knitted, of course, but made of cotton—were thus manufactured. What a comfort it was to the settlers to clothe themselves again in clean linen, which was doubtless rather rough, but they were not troubled about that! and then to go to sleep between sheets, which made the couches at Granite House into quite comfortable beds!

It was about this time also that they made boots of seal-leather, which were greatly needed to replace the shoes and boots brought from America. We may be sure that these new shoes were large enough and never pinched the feet of the wearers.

With the beginning of the year 1866 the heat was very great, but the hunting in the forests did not stand still. Agouties, peccaries, capybaras, kangaroos, game of all sorts, actually swarmed there, and Spilett and Herbert were too good marksmen ever to throw away their shot uselessly.

Cyrus Harding still recommended them to husband the ammunition, and he took measures to replace the powder and shot which had been found in the box, and which he wished to reserve for the future. How did he know where chance might one day cast his companions and himself in the event of their leaving their domain? They should, then, prepare for the unknown future by husbanding their ammunition and by substituting for it some easily renewable substance.

To replace lead, of which Harding had found no traces in the island, he employed granulated iron, which was easy to manufacture. These bullets, not having the weight of leaden bullets, were made larger, and each charge contained less, but the skill of the sportsmen made up this deficiency. As to powder, Cyrus Harding would have been able to make that also, for he had at his disposal saltpeter, sulphur, and coal; but this preparation requires extreme care, and without special tools it is difficult to produce it of a good quality. Harding preferred, therefore, to manufacture pyroxyle, that is to say gun-cotton, a substance in which cotton is not indispensable, as the elementary tissue of vegetables may be used, and this is found in an almost pure state, not only in cotton, but in the textile fiber of hemp and flax, in paper, the pith of the elder, etc. Now, the elder abounded in the island towards the mouth of Red Creek, and the colonists had already made coffee of the berries of these shrubs, which belong to the family of the caprifoliaceae.

The only thing to be collected, therefore, was elder-pith, for as to the other substance necessary for the manufacture of pyroxyle, it was only fuming azotic acid. Now, Harding having sulphuric acid at his disposal, had already been easily able to produce azotic acid by attacking the saltpeter with which nature supplied him. He accordingly resolved to manufacture and employ pyroxyle, although it has some inconveniences, that is to say, a great inequality of effect, an excessive inflammability, since it takes fire at one hundred and seventy degrees instead of two hundred and forty, and lastly, an instantaneous deflagration which might damage the firearms. On the other hand, the advantages of pyroxyle consist in this, that it is not injured by damp, that it does not make the gun-barrels dirty, and that its force is four times that of ordinary powder.

To make pyroxyle, the cotton must be immersed in the fuming azotic acid for a quarter of an hour, then washed in cold water and dried. Nothing could be more simple.

Cyrus Harding had only at his disposal the ordinary azotic acid and not the fuming or monohydrate azotic acid, that is to say, acid which emits white vapors when it comes in contact with damp air; but by substituting for the latter ordinary azotic acid, mixed, in the proportion of from three to five volumes of concentrated sulphuric acid, the engineer obtained the same result. The sportsmen of the island therefore soon had a perfectly prepared substance, which, employed discreetly, produced admirable results.

About this time the settlers cleared three acres of the plateau, and the rest was preserved in a wild state, for the benefit of the onagers. Several excursions were made into the Jacamar Wood and the forests of the Far West, and they brought back from thence a large collection of wild vegetables, spinach, cress, radishes, and turnips, which careful culture would soon improve, and which would temper the regimen on which the settlers had till then subsisted. Supplies of wood and coal were also carted. Each excursion was at the same time a means of improving the roads, which gradually became smoother under the wheels of the cart.

The rabbit-warren still continued to supply the larder of Granite House. As fortunately it was situated on the other side of Creek Glycerine, its inhabitants could not reach the plateau nor ravage the newly-made plantation. The oyster-bed among the rocks was frequently renewed and furnished excellent molluscs. Besides that, the fishing, either in the lake or the Mercy, was very profitable, for Pencroft had made some lines, armed with iron hooks, with which they frequently caught fine trout, and a species of fish whose silvery sides were speckled with yellow, and which were also extremely savory. Master Neb, who was skilled in the culinary art, knew how to vary agreeably the bill of fare. Bread alone was wanting at the table of the settlers, and as has been said, they felt this privation greatly.

The settlers hunted too the turtles which frequented the shores of Cape Mandible. At this place the beach was covered with little mounds, concealing perfectly spherical turtles' eggs, with white hard shells, the albumen of which does not coagulate as that of birds' eggs. They were hatched by the sun, and their number was naturally considerable, as each turtle can lay annually two hundred and fifty.

"A regular egg-field," observed Gideon Spilett, "and we have nothing to do but to pick them up."

But not being contented with simply the produce, they made chase after the producers, the result of which was that they were able to bring back to Granite House a dozen of these chelonians, which were really valuable from an alimentary point of view. The turtle soup, flavored with aromatic herbs, often gained well-merited praises for its preparer, Neb.

We must here mention another fortunate circumstance by which new stores for the winter were laid in. Shoals of salmon entered the Mercy, and ascended the country for several miles. It was the time at which the females, going to find suitable places in which to spawn, precede the males and make a great noise through the fresh water. A thousand of these fish, which measured about two feet and a half in length, came up the river, and a large quantity were retained by fixing dams across the stream. More than a hundred were thus taken, which were salted and stored for the time when winter, freezing up the streams, would render fishing impracticable. By this time the intelligent Jup was raised to the duty of valet. He had been dressed in a jacket, white linen breeches, and an apron, the pockets of which were his delight. The clever orang had been marvelously trained by Neb, and any one would have said that the Negro and the ape understood each other when they talked together. Jup had besides a real affection for Neb, and Neb returned it. When his services were not required, either for carrying wood or for climbing to the top of some tree, Jup passed the greatest part of his time in the kitchen, where he endeavored to imitate Neb in all that he saw him do. The black showed the greatest patience and even extreme zeal in instructing his pupil, and the pupil exhibited remarkable intelligence in profiting by the lessons he received from his master.

Judge then of the pleasure Master Jup gave to the inhabitants of Granite House when, without their having had any idea of it, he appeared one day, napkin on his arm, ready to wait at table. Quick, attentive, he acquitted himself perfectly, changing the plates, bringing dishes, pouring out water, all with a gravity which gave intense amusement to the settlers, and which enraptured Pencroft.

"Jup, some soup!"

"Jup, a little agouti!"

"Jup, a plate!"

"Jup! Good Jup! Honest Jup!"

Nothing was heard but that, and Jup without ever being disconcerted, replied to every one, watched for everything, and he shook his head in a knowing way when Pencroft, referring to his joke of the first day, said to him,—

"Decidedly, Jup, your wages must be doubled."

It is useless to say that the orang was now thoroughly domesticated at Granite House, and that he often accompanied his masters to the forest without showing any wish to leave them. It was most amusing to see him walking with a stick which Pencroft had given him, and which he carried on his shoulder like a gun. If they wished to gather some fruit from the summit of a tree, how quickly he climbed for it. If the wheel of the cart stuck in the mud, with what energy did Jup with a single heave of his shoulder put it right again.

"What a jolly fellow he is!" cried Pencroft often. "If he was as mischievous as he is good, there would be no doing anything with him!"

It was towards the end of January the colonists began their labors in the center of the island. It had been decided that a corral should be established near the sources of the Red Creek, at the foot of Mount Franklin, destined to contain the ruminants, whose presence would have been troublesome at Granite House, and especially for the musmons, who were to supply the wool for the settlers' winter garments.

Each morning, the colony, sometimes entire, but more often represented only by Harding, Herbert, and Pencroft, proceeded to the sources of the Creek, a distance of not more than five miles, by the newly beaten road to which the name of Corral Road had been given.

There a site was chosen, at the back of the southern ridge of the mountain. It was a meadow land, dotted here and there with clumps of trees, and watered by a little stream, which sprung from the slopes which closed it in on one side. The grass was fresh, and it was not too much shaded by the trees which grew about it. This meadow was to be surrounded by a palisade, high enough to prevent even the most agile animals from leaping over. This enclosure would be large enough to contain a hundred musmons and wild goats, with all the young ones they might produce.

The perimeter of the corral was then traced by the engineer, and they would then have proceeded to fell the trees necessary for the construction of the palisade, but as the opening up of the road had already necessitated the sacrifice of a considerable number, those were brought and supplied a hundred stakes, which were firmly fixed in the ground.

The construction of this corral did not take less than three weeks, for besides the palisade, Cyrus Harding built large sheds, in which the animals could take shelter. These buildings had also to be made very strong, for musmons are powerful animals, and their first fury was to be feared. The stakes, sharpened at their upper end and hardened by fire, had been fixed by means of cross-bars, and at regular distances props assured the solidity of the whole.

The corral finished, a raid had to be made on the pastures frequented by the ruminants. This was done on the 7th of February, on a beautiful summer's day, and every one took part in it. The onagers, already well trained, were ridden by Spilett and Herbert, and were of great use.

The maneuver consisted simply in surrounding the musmons and goats, and gradually narrowing the circle around them. Cyrus Harding, Pencroft, Neb, and Jup, posted themselves in different parts of the wood, while the two cavaliers and Top galloped in a radius of half a mile round the corral.

The musmons were very numerous in this part of the island. These fine animals were as large as deer; their horns were stronger than those of the ram, and their gray-colored fleece was mixed with long hair.

This hunting day was very fatiguing. Such going and coming, and running and riding and shouting! Of a hundred musmons which had been surrounded, more than two-thirds escaped, but at last, thirty of these animals and ten wild goats were gradually driven back towards the corral, the open door of which appearing to offer a means of escape, they rushed in and were prisoners.

In short, the result was satisfactory, and the settlers had no reason to complain. There was no doubt that the flock would prosper, and that at no distant time not only wool but hides would be abundant.

That evening the hunters returned to Granite House quite exhausted. However, notwithstanding their fatigue, they returned the next day to visit the corral. The prisoners had been trying to overthrow the palisade, but of course had not succeeded, and were not long in becoming more tranquil.

During the month of February, no event of any importance occurred. The daily labors were pursued methodically, and, as well as improving the roads to the corral and to Port Balloon, a third was commenced, which, starting from the enclosure, proceeded towards the western coast. The yet unknown portion of Lincoln Island was that of the wood-covered Serpentine Peninsula, which sheltered the wild beasts, from which Gideon Spilett was so anxious to clear their domain.

Before the cold season should appear the most assiduous care was given to the cultivation of the wild plants which had been transplanted from the forest to Prospect Heights. Herbert never returned from an excursion without bringing home some useful vegetable. One day, it was some specimens of the chicory tribe,

Jules Verne

the seeds of which by pressure yield an excellent oil; another, it was some common sorrel, whose antiscorbutic qualities were not to be despised; then, some of those precious tubers, which have at all times been cultivated in South America, potatoes, of which more than two hundred species are now known. The kitchen garden, now well stocked and carefully defended from the birds, was divided into small beds, where grew lettuces, kidney potatoes, sorrel, turnips, radishes, and other coneiferae. The soil on the plateau was particularly fertile, and it was hoped that the harvests would be abundant.

They had also a variety of different beverages, and so long as they did not demand wine, the most hard to please would have had no reason to complain. To the Oswego tea, and the fermented liquor extracted from the roots of the dragonnier, Harding had added a regular beer, made from the young shoots of the spruce-fir, which, after having been boiled and fermented, made that agreeable drink called by the Anglo-Americans spring-beer.

Towards the end of the summer, the poultry-yard was possessed of a couple of fine bustards, which belonged to the houbara species, characterized by a sort of feathery mantle; a dozen shovelers, whose upper mandible was prolonged on each side by a membraneous appendage; and also some magnificent cocks, similar to the Mozambique cocks, the comb, caruncle, and epidermis being black. So far, everything had succeeded, thanks to the activity of these courageous and intelligent men. Nature did much for them, doubtless; but faithful to the great precept, they made a right use of what a bountiful Providence gave them.

After the heat of these warm summer days, in the evening when their work was finished and the sea-breeze began to blow, they liked to sit on the edge of Prospect Heights, in a sort of veranda, covered with creepers, which Neb had made with his own hands. There they talked, they instructed each other, they made plans, and the rough good-humor of the sailor always amused this little world, in which the most perfect harmony had never ceased to reign.

They often spoke of their country, of their dear and great America. What was the result of the War of Secession? It could not have been greatly prolonged. Richmond had doubtless soon fallen into the hands of General Grant. The taking of the capital of the Confederates must have been the last action of this terrible struggle. Now the North had triumphed in the good cause, how welcome would have been a newspaper to the exiles in Lincoln Island! For eleven months all communication between them and the rest of their fellow-creatures had been interrupted, and in a short time the 24th of March would arrive, the anniversary of the day on which the balloon had thrown them on this unknown coast. They were then mere castaways, not even knowing how they should preserve their miserable lives from the fury of the elements! And now, thanks to the knowledge of their captain, and their own intelligence, they were regular colonists, furnished with arms, tools, and instruments; they had been able to turn to their profit the animals, plants, and minerals of the island, that is to say, the three kingdoms of Nature.

Yes; they often talked of all these things and formed still more plans.

As to Cyrus Harding he was for the most part silent, and listened to his companions more often than he spoke to them. Sometimes he smiled at Herbert's ideas or Pencroft's nonsense, but always and everywhere he pondered over those inexplicable facts, that strange enigma, of which the secret still escaped him!

Chapter 9

The weather changed during the first week of March. There had been a full moon at the commencement of the month, and the heat was excessive. The atmosphere was felt to be full of electricity, and a period of some length of tempestuous weather was to be feared.

Indeed, on the 2nd, peals of thunder were heard, the wind blew from the east, and hail rattled against the facade of Granite House like volleys of grape-shot. The door and windows were immediately closed, or everything in the rooms would have been drenched. On seeing these hailstones, some of which were the size of a pigeon's egg, Pencroft's first thought was that his cornfield was in serious danger.

He directly rushed to his field, where little green heads were already appearing, and by means of a great cloth, he managed to protect his crop.

This bad weather lasted a week, during which time the thunder rolled without cessation in the depths of the sky.

The colonists, not having any pressing work out of doors, profited by the bad weather to work at the interior of Granite House, the arrangement of which was becoming more complete from day to day. The engineer made a turning-lathe, with which he turned several articles both for the toilet and the kitchen, particularly buttons, the want of which was greatly felt. A gunrack had been made for the firearms, which were kept with extreme care, and neither tables nor cupboards were left incomplete. They sawed, they planed, they filed, they turned; and during the whole of this bad season, nothing was heard but the grinding of tools or the humming of the turning-lathe which responded to the growling of the thunder.

Master Jup had not been forgotten, and he occupied a room at the back, near the storeroom, a sort of cabin with a cot always full of good litter, which perfectly suited his taste.

"With good old Jup there is never any quarreling," often repeated Pencroft, "never any improper reply. What a servant, Neb, what a servant!"

Of course Jup was now well used to service. He brushed their clothes, he turned the spit, he waited at table, he swept the rooms, he gathered wood, and he performed another admirable piece of service which delighted Pencroft—he never went to sleep without first coming to tuck up the worthy sailor in his bed.

As to the health of the members of the colony, bipeds or bimana, quadrumana or quadrupeds, it left nothing to be desired. With their life in the open air, on this salubrious soil, under that temperate zone, working both with head and hands, they could not suppose that illness would ever attack them.

All were indeed wonderfully well. Herbert had already grown two inches in the year. His figure was forming and becoming more manly, and he promised to be an accomplished man, physically as well as morally. Besides he improved himself during the leisure hours which manual occupations left to him; he read the books found in the case; and after the practical lessons which were taught by the very necessity of their position, he found in the engineer for science, and the reporter for languages, masters who were delighted to complete his education.

The tempest ended about the 9th of March, but the sky remained covered with clouds during the whole of this last summer month. The atmosphere, violently agitated by the electric commotions, could not recover its former purity, and there was almost invariably rain and fog, except for three or four fine days on which several excursions were made. About this time the female onager gave birth to a young one which belonged to the same sex as its mother, and which throve capitally. In the corral, the flock of musmons had also increased, and several lambs already bleated in the sheds, to the great delight of Neb and Herbert, who had each their favorite among these newcomers. An attempt was also made for the domestication of the peccaries, which succeeded well. A sty was constructed under the poultry-yard, and soon contained several young ones in the way to become civilized, that is to say, to become fat under Neb's care. Master Jup, entrusted with carrying them their daily nourishment, leavings from the kitchen, etc., acquitted himself conscientiously of his task. He sometimes amused himself at the expense of his little pensioners by tweaking their tails; but this was mischief, and not wickedness, for these little twisted tails amused him like a plaything, and his instinct was that of a child. One day in this month of March, Pencroft, talking to the engineer, reminded Cyrus Harding of a promise which the latter had not as yet had time to fulfil.

"You once spoke of an apparatus which would take the place of the long ladders at Granite House, captain," said he; "won't you make it some day?"

"Nothing will be easier; but is this a really useful thing?"

"Certainly, captain. After we have given ourselves necessaries, let us think a little of luxury. For us it may be luxury, if you like, but for things it is necessary. It isn't very convenient to climb up a long ladder when one is heavily loaded."

"Well, Pencroft, we will try to please you," replied Cyrus Harding.

"But you have no machine at your disposal."

"We will make one."

"A steam machine?"

"No, a water machine."

And, indeed, to work his apparatus there was already a natural force at the disposal of the engineer which could be used without great difficulty. For this, it was enough to augment the flow of the little stream which supplied the interior of Granite House with water. The opening among the stones and grass was then increased, thus producing a strong fall at the bottom of the passage, the overflow from which escaped by the inner well. Below this fall the engineer fixed a cylinder with paddles, which was joined on the exterior with a strong cable rolled on a wheel, supporting a basket. In this way, by means of a long rope reaching to the ground, which enabled them to regulate the motive power, they could rise in the basket to the door of Granite House.

It was on the 17th of March that the lift acted for the first time, and gave universal satisfaction. Henceforward all the loads, wood, coal, provisions, and even the settlers themselves, were hoisted by this simple system, which replaced the primitive ladder, and, as may be supposed, no one thought of regretting the change. Top particularly was enchanted with this improvement, for he had not, and never could have possessed Master Jup's skill in climbing ladders, and often it was on Neb's back, or even on that of the orang that he had been obliged to make the ascent to Granite House. About this time, too, Cyrus Harding attempted to manufacture glass, and he at first put the old pottery-kiln to this new use. There were some difficulties to be encountered; but, after several fruitless attempts, he succeeded in setting up a glass manufactory, which Gideon Spilett and Herbert, his usual assistants, did not leave for several days. As to the substances used in the composition of glass, they are simply sand, chalk, and soda, either carbonate or sulphate. Now the beach supplied sand, lime supplied chalk, sea-weeds supplied soda, pyrites supplied sulphuric acid, and the ground supplied coal to heat the kiln to the wished-for temperature. Cyrus Harding thus soon had everything ready for setting to work.

The tool, the manufacture of which presented the most difficulty, was the pipe of the glass-maker, an iron tube, five or six feet long, which collects on one end the material in a state of fusion. But by means of a long, thin piece of iron rolled up like the barrel of a gun, Pencroft succeeded in making a tube soon ready for use.

On the 28th of March the tube was heated. A hundred parts of sand, thirty-five of chalk, forty of sulphate of soda, mixed with two or three parts of powdered coal, composed the substance, which was placed in crucibles. When the high temperature of the oven had reduced it to a liquid, or rather a pasty state, Cyrus Harding collected with the tube a quantity of the paste: he turned it about on a metal plate, previously arranged, so as to give it a form suitable for blowing, then he passed the tube to Herbert, telling him to blow at the other extremity.

And Herbert, swelling out his cheeks, blew so much and so well into the tube-taking care to twirl it round at the same time—that his breath dilated the glassy mass. Other quantities of the substance in a state of fusion were added to the first, and in a short time the result was a bubble which measured a foot in diameter. Harding then took the tube out of Herbert's hands, and, giving it a pendulous motion, he ended by lengthening the malleable bubble so as to give it a cylindroconic shape.

The blowing operation had given a cylinder of glass terminated by two hemispheric caps, which were easily detached by means of a sharp iron dipped in cold water; then, by the same proceeding, this cylinder was cut lengthways, and after having been rendered malleable by a second heating, it was extended on a plate and spread out with a wooden roller.

The first pane was thus manufactured, and they had only to perform this operation fifty times to have fifty panes. The windows at Granite House were soon furnished with panes; not very white, perhaps, but still sufficiently transparent.

As to bottles and tumblers, that was only play. They were satisfied with them, besides, just as they came from the end of the tube. Pencroft had asked to be allowed to "blow" in his turn, and it was great fun for him; but he blew so hard that his productions took the most ridiculous shapes, which he admired immensely.

Cyrus Harding and Herbert, while hunting one day, had entered the forest of the Far West, on the left bank of the Mercy, and, as usual, the lad was asking a thousand questions of the engineer, who answered them heartily. Now, as Harding was not a sportsman, and as, on the other side, Herbert was talking chemistry and natural philosophy, numbers of kangaroos, capybaras, and agouties came within range, which, however, escaped the lad's gun; the consequence was that the day was already advanced, and the two hunters were in danger of having made a useless excursion, when Herbert, stopping, and uttering a cry of joy, exclaimed,—

"Oh, Captain Harding, do you see that tree?" and he pointed to a shrub, rather than a tree, for it was composed of a single stem, covered with a scaly bark, which bore leaves streaked with little parallel veins.

"And what is this tree which resembles a little palm?" asked Harding.

"It is a 'cycas revoluta,' of which I have a picture in our dictionary of Natural History!" said Herbert.

"But I can't see any fruit on this shrub!" observed his companion.

"No, captain," replied Herbert; "but its stem contains a flour with which nature has provided us all ready ground."

"It is, then, the bread-tree?"

"Yes, the bread-tree."

"Well, my boy," replied the engineer, "this is a valuable discovery, since our wheat harvest is not yet ripe; I hope that you are not mistaken!"

Herbert was not mistaken: he broke the stem of a cycas, which was composed of a glandulous tissue, containing a quantity of floury pith, traversed with woody fiber, separated by rings of the same substance, arranged concentrically. With this fecula was mingled a mucilaginous juice of disagreeable flavor, but which it would be easy to get rid of by pressure. This cellular substance was regular flour of a superior quality, extremely nourishing; its exportation was formerly forbidden by the Japanese laws.

Cyrus Harding and Herbert, after having examined that part of the Far West where the cycas grew, took their bearings, and returned to Granite House, where they made known their discovery.

The next day the settlers went to collect some, and returned to Granite House with an ample supply of cycas stems. The engineer constructed a press, with which to extract the mucilaginous juice mingled with the fecula, and he obtained a large quantity of flour, which Neb soon transformed into cakes and puddings. This was not quite real wheaten bread, but it was very like it.

Now, too, the onager, the goats, and the sheep in the corral furnished daily the milk necessary to the colony. The cart, or rather a sort of light carriole which had replaced it, made frequent journeys to the corral, and when it was Pencroft's turn to go he took Jup, and let him drive, and Jup, cracking his whip, acquitted himself with his customary intelligence.

Everything prospered, as well in the corral as in Granite House, and certainly the settlers, if it had not been that they were so far from their native land, had no reason to complain. They were so well suited to this life, and were, besides, so accustomed to the island, that they could not have left its hospitable soil without regret!

And yet so deeply is the love of his country implanted in the heart of man, that if a ship had unexpectedly come in sight of the island, the colonists would have made signals, would have attracted her attention, and would have departed!

It was the 1st of April, a Sunday, Easter Day, which Harding and his companions sanctified by rest and prayer. The day was fine, such as an October day in the Northern Hemisphere might be.

All, towards the evening after dinner, were seated under the veranda on the edge of Prospect Heights, and they were watching the darkness creeping up from the horizon. Some cups of the infusion of elder-berries, which took the place of coffee, had been served by Neb. They were speaking of the island and of its isolated situation in the Pacific, which led Gideon Spilett to say,—

"My dear Cyrus, have you ever, since you possessed the sextant found in the case, again taken the position of our island?"

"No," replied the engineer.

"But it would perhaps be a good thing to do it with this instrument, which is more perfect than that which you before used."

"What is the good?" said Pencroft. "The island is quite comfortable where it is!"

"Well, who knows," returned the reporter, "who knows but that we may be much nearer inhabited land than we think?"

"We shall know to-morrow," replied Cyrus Harding, "and if it had not been for the occupations which left me no leisure, we should have known it already."

"Good!" said Pencroft. "The captain is too good an observer to be mistaken, and, if it has not moved from its place, the island is just where he put it."

"We shall see."

On the next day, therefore, by means of the sextant, the engineer made the necessary observations to verify the position which he had already obtained, and this was the result of his operation. His first observation had given him the situation of Lincoln Island,—

In west longitude: from 1500 to 1550;

In south latitude: from 300 to 350

   The second gave exactly:

In longitude: 1500 30'

In south latitude: 340 57'

So then, notwithstanding the imperfection of his apparatus, Cyrus Harding had operated with so much skill that his error did not exceed five degrees.

"Now," said Gideon Spilett, "since we possess an atlas as well as a sextant, let us see, my dear Cyrus, the exact position which Lincoln Island occupies in the Pacific."

Herbert fetched the atlas, and the map of the Pacific was opened, and the engineer, compass in hand, prepared to determine their position.

Suddenly the compasses stopped, and he exclaimed,

"But an island exists in this part of the Pacific already!"

"An island?" cried Pencroft.

"Tabor Island."

"An important island?"

"No, an islet lost in the Pacific, and which perhaps has never been visited."

"Well, we will visit it," said Pencroft.

"We?"

"Yes, captain. We will build a decked boat, and I will undertake to steer her. At what distance are we from this Tabor Island?"

"About a hundred and fifty miles to the northeast," replied Harding.

"A hundred and fifty miles! And what's that?" returned Pencroft. "In forty-eight hours, with a good wind, we should sight it!"

And, on this reply, it was decided that a vessel should be constructed in time to be launched towards the month of next October, on the return of the fine season.

Chapter 10

When Pencroft had once got a plan in his head, he had no peace till it was executed. Now he wished to visit Tabor Island, and as a boat of a certain size was necessary for this voyage, he determined to build one.

What wood should he employ? Elm or fir, both of which abounded in the island? They decided for the fir, as being easy to work, but which stands water as well as the elm.

These details settled, it was agreed that since the fine season would not return before six months, Cyrus Harding and Pencroft should work alone at the boat. Gideon Spilett and Herbert were to continue to hunt, and neither Neb nor Master Jup, his assistant, were to leave the domestic duties which had devolved upon them.

Directly the trees were chosen, they were felled, stripped of their branches, and sawn into planks as well as sawyers would have been able to do it. A week after, in the recess between the Chimneys and the cliff, a dockyard was prepared, and a keel five-and-thirty feet long, furnished with a stern-post at the stern and a stem at the bows, lay along the sand.

Cyrus Harding was not working in the dark at this new trade. He knew as much about ship-building as about nearly everything else, and he had at first drawn the model of his ship on paper. Besides, he was ably seconded by Pencroft, who, having worked for several years in a dockyard in Brooklyn, knew the practical part of the trade. It was not until after careful calculation and deep thought that the timbers were laid on the keel.

Pencroft, as may be believed, was all eagerness to carry out his new enterprise, and would not leave his work for an instant.

A single thing had the honor of drawing him, but for one day only, from his dockyard. This was the second wheat-harvest, which was gathered in on the 15th of April. It was as much a success as the first, and yielded the number of grains which had been predicted.

"Five bushels, captain," said Pencroft, alter having scrupulously measured his treasure.

"Five bushels," replied the engineer; "and a hundred and thirty thousand grains a bushel will make six hundred and fifty thousand grains."

"Well, we will sow them all this time," said the sailor, "except a little in reserve."

"Yes, Pencroft, and if the next crop gives a proportionate yield, we shall have four thousand bushels."

"And shall we eat bread?"

"We shall eat bread."

"But we must have a mill."

"We will make one."

The third corn-field was very much larger than the two first, and the soil, prepared with extreme care, received the precious seed. That done, Pencroft returned to his work.

During this time Spilett and Herbert hunted in the neighborhood, and they ventured deep into the still unknown parts of the Far West, their guns loaded with ball, ready for any dangerous emergency. It was a vast thicket of magnificent trees, crowded together as if pressed for room. The exploration of these dense masses of wood was difficult in the extreme, and the reporter never ventured there without the pocket-compass, for the sun scarcely pierced through the thick foliage and it would have been very difficult for them to retrace their way. It naturally happened that game was more rare in those situations where there was hardly sufficient room to move; two or three large herbivorous animals were however killed during the last fortnight of April. These were koalas, specimens of which the settlers had already seen to the north of the lake, and which stupidly allowed themselves to be killed among the thick branches of the trees in which they took refuge. Their skins were brought back to Granite House, and there, by the help of sulphuric acid, they were subjected to a sort of tanning process which rendered them capable of being used.

On the 30th of April, the two sportsmen were in the depth of the Far West, when the reporter, preceding Herbert a few paces, arrived in a sort of clearing, into which the trees more sparsely scattered had permitted a few rays to penetrate. Gideon Spilett was at first surprised at the odor which exhaled from certain plants with straight stalks, round and branchy, bearing grape-like clusters of flowers and very small berries. The reporter broke off one or two of these stalks and returned to the lad, to whom he said,—

"What can this be, Herbert?"

"Well, Mr. Spilett," said Herbert, "this is a treasure which will secure you Pencroft's gratitude forever."

"Is it tobacco?"

"Yes, and though it may not be of the first quality, it is none the less tobacco!"

"Oh, good old Pencroft! Won't he be pleased! But we must not let him smoke it all, he must give us our share."

"Ah! an idea occurs to me, Mr. Spilett," replied Herbert. "Don't let us say anything to Pencroft yet; we will prepare these leaves, and one fine day we will present him with a pipe already filled!"

"All right, Herbert, and on that day our worthy companion will have nothing left to wish for in this world."

The reporter and the lad secured a good store of the precious plant, and then returned to Granite House, where they smuggled it in with as much precaution as if Pencroft had been the most vigilant and severe of custom-house officers.

Cyrus Harding and Neb were taken into confidence, and the sailor suspected nothing during the whole time, necessarily somewhat long, which was required in order to dry the small leaves, chop them up, and subject them to a certain torrefaction on hot stones. This took two months; but all these manipulations were successfully carried on unknown to Pencroft, for, occupied with the construction of his boat, he only returned to Granite House at the hour of rest.

For some days they had observed an enormous animal two or three miles out in the open sea swimming around Lincoln Island. This was a whale of the largest size, which apparently belonged to the southern species, called the "Cape Whale."

"What a lucky chance it would be if we could capture it!" cried the sailor. "Ah! if we only had a proper boat and a good harpoon, I would say 'After the beast,' for he would be well worth the trouble of catching!"

"Well, Pencroft," observed Harding, "I should much like to watch you handling a harpoon. It would be very interesting."

"I am astonished," said the reporter, "to see a whale in this comparatively high latitude."

"Why so, Mr. Spilett?" replied Herbert. "We are exactly in that part of the Pacific which English and American whalemen call the whale field, and it is here, between New Zealand and South America, that the whales of the Southern Hemisphere are met with in the greatest numbers."

And Pencroft returned to his work, not without uttering a sigh of regret, for every sailor is a born fisherman, and if the pleasure of fishing is in exact proportion to the size of the animal, one can judge how a whaler feels in sight of a whale. And if this had only been for pleasure! But they could not help feeling how valuable such a prize would have been to the colony, for the oil, fat, and bones would have been put to many uses.

Now it happened that this whale appeared to have no wish to leave the waters of the island. Therefore, whether from the windows of Granite House, or from Prospect Heights, Herbert and Gideon Spilett, when they were not hunting, or Neb, unless presiding over his fires, never left the telescope, but watched all the animal's movements. The cetacean, having entered far into Union Bay, made rapid furrows across it from Mandible Cape to Claw Cape, propelled by its enormously powerful flukes, on which it supported itself, and making its way through the water at the rate little short of twelve knots an hour. Sometimes also it approached so near to the island that it could be clearly distinguished. It was the southern whale, which is completely black, the head being more depressed than that of the northern whale.

They could also see it throwing up from its air-holes to a great height a cloud of vapor, or of water, for, strange as it may appear, naturalists and whalers are not agreed on this subject. Is it air or is it water which is thus driven out? It is generally admitted to be vapor, which, condensing suddenly by contact with the cold air, falls again as rain.

However, the presence of this mammifer preoccupied the colonists. It irritated Pencroft especially, as he could think of nothing else while at work. He ended by longing for it, like a child for a thing which it has been denied. At night he talked about it in his sleep, and certainly if he had had the means of attacking it, if the sloop had been in a fit state to put to sea, he would not have hesitated to set out in pursuit.

But what the colonists could not do for themselves chance did for them, and on the 3rd of May shouts from Neb, who had stationed himself at the kitchen window, announced that the whale was stranded on the beach of the island.

Herbert and Gideon Spilett, who were just about to set out hunting, left their guns, Pencroft threw down his ax, and Harding and Neb joining their companions, all rushed towards the scene of action.

The stranding had taken place on the beach of Flotsam Point, three miles from Granite House, and at high tide. It was therefore probable that the cetacean would not be able to extricate itself easily; at any rate it was best to hasten, so as to cut off its retreat if necessary. They ran with pick-axes and iron-tipped poles in their hands, passed over the Mercy bridge, descended the right bank of the river, along the beach, and in less than twenty minutes the settlers were close to the enormous animal, above which flocks of birds already hovered.

"What a monster!" cried Neb.

And the exclamation was natural, for it was a southern whale, eighty feet long, a giant of the species, probably not weighing less than a hundred and fifty thousand pounds!

In the meanwhile, the monster thus stranded did not move, nor attempt by struggling to regain the water while the tide was still high.

It was dead, and a harpoon was sticking out of its left side.

"There are whalers in these quarters, then?" said Gideon Spilett directly.

"Oh, Mr. Spilett, that doesn't prove anything!" replied Pencroft. "Whales have been known to go thousands of miles with a harpoon in the side, and this one might even have been struck in the north of the Atlantic and come to die in the south of the Pacific, and it would be nothing astonishing."

Pencroft, having torn the harpoon from the animal's side, read this inscription on it:

MARIA STELLA, VINEYARD

"A vessel from the Vineyard! A ship from my country!" he cried. "The 'Maria Stella!' A fine whaler, 'pon my word; I know her well! Oh, my friends, a vessel from the Vineyard!—a whaler from the Vineyard!"

And the sailor brandishing the harpoon, repeated, not without emotion, the name which he loved so well—the name of his birthplace.

But as it could not be expected that the "Maria Stella" would come to reclaim the animal harpooned by her, they resolved to begin cutting it up before decomposition should commence. The birds, who had watched this rich prey for several days, had determined to take possession of it without further delay, and it was necessary to drive them off by firing at them repeatedly.

The whale was a female, and a large quantity of milk was taken from it, which, according to the opinion of the naturalist Duffenbach, might pass for cow's milk, and, indeed, it differs from it neither in taste, color, nor density.

Pencroft had formerly served on board a whaling-ship, and he could methodically direct the operation of cutting up, a sufficiently disagreeable operation lasting three days, but from which the settlers did not flinch, not even Gideon Spilett, who, as the sailor said, would end by making a "real good castaway."

The blubber, cut in parallel slices of two feet and a half in thickness, then divided into pieces which might weigh about a thousand pounds each, was melted down in large earthen pots brought to the spot, for they did not wish to taint the environs of Granite House, and in this fusion it lost nearly a third of its weight.

But there was an immense quantity of it; the tongue alone yielded six thousand pounds of oil, and the lower lip four thousand. Then, besides the fat, which would insure for a long time a store of stearine and glycerine, there were still the bones, for which a use could doubtless be found, although there were neither umbrellas nor stays used at Granite House. The upper part of the mouth of the cetacean was, indeed, provided on both sides with eight hundred horny blades, very elastic, of a fibrous texture, and fringed at the edge like great combs, at which the teeth, six feet long, served to retain the thousands of animalculae, little fish, and molluscs, on which the whale fed.

The operation finished, to the great satisfaction of the operators, the remains of the animal were left to the birds, who would soon make every vestige of it disappear, and their usual daily occupations were resumed by the inmates of Granite House.

However, before returning to the dockyard, Cyrus Harding conceived the idea of fabricating certain machines, which greatly excited the curiosity of his companions. He took a dozen of the whale's bones, cut them into six equal parts, and sharpened their ends.

"This machine is not my own invention, and it is frequently employed by the Aleutian hunters in Russian America. You see these bones, my friends; well, when it freezes, I will bend them, and then wet them with water till they are entirely covered with ice, which will keep them bent, and I will strew them on the snow, having previously covered them with fat. Now, what will happen if a hungry animal swallows one of these baits? Why, the heat of his stomach will melt the ice, and the bone, springing straight, will pierce him with its sharp points."

"Well! I do call that ingenious!" said Pencroft.

"And it will spare the powder and shot," rejoined Cyrus Harding.

"That will be better than traps!" added Neb.

In the meanwhile the boat-building progressed, and towards the end of the month half the planking was completed. It could already be seen that her shape was excellent, and that she would sail well.

Pencroft worked with unparalleled ardor, and only a sturdy frame could have borne such fatigue; but his companions were preparing in secret a reward for his labors, and on the 31st of May he was to meet with one of the greatest joys of his life.

On that day, after dinner, just as he was about to leave the table, Pencroft felt a hand on his shoulder.

It was the hand of Gideon Spilett, who said,—

"One moment, Master Pencroft, you mustn't sneak off like that! You've forgotten your dessert."

"Thank you, Mr. Spilett," replied the sailor, "I am going back to my work."

"Well, a cup of coffee, my friend?"

"Nothing more."

"A pipe, then?"

Pencroft jumped up, and his great good-natured face grew pale when he saw the reporter presenting him with a ready-filled pipe, and Herbert with a glowing coal.

The sailor endeavored to speak, but could not get out a word; so, seizing the pipe, he carried it to his lips, then applying the coal, he drew five or six great whiffs. A fragrant blue cloud soon arose, and from its depths a voice was heard repeating excitedly,—

"Tobacco! real tobacco!"

"Yes, Pencroft," returned Cyrus Harding, "and very good tobacco too!"

"O, divine Providence; sacred Author of all things!" cried the sailor. "Nothing more is now wanting to our island."

And Pencroft smoked, and smoked, and smoked.

"And who made this discovery?" he asked at length. "You, Herbert, no doubt?"

"No, Pencroft, it was Mr. Spilett."

"Mr. Spilett!" exclaimed the sailor, seizing the reporter, and clasping him to his breast with such a squeeze that he had never felt anything like it before.

"Oh Pencroft," said Spilett, recovering his breath at last, "a truce for one moment. You must share your gratitude with Herbert, who recognized the plant, with Cyrus, who prepared it, and with Neb, who took a great deal of trouble to keep our secret."

"Well, my friends, I will repay you some day," replied the sailor. "Now we are friends for life."

Chapter 11

Winter arrived with the month of June, which is the December of the northern zones, and the great business was the making of warm and solid clothing.

The musmons in the corral had been stripped of their wool, and this precious textile material was now to be transformed into stuff.

Of course Cyrus Harding, having at his disposal neither carders, combers, polishers, stretchers, twisters, mule-jenny, nor self-acting machine to spin the wool, nor loom to weave it, was obliged to proceed in a simpler way, so as to do without spinning and weaving. And indeed he proposed to make use of the property which the filaments of wool possess when subjected to a powerful pressure of mixing together, and of manufacturing by this simple process the material called felt. This felt could then be obtained by a simple operation which, if it diminished the flexibility of the stuff, increased its power of retaining heat in proportion. Now the wool furnished by the musmons was composed of very short hairs, and was in a good condition to be felted.

The engineer, aided by his companions, including Pencroft, who was once more obliged to leave his boat, commenced the preliminary operations, the subject of which was to rid the wool of that fat and oily substance with which it is impregnated, and which is called grease. This cleaning was done in vats filled with water, which was maintained at the temperature of seventy degrees, and in which the wool was soaked for four-and-twenty hours; it was then thoroughly washed in baths of soda, and, when sufficiently dried by pressure, it was in a state to be compressed, that is to say, to produce a solid material, rough, no doubt, and such as would have no value in a manufacturing center of Europe or America, but which would be highly esteemed in the Lincoln Island markets.

This sort of material must have been known from the most ancient times, and, in fact, the first woolen stuffs were manufactured by the process which Harding was now about to employ. Where Harding's engineering qualifications now came into play was in the construction of the machine for pressing the wool; for he knew how to turn ingeniously to profit the mechanical force, hitherto unused, which the waterfall on the beach possessed to move a fulling-mill.

Nothing could be more rudimentary. The wool was placed in troughs, and upon it fell in turns heavy wooden mallets; such was the machine in question, and such it had been for centuries until the time when the mallets were replaced by cylinders of compression, and the material was no longer subjected to beating, but to regular rolling.

The operation, ably directed by Cyrus Harding, was a complete success. The wool, previously impregnated with a solution of soap, intended on the one hand to facilitate the interlacing, the compression, and the softening of the wool, and on the other to prevent its diminution by the beating, issued from the mill in the shape of thick felt cloth. The roughnesses with which the staple of wool is naturally filled were so thoroughly entangled and interlaced together that a material was formed equally suitable either for garments or bedclothes. It was certainly neither merino, muslin, cashmere, rep, satin, alpaca, cloth, nor flannel. It was "Lincolnian felt," and Lincoln Island possessed yet another manufacture.

The colonists had now warm garments and thick bedclothes, and they could without fear await the approach of the winter of 1866-67.

The severe cold began to be felt about the 20th of June, and, to his great regret, Pencroft was obliged to suspend his boat-building, which he hoped to finish in time for next spring.

The sailor's great idea was to make a voyage of discovery to Tabor Island, although Harding could not approve of a voyage simply for curiosity's sake, for there was evidently nothing to be found on this desert and almost arid rock. A voyage of a hundred and fifty miles in a comparatively small vessel, over unknown seas, could not but cause him some anxiety. Suppose that their vessel, once out at sea, should be unable to reach Tabor Island, and could not return to Lincoln Island, what would become of her in the midst of the Pacific, so fruitful of disasters?

Harding often talked over this project with Pencroft, and he found him strangely bent upon undertaking this voyage, for which determination he himself could give no sufficient reason.

"Now," said the engineer one day to him, "I must observe, my friend, that after having said so much, in praise of Lincoln Island, after having spoken so often of the sorrow you would feel if you were obliged to forsake it, you are the first to wish to leave it."

"Only to leave it for a few days," replied Pencroft, "only for a few days, captain. Time to go and come back, and see what that islet is like!"

"But it is not nearly as good as Lincoln Island."

"I know that beforehand."

"Then why venture there?"

"To know what is going on in Tabor Island."

"But nothing is going on there; nothing could happen there."

"Who knows?"

"And if you are caught in a hurricane?"

"There is no fear of that in the fine season," replied Pencroft. "But, captain, as we must provide against everything, I shall ask your permission to take Herbert only with me on this voyage."

"Pencroft," replied the engineer, placing his hand on the sailor's shoulder, "if any misfortune happens to you, or to this lad, whom chance has made our child, do you think we could ever cease to blame ourselves?"

"Captain Harding," replied Pencroft, with unshaken confidence, "we shall not cause you that sorrow. Besides, we will speak further of this voyage, when the time comes to make it. And I fancy, when you have seen our tight-rigged little craft, when you have observed how she behaves at sea, when we sail round our island, for we will do so together—I fancy, I say, that you will no longer hesitate to let me go. I don't conceal from you that your boat will be a masterpiece."

"Say 'our' boat, at least, Pencroft," replied the engineer, disarmed for the moment. The conversation ended thus, to be resumed later on, without convincing either the sailor or the engineer.

The first snow fell towards the end of the month of June. The corral had previously been largely supplied with stores, so that daily visits to it were not requisite; but it was decided that more than a week should never be allowed to pass without someone going to it.

Traps were again set, and the machines manufactured by Harding were tried. The bent whalebones, imprisoned in a case of ice, and covered with a thick outer layer of fat, were placed on the border of the forest at a spot where animals usually passed on their way to the lake.

To the engineer's great satisfaction, this invention, copied from the Aleutian fishermen, succeeded perfectly. A dozen foxes, a few wild boars, and even a jaguar, were taken in this way, the animals being found dead, their stomachs pierced by the unbent bones.

An incident must here be related, not only as interesting in itself, but because it was the first attempt made by the colonists to communicate with the rest of mankind.

Gideon Spilett had already several times pondered whether to throw into the sea a letter enclosed in a bottle, which currents might perhaps carry to an inhabited coast, or to confide it to pigeons.

But how could it be seriously hoped that either pigeons or bottles could cross the distance of twelve hundred miles which separated the island from any inhabited land? It would have been pure folly.

But on the 30th of June the capture was effected, not without difficulty, of an albatross, which a shot from Herbert's gun had slightly wounded in the foot. It was a magnificent bird, measuring ten feet from wing to wing, and which could traverse seas as wide as the Pacific.

Herbert would have liked to keep this superb bird, as its wound would soon heal, and he thought he could tame it; but Spilett explained to him that they should not neglect this opportunity of attempting to communicate by this messenger with the lands of the Pacific; for if the albatross had come from some inhabited region, there was no doubt but that it would return there so soon as it was set free.

Perhaps in his heart Gideon Spilett, in whom the journalist sometimes came to the surface, was not sorry to have the opportunity of sending forth to take its chance an exciting article relating the adventures of the settlers in Lincoln Island. What a success for the authorized reporter of the New York Herald, and for the number which should contain the article, if it should ever reach the address of its editor, the Honorable James Bennett!

Gideon Spilett then wrote out a concise account, which was placed in a strong waterproof bag, with an earnest request to whoever might find it to forward it to the office of the New York Herald. This little bag was fastened to the neck of the albatross, and not to its foot, for these birds are in the habit of resting on the surface of the sea; then liberty was given to this swift courier of the air, and it was not without some emotion that the colonists watched it disappear in the misty west.

"Where is he going to?" asked Pencroft.

"Towards New Zealand," replied Herbert.

"A good voyage to you," shouted the sailor, who himself did not expect any great result from this mode of correspondence.

With the winter, work had been resumed in the interior of Granite House, mending clothes and different occupations, among others making the sails for their vessel, which were cut from the inexhaustible balloon-case.

During the month of July the cold was intense, but there was no lack of either wood or coal. Cyrus Harding had established a second fireplace in the dining-room, and there the long winter evenings were spent. Talking while they worked, reading when the hands remained idle, the time passed with profit to all.

It was real enjoyment to the settlers when in their room, well lighted with candles, well warmed with coal, after a good dinner, elderberry coffee smoking in the cups, the pipes giving forth an odoriferous smoke, they could hear the storm howling without. Their comfort would have been complete, if complete comfort could ever exist for those who are far from their fellow-creatures, and without any means of communication with them. They often talked of their country, of the friends whom they had left, of the grandeur of the American Republic, whose influence could not but increase; and Cyrus Harding, who had been much mixed up with the affairs of the Union, greatly interested his auditors by his recitals, his views, and his prognostics.

It chanced one day that Spilett was led to say—

"But now, my dear Cyrus, all this industrial and commercial movement to which you predict a continual advance, does it not run the danger of being sooner or later completely stopped?"

"Stopped! And by what?"

"By the want of coal, which may justly be called the most precious of minerals."

"Yes, the most precious indeed," replied the engineer; "and it would seem that nature wished to prove that it was so by making the diamond, which is simply pure carbon crystallized."

"You don't mean to say, captain," interrupted Pencroft, "that we burn diamonds in our stoves in the shape of coal?"

"No, my friend," replied Harding.

"However," resumed Gideon Spilett, "you do not deny that some day the coal will be entirely consumed?"

"Oh! the veins of coal are still considerable, and the hundred thousand miners who annually extract from them a hundred millions of hundredweights have not nearly exhausted them."

"With the increasing consumption of coal," replied Gideon Spilett, "it can be foreseen that the hundred thousand workmen will soon become two hundred thousand, and that the rate of extraction will be doubled."

"Doubtless; but after the European mines, which will be soon worked more thoroughly with new machines, the American and Australian mines will for a long time yet provide for the consumption in trade."

"For how long a time?" asked the reporter.

"For at least two hundred and fifty or three hundred years."

"That is reassuring for us, but a bad look-out for our great-grandchildren!" observed Pencroft.

"They will discover something else," said Herbert.

"It is to be hoped so," answered Spilett, "for without coal there would be no machinery, and without machinery there would be no railways, no steamers, no manufactures, nothing of that which is indispensable to modern civilization!"

"But what will they find?" asked Pencroft. "Can you guess, captain?"

"Nearly, my friend."

"And what will they burn instead of coal?"

"Water," replied Harding.

"Water!" cried Pencroft, "water as fuel for steamers and engines! water to heat water!"

"Yes, but water decomposed into its primitive elements," replied Cyrus Harding, "and decomposed doubtless, by electricity, which will then have become a powerful and manageable force, for all great discoveries, by some inexplicable laws, appear to agree and become complete at the same time. Yes, my friends, I believe that water will one day be employed as fuel, that hydrogen and oxygen which constitute it, used singly or together, will furnish an inexhaustible source of heat and light, of an intensity of which coal is not capable. Some day the coalrooms of steamers and the tenders of locomotives will, instead of coal, be stored with these two condensed gases, which will burn in the furnaces with enormous calorific power. There is, therefore, nothing to fear. As long as the earth is inhabited it will supply the wants of its inhabitants, and there will be no want of either light or heat as long as the productions of the vegetable, mineral or animal kingdoms do not fail us. I believe, then, that when the deposits of coal are exhausted we shall heat and warm ourselves with water. Water will be the coal of the future."

"I should like to see that," observed the sailor.

"You were born too soon, Pencroft," returned Neb, who only took part in the discussion by these words.

However, it was not Neb's speech which interrupted the conversation, but Top's barking, which broke out again with that strange intonation which had before perplexed the engineer. At the same time Top began to run round the mouth of the well, which opened at the extremity of the interior passage.

"What can Top be barking in that way for?" asked Pencroft.

"And Jup be growling like that?" added Herbert.

In fact the orang, joining the dog, gave unequivocal signs of agitation, and, singular to say, the two animals appeared more uneasy than angry.

"It is evident," said Gideon Spilett, "that this well is in direct communication with the sea, and that some marine animal comes from time to time to breathe at the bottom."

"That's evident," replied the sailor, "and there can be no other explanation to give. Quiet there, Top!" added Pencroft, turning to the dog, "and you, Jup, be off to your room!"

The ape and the dog were silent. Jup went off to bed, but Top remained in the room, and continued to utter low growls at intervals during the rest of the evening. There was no further talk on the subject, but the incident, however, clouded the brow of the engineer.

During the remainder of the month of July there was alternate rain and frost. The temperature was not so low as during the preceding winter, and its maximum did not exceed eight degrees Fahrenheit. But although this winter was less cold, it was more troubled by storms and squalls; the sea besides often endangered the safety of the Chimneys. At times it almost seemed as if an under-current raised these monstrous billows which thundered against the wall of Granite House.

When the settlers, leaning from their windows, gazed on the huge watery masses breaking beneath their eyes, they could not but admire the magnificent spectacle of the ocean in its impotent fury. The waves rebounded in dazzling foam, the beach entirely disapppearing under the raging flood, and the cliff appearing to emerge from the sea itself, the spray rising to a height of more than a hundred feet.

During these storms it was difficult and even dangerous to venture out, owing to the frequently falling trees; however, the colonists never allowed a week to pass without having paid a visit to the corral. Happily, this enclosure, sheltered by the southeastern spur of Mount Franklin, did not greatly suffer from the violence of the hurricanes, which spared its trees, sheds, and palisades; but the poultry-yard on Prospect Heights, being directly exposed to the gusts of wind from the east, suffered considerable damage. The pigeon-house was twice unroofed and the paling blown down. All this required to be remade more solidly than before, for, as may be clearly seen, Lincoln Island was situated in one of the most dangerous parts of the Pacific. It really appeared as if it formed the central point of vast cyclones, which beat it perpetually as the whip does the top, only here it was the top which was motionless and the whip which moved. During the first week of the month of August the weather became more moderate, and the atmosphere recovered the calm which it appeared to have lost forever. With the calm the cold again became intense, and the thermometer fell to eight degrees Fahrenheit, below zero.

On the 3rd of August an excursion which had been talked of for several days was made into the southeastern part of the island, towards Tadorn Marsh. The hunters were tempted by the aquatic game which took up their winter quarters there. Wild duck, snipe, teal and grebe abounded there, and it was agreed that a day should be devoted to an expedition against these birds.

Not only Gideon Spilett and Herbert, but Pencroft and Neb also took part in this excursion. Cyrus Harding alone, alleging some work as an excuse, did not join them, but remained at Granite House.

The hunters proceeded in the direction of Port Balloon, in order to reach the marsh, after having promised to be back by the evening. Top and Jup accompanied them. As soon as they had passed over the Mercy Bridge, the engineer raised it and returned, intending to put into execution a project for the performance of which he wished to be alone.

Now this project was to minutely explore the interior well, the mouth of which was on a level with the passage of Granite House, and which communicated with the sea, since it formerly supplied a way to the waters of the lake.

Why did Top so often run round this opening? Why did he utter such strange barks when a sort of uneasiness seemed to draw him towards this well? Why did Jup join Top in a sort of common anxiety? Had this well branches besides the communication with the sea? Did it spread towards other parts of the island? This is what Cyrus Harding wished to know. He had resolved, therefore, to attempt the exploration of the well during the absence of his companions, and an opportunity for doing so had now presented itself.

It was easy to descend to the bottom of the well by employing the rope ladder which had not been used since the establishment of the lift. The engineer drew the ladder to the hole, the diameter of which measured nearly six feet, and allowed it to unroll itself after having securely fastened its upper extremity. Then, having lighted a lantern, taken a revolver, and placed a cutlass in his belt, he began the descent.

The sides were everywhere entire; but points of rock jutted out here and there, and by means of these points it would have been quite possible for an active creature to climb to the mouth of the well.

The engineer remarked this; but although he carefully examined these points by the light of his lantern, he could find no impression, no fracture which could give any reason to suppose that they had either recently or at any former time been used as a staircase. Cyrus Harding descended deeper, throwing the light of his lantern on all sides.

He saw nothing suspicious.

When the engineer had reached the last rounds he came upon the water, which was then perfectly calm. Neither at its level nor in any other part of the well, did any passage open, which could lead to the interior of the cliff. The wall which Harding struck with the hilt of his cutlass sounded solid. It was compact granite, through which no living being could force a way. To arrive at the bottom of the well and then climb up to its mouth it was necessary to pass through the channel under the rocky subsoil of the beach, which placed it in communication with the sea, and this was only possible for marine animals. As to the question of knowing where this channel ended, at what point of the shore, and at what depth beneath the water, it could not be answered.

Then Cyrus Harding, having ended his survey, re-ascended, drew up the ladder, covered the mouth of the well, and returned thoughtfully to the diningroom, saying to himself,—

"I have seen nothing, and yet there is something there!"

Chapter 12

In the evening the hunters returned, having enjoyed good sport, and being literally loaded with game; indeed, they had as much as four men could possibly carry. Top wore a necklace of teal and Jup wreaths of snipe round his body.

"Here, master," cried Neb; "here's something to employ our time! Preserved and made into pies we shall have a welcome store! But I must have some one to help me. I count on you, Pencroft."

"No, Neb," replied the sailor; "I have the rigging of the vessel to finish and to look after, and you will have to do without me."

"And you, Mr. Herbert?"

"I must go to the corral to-morrow, Neb," replied the lad.

"It will be you then, Mr. Spilett, who will help me?"

"To oblige you, Neb, I will," replied the reporter; "but I warn you that if you disclose your receipts to me, I shall publish them."

"Whenever you like, Mr. Spilett," replied Neb; "whenever you like."

And so the next day Gideon Spilett became Neb's assistant and was installed in his culinary laboratory. The engineer had previously made known to him the result of the exploration which he had made the day before, and on this point the reporter shared Harding's opinion, that although he had found nothing, a secret still remained to be discovered!

The frost continued for another week, and the settlers did not leave Granite House unless to look after the poultry-yard. The dwelling was filled with appetizing odors, which were emitted from the learned manipulation of Neb and the reporter. But all the results of the chase were not made into preserved provisions; and as the game kept perfectly in the intense cold, wild duck and other fowl were eaten fresh, and declared superior to all other aquatic birds in the known world.

During this week, Pencroft, aided by Herbert, who handled the sailmaker's needle with much skill, worked with such energy that the sails of the vessel were finished. There was no want of cordage. Thanks to the rigging which had been discovered with the case of the balloon, the ropes and cables from the net were all of good quality, and the sailor turned them all to account. To the sails were attached strong bolt ropes, and there still remained enough from which to make the halyards, shrouds, and sheets, etc. The blocks were manufactured by Cyrus Harding under Pencroft's directions by means of the turning lathe. It therefore happened that the rigging was entirely prepared before the vessel was finished. Pencroft also manufactured a flag, that flag so dear to every true American, containing the stars and stripes of their glorious Union. The colors for it were supplied from certain plants used in dyeing, and which were very abundant in the island; only to the thirty-seven stars, representing the thirty-seven States of the Union, which shine on the American flag, the sailor added a thirty-eighth, the star of "the State of Lincoln," for he considered his island as already united to the great republic. "And," said he, "it is so already in heart, if not in deed!"

In the meantime, the flag was hoisted at the central window of Granite House, and the settlers saluted it with three cheers.

The cold season was now almost at an end, and it appeared as if this second winter was to pass without any unusual occurrence, when on the night of the 11th of August, the plateau of Prospect Heights was menaced with complete destruction.

After a busy day the colonists were sleeping soundly, when towards four o'clock in the morning they were suddenly awakened by Top's barking.

The dog was not this time barking near the mouth of the well, but at the threshold of the door, at which he was scratching as if he wished to burst it open. Jup was also uttering piercing cries.

"Hello, Top!" cried Neb, who was the first awake. But the dog continued to bark more furiously than ever.

"What's the matter now?" asked Harding.

And all dressing in haste rushed to the windows, which they opened.

Beneath their eyes was spread a sheet of snow which looked gray in the dim light. The settlers could see nothing, but they heard a singular yelping noise away in the darkness. It was evident that the beach had been invaded by a number of animals which could not be seen.

"What are they?" cried Pencroft.

"Wolves, jaguars, or apes?" replied Neb.

"They have nearly reached the plateau," said the reporter.

"And our poultry-yard," exclaimed Herbert, "and our garden!"

"Where can they have crossed?" asked Pencroft.

"They must have crossed the bridge on the shore," replied the engineer, "which one of us must have forgotten to close."

"True," said Spilett, "I remember having left it open."

"A fine job you have made of it, Mr. Spilett," cried the sailor.

"What is done cannot be undone," replied Cyrus Harding. "We must consult what it will now be best to do."

Such were the questions and answers which were rapidly exchanged between Harding and his companions. It was certain that the bridge had been crossed, that the shore had been invaded by animals, and that whatever they might be they could by ascending the left bank of the Mercy reach Prospect Heights. They must therefore be advanced against quickly and fought with if necessary.

"But what are these beasts?" was asked a second time, as the yelpings were again heard more loudly than before. These yelps made Herbert start, and he remembered having heard them before during his first visit to the sources of the Red Creek.

"They are colpeo foxes!" he exclaimed.

"Forward!" shouted the sailor.

And all arming themselves with hatchets, carbines, and revolvers, threw themselves into the lift and soon set foot on the shore.

Colpeos are dangerous animals when in great numbers and irritated by hunger, nevertheless the colonists did not hesitate to throw themselves into the midst of the troop, and their first shots vividly lighting up the darkness made their assailants draw back.

The chief thing was to hinder these plunderers from reaching the plateau, for the garden and the poultry-yard would then have been at their mercy, and immense, perhaps irreparable mischief, would inevitably be the result, especially with regard to the corn-field. But as the invasion of the plateau could only be made by the left bank of the Mercy, it was sufficient to oppose the colpeos on the narrow bank between the river and the cliff of granite.

This was plain to all, and, by Cyrus Harding's orders, they reached the spot indicated by him, while the colpeos rushed fiercely through the gloom. Harding, Gideon Spilett, Herbert, Pencroft and Neb posted themselves in impregnable line. Top, his formidable jaws open, preceded the colonists, and he was followed by Jup, armed with knotty cudgel, which he brandished like a club.

The night was extremely dark, it was only by the flashes from the revolvers as each person fired that they could see their assailants, who were at least a hundred in number, and whose eyes were glowing like hot coals.

"They must not pass!" shouted Pencroft.

"They shall not pass!" returned the engineer.

But if they did not pass it was not for want of having attempted it. Those in the rear pushed on the foremost assailants, and it was an incessant struggle with revolvers and hatchets. Several colpeos already lay dead on the ground, but their number did not appear to diminish, and it might have been supposed that reinforcements were continually arriving over the bridge.

The colonists were soon obliged to fight at close quarters, not without receiving some wounds, though happily very slight ones. Herbert had, with a shot from his revolver, rescued Neb, on whose back a colpeo had sprung like a tiger cat. Top fought with actual fury, flying at the throats of the foxes and strangling them instantaneously. Jup wielded his weapon valiantly, and it was in vain that they endeavored to keep him in the rear. Endowed doubtless with sight which enabled him to pierce the obscurity, he was always in the thick of the fight uttering from time to time—a sharp hissing sound, which was with him the sign of great rejoicing.

At one moment he advanced so far, that by the light from a revolver he was seen surrounded by five or six large colpeos, with whom he was coping with great coolness.

However, the struggle was ended at last, and victory was on the side of the settlers, but not until they had fought for two long hours! The first signs of the approach of day doubtless determined the retreat of their assailants, who scampered away towards the North, passing over the bridge, which Neb ran immediately to raise. When day had sufficiently lighted up the field of battle, the settlers counted as many as fifty dead bodies scattered about on the shore.

"And Jup!" cried Pencroft; "where is Jup?" Jup had disappeared. His friend Neb called him, and for the first time Jup did not reply to his friend's call.

Everyone set out in search of Jup, trembling lest he should be found among the slain; they cleared the place of the bodies which stained the snow with their blood. Jup was found in the midst of a heap of colpeos whose broken jaws and crushed bodies showed that they had to do with the terrible club of the intrepid animal.

Poor Jup still held in his hand the stump of his broken cudgel, but deprived of his weapon he had been overpowered by numbers, and his chest was covered with severe wounds.

"He is living," cried Neb, who was bending over him.

"And we will save him," replied the sailor. "We will nurse him as if he was one of ourselves."

It appeared as if Jup understood, for he leaned his head on Pencroft's shoulder as if to thank him. The sailor was wounded himself, but his wound was insignificant, as were those of his companions; for thanks to their firearms they had been almost always able to keep their assailants at a distance. It was therefore only the orang whose condition was serious.

Jup, carried by Neb and Pencroft, was placed in the lift, and only a slight moan now and then escaped his lips. He was gently drawn up to Granite House. There he was laid on a mattress taken from one of the beds, and his wounds were bathed with the greatest care. It did not appear that any vital part had been reached, but Jup was very weak from loss of blood, and a high fever soon set in after his wounds had been dressed. He was laid down, strict diet was imposed, "just like a real person," as Neb said, and they made him swallow several cups of a cooling drink, for which the ingredients were supplied from the vegetable medicine chest of Granite House. Jup was at first restless, but his breathing gradually became more regular, and he was left sleeping quietly. From time to time Top, walking on tip-toe, as one might say, came to visit his friend, and seemed to approve of all the care that had been taken of him. One of Jup's hands hung over the side of his bed, and Top licked it with a sympathizing air.

They employed the day in interring the dead, who were dragged to the forest of the Far West, and there buried deep.

This attack, which might have had such serious consequences, was a lesson to the settlers, who from this time never went to bed until one of their number had made sure that all the bridges were raised, and that no invasion was possible.

However, Jup, after having given them serious anxiety for several days, began to recover. His constitution brought him through, the fever gradually subsided, and Gideon Spilett, who was a bit of a doctor, pronounced him quite out of danger. On the 16th of August, Jup began to eat. Neb made him nice little sweet dishes, which the invalid devoured with great relish, for if he had a pet failing it was that of being somewhat of a gourmend, and Neb had never done anything to cure him of this fault.

"What would you have?" said he to Gideon Spilett, who sometimes expostulated with him for spoiling the ape. "Poor Jup has no other pleasure than that of the palate, and I am only too glad to be able to reward his services in this way!"

Ten days after taking to his bed, on the 21st of August, Master Jup arose. His wounds were healed, and it was evident that he would not be long in regaining his usual strength and agility. Like all convalescents, he was tremendously hungry, and the reporter allowed him to eat as much as he liked, for he trusted to that instinct, which is too often wanting in reasoning beings, to keep the orang from any excess. Neb was delighted to see his pupil's appetite returning.

"Eat away, my Jup," said he, "and don't spare anything; you have shed your blood for us, and it is the least I can do to make you strong again!"

On the 25th of August Neb's voice was heard calling to his companions.

"Captain, Mr. Spilett, Mr. Herbert, Pencroft, come! come!"

The colonists, who were together in the dining-room, rose at Neb's call, who was then in Jup's room.

"What's the matter?" asked the reporter.

"Look," replied Neb, with a shout of laughter. And what did they see? Master Jup smoking calmly and seriously, sitting crosslegged like a Turk at the entrance to Granite House!

"My pipe," cried Pencroft. "He has taken my pipe! Hello, my honest Jup, I make you a present of it! Smoke away, old boy, smoke away!"

And Jup gravely puffed out clouds of smoke which seemed to give him great satisfaction. Harding did not appear to be much astonished at this incident, and he cited several examples of tame apes, to whom the use of tobacco had become quite familiar.

But from this day Master Jup had a pipe of his own, the sailor's ex-pipe, which was hung in his room near his store of tobacco. He filled it himself, lighted it with a glowing coal, and appeared to be the happiest of quadrumana. It may readily be understood that this similarity of tastes of Jup and Pencroft served to tighten the bonds of friendship which already existed between the honest ape and the worthy sailor.

"Perhaps he is really a man," said Pencroft sometimes to Neb. "Should you be surprised to hear him beginning to speak to us some day?"

"My word, no," replied Neb. "What astonishes me is that he hasn't spoken to us before, for now he wants nothing but speech!"

"It would amuse me all the same," resumed the sailor, "if some fine day he said to me, 'Suppose we change pipes, Pencroft.'"

"Yes," replied Neb, "what a pity he was born dumb!"

With the month of September the winter ended, and the works were again eagerly commenced. The building of the vessel advanced rapidly, she was already completely decked over, and all the inside parts of the hull were firmly united with ribs bent by means of steam, which answered all the purposes of a mold.

As there was no want of wood, Pencroft proposed to the engineer to give a double lining to the hull, to insure the strength of the vessel.

Harding, not knowing what the future might have in store for them, approved the sailor's idea of making the craft as strong as possible. The interior and deck of the vessel was entirely finished towards the 15th of September. For calking the seams they made oakum of dry seaweed, which was hammered in between the planks; then these seams were covered with boiling tar, which was obtained in great abundance from the pines in the forest.

The management of the vessel was very simple. She had from the first been ballasted with heavy blocks of granite walled up, in a bed of lime, twelve thousand pounds of which they stowed away.

A deck was placed over this ballast, and the interior was divided into two cabins; two benches extended along them and served also as lockers. The foot of the mast supported the partition which separated the two cabins, which were reached by two hatchways let into the deck.

Pencroft had no trouble in finding a tree suitable for the mast. He chose a straight young fir, with no knots, and which he had only to square at the step, and round off at the top. The ironwork of the mast, the rudder and the hull had been roughly but strongly forged at the Chimneys. Lastly, yards, masts, boom, spars, oars, etc., were all furnished by the first week in October, and it was agreed that a trial trip should be taken round the island, so as to ascertain how the vessel would behave at sea, and how far they might depend upon her.

During all this time the necessary works had not been neglected. The corral was enlarged, for the flock of musmons and goats had been increased by a number of young ones, who had to be housed and fed. The colonists had paid visits also to the oyster bed, the warren, the coal and iron mines, and to the till then unexplored districts of the Far West forest, which abounded in game. Certain indigenous plants were discovered, and those fit for immediate use contributed to vary the vegetable stores of Granite House.

They were a species of ficoide, some similar to those of the Cape, with eatable fleshy leaves, others bearing seeds containing a sort of flour.

On the 10th of October the vessel was launched. Pencroft was radiant with joy, the operation was perfectly successful; the boat completely rigged, having been pushed on rollers to the water's edge, was floated by the rising tide, amid the cheers of the colonists, particularly of Pencroft, who showed no modesty on this occasion. Besides his importance was to last beyond the finishing of the vessel, since, after having built her, he was to command her. The grade of captain was bestowed upon him with the approbation of all. To satisfy Captain Pencroft, it was now necessary to give a name to the vessel, and, after many propositions had been discussed, the votes were all in favor of the "Bonadventure." As soon as the "Bonadventure" had been lifted by the rising tide, it was seen that she lay evenly in the water, and would be easily navigated. However, the trial trip was to be made that very day, by an excursion off the coast. The weather was fine, the breeze fresh, and the sea smooth, especially towards the south coast, for the wind was blowing from the northwest.

"All hands on board," shouted Pencroft; but breakfast was first necessary, and it was thought best to take provisions on board, in the event of their excursion being prolonged until the evening.

Cyrus Harding was equally anxious to try the vessel, the model of which had originated with him, although on the sailor's advice he had altered some parts of it, but he did not share Pencroft's confidence in her, and as the latter had not again spoken of the voyage to Tabor Island, Harding hoped he had given it up. He would have indeed great reluctance in letting two or three of his companions venture so far in so small a boat, which was not of more than fifteen tons' burden.

At half-past ten everybody was on board, even Top and Jup, and Herbert weighed the anchor, which was fast in the sand near the mouth of the Mercy. The sail was hoisted, the Lincolnian flag floated from the masthead, and the "Bonadventure," steered by Pencroft, stood out to sea.

The wind blowing out of Union Bay she ran before it, and thus showed her owners, much to their satisfaction, that she possessed a remarkably fast pair of heels, according to Pencroft's mode of speaking. After having doubled Flotsam Point and Claw Cape, the captain kept her close hauled, so as to sail along the southern coast of the island, when it was found she sailed admirably within five points of the wind. All hands were enchanted, they had a good vessel, which, in case of need, would be of great service to them, and with fine weather and a fresh breeze the voyage promised to be charming.

Pencroft now stood off the shore, three or four miles across from Port Balloon. The island then appeared in all its extent and under a new aspect, with the varied panorama of its shore from Claw Cape to Reptile End, the forests in which dark firs contrasted with the young foliage of other trees and overlooked the whole, and Mount Franklin whose lofty head was still whitened with snow.

"How beautiful it is!" cried Herbert.

"Yes, our island is beautiful and good," replied Pencroft. "I love it as I loved my poor mother. It received us poor and destitute, and now what is wanting to us five fellows who fell on it from the sky?"

"Nothing," replied Neb; "nothing, captain."

And the two brave men gave three tremendous cheers in honor of their island!

During all this time Gideon Spilett, leaning against the mast, sketched the panorama which was developed before his eyes.

Cyrus Harding gazed on it in silence.

"Well, Captain Harding," asked Pencroft, "what do you think of our vessel?"

"She appears to behave well," replied the engineer.

"Good! And do you think now that she could undertake a voyage of some extent?"

"What voyage, Pencroft?"

"One to Tabor Island, for instance."

"My friend," replied Harding, "I think that in any pressing emergency we need not hesitate to trust ourselves to the 'Bonadventure' even for a longer voyage; but you know I should see you set off to Tabor Island with great uneasiness, since nothing obliges you to go there."

"One likes to know one's neighbors," returned the sailor, who was obstinate in his idea. "Tabor Island is our neighbor, and the only one! Politeness requires us to go at least to pay a visit."

"By Jove," said Spilett, "our friend Pencroft has become very particular about the proprieties all at once!"

"I am not particular about anything at all," retorted the sailor, who was rather vexed by the engineer's opposition, but who did not wish to cause him anxiety.

"Consider, Pencroft," resumed Harding, "you cannot go alone to Tabor Island."

"One companion will be enough for me."

"Even so," replied the engineer, "you will risk depriving the colony of Lincoln Island of two settlers out of five."

"Out of six," answered Pencroft; "you forget Jup."

"Out of seven," added Neb; "Top is quite worth another."

"There is no risk at all in it, captain," replied Pencroft.

"That is possible, Pencroft; but I repeat it is to expose ourselves uselessly."

The obstinate sailor did not reply, and let the conversation drop, quite determined to resume it again. But he did not suspect that an incident would come to his aid and change into an act of humanity that which was at first only a doubtful whim.

After standing off the shore the "Bonadventure" again approached it in the direction of Port Balloon. It was important to ascertain the channels between the sandbanks and reefs, that buoys might be laid down since this little creek was to be the harbor.

They were not more than half a mile from the coast, and it was necessary to tack to beat against the wind. The "Bonadventure" was then going at a very moderate rate, as the breeze, partly intercepted by the high land, scarcely swelled her sails, and the sea, smooth as glass, was only rippled now and then by passing gusts.

Herbert had stationed himself in the bows that he might indicate the course to be followed among the channels, when all at once he shouted,—

"Luff, Pencroft, luff!"

"What's the matter," replied the sailor; "a rock?"

"No—wait," said Herbert; "I don't quite see. Luff again—right—now."

So saying, Herbert, leaning over the side, plunged his arm into the water, and pulled it out, exclaiming,—

"A bottle!"

He held in his hand a corked bottle which he had just seized a few cables' length from the shore.

Cyrus Harding took the bottle. Without uttering a single word he drew the cork, and took from it a damp paper, on which were written these words:—

"Castaway.... Tabor island: 153deg W. long., 37deg 11' S. lat."

Chapter 13

"A castaway!" exclaimed Pencroft; "left on this Tabor Island not two hundred miles from us! Ah, Captain Harding, you won't now oppose my going."

"No, Pencroft," replied Cyrus Harding; "and you shall set out as soon as possible."

"To-morrow?"

"To-morrow!"

The engineer still held in his hand the paper which he had taken from the bottle. He contemplated it for some instants, then resumed,

"From this document, my friends, from the way in which it is worded, we may conclude this: first, that the castaway on Tabor Island is a man possessing a considerable knowledge of navigation, since he gives the latitude and longitude of the island exactly as we ourselves found it, and to a second of approximation; secondly, that he is either English or American, as the document is written in the English language."

"That is perfectly logical," answered Spilett; "and the presence of this castaway explains the arrival of the case on the shores of our island. There must have been a wreck, since there is a castaway. As to the latter, whoever he may be, it is lucky for him that Pencroft thought of building this boat and of trying her this very day, for a day later and this bottle might have been broken on the rocks."

"Indeed," said Herbert, "it is a fortunate chance that the 'Bonadventure' passed exactly where the bottle was still floating!"

"Does not this appear strange to you?" asked Harding of Pencroft.

"It appears fortunate, that's all," answered the sailor. "Do you see anything extraordinary in it, captain? The bottle must go somewhere, and why not here as well as anywhere else?"

"Perhaps you are right, Pencroft," replied the engineer; "and yet—"

"But," observed Herbert, "there's nothing to prove that this bottle has been floating long in the sea."

"Nothing," replied Gideon Spilett, "and the document appears even to have been recently written. What do you think about it, Cyrus?"

During this conversation Pencroft had not remained inactive. He had put the vessel about, and the "Bonadventure," all sails set, was running rapidly towards Claw Cape.

Every one was thinking of the castaway on Tabor Island. Should they be in time to save him? This was a great event in the life of the colonists! They themselves were but castaways, but it was to be feared that another might not have been so fortunate, and their duty was to go to his succor.

Claw Cape was doubled, and about four o'clock the "Bonadventure" dropped her anchor at the mouth of the Mercy.

That same evening the arrangements for the new expedition were made. It appeared best that Pencroft and Herbert, who knew how to work the vessel, should undertake the voyage alone. By setting out the next day, the 10th of October, they would arrive on the 13th, for with the present wind it would not take more than forty-eight hours to make this passage of a hundred and fifty miles. One day in the island, three or four to return, they might hope therefore that on the 17th they would again reach Lincoln Island. The weather was fine, the barometer was rising, the wind appeared settled, everything then was in favor of these brave men whom an act of humanity was taking far from their island.

Thus it had been agreed that Cyrus Harding, Neb, and Gideon Spilett should remain at Granite House, but an objection was raised, and Spilett, who had not forgotten his business as reporter to the New York Herald, having declared that he would go by swimming rather than lose such an opportunity, he was admitted to take a part in the voyage.

The evening was occupied in transporting on board the "Bonadventure," articles of bedding, utensils, arms, ammunition, a compass, provisions for a week; this being rapidly done, the colonists ascended to Granite House.

The next day, at five o'clock in the morning, the farewells were said, not without some emotion on both sides, and Pencroft setting sail made towards Claw Cape, which had to be doubled in order to proceed to the southwest.

The "Bonadventure" was already a quarter of a mile from the coast when the passengers perceived on the heights of Granite House two men waving their farewells; they were Cyrus Harding and Neb.

"Our friends," exclaimed Spilett, "this is our first separation in fifteen months."

Pencroft, the reporter and Herbert waved in return, and Granite House soon disappeared behind the high rocks of the Cape.

During the first part of the day the "Bonadventure" was still in sight of the southern coast of Lincoln Island, which soon appeared just like a green basket, with Mount Franklin rising from the center. The heights, diminished by distance, did not present an appearance likely to tempt vessels to touch there. Reptile End was passed in about an hour, though at a distance of about ten miles.

At this distance it was no longer possible to distinguish anything of the Western Coast, which stretched away to the ridges of Mount Franklin, and three hours after the last of Lincoln Island sank below the horizon.

The "Bonadventure" behaved capitally. Bounding over the waves she proceeded rapidly on her course. Pencroft had hoisted the foresail, and steering by the compass followed a rectilinear direction. From time to time Herbert relieved him at the helm, and the lad's hand was so firm that the sailor had not a point to find fault with.

Gideon Spilett chatted sometimes with one, sometimes with the other, if wanted he lent a hand with the ropes, and Captain Pencroft was perfectly satisfied with his crew.

In the evening the crescent moon, which would not be in its first quarter until the 16th, appeared in the twilight and soon set again. The night was dark but starry, and the next day again promised to be fine.

Pencroft prudently lowered the foresail, not wishing to be caught by a sudden gust while carrying too much canvas; it was perhaps an unnecessary precaution on such a calm night, but Pencroft was a prudent sailor and cannot be blamed for it.

The reporter slept part of the night. Pencroft and Herbert took turns for a spell of two hours each at the helm. The sailor trusted Herbert as he would himself, and his confidence was justified by the coolness and judgment of the lad. Pencroft gave him his directions as a commander to his steersman, and Herbert never allowed the "Bonadventure" to swerve even a point. The night passed quickly, as did the day of the 12th of October. A south-easterly direction was strictly maintained. Unless the "Bonadventure" fell in with some unknown current she would come exactly within sight of Tabor Island.

As to the sea over which the vessel was then sailing, it was absolutely deserted. Now and then a great albatross or frigate bird passed within gunshot, and Gideon Spilett wondered if it was to one of them that he had confided his last letter addressed to the New York Herald. These birds were the only beings that appeared to frequent this part of the ocean between Tabor and Lincoln Islands.

"And yet," observed Herbert, "this is the time that whalers usually proceed towards the southern part of the Pacific. Indeed I do not think there could be a more deserted sea than this."

"It is not quite so deserted as all that," replied Pencroft.

"What do you mean?" asked the reporter.

"We are on it. Do you take our vessel for a wreck and us for porpoises?"

And Pencroft laughed at his joke.

By the evening, according to calculation, it was thought that the "Bonadventure" had accomplished a distance of a hundred and twenty miles since her departure from Lincoln Island, that is to say in thirty-six hours, which would give her a speed of between three and four knots an hour. The breeze was very slight and might soon drop altogether. However, it was hoped that the next morning by break of day, if the calculation had been correct and the course true, they would sight Tabor Island.

Neither Gideon Spilett, Herbert, nor Pencroft slept that night. In the expectation of the next day they could not but feel some emotion. There was so much uncertainty in their enterprise! Were they near Tabor Island? Was the island still inhabited by the castaway to whose succor they had come? Who was this man? Would not his presence disturb the little colony till then so united? Besides, would he be content to exchange his prison for another? All these questions, which would no doubt be answered the next day, kept them in suspense, and at the dawn of day they all fixed their gaze on the western horizon.

"Land!" shouted Pencroft at about six o'clock in the morning.

And it was impossible that Pencroft should be mistaken, it was evident that land was there. Imagine the joy of the little crew of the "Bonadventure." In a few hours they would land on the beach of the island!

The low coast of Tabor Island, scarcely emerging from the sea, was not more than fifteen miles distant.

The head of the "Bonadventure," which was a little to the south of the island, was set directly towards it, and as the sun mounted in the east, its rays fell upon one or two headlands.

"This is a much less important isle than Lincoln Island," observed Herbert, "and is probably due like ours to some submarine convulsion."

At eleven o'clock the "Bonadventure" was not more than two miles off, and Pencroft, while looking for a suitable place at which to land, proceeded very cautiously through the unknown waters. The whole of the island could now be surveyed, and on it could be seen groups of gum and other large trees, of the same species as those growing on Lincoln Island. But the astonishing thing was that no smoke arose to show that the island was inhabited, no signal whatever appeared on the shore!

And yet the document was clear enough; there was a castaway, and this castaway should have been on the watch.

In the meanwhile the "Bonadventure" entered the winding channels among the reefs, and Pencroft observed every turn with extreme care. He had put

Herbert at the helm, posting himself in the bows, inspecting the water, while he held the halliard in his hand, ready to lower the sail at a moment's notice. Gideon Spilett with his glass eagerly scanned the shore, though without perceiving anything.

However, at about twelve o'clock the keel of the "Bonadventure" grated on the bottom. The anchor was let go, the sails furled, and the crew of the little vessel landed.

And there was no reason to doubt that this was Tabor Island, since according to the most recent charts there was no island in this part of the Pacific between New Zealand and the American Coast.

The vessel was securely moored, so that there should be no danger of her being carried away by the receding tide; then Pencroft and his companions, well armed, ascended the shore, so as to gain an elevation of about two hundred and fifty or three hundred feet which rose at a distance of half a mile.

"From the summit of that hill," said Spilett, "we can no doubt obtain a complete view of the island, which will greatly facilitate our search."

"So as to do here," replied Herbert, "that which Captain Harding did the very first thing on Lincoln Island, by climbing Mount Franklin."

"Exactly so," answered the reporter, "and it is the best plan."

While thus talking the explorers had advanced along a clearing which terminated at the foot of the hill. Flocks of rock-pigeons and sea-swallows, similar to those of Lincoln Island, fluttered around them. Under the woods which skirted the glade on the left they could hear the bushes rustling and see the grass waving, which indicated the presence of timid animals, but still nothing to show that the island was inhabited.

Arrived at the foot of the hill, Pencroft, Spilett, and Herbert climbed it in a few minutes, and gazed anxiously round the horizon.

They were on an islet, which did not measure more than six miles in circumference, its shape not much bordered by capes or promontories, bays or creeks, being a lengthened oval. All around, the lonely sea extended to the limits of the horizon. No land nor even a sail was in sight.

This woody islet did not offer the varied aspects of Lincoln Island, arid and wild in one part, but fertile and rich in the other. On the contrary this was a uniform mass of verdure, out of which rose two or three hills of no great height. Obliquely to the oval of the island ran a stream through a wide meadow falling into the sea on the west by a narrow mouth.

"The domain is limited," said Herbert.

"Yes," rejoined Pencroft: "It would have been too small for us."

"And moreover," said the reporter, "it appears to be uninhabited."

"Indeed," answered Herbert, "nothing here betrays the presence of man."

"Let us go down," said Pencroft, "and search."

The sailor and his two companions returned to the shore, to the place where they had left the "Bonadventure."

They had decided to make the tour of the island on foot, before exploring the interior; so that not a spot should escape their investigations. The beach was easy to follow, and only in some places was their way barred by large rocks, which, however, they easily passed round. The explorers proceeded towards the south, disturbing numerous flocks of sea-birds and herds of seals, which threw themselves into the sea as soon as they saw the strangers at a distance.

"Those beasts yonder," observed the reporter, "do not see men for the first time. They fear them, therefore they must know them."

An hour after their departure they arrived on the southern point of the islet, terminated by a sharp cape, and proceeded towards the north along the western coast, equally formed by sand and rocks, the background bordered with thick woods.

There was not a trace of a habitation in any part, not the print of a human foot on the shore of the island, which after four hours' walking had been gone completely round.

It was to say the least very extraordinary, and they were compelled to believe that Tabor Island was not or was no longer inhabited. Perhaps, after all the document was already several months or several years old, and it was possible in this case, either that the castaway had been enabled to return to his country, or that he had died of misery.

Pencroft, Spilett, and Herbert, forming more or less probable conjectures, dined rapidly on board the "Bonadventure" so as to be able to continue their excursion until nightfall. This was done at five o'clock in the evening, at which hour they entered the wood.

Numerous animals fled at their approach, being principally, one might say, only goats and pigs, which were obviously European species.

Doubtless some whaler had landed them on the island, where they had rapidly increased. Herbert resolved to catch one or two living, and take them back to Lincoln Island.

It was no longer doubtful that men at some period or other had visited this islet, and this became still more evident when paths appeared trodden through the forest, felled trees, and everywhere traces of the hand of man; but the trees were becoming rotten, and had been felled many years ago; the marks of the axe were velveted with moss, and the grass grew long and thick on the paths, so that it was difficult to find them.

"But," observed Gideon Spilett, "this not only proves that men have landed on the island, but also that they lived on it for some time. Now, who were these men? How many of them remain?"

"The document," said Herbert, "only spoke of one castaway."

"Well, if he is still on the island," replied Pencroft, "it is impossible but that we shall find him."

The exploration was continued. The sailor and his companions naturally followed the route which cut diagonally across the island, and they were thus obliged to follow the stream which flowed towards the sea.

If the animals of European origin, if works due to a human hand, showed incontestably that men had already visited the island, several specimens of the vegetable kingdom did not prove it less. In some places, in the midst of clearings, it was evident that the soil had been planted with culinary plants, at probably the same distant period.

What, then, was Herbert's joy, when he recognized potatoes, chicory, sorrel, carrots, cabbages, and turnips, of which it was sufficient to collect the seed to enrich the soil of Lincoln Island.

"Capital, jolly!" exclaimed Pencroft. "That will suit Neb as well as us. Even if we do not find the castaway, at least our voyage will not have been useless, and God will have rewarded us."

"Doubtless," replied Gideon Spilett, "but to see the state in which we find these plantations, it is to be feared that the island has not been inhabited for some time."

"Indeed," answered Herbert, "an inhabitant, whoever he was, could not have neglected such an important culture!"

"Yes," said Pencroft, "the castaway has gone."

"We must suppose so."

"It must then be admitted that the document has already a distant date?"

"Evidently."

"And that the bottle only arrived at Lincoln Island after having floated in the sea a long time."

"Why not?" returned Pencroft. "But night is coming on," added he, "and I think that it will be best to give up the search for the present."

"Let us go on board, and to-morrow we will begin again," said the reporter.

This was the wisest course, and it was about to be followed when Herbert, pointing to a confused mass among the trees, exclaimed,—

"A hut!"

All three immediately ran towards the dwelling. In the twilight it was just possible to see that it was built of planks and covered with a thick tarpaulin.

The half-closed door was pushed open by Pencroft, who entered with a rapid step.

The hut was empty!

Chapter 14

Pencroft, Herbert, and Gideon Spilett remained silent in the midst of the darkness.

Pencroft shouted loudly.

No reply was made.

The sailor then struck a light and set fire to a twig. This lighted for a minute a small room, which appeared perfectly empty. At the back was a rude fireplace, with a few cold cinders, supporting an armful of dry wood. Pencroft threw the blazing twig on it, the wood crackled and gave forth a bright light.

The sailor and his two companions then perceived a disordered bed, of which the damp and yellow coverlets proved that it had not been used for a long time. In the corner of the fireplace were two kettles, covered with rust, and an overthrown pot. A cupboard, with a few moldy sailor's clothes; on the table a tin plate and a Bible, eaten away by damp; in a corner a few tools, a spade, pickaxe, two fowling-pieces, one of which was broken; on a plank, forming a shelf, stood a barrel of powder, still untouched, a barrel of shot, and several boxes of caps, all thickly covered with dust, accumulated, perhaps, by many long years.

"There is no one here," said the reporter.

"No one," replied Pencroft.

"It is a long time since this room has been inhabited," observed Herbert.

"Yes, a very long time!" answered the reporter.

"Mr. Spilett," then said Pencroft, "instead of returning on board, I think that it would be well to pass the night in this hut."

"You are right, Pencroft," answered Gideon Spilett, "and if its owner returns, well! perhaps he will not be sorry to find the place taken possession of."

"He will not return," said the sailor, shaking his head.

"You think that he has quitted the island?" asked the reporter.

"If he had quitted the island he would have taken away his weapons and his tools," replied Pencroft. "You know the value which castaways set on such articles as these the last remains of a wreck. No! no!" repeated the sailor, in a tone of conviction; "no, he has not left the island! If he had escaped in a boat made by himself, he would still less have left these indispensable and necessary articles. No! he is on the island!"

"Living?" asked Herbert.

"Living or dead. But if he is dead, I suppose he has not buried himself, and so we shall at least find his remains!"

It was then agreed that the night should be passed in the deserted dwelling, and a store of wood found in a corner was sufficient to warm it. The door closed, Pencroft, Herbert and Spilett remained there, seated on a bench, talking little but wondering much. They were in a frame of mind to imagine anything or expect anything. They listened eagerly for sounds outside. The door might have opened suddenly, and a man presented himself to them without their being in the least surprised, notwithstanding all that the hut revealed of abandonment, and they had their hands ready to press the hands of this man, this castaway, this unknown friend, for whom friends were waiting.

But no voice was heard, the door did not open. The hours thus passed away.

How long the night appeared to the sailor and his companions! Herbert alone slept for two hours, for at his age sleep is a necessity. They were all three anxious to continue their exploration of the day before, and to search the most secret recesses of the islet! The inferences deduced by Pencroft were perfectly reasonable, and it was nearly certain that, as the hut was deserted, and the tools, utensils, and weapons were still there, the owner had succumbed. It was agreed, therefore, that they should search for his remains, and give them at least Christian burial.

Day dawned; Pencroft and his companions immediately proceeded to survey the dwelling. It had certainly been built in a favorable situation, at the back of a little hill, sheltered by five or six magnificent gum-trees. Before its front and through the trees the axe had prepared a wide clearing, which allowed the view to extend to the sea. Beyond a lawn, surrounded by a wooden fence falling to pieces, was the shore, on the left of which was the mouth of the stream.

The hut had been built of planks, and it was easy to see that these planks had been obtained from the hull or deck of a ship. It was probable that a disabled vessel had been cast on the coast of the island, that one at least of the crew had been saved, and that by means of the wreck this man, having tools at his disposal, had built the dwelling.

And this became still more evident when Gideon Spilett, after having walked around the hut, saw on a plank, probably one of those which had formed the armor of the wrecked vessel, these letters already half effaced:

BR—TAN—A

"Britannia," exclaimed Pencroft, whom the reporter had called; "it is a common name for ships, and I could not say if she was English or American!"

"It matters very little, Pencroft!"

"Very little indeed," answered the sailor, "and we will save the survivor of her crew if he is still living, to whatever country he may belong. But before beginning our search again let us go on board the 'Bonadventure'."

A sort of uneasiness had seized Pencroft upon the subject of his vessel. Should the island be inhabited after all, and should some one have taken possession of her? But he shrugged his shoulders at such an unreasonable supposition. At any rate the sailor was not sorry to go to breakfast on board. The road already trodden was not long, scarcely a mile. They set out on their walk, gazing into the wood and thickets through which goats and pigs fled in hundreds.

Twenty minutes after leaving the hut Pencroft and his companions reached the western coast of the island, and saw the "Bonadventure" held fast by her anchor, which was buried deep in the sand.

Pencroft could not restrain a sigh of satisfaction. After all this vessel was his child, and it is the right of fathers to be often uneasy when there is no occasion for it.

They returned on board, breakfasted, so that it should not be necessary to dine until very late; then the repast being ended, the exploration was continued and conducted with the most minute care. Indeed, it was very probable that the only inhabitant of the island had perished. It was therefore more for the traces of a dead than of a living man that Pencroft and his companions searched. But their searches were vain, and during the half of that day they sought to no purpose among the thickets of trees which covered the islet. There was then scarcely any doubt that, if the castaway was dead, no trace of his body now remained, but that some wild beast had probably devoured it to the last bone.

"We will set off to-morrow at daybreak," said Pencroft to his two companions, as about two o'clock they were resting for a few minutes under the shade of a clump of firs.

"I should think that we might without scruple take the utensils which belonged to the castaway," added Herbert.

"I think so, too," returned Gideon Spilett, "and these arms and tools will make up the stores of Granite House. The supply of powder and shot is also most important."

"Yes," replied Pencroft, "but we must not forget to capture a couple or two of those pigs, of which Lincoln Island is destitute."

"Nor to gather those seeds," added Herbert, "which will give us all the vegetables of the Old and the New Worlds."

"Then perhaps it would be best," said the reporter, "to remain a day longer on Tabor Island, so as to collect all that may be useful to us."

"No, Mr. Spilett," answered Pencroft, "I will ask you to set off to-morrow at daybreak. The wind seems to me to be likely to shift to the west, and after having had a fair wind for coming we shall have a fair wind for going back."

"Then do not let us lose time," said Herbert, rising.

"We won't waste time," returned Pencroft. "You, Herbert, go and gather the seeds, which you know better than we do. While you do that, Mr. Spilett and I will go and have a pig hunt, and even without Top I hope we shall manage to catch a few!"

Herbert accordingly took the path which led towards the cultivated part of the islet, while the sailor and the reporter entered the forest.

Many specimens of the porcine race fled before them, and these animals, which were singularly active, did not appear to be in a humor to allow themselves to be approached.

However, after an hour's chase, the hunters had just managed to get hold of a couple lying in a thicket, when cries were heard resounding from the north part of the island, With the cries were mingled terrible yells, in which there was nothing human.

Pencroft and Gideon Spilett were at once on their feet, and the pigs by this movement began to run away, at the moment when the sailor was getting ready the rope to bind them.

"That's Herbert's voice," said the reporter.

"Run!" exclaimed Pencroft.

And the sailor and Spilett immediately ran at full speed towards the spot from whence the cries proceeded.

They did well to hasten, for at a turn of the path near a clearing they saw the lad thrown on the ground and in the grasp of a savage being, apparently a gigantic ape, who was about to do him some great harm.

To rush on this monster, throw him on the ground in his turn, snatch Herbert from him, then bind him securely, was the work of a minute for Pencroft and Gideon Spilett. The sailor was of Herculean strength, the reporter also very powerful, and in spite of the monster's resistance he was firmly tied so that he could not even move.

"You are not hurt, Herbert?" asked Spilett.

"No, no!"

"Oh, if this ape had wounded him!" exclaimed Pencroft.

"But he is not an ape," answered Herbert.

At these words Pencroft and Gideon Spilett looked at the singular being who lay on the ground. Indeed it was not an ape; it was a human being, a man. But what a man! A savage in all the horrible acceptation of the word, and so much the more frightful that he seemed fallen to the lowest degree of brutishness!

Shaggy hair, untrimmed beard descending to the chest, the body almost naked except a rag round the waist, wild eyes, enormous hands with immensely long nails, skin the color of mahogany, feet as hard as if made of horn, such was the miserable creature who yet had a claim to be called a man. But it might justly be asked if there were yet a soul in this body, or if the brute instinct alone survived in it!

"Are you quite sure that this is a man, or that he has ever been one?" said Pencroft to the reporter.

"Alas! there is no doubt about it," replied Spilett.

"Then this must be the castaway?" asked Herbert.

"Yes," replied Gideon Spilett, "but the unfortunate man has no longer anything human about him!"

The reporter spoke the truth. It was evident that if the castaway had ever been a civilized being, solitude had made him a savage, or worse, perhaps a regular man of the woods. Hoarse sounds issued from his throat between his teeth, which were sharp as the teeth of a wild beast made to tear raw flesh.

Memory must have deserted him long before, and for a long time also he had forgotten how to use his gun and tools, and he no longer knew how to make a fire! It could be seen that he was active and powerful, but the physical qualities had been developed in him to the injury of the moral qualities. Gideon Spilett spoke to him. He did not appear to understand or even to hear. And yet on looking into his eyes, the reporter thought he could see that all reason was not extinguished in him. However, the prisoner did not struggle, nor even attempt to break his bonds. Was he overwhelmed by the presence of men whose fellow he had once been? Had he found in some corner of his brain a fleeting remembrance which recalled him to humanity? If free, would he attempt to fly, or would he remain? They could not tell, but they did not make the experiment; and after gazing attentively at the miserable creature,—

"Whoever he may be," remarked Gideon Spilett, "whoever he may have been, and whatever he may become, it is our duty to take him with us to Lincoln Island."

"Yes, yes!" replied Herbert, "and perhaps with care we may arouse in him same gleam of intelligence."

"The soul does not die," said the reporter, "and it would be a great satisfaction to rescue one of God's creatures from brutishness."

Pencroft shook his head doubtfully.

"We must try at any rate," returned the reporter; "humanity commands us."

It was indeed their duty as Christians and civilized beings. All three felt this, and they well knew that Cyrus Harding would approve of their acting thus.

"Shall we leave him bound?" asked the sailor.

"Perhaps he would walk if his feet were unfastened," said Herbert.

"Let us try," replied Pencroft.

The cords which shackled the prisoner's feet were cut off, but his arms remained securely fastened. He got up by himself and did not manifest any desire to run away. His hard eyes darted a piercing glance at the three men, who walked near him, but nothing denoted that he recollected being their fellow, or at least having been so. A continual hissing sound issued from his lips, his aspect was wild, but he did not attempt to resist.

By the reporter's advice the unfortunate man was taken to the hut. Perhaps the sight of the things that belonged to him would make some impression on him! Perhaps a spark would be sufficient to revive his obscured intellect, to rekindle his dulled soul. The dwelling was not far off. In a few minutes they arrived there, but the prisoner remembered nothing, and it appeared that he had lost consciousness of everything.

What could they think of the degree of brutishness into which this miserable being had fallen, unless that his imprisonment on the islet dated from a very distant period and after having arrived there a rational being solitude had reduced him to this condition.

The reporter then thought that perhaps the sight of fire would have some effect on him, and in a moment one of those beautiful flames, that attract even animals, blazed up on the hearth. The sight of the flame seemed at first to fix the attention of the unhappy object, but soon he turned away and the look of intelligence faded. Evidently there was nothing to be done, for the time at least, but to take him on board the "Bonadventure." This was done, and he remained there in Pencroft's charge.

Herbert and Spilett returned to finish their work; and some hours after they came back to the shore, carrying the utensils and guns, a store of vegetables, of seeds, some game, and two couple of pigs.

All was embarked, and the "Bonadventure" was ready to weigh anchor and sail with the morning tide.

The prisoner had been placed in the fore-cabin, where he remained quiet, silent, apparently deaf and dumb.

Pencroft offered him something to eat, but he pushed away the cooked meat that was presented to him and which doubtless did not suit him. But on the sailor showing him one of the ducks which Herbert had killed, he pounced on it like a wild beast, and devoured it greedily.

"You think that he will recover his senses?" asked Pencroft. "It is not impossible that our care will have an effect upon him, for it is solitude that has made him what he is, and from this time forward he will be no longer alone."

"The poor man must no doubt have been in this state for a long time," said Herbert.

"Perhaps," answered Gideon Spilett.

"About what age is he?" asked the lad.

"It is difficult to say," replied the reporter, "for it is impossible to see his features under the thick beard which covers his face, but he is no longer young, and I suppose he might be about fifty."

"Have you noticed, Mr. Spilett, how deeply sunk his eyes are?" asked Herbert.

"Yes, Herbert, but I must add that they are more human than one could expect from his appearance."

"However, we shall see," replied Pencroft, "and I am anxious to know what opinion Captain Harding will have of our savage. We went to look for a human creature, and we are bringing back a monster! After all, we did what we could."

The night passed, and whether the prisoner slept or not could not be known, but at any rate, although he had been unbound, he did not move. He was like a wild animal, which appears stunned at first by its capture, and becomes wild again afterwards.

At daybreak the next morning, the 15th of October, the change of weather predicted by Pencroft occurred. The wind having shifted to the northwest favored the return of the "Bonadventure," but at the same time it freshened, which might render navigation more difficult.

At five o'clock in the morning the anchor was weighed. Pencroft took a reef in the mainsail, and steered towards the north-east, so as to sail straight for Lincoln Island.

The first day of the voyage was not marked by any incident. The prisoner remained quiet in the fore-cabin, and as he had been a sailor it appeared that the motion of the vessel might produce on him a salutary reaction. Did some recollection of his former calling return to him? However that might be, he remained tranquil, astonished rather than depressed.

The next day the wind increased, blowing more from the north, consequently in a less favorable direction for the "Bonadventure." Pencroft was soon obliged to sail close-hauled, and without saying anything about it he began to be uneasy at the state of the sea, which frequently broke over the bows. Certainly, if the wind did not moderate, it would take a longer time to reach Lincoln Island than it had taken to make Tabor Island.

Indeed, on the morning of the 17th, the "Bonadventure" had been forty-eight hours at sea, and nothing showed that she was near the island. It was impossible, besides, to estimate the distance traversed, or to trust to the reckoning for the direction, as the speed had been very irregular.

Twenty-four hours after there was yet no land in sight. The wind was right ahead and the sea very heavy. The sails were close-reefed, and they tacked frequently. On the 18th, a wave swept completely over the "Bonadventure"; and if the crew had not taken the precaution of lashing themselves to the deck, they would have been carried away.

On this occasion Pencroft and his companions, who were occupied with loosing themselves, received unexpected aid from the prisoner, who emerged from the hatchway as if his sailor's instinct had suddenly returned, broke a piece out of the bulwarks with a spar so as to let the water which filled the deck escape. Then the vessel being clear, he descended to his cabin without having uttered a word. Pencroft, Gideon Spilett, and Herbert, greatly astonished, let him proceed.

Their situation was truly serious, and the sailor had reason to fear that he was lost on the wide sea without any possibility of recovering his course.

The night was dark and cold. However, about eleven o'clock, the wind fell, the sea went down, and the speed of the vessel, as she labored less, greatly increased.

Neither Pencroft, Spilett, nor Herbert thought of taking an hour's sleep. They kept a sharp look-out, for either Lincoln Island could not be far distant and would be sighted at daybreak, or the "Bonadventure," carried away by currents, had drifted so much that it would be impossible to rectify her course. Pencroft, uneasy to the last degree, yet did not despair, for he had a gallant heart, and grasping the tiller he anxiously endeavored to pierce the darkness which surrounded them.

About two o'clock in the morning he started forward,—

"A light! a light!" he shouted.

Indeed, a bright light appeared twenty miles to the northeast. Lincoln Island was there, and this fire, evidently lighted by Cyrus Harding, showed them the course to be followed. Pencroft, who was bearing too much to the north, altered his course and steered towards the fire, which burned brightly above the horizon like a star of the first magnitude.

Chapter 15

The next day, the 20th of October, at seven o'clock in the morning, after a voyage of four days, the "Bonadventure" gently glided up to the beach at the mouth of the Mercy.

Cyrus Harding and Neb, who had become very uneasy at the bad weather and the prolonged absence of their companions, had climbed at daybreak to the plateau of Prospect Heights, and they had at last caught sight of the vessel which had been so long in returning.

"God be praised! there they are!" exclaimed Cyrus Harding.

As to Neb in his joy, he began to dance, to twirl round, clapping his hands and shouting, "Oh! my master!" A more touching pantomime than the finest discourse.

The engineer's first idea, on counting the people on the deck of the "Bonadventure," was that Pencroft had not found the castaway of Tabor Island, or at any rate that the unfortunate man had refused to leave his island and change one prison for another.

Indeed Pencroft, Gideon Spilett, and Herbert were alone on the deck of the "Bonadventure."

The moment the vessel touched, the engineer and Neb were waiting on the beach, and before the passengers had time to leap on to the sand, Harding said: "We have been very uneasy at your delay, my friends! Did you meet with any accident?"

"No," replied Gideon Spilett; "on the contrary, everything went wonderfully well. We will tell you all about it."

"However," returned the engineer, "your search has been unsuccessful, since you are only three, just as you went!"

"Excuse me, captain," replied the sailor, "we are four."

"You have found the castaway?"

"Yes."

"And you have brought him?"

"Yes."

"Living?"

"Yes."

"Where is he? Who is he?"

"He is," replied the reporter, "or rather he was a man! There, Cyrus, that is all we can tell you!"

The engineer was then informed of all that had passed during the voyage, and under what conditions the search had been conducted; how the only dwelling in the island had long been abandoned; how at last a castaway had been captured, who appeared no longer to belong to the human species.

"And that's just the point," added Pencroft, "I don't know if we have done right to bring him here."

"Certainly you have, Pencroft," replied the engineer quickly.

"But the wretched creature has no sense!"

"That is possible at present," replied Cyrus Harding, "but only a few months ago the wretched creature was a man like you and me. And who knows what will become of the survivor of us after a long solitude on this island? It is a great misfortune to be alone, my friends; and it must be believed that solitude can quickly destroy reason, since you have found this poor creature in such a state!"

"But, captain," asked Herbert, "what leads you to think that the brutishness of the unfortunate man began only a few months back?"

"Because the document we found had been recently written," answered the engineer, "and the castaway alone can have written it."

"Always supposing," observed Gideon Spilett, "that it had not been written by a companion of this man, since dead."

"That is impossible, my dear Spilett."

"Why so?" asked the reporter.

"Because the document would then have spoken of two castaways," replied Harding, "and it mentioned only one."

Herbert then in a few words related the incidents of the voyage, and dwelt on the curious fact of the sort of passing gleam in the prisoner's mind, when for an instant in the height of the storm he had become a sailor.

"Well, Herbert," replied the engineer, "you are right to attach great importance to this fact. The unfortunate man cannot be incurable, and despair has made him what he is; but here he will find his fellow-men, and since there is still a soul in him, this soul we shall save!"

The castaway of Tabor Island, to the great pity of the engineer and the great astonishment of Neb, was then brought from the cabin which he occupied in the fore part of the "Bonadventure"; when once on land he manifested a wish to run away.

But Cyrus Harding approaching, placed his hand on his shoulder with a gesture full of authority, and looked at him with infinite tenderness. Immediately the unhappy man, submitting to a superior will, gradually became calm, his eyes fell, his head bent, and he made no more resistance.

"Poor fellow!" murmured the engineer.

Cyrus Harding had attentively observed him. To judge by his appearance this miserable being had no longer anything human about him, and yet Harding, as had the reporter already, observed in his look an indefinable trace of intelligence.

It was decided that the castaway, or rather the stranger as he was thenceforth termed by his companions, should live in one of the rooms of Granite House, from which, however, he could not escape. He was led there without difficulty, and with careful attention, it might, perhaps, be hoped that some day he would be a companion to the settlers in Lincoln Island.

Cyrus Harding, during breakfast, which Neb had hastened to prepare, as the reporter, Herbert, and Pencroft were dying of hunger, heard in detail all the incidents which had marked the voyage of exploration to the islet. He agreed with his friends on this point, that the stranger must be either English or American, the name Britannia leading them to suppose this, and, besides, through the bushy beard, and under the shaggy, matted hair, the engineer thought he could recognize the characteristic features of the Anglo-Saxon.

"But, by the bye," said Gideon Spilett, addressing Herbert, "you never told us how you met this savage, and we know nothing, except that you would have been strangled, if we had not happened to come up in time to help you!"

"Upon my word," answered Herbert, "it is rather difficult to say how it happened. I was, I think, occupied in collecting my plants, when I heard a noise like an avalanche falling from a very tall tree. I scarcely had time to look round. This unfortunate man, who was without doubt concealed in a tree, rushed upon me in less time than I take to tell you about it, and unless Mr. Spilett and Pencroft—"

"My boy!" said Cyrus Harding, "you ran a great danger, but, perhaps, without that, the poor creature would have still hidden himself from your search, and we should not have had a new companion."

"You hope, then, Cyrus, to succeed in reforming the man?" asked the reporter.

"Yes," replied the engineer.

Breakfast over, Harding and his companions left Granite House and returned to the beach. They there occupied themselves in unloading the "Bonadventure," and the engineer, having examined the arms and tools, saw nothing which could help them to establish the identity of the stranger.

The capture of pigs, made on the islet, was looked upon as being very profitable to Lincoln Island, and the animals were led to the sty, where they soon became at home.

The two barrels, containing the powder and shot, as well as the box of caps, were very welcome. It was agreed to establish a small powder-magazine, either outside Granite House or in the Upper Cavern, where there would be no fear of explosion. However, the use of pyroxyle was to be continued, for this substance giving excellent results, there was no reason for substituting ordinary powder.

When the unloading of the vessel was finished,—

"Captain," said Pencroft, "I think it would be prudent to put our 'Bonadventure' in a safe place."

"Is she not safe at the mouth of the Mercy?" asked Cyrus Harding.

"No, captain," replied the sailor. "Half of the time she is stranded on the sand, and that works her. She is a famous craft, you see, and she behaved admirably during the squall which struck us on our return."

"Could she not float in the river?"

"No doubt, captain, she could; but there is no shelter there, and in the east winds, I think that the 'Bonadventure' would suffer much from the surf."

"Well, where would you put her, Pencroft?"

"In Port Balloon," replied the sailor. "That little creek, shut in by rocks, seems to me to be just the harbor we want."

"Is it not rather far?"

"Pooh! it is not more than three miles from Granite House, and we have a fine straight road to take us there!"

"Do it then, Pencroft, and take your 'Bonadventure' there," replied the engineer, "and yet I would rather have her under our more immediate protection. When we have time, we must make a little harbor for her."

"Famous!" exclaimed Pencroft. "A harbor with a lighthouse, a pier, and dock! Ah! really with you, captain, everything becomes easy."

"Yes, my brave Pencroft," answered the engineer, "but on condition, however, that you help me, for you do as much as three men in all our work."

Herbert and the sailor then re-embarked on board the "Bonadventure," the anchor was weighed, the sail hoisted, and the wind drove her rapidly towards Claw Cape. Two hours after, she was reposing on the tranquil waters of Port Balloon.

During the first days passed by the stranger in Granite House, had he already given them reason to think that his savage nature was becoming tamed? Did a brighter light burn in the depths of that obscured mind? In short, was the soul returning to the body?

Yes, to a certainty, and to such a degree, that Cyrus Harding and the reporter wondered if the reason of the unfortunate man had ever been totally extinguished. At first, accustomed to the open air, to the unrestrained liberty which he had enjoyed on Tabor Island, the stranger manifested a sullen fury, and it was feared that he might throw himself onto the beach, out of one of the windows of Granite House. But gradually he became calmer, and more freedom was allowed to his movements.

They had reason to hope, and to hope much. Already, forgetting his carnivorous instincts, the stranger accepted a less bestial nourishment than that on which he fed on the islet, and cooked meat did not produce in him the same sentiment of repulsion which he had showed on board the "Bonadventure." Cyrus Harding had profited by a moment when he was sleeping, to cut his hair and matted beard, which formed a sort of mane and gave him such a savage aspect. He had also been clothed more suitably, after having got rid of the rag which covered him. The result was that, thanks to these attentions, the stranger resumed a more human appearance, and it even seemed as if his eyes had become milder. Certainly, when formerly lighted up by intelligence, this man's face must have had a sort of beauty.

Every day, Harding imposed on himself the task of passing some hours in his company. He came and worked near him, and occupied himself in different things, so as to fix his attention. A spark, indeed, would be sufficient to reillumine that soul, a recollection crossing that brain to recall reason. That had been seen, during the storm, on board the "Bonadventure!" The engineer did not neglect either to speak aloud, so as to penetrate at the same time by the organs of hearing and sight the depths of that torpid intelligence. Sometimes one of his companions, sometimes another, sometimes all joined him. They spoke most often of things belonging to the navy, which must interest a sailor.

At times, the stranger gave some slight attention to what was said, and the settlers were soon convinced that he partly understood them. Sometimes the expression of his countenance was deeply sorrowful, a proof that he suffered mentally, for his face could not be mistaken; but he did not speak, although at different times, however, they almost thought that words were about to issue from his lips. At all events, the poor creature was quite quiet and sad!

But was not his calm only apparent? Was not his sadness only the result of his seclusion? Nothing could yet be ascertained. Seeing only certain objects and in a limited space, always in contact with the colonists, to whom he would soon become accustomed, having no desires to satisfy, better fed, better clothed, it was natural that his physical nature should gradually improve; but was he penetrated with the sense of a new life? or rather, to employ a word which would be exactly applicable to him, was he not becoming tamed, like an animal in company with his master? This was an important question, which Cyrus Harding was anxious to answer, and yet he did not wish to treat his invalid roughly! Would he ever be a convalescent?

How the engineer observed him every moment! How he was on the watch for his soul, if one may use the expression! How he was ready to grasp it! The settlers followed with real sympathy all the phases of the cure undertaken by Harding. They aided him also in this work of humanity, and all, except perhaps the incredulous Pencroft, soon shared both his hope and his faith.

The calm of the stranger was deep, as has been said, and he even showed a sort of attachment for the engineer, whose influence he evidently felt. Cyrus Harding resolved then to try him, by transporting him to another scene, from that ocean which formerly his eyes had been accustomed to contemplate, to the border of the forest, which might perhaps recall those where so many years of his life had been passed!

"But," said Gideon Spilett, "can we hope that he will not escape, if once set at liberty?"

"The experiment must be tried," replied the engineer.

"Well!" said Pencroft. "When that fellow is outside, and feels the fresh air, he will be off as fast as his legs can carry him!"

"I do not think so," returned Harding.

"Let us try," said Spilett.

"We will try," replied the engineer.

This was on the 30th of October, and consequently the castaway of Tabor Island had been a prisoner in Granite House for nine days. It was warm, and a bright sun darted its rays on the island. Cyrus Harding and Pencroft went to the room occupied by the stranger, who was found lying near the window and gazing at the sky.

"Come, my friend," said the engineer to him.

The stranger rose immediately. His eyes were fixed on Cyrus Harding, and he followed him, while the sailor marched behind them, little confident as to the result of the experiment.

Arrived at the door, Harding and Pencroft made him take his place in the lift, while Neb, Herbert, and Gideon Spilett waited for them before Granite House. The lift descended, and in a few moments all were united on the beach.

The settlers went a short distance from the stranger, so as to leave him at liberty.

He then made a few steps toward the sea, and his look brightened with extreme animation, but he did not make the slightest attempt to escape. He was gazing at the little waves which, broken by the islet, rippled on the sand.

"This is only the sea," observed Gideon Spilett, "and possibly it does not inspire him with any wish to escape!"

"Yes," replied Harding, "we must take him to the plateau, on the border of the forest. There the experiment will be more conclusive."

"Besides, he could not run away," said Neb, "since the bridge is raised."

"Oh!" said Pencroft, "that isn't a man to be troubled by a stream like Creek Glycerine! He could cross it directly, at a single bound!"

"We shall soon see," Harding contented himself with replying, his eyes not quitting those of his patient.

The latter was then led towards the mouth of the Mercy, and all climbing the left bank of the river, reached Prospect Heights.

Arrived at the spot on which grew the first beautiful trees of the forest, their foliage slightly agitated by the breeze, the stranger appeared greedily to drink in the penetrating odor which filled the atmosphere, and a long sigh escaped from his chest.

The settlers kept behind him, ready to seize him if he made any movement to escape!

And, indeed, the poor creature was on the point of springing into the creek which separated him from the forest, and his legs were bent for an instant as if for a spring, but almost immediately he stepped back, half sank down, and a large tear fell from his eyes.

"Ah!" exclaimed Cyrus Harding, "you have become a man again, for you can weep!"

Chapter 16

Yes! the unfortunate man had wept! Some recollection doubtless had flashed across his brain, and to use Cyrus Harding's expression, by those tears he was once more a man.

The colonists left him for some time on the plateau, and withdrew themselves to a short distance, so that he might feel himself free; but he did not think of profiting by this liberty, and Harding soon brought him back to Granite House. Two days after this occurrence, the stranger appeared to wish gradually to mingle with their common life. He evidently heard and understood, but no less evidently was he strangely determined not to speak to the colonists; for one evening, Pencroft, listening at the door of his room, heard these words escape from his lips:—

"No! here! I! never!"

The sailor reported these words to his companions.

"There is some painful mystery there!" said Harding.

The stranger had begun to use the laboring tools, and he worked in the garden. When he stopped in his work, as was often the case, he remained retired within himself, but on the engineer's recommendation, they respected the reserve which he apparently wished to keep. If one of the settlers approached him, he drew back, and his chest heaved with sobs, as if overburdened!

Was it remorse that overwhelmed him thus? They were compelled to believe so, and Gideon Spilett could not help one day making this observation,—

"If he does not speak it is because he has, I fear, things too serious to be told!"

They must be patient and wait.

A few days later, on the 3rd of November, the stranger, working on the plateau, had stopped, letting his spade drop to the ground, and Harding, who was observing him from a little distance, saw that tears were again flowing from his eyes. A sort of irresistible pity led him towards the unfortunate man, and he touched his arm lightly.

"My friend!" said he.

The stranger tried to avoid his look, and Cyrus Harding having endeavored to take his hand, he drew back quickly.

"My friend," said Harding in a firmer voice, "look at me, I wish it!"

The stranger looked at the engineer, and seemed to be under his power, as a subject under the influence of a mesmerist. He wished to run away. But then his countenance suddenly underwent a transformation. His eyes flashed. Words struggled to escape from his lips. He could no longer contain himself! At last he folded his arms; then, in a hollow voice,—"Who are you?" he asked Cyrus Harding.

"Castaways, like you," replied the engineer, whose emotion was deep. "We have brought you here, among your fellow-men."

"My fellow-men!.... I have none!"

"You are in the midst of friends."

"Friends!—for me! friends!" exclaimed the stranger, hiding his face in his hands. "No—never—leave me! leave me!"

Then he rushed to the side of the plateau which overlooked the sea, and remained there a long time motionless.

Harding rejoined his companions and related to them what had just happened.

"Yes! there is some mystery in that man's life," said Gideon Spilett, "and it appears as if he had only re-entered society by the path of remorse."

"I don't know what sort of a man we have brought here," said the sailor. "He has secrets—"

"Which we will respect," interrupted Cyrus Harding quickly. "If he has committed any crime, he has most fearfully expiated it, and in our eyes he is absolved."

For two hours the stranger remained alone on the shore, evidently under the influence of recollections which recalled all his past life—a melancholy life doubtless—and the colonists, without losing sight of him, did not attempt to disturb his solitude. However, after two hours, appearing to have formed a resolution, he came to find Cyrus Harding. His eyes were red with the tears he had shed, but he wept no longer. His countenance expressed deep humility. He appeared anxious, timorous, ashamed, and his eyes were constantly fixed on the ground.

"Sir," said he to Harding, "your companions and you, are you English?"

"No," answered the engineer, "we are Americans."

"Ah!" said the stranger, and he murmured, "I prefer that!"

"And you, my friend?" asked the engineer.

"English," replied he hastily.

And as if these few words had been difficult to say, he retreated to the beach, where he walked up and down between the cascade and the mouth of the Mercy, in a state of extreme agitation.

Then, passing one moment close to Herbert, he stopped and in a stifled voice,—

"What month?" he asked.

"December," replied Herbert.

"What year?"

"1866."

"Twelve years! twelve years!" he exclaimed.

Then he left him abruptly.

Herbert reported to the colonists the questions and answers which had been made.

"This unfortunate man," observed Gideon Spilett, "was no longer acquainted with either months or years!"

"Yes!" added Herbert, "and he had been twelve years already on the islet when we found him there!"

"Twelve years!" rejoined Harding. "Ah! twelve years of solitude, after a wicked life, perhaps, may well impair a man's reason!"

"I am induced to think," said Pencroft, "that this man was not wrecked on Tabor Island, but that in consequence of some crime he was left there."

"You must be right, Pencroft," replied the reporter, "and if it is so it is not impossible that those who left him on the island may return to fetch him some day!"

"And they will no longer find him," said Herbert.

"But then," added Pencroft, "they must return, and—"

"My friends," said Cyrus Harding, "do not let us discuss this question until we know more about it. I believe that the unhappy man has suffered, that he has severely expiated his faults, whatever they may have been, and that the wish to unburden himself stifles him. Do not let us press him to tell us his history! He will tell it to us doubtless, and when we know it, we shall see what course it will be best to follow. He alone besides can tell us, if he has more than a hope, a certainty, of returning some day to his country, but I doubt it!"

"And why?" asked the reporter.

"Because that, in the event of his being sure of being delivered at a certain time, he would have waited the hour of his deliverance and would not have thrown this document into the sea. No, it is more probable that he was condemned to die on that islet, and that he never expected to see his fellow-creatures again!"

"But," observed the sailor, "there is one thing which I cannot explain."

"What is it?"

"If this man had been left for twelve years on Tabor Island, one may well suppose that he had been several years already in the wild state in which we found him!"

"That is probable," replied Cyrus Harding.

"It must then be many years since he wrote that document!"

"No doubt," and yet the document appears to have been recently written!

"Besides, how do you know that the bottle which enclosed the document may not have taken several years to come from Tabor Island to Lincoln Island?"

"That is not absolutely impossible," replied the reporter.

"Might it not have been a long time already on the coast of the island?"

"No," answered Pencroft, "for it was still floating. We could not even suppose that after it had stayed for any length of time on the shore, it would have been swept off by the sea, for the south coast is all rocks, and it would certainly have been smashed to pieces there!"

"That is true," rejoined Cyrus Harding thoughtfully.

"And then," continued the sailor, "if the document was several years old, if it had been shut up in that bottle for several years, it would have been injured by damp. Now, there is nothing of the kind, and it was found in a perfect state of preservation."

The sailor's reasoning was very just, and pointed out an incomprehensible fact, for the document appeared to have been recently written, when the colonists found it in the bottle. Moreover, it gave the latitude and longitude of Tabor Island correctly, which implied that its author had a more complete knowledge of hydrography than could be expected of a common sailor.

"There is in this, again, something unaccountable," said the engineer, "but we will not urge our companions to speak. When he likes, my friends, then we shall be ready to hear him!"

During the following days the stranger did not speak a word, and did not once leave the precincts of the plateau. He worked away, without losing a moment, without taking a minute's rest, but always in a retired place. At meal times he never came to Granite House, although invited several times to do so, but contented himself with eating a few raw vegetables. At nightfall he did not return to the room assigned to him, but remained under some clump of trees, or when the weather was bad crouched in some cleft of the rocks. Thus he lived in the same manner as when he had no other shelter than the forests of Tabor Island, and as all persuasion to induce him to improve his life was in vain, the colonists waited patiently. And the time was near, when, as it seemed, almost involuntarily urged by his conscience, a terrible confession escaped him.

On the 10th of November, about eight o'clock in the evening, as night was coming on, the stranger appeared unexpectedly before the settlers, who were assembled under the veranda. His eyes burned strangely, and he had quite resumed the wild aspect of his worst days.

Cyrus Harding and his companions were astounded on seeing that, overcome by some terrible emotion, his teeth chattered like those of a person in a fever. What was the matter with him? Was the sight of his fellow-creatures insupportable to him? Was he weary of this return to a civilized mode of existence? Was he pining for his former savage life? It appeared so, as soon he was heard to express himself in these incoherent sentences:—

"Why am I here?.... By what right have you dragged me from my islet?.... Do you think there could be any tie between you and me?.... Do you know who I am—what I have done—why I was there—alone? And who told you that I was not abandoned there—that I was not condemned to die there?.... Do you know my past?.... How do you know that I have not stolen, murdered—that I am not a wretch—an accursed being—only fit to live like a wild beast, far from all—speak—do you know it?"

The colonists listened without interrupting the miserable creature, from whom these broken confessions escaped, as it were, in spite of himself. Harding wishing to calm him, approached him, but he hastily drew back.

"No! no!" he exclaimed; "one word only—am I free?"

"You are free," answered the engineer.

"Farewell, then!" he cried, and fled like a madman.

Neb, Pencroft, and Herbert ran also towards the edge of the wood—but they returned alone.

"We must let him alone!" said Cyrus Harding.

"He will never come back!" exclaimed Pencroft.

"He will come back," replied the engineer.

Many days passed; but Harding—was it a sort of presentiment?—presentiment in the fixed idea that sooner or later the unhappy man would return.

"It is the last revolt of his wild nature," said he, "which remorse has touched, and which renewed solitude will terrify."

In the meanwhile, works of all sorts were continued, as well on Prospect Heights as at the corral, where Harding intended to build a farm. It is unnecessary to say that the seeds collected by Herbert on Tabor Island had been carefully sown. The plateau thus formed one immense kitchen-garden, well laid out and carefully tended, so that the arms of the settlers were never in want of work. There was always something to be done. As the esculents increased in number, it became necessary to enlarge the simple beds, which threatened to grow into regular fields and replace the meadows. But grass abounded in other parts of the island, and there was no fear of the onagers being obliged to go on short allowance. It was well worth while, besides, to turn Prospect Heights into a kitchen-garden, defended by its deep belt of creeks, and to remove them to the meadows, which had no need of protection against the depredations of quadrumana and quadrupeds.

On the 15th of November, the third harvest was gathered in. How wonderfully had the field increased in extent, since eighteen months ago, when the first grain of wheat was sown! The second crop of six hundred thousand grains produced this time four thousand bushels, or five hundred millions of grains!

The colony was rich in corn, for ten bushels alone were sufficient for sowing every year to produce an ample crop for the food both of men and beasts. The harvest was completed, and the last fortnight of the month of November was devoted to the work of converting it into food for man. In fact, they had corn, but not flour, and the establishment of a mill was necessary. Cyrus Harding could have utilized the second fall which flowed into the Mercy to establish his motive power, the first being already occupied with moving the felting mill, but, after some consultation, it was decided that a simple windmill should be built on Prospect Heights. The building of this presented no more difficulty than the building of the former, and it was moreover certain that there would be no want of wind on the plateau, exposed as it was to the sea breezes.

"Not to mention," said Pencroft, "that the windmill will be more lively and will have a good effect in the landscape!"

They set to work by choosing timber for the frame and machinery of the mill. Some large stones, found at the north of the lake, could be easily transformed into millstones, and as to the sails, the inexhaustible case of the balloon furnished the necessary material.

Cyrus Harding made his model, and the site of the mill was chosen a little to the right of the poultry-yard, near the shore of the lake. The frame was to rest on a pivot supported with strong timbers, so that it could turn with all the machinery it contained according as the wind required it. The work advanced rapidly. Neb and Pencroft had become very skilful carpenters, and had nothing to do but to copy the models provided by the engineer.

Soon a sort of cylindrical box, in shape like a pepper-pot, with a pointed roof, rose on the spot chosen. The four frames which formed the sails had been firmly fixed in the center beam, so as to form a certain angle with it, and secured with iron clamps. As to the different parts of the internal mechanism, the box destined to contain the two millstones, the fixed stone and the moving stone, the hopper, a sort of large square trough, wide at the top, narrow at the bottom, which would allow the grain to fall on the stones, the oscillating spout intended to regulate the passing of the grain, and lastly the bolting machine, which by the operation of sifting, separates the bran from the flour, were made without difficulty. The tools were good, and the work not difficult, for in reality, the machinery of a mill is very simple. This was only a question of time.

Every one had worked at the construction of the mill, and on the 1st of December it was finished. As usual, Pencroft was delighted with his work, and had no doubt that the apparatus was perfect.

"Now for a good wind," said he, "and we shall grind our first harvest splendidly!"

"A good wind, certainly," answered the engineer, "but not too much, Pencroft."

"Pooh! our mill would only go the faster!"

"There is no need for it to go so very fast," replied Cyrus Harding. "It is known by experience that the greatest quantity of work is performed by a mill when the number of turns made by the sails in a minute is six times the number of feet traversed by the wind in a second. A moderate breeze, which passes over twenty-four feet to the second, will give sixteen turns to the sails during a minute, and there is no need of more."

"Exactly!" cried Herbert, "a fine breeze is blowing from the northeast, which will soon do our business for us."

There was no reason for delaying the inauguration of the mill, for the settlers were eager to taste the first piece of bread in Lincoln Island. On this morning two or three bushels of wheat were ground, and the next day at breakfast a magnificent loaf, a little heavy perhaps, although raised with yeast, appeared on the table at Granite House. Every one munched away at it with a pleasure which may be easily understood.

In the meanwhile, the stranger had not reappeared. Several times Gideon Spilett and Herbert searched the forest in the neighborhood of Granite House, without meeting or finding any trace of him. They became seriously uneasy at this prolonged absence. Certainly, the former savage of Tabor island could not be perplexed how to live in the forest, abounding in game, but was it not to be feared that he had resumed his habits, and that this freedom would revive in him his wild instincts? However, Harding, by a sort of presentiment, doubtless, always persisted in saying that the fugitive would return.

"Yes, he will return!" he repeated with a confidence which his companions could not share. "When this unfortunate man was on Tabor Island, he knew himself to be alone! Here, he knows that fellow-men are awaiting him! Since he has partially spoken of his past life, the poor penitent will return to tell the whole, and from that day he will belong to us!"

The event justified Cyrus Harding's predictions. On the 3rd of December, Herbert had left the plateau to go and fish on the southern bank of the lake. He was unarmed, and till then had never taken any precautions for defense, as dangerous animals had not shown themselves on that part of the island.

Meanwhile, Pencroft and Neb were working in the poultry-yard, while Harding and the reporter were occupied at the Chimneys in making soda, the store of soap being exhausted.

Suddenly cries resounded,—

"Help! help!"

Cyrus Harding and the reporter, being at too great a distance, had not been able to hear the shouts. Pencroft and Neb, leaving the poultry-yard in all haste, rushed towards the lake.

But before then, the stranger, whose presence at this place no one had suspected, crossed Creek Glycerine, which separated the plateau from the forest, and bounded up the opposite bank.

Herbert was there face to face with a fierce jaguar, similar to the one which had been killed on Reptile End. Suddenly surprised, he was standing with his back against a tree, while the animal gathering itself together was about to spring.

But the stranger, with no other weapon than a knife, rushed on the formidable animal, who turned to meet this new adversary.

The struggle was short. The stranger possessed immense strength and activity. He seized the jaguar's throat with one powerful hand, holding it as in a vise, without heeding the beast's claws which tore his flesh, and with the other he plunged his knife into its heart.

The jaguar fell. The stranger kicked away the body, and was about to fly at the moment when the settlers arrived on the field of battle, but Herbert, clinging to him, cried,—

"No, no! you shall not go!"

Harding advanced towards the stranger, who frowned when he saw him approaching. The blood flowed from his shoulder under his torn shirt, but he took no notice of it.

"My friend," said Cyrus Harding, "we have just contracted a debt of gratitude to you. To save our boy you have risked your life!"

"My life!" murmured the stranger. "What is that worth? Less than nothing!"

"You are wounded?"

"It is no matter."

"Will you give me your hand?"

And as Herbert endeavored to seize the hand which had just saved him, the stranger folded his arms, his chest heaved, his look darkened, and he appeared to wish to escape, but making a violent effort over himself, and in an abrupt tone,—

"Who are you?" he asked, "and what do you claim to be to me?"

It was the colonists' history which he thus demanded, and for the first time. Perhaps this history recounted, he would tell his own.

In a few words Harding related all that had happened since their departure from Richmond; how they had managed, and what resources they now had at their disposal.

The stranger listened with extreme attention.

Then the engineer told who they all were, Gideon Spilett, Herbert, Pencroft, Neb, himself, and, he added, that the greatest happiness they had felt since their arrival in Lincoln Island was on the return of the vessel from Tabor Island, when they had been able to include among them a new companion.

At these words the stranger's face flushed, his head sunk on his breast, and confusion was depicted on his countenance.

"And now that you know us," added Cyrus Harding, "will you give us your hand?"

"No," replied the stranger in a hoarse voice; "no! You are honest men! And I—"

Chapter 17

These last words justified the colonists' presentiment. There had been some mournful past, perhaps expiated in the sight of men, but from which his conscience had not yet absolved him. At any rate the guilty man felt remorse, he repented, and his new friends would have cordially pressed the hand which they sought; but he did not feel himself worthy to extend it to honest men! However, after the scene with the jaguar, he did not return to the forest, and from that day did not go beyond the enclosure of Granite House.

What was the mystery of his life? Would the stranger one day speak of it? Time alone could show. At any rate, it was agreed that his secret should never be asked from him, and that they would live with him as if they suspected nothing.

For some days their life continued as before. Cyrus Harding and Gideon Spilett worked together, sometimes chemists, sometimes experimentalists. The reporter never left the engineer except to hunt with Herbert, for it would not have been prudent to allow the lad to ramble alone in the forest; and it was very necessary to be on their guard. As to Neb and Pencroft, one day at the stables and poultry-yard, another at the corral, without reckoning work in Granite House, they were never in want of employment.

The stranger worked alone, and he had resumed his usual life, never appearing at meals, sleeping under the trees in the plateau, never mingling with his companions. It really seemed as if the society of those who had saved him was insupportable to him!

"But then," observed Pencroft, "why did he entreat the help of his fellow-creatures? Why did he throw that paper into the sea?"

"He will tell us why," invariably replied Cyrus Harding.

"When?"

"Perhaps sooner than you think, Pencroft."

And, indeed, the day of confession was near.

On the 10th of December, a week after his return to Granite House, Harding saw the stranger approaching, who, in a calm voice and humble tone, said to him: "Sir, I have a request to make of you."

"Speak," answered the engineer, "but first let me ask you a question."

At these words the stranger reddened, and was on the point of withdrawing. Cyrus Harding understood what was passing in the mind of the guilty man, who doubtless feared that the engineer would interrogate him on his past life.

Harding held him back.

"Comrade," said he, "we are not only your companions but your friends. I wish you to believe that, and now I will listen to you."

The stranger pressed his hand over his eyes. He was seized with a sort of trembling, and remained a few moments without being able to articulate a word.

"Sir," said he at last, "I have come to beg you to grant me a favor."

"What is it?"

"You have, four or five miles from here, a corral for your domesticated animals. These animals need to be taken care of. Will you allow me to live there with them?"

Cyrus Harding gazed at the unfortunate man for a few moments with a feeling of deep commiseration; then,—

"My friend," said he, "the corral has only stables hardly fit for animals."

"It will be good enough for me, sir."

"My friend," answered Harding, "we will not constrain you in anything. You wish to live at the corral, so be it. You will, however, be always welcome at Granite House. But since you wish to live at the corral we will make the necessary arrangements for your being comfortably established there."

"Never mind that, I shall do very well."

"My friend," answered Harding, who always intentionally made use of this cordial appellation, "you must let us judge what it will be best to do in this respect."

"Thank you, sir," replied the stranger as he withdrew.

The engineer then made known to his companions the proposal which had been made to him, and it was agreed that they should build a wooden house at the corral, which they would make as comfortable as possible.

That very day the colonists repaired to the corral with the necessary tools, and a week had not passed before the house was ready to receive its tenant. It was built about twenty feet from the sheds, and from there it was easy to overlook the flock of sheep, which then numbered more than eighty. Some furniture, a bed, table, bench, cupboard, and chest were manufactured, and a gun, ammunition, and tools were carried to the corral.

The stranger, however, had seen nothing of his new dwelling, and he had allowed the settlers to work there without him, while he occupied himself on the plateau, wishing, doubtless, to put the finishing stroke to his work. Indeed, thanks to him, all the ground was dug up and ready to he sowed when the time came.

It was on the 20th of December that all the arrangements at the corral were completed. The engineer announced to the stranger that his dwelling was ready to receive him, and the latter replied that he would go and sleep there that very evening.

On this evening the colonists were gathered in the diningroom of Granite House. It was then eight o'clock, the hour at which their companion was to leave them. Not wishing to trouble him by their presence, and thus imposing on him the necessity of saying farewells which might perhaps be painful to him, they had left him alone and ascended to Granite House.

Now, they had been talking in the room for a few minutes, when a light knock was heard at the door. Almost immediately the stranger entered, and without any preamble,—

"Gentlemen," said he, "before I leave you, it is right that you should know my history. I will tell it you."

These simple words profoundly impressed Cyrus Harding and his companions. The engineer rose.

"We ask you nothing, my friend," said he; "it is your right to be silent."

"It is my duty to speak."

"Sit down, then."

"No, I will stand."

"We are ready to hear you," replied Harding.

The stranger remained standing in a corner of the room, a little in the shade. He was bareheaded, his arms folded across his chest, and it was in this posture that in a hoarse voice, speaking like some one who obliges himself to speak, he gave the following recital, which his auditors did not once interrupt:—

"On the 20th of December, 1854, a steam-yacht, belonging to a Scotch nobleman, Lord Glenarvan, anchored off Cape Bernouilli, on the western coast of Australia, in the thirty-seventh parallel. On board this yacht were Lord

Glenarvan and his wife, a major in the English army, a French geographer, a young girl, and a young boy. These two last were the children of Captain Grant, whose ship, the 'Britannia,' had been lost, crew and cargo, a year before. The 'Duncan' was commanded by Captain John Mangles, and manned by a crew of fifteen men.

"This is the reason the yacht at this time lay off the coast of Australia. Six months before, a bottle, enclosing a document written in English, German, and French, had been found in the Irish Sea, and picked up by the 'Duncan.' This document stated in substance that there still existed three survivors from the wreck of the 'Britannia,' that these survivors were Captain Grant and two of his men, and that they had found refuge on some land, of which the document gave the latitude, but of which the longitude, effaced by the sea, was no longer legible.

"This latitude was 37deg 11' south; therefore, the longitude being unknown, if they followed the thirty-seventh parallel over continents and seas, they would be certain to reach the spot inhabited by Captain Grant and his two companions. The English Admiralty having hesitated to undertake this search, Lord Glenarvan resolved to attempt everything to find the captain. He communicated with Mary and Robert Grant, who joined him. The 'Duncan' yacht was equipped for the distant voyage, in which the nobleman's family and the captain's children wished to take part, and the 'Duncan,' leaving Glasgow, proceeded towards the Atlantic, passed through the Straits of Magellan, and ascended the Pacific as far as Patagonia, where, according to a previous interpretation of the document, they supposed that Captain Grant was a prisoner among the Indians.

"The 'Duncan' disembarked her passengers on the western coast of Patagonia, and sailed to pick them up again on the eastern coast at Cape Corrientes. Lord Glenarvan traversed Patagonia, following the thirty-seventh parallel, and having found no trace of the captain, he re-embarked on the 13th of November, so as to pursue his search through the Ocean.

"After having unsuccessfully visited the islands of Tristan d'Acunha and Amsterdam, situated in her course, the 'Duncan,' as I have said, arrived at Cape Bernouilli, on the Australian coast, on the 20th of December, 1854.

"It was Lord Glenarvan's intention to traverse Australia as he had traversed America, and he disembarked. A few miles from the coast was established a farm, belonging to an Irishman, who offered hospitality to the travelers. Lord Glenarvan made known to the Irishman the cause which had brought him to these parts, and asked if he knew whether a three-masted English vessel, the 'Britannia,' had been lost less than two years before on the west coast of Australia.

"The Irishman had never heard of this wreck, but, to the great surprise of the bystanders, one of his servants came forward and said,—

"'My lord, praise and thank God! If Captain Grant is still living, he is living on the Australian shores.'

"'Who are you?' asked Lord Glenarvan.

"'A Scotchman like yourself, my lord,' replied the man; 'I am one of Captain Grant's crew—one of the castaways of the "Britannia."'

"This man was called Ayrton. He was, in fact, the boatswain's mate of the 'Britannia,' as his papers showed. But, separated from Captain Grant at the moment when the ship struck upon the rocks, he had till then believed that the captain with all his crew had perished, and that he, Ayrton, was the sole survivor of the 'Britannia.'

"'Only,' he added, 'it was not on the west coast, but on the east coast of Australia that the vessel was lost, and if Captain Grant is still living, as his document indicates, he is a prisoner among the natives, and it is on the other coast that he must be looked for.'

"This man spoke in a frank voice and with a confident look; his words could not be doubted. The irishman, in whose service he had been for more than a year, answered for his trustworthiness. Lord Glenarvan, therefore, believed in the fidelity of this man and, by his advice, resolved to cross Australia, following the thirty-seventh parallel. Lord Glenarvan, his wife, the two children, the major, the Frenchman, Captain Mangles, and a few sailors composed the little band under the command of Ayrton, while the 'Duncan,' under charge of the mate, Tom Austin, proceeded to Melbourne, there to await Lord Glenarvan's instructions.

"They set out on the 23rd of December, 1854.

"It is time to say that Ayrton was a traitor. He was, indeed, the boatswain's mate of the 'Britannia,' but, after some dispute with his captain, he endeavored to incite the crew to mutiny and seize the ship, and Captain Grant had landed him, on the 8th of April, 1852, on the west coast of Australia, and then sailed, leaving him there, as was only just.

"Therefore this wretched man knew nothing of the wreck of the 'Britannia'; he had just heard of it from Glenarvan's account. Since his abandonment, he had become, under the name of Ben Joyce, the leader of the escaped convicts; and if he boldly maintained that the wreck had taken place on the east coast, and led Lord Glenarvan to proceed in that direction, it was that he hoped to separate him from his ship, seize the 'Duncan,' and make the yacht a pirate in the Pacific."

Here the stranger stopped for a moment. His voice trembled, but he continued,—

"The expedition set out and proceeded across Australia. It was inevitably unfortunate, since Ayrton, or Ben Joyce, as he may be called, guided it, sometimes preceded, sometimes followed by his band of convicts, who had been told what they had to do.

"Meanwhile, the 'Duncan' had been sent to Melbourne for repairs. It was necessary, then, to get Lord Glenarvan to order her to leave Melbourne and go to the east coast of Australia, where it would be easy to seize her. After having led the expedition near enough to the coast, in the midst of vast forests with no resources, Ayrton obtained a letter, which he was charged to carry to the mate of the 'Duncan'—a letter which ordered the yacht to repair immediately to the east coast, to Twofold Bay, that is to say a few days' journey from the place where the expedition had stopped. It was there that Ayrton had agreed to meet his accomplices, and two days after gaining possession of the letter, he arrived at Melbourne.

"So far the villain had succeeded in his wicked design. He would be able to take the 'Duncan' into Twofold Bay, where it would be easy for the convicts to seize her, and her crew massacred, Ben Joyce would become master of the seas. But it pleased God to prevent the accomplishment of these terrible projects.

"Ayrton, arrived at Melbourne, delivered the letter to the mate, Tom Austin, who read it and immediately set sail, but judge of Ayrton's rage and disappointment, when the next day he found that the mate was taking the vessel, not to the east coast of Australia, to Twofold Bay, but to the east coast of New Zealand. He wished to stop him, but Austin showed him the letter!... And indeed, by a providential error of the French geographer, who had written the letter, the east coast of New Zealand was mentioned as the place of destination.

"All Ayrton's plans were frustrated! He became outrageous. They put him in irons. He was then taken to the coast of New Zealand, not knowing what would become of his accomplices, or what would become of Lord Glenarvan.

"The 'Duncan' cruised about on this coast until the 3rd of March. On that day Ayrton heard the report of guns. The guns on the 'Duncan' were being fired, and soon Lord Glenarvan and his companions came on board.

"This is what had happened.

"After a thousand hardships, a thousand dangers, Lord Glenarvan had accomplished his journey, and arrived on the east coast of Australia, at Twofold Bay. 'Not "Duncan!' He telegraphed to Melbourne. They answered, "Duncan" sailed on the 18th instant. Destination unknown.'

"Lord Glenarvan could only arrive at one conclusion; that his honest yacht had fallen into the hands of Ben Joyce, and had become a pirate vessel!

"However, Lord Glenarvan would not give up. He was a bold and generous man. He embarked in a merchant vessel, sailed to the west coast of New Zealand, traversed it along the thirty-seventh parallel, without finding any trace of Captain Grant; but on the other side, to his great surprise, and by the will of Heaven, he found the 'Duncan,' under command of the mate, who had been waiting for him for five weeks!

"This was on the 3rd of March, 1855. Lord Glenarvan was now on board the 'Duncan,' but Ayrton was there also. He appeared before the nobleman, who wished to extract from him all that the villain knew about Captain Grant. Ayrton refused to speak. Lord Glenarvan then told him, that at the first port they put into, he would be delivered up to the English authorities. Ayrton remained mute.

"The 'Duncan' continued her voyage along the thirty-seventh parallel. In the meanwhile, Lady Glenarvan undertook to vanquish the resistance of the ruffian.

"At last, her influence prevailed, and Ayrton, in exchange for what he could tell, proposed that Lord Glenarvan should leave him on some island in the Pacific, instead of giving him up to the English authorities. Lord Glenarvan, resolving to do anything to obtain information about Captain Grant, consented.

"Ayrton then related all his life, and it was certain that he knew nothing from the day on which Captain Grant had landed him on the Australian coast.

"Nevertheless, Lord Glenarvan kept the promise which he had given. The 'Duncan' continued her voyage and arrived at Tabor Island. It was there that Ayrton was to be landed, and it was there also that, by a veritable miracle, they found Captain Grant and two men, exactly on the thirty-seventh parallel.

"The convict, then, went to take their place on this desert islet, and at the moment he left the yacht these words were pronounced by Lord Glenarvan:—

"'Here, Ayrton, you will be far from any land, and without any possible communication with your fellow-creatures. You can-not escape from this islet on which the 'Duncan' leaves you. You will be alone, under the eye of a God who reads the depths of the heart, but you will be neither lost nor forgotten, as was Captain Grant. Unworthy as you are to be remembered by men, men will remember you. I know where you are Ayrton, and I know where to find you. I will never forget it!

"And the 'Duncan,' making sail, soon disappeared. This was 18th of March, 1855.

(The events which have just been briefly related are taken from a work which some of our readers have no doubt read, and which is entitled, "Captain Grant's children." They will remark on this occasion, as well as later, some discrepancy in the dates; but later again, they will understand why the real dates were not at first given.)

"Ayrton was alone, but he had no want of either ammunition, weapons, tools, or seeds.

"At his, the convict's disposal, was the house built by honest Captain Grant. He had only to live and expiate in solitude the crimes which he had committed.

"Gentlemen, he repented, he was ashamed of his crimes and was very miserable! He said to himself, that if men came some day to take him from that islet, he must be worthy to return among them! How he suffered, that wretched man! How he labored to recover himself by work! How he prayed to be reformed by prayer! For two years, three years, this went on, but Ayrton, humbled by solitude, always looking for some ship to appear on the horizon, asking himself if the time of expiation would soon be complete, suffered as none other suffered! Oh! how dreadful was this solitude, to a heart tormented by remorse!

"But doubtless Heaven had not sufficiently punished this unhappy man, for he felt that he was gradually becoming a savage! He felt that brutishness was gradually gaining on him!

"He could not say if it was after two or three years of solitude, but at last he became the miserable creature you found!

"I have no need to tell you, gentlemen, that Ayrton, Ben Joyce, and I, are the same."

Cyrus Harding and his companions rose at the end of this account. It is impossible to say how much they were moved! What misery, grief, and despair lay revealed before them!

"Ayrton," said Harding, rising, "you have been a great criminal, but Heaven must certainly think that you have expiated your crimes! That has been proved by your having been brought again among your fellow-creatures. Ayrton, you are forgiven! And now you will be our companion?"

Ayrton drew back.

"Here is my hand!" said the engineer.

Ayrton grasped the hand which Harding extended to him, and great tears fell from his eyes.

"Will you live with us?" asked Cyrus Harding.

"Captain Harding, leave me some time longer," replied Ayrton, "leave me alone in the hut in the corral!"

"As you like, Ayrton," answered Cyrus Harding. Ayrton was going to withdraw, when the engineer addressed one more question to him:—

"One word more, my friend. Since it was your intention to live alone, why did you throw into the sea the document which put us on your track?"

"A document?" repeated Ayrton, who did not appear to know what he meant.

"Yes, the document which we found enclosed in a bottle, giving us the exact position of Tabor Island!"

Ayrton passed his hand over his brow, then after having thought, "I never threw any document into the sea!" he answered.

"Never?" exclaimed Pencroft.

"Never!"

And Ayrton, bowing, reached the door and departed.

Chapter 18

"Poor man!" said Herbert, who had rushed to the door, but returned, having seen Ayrton slide down the rope on the lift and disappear in the darkness.

"He will come back," said Cyrus Harding.

"Come, now, captain," exclaimed Pencroft, "what does that mean? What! wasn't it Ayrton who threw that bottle into the sea? Who was it then?"

Certainly, if ever a question was necessary to be made, it was that one!

"It was he," answered Neb, "only the unhappy man was half-mad."

"Yes!" said Herbert, "and he was no longer conscious of what he was doing."

"It can only be explained in that way, my friends," replied Harding quickly, "and I understand now how Ayrton was able to point out exactly the situation of Tabor Island, since the events which had preceded his being left on the island had made it known to him."

"However," observed Pencroft, "if he was not yet a brute when he wrote that document, and if he threw it into the sea seven or eight years ago, how is it that the paper has not been injured by damp?"

"That proves," answered Cyrus Harding, "that Ayrton was deprived of intelligence at a more recent time than he thinks."

"Of course it must be so," replied Pencroft, "without that the fact would be unaccountable."

"Unaccountable indeed," answered the engineer, who did not appear desirous to prolong the conversation.

"But has Ayrton told the truth?" asked the sailor.

"Yes," replied the reporter. "The story which he has told is true in every point. I remember quite well the account in the newspapers of the yacht expedition undertaken by Lord Glenarvan, and its result."

"Ayrton has told the truth," added Harding. "Do not doubt it, Pencroft, for it was painful to him. People tell the truth when they accuse themselves like that!"

The next day—the 21st of December—the colonists descended to the beach, and having climbed the plateau they found nothing of Ayrton. He had reached his house in the corral during the night and the settlers judged it best not to agitate him by their presence. Time would doubtless perform what sympathy had been unable to accomplish.

Herbert, Pencroft, and Neb resumed their ordinary occupations. On this day the same work brought Harding and the reporter to the workshop at the Chimneys.

"Do you know, my dear Cyrus," said Gideon Spilett, "that the explanation you gave yesterday on the subject of the bottle has not satisfied me at all! How can it be supposed that the unfortunate man was able to write that document and throw the bottle into the sea without having the slightest recollection of it?"

"Nor was it he who threw it in, my dear Spilett."

"You think then—"

"I think nothing, I know nothing!" interrupted Cyrus Harding. "I am content to rank this incident among those which I have not been able to explain to this day!"

"Indeed, Cyrus," said Spilett, "these things are incredible! Your rescue, the case stranded on the sand, Top's adventure, and lastly this bottle... Shall we never have the answer to these enigmas?"

"Yes!" replied the engineer quickly, "yes, even if I have to penetrate into the bowels of this island!"

"Chance will perhaps give us the key to this mystery!"

"Chance! Spilett! I do not believe in chance, any more than I believe in mysteries in this world. There is a reason for everything unaccountable which has happened here, and that reason I shall discover. But in the meantime we must work and observe."

The month of January arrived. The year 1867 commenced. The summer occupations were assiduously continued. During the days which followed, Herbert and Spilett having gone in the direction of the corral, ascertained that Ayrton had taken possession of the habitation which had been prepared for him. He busied himself with the numerous flock confided to his care, and spared his companions the trouble of coming every two or three days to visit the corral. Nevertheless, in order not to leave Ayrton in solitude for too long a time, the settlers often paid him a visit.

It was not unimportant either, in consequence of some suspicions entertained by the engineer and Gideon Spilett, that this part of the island should be subject to a surveillance of some sort, and that Ayrton, if any incident occurred unexpectedly, should not neglect to inform the inhabitants of Granite House of it.

Nevertheless it might happen that something would occur which it would be necessary to bring rapidly to the engineer's knowledge. Independently of facts bearing on the mystery of Lincoln Island, many others might happen, which would call for the prompt interference of the colonists,—such as the sighting of a vessel, a wreck on the western coast, the possible arrival of pirates, etc.

Therefore Cyrus Harding resolved to put the corral in instantaneous communication with Granite House.

It was on the 10th of January that he made known his project to his companions.

"Why! how are you going to manage that, captain?" asked Pencroft. "Do you by chance happen to think of establishing a telegraph?"

"Exactly so," answered the engineer.

"Electric?" cried Herbert.

"Electric," replied Cyrus Harding. "We have all the necessary materials for making a battery, and the most difficult thing will be to stretch the wires, but by means of a drawplate I think we shall manage it."

"Well, after that," returned the sailor, "I shall never despair of seeing ourselves some day rolling along on a railway!"

They then set to work, beginning with the most difficult thing, for, if they failed in that, it would be useless to manufacture the battery and other accessories.

The iron of Lincoln Island, as has been said, was of excellent quality, and consequently very fit for being drawn out. Harding commenced by manufacturing a drawplate, that is to say, a plate of steel, pierced with conical holes of different sizes, which would successively bring the wire to the wished-for tenacity. This piece of steel, after having been tempered, was fixed in as firm a way as possible in a solid framework planted in the ground, only a few feet from the great fall, the motive power of which the engineer intended to utilize. In fact as the fulling-mill was there, although not then in use, its beam moved with extreme power would serve to stretch out the wire by rolling it round itself. It was a delicate operation, and required much care. The iron, prepared previously in long thin rods, the ends of which were sharpened with the file, having been introduced into the largest hole of the drawplate, was drawn out by the beam which wound it round itself, to a length of twenty-five or thirty feet, then unrolled, and the same operation was performed successively through the holes of a less size. Finally, the engineer obtained wires from forty to fifty feet long, which could be easily fastened together and stretched over the distance of five miles, which separated the corral from the bounds of Granite House.

It did not take more than a few days to perform this work, and indeed as soon as the machine had been commenced, Cyrus Harding left his companions to follow the trade of wiredrawers, and occupied himself with manufacturing his battery.

It was necessary to obtain a battery with a constant current. It is known that the elements of modern batteries are generally composed of retort coal, zinc, and copper. Copper was absolutely wanting to the engineer, who, notwithstanding all his researches, had never been able to find any trace of it in Lincoln Island, and was therefore obliged to do without it. Retort coal, that is to say, the hard graphite which is found in the retorts of gas manufactories, after the coal has been dehydrogenized, could have been obtained, but it would have been necessary to establish a special apparatus, involving great labor. As to zinc, it may be remembered that the case found at Flotsam Point was lined with this metal, which could not be better utilized than for this purpose.

Cyrus Harding, after mature consideration, decided to manufacture a very simple battery, resembling as nearly as possible that invented by Becquerel in 1820, and in which zinc only is employed. The other substances, azotic acid and potash, were all at his disposal.

The way in which the battery was composed was as follows, and the results were to be attained by the reaction of acid and potash on each other. A number of glass bottles were made and filled with azotic acid. The engineer corked them by means of a stopper through which passed a glass tube, bored at its lower extremity, and intended to be plunged into the acid by means of a clay stopper secured by a rag. Into this tube, through its upper extremity, he poured a solution of potash, previously obtained by burning and reducing to ashes various plants, and in this way the acid and potash could act on each other through the clay.

Cyrus Harding then took two slips of zinc, one of which was plunged into azotic acid, the other into a solution of potash. A current was immediately produced, which was transmitted from the slip of zinc in the bottle to that in the tube, and the two slips having been connected by a metallic wire the slip in the tube became the positive pole, and that in the bottle the negative pole of the apparatus. Each bottle, therefore, produced as many currents as united would be sufficient to produce all the phenomena of the electric telegraph. Such was the ingenious and very simple apparatus constructed by Cyrus Harding, an apparatus which would allow them to establish a telegraphic communication between Granite House and the corral.

On the 6th of February was commenced the planting along the road to the corral, of posts furnished with glass insulators, and intended to support the wire. A few days after, the wire was extended, ready to produce the electric current at a rate of twenty thousand miles a second.

Two batteries had been manufactured, one for Granite House, the other for the corral; for if it was necessary the corral should be able to communicate with Granite House it might also be useful that Granite House should be able to communicate with the corral.

As to the receiver and manipulator, they were very simple. At the two stations the wire was wound round a magnet, that is to say, round a piece of soft iron surrounded with a wire. The communication was thus established between the two poles; the current, starting from the positive pole, traversed the wire, passed through the magnet which was temporarily magnetized, and returned through the earth to the negative pole. If the current was interrupted, the magnet immediately became unmagnetized. It was sufficient to place a plate of soft iron before the magnet, which, attracted during the passage of the current, would fall back when the current was interrupted. This movement of the plate thus obtained, Harding could easily fasten to it a needle arranged on a dial, bearing the letters of the alphabet, and in this way communicate from one station to the other.

All was completely arranged by the 12th of February. On this day, Harding, having sent the current through the wire, asked if all was going on well at the corral, and received in a few moments a satisfactory reply from Ayrton. Pencroft was wild with joy, and every morning and evening he sent a telegram to the corral, which always received an answer.

This mode of communication presented two very real advantages: firstly, because it enabled them to ascertain that Ayrton was at the corral; and secondly, that he was thus not left completely isolated. Besides, Cyrus Harding never allowed a week to pass without going to see him, and Ayrton came from time to time to Granite House, where he always found a cordial welcome.

The fine season passed away in the midst of the usual work. The resources of the colony, particularly in vegetables and corn, increased from day to day, and the plants brought from Tabor Island had succeeded perfectly.

The plateau of Prospect Heights presented an encouraging aspect. The fourth harvest had been admirable and it may be supposed that no one thought of counting whether the four hundred thousand millions of grains duly appeared in the crop. However, Pencroft had thought of doing so, but Cyrus Harding having told him that even if he managed to count three hundred grains a minute, or nine thousand an hour, it would take him nearly five thousand five-hundred years to finish his task, the honest sailor considered it best to give up the idea.

The weather was splendid, the temperature very warm in the day time, but in the evening the sea-breezes tempered the heat of the atmosphere and procured cool nights for the inhabitants of Granite House. There were, however, a few storms, which, although they were not of long duration, swept over Lincoln Island with extraordinary fury. The lightning blazed and the thunder continued to roll for some hours.

At this period the little colony was extremely prosperous.

The tenants of the poultry-yard swarmed, and they lived on the surplus, but it became necessary to reduce the population to a more moderate number. The pigs had already produced young, and it may be understood that their care for these animals absorbed a great part of Neb and Pencroft's time. The onagers, who had two pretty colts, were most often mounted by Gideon Spilett and Herbert, who had become an excellent rider under the reporter's instruction, and they also harnessed them to the cart either for carrying wood and coal to Granite House, or different mineral productions required by the engineer.

Several expeditions were made about this time into the depths of the Far West Forests. The explorers could venture there without having anything to fear from the heat, for the sun's rays scarcely penetrated through the thick foliage spreading above their heads. They thus visited all the left bank of the Mercy, along which ran the road from the corral to the mouth of Falls River.

But in these excursions the settlers took care to be well armed, for they met with savage wild boars, with which they often had a tussle. They also, during this season, made fierce war against the jaguars. Gideon Spilett had vowed a special hatred against them, and his pupil Herbert seconded him well. Armed as they were, they no longer feared to meet one of those beasts. Herbert's courage was superb, and the reporter's sang-froid astonishing. Already twenty magnificent skins ornamented the dining-room of Granite House, and if this continued, the jaguar race would soon be extinct in the island, the object aimed at by the hunters.

The engineer sometimes took part in the expeditions made to the unknown parts of the island, which he surveyed with great attention. It was for other traces than those of animals that he searched the thickets of the vast forest, but nothing suspicious ever appeared. Neither Top nor Jup, who accompanied him, ever betrayed by their behavior that there was anything strange there, and yet more than once again the dog barked at the mouth of the well, which the engineer had before explored without result.

At this time Gideon Spilett, aided by Herbert, took several views of the most picturesque parts of the island, by means of the photographic apparatus found in the cases, and of which they had not as yet made any use.

This apparatus, provided with a powerful object-glass, was very complete. Substances necessary for the photographic reproduction, collodion for preparing the glass plate, nitrate of silver to render it sensitive, hyposulfate of soda to fix the prints obtained, chloride of ammonium in which to soak the paper destined to give the positive proof, acetate of soda and chloride of gold in which to immerse the paper, nothing was wanting. Even the papers were there, all prepared, and before laying in the printing-frame upon the negatives, it was sufficient to soak them for a few minutes in the solution of nitrate of silver.

The reporter and his assistant became in a short time very skilful operators, and they obtained fine views of the country, such as the island, taken from Prospect Heights with Mount Franklin in the distance, the mouth of the Mercy, so picturesquely framed in high rocks, the glade and the corral, with the spurs of the mountain in the background, the curious development of Claw Cape, Flotsam Point, etc.

Nor did the photographers forget to take the portraits of all the inhabitants of the island, leaving out no one.

"It multiplies us," said Pencroft.

And the sailor was enchanted to see his own countenance, faithfully reproduced, ornamenting the walls of Granite House, and he stopped as willingly before this exhibition as he would have done before the richest shop-windows in Broadway.

But it must be acknowledged that the most successful portrait was incontestably that of Master Jup. Master Jup had sat with a gravity not to be described, and his portrait was lifelike!

"He looks as if he was just going to grin!" exclaimed Pencroft.

And if Master Jup had not been satisfied, he would have been very difficult to please; but he was quite contented and contemplated his own countenance with a sentimental air which expressed some small amount of conceit.

The summer heat ended with the month of March. The weather was sometimes rainy, but still warm. The month of March, which corresponds to the

September of northern latitudes, was not so fine as might have been hoped. Perhaps it announced an early and rigorous winter.

It might have been supposed one morning—the 21 st—that the first snow had already made its appearance. In fact Herbert looking early from one of the windows of Granite House, exclaimed,—

"Hallo! the islet is covered with snow!"

"Snow at this time?" answered the reporter, joining the boy.

Their companions were soon beside them, but could only ascertain one thing, that not only the islet but all the beach below Granite House was covered with one uniform sheet of white.

"It must be snow!" said Pencroft.

"Or rather it's very like it!" replied Neb.

"But the thermometer marks fifty-eight degrees!" observed Gideon Spilett.

Cyrus Harding gazed at the sheet of white without saying anything, for he really did not know how to explain this phenomenon, at this time of year and in such a temperature.

"By Jove!" exclaimed Pencroft, "all our plants will be frozen!"

And the sailor was about to descend, when he was preceded by the nimble Jup, who slid down to the sand.

But the orang had not touched the ground, when the snowy sheet arose and dispersed in the air in such innumerable flakes that the light of the sun was obscured for some minutes.

"Birds!" cried Herbert.

They were indeed swarms of sea-birds, with dazzling white plumage. They had perched by thousands on the islet and on the shore, and they disappeared in the distance, leaving the colonists amazed as if they had been present at some transformation scene, in which summer succeeded winter at the touch of a fairy's wand. Unfortunately the change had been so sudden, that neither the reporter nor the lad had been able to bring down one of these birds, of which they could not recognize the species.

A few days after came the 26th of March, the day on which, two years before, the castaways from the air had been thrown upon Lincoln Island.

Chapter 19

Two years already! and for two years the colonists had had no communication with their fellow-creatures! They were without news from the civilized world, lost on this island, as completely as if they had been on the most minute star of the celestial hemisphere!

What was now happening in their country? The picture of their native land was always before their eyes, the land torn by civil war at the time they left it, and which the Southern rebellion was perhaps still staining with blood! It was a great sorrow to them, and they often talked together of these things, without ever doubting however that the cause of the North must triumph, for the honor of the American Confederation.

During these two years not a vessel had passed in sight of the island; or, at least, not a sail had been seen. It was evident that Lincoln Island was out of the usual track, and also that it was unknown,—as was besides proved by the maps,—for though there was no port, vessels might have visited it for the purpose of renewing their store of water. But the surrounding ocean was deserted as far as the eye could reach, and the colonists must rely on themselves for regaining their native land.

However, one chance of rescue existed, and this chance was discussed one day on the first week of April, when the colonists were gathered together in the dining-room of Granite House.

They had been talking of America, of their native country, which they had so little hope of ever seeing again.

"Decidedly we have only one way," said Spilett, "one single way for leaving Lincoln Island, and that is, to build a vessel large enough to sail several hundred miles. It appears to me, that when one has built a boat it is just as easy to build a ship!"

"And in which we might go to the Pomoutous," added Herbert, "just as easily as we went to Tabor Island."

"I do not say no," replied Pencroft, who had always the casting vote in maritime questions; "I do not say no, although it is not exactly the same thing to make a long as a short voyage! If our little craft had been caught in any heavy gale of wind during the voyage to Tabor Island, we should have known that land was at no great distance either way; but twelve hundred miles is a pretty long way, and the nearest land is at least that distance!"

"Would you not, in that case, Pencroft, attempt the adventure?" asked the reporter.

"I will attempt anything that is desired, Mr. Spilett," answered the sailor, "and you know well that I am not a man to flinch!"

"Remember, besides, that we number another sailor amongst us now," remarked Neb.

"Who is that?" asked Pencroft.

"Ayrton."

"If he will consent to come," said Pencroft.

"Nonsense!" returned the reporter; "do you think that if Lord Glenarvan's yacht had appeared at Tabor Island, while he was still living there, Ayrton would have refused to depart?"

"You forget, my friends," then said Cyrus Harding, "that Ayrton was not in possession of his reason during the last years of his stay there. But that is not the question. The point is to know if we may count among our chances of being rescued, the return of the Scotch vessel. Now, Lord Glenarvan promised Ayrton that he would return to take him off from Tabor Island when he considered that his crimes were expiated, and I believe that he will return."

"Yes," said the reporter, "and I will add that he will return soon, for it is twelve years since Ayrton was abandoned."

"Well!" answered Pencroft, "I agree with you that the nobleman will return, and soon too. But where will he touch? At Tabor Island, and not at Lincoln Island."

"That is the more certain," replied Herbert, "as Lincoln Island is not even marked on the map."

"Therefore, my friends," said the engineer, "we ought to take the necessary precautions for making our presence and that of Ayrton on Lincoln Island known at Tabor Island."

"Certainly," answered the reporter, "and nothing is easier than to place in the hut, which was Captain Grant's and Ayrton's dwelling, a notice which Lord Glenarvan and his crew cannot help finding, giving the position of our island."

"It is a pity," remarked the sailor, "that we forgot to take that precaution on our first visit to Tabor Island."

"And why should we have done it?" asked Herbert. "At that time we did not know Ayrton's history; we did not know that any one was likely to come some day to fetch him, and when we did know his history, the season was too advanced to allow us to return then to Tabor Island."

"Yes," replied Harding, "it was too late, and we must put off the voyage until next spring."

"But suppose the Scotch yacht comes before that," said Pencroft.

"That is not probable," replied the engineer, "for Lord Glenarvan would not choose the winter season to venture into these seas. Either he has already returned to Tabor Island, since Ayrton has been with us, that is to say, during the last five months and has left again; or he will not come till later, and it will be time enough in the first fine October days to go to Tabor Island, and leave a notice there."

"We must allow," said Neb, "that it will be very unfortunate if the 'Duncan' has returned to these parts only a few months ago!"

"I hope that it is not so," replied Cyrus Harding, "and that Heaven has not deprived us of the best chance which remains to us."

"I think," observed the reporter, "that at any rate we shall know what we have to depend on when we have been to Tabor Island, for if the yacht has returned there, they will necessarily have left some traces of their visit."

"That is evident," answered the engineer. "So then, my friends, since we have this chance of returning to our country, we must wait patiently, and if it is taken from us we shall see what will be best to do."

"At any rate," remarked Pencroft, "it is well understood that if we do leave Lincoln Island, it will not be because we were uncomfortable there!"

"No, Pencroft," replied the engineer, "it will be because we are far from all that a man holds dearest in the world, his family, his friends, his native land!"

Matters being thus decided, the building of a vessel large enough to sail either to the Archipelagoes in the north, or to New Zealand in the west, was no longer talked of, and they busied themselves in their accustomed occupations, with a view to wintering a third time in Granite House.

However, it was agreed that before the stormy weather came on, their little vessel should be employed in making a voyage round the island. A complete survey of the coast had not yet been made, and the colonists had but an imperfect idea of the shore to the west and north, from the mouth of Falls River to the Mandible Capes, as well as of the narrow bay between them, which opened like a shark's jaws.

The plan of this excursion was proposed by Pencroft, and Cyrus Harding fully acquiesced in it, for he himself wished to see this part of his domain.

The weather was variable, but the barometer did not fluctuate by sudden movements, and they could therefore count on tolerable weather. However, during the first week of April, after a sudden barometrical fall, a renewed rise was marked by a heavy gale of wind, lasting five or six days; then the needle of the instrument remained stationary at a height of twenty-nine inches and nine-tenths, and the weather appeared propitious for an excursion.

The departure was fixed for the 16th of April, and the "Bonadventure," anchored in Port Balloon, was provisioned for a voyage which might be of some duration.

Cyrus Harding informed Ayrton of the projected expedition, and proposed that he should take part in it, but Ayrton preferring to remain on shore, it was decided that he should come to Granite House during the absence of his companions. Master Jup was ordered to keep him company, and made no remonstrance.

On the morning of the 16th of April all the colonists, including Top, embarked. A fine breeze blew from the south-west, and the "Bonadventure" tacked on leaving Port Balloon so as to reach Reptile End. Of the ninety miles which the perimeter of the island measured, twenty included the south coast between the port and the promontory. The wind being right ahead it was necessary to hug the shore.

It took the whole day to reach the promontory, for the vessel on leaving port had only two hours of ebb tide and had therefore to make way for six hours against the flood. It was nightfall before the promontory was doubled.

The sailor then proposed to the engineer that they should continue sailing slowly with two reefs in the sail. But Harding preferred to anchor a few cable-lengths from the shore, so as to survey that part of the coast during the day. It was agreed also that as they were anxious for a minute exploration of the coast they should not sail during the night, but would always, when the weather permitted it, be at anchor near the shore.

The night was passed under the promontory, and the wind having fallen, nothing disturbed the silence. The passengers, with the exception of the sailor, scarcely slept as well on board the "Bonadventure" as they would have done in their rooms at Granite House, but they did sleep however. Pencroft set sail at break of day, and by going on the larboard tack they could keep close to the shore.

The colonists knew this beautiful wooded coast, since they had already explored it on foot, and yet it again excited their admiration. They coasted along as close in as possible, so as to notice everything, avoiding always the trunks of trees which floated here and there. Several times also they anchored, and Gideon Spilett took photographs of the superb scenery.

About noon the "Bonadventure" arrived at the mouth of Falls River. Beyond, on the left bank, a few scattered trees appeared, and three miles further even these dwindled into solitary groups among the western spurs of the mountain, whose arid ridge sloped down to the shore.

What a contrast between the northern and southern part of the coast! In proportion as one was woody and fertile so was the other rugged and barren! It might have been designated as one of those iron coasts, as they are called in some countries, and its wild confusion appeared to indicate that a sudden crystallization had been produced in the yet liquid basalt of some distant geological sea. These stupendous masses would have terrified the settlers if they had been cast at first on this part of the island! They had not been able to perceive the sinister aspect of this shore from the summit of Mount Franklin, for they overlooked it from too great a height, but viewed from the sea it presented a wild appearance which could not perhaps be equaled in any corner of the globe.

The "Bonadventure" sailed along this coast for the distance of half a mile. It was easy to see that it was composed of blocks of all sizes, from twenty to three hundred feet in height, and of all shapes, round like towers, prismatic like steeples, pyramidal like obelisks, conical like factory chimneys. An iceberg of the Polar seas could not have been more capricious in its terrible sublimity! Here, bridges were thrown from one rock to another; there, arches like those of a wave, into the depths of which the eye could not penetrate; in one place, large vaulted excavations presented a monumental aspect; in another, a crowd of columns, spires, and arches, such as no Gothic cathedral ever possessed. Every caprice of nature, still more varied than those of the imagination, appeared on this grand coast, which extended over a length of eight or nine miles.

Cyrus Harding and his companions gazed, with a feeling of surprise bordering on stupefaction. But, although they remained silent, Top, not being troubled with feelings of this sort, uttered barks which were repeated by the thousand echoes of the basaltic cliff. The engineer even observed that these barks had something strange in them, like those which the dog had uttered at the mouth of the well in Granite House.

"Let us go close in," said he.

And the "Bonadventure" sailed as near as possible to the rocky shore. Perhaps some cave, which it would be advisable to explore, existed there? But Harding saw nothing, not a cavern, not a cleft which could serve as a retreat to any being whatever, for the foot of the cliff was washed by the surf. Soon Top's barks ceased, and the vessel continued her course at a few cables-length from the coast.

In the northwest part of the island the shore became again flat and sandy. A few trees here and there rose above a low, marshy ground, which the colonists had already surveyed, and in violent contrast to the other desert shore, life was again manifested by the presence of myriads of water-fowl. That evening the "Bonadventure" anchored in a small bay to the north of the island, near the land, such was the depth of water there. The night passed quietly, for the breeze died away with the last light of day, and only rose again with the first streaks of dawn.

As it was easy to land, the usual hunters of the colony, that is to say, Herbert and Gideon Spilett, went for a ramble of two hours or so, and returned with several strings of wild duck and snipe. Top had done wonders, and not a bird had been lost, thanks to his zeal and cleverness.

At eight o'clock in the morning the "Bonadventure" set sail, and ran rapidly towards North Mandible Cape, for the wind was right astern and freshening rapidly.

"However," observed Pencroft, "I should not be surprised if a gale came up from the west. Yesterday the sun set in a very red-looking horizon, and now, this morning, those mares-tails don't forbode anything good."

These mares-tails are cirrus clouds, scattered in the zenith, their height from the sea being less than five thousand feet. They look like light pieces of cotton wool, and their presence usually announces some sudden change in the weather.

"Well," said Harding, "let us carry as much sail as possible, and run for shelter into Shark Gulf. I think that the 'Bonadventure' will be safe there."

"Perfectly," replied Pencroft, "and besides, the north coast is merely sand, very uninteresting to look at."

"I shall not be sorry," resumed the engineer, "to pass not only to-night but to-morrow in that bay, which is worth being carefully explored."

"I think that we shall be obliged to do so, whether we like it or not," answered Pencroft, "for the sky looks very threatening towards the west. Dirty weather is coming on!"

"At any rate we have a favorable wind for reaching Cape Mandible," observed the reporter.

"A very fine wind," replied the sailor; "but we must tack to enter the gulf, and I should like to see my way clear in these unknown quarters."

"Quarters which appear to be filled with rocks," added Herbert, "if we judge by what we saw on the south coast of Shark Gulf."

"Pencroft," said Cyrus Harding, "do as you think best, we will leave it to you."

"Don't make your mind uneasy, captain," replied the sailor, "I shall not expose myself needlessly! I would rather a knife were run into my ribs than a sharp rock into those of my 'Bonadventure!'"

That which Pencroft called ribs was the pan of his vessel under water, and he valued it more than his own skin.

"What o'clock is it?" asked Pencroft.

"Ten o'clock," replied Gideon Spilett.

"And what distance is it to the Cape, captain?"

"About fifteen miles," replied the engineer.

"That's a matter of two hours and a half," said the sailor, "and we shall be off the Cape between twelve and one o'clock. Unluckily, the tide will be turning at that moment, and will be ebbing out of the gulf. I am afraid that it will be very difficult to get in, having both wind and tide against us."

"And the more so that it is a full moon to-day," remarked Herbert, "and these April tides are very strong."

"Well, Pencroft," asked Harding, "can you not anchor off the Cape?"

"Anchor near land, with bad weather coming on!" exclaimed the sailor. "What are you thinking of, captain? We should run aground, of a certainty!"

"What will you do then?"

"I shall try to keep in the offing until the flood, that is to say, till about seven in the evening, and if there is still light enough I will try to enter the gulf; if not, we must stand off and on during the night, and we will enter to-morrow at sunrise."

"As I told you, Pencroft, we will leave it to you," answered Harding.

"Ah!" said Pencroft, "if there was only a lighthouse on the coast, it would be much more convenient for sailors."

"Yes," replied Herbert, "and this time we shall have no obliging engineer to light a fire to guide us into port!"

"Why, indeed, my dear Cyrus," said Spilett, "we have never thanked you; but frankly, without that fire we should never have been ableV

"A fire?" asked Harding, much astonished at the reporter's words.

"We mean, captain," answered Pencroft, "that on board the 'Bonadventure' we were very anxious during the few hours before our return, and we should have passed to windward of the island, if it had not been for the precaution you took of lighting a fire the night of the 19th of October, on Prospect Heights."

"Yes, yes! That was a lucky idea of mine!" replied the engineer.

"And this time," continued the sailor, "unless the idea occurs to Ayrton, there will be no one to do us that little service!"

"No! No one!" answered Cyrus Harding.

A few minutes after, finding himself alone in the bows of the vessel, with the reporter, the engineer bent down and whispered,—

"If there is one thing certain in this world, Spilett, it is that I never lighted any fire during the night of the 19th of October, neither on Prospect Heights nor on any other part of the island!"

Chapter 20

Things happened as Pencroft had predicted, he being seldom mistaken in his prognostications. The wind rose, and from a fresh breeze it soon increased to a regular gale; that is to say, it acquired a speed of from forty to forty-five miles an hour, before which a ship in the open sea would have run under close-reefed topsails. Now, as it was nearly six o'clock when the "Bonadventure" reached the gulf, and as at that moment the tide turned, it was impossible to enter. They were therefore compelled to stand off, for even if he had wished to do so, Pencroft could not have gained the mouth of the Mercy. Hoisting the jib to the mainmast by way of a storm-sail, he hove to, putting the head of the vessel towards the land.

Fortunately, although the wind was strong the sea, being sheltered by the land, did not run very high. They had then little to fear from the waves, which always endanger small craft. The "Bonadventure" would doubtlessly not have capsized, for she was well ballasted, but enormous masses of water falling on the deck might injure her if her timbers could not sustain them. Pencroft, as a good sailor, was prepared for anything. Certainly, he had great confidence in his vessel, but nevertheless he awaited the return of day with some anxiety.

During the night, Cyrus Harding and Gideon Spilett had no opportunity for talking together, and yet the words pronounced in the reporter's ear by the engineer were well worth being discussed, together with the mysterious influence which appeared to reign over Lincoln Island. Gideon Spilett did not cease from pondering over this new and inexplicable incident, the appearance of a fire on the coast of the island. The fire had actually been seen! His companions, Herbert and Pencroft, had seen it with him! The fire had served to signalize the position of the island during that dark night, and they had not doubted that it was lighted by the engineer's hand; and here was Cyrus Harding expressly declaring that he had never done anything of the sort! Spilett resolved to recur to this incident as soon as the "Bonadventure" returned, and to urge Cyrus Harding to acquaint their companions with these strange facts. Perhaps it would be decided to make in common a complete investigation of every part of Lincoln Island.

However that might be, on this evening no fire was lighted on these yet unknown shores, which formed the entrance to the gulf, and the little vessel stood off during the night.

When the first streaks of dawn appeared in the western horizon, the wind, which had slightly fallen, shifted two points, and enabled Pencroft to enter the narrow gulf with greater ease. Towards seven o'clock in the morning, the "Bonadventure," weathering the North Mandible Cape, entered the strait and glided on to the waters, so strangely enclosed in the frame of lava.

"Well," said Pencroft, "this bay would make admirable roads, in which a whole fleet could lie at their ease!"

"What is especially curious," observed Harding, "is that the gulf has been formed by two rivers of lava, thrown out by the volcano, and accumulated by successive eruptions. The result is that the gulf is completely sheltered on all sides, and I believe that even in the stormiest weather, the sea here must be as calm as a lake."

"No doubt," returned the sailor, "since the wind has only that narrow entrance between the two capes to get in by, and, besides, the north cape protects that of the south in a way which would make the entrance of gusts very difficult. I declare our 'Bonadventure' could stay here from one end of the year to the other, without even dragging at her anchor!"

"It is rather large for her!" observed the reporter.

"Well! Mr. Spilett," replied the sailor, "I agree that it is too large for the 'Bonadventure,' but if the fleets of the Union were in want of a harbor in the Pacific, I don't think they would ever find a better place than this!"

"We are in the shark's mouth," remarked Nab, alluding to the form of the gulf.

"Right into its mouth, my honest Nab!" replied Herbert, "but you are not afraid that it will shut upon us, are you?"

"No, Mr. Herbert," answered Neb, "and yet this gulf here doesn't please me much! It has a wicked look!"

"Hallo!" cried Pencroft, "here is Neb turning up his nose at my gulf, just as I was thinking of presenting it to America!"

"But, at any rate, is the water deep enough?" asked the engineer, "for a depth sufficient for the keel of the 'Bonadventure' would not be enough for those of our iron-clads."

"That is easily found out," replied Pencroft.

And the sailor sounded with a long cord, which served him as a lead-line, and to which was fastened a lump of iron. This cord measured nearly fifty fathoms, and its entire length was unrolled without finding any bottom.

"There," exclaimed Pencroft, "our iron-clads can come here after all! They would not run aground!"

"Indeed," said Gideon Spilett, "this gulf is a regular abyss, but, taking into consideration the volcanic origin of the island, it is not astonishing that the sea should offer similar depressions."

"One would say too," observed Herbert, "that these cliffs were perfectly perpendicular; and I believe that at their foot, even with a line five or six times longer, Pencroft would not find bottom."

"That is all very well," then said the reporter, "but I must point out to Pencroft that his harbor is wanting in one very important respect!"

"And what is that, Mr. Spilett?"

"An opening, a cutting of some sort, to give access to the interior of the island. I do not see a spot on which we could land." And, in fact, the steep lava cliffs did not afford a single place suitable for landing. They formed an insuperable barrier, recalling, but with more wildness, the fiords of Norway. The "Bonadventure," coasting as close as possible along the cliffs, did not discover even a projection which would allow the passengers to leave the deck.

Pencroft consoled himself by saying that with the help of a mine they could soon open out the cliff when that was necessary, and then, as there was evidently nothing to be done in the gulf, he steered his vessel towards the strait and passed out at about two o'clock in the afternoon.

"Ah!" said Nab, uttering a sigh of satisfaction.

One might really say that the honest Negro did not feel at his ease in those enormous jaws.

The distance from Mandible Cape to the mouth of the Mercy was not more than eight miles. The head of the "Bonadventure" was put towards Granite House, and a fair wind filling her sails, she ran rapidly along the coast.

To the enormous lava rocks succeeded soon those capricious sand dunes, among which the engineer had been so singularly recovered, and which seabirds frequented in thousands.

About four o'clock, Pencroft leaving the point of the islet on his left, entered the channel which separated it from the coast, and at five o'clock the anchor of the "Bonadventure" was buried in the sand at the mouth of the Mercy.

The colonists had been absent three days from their dwelling. Ayrton was waiting for them on the beach, and Jup came joyously to meet them, giving vent to deep grunts of satisfaction.

A complete exploration of the coast of the island had now been made, and no suspicious appearances had been observed. If any mysterious being resided on it, it could only be under cover of the impenetrable forest of the Serpentine Peninsula, to which the colonists had not yet directed their investigations.

Gideon Spilett discussed these things with the engineer, and it was agreed that they should direct the attention of their companions to the strange character of certain incidents which had occurred on the island, and of which the last was the most unaccountable.

However, Harding, returning to the fact of a fire having been kindled on the shore by an unknown hand, could not refrain from repeating for the twentieth time to the reporter,—

"But are you quite sure of having seen it? Was it not a partial eruption of the volcano, or perhaps some meteor?"

"No, Cyrus," answered the reporter, "it was certainly a fire lighted by the hand of man. Besides; question Pencroft and Herbert. They saw it as I saw it myself, and they will confirm my words."

In consequence, therefore, a few days after, on the 25th of April, in the evening, when the settlers were all collected on Prospect Heights, Cyrus Harding began by saying,—

"My friends, I think it my duty to call your attention to certain incidents which have occurred in the island, on the subject of which I shall be happy to have your advice. These incidents are, so to speak, supernatural—"

"Supernatural!" exclaimed the sailor, emitting a volume of smoke from his mouth. "Can it be possible that our island is supernatural?"

"No, Pencroft, but mysterious, most certainly," replied the engineer; "unless you can explain that which Spilett and I have until now failed to understand."

"Speak away, captain," answered the sailor.

"Well, have you understood," then said the engineer, "how was it that after falling into the sea, I was found a quarter of a mile into the interior of the island, and that, without my having any consciousness of my removal there?"

"Unless, being unconscious—" said Pencroft.

"That is not admissible," replied the engineer. "But to continue. Have you understood how Top was able to discover your retreat five miles from the cave in which I was lying?"

"The dog's instinct—" observed Herbert.

"Singular instinct!" returned the reporter, "since notwithstanding the storm of rain and wind which was raging during that night, Top arrived at the Chimneys, dry and without a speck of mud!"

"Let us continue," resumed the engineer. "Have you understood how our dog was so strangely thrown up out of the water of the lake, after his struggle with the dugong?"

"No! I confess, not at all," replied Pencroft, "and the wound which the dugong had in its side, a wound which seemed to have been made with a sharp instrument; that can't be understood, either."

"Let us continue again," said Harding. "Have you understood, my friends, how that bullet got into the body of the young peccary; how that case happened to be so fortunately stranded, without there being any trace of a wreck; how that bottle containing the document presented itself so opportunely, during our first sea-excursion; how our canoe, having broken its moorings, floated down the current of the Mercy and rejoined us at the very moment we needed it; how after the ape invasion the ladder was so obligingly thrown down from Granite House; and lastly, how the document, which Ayrton asserts was never written by him, fell into our hands?"

As Cyrus Harding thus enumerated, without forgetting one, the singular incidents which had occurred in the island, Herbert, Neb, and Pencroft stared at each other, not knowing what to reply, for this succession of incidents, grouped thus for the first time, could not but excite their surprise to the highest degree.

"'Pon my word," said Pencroft at last, "you are right, captain, and it is difficult to explain all these things!"

"Well, my friends," resumed the engineer, "a last fact has just been added to these, and it is no less incomprehensible than the others!"

"What is it, captain?" asked Herbert quickly.

"When you were returning from Tabor Island, Pencroft," continued the engineer, "you said that a fire appeared on Lincoln Island?"

"Certainly," answered the sailor.

"And you are quite certain of having seen this fire?"

"As sure as I see you now."

"You also, Herbert?"

"Why, captain," cried Herbert, "that fire was blazing like a star of the first magnitude!"

"But was it not a star?" urged the engineer.

"No," replied Pencroft, "for the sky was covered with thick clouds, and at any rate a star would not have been so low on the horizon. But Mr. Spilett saw it as well as we, and he will confirm our words."

"I will add," said the reporter, "that the fire was very bright, and that it shot up like a sheet of lightning."

"Yes, yes! exactly," added Herbert, "and it was certainly placed on the heights of Granite House."

"Well, my friends," replied Cyrus Harding, "during the night of the 19th of October, neither Neb nor I lighted any fire on the coast."

"You did not!" exclaimed Pencroft, in the height of his astonishment, not being able to finish his sentence.

"We did not leave Granite House," answered Cyrus Harding, "and if a fire appeared on the coast, it was lighted by another hand than ours!"

Pencroft, Herbert, and Neb were stupefied. No illusion could be possible, and a fire had actually met their eyes during the night of the 19th of October. Yes! they had to acknowledge it, a mystery existed! An inexplicable influence, evidently favorable to the colonists, but very irritating to their curiosity, was executed always in the nick of time on Lincoln Island. Could there be some being hidden in its profoundest recesses? It was necessary at any cost to ascertain this.

Harding also reminded his companions of the singular behavior of Top and Jup when they prowled round the mouth of the well, which placed Granite House in communication with the sea, and he told them that he had explored the well, without discovering anything suspicious. The final resolve taken, in consequence of this conversation, by all the members of the colony, was that as soon as the fine season returned they would thoroughly search the whole of the island.

But from that day Pencroft appeared to be anxious. He felt as if the island which he had made his own personal property belonged to him entirely no longer, and that he shared it with another master, to whom, willing or not, he felt subject. Neb and he often talked of those unaccountable things, and both, their natures inclining them to the marvelous, were not far from believing that Lincoln Island was under the dominion of some supernatural power.

In the meanwhile, the bad weather came with the month of May, the November of the northern zones. It appeared that the winter would be severe and forward. The preparations for the winter season were therefore commenced without delay.

Nevertheless, the colonists were well prepared to meet the winter, however hard it might be. They had plenty of felt clothing, and the musmons, very numerous by this time, had furnished an abundance of wool necessary for the manufacture of this warm material.

It is unnecessary to say that Ayrton had been provided with this comfortable clothing. Cyrus Harding proposed that he should come to spend the bad season with them in Granite House, where he would be better lodged than at the corral, and Ayrton promised to do so, as soon as the last work at the corral was finished. He did this towards the middle of April. From that time Ayrton shared the common life, and made himself useful on all occasions; but still humble and sad, he never took part in the pleasures of his companions.

For the greater part of this, the third winter which the settlers passed in Lincoln Island, they were confined to Granite House. There were many violent storms and frightful tempests, which appeared to shake the rocks to their very foundations. Immense waves threatened to overwhelm the island, and certainly any vessel anchored near the shore would have been dashed to pieces. Twice, during one of these hurricanes, the Mercy swelled to such a degree as to give reason to fear that the bridges would be swept away, and it was necessary to strengthen those on the shore, which disappeared under the foaming waters, when the sea beat against the beach.

It may well be supposed that such storms, comparable to water-spouts in which were mingled rain and snow, would cause great havoc on the plateau of Prospect Heights. The mill and the poultry-yard particularly suffered. The colonists were often obliged to make immediate repairs, without which the safety of the birds would have been seriously threatened.

During the worst weather, several jaguars and troops of quadrumana ventured to the edge of the plateau, and it was always to be feared that the most active and audacious would, urged by hunger, manage to cross the stream, which besides, when frozen, offered them an easy passage. Plantations and domestic animals would then have been infallibly destroyed, without a constant watch, and it was often necessary to make use of the guns to keep those dangerous visitors at a respectful distance. Occupation was not wanting to the colonists, for without reckoning their out-door cares, they had always a thousand plans for the fitting up of Granite House.

They had also some fine sporting excursions, which were made during the frost in the vast Tadorn Marsh. Gideon Spilett and Herbert, aided by Jup and Top, did not miss a shot in the midst of myriads of wild-duck, snipe, teal, and others. The access to these hunting-grounds was easy; besides, whether they reached them by the road to Port Balloon, after having passed the Mercy Bridge, or by turning the rocks from Flotsam Point, the hunters were never distant from Granite House more than two or three miles.

Thus passed the four winter months, which were really rigorous, that is to say, June, July, August, and September. But, in short, Granite House did not suffer much from the inclemency of the weather, and it was the same with the corral, which, less exposed than the plateau, and sheltered partly by Mount Franklin, only received the remains of the hurricanes, already broken by the forests and the high rocks of the shore. The damages there were consequently of small importance, and the activity and skill of Ayrton promptly repaired them, when some time in October he returned to pass a few days in the corral.

During this winter, no fresh inexplicable incident occurred. Nothing strange happened, although Pencroft and Neb were on the watch for the most insignificant facts to which they attached any mysterious cause. Top and Jup themselves no longer growled round the well or gave any signs of uneasiness. It appeared, therefore, as if the series of supernatural incidents was interrupted, although they often talked of them during the evenings in Granite House, and they remained thoroughly resolved that the island should be searched, even in those parts the most difficult to explore. But an event of the highest importance, and of which the consequences might be terrible, momentarily diverted from their projects Cyrus Harding and his companions.

It was the month of October. The fine season was swiftly returning. Nature was reviving; and among the evergreen foliage of the coniferae which formed the border of the wood, already appeared the young leaves of the banksias, deodars, and other trees.

It may be remembered that Gideon Spilett and Herbert had, at different times, taken photographic views of Lincoln Island.

Now, on the 17th of this month of October, towards three o'clock in the afternoon, Herbert, enticed by the charms of the sky, thought of reproducing Union Bay, which was opposite to Prospect Heights, from Cape Mandible to Claw Cape.

The horizon was beautifully clear, and the sea, undulating under a soft breeze, was as calm as the waters of a lake, sparkling here and there under the sun's rays.

The apparatus had been placed at one of the windows of the dining-room at Granite House, and consequently overlooked the shore and the bay. Herbert proceeded as he was accustomed to do, and the negative obtained, he went away to fix it by means of the chemicals deposited in a dark nook of Granite House.

Returning to the bright light, and examining it well, Herbert perceived on his negative an almost imperceptible little spot on the sea horizon. He endeavored to make it disappear by reiterated washing, but could not accomplish it.

"It is a flaw in the glass," he thought.

And then he had the curiosity to examine this flaw with a strong magnifier which he unscrewed from one of the telescopes.

But he had scarcely looked at it, when he uttered a cry, and the glass almost fell from his hands.

Immediately running to the room in which Cyrus Harding then was, he extended the negative and magnifier towards the engineer, pointing out the little spot.

Harding examined it; then seizing his telescope he rushed to the window.

The telescope, after having slowly swept the horizon, at last stopped on the looked-for spot, and Cyrus Harding, lowering it, pronounced one word only,—

"A vessel!"

And in fact a vessel was in sight, off Lincoln Island!

Part 3. The Secret of the Island

Chapter 1

It was now two years and a half since the castaways from the balloon had been thrown on Lincoln Island, and during that period there had been no communication between them and their fellow-creatures. Once the reporter had attempted to communicate with the inhabited world by confiding to a bird a letter which contained the secret of their situation, but that was a chance on which it was impossible to reckon seriously. Ayrton, alone, under the circumstances which have been related, had come to join the little colony. Now, suddenly, on this day, the 17th of October, other men had unexpectedly appeared in sight of the island, on that deserted sea!

There could be no doubt about it! A vessel was there! But would she pass on, or would she put into port? In a few hours the colonists would definitely know what to expect.

Cyrus Harding and Herbert having immediately called Gideon Spilett, Pencroft, and Neb into the dining-room of Granite House, told them what had happened. Pencroft, seizing the telescope, rapidly swept the horizon, and stopping on the indicated point, that is to say, on that which had made the almost imperceptible spot on the photographic negative,—

"I'm blessed but it is really a vessel!" he exclaimed, in a voice which did not express any great amount of satisfaction.

"Is she coming here?" asked Gideon Spilett.

"Impossible to say anything yet," answered Pencroft, "for her rigging alone is above the horizon, and not a bit of her hull can be seen."

"What is to be done?" asked the lad.

"Wait," replied Harding.

And for a considerable time the settlers remained silent, given up to all the thoughts, and the emotions, all the fears, all the hopes, which were aroused by this incident—the most important which had occurred since their arrival in Lincoln Island. Certainly, the colonists were not in the situation of castaways abandoned on a sterile islet, constantly contending against a cruel nature for their miserable existence, and incessantly tormented by the longing to return to inhabited countries. Pencroft and Neb, especially, who felt themselves at once so happy and so rich, would not have left their island without regret. They were accustomed, besides, to this new life in the midst of the domain which their intelligence had as it were civilized. But at any rate this ship brought news from the world, perhaps even from their native land. It was bringing fellow-creatures to them, and it may be conceived how deeply their hearts were moved at the sight!

From time to time Pencroft took the glass and rested himself at the window. From thence he very attentively examined the vessel, which was at a distance of twenty miles to the east. The colonists had as yet, therefore, no means of signalizing their presence. A flag would not have been perceived; a gun would not have been heard; a fire would not have been visible. However, it was certain that the island, overtopped by Mount Franklin, could not escape the notice of the vessel's lookout. But why was the ship coming there? Was it simple chance which brought it to that part of the Pacific, where the maps mentioned no land except Tabor Island, which itself was out of the route usually followed by vessels from the Polynesian Archipelagoes, from New Zealand, and from the American coast? To this question, which each one asked himself, a reply was suddenly made by Herbert.

"Can it be the 'Duncan'?" he cried.

The "Duncan," as has been said, was Lord Glenarvan's yacht, which had left Ayrton on the islet, and which was to return there someday to fetch him. Now, the islet was not so far distant from Lincoln Island, but that a vessel, standing for the one, could pass in sight of the other. A hundred and fifty miles only separated them in longitude, and seventy in latitude.

"We must tell Ayrton," said Gideon Spilett, "and send for him immediately. He alone can say if it is the 'Duncan.'"

This was the opinion of all, and the reporter, going to the telegraphic apparatus which placed the corral in communication with Granite House, sent this telegram:—" Come with all possible speed."

In a few minutes the bell sounded.

"I am coming," replied Ayrton.

Then the settlers continued to watch the vessel.

"If it is the 'Duncan,'" said Herbert, "Ayrton will recognize her without difficulty, since he sailed on board her for some time."

"And if he recognizes her," added Pencroft, "it will agitate him exceedingly!"

"Yes," answered Cyrus Harding; "but now Ayrton is worthy to return on board the 'Duncan,' and pray Heaven that it is indeed Lord Glenarvan's yacht, for I should be suspicious of any other vessel. These are ill-famed seas, and I have always feared a visit from Malay pirates to our island."

"We could defend it,', cried Herbert.

"No doubt, my boy," answered the engineer smiling, "but it would be better not to have to defend it."

"A useless observation," said Spilett. "Lincoln Island is unknown to navigators, since it is not marked even on the most recent maps. Do you think, Cyrus, that that is a sufficient motive for a ship, finding herself unexpectedly in sight of new land, to try and visit rather than avoid it?"

"Certainly," replied Pencroft.

"I think so too," added the engineer. "It may even be said that it is the duty of a captain to come and survey any land or island not yet known, and Lincoln Island is in this position."

"Well," said Pencroft, "suppose this vessel comes and anchors there a few cables-lengths from our island, what shall we do?"

This sudden question remained at first without any reply. But Cyrus Harding, after some moments' thought, replied in the calm tone which was usual to him,—

"What we shall do, my friends? What we ought to do is this:—we will communicate with the ship, we will take our passage on board her, and we will leave our island, after having taken possession of it in the name of the United States. Then we will return with any who may wish to follow us to colonize it definitely, and endow the American Republic with a useful station in this part of the Pacific Ocean!"

"Hurrah!" exclaimed Pencroft, "and that will be no small present which we shall make to our country! The colonization is already almost finished; names are given to every part of the island; there is a natural port, fresh water, roads, a telegraph, a dockyard, and manufactories; and there will be nothing to be done but to inscribe Lincoln Island on the maps!"

"But if anyone seizes it in our absence?" observed Gideon Spilett.

"Hang it!" cried the sailor. "I would rather remain all alone to guard it: and trust to Pencroft, they shouldn't steal it from him, like a watch from the pocket of a swell!"

For an hour it was impossible to say with any certainty whether the vessel was or was not standing towards Lincoln Island. She was nearer, but in what direction was she sailing? This Pencroft could not determine. However, as the wind was blowing from the northeast, in all probability the vessel was sailing on the starboard tack. Besides, the wind was favorable for bringing her towards the island, and, the sea being calm, she would not be afraid to approach although the shallows were not marked on the chart.

Towards four o'clock—an hour after he had been sent for—Ayrton arrived at Granite House. He entered the dining-room saying,—

"At your service, gentlemen."

Cyrus Harding gave him his hand, as was his custom to do, and, leading him to the window,—

"Ayrton," said he, "we have begged you to come here for an important reason. A ship is in sight of the island."

Ayrton at first paled slightly, and for a moment his eyes became dim; then, leaning out the window, he surveyed the horizon, but could see nothing.

"Take this telescope," said Spilett, "and look carefully, Ayrton, for it is possible that this ship may be the 'Duncan' come to these seas for the purpose of taking you home again."

"The 'Duncan!'" murmured Ayrton. "Already?" This last word escaped Ayrton's lips as if involuntarily, and his head drooped upon his hands.

Did not twelve years' solitude on a desert island appear to him a sufficient expiation? Did not the penitent yet feel himself pardoned, either in his own eyes or in the eyes of others?

"No," said he, "no! it cannot be the 'Duncan'!"

"Look, Ayrton," then said the engineer, "for it is necessary that we should know beforehand what to expect."

Ayrton took the glass and pointed it in the direction indicated. During some minutes he examined the horizon without moving, without uttering a word. Then,—

"It is indeed a vessel," said he, "but I do not think she is the 'Duncan.'"

"Why do you not think so?" asked Gideon Spilett.

"Because the 'Duncan' is a steam-yacht, and I cannot perceive any trace of smoke either above or near that vessel."

"Perhaps she is simply sailing," observed Pencroft. "The wind is favorable for the direction which she appears to be taking, and she may be anxious to economize her coal, being so far from land."

"It is possible that you may be right, Mr. Pencroft," answered Ayrton, "and that the vessel has extinguished her fires. We must wait until she is nearer, and then we shall soon know what to expect."

So saying, Ayrton sat down in a corner of the room and remained silent. The colonists again discussed the strange ship, but Ayrton took no part in the conversation. All were in such a mood that they found it impossible to continue their work. Gideon Spilett and Pencroft were particularly nervous, going, coming, not able to remain still in one place. Herbert felt more curiosity. Neb alone maintained his usual calm manner. Was not his country that where his master was? As to the engineer, he remained plunged in deep thought, and in his heart feared rather than desired the arrival of the ship. In the meanwhile, the vessel was a little nearer the island. With the aid of the glass, it was ascertained that she was a brig, and not one of those Malay proas, which are generally used by the pirates of the Pacific. It was, therefore, reasonable to believe that the engineer's apprehensions would not be justified, and that the presence of this vessel in the vicinity of the island was fraught with no danger.

Pencroft, after a minute examination, was able positively to affirm that the vessel was rigged as a brig, and that she was standing obliquely towards the coast, on the starboard tack, under her topsails and top-gallant-sails. This was confirmed by Ayrton. But by continuing in this direction she must soon disappear behind Claw Cape, as the wind was from the southwest, and to watch her it would be then necessary to ascend the height of Washington Bay, near Port Balloon—a provoking circumstance, for it was already five o'clock in the evening, and the twilight would soon make any observation extremely difficult.

"What shall we do when night comes on?" asked Gideon Spilett. "Shall we light a fire, so as to signal our presence on the coast?"

This was a serious question, and yet, although the engineer still retained some of his presentiments, it was answered in the affirmative. During the night the ship might disappear and leave for ever, and, this ship gone, would another ever return to the waters of Lincoln Island? Who could foresee what the future would then have in store for the colonists?

"Yes," said the reporter, "we ought to make known to that vessel, whoever she may be, that the island is inhabited. To neglect the opportunity which is offered to us might be to create everlasting regrets."

It was therefore decided that Neb and Pencroft should go to Port Balloon, and that there, at nightfall, they should light an immense fire, the blaze of which would necessarily attract the attention of the brig.

But at the moment when Neb and the sailor were preparing to leave Granite House, the vessel suddenly altered her course, and stood directly for Union Bay. The brig was a good sailer, for she approached rapidly. Neb and Pencroft put off their departure, therefore, and the glass was put into Ayrton's hands, that he might ascertain for certain whether the ship was or was not the "Duncan." The Scotch yacht was also rigged as a brig. The question was, whether a chimney could be discerned between the two masts of the vessel, which was now at a distance of only five miles.

The horizon was still very clear. The examination was easy, and Ayrton soon let the glass fall again, saying—

"It is not the 'Duncan'! It could not be!"

Pencroft again brought the brig within the range of the telescope, and could see that she was of between three and four hundred tons burden, wonderfully narrow, well-masted, admirably built, and must be a very rapid sailer. But to what nation did she belong? That was difficult to say.

"And yet," added the sailor, "a flag is floating from her peak, but I cannot distinguish the colors of it."

"In half an hour we shall be certain about that," answered the reporter. "Besides, it is very evident that the intention of the captain of this ship is to land, and, consequently, if not today, to-morrow at the latest, we shall make his acquaintance."

"Never mind!" said Pencroft. "It is best to know whom we have to deal with, and I shall not be sorry to recognize that fellow's colors!"

And, while thus speaking, the sailor never left the glass. The day began to fade, and with the day the breeze fell also. The brig's ensign hung in folds, and it became more and more difficult to observe it.

"It is not the American flag," said Pencroft from time to time, "nor the English, the red of which could be easily seen, nor the French or German colors, nor the white flag of Russia, nor the yellow of Spain. One would say it was all one color. Let's see: in these seas, what do we generally meet with? The Chilean flag?—but that is tri-color. Brazilian?—it is green. Japanese?—it is yellow and black, while this—"

At that moment the breeze blew out the unknown flag. Ayrton seizing the telescope which the sailor had put down, put it to his eye, and in a hoarse voice,—

"The black flag!" he exclaimed.

And indeed the somber bunting was floating from the mast of the brig, and they had now good reason for considering her to be a suspicious vessel!

Had the engineer, then, been right in his presentiments? Was this a pirate vessel? Did she scour the Pacific, competing with the Malay proas which still infest it? For what had she come to look at the shores of Lincoln Island? Was it to them an unknown island, ready to become a magazine for stolen cargoes? Had she come to find on the coast a sheltered port for the winter months? Was the settlers' honest domain destined to be transformed into an infamous refuge—the headquarters of the piracy of the Pacific?

All these ideas instinctively presented themselves to the colonists' imaginations. There was no doubt, besides, of the signification which must be attached to the color of the hoisted flag. It was that of pirates! It was that which the "Duncan" would have carried, had the convicts succeeded in their criminal design! No time was lost before discussing it.

"My friends," said Cyrus Harding, "perhaps this vessel only wishes to survey the coast of the island. Perhaps her crew will not land. There is a chance of it. However that may be, we ought to do everything we can to hide our presence here. The windmill on Prospect Heights is too easily seen. Let Ayrton and Neb go and take down the sails. We must also conceal the windows of Granite House with thick branches. All the fires must be extinguished, so that nothing may betray the presence of men on the island."

"And our vessel?" said Herbert.

"Oh," answered Pencroft, "she is sheltered in Port Balloon, and I defy any of those rascals there to find her!"

The engineer's orders were immediately executed. Neb and Ayrton ascended the plateau, and took the necessary precautions to conceal any indication of a settlement. While they were thus occupied, their companions went to the border of Jacamar Wood, and brought back a large quantity of branches and creepers, which would at some distance appear as natural foliage, and thus disguise the windows in the granite cliff. At the same time, the ammunition and guns were placed ready so as to be at hand in case of an unexpected attack.

When all these precautions had been taken,—

"My friends," said Harding, and his voice betrayed some emotion, "if the wretches endeavor to seize Lincoln Island, we shall defend it—shall we not?"

"Yes, Cyrus," replied the reporter, "and if necessary we will die to defend it!"

The engineer extended his hand to his companions, who pressed it warmly. Ayrton remained in his corner, not joining the colonists. Perhaps he, the former convict, still felt himself unworthy to do so!

Cyrus Harding understood what was passing in Ayrton's mind, and going to him—

"And you, Ayrton," he asked, "what will you do?"

"My duty," answered Ayrton.

He then took up his station near the window and gazed through the foliage.

It was now half-past seven. The sun had disappeared twenty minutes ago behind Granite House. Consequently the Eastern horizon was becoming obscured. In the meanwhile the brig continued to advance towards Union Bay. She was now not more than two miles off, and exactly opposite the plateau of Prospect Heights, for after having tacked off Claw Cape, she had drifted towards the north in the current of the rising tide. One might have said that at this distance she had already entered the vast bay, for a straight line drawn from Claw Cape to Cape Mandible would have rested on her starboard quarter.

Was the brig about to penetrate far into the bay? That was the first question. When once in the bay, would she anchor there? That was the second. Would she not content herself with only surveying the coast, and stand out to sea again without landing her crew? They would know this in an hour. The colonists could do nothing but wait.

Cyrus Harding had not seen the suspected vessel hoist the black flag without deep anxiety. Was it not a direct menace against the work which he and his companions had till now conducted so successfully? Had these pirates—for the sailors of the brig could be nothing else—already visited the island, since on approaching it they had hoisted their colors. Had they formerly invaded it, so that certain unaccountable peculiarities might be explained in this way? Did there exist in the as yet unexplored parts some accomplice ready to enter into communication with them?

To all these questions which he mentally asked himself, Harding knew not what to reply; but he felt that the safety of the colony could not but be seriously threatened by the arrival of the brig.

However, he and his companions were determined to fight to the last gasp. It would have been very important to know if the pirates were numerous and better armed than the colonists. But how was this information to be obtained?

Night fell. The new moon had disappeared. Profound darkness enveloped the island and the sea. No light could pierce through the heavy piles of clouds on the horizon. The wind had died away completely with the twilight. Not a leaf rustled on the trees, not a ripple murmured on the shore. Nothing could be seen of the ship, all her lights being extinguished, and if she was still in sight of the island, her whereabouts could not be discovered.

"Well! who knows?" said Pencroft. "Perhaps that cursed craft will stand off during the night, and we shall see nothing of her at daybreak."

As if in reply to the sailor's observation, a bright light flashed in the darkness, and a cannon-shot was heard.

The vessel was still there and had guns on board.

Six seconds elapsed between the flash and the report.

Therefore the brig was about a mile and a quarter from the coast.

At the same time, the chains were heard rattling through the hawse-holes.

The vessel had just anchored in sight of Granite House!

Chapter 2

There was no longer any doubt as to the pirates' intentions. They had dropped anchor at a short distance from the island, and it was evident that the next day by means of their boats they purposed to land on the beach!

Cyrus Harding and his companions were ready to act, but, determined though they were, they must not forget to be prudent. Perhaps their presence might still be concealed in the event of the pirates contenting themselves with landing on the shore without examining the interior of the island. It might be, indeed, that their only intention was to obtain fresh water from the Mercy, and it was not impossible that the bridge, thrown across a mile and a half from the mouth, and the manufactory at the Chimneys might escape their notice.

But why was that flag hoisted at the brig's peak? What was that shot fired for? Pure bravado doubtless, unless it was a sign of the act of taking possession. Harding knew now that the vessel was well armed. And what had the colonists of Lincoln Island to reply to the pirates' guns? A few muskets only.

"However," observed Cyrus Harding, "here we are in an impregnable position. The enemy cannot discover the mouth of the outlet, now that it is hidden under reeds and grass, and consequently it would be impossible for them to penetrate into Granite House."

"But our plantations, our poultry-yard, our corral, all, everything!" exclaimed Pencroft, stamping his foot. "They may spoil everything, destroy everything in a few hours!"

"Everything, Pencroft," answered Harding, "and we have no means of preventing them."

"Are they numerous? that is the question," said the reporter. "If they are not more than a dozen, we shall be able to stop them, but forty, fifty, more perhaps!"

"Captain Harding," then said Ayrton, advancing towards the engineer, "will you give me leave?"

"For what, my friend?"

"To go to that vessel to find out the strength of her crew."

"But Ayrton—" answered the engineer, hesitating, "you will risk your life—"

"Why not, sir?"

"That is more than your duty."

"I have more than my duty to do," replied Ayrton.

"Will you go to the ship in the boat?" asked Gideon Spilett.

"No, sir, but I will swim. A boat would be seen where a man may glide between wind and water."

"Do you know that the brig is a mile and a quarter from the shore?" said Herbert.

"I am a good swimmer, Mr. Herbert."

"I tell you it is risking your life," said the engineer.

"That is no matter," answered Ayrton. "Captain Harding, I ask this as a favor. Perhaps it will be a means of raising me in my own eyes!"

"Go, Ayrton," replied the engineer, who felt sure that a refusal would have deeply wounded the former convict, now become an honest man.

"I will accompany you," said Pencroft.

"You mistrust me!" said Ayrton quickly.

Then more humbly,—

"Alas!"

"No! no!" exclaimed Harding with animation, "no, Ayrton, Pencroft does not mistrust you. You interpret his words wrongly."

"Indeed," returned the sailor, "I only propose to accompany Ayrton as far as the islet. It may be, although it is scarcely possible, that one of these villains has landed, and in that case two men will not be too many to hinder him from giving the alarm. I will wait for Ayrton on the islet, and he shall go alone to the vessel, since he has proposed to do so." These things agreed to, Ayrton made preparations for his departure. His plan was bold, but it might succeed, thanks to the darkness of the night. Once arrived at the vessel's side, Ayrton, holding on to the main chains, might reconnoiter the number and perhaps overhear the intentions of the pirates.

Ayrton and Pencroft, followed by their companions, descended to the beach. Ayrton undressed and rubbed himself with grease, so as to suffer less from the temperature of the water, which was still cold. He might, indeed, be obliged to remain in it for several hours.

Pencroft and Neb, during this time, had gone to fetch the boat, moored a few hundred feet higher up, on the bank of the Mercy, and by the time they returned,

Ayrton was ready to start. A coat was thrown over his shoulders, and the settlers all came round him to press his hand.

Ayrton then shoved off with Pencroft in the boat.

It was half-past ten in the evening when the two adventurers disappeared in the darkness. Their companions returned to wait at the Chimneys.

The channel was easily traversed, and the boat touched the opposite shore of the islet. This was not done without precaution, for fear lest the pirates might be roaming about there. But after a careful survey, it was evident that the islet was deserted. Ayrton then, followed by Pencroft, crossed it with a rapid step, scaring the birds nestled in the holes of the rocks; then, without hesitating, he plunged into the sea, and swam noiselessly in the direction of the ship, in which a few lights had recently appeared, showing her exact situation. As to Pencroft, he crouched down in a cleft of the rock, and awaited the return of his companion.

In the meanwhile, Ayrton, swimming with a vigorous stroke, glided through the sheet of water without producing the slightest ripple. His head just emerged above it and his eyes were fixed on the dark hull of the brig, from which the lights were reflected in the water. He thought only of the duty which he had promised to accomplish, and nothing of the danger which he ran, not only on board the ship, but in the sea, often frequented by sharks. The current bore him along and he rapidly receded from the shore.

Half an hour afterwards, Ayrton, without having been either seen or heard, arrived at the ship and caught hold of the main-chains. He took breath, then, hoisting himself up, he managed to reach the extremity of the cutwater. There were drying several pairs of sailors' trousers. He put on a pair. Then settling himself firmly, he listened. They were not sleeping on board the brig. On the contrary, they were talking, singing, laughing. And these were the sentences, accompanied with oaths, which principally struck Ayrton:—

"Our brig is a famous acquisition."

"She sails well, and merits her name of the 'Speedy.'"

"She would show all the navy of Norfolk a clean pair of heels."

"Hurrah for her captain!"

"Hurrah for Bob Harvey!"

What Ayrton felt when he overheard this fragment of conversation may be understood when it is known that in this Bob Harvey he recognized one of his old Australian companions, a daring sailor, who had continued his criminal career. Bob Harvey had seized, on the shores of Norfolk Island this brig, which was loaded with arms, ammunition, utensils, and tools of all sorts, destined for one of the Sandwich Islands. All his gang had gone on board, and pirates after having been convicts, these wretches, more ferocious than the Malays themselves, scoured the Pacific, destroying vessels, and massacring their crews.

The convicts spoke loudly, they recounted their deeds, drinking deeply at the same time, and this is what Ayrton gathered. The actual crew of the "Speedy" was composed solely of English prisoners, escaped from Norfolk Island.

Here it may be well to explain what this island was. In 29deg 2' south latitude, and 165deg 42' east longitude, to the east of Australia, is found a little island, six miles in circumference, overlooked by Mount Pitt, which rises to a height of 1,100 feet above the level of the sea. This is Norfolk Island, once the seat of an establishment in which were lodged the most intractable convicts from the English penitentiaries. They numbered 500, under an iron discipline, threatened with terrible punishments, and were guarded by 150 soldiers, and 150 employed under the orders of the governor. It would be difficult to imagine a collection of greater ruffians. Sometimes,—although very rarely,—notwithstanding the extreme surveillance of which they were the object, many managed to escape, and seizing vessels which they surprised, they infested the Polynesian Archipelagoes.

Thus had Bob Harvey and his companions done. Thus had Ayrton formerly wished to do. Bob Harvey had seized the brig "Speedy," anchored in sight of Norfolk Island; the crew had been massacred; and for a year this ship had scoured the Pacific, under the command of Harvey, now a pirate, and well known to Ayrton!

The convicts were, for the most part, assembled under the poop; but a few, stretched on the deck, were talking loudly.

The conversation still continued amid shouts and libations. Ayrton learned that chance alone had brought the "Speedy" in sight of Lincoln Island; Bob Harvey had never yet set foot on it; but, as Cyrus Harding had conjectured, finding this unknown land in his course, its position being marked on no chart, he had formed the project of visiting it, and, if he found it suitable, of making it the brig's headquarters.

As to the black flag hoisted at the "Speedy's" peak, and the gun which had been fired, in imitation of men-of-war when they lower their colors, it was pure piratical bravado. It was in no way a signal, and no communication yet existed between the convicts and Lincoln Island.

The settlers' domain was now menaced with terrible danger. Evidently the island, with its water, its harbor, its resources of all kinds so increased in value by the colonists, and the concealment afforded by Granite House, could not but be convenient for the convicts; in their hands it would become an excellent place of refuge, and, being unknown, it would assure them, for a long time perhaps, impunity and security. Evidently, also, the lives of the settlers would not be respected, and Bob Harvey and his accomplices' first care would be to massacre them without mercy. Harding and his companions had, therefore, not even the choice of flying and hiding themselves in the island, since the convicts intended to reside there, and since, in the event of the "Speedy" departing on an expedition, it was probable that some of the crew would remain on shore, so as to settle themselves there. Therefore, it would be necessary to fight, to destroy every one of these scoundrels, unworthy of pity, and against whom any means would be right. So thought Ayrton, and he well knew that Cyrus Harding would be of his way of thinking.

But was resistance and, in the last place, victory possible? That would depend on the equipment of the brig, and the number of men which she carried.

This Ayrton resolved to learn at any cost, and as an hour after his arrival the vociferations had begun to die away, and as a large number of the convicts were already buried in a drunken sleep, Ayrton did not hesitate to venture onto the "Speedy's" deck, which the extinguished lanterns now left in total darkness. He hoisted himself onto the cutwater, and by the bowsprit arrived at the forecastle. Then, gliding among the convicts stretched here and there, he made the round of the ship, and found that the "Speedy" carried four guns, which would throw shot of from eight to ten pounds in weight. He found also, on touching them that these guns were breech-loaders. They were therefore, of modern make, easily used, and of terrible effect.

As to the men lying on the deck, they were about ten in number, but it was to be supposed that more were sleeping down below. Besides, by listening to them, Ayrton had understood that there were fifty on board. That was a large number for the six settlers of Lincoln Island to contend with! But now, thanks to Ayrton's devotion, Cyrus Harding would not be surprised, he would know the strength of his adversaries, and would make his arrangements accordingly.

There was nothing more for Ayrton to do but to return, and render to his companions an account of the mission with which he had charged himself, and he prepared to regain the bows of the brig, so that he might let himself down into the water. But to this man, whose wish was, as he had said, to do more than his duty, there came an heroic thought. This was to sacrifice his own life, but save the island and the colonists. Cyrus Harding evidently could not resist fifty ruffians, all well armed, who, either by penetrating by main force into Granite House, or by starving out the besieged, could obtain from them what they wanted. And then he thought of his preservers—those who had made him again a man, and an honest mm, those to whom he owed all—murdered without pity, their works destroyed, their island turned into a pirates' den! He said to himself that he, Ayrton, was the principal cause of so many disasters, since his old companion, Bob Harvey, had but realized his own plans, and a feeling of horror took possession of him. Then he was seized with an irresistible desire to blow up the brig and with her, all whom she had on board. He would perish in the explosion, but he would have done his duty.

Ayrton did not hesitate. To reach the powder-room, which is always situated in the after-part of a vessel, was easy. There would be no want of powder in a vessel which followed such a trade, and a spark would be enough to destroy it in an instant.

Ayrton stole carefully along the between-decks, strewn with numerous sleepers, overcome more by drunkenness than sleep. A lantern was lighted at the foot of the mainmast, round which was hung a gun-rack, furnished with weapons of all sorts.

Ayrton took a revolver from the rack, and assured himself that it was loaded and primed. Nothing more was needed to accomplish the work of destruction. He then glided towards the stern, so as to arrive under the brig's poop at the powder-magazine.

It was difficult to proceed along the dimly lighted deck without stumbling over some half-sleeping convict, who retorted by oaths and kicks. Ayrton was, therefore, more than once obliged to halt. But at last he arrived at the partition dividing the aftercabin, and found the door opening into the magazine itself.

Ayrton, compelled to force it open, set to work. It was a difficult operation to perform without noise, for he had to break a padlock. But under his vigorous hand, the padlock broke, and the door was open.

At that moment a hand was laid on Ayrton's shoulder.

"What are you doing here?" asked a tall man, in a harsh voice, who, standing in the shadow, quickly threw the light of a lantern in Ayrton's face.

Ayrton drew beck. In the rapid flash of the lantern, he had recognized his former accomplice, Bob Harvey, who could not have known him, as he must have thought Ayrton long since dead.

"What are you doing here?" again said Bob Harvey, seizing Ayrton by the waistband.

But Ayrton, without replying, wrenched himself from his grasp and attempted to rush into the magazine. A shot fired into the midst of the powder-casks, and all would be over!

"Help, lads!" shouted Bob Harvey.

At his shout two or three pirates awoke, jumped up, and, rushing on Ayrton, endeavored to throw him down. He soon extricated himself from their grasp. He fired his revolver, and two of the convicts fell, but a blow from a knife which he could not ward off made a gash in his shoulder.

Ayrton perceived that he could no longer hope to carry out his project. Bob Harvey had reclosed the door of the powder-magazine, and a movement on the deck indicated a general awakening of the pirates. Ayrton must reserve himself to fight at the side of Cyrus Harding. There was nothing for him but flight!

But was flight still possible? It was doubtful, yet Ayrton resolved to dare everything in order to rejoin his companions.

Four barrels of the revolver were still undischarged. Two were fired—one, aimed at Bob Harvey, did not wound him, or at any rate only slightly, and Ayrton, profiting by the momentary retreat of his adversaries, rushed towards the companion-ladder to gain the deck. Passing before the lantern, he smashed it with a blow from the butt of his revolver. A profound darkness ensued, which favored his flight. Two or three pirates, awakened by the noise, were descending the ladder at the same moment.

A fifth shot from Ayrton laid one low, and the others drew back, not understanding what was going on. Ayrton was on deck in two bounds, and three seconds later, having discharged his last barrel in the face of a pirate who was about to seize him by the throat, he leaped over the bulwarks into the sea.

Ayrton had not made six strokes before shots were splashing around him like hail.

What were Pencroft's feelings, sheltered under a rock on the islet! What were those of Harding, the reporter, Herbert, and Neb, crouched in the Chimneys, when they heard the reports on board the brig! They rushed out on to the beach, and, their guns shouldered, they stood ready to repel any attack.

They had no doubt about it themselves! Ayrton, surprised by the pirates, had been murdered, and, perhaps, the wretches would profit by the night to make a descent on the island!

Half an hour was passed in terrible anxiety. The firing had ceased, and yet neither Ayrton nor Pencroft had reappeared. Was the islet invaded? Ought they not to fly to the help of Ayrton and Pencroft? But how? The tide being high at that time, rendered the channel impassable. The boat was not there! We may imagine the horrible anxiety which took possession of Harding and his companions!

At last, towards half-past twelve, a boat, carrying two men, touched the beach. It was Ayrton, slightly wounded in the shoulder, and Pencroft, safe and sound, whom their friends received with open arms.

All immediately took refuge in the Chimneys. There Ayrton recounted all that had passed, even to his plan for blowing up the brig, which he had attempted to put into execution.

All hands were extended to Ayrton, who did not conceal from them that their situation was serious. The pirates had been alarmed. They knew that Lincoln Island was inhabited. They would land upon it in numbers and well armed. They would respect nothing. Should the settlers fall into their hands, they must expect no mercy!

"Well, we shall know how to die!" said the reporter.

"Let us go in and watch," answered the engineer.

"Have we any chance of escape, captain?" asked the sailor.

"Yes, Pencroft."

"Hum! six against fifty!"

"Yes! six! without counting—"

"Who?" asked Pencroft.

Cyrus did not reply, but pointed upwards.

Chapter 3

The night passed without incident. The colonists were on the qui vive, and did not leave their post at the Chimneys. The pirates, on their side, did not appear to have made any attempt to land. Since the last shots fired at Ayrton not a report, not even a sound, had betrayed the presence of the brig in the neighborhood of the island. It might have been fancied that she had weighed anchor, thinking that she had to deal with her match, and had left the coast.

But it was no such thing, and when day began to dawn the settlers could see a confused mass through the morning mist. It was the "Speedy."

"These, my friends," said the engineer, "are the arrangements which appear to me best to make before the fog completely clears away. It hides us from the eyes of the pirates, and we can act without attracting their attention. The most important thing is, that the convicts should believe that the inhabitants of the island are numerous, and consequently capable of resisting them. I therefore propose that we divide into three parties. The first of which shall be posted at the Chimneys, the second at the mouth of the Mercy. As to the third, I think it would be best to place it on the islet, so as to prevent, or at all events delay, any attempt at landing. We have the use of two rifles and four muskets. Each of us will be armed, and, as we are amply provided with powder and shot, we need not spare our fire. We have nothing to fear from the muskets nor even from the guns of the brig. What can they do against these rocks? And, as we shall not fire from the windows of Granite House, the pirates will not think of causing irreparable damage by throwing shell against it. What is to be feared is, the necessity of meeting hand-to-hand, since the convicts have numbers on their side. We must therefore try to prevent them from landing, but without discovering ourselves. Therefore, do not economize the ammunition. Fire often, but with a sure aim. We have each eight or ten enemies to kill, and they must be killed!"

Cyrus Harding had clearly represented their situation, although he spoke in the calmest voice, as if it was a question of directing a piece of work and not ordering a battle. His companions approved these arrangements without even uttering a word. There was nothing more to be done but for each to take his place before the fog should be completely dissipated. Neb and Pencroft immediately ascended to Granite House and brought back a sufficient quantity of ammunition. Gideon Spilett and Ayrton, both very good marksmen, were armed with the two rifles, which carried nearly a mile. The four other muskets were divided among Harding, Neb, Pencroft, and Herbert.

The posts were arranged in the following manner:—

Cyrus Harding and Herbert remained in ambush at the Chimneys, thus commanding the shore to the foot of Granite House.

Gideon Spilett and Neb crouched among the rocks at the mouth of the Mercy, from which the drawbridges had been raised, so as to prevent any one from crossing in a boat or landing on the opposite shore.

As to Ayrton and Pencroft, they shoved off in the boat, and prepared to cross the channel and to take up two separate stations on the islet. In this way, shots being fired from four different points at once, the convicts would be led to believe that the island was both largely peopled and strongly defended.

In the event of a landing being effected without their having been able to prevent it, and also if they saw that they were on the point of being cut off by the brig's boat, Ayrton and Pencroft were to return in their boat to the shore and proceed towards the threatened spot.

Before starting to occupy their posts, the colonists for the last time wrung each other's hands.

Pencroft succeeded in controlling himself sufficiently to suppress his emotion when he embraced Herbert, his boy! and then they separated.

In a few moments Harding and Herbert on one side, the reporter and Neb on the other, had disappeared behind the rocks, and five minutes later Ayrton and Pencroft, having without difficulty crossed the channel, disembarked on the islet and concealed themselves in the clefts of its eastern shore.

None of them could have been seen, for they themselves could scarcely distinguish the brig in the fog.

It was half-past six in the morning.

Soon the fog began to clear away, and the topmasts of the brig issued from the vapor. For some minutes great masses rolled over the surface of the sea, then a breeze sprang up, which rapidly dispelled the mist.

The "Speedy" now appeared in full view, with a spring on her cable, her head to the north, presenting her larboard side to the island. Just as Harding had calculated, she was not more than a mile and a quarter from the coast.

The sinister black flag floated from the peak.

The engineer, with his telescope, could see that the four guns on board were pointed at the island. They were evidently ready to fire at a moment's notice.

In the meanwhile the "Speedy" remained silent. About thirty pirates could be seen moving on the deck. A few more on the poop; two others posted in the shrouds, and armed with spyglasses, were attentively surveying the island.

Certainly, Bob Harvey and his crew would not be able easily to give an account of what had happened during the night on board the brig. Had this half-naked man, who had forced the door of the powder-magazine, and with whom they had struggled, who had six times discharged his revolver at them, who had killed one and wounded two others, escaped their shot? Had he been able to swim to shore?

Whence did he come? What had been his object? Had his design really been to blow up the brig, as Bob Harvey had thought? All this must be confused enough to the convicts' minds. But what they could no longer doubt was that the unknown island before which the "Speedy" had cast anchor was inhabited, and that there was, perhaps, a numerous colony ready to defend it. And yet no one was to be seen, neither on the shore, nor on the heights. The beach appeared to be absolutely deserted. At any rate, there was no trace of dwellings. Had the inhabitants fled into the interior? Thus probably the pirate captain reasoned, and doubtless, like a prudent man, he wished to reconnoiter the locality before he allowed his men to venture there.

During an hour and a half, no indication of attack or landing could be observed on board the brig. Evidently Bob Harvey was hesitating. Even with his strongest telescopes he could not have perceived one of the settlers crouched among the rocks. It was not even probable that his attention had been awakened by the screen of green branches and creepers hiding the windows of Granite House, and showing rather conspicuously on the bare rock. Indeed, how could he imagine that a dwelling was hollowed out, at that height, in the solid granite? From Claw Cape to the Mandible Capes, in all the extent of Union Bay, there was nothing to lead him to suppose that the island was or could be inhabited.

At eight o'clock, however, the colonists observed a movement on board the "Speedy." A boat was lowered, and seven men jumped into her. They were armed with muskets; one took the yoke-lines, four others the oars, and the two others, kneeling in the bows, ready to fire, reconnoitered the island. Their object was no doubt to make an examination but not to land, for in the latter case they would have come in larger numbers. The pirates from their look-out could have seen that the coast was sheltered by an islet, separated from it by a channel half a mile in width. However, it was soon evident to Cyrus Harding, on observing the direction followed by the boat, that they would not attempt to penetrate into the channel, but would land on the islet.

Pencroft and Ayrton, each hidden in a narrow cleft of the rock, saw them coming directly towards them, and waited till they were within range.

The boat advanced with extreme caution. The oars only dipped into the water at long intervals. It could now be seen that one of the convicts held a lead-line in his hand, and that he wished to fathom the depth of the channel hollowed out by the current of the Mercy. This showed that it was Bob Harvey's intention to bring his brig as near as possible to the coast. About thirty pirates, scattered in the rigging, followed every movement of the boat, and took the bearings of certain landmarks which would allow them to approach without danger. The boat was not more than two cables-lengths off the islet when she stopped. The man at the tiller stood up and looked for the best place at which to land.

At that moment two shots were heard. Smoke curled up from among the rocks of the islet. The man at the helm and the man with the lead-line fell backwards into the boat. Ayrton's and Pencroft's balls had struck them both at the same moment.

Almost immediately a louder report was heard, a cloud of smoke issued from the brig's side, and a ball, striking the summit of the rock which sheltered Ayrton and Pencroft, made it fly in splinters, but the two marksmen remained unhurt.

Horrible imprecations burst from the boat, which immediately continued its way. The man who had been at the tiller was replaced by one of his comrades, and the oars were rapidly plunged into the water. However, instead of returning on board as might have been expected, the boat coasted along the islet, so as to round its southern point. The pirates pulled vigorously at their oars that they might get out of range of the bullets.

They advanced to within five cables-lengths of that part of the shore terminated by Flotsam Point, and after having rounded it in a semicircular line, still protected by the brig's guns, they proceeded towards the mouth of the Mercy.

Their evident intention was to penetrate into the channel, and cut off the colonists posted on the islet, in such a way, that whatever their number might be, being placed between the fire from the boat and the fire from the brig, they would find themselves in a very disadvantageous position.

A quarter of an hour passed while the boat advanced in this direction. Absolute silence, perfect calm reigned in the air and on the water.

Pencroft and Ayrton, although they knew they ran the risk of being cut off, had not left their post, both that they did not wish to show themselves as yet to their assailants, and expose themselves to the "Speedy's" guns, and that they relied on Neb and Gideon Spilett, watching at the mouth of the river, and on Cyrus Harding and Herbert, in ambush among the rocks at the Chimneys.

Twenty minutes after the first shots were fired, the boat was less than two cables-lengths off the Mercy. As the tide was beginning to rise with its accustomed violence, caused by the narrowness of the straits, the pirates were drawn towards the river, and it was only by dint of hard rowing that they were able to keep in the middle of the channel. But, as they were passing within good range of the mouth of the Mercy, two balls saluted them, and two more of their number were laid in the bottom of the boat. Neb and Spilett had not missed their aim.

The brig immediately sent a second ball on the post betrayed by the smoke, but without any other result than that of splintering the rock.

The boat now contained only three able men. Carried on by the current, it shot through the channel with the rapidity of an arrow, passed before Harding and Herbert, who, not thinking it within range, withheld their fire, then, rounding the

Jules Verne

northern point of the islet with the two remaining oars, they pulled towards the brig.

Hitherto the settlers had nothing to complain of. Their adversaries had certainly had the worst of it. The latter already counted four men seriously wounded if not dead; they, on the contrary, unwounded, had not missed a shot. If the pirates continued to attack them in this way, if they renewed their attempt to land by means of a boat, they could be destroyed one by one.

It was now seen how advantageous the engineer's arrangements had been. The pirates would think that they had to deal with numerous and well-armed adversaries, whom they could not easily get the better of.

Half an hour passed before the boat, having to pull against the current, could get alongside the "Speedy." Frightful cries were heard when they returned on board with the wounded, and two or three guns were fired with no results.

But now about a dozen other convicts, maddened with rage, and possibly by the effect of the evening's potations, threw themselves into the boat. A second boat was also lowered, in which eight men took their places, and while the first pulled straight for the islet, to dislodge the colonists from thence the second maneuvered so as to force the entrance of the Mercy.

The situation was evidently becoming very dangerous for Pencroft and Ayrton, and they saw that they must regain the mainland.

However, they waited till the first boat was within range, when two well-directed balls threw its crew into disorder. Then, Pencroft and Ayrton, abandoning their posts, under fire from the dozen muskets, ran across the islet at full speed, jumped into their boat, crossed the channel at the moment the second boat reached the southern end, and ran to hide themselves in the Chimneys.

They had scarcely rejoined Cyrus Harding and Herbert, before the islet was overrun with pirates in every direction. Almost at the same moment, fresh reports resounded from the Mercy station, to which the second boat was rapidly approaching. Two, out of the eight men who manned her, were mortally wounded by Gideon Spilett and Neb, and the boat herself, carried irresistibly onto the reefs, was stove in at the mouth of the Mercy. But the six survivors, holding their muskets above their heads to preserve them from contact with the water, managed to land on the right bank of the river. Then, finding they were exposed to the fire of the ambush there, they fled in the direction of Flotsam Point, out of range of the balls.

The actual situation was this: on the islet were a dozen convicts, of whom some were no doubt wounded, but who had still a boat at their disposal; on the island were six, but who could not by any possibility reach Granite House, as they could not cross the river, all the bridges being raised.

"Hallo," exclaimed Pencroft as he rushed into the Chimneys, "hallo, captain! What do you think of it, now?"

"I think," answered the engineer, "that the combat will now take a new form, for it cannot be supposed that the convicts will be so foolish as to remain in a position so unfavorable for them!"

"They won't cross the channel," said the sailor. "Ayrton and Mr. Spilett's rifles are there to prevent them. You know that they carry more than a mile!"

"No doubt," replied Herbert; "but what can two rifles do against the brig's guns?"

"Well, the brig isn't in the channel yet, I fancy!" said Pencroft.

"But suppose she does come there?" said Harding.

"That's impossible, for she would risk running aground and being lost!"

"It is possible," said Ayrton. "The convicts might profit by the high tide to enter the channel, with the risk of grounding at low tide, it is true; but then, under the fire from her guns, our posts would be no longer tenable."

"Confound them!" exclaimed Pencroft, "it really seems as if the blackguards were preparing to weigh anchor."

"Perhaps we shall be obliged to take refuge in Granite House!" observed Herbert.

"We must wait!" answered Cyrus Harding.

"But Mr. Spilett and Neb?" said Pencroft.

"They will know when it is best to rejoin us. Be ready, Ayrton. It is yours and Spilett's rifles which must speak now."

It was only too true. The "Speedy" was beginning to weigh her anchor, and her intention was evidently to approach the islet. The tide would be rising for an hour and a half, and the ebb current being already weakened, it would be easy for the brig to advance. But as to entering the channel, Pencroft, contrary to Ayrton's opinion, could not believe that she would dare to attempt it.

In the meanwhile, the pirates who occupied the islet had gradually advanced to the opposite shore, and were now only separated from the mainland by the channel.

Being armed with muskets alone, they could do no harm to the settlers, in ambush at the Chimneys and the mouth of the Mercy; but, not knowing the latter to be supplied with long-range rifles, they on their side did not believe themselves to be exposed. Quite uncovered, therefore, they surveyed the islet, and examined the shore.

Their illusion was of short duration. Ayrton's and Gideon Spilett's rifles then spoke, and no doubt imparted some very disagreeable intelligence to two of the convicts, for they fell backwards.

Then there was a general helter-skelter. The ten others, not even stopping to pick up their dead or wounded companions, fled to the other side of the islet, tumbled into the boat which had brought them, and pulled away with all their strength.

"Eight less!" exclaimed Pencroft. "Really, one would have thought that Mr. Spilett and Ayrton had given the word to fire together!"

"Gentlemen," said Ayrton, as he reloaded his gun, "this is becoming more serious. The brig is making sail!"

"The anchor is weighed!" exclaimed Pencroft.

"Yes, and she is already moving."

In fact, they could distinctly hear the creaking of the windlass. The "Speedy" was at first held by her anchor; then, when that had been raised, she began to drift towards the shore. The wind was blowing from the sea; the jib and the foretopsail were hoisted, and the vessel gradually approached the island.

From the two posts of the Mercy and the Chimneys they watched her without giving a sign of life, but not without some emotion. What could be more terrible for the colonists than to be exposed, at a short distance, to the brig's guns, without being able to reply with any effect? How could they then prevent the pirates from landing?

Cyrus Harding felt this strongly, and he asked himself what it would be possible to do. Before long, he would be called upon for his determination. But what was it to be? To shut themselves up in Granite House, to be besieged there, to remain there for weeks, for months even, since they had an abundance of provisions? So far good! But after that? The pirates would not the less be masters of the island, which they would ravage at their pleasure, and in time, they would end by having their revenge on the prisoners in Granite House.

However, one chance yet remained; it was that Bob Harvey, after all, would not venture his ship into the channel, and that he would keep outside the islet. He would be still separated from the coast by half a mile, and at that distance his shot could not be very destructive.

"Never!" repeated Pencroft, "Bob Harvey will never, if he is a good seaman, enter that channel! He knows well that it would risk the brig, if the sea got up ever so little! And what would become of him without his vessel?"

In the meanwhile the brig approached the islet, and it could be seen that she was endeavoring to make the lower end. The breeze was light, and as the current had then lost much of its force, Bob Harvey had absolute command over his vessel.

The route previously followed by the boats had allowed her to reconnoiter the channel, and she boldly entered it.

The pirate's design was now only too evident; he wished to bring her broadside to bear on the Chimneys and from there to reply with shell and ball to the shot which had till then decimated her crew.

Soon the "Speedy" reached the point of the islet; she rounded it with ease; the mainsail was braced up, and the brig hugging the wind, stood across the mouth of the Mercy.

"The scoundrels! they are coming!" said Pencroft.

At that moment, Cyrus Harding, Ayrton, the sailor, and Herbert, were rejoined by Neb and Gideon Spilett.

The reporter and his companion had judged it best to abandon the post at the Mercy, from which they could do nothing against the ship, and they had acted wisely. It was better that the colonists should be together at the moment when they were about to engage in a decisive action. Gideon Spilett and Neb had arrived by dodging behind the rocks, though not without attracting a shower of bullets, which had not, however, reached them.

"Spilett! Neb!" cried the engineer. "You are not wounded?"

"No," answered the reporter, "a few bruises only from the ricochet! But that cursed brig has entered the channel!"

"Yes," replied Pencroft, "and in ten minutes she will have anchored before Granite House!"

"Have you formed any plan, Cyrus?" asked the reporter.

"We must take refuge in Granite House while there is still time, and the convicts cannot see us."

"That is, my opinion, too," replied Gideon Spilett, "but once shut up—"

"We must be guided by circumstances," said the engineer.

"Let us be off, then, and make haste!" said the reporter.

"Would you not wish, captain, that Ayrton and I should remain here?" asked the sailor.

"What would be the use of that, Pencroft?" replied Harding. "No. We will not separate!"

There was not a moment to be lost. The colonists left the Chimneys. A bend of the cliff prevented them from being seen by those in the brig, but two or three reports, and the crash of bullets on the rock, told them that the "Speedy" was at no great distance.

To spring into the lift, hoist themselves up to the door of Granite House, where Top and Jup had been shut up since the evening before, to rush into the large room, was the work of a minute only.

It was quite time, for the settlers, through the branches, could see the "Speedy," surrounded with smoke, gliding up the channel. The firing was incessant, and shot from the four guns struck blindly, both on the Mercy post, although it was not occupied, and on the Chimneys. The rocks were splintered, and cheers accompanied each discharge. However, they were hoping that Granite House would be spared, thanks to Harding's precaution of concealing the windows when a shot, piercing the door, penetrated into the passage.

"We are discovered!" exclaimed Pencroft.

The colonists had not, perhaps, been seen, but it was certain that Bob Harvey had thought proper to send a ball through the suspected foliage which concealed that part of the cliff. Soon he redoubled his attack, when another ball having torn away the leafy screen, disclosed a gaping aperture in the granite.

The colonists' situation was desperate. Their retreat was discovered. They could not oppose any obstacle to these missiles, nor protect the stone, which flew in splinters around them. There was nothing to be done but to take refuge in the upper passage of Granite House, and leave their dwelling to be devastated, when a deep roar was heard, followed by frightful cries!

Cyrus Harding and his companions rushed to one of the windows—

The brig, irresistibly raised on a sort of water-spout, had just split in two, and in less than ten seconds she was swallowed up with all her criminal crew!

Chapter 4

"She has blown up!" cried Herbert.

"Yes! blown up, just as if Ayrton had set fire to the powder!" returned Pencroft, throwing himself into the lift together with Neb and the lad.

"But what has happened?" asked Gideon Spilett, quite stunned by this unexpected catastrophe.

"Oh! this time, we shall know—" answered the engineer quickly.

"What shall we know?—"

"Later! later! Come, Spilett. The main point is that these pirates have been exterminated!"

And Cyrus Harding, hurrying away the reporter and Ayrton, joined Pencroft, Neb, and Herbert on the beach.

Nothing could be seen of the brig, not even her masts. After having been raised by the water-spout, she had fallen on her side, and had sunk in that position, doubtless in consequence of some enormous leak. But as in that place the channel was not more than twenty feet in depth, it was certain that the sides of the submerged brig would reappear at low water.

A few things from the wreck floated on the surface of the water, a raft could be seen consisting of spare spars, coops of poultry with their occupants still living, boxes and barrels, which gradually came to the surface, after having escaped through the hatchways, but no pieces of the wreck appeared, neither planks from the deck, nor timber from the hull,—which rendered the sudden disappearance of the "Speedy" perfectly inexplicable.

However, the two masts, which had been broken and escaped from the shrouds and stays came up, and with their sails, some furled and the others spread. But it was not necessary to wait for the tide to bring up these riches, and Ayrton and Pencroft jumped into the boat with the intention of towing the pieces of wreck either to the beach or to the islet. But just as they were shoving off, an observation from Gideon Spilett arrested them.

"What about those six convicts who disembarked on the right bank of the Mercy?" said he.

In fact, it would not do to forget that the six men whose boat had gone to pieces on the rocks had landed at Flotsam Point.

They looked in that direction. None of the fugitives were visible. It was probable that, having seen their vessel engulfed in the channel, they had fled into the interior of the island.

"We will deal with them later," said Harding. "As they are armed, they will still be dangerous; but as it is six against six, the chances are equal. To the most pressing business first."

Ayrton and Pencroft pulled vigorously towards the wreck.

The sea was calm and the tide very high, as there had been a new moon but two days before. A whole hour at least would elapse before the hull of the brig could emerge from the water of the channel.

Ayrton and Pencroft were able to fasten the masts and spars by means of ropes, the ends of which were carried to the beach. There, by the united efforts of the settlers the pieces of wreck were hauled up. Then the boat picked up all that was floating, coops, barrels, and boxes, which were immediately carried to the Chimneys.

Several bodies floated also. Among them, Ayrton recognized that of Bob Harvey, which he pointed out to his companion, saying with some emotion,—

"That is what I have been, Pencroft."

"But what you are no longer, brave Ayrton!" returned the sailor warmly.

It was singular enough that so few bodies floated. Only five or six were counted, which were already being carried by the current towards the open sea. Very probably the convicts had not had time to escape, and the ship lying over on her side, the greater number of them had remained below. Now the current, by carrying the bodies of these miserable men out to sea, would spare the colonists the sad task of burying them in some corner of their island.

For two hours, Cyrus Harding and his companions were solely occupied in hauling up the spars on to the sand, and then in spreading the sails which were perfectly uninjured, to dry. They spoke little, for they were absorbed in their work, but what thoughts occupied their minds!

The possession of this brig, or rather all that she contained, was a perfect mine of wealth. In fact, a ship is like a little world in miniature, and the stores of the colony would be increased by a large number of useful articles. It would be, on a large scale, equivalent to the chest found at Flotsam Point.

"And besides," thought Pencroft, "why should it be impossible to refloat the brig? If she has only a leak, that may be stopped up; a vessel from three to four hundred tons, why she is a regular ship compared to our 'Bonadventure'! And we could go a long distance in her! We could go anywhere we liked! Captain Harding, Ayrton and I must examine her! She would be well worth the trouble!"

In fact, if the brig was still fit to navigate, the colonists' chances of returning to their native land were singularly increased. But, to decide this important question, it was necessary to wait until the tide was quite low, so that every part of the brig's hull might be examined.

When their treasures had been safely conveyed on shore, Harding and his companions agreed to devote some minutes to breakfast. They were almost famished; fortunately, the larder was not far off, and Neb was noted for being an expeditious cook. They breakfasted, therefore, near the Chimneys, and during their repast, as may be supposed, nothing was talked of but the event which had so miraculously saved the colony.

"Miraculous is the word," repeated Pencroft, "for it must be acknowledged that those rascals blew up just at the right moment! Granite House was beginning to be uncomfortable as a habitation!"

"And can you guess, Pencroft," asked the reporter, "how it happened, or what can have occasioned the explosion?"

"Oh! Mr. Spilett, nothing is more simple," answered Pencroft. "A convict vessel is not disciplined like a man-of-war! Convicts are not sailors. Of course the powder-magazine was open, and as they were firing incessantly, some careless or clumsy fellow just blew up the vessel!"

"Captain Harding," said Herbert, "what astonishes me is that the explosion has not produced more effect. The report was not loud, and besides there are so few planks and timbers torn out. It seems as if the ship had rather foundered than blown up."

"Does that astonish you, my boy?" asked the engineer.

"Yes, captain."

"And it astonishes me also, Herbert," replied he, "but when we visit the hull of the brig, we shall no doubt find the explanation of the matter."

"Why, captain," said Pencroft, "you don't suppose that the 'Speedy' simply foundered like a ship which has struck on a rock?"

"Why not," observed Neb, "if there are rocks in the channel?"

"Nonsense, Neb," answered Pencroft, "you did not look at the right moment. An instant before she sank, the brig, as I saw perfectly well, rose on an enormous wave, and fell back on her larboard side. Now, if she had only struck, she would have sunk quietly and gone to the bottom like an honest vessel."

"It was just because she was not an honest vessel!" returned Neb.

"Well, we shall soon see, Pencroft," said the engineer.

"We shall soon see," rejoined the sailor, "but I would wager my head there are no rocks in the channel. Look here, captain, to speak candidly, do you mean to say that there is anything marvelous in the occurrence?"

Cyrus Harding did not answer.

"At any rate," said Gideon Spilett, "whether rock or explosion, you will agree, Pencroft, that it occurred just in the nick of time!"

"Yes! yes!" replied the sailor, "but that is not the question. I ask Captain Harding if he sees anything supernatural in all this."

"I cannot say, Pencroft," said the engineer. "That is all the answer I can make."

A reply which did not satisfy Pencroft at all. He stuck to "an explosion," and did not wish to give it up. He would never consent to admit that in that channel, with its fine sandy bed, just like the beach, which he had often crossed at low water, there could be an unknown rock.

And besides, at the time the brig foundered, it was high water, that is to say, there was enough water to carry the vessel clear over any rocks which would not be uncovered at low tide. Therefore, there could not have been a collision. Therefore, the vessel had not struck. So she had blown up.

And it must be confessed that the sailor's arguments were reasonable.

Towards half-past one, the colonists embarked in the boat to visit the wreck. It was to be regretted that the brig's two boats had not been saved; but one, as has been said, had gone to pieces at the mouth of the Mercy, and was absolutely useless; the other had disappeared when the brig went down, and had not again been seen, having doubtless been crushed.

The hull of the "Speedy" was just beginning to issue from the water. The brig was lying right over on her side, for her masts being broken, pressed down by the weight of the ballast displaced by the shock, the keel was visible along her whole length. She had been regularly turned over by the inexplicable but frightful submarine action, which had been at the same time manifested by an enormous water-spout.

The settlers rowed round the hull, and in proportion as the tide went down, they could ascertain, if not the cause which had occasioned the catastrophe, at least the effect produced.

Towards the bows, on both sides of the keel, seven or eight feet from the beginning of the stem, the sides of the brig were frightfully torn. Over a length of at least twenty feet there opened two large leaks, which would be impossible to stop up. Not only had the copper sheathing and the planks disappeared, reduced, no doubt, to powder, but also the ribs, the iron bolts, and treenalls which united them. From the entire length of the hull to the stern the false keel had been separated with an unaccountable violence, and the keel itself, torn from the carline in several places, was split in all its length.

"I've a notion!" exclaimed Pencroft, "that this vessel will be difficult to get afloat again."

"It will be impossible," said Ayrton.

"At any rate," observed Gideon Spilett to the sailor, "the explosion, if there has been one, has produced singular effects! It has split the lower part of the hull, instead of blowing up the deck and topsides! These great rents appear rather to have been made by a rock than by the explosion of a powder-magazine."

"There is not a rock in the channel!" answered the sailor. "I will admit anything you like, except the rock."

"Let us try to penetrate into the interior of the brig," said the engineer; "perhaps we shall then know what to think of the cause of her destruction."

This was the best thing to be done, and it was agreed, besides, to take an inventory of all the treasures on board, and to arrange their preservation.

Access to the interior of the brig was now easy. The tide was still going down and the deck was practicable. The ballast, composed of heavy masses of iron, had broken through in several places. The noise of the sea could be heard as it rushed out at the holes in the hull.

Cyrus Harding and his companions, hatchets in hand, advanced along the shattered deck. Cases of all sorts encumbered it, and, as they had been but a very short time in the water, their contents were perhaps uninjured.

They then busied themselves in placing all this cargo in safety. The water would not return for several hours, and these hours must be employed in the most profitable way. Ayrton and Pencroft had, at the entrance made in the hull, discovered tackle, which would serve to hoist up the barrels and chests. The boat received them and transported them to the shore. They took the articles as they came, intending to sort them afterwards.

At any rate, the settlers saw at once, with extreme satisfaction, that the brig possessed a very varied cargo—an assortment of all sorts of articles, utensils, manufactured goods, and tools—such as the ships which make the great coasting-trade of Polynesia are usually laden with. It was probable that they would find a little of everything, and they agreed that it was exactly what was necessary for the colony of Lincoln Island.

However—and Cyrus Harding observed it in silent astonishment—not only, as has been said, had the hull of the brig enormously suffered from the shock, whatever it was, that had occasioned the catastrophe, but the interior arrangements had been destroyed, especially towards the bows. Partitions and stanchions were smashed, as if some tremendous shell had burst in the interior of the brig. The colonists could easily go fore and aft, after having removed the cases as they were extricated. They were not heavy bales, which would have been difficult to remove, but simple packages, of which the stowage, besides, was no longer recognizable.

The colonists then reached the stern of the brig—the part formerly surmounted by the poop. It was there that, following Ayrton's directions, they must look for the powder-magazine. Cyrus Harding thought that it had not exploded; that it was possible some barrels might be saved, and that the powder, which is usually enclosed in metal coverings might not have suffered from contact with the water.

This, in fact, was just what had happened. They extricated from among a large number of shot twenty barrels, the insides of which were lined with copper. Pencroft was convinced by the evidence of his own eyes that the destruction of the "Speedy" could not be attributed to an explosion. That part of the hull in which the magazine was situated was, moreover, that which had suffered least.

"It may be so," said the obstinate sailor; "but as to a rock, there is not one in the channel!"

"Then, how did it happen?" asked Herbert.

"I don't know," answered Pencroft, "Captain Harding doesn't know, and nobody knows or ever will know!"

Several hours had passed during these researches, and the tide began to flow. Work must be suspended for the present. There was no fear of the brig being carried away by the sea, for she was already fixed as firmly as if moored by her anchors.

They could, therefore, without inconvenience, wait until the next day to resume operations; but, as to the vessel itself, she was doomed, and it would be best to hasten to save the remains of her hull, as she would not be long in disappearing in the quicksands of the channel.

It was now five o'clock in the evening. It had been a hard day's work for the men. They ate with good appetite, and notwithstanding their fatigue, they could not resist, after dinner, their desire of inspecting the cases which composed the cargo of the "Speedy."

Most of them contained clothes, which, as may be believed, was well received. There were enough to clothe a whole colony—linen for every one's use, shoes for every one's feet.

"We are too rich!" exclaimed Pencroft, "But what are we going to do with all this?"

And every moment burst forth the hurrahs of the delighted sailor when he caught sight of the barrels of gunpowder, firearms and sidearms, balls of cotton, implements of husbandry, carpenter's, joiner's, and blacksmith's tools, and boxes of all kinds of seeds, not in the least injured by their short sojourn in the water. Ah, two years before, how these things would have been prized! And now, even though the industrious colonists had provided themselves with tools, these treasures would find their use.

There was no want of space in the store-rooms of Granite House, but that daytime would not allow them to stow away the whole. It would not do also to forget that the six survivors of the "Speedy's" crew had landed on the island, for they were in all probability scoundrels of the deepest dye, and it was necessary that the colonists should be on their guard against them. Although the bridges over the Mercy were raised, the convicts would not be stopped by a river or a stream and, rendered desperate, these wretches would be capable of anything.

They would see later what plan it would be best to follow; but in the meantime it was necessary to mount guard over cases and packages heaped up near the Chimneys, and thus the settlers employed themselves in turn during the night.

The morning came, however, without the convicts having attempted any attack. Master Jup and Top, on guard at the foot of Granite House, would have quickly given the alarm. The three following day—the 19th, 20th, and 21st of October—were employed in saving everything of value, or of any use whatever, either from the cargo or rigging of the brig. At low tide they overhauled the hold—at high tide they stowed away the rescued articles. A great part of the copper sheathing had been torn from the hull, which every day sank lower. But before the sand had swallowed the heavy things which had fallen through the bottom, Ayrton and Pencroft, diving to the bed of the channel, recovered the chains and anchors of the brig, the iron of her ballast, and even four guns, which, floated by means of empty casks, were brought to shore.

It may be seen that the arsenal of the colony had gained by the wreck, as well as the storerooms of Granite House. Pencroft, always enthusiastic in his projects, already spoke of constructing a battery to command the channel and the mouth of the river. With four guns, he engaged to prevent any fleet, "however powerful it might be," from venturing into the waters of Lincoln Island!

In the meantime, when nothing remained of the brig but a useless hulk, bad weather came on, which soon finished her. Cyrus Harding had intended to blow her up, so as to collect the remains on the shore, but a strong gale from the northeast and a heavy sea compelled him to economize his powder.

In fact, on the night of the 23rd, the hull entirely broke up, and some of the wreck was cast up on the beach.

As to the papers on board, it is useless to say that, although he carefully searched the lockers of the poop, Harding did not discover any trace of them. The pirates had evidently destroyed everything that concerned either the captain or the owners of the "Speedy," and, as the name of her port was not painted on her counter, there was nothing which would tell them her nationality. However, by the shape of her boats Ayrton and Pencroft believed that the brig was of English build.

A week after the castrophe—or, rather, after the fortunate, though inexplicable, event to which the colony owed its preservation—nothing more could be seen of the vessel, even at low tide. The wreck had disappeared, and Granite House was enriched by nearly all it had contained.

However, the mystery which enveloped its strange destruction would doubtless never have been cleared away if, on the 30th of November, Neb, strolling on the beach, had not found a piece of a thick iron cylinder, bearing traces of explosion.

The edges of this cylinder were twisted and broken, as if they had been subjected to the action of some explosive substance.

Neb brought this piece of metal to his master, who was then occupied with his companions in the workshop of the Chimneys.

Cyrus Harding examined the cylinder attentively, then, turning to Pencroft,—

"You persist, my friend," said he, "in maintaining that the 'Speedy' was not lost in consequence of a collision?"

"Yes, captain," answered the sailor. "You know as well as I do that there are no rocks in the channel."

"But suppose she had run against this piece of iron?" said the engineer, showing the broken cylinder.

"What, that bit of pipe!" exclaimed Pencroft in a tone of perfect incredulity.

"My friends," resumed Harding, "you remember that before she foundered the brig rose on the summit of a regular waterspout?"

"Yes, captain," replied Herbert.

"Well, would you like to know what occasioned that waterspout? It was this," said the engineer, holding up the broken tube.

"That?" returned Pencroft.

"Yes! This cylinder is all that remains of a torpedo!"

"A torpedo!" exclaimed the engineer's companions.

"And who put the torpedo there?" demanded Pencroft, who did not like to yield.

"All that I can tell you is, that it was not I," answered Cyrus Harding; "but it was there, and you have been able to judge of its incomparable power!"

Chapter 5

So, then, all was explained by the submarine explosion of this torpedo. Cyrus Harding could not be mistaken, as, during the war of the Union, he had had occasion to try these terrible engines of destruction. It was under the action of this cylinder, charged with some explosive substance, nitro-glycerine, picrate, or some other material of the same nature, that the water of the channel had been raised like a dome, the bottom of the brig crushed in, and she had sunk instantly, the damage done to her hull being so considerable that it was impossible to refloat her. The "Speedy" had not been able to withstand a torpedo that would have destroyed an ironclad as easily as a fishing-boat!

Yes! all was explained, everything—except the presence of the torpedo in the waters of the channel!

"My friends, then," said Cyrus Harding, "we can no longer be in doubt as to the presence of a mysterious being, a castaway like us, perhaps, abandoned on our island, and I say this in order that Ayrton may be acquainted with all the strange events which have occurred during these two years. Who this beneficent stranger is, whose intervention has, so fortunately for us, been manifested on many occasions, I cannot imagine. What his object can be in acting thus, in concealing himself after rendering us so many services, I cannot understand: But his services are not the less real, and are of such a nature that only a man possessed of prodigious power, could render them. Ayrton is indebted to him as much as we are, for, if it was the stranger who saved me from the waves after the fall from the balloon, evidently it was he who wrote the document, who placed the bottle in the channel, and who has made known to us the situation of our companion. I will add that it was he who guided that chest, provided with everything we wanted, and stranded it on Flotsam Point; that it was he who lighted that fire on the heights of the island, which permitted you to land; that it was he who fired that bullet found in the body of the peccary; that it was he who plunged that torpedo into the channel, which destroyed the brig; in a word, that all those inexplicable events, for which we could not assign a reason, are due to this mysterious being. Therefore, whoever he may be, whether shipwrecked, or exiled on our island, we shall be ungrateful, if we think ourselves freed from gratitude towards him. We have contracted a debt, and I hope that we shall one day pay it."

"You are right in speaking thus, my dear Cyrus," replied Gideon Spilett. "Yes, there is an almost all-powerful being, hidden in some part of the island, and whose influence has been singularly useful to our colony. I will add that the unknown appears to possess means of action which border on the supernatural, if in the events of practical life the supernatural were recognizable. Is it he who is in secret communication with us by the well in Granite House, and has he thus a knowledge of all our plans? Was it he who threw us that bottle, when the vessel made her first cruise? Was it he who threw Top out of the lake, and killed the dugong? Was it he, who as everything leads us to believe, saved you from the waves, and that under circumstances in which any one else would not have been able to act? If it was he, he possesses a power which renders him master of the elements."

The reporter's reasoning was just, and every one felt it to be so.

"Yes," rejoined Cyrus Harding, "if the intervention of a human being is not more questionable for us, I agree that he has at his disposal means of action beyond those possessed by humanity. There is a mystery still, but if we discover the man, the mystery will be discovered also. The question, then, is, ought we to respect the incognito of this generous being, or ought we to do everything to find him out? What is your opinion on the matter?"

"My opinion," said Pencroft, "is that, whoever he may be, he is a brave man, and he has my esteem!"

"Be it so," answered Harding, "but that is not an answer, Pencroft."

"Master," then said Neb, "my idea is, that we may search as long as we like for this gentleman whom you are talking about, but that we shall not discover him till he pleases."

"That's not bad, what you say, Neb," observed Pencroft.

"I am of Neb's opinion," said Gideon Spilett, "but that is no reason for not attempting the adventure. Whether we find this mysterious being or not, we shall at least have fulfilled our duty towards him."

"And you, my boy, give us your opinion," said the engineer, turning to Herbert.

"Oh," cried Herbert, his countenance full of animation, "how I should like to thank him, he who saved you first, and who has now saved us!"

"Of course, my boy," replied Pencroft, "so would I and all of us. I am not inquisitive, but I would give one of my eyes to see this individual face to face! It seems to me that he must be handsome, tall, strong, with a splendid beard, radiant hair, and that he must be seated on clouds, a great ball in his hands!"

"But, Pencroft," answered Spilett, "you are describing a picture of the Creator."

"Possibly, Mr. Spilett," replied the sailor, "but that is how I imagine him!"

"And you, Ayrton?" asked the engineer.

"Captain Harding," replied Ayrton, "I can give you no better advice in this matter. Whatever you do will be best; when you wish me to join you in your researches, I am ready to follow you.

"I thank you, Ayrton," answered Cyrus Harding, "but I should like a more direct answer to the question I put to you. You are our companion; you have already endangered your life several times for us, and you, as well as the rest, ought to be consulted in the matter of any important decision. Speak, therefore."

"Captain Harding," replied Ayrton, "I think that we ought to do everything to discover this unknown benefactor. Perhaps he is alone. Perhaps he is suffering. Perhaps he has a life to be renewed. I, too, as you said, have a debt of gratitude to pay him. It was he, it could be only he who must have come to Tabor Island, who found there the wretch you knew, and who made known to you that there was an unfortunate man there to be saved. Therefore it is, thanks to him, that I have become a man again. No, I will never forget him!"

"That is settled, then," said Cyrus Harding. "We will begin our researches as soon as possible. We will not leave a corner of the island unexplored. We will search into its most secret recesses, and will hope that our unknown friend will pardon us in consideration of our intentions!"

For several days the colonists were actively employed in haymaking and the harvest. Before putting their project of exploring the yet unknown parts of the island into execution, they wished to get all possible work finished. It was also the time for collecting the various vegetables from the Tabor Island plants. All was stowed away, and happily there was no want of room in Granite House, in which they might have housed all the treasures of the island. The products of the colony were there, methodically arranged, and in a safe place, as may be believed, sheltered as much from animals as from man.

There was no fear of damp in the middle of that thick mass of granite. Many natural excavations situated in the upper passage were enlarged either by pick-axe or mine, and Granite House thus became a general warehouse, containing all the provisions, arms, tools, and spare utensils—in a word, all the stores of the colony.

As to the guns obtained from the brig, they were pretty pieces of ordnance, which, at Pencroft's entreaty, were hoisted by means of tackle and pulleys, right up into Granite House; embrasures were made between the windows, and the shining muzzles of the guns could soon be seen through the granite cliff. From this height they commanded all Union Bay. It was like a little Gibraltar, and any vessel anchored off the islet would inevitably be exposed to the fire of this aerial battery.

"Captain," said Pencroft one day, it was the 8th of November, "now that our fortifications are finished, it would be a good thing if we tried the range of our guns."

"Do you think that is useful?" asked the engineer.

"It is more than useful, it is necessary! Without that how are we to know to what distance we can send one of those pretty shot with which we are provided?"

"Try them, Pencroft," replied the engineer. "However, I think that in making the experiment, we ought to employ, not the ordinary powder, the supply of which, I think, should remain untouched, but the pyroxyle which will never fail us."

"Can the cannon support the shock of the pyroxyle?" asked the reporter, who was not less anxious than Pencroft to try the artillery of Granite House.

"I believe so. However," added the engineer, "we will be prudent." The engineer was right in thinking that the guns were of excellent make. Made of forged steel, and breech-loaders, they ought consequently to be able to bear a considerable charge, and also have an enormous range. In fact, as regards practical effect, the transit described by the ball ought to be as extended as possible, and this tension could only be obtained under the condition that the projectile should be impelled with a very great initial velocity.

"Now," said Harding to his companions, "the initial velocity is in proportion to the quantity of powder used. In the fabrication of these pieces, everything depends on employing a metal with the highest possible power of resistance, and steel is incontestably that metal of all others which resists the best. I have, therefore, reason to believe that our guns will bear without risk the expansion of the pyroxyle gas, and will give excellent results."

"We shall be a great deal more certain of that when we have tried them!" answered Pencroft.

It is unnecessary to say that the four cannons were in perfect order. Since they had been taken from the water, the sailor had bestowed great care upon them.

How many hours he had spent, in rubbing, greasing, and polishing them, and in cleaning the mechanism! And now the pieces were as brilliant as if they had been on board a frigate of the United States Navy.

On this day, therefore, in presence of all the members of the colony, including Master Jup and Top, the four cannon were successively tried. They were charged with pyroxyle, taking into consideration its explosive power, which, as has been said, is four times that of ordinary powder: the projectile to be fired was cylindroconic.

Pencroft, holding the end of the quick-match, stood ready to fire.

At Harding's signal, he fired. The shot, passing over the islet, fell into the sea at a distance which could not be calculated with exactitude.

The second gun was pointed at the rocks at the end of Flotsam Point, and the shot striking a sharp rock nearly three miles from Granite House, made it fly into splinters. It was Herbert who had pointed this gun and fired it, and very proud he was of his first shot. Pencroft only was prouder than he! Such a shot, the honor of which belonged to his dear boy.

The third shot, aimed this time at the downs forming the upper side of Union Bay, struck the sand at a distance of four miles, then having ricocheted: was lost in the sea in a cloud of spray.

For the fourth piece Cyrus Harding slightly increased the charge, so as to try its extreme range. Then, all standing aside for fear of its bursting, the match was lighted by means of a long cord.

A tremendous report was heard, but the piece had held good, and the colonists rushing to the windows, saw the shot graze the rocks of Mandible Cape, nearly five miles from Granite House, and disappear in Shark Gulf.

"Well, captain," exclaimed Pencroft, whose cheers might have rivaled the reports themselves, "what do you say of our battery? All the pirates in the Pacific have only to present themselves before Granite House! Not one can land there now without our permission!"

"Believe me, Pencroft," replied the engineer, "it would be better not to have to make the experiment."

"Well," said the sailor, "what ought to be done with regard to those six villains who are roaming about the island? Are we to leave them to overrun our forests, our fields, our plantations? These pirates are regular jaguars, and it seems to me we ought not to hesitate to treat them as such! What do you think, Ayrton?" added Pencroft, turning to his companion.

Ayrton hesitated at first to reply, and Cyrus Harding regretted that Pencroft had so thoughtlessly put this question. And he was much moved when Ayrton replied in a humble tone,—

"I have been one of those jaguars, Mr. Pencroft. I have no right to speak."

And with a slow step he walked away.

Pencroft understood.

"What a brute I am!" he exclaimed. "Poor Ayrton! He has as much right to speak here as any one!"

"Yes," said Gideon Spilett, "but his reserve does him honor, and it is right to respect the feeling which he has about his sad past."

"Certainly, Mr. Spilett," answered the sailor, "and there is no fear of my doing so again. I would rather bite my tongue off than cause Ayrton any pain! But to return to the question. It seems to me that these ruffians have no right to any pity, and that we ought to rid the island of them as soon as possible."

"Is that your opinion, Pencroft?" asked the engineer.

"Quite my opinion."

"And before hunting them mercilessly, you would not wait until they had committed some fresh act of hostility against us?"

"Isn't what they have done already enough?" asked Pencroft, who did not understand these scruples.

"They may adopt other sentiments!" said Harding, "and perhaps repent."

"They repent!" exclaimed the sailor, shrugging his shoulders.

"Pencroft, think of Ayrton!" said Herbert, taking the sailor's hand. "He became an honest man again!"

Pencroft looked at his companions one after the other. He had never thought of his proposal being met with any objection. His rough nature could not allow that they ought to come to terms with the rascals who had landed on the island with Bob Harvey's accomplices, the murderers of the crew of the "Speedy," and he looked upon them as wild beasts which ought to be destroyed without delay and without remorse.

"Come!" said he. "Everybody is against me! You wish to be generous to those villains! Very well; I hope we mayn't repent it!"

"What danger shall we run," said Herbert, "if we take care to be always on our guard?"

"Hum!" observed the reporter, who had not given any decided opinion. "They are six and well armed. If they each lay hid in a corner, and each fired at one of us, they would soon be masters of the colony!"

"Why have they not done so?" said Herbert. "No doubt because it was not their interest to do it. Besides, we are six also."

"Well, well!" replied Pencroft, whom no reasoning could have convinced. "Let us leave these good people to do what they like, and don't think anything more about them!"

"Come, Pencroft," said Neb, "don't make yourself out so bad as all that! Suppose one of these unfortunate men were here before you, within good range of your guns, you would not fire."

"I would fire on him as I would on a mad dog, Neb," replied Pencroft coldly.

"Pencroft," said the engineer, "you have always shown much deference to my advice; will you, in this matter, yield to me?"

"I will do as you please, Captain Harding," answered the sailor, who was not at all convinced.

"Very well, wait, and we will not attack them unless we are attacked first."

Thus their behavior towards the pirates was agreed upon, although Pencroft augured nothing good from it. They were not to attack them, but were to be on their guard. After all, the island was large and fertile. If any sentiment of honesty yet remained in the bottom of their hearts, these wretches might perhaps be reclaimed. Was it not their interest in the situation in which they found themselves to begin a new life? At any rate, for humanity's sake alone, it would be right to wait. The colonists would no longer as before, be able to go and come without fear. Hitherto they had only wild beasts to guard against, and now six convicts of the worst description, perhaps, were roaming over their island. It was serious, certainly, and to less brave men, it would have been security lost! No matter! At present, the colonists had reason on their side against Pencroft. Would they be right in the future? That remained to be seen.

Chapter 6

However, the chief business of the colonists was to make that complete exploration of the island which had been decided upon, and which would have two objects: to discover the mysterious being whose existence was now indisputable, and at the same time to find out what had become of the pirates, what retreat they had chosen, what sort of life they were leading, and what was to be feared from them. Cyrus Harding wished to set out without delay; but as the expedition would be of some days duration, it appeared best to load the cart with different materials and tools in order to facilitate the organization of the encampments. One of the onagers, however, having hurt its leg, could not be harnessed at present, and a few days' rest was necessary. The departure was, therefore, put off for a week, until the 20th of November. The month of November in this latitude corresponds to the month of May in the northern zones. It was, therefore, the fine season. The sun was entering the tropic of Capricorn, and gave the longest days in the year. The time was, therefore, very favorable for the projected expedition, which, if it did not accomplish its principal object, would at any rate be fruitful in discoveries, especially of natural productions, since Harding proposed to explore those dense forests of the Far West, which stretched to the extremity of the Serpentine Peninsula.

During the nine days which preceded their departure, it was agreed that the work on Prospect Heights should be finished off.

Moreover, it was necessary for Ayrton to return to the corral, where the domesticated animals required his care. It was decided that he should spend two days there, and return to Granite House after having liberally supplied the stables.

As he was about to start, Harding asked him if he would not like one of them to accompany him, observing that the island was less safe than formerly. Ayrton replied that this was unnecessary, as he was enough for the work, and that besides he apprehended no danger. If anything occurred at the corral, or in the neighborhood, he could instantly warn the colonists by sending a telegram to Granite House.

Ayrton departed at dawn on the 9th, taking the cart drawn by one onager, and two hours after, the electric wire announced that he had found all in order at the corral.

During these two days Harding busied himself in executing a project which would completely guard Granite House against any surprise. It was necessary to completely conceal the opening of the old outlet, which was already walled up and partly hidden under grass and plants, at the southern angle of Lake Grant. Nothing was easier, since if the level of the lake was raised two or three feet, the opening would be quite beneath it. Now, to raise this level they had only to establish a dam at the two openings made by the lake, and by which were fed Creek Glycerine and Falls River.

The colonists worked with a will, and the two dams which besides did not exceed eight feet in width by three in height, were rapidly erected by means of well-cemented blocks of stone.

This work finished, it would have been impossible to guess that at that part of the lake, there existed a subterranean passage through which the overflow of the lake formerly escaped.

Of course the little stream which fed the reservoir of Granite House and worked the lift, had been carefully preserved, and the water could not fail. The lift once raised, this sure and comfortable retreat would be safe from any surprise.

This work had been so quickly done, that Pencroft, Gideon Spilett, and Herbert found time to make an expedition to Port Balloon, The sailor was very anxious to know if the little creek in which the "Bonadventure" was moored, had been visited by the convicts.

"These gentlemen," he observed, "landed on the south coast, and if they followed the shore, it is to be feared that they may have discovered the little harbor, and in that case, I wouldn't give half-a-dollar for our 'Bonadventure.'"

Pencroft's apprehensions were not without foundation, and a visit to Port Balloon appeared to be very desirable. The sailor and his companions set off on the 10th of November, after dinner, well armed. Pencroft, ostentatiously slipping two bullets into each barrel of his rifle, shook his head in a way which betokened nothing good to any one who approached too near him, whether "man or beast," as he said. Gideon Spilett and Herbert also took their guns, and about three o'clock all three left Granite House.

Neb accompanied them to the turn of the Mercy, and after they had crossed, he raised the bridge. It was agreed that a gunshot should announce the colonists' return, and that at the signal Neb should return and reestablish the communication between the two banks of the river.

The little band advanced directly along the road which led to the southern coast of the island. This was only a distance of three miles and a half, but Gideon Spilett and his companions took two hours to traverse it. They examined all the border of the road, the thick forest, as well as Tabor Marsh. They found no trace of the fugitives who, no doubt, not having yet discovered the number of the colonists, or the means of defense which they had at their disposal, had gained the less accessible parts of the island.

Arrived at Port Balloon, Pencroft saw with extreme satisfaction that the "Bonadventure" was tranquilly floating in the narrow creek. However, Port Balloon was so well hidden among high rocks, that it could scarcely be discovered either from the land or the sea.

"Come," said Pencroft, "the blackguards have not been there yet. Long grass suits reptiles best, and evidently we shall find them in the Far West."

"And it's very lucky, for if they had found the 'Bonadventure'," added Herbert, "they would have gone off in her, and we should have been prevented from returning to Tabor Island."

"Indeed," remarked the reporter, "it will be important to take a document there which will make known the situation of Lincoln Island, and Ayrton's new residence, in case the Scotch yacht returns to fetch him."

"Well, the 'Bonadventure' is always there, Mr. Spilett," answered the sailor. "She and her crew are ready to start at a moment's notice!"

"I think, Pencroft, that that is a thing to be done after our exploration of the island is finished. It is possible after all that the stranger, if we manage to find him, may know as much about Tabor Island as about Lincoln Island. Do not forget that he is certainly the author of the document, and he may, perhaps, know how far we may count on the return of the yacht!"

"But!" exclaimed Pencroft, "who in the world can he be? The fellow knows us and we know nothing about him! If he is a simple castaway, why should he conceal himself! We are honest men, I suppose, and the society of honest men isn't unpleasant to any one. Did he come here voluntarily? Can he leave the island if he likes? Is he here still? Will he remain any longer?"

Chatting thus, Pencroft, Gideon Spilett, and Herbert got on board and looked about the deck of the "Bonadventure." All at once, the sailor having examined the bitts to which the cable of the anchor was secured,—

"Hallo," he cried, "this is queer!"

"What is the matter, Pencroft?" asked the reporter.

"The matter is, that it was not I who made this knot!"

And Pencroft showed a rope which fastened the cable to the bitt itself.

"What, it was not you?" asked Gideon Spilett.

"No! I can swear to it. This is a reef knot, and I always make a running bowline."

"You must be mistaken, Pencroft."

"I am not mistaken!" declared the sailor. "My hand does it so naturally, and one's hand is never mistaken!"

"Then can the convicts have been on board?" asked Herbert.

"I know nothing about that," answered Pencroft, "but what is certain, is that some one has weighed the 'Bonadventure's' anchor and dropped it again! And look here, here is another proof! The cable of the anchor has been run out, and its service is no longer at the hawse-hole. I repeat that some one has been using our vessel!"

"But if the convicts had used her, they would have pillaged her, or rather gone off with her."

"Gone off! where to—to Tabor Island?" replied Pencroft. "Do you think, they would risk themselves in a boat of such small tonnage?"

"We must, besides, be sure that they know of the islet," rejoined the reporter.

"However that may be," said the sailor, "as sure as my name is Bonadventure Pencroft, of the Vineyard, our 'Bonadventure' has sailed without us!"

The sailor was positive that neither Gideon Spilett nor Herbert could dispute his statement. It was evident that the vessel had been moved, more or less, since Pencroft had brought her to Port Balloon. As to the sailor, he had not the slightest doubt that the anchor had been raised and then dropped again. Now, what was the use of these two maneuvers, unless the vessel had been employed in some expedition?

"But how was it we did not see the 'Bonadventure' pass in the sight of the island?" observed the reporter, who was anxious to bring forward every possible objection.

"Why, Mr. Spilett," replied the sailor, "they would only have to start in the night with a good breeze, and they would be out of sight of the island in two hours."

"Well," resumed Gideon Spilett, "I ask again, what object could the convicts have had in using the 'Bonadventure,' and why, after they had made use of her, should they have brought her back to port?"

"Why, Mr. Spilett," replied the sailor, "we must put that among the unaccountable things, and not think anything more about it. The chief thing is that the 'Bonadventure' was there, and she is there now. Only, unfortunately, if the convicts take her a second time, we shall very likely not find her again in her place!"

"Then, Pencroft," said Herbert, "would it not be wisest to bring the 'Bonadventure' off to Granite House?"

"Yes and no," answered Pencroft, "or rather no. The mouth of the Mercy is a bad place for a vessel, and the sea is heavy there."

"But by hauling her up on the sand, to the foot of the Chimneys?"

"Perhaps yes," replied Pencroft. "At any rate, since we must leave Granite House for a long expedition, I think the 'Bonadventure' will be safer here during our absence, and we shall do best to leave her here until the island is rid of these blackguards."

"That is exactly my opinion," said the reporter. "At any rate in the event of bad weather, she will not be exposed here as she would be at the mouth of the Mercy."

"But suppose the convicts pay her another visit," said Herbert.

"Well, my boy," replied Pencroft, "not finding her here, they would not be long in finding her on the sands of Granite House, and, during our absence, nothing could hinder them from seizing her! I agree, therefore, with Mr. Spilett, that she must be left in Port Balloon. But, if on our return we have not rid the island of those rascals, it will be prudent to bring our boat to Granite House, until the time when we need not fear any unpleasant visits."

"That's settled. Let us be off," said the reporter.

Pencroft, Herbert, and Gideon Spilett, on their return to Granite House, told the engineer all that had passed, and the latter approved of their arrangements both for the present and the future. He also promised the sailor that he would study that part of the channel situated between the islet and the coast, so as to ascertain if it would not be possible to make an artificial harbor there by means of dams. In this way, the "Bonadventure" would be always within reach, under the eyes of the colonists, and if necessary, under lock and key.

That evening a telegram was sent to Ayrton, requesting him to bring from the corral a couple of goats, which Neb wished to acclimatize to the plateau. Singularly enough, Ayrton did not acknowledge the receipt of the despatch, as he was accustomed to do. This could not but astonish the engineer. But it might be that Ayrton was not at that moment in the corral, or even that he was on his way back to Granite House. In fact, two days had already passed since his departure, and it had been decided that on the evening of the 10th or at the latest the morning of the 11th, he should return. The colonists waited, therefore, for Ayrton to appear on Prospect Heights. Neb and Herbert even watched at the bridge so as to be ready to lower it the moment their companion presented himself.

But up to ten in the evening, there were no signs of Ayrton. It was, therefore, judged best to send a fresh despatch, requiring an immediate reply.

The bell of the telegraph at Granite House remained mute.

The colonists' uneasiness was great. What had happened? Was Ayrton no longer at the corral, or if he was still there, had he no longer control over his movements? Could they go to the corral in this dark night?

They consulted. Some wished to go, the others to remain.

"But," said Herbert, "perhaps some accident has happened to the telegraphic apparatus, so that it works no longer?"

"That may be," said the reporter.

"Wait till to-morrow," replied Cyrus Harding. "It is possible, indeed, that Ayrton has not received our despatch, or even that we have not received his."

They waited, of course not without some anxiety.

At dawn of day, the 11th of November, Harding again sent the electric current along the wire and received no reply.

He tried again: the same result.

"Off to the corral," said he.

"And well armed!" added Pencroft.

It was immediately decided that Granite House should not be left alone and that Neb should remain there. After having accompanied his friends to Creek Glycerine, he raised the bridge; and waiting behind a tree he watched for the return of either his companions or Ayrton.

In the event of the pirates presenting themselves and attempting to force the passage, he was to endeavor to stop them by firing on them, and as a last resource he was to take refuge in Granite House, where, the lift once raised, he would be in safety.

Cyrus Harding, Gideon Spilett, Herbert, and Pencroft were to repair to the corral, and if they did not find Ayrton, search the neighboring woods.

At six o'clock in the morning, the engineer and his three companions had passed Creek Glycerine, and Neb posted himself behind a small mound crowned by several dragon trees, on the left bank of the stream.

The colonists, after leaving the plateau of Prospect Heights, immediately took the road to the corral. They shouldered their guns, ready to fire on the slightest hostile demonstration. The two rifles and the two guns had been loaded with ball.

The wood was thick on each side of the road and might easily have concealed the convicts, who owing to their weapons would have been really formidable.

The colonists walked rapidly and in silence. Top preceded them, sometimes running on the road, sometimes taking a ramble into the wood, but always quiet and not appearing to fear anything unusual. And they could be sure that the faithful dog would not allow them to be surprised, but would bark at the least appearance of danger.

Cyrus Harding and his companions followed beside the road the wire which connected the corral with Granite House. After walking for nearly two miles, they had not as yet discovered any explanation of the difficulty. The posts were in good order, the wire regularly extended. However, at that moment the engineer observed that the wire appeared to be slack, and on arriving at post No. 74, Herbert, who was in advance stopped, exclaiming,—

"The wire is broken!"

His companions hurried forward and arrived at the spot where the lad was standing. The post was rooted up and lying across the path. The unexpected explanation of the difficulty was here, and it was evident that the despatches from Granite House had not been received at the corral, nor those from the corral at Granite House.

"It wasn't the wind that blew down this post," observed Pencroft.

"No," replied Gideon Spilett. "The earth has been dug up round its foot, and it has been torn up by the hand of man."

"Besides, the wire is broken," added Herbert, showing that the wire had been snapped.

"Is the fracture recent?" asked Harding.

"Yes," answered Herbert, "it has certainly been done quite lately."

"To the corral! to the corral!" exclaimed the sailor.

The colonists were now half way between Granite House and the corral, having still two miles and a half to go. They pressed forward with redoubled speed.

Indeed, it was to be feared that some serious accident had occurred in the corral. No doubt, Ayrton might have sent a telegram which had not arrived, but this was not the reason why his companions were so uneasy, for, a more unaccountable circumstance, Ayrton, who had promised to return the evening before, had not reappeared. In short, it was not without a motive that all communication had been stopped between the corral and Granite House, and who but the convicts could have any interest in interrupting this communication?

The settlers hastened on, their hearts oppressed with anxiety. They were sincerely attached to their new companion. Were they to find him struck down by the hands of those of whom he was formerly the leader?

Soon they arrived at the place where the road led along the side of the little stream which flowed from the Red Creek and watered the meadows of the corral. They then moderated their pace so that they should not be out of breath at the moment when a struggle might be necessary. Their guns were in their hands ready cocked. The forest was watched on every side. Top uttered sullen groans which were rather ominous.

At last the palisade appeared through the trees. No trace of any damage could be seen. The gate was shut as usual. Deep silence reigned in the corral. Neither the accustomed bleating of the sheep nor Ayrton's voice could be heard.

"Let us enter," said Cyrus Harding.

And the engineer advanced, while his companions, keeping watch about twenty paces behind him, were ready to fire at a moment's notice.

Harding raised the inner latch of the gate and was about to push it back, when Top barked loudly. A report sounded and was responded to by a cry of pain.

Herbert, struck by a bullet, lay stretched on the ground.

Chapter 7

At Herbert's cry, Pencroft, letting his gun fall, rushed towards him.

"They have killed him!" he cried. "My boy! They have killed him!"

Cyrus Harding and Gideon Spilett ran to Herbert.

The reporter listened to ascertain if the poor lad's heart was still beating.

"He lives," said he, "but he must be carried—"

"To Granite House? that is impossible!" replied the engineer.

"Into the corral, then!" said Pencroft.

"In a moment," said Harding.

And he ran round the left corner of the palisade. There he found a convict, who aiming at him, sent a ball through his hat. In a few seconds, before he had even time to fire his second barrel, he fell, struck to the heart by Harding's dagger, more sure even than his gun.

During this time, Gideon Spilett and the sailor hoisted themselves over the palisade, leaped into the enclosure, threw down the props which supported the inner door, ran into the empty house, and soon, poor Herbert was lying on Ayrton's bed. In a few moments, Harding was by his side.

On seeing Herbert senseless, the sailor's grief was terrible.

He sobbed, he cried, he tried to beat his head against the wall.

Neither the engineer nor the reporter could calm him. They themselves were choked with emotion. They could not speak.

However, they knew that it depended on them to rescue from death the poor boy who was suffering beneath their eyes. Gideon Spilett had not passed through the many incidents by which his life had been checkered without acquiring some slight knowledge of medicine. He knew a little of everything, and several times he had been obliged to attend to wounds produced either by a sword-bayonet or shot. Assisted by Cyrus Harding, he proceeded to render the aid Herbert required.

The reporter was immediately struck by the complete stupor in which Herbert lay, a stupor owing either to the hemorrhage, or to the shock, the ball having struck a bone with sufficient force to produce a violent concussion.

Herbert was deadly pale, and his pulse so feeble that Spilett only felt it beat at long intervals, as if it was on the point of stopping.

These symptoms were very serious.

Herbert's chest was laid bare, and the blood having been stanched with handkerchiefs, it was bathed with cold water.

The contusion, or rather the contused wound appeared,—an oval below the chest between the third and fourth ribs. It was there that Herbert had been hit by the bullet.

Cyrus Harding and Gideon Spilett then turned the poor boy over; as they did so, he uttered a moan so feeble that they almost thought it was his last sigh.

Herberts back was covered with blood from another contused wound, by which the ball had immediately escaped.

"God be praised!" said the reporter, "the ball is not in the body, and we shall not have to extract it."

"But the heart?" asked Harding.

"The heart has not been touched; if it had been, Herbert would be dead!"

"Dead!" exclaimed Pencroft, with a groan.

The sailor had only heard the last words uttered by the reporter.

"No, Pencroft," replied Cyrus Harding, "no! He is not dead. His pulse still beats. He has even uttered a moan. But for your boy's sake, calm yourself. We have need of all our self-possession."

"Do not make us lose it, my friend."

Pencroft was silent, but a reaction set in, and great tears rolled down his cheeks.

In the meanwhile, Gideon Spilett endeavored to collect his ideas, and proceed methodically. After his examination he had no doubt that the ball, entering in front, between the seventh and eighth ribs, had issued behind between the third and fourth. But what mischief had the ball committed in its passage? What important organs had been reached? A professional surgeon would have had difficulty in determining this at once, and still more so the reporter.

However, he knew one thing, this was that he would have to prevent the inflammatory strangulation of the injured parts, then to contend with the local inflammation and fever which would result from the wound, perhaps mortal! Now, what styptics, what antiphiogistics ought to be employed? By what means could inflammation be prevented?

At any rate, the most important thing was that the two wounds should be dressed without delay. It did not appear necessary to Gideon Spilett that a fresh flow of blood should be caused by bathing them in tepid water, and compressing their lips. The hemorrhage had been very abundant, and Herbert was already too much enfeebled by the loss of blood.

The reporter, therefore, thought it best to simply bathe the two wounds with cold water.

Herbert was placed on his left side, and was maintained in that position.

"He must not be moved." said Gideon Spilett. "He is in the most favorable position for the wounds in his back and chest to suppurate easily, and absolute rest is necessary."

"What! can't we carry him to Granite House?" asked Pencroft.

"No, Pencroft," replied the reporter.

"I'll pay the villains off!" cried the sailor, shaking his fist in a menacing manner.

"Pencroft!" said Cyrus Harding.

Gideon Spilett had resumed his examination of the wounded boy. Herbert was still so frightfully pale, that the reporter felt anxious.

"Cyrus," said he, "I am not a surgeon. I am in terrible perplexity. You must aid me with your advice, your experience!"

"Take courage, my friend," answered the engineer, pressing the reporter's hand. "Judge coolly. Think only of this: Herbert must be saved!"

These words restored to Gideon Spilett that self-possession which he had lost in a moment of discouragement on feeling his great responsibility. He seated himself close to the bed. Cyrus Harding stood near. Pencroft had torn up his shirt, and was mechanically making lint.

Spilett then explained to Cyrus Harding that he thought he ought first of all to stop the hemorrhage, but not close the two wounds, or cause their immediate cicatrization, for there had been internal perforation, and the suppuration must not be allowed to accumulate in the chest.

Harding approved entirely, and it was decided that the two wounds should be dressed without attempting to close them by immediate coaptation.

And now did the colonists possess an efficacious agent to act against the inflammation which might occur?

Yes. They had one, for nature had generously lavished it. They had cold water, that is to say, the most powerful sedative that can be employed against inflammation of wounds, the most efficacious therapeutic agent in grave cases, and the one which is now adopted by all physicians. Cold water has, moreover, the advantage of leaving the wound in absolute rest, and preserving it from all premature dressing, a considerable advantage, since it has been found by experience that contact with the air is dangerous during the first days.

Gideon Spilett and Cyrus Harding reasoned thus with their simple good sense, and they acted as the best surgeon would have done. Compresses of linen were applied to poor Herbert's two wounds, and were kept constantly wet with cold water.

The sailor had at first lighted a fire in the hut, which was not wanting in things necessary for life. Maple sugar, medicinal plants, the same which the lad had gathered on the banks of Lake Grant, enabled them to make some refreshing drinks, which they gave him without his taking any notice of it. His fever was extremely high, and all that day and night passed without his becoming conscious.

Herbert's life hung on a thread, and this thread might break at any moment. The next day, the 12th of November, the hopes of Harding and his companions slightly revived. Herbert had come out of his long stupor. He opened his eyes, he recognized Cyrus Harding, the reporter, and Pencroft. He uttered two or three words. He did not know what had happened. They told him, and Spilett begged him to remain perfectly still, telling him that his life was not in danger, and that his wounds would heal in a few days. However, Herbert scarcely suffered at all, and the cold water with which they were constantly bathed, prevented any inflammation of the wounds. The suppuration was established in a regular way, the fever did not increase, and it might now be hoped that this terrible wound would not involve any catastrophe. Pencroft felt the swelling of his heart gradually subside. He was like a sister of mercy, like a mother by the bed of her child.

Herbert dozed again, but his sleep appeared more natural.

"Tell me again that you hope, Mr. Spilett," said Pencroft. "Tell me again that you will save Herbert!"

"Yes, we will save him!" replied the reporter. "The wound is serious, and, perhaps, even the ball has traversed the lungs, but the perforation of this organ is not fatal."

"God bless you!" answered Pencroft.

As may be believed, during the four-and-twenty hours they had been in the corral, the colonists had no other thought than that of nursing Herbert. They did not think either of the danger which threatened them should the convicts return, or of the precautions to be taken for the future.

But on this day, while Pencroft watched by the sick-bed, Cyrus Harding and the reporter consulted as to what it would be best to do.

First of all they examined the corral. There was not a trace of Ayrton. Had the unhappy man been dragged away by his former accomplices? Had he resisted, and been overcome in the struggle? This last supposition was only too probable. Gideon Spilett, at the moment he scaled the palisade, had clearly seen some one of the convicts running along the southern spur of Mount Franklin, towards whom Top had sprung. It was one of those whose object had been so completely defeated by the rocks at the mouth of the Mercy. Besides, the one killed by Harding, and whose body was found outside the enclosure, of course belonged to Bob Harvey's crew.

As to the corral, it had not suffered any damage. The gates were closed, and the animals had not been able to disperse in the forest. Nor could they see traces of any struggle, any devastation, either in the hut, or in the palisade. The ammunition only, with which Ayrton had been supplied, had disappeared with him.

"The unhappy man has been surprised," said Harding, "and as he was a man to defend himself, he must have been overpowered."

"Yes, that is to be feared!" said the reporter. "Then, doubtless, the convicts installed themselves in the corral where they found plenty of everything, and only fled when they saw us coming. It is very evident, too, that at this moment Ayrton, whether living or dead, is not here!"

"We shall have to beat the forest," said the engineer, "and rid the island of these wretches. Pencroft's presentiments were not mistaken, when he wished to hunt them as wild beasts. That would have spared us all these misfortunes!"

"Yes," answered the reporter, "but now we have the right to be merciless!"

"At any rate," said the engineer, "we are obliged to wait some time, and to remain at the corral until we can carry Herbert without danger to Granite House."

"But Neb?" asked the reporter.

"Neb is in safety."

"But if, uneasy at our absence, he would venture to come?"

"He must not come!" returned Cyrus Harding quickly. "He would be murdered on the road!"

"It is very probable, however, that he will attempt to rejoin us!"

"Ah, if the telegraph still acted, he might be warned! But that is impossible now! As to leaving Pencroft and Herbert here alone, we could not do it! Well, I will go alone to Granite House."

"No, no! Cyrus," answered the reporter, "you must not expose yourself! Your courage would be of no avail. The villains are evidently watching the corral, they are hidden in the thick woods which surround it, and if you go we shall soon have to regret two misfortunes instead of one!"

"But Neb?" repeated the engineer. "It is now four-and-twenty hours since he has had any news of us! He will be sure to come!"

"And as he will be less on his guard than we should be ourselves," added Spilett, "he will be killed!"

"Is there really no way of warning him?"

While the engineer thought, his eyes fell on Top, who, going backwards and forwards seemed to say,—

"Am not I here?"

"Top!" exclaimed Cyrus Harding.

The animal sprang at his master's call.

"Yes, Top will go," said the reporter, who had understood the engineer.

"Top can go where we cannot! He will carry to Granite House the news of the corral, and he will bring back to us that from Granite House!"

"Quick!" said Harding. "Quick!"

Spilett rapidly tore a leaf from his note-book, and wrote these words:—

"Herbert wounded. We are at the corral. Be on your guard. Do not leave Granite House. Have the convicts appeared in the neighborhood? Reply by Top."

This laconic note contained all that Neb ought to know, and at the same time asked all that the colonists wished to know. It was folded and fastened to Top's collar in a conspicuous position.

"Top, my dog," said the engineer, caressing the animal, "Neb, Top! Neb! Go, go!"

Top bounded at these words. He understood, he knew what was expected of him. The road to the corral was familiar to him. In less than an hour he could clear it, and it might be hoped that where neither Cyrus Harding nor the reporter could have ventured without danger, Top, running among the grass or in the wood, would pass unperceived.

The engineer went to the gate of the corral and opened it.

"Neb, Top! Neb!" repeated the engineer, again pointing in the direction of Granite House.

Top sprang forwards, then almost immediately disappeared.

"He will get there!" said the reporter.

"Yes, and he will come back, the faithful animal!"

"What o'clock is it?" asked Gideon Spilett.

"Ten."

"In an hour he may be here. We will watch for his return."

The gate of the corral was closed. The engineer and the reporter re-entered the house. Herbert was still in a sleep. Pencroft kept the compresser always wet. Spilett, seeing there was nothing he could do at that moment, busied himself in preparing some nourishment, while attentively watching that part of the enclosure against the hill, at which an attack might be expected.

The settlers awaited Top's return with much anxiety. A little before eleven o'clock, Cyrus Harding and the reporter, rifle in hand, were behind the gate, ready to open it at the first bark of their dog.

They did not doubt that if Top had arrived safely at Granite House, Neb would have sent him back immediately.

They had both been there for about ten minutes, when a report was heard, followed by repeated barks.

The engineer opened the gate, and seeing smoke a hundred feet off in the wood, he fired in that direction.

Almost immediately Top bounded into the corral, and the gate was quickly shut.

"Top, Top!" exclaimed the engineer, taking the dog's great honest head between his hands.

A note was fastened to his neck, and Cyrus Harding read these words, traced in Neb's large writing:—"No pirates in the neighborhood of Granite House. I will not stir. Poor Mr. Herbert!"

Chapter 8

So the convicts were still there, watching the corral, and determined to kill the settlers one after the other. There was nothing to be done but to treat them as wild beasts. But great precautions must be taken, for just now the wretches had the advantage on their side, seeing, and not being seen, being able to surprise by the suddenness of their attack, yet not to be surprised themselves. Harding made arrangements, therefore, for living in the corral, of which the provisions would last for a tolerable length of time. Ayrton's house had been provided with all that was necessary for existence, and the convicts, scared by the arrival of the settlers, had not had time to pillage it. It was probable, as Gideon Spilett observed, that things had occurred as follows:

The six convicts, disembarking on the island, had followed the southern shore, and after having traversed the double shore of the Serpentine Peninsula, not being inclined to venture into the Far West woods, they had reached the mouth of Falls River. From this point, by following the right bank of the watercourse, they would arrive at the spurs of Mount Franklin, among which they would naturally seek a retreat, and they could not have been long in discovering the corral, then uninhabited. There they had regularly installed themselves, awaiting the moment to put their abominable schemes into execution. Ayrton's arrival had surprised them, but they had managed to overpower the unfortunate man, and—the rest may be easily imagined!

Now, the convicts,—reduced to five, it is true, but well armed,—were roaming the woods, and to venture there was to expose themselves to their attacks, which could be neither guarded against nor prevented.

"Wait! There is nothing else to be done!" repeated Cyrus Harding. "When Herbert is cured, we can organize a general battle of the island, and have satisfaction of these convicts. That will be the object of our grand expedition at the same time—"

"As the search for our mysterious protector," added Gideon Spilett, finishing the engineer's sentence. "And it must be acknowledged, my dear Cyrus, that this time his protection was wanting at the very moment when it was most necessary to us!"

"Who knows?" replied the engineer.

"What do you mean?" asked the reporter.

"That we are not at the end of our trouble yet, my dear Spilett, and that his powerful intervention may have another opportunity of exercising itself. But that is not the question now. Herbert's life before everything."

This was the colonists' saddest thought. Several days passed, and the poor boy's state was happily no worse. Cold water, always kept at a suitable temperature, had completely prevented the inflammation of the wounds. It even seemed to the reporter that this water, being slightly sulphurous,—which was explained by the neighborhood of the volcano, had a more direct action on the healing. The suppuration was much less abundant, and thanks to the incessant care by which he was surrounded!—Herbert returned to life, and his fever abated. He was besides subjected to a severe diet, and consequently his weakness was and would be extreme; but there was no want of refreshing drinks, and absolute rest was of the greatest benefit to him. Cyrus Harding, Gideon Spilett, and Pencroft had become very skilful in dressing the lad's wounds. All the linen in the house had been sacrificed. Herbert's wounds, covered with compresses and lint, were pressed neither too much nor too little, so as to cause their cicatrization without effecting any inflammatory reaction. The reporter used extreme care in the dressing, knowing well the importance of it, and repeating to his companions that which most surgeons willingly admit, that it is perhaps rarer to see a dressing well done than an operation well performed.

In ten days, on the 22nd of November, Herbert was considerably better. He had begun to take some nourishment.

The color was returning to his cheeks, and his bright eyes smiled at his nurses. He talked a little, notwithstanding Pencroft's efforts, who talked incessantly to prevent him from beginning to speak, and told him the most improbable stories. Herbert had questioned him on the subject of Ayrton, whom he was astonished not to see near him, thinking that he was at the corral. But the sailor, not wishing to distress Herbert, contented himself by replying that Ayrton had rejoined Neb, so as to defend Granite House.

"Humph!" said Pencroft, "these pirates! they are gentlemen who have no right to any consideration! And the captain wanted to win them by kindness! I'll send them some kindness, but in the shape of a good bullet!"

"And have they not been seen again?" asked Herbert.

"No, my boy," answered the sailor, "but we shall find them, and when you are cured we shall see if the cowards who strike us from behind will dare to meet us face to face!"

"I am still very weak, my poor Pencroft!"

"Well! your strength will return gradually! What's a ball through the chest? Nothing but a joke! I've seen many, and I don't think much of them!"

At last things appeared to be going on well, and if no complication occurred, Herbert's recovery might be regarded as certain. But what would have been the condition of the colonists if his state had been aggravated,—if, for example, the ball had remained in his body, if his arm or his leg had had to be amputated?

"No," said Spilett more than once, "I have never thought of such a contingency without shuddering!"

"And yet, if it had been necessary to operate," said Harding one day to him, "you would not have hesitated?"

Jules Verne

"No, Cyrus!" said Gideon Spilett, "but thank God that we have been spared this complication!"

As in so many other conjectures, the colonists had appealed to the logic of that simple good sense of which they had made use so often, and once more, thanks to their general knowledge, it had succeeded! But might not a time come when all their science would be at fault? They were alone on the island. Now, men in all states of society are necessary to each other. Cyrus Harding knew this well, and sometimes he asked if some circumstance might not occur which they would be powerless to surmount. It appeared to him besides, that he and his companions, till then so fortunate, had entered into an unlucky period. During the two years and a half which had elapsed since their escape from Richmond, it might be said that they had had everything their own way. The island had abundantly supplied them with minerals, vegetables, animals, and as Nature had constantly loaded them, their science had known how to take advantage of what she offered them.

The wellbeing of the colony was therefore complete. Moreover, in certain occurrences an inexplicable influence had come to their aid!... But all that could only be for a time.

In short, Cyrus Harding believed that fortune had turned against them.

In fact, the convicts' ship had appeared in the waters of the island, and if the pirates had been, so to speak, miraculously destroyed, six of them, at least, had escaped the catastrophe. They had disembarked on the island, and it was almost impossible to get at the five who survived. Ayrton had no doubt been murdered by these wretches, who possessed firearms, and at the first use that they had made of them, Herbert had fallen, wounded almost mortally. Were these the first blows aimed by adverse fortune at the colonists? This was often asked by Harding. This was often repeated by the reporter; and it appeared to him also that the intervention, so strange, yet so efficacious, which till then had served them so well, had now failed them. Had this mysterious being, whatever he was, whose existence could not be denied, abandoned the island? Had he in his turn succumbed?

No reply was possible to these questions. But it must not be imagined that because Harding and his companions spoke of these things, they were men to despair. Far from that. They looked their situation in the face, they analyzed the chances, they prepared themselves for any event, they stood firm and straight before the future, and if adversity was at last to strike them, it would find in them men prepared to struggle against it.

Chapter 9

The convalescence of the young invalid was regularly progressing. One thing only was now to be desired, that his state would allow him to be brought to

Granite House. However well built and supplied the corral house was, it could not be so comfortable as the healthy granite dwelling. Besides, it did not offer the same security, and its tenants, notwithstanding their watchfulness, were here always in fear of some shot from the convicts. There, on the contrary, in the middle of that impregnable and inaccessible cliff, they would have nothing to fear, and any attack on their persons would certainly fail. They therefore waited impatiently for the moment when Herbert might be moved without danger from his wound, and they were determined to make this move, although the communication through Jacamar Wood was very difficult.

They had no news from Neb, but were not uneasy on that account. The courageous Negro, well entrenched in the depths of Granite House, would not allow himself to be surprised. Top had not been sent again to him, as it appeared useless to expose the faithful dog to some shot which might deprive the settlers of their most useful auxiliary.

They waited, therefore, although they were anxious to be reunited at Granite House. It pained the engineer to see his forces divided, for it gave great advantage to the pirates. Since Ayrton's disappearance they were only four against five, for Herbert could not yet be counted, and this was not the least care of the brave boy, who well understood the trouble of which he was the cause.

The question of knowing how, in their condition, they were to act against the pirates, was thoroughly discussed on the 29th of November by Cyrus Harding, Gideon Spilett, and Pencroft, at a moment when Herbert was asleep and could not hear them.

"My friends," said the reporter, after they had talked of Neb and of the impossibility of communicating with him, "I think,—like you, that to venture on the road to the corral would be to risk receiving a gunshot without being able to return it. But do you not think that the best thing to be done now is to openly give chase to these wretches?"

"That is just what I was thinking," answered Pencroft. "I believe we're not fellows to be afraid of a bullet, and as for me, if Captain Harding approves, I'm ready to dash into the forest! Why, hang it, one man is equal to another!"

"But is he equal to five?" asked the engineer.

"I will join Pencroft," said the reporter, "and both of us, well-armed and accompanied by Top—"

"My dear Spilett, and you, Pencroft," answered Harding, "let us reason coolly. If the convicts were hid in one spot of the island, if we knew that spot, and had only to dislodge them, I would undertake a direct attack; but is there not occasion to fear, on the contrary, that they are sure to fire the first shot?"

"Well, captain," cried Pencroft, "a bullet does not always reach its mark."

"That which struck Herbert did not miss, Pencroft," replied the engineer. "Besides, observe that if both of you left the corral I should remain here alone to defend it. Do you imagine that the convicts will not see you leave it, that they will not allow you to enter the forest, and that they will not attack it during your absence, knowing that there is no one here but a wounded boy and a man?"

"You are right, captain," replied Pencroft, his chest swelling with sullen anger. "You are right; they will do all they can to retake the corral, which they know to be well stored; and alone you could not hold it against them."

"Oh, if we were only at Granite House!"

"If we were at Granite House," answered the engineer, "the case would be very different. There I should not be afraid to leave Herbert with one, while the other three went to search the forests of the island. But we are at the corral, and it is best to stay here until we can leave it together."

Cyrus Harding's reasoning was unanswerable, and his companions understood it well.

"If only Ayrton was still one of us!" said Gideon Spilett. "Poor fellow! his return to social life will have been but of short duration."

"If he is dead," added Pencroft, in a peculiar tone.

"Do you hope, then, Pencroft, that the villains have spared him?" asked Gideon Spilett.

"Yes, if they had any interest in doing so."

"What! you suppose that Ayrton finding his old companions, forgetting all that he owes us—"

"Who knows?" answered the sailor, who did not hazard this shameful supposition without hesitating.

"Pencroft," said Harding, taking the sailor's arm, "that is a wicked idea of yours, and you will distress me much if you persist in speaking thus. I will answer for Ayrton's fidelity."

"And I also," added the reporter quickly.

"Yes, yes, captain, I was wrong," replied Pencroft; "it was a wicked idea indeed that I had, and nothing justifies it. But what can I do? I'm not in my senses. This imprisonment in the corral wearies me horribly, and I have never felt so excited as I do now."

"Be patient, Pencroft," replied the engineer. "How long will it be, my dear Spilett, before you think Herbert may be carried to Granite House?"

"That is difficult to say, Cyrus," answered the reporter, "for any imprudence might involve terrible consequences. But his convalescence is progressing, and if he continues to gain strength, in eight days from now—well, we shall see."

Eight days! That would put off the return to Granite House until the first days of December. At this time two months of spring had already passed. The weather was fine, and the heat began to be great. The forests of the island were in full leaf, and the time was approaching when the usual crops ought to be gathered. The return to the plateau of Prospect Heights would, therefore, be followed by extensive agricultural labors, interrupted only by the projected expedition through the island.

It can, therefore, be well understood how injurious this seclusion in the corral must have been to the colonists.

But if they were compelled to bow before necessity, they did not do so without impatience.

Once or twice the reporter ventured out into the road and made the tour of the palisade. Top accompanied him, and Gideon Spilett, his gun cocked, was ready for any emergency.

He met with no misadventure and found no suspicious traces. His dog would have warned him of any danger, and, as Top did not bark, it might be concluded that there was nothing to fear at the moment at least, and that the convicts were occupied in another part of the island.

However, on his second sortie, on the 27th of November, Gideon Spilett, who had ventured a quarter of a mile into the woods, towards the south of the mountain, remarked that Top scented something. The dog had no longer his unconcerned manner; he went backwards and forwards, ferreting among the grass and bushes as if his smell had revealed some suspicious object to him.

Gideon Spilett followed Top, encouraged him, excited him by his voice, while keeping a sharp look-out, his gun ready to fire, and sheltering himself behind the trees. It was not probable that Top scented the presence of man, for in that case, he would have announced it by half-uttered, sullen, angry barks. Now, as he did not growl, it was because danger was neither near nor approaching.

Nearly five minutes passed thus, Top rummaging, the reporter following him prudently when, all at once, the dog rushed towards a thick bush, and drew out a rag.

It was a piece of cloth, stained and torn, which Spilett immediately brought back to the corral. There it was examined by the colonists, who found that it was a fragment of Ayrton's waistcoat, a piece of that felt, manufactured solely by the Granite House factory.

"You see, Pencroft," observed Harding, "there has been resistance on the part of the unfortunate Ayrton. The convicts have dragged him away in spite of himself! Do you still doubt his honesty?"

"No, captain," answered the sailor, "and I repented of my suspicion a long time ago! But it seems to me that something may be learned from the incident."

"What is that?" asked the reporter.

"It is that Ayrton was not killed at the corral! That they dragged him away living, since he has resisted. Therefore, perhaps, he is still living!"

"Perhaps, indeed," replied the engineer, who remained thoughtful.

This was a hope, to which Ayrton's companions could still hold. Indeed, they had before believed that, surprised in the corral, Ayrton had fallen by a bullet, as

Herbert had fallen. But if the convicts had not killed him at first, if they had brought him living to another part of the island, might it not be admitted that he was still their prisoner? Perhaps, even, one of them had found in Ayrton his old Australian companion Ben Joyce, the chief of the escaped convicts. And who knows but that they had conceived the impossible hope of bringing back Ayrton to themselves? He would have been very useful to them, if they had been able to make him turn traitor!

This incident was, therefore, favorably interpreted at the corral, and it no longer appeared impossible that they should find Ayrton again. On his side, if he was only a prisoner, Ayrton would no doubt do all he could to escape from the hands of the villains, and this would be a powerful aid to the settlers!

"At any rate," observed Gideon Spilett, "if happily Ayrton did manage to escape, he would go directly to Granite House, for he could not know of the attempted assassination of which Herbert has been a victim, and consequently would never think of our being imprisoned in the corral."

"Oh! I wish that he was there, at Granite House!" cried Pencroft, "and that we were there, too! For, although the rascals can do nothing to our house, they may plunder the plateau, our plantations, our poultry-yard!"

Pencroft had become a thorough farmer, heartily attached to his crops. But it must be said that Herbert was more anxious than any to return to Granite House, for he knew how much the presence of the settlers was needed there. And it was he who was keeping them at the corral! Therefore, one idea occupied his mind—to leave the corral, and when! He believed he could bear removal to Granite House. He was sure his strength would return more quickly in his room, with the air and sight of the sea!

Several times he pressed Gideon Spilett, but the latter, fearing, with good reason, that Herbert's wounds, half healed, might reopen on the way, did not give the order to start.

However, something occurred which compelled Cyrus Harding and his two friends to yield to the lad's wish, and God alone knew that this determination might cause them grief and remorse.

It was the 29th of November, seven o'clock in the evening. The three settlers were talking in Herbert's room, when they heard Top utter quick barks.

Harding, Pencroft, and Spilett seized their guns and ran out of the house. Top, at the foot of the palisade, was jumping, barking, but it was with pleasure, not anger.

"Some one is coming."

"Yes."

"It is not an enemy!"

"Neb, perhaps?"

"Or Ayrton?"

These words had hardly been exchanged between the engineer and his two companions when a body leaped over the palisade and fell on the ground inside the corral.

It was Jup, Master Jup in person, to whom Top immediately gave a most cordial reception.

"Jup!" exclaimed Pencroft.

"Neb has sent him to us," said the reporter.

"Then," replied the engineer, "he must have some note on him."

Pencroft rushed up to the orang. Certainly if Neb had any important matter to communicate to his master he could not employ a more sure or more rapid messenger, who could pass where neither the colonists could, nor even Top himself.

Cyrus Harding was not mistaken. At Jup's neck hung a small bag, and in this bag was found a little note traced by Neb's hand.

The despair of Harding and his companions may be imagined when they read these words:—

"Friday, six o'clock in the morning.

"Plateau invaded by convicts.

"Neb."

They gazed at each other without uttering a word, then they re-entered the house. What were they to do? The convicts on Prospect Heights! that was disaster, devastation, ruin.

Herbert, on seeing the engineer, the reporter, and Pencroft re-enter, guessed that their situation was aggravated, and when he saw Jup, he no longer doubted that some misfortune menaced Granite House.

"Captain Harding," said he, "I must go; I can bear the journey. I must go."

Gideon Spilett approached Herbert; then, having looked at him,—

"Let us go, then!" said he.

The question was quickly decided whether Herbert should be carried on a litter or in the cart which had brought Ayrton to the corral. The motion of the litter would have been more easy for the wounded lad, but it would have necessitated two bearers, that is to say, there would have been two guns less for defense if an attack was made on the road. Would they not, on the contrary, by employing the cart leave every arm free? Was it impossible to place the mattress on which Herbert was lying in it, and to advance with so much care that any jolt should be avoided? It could be done.

The cart was brought. Pencroft harnessed the onager. Cyrus Harding and the reporter raised Herbert's mattress and placed it on the bottom of the cart. The weather was fine. The sun's bright rays glanced through the trees.

"Are the guns ready?" asked Cyrus Harding.

They were. The engineer and Pencroft, each armed with a double-barreled gun, and Gideon Spilett carrying his rifle, had nothing to do but start.

"Are you comfortable, Herbert?" asked the engineer.

"Ah, captain," replied the lad, "don't be uneasy, I shall not die on the road!"

While speaking thus, it could be seen that the poor boy had called up all his energy, and by the energy of a powerful will had collected his failing strength.

The engineer felt his heart sink painfully. He still hesitated to give the signal for departure; but that would have driven Herbert to despair—killed him perhaps.

"Forward!" said Harding.

The gate of the corral was opened. Jup and Top, who knew when to be silent, ran in advance. The cart came out, the gate was reclosed, and the onager, led by Pencroft, advanced at a slow pace.

Certainly, it would have been safer to have taken a different road than that which led straight from the corral to Granite House, but the cart would have met with great difficulties in moving under the trees. It was necessary, therefore, to follow this way, although it was well known to the convicts.

Cyrus Harding and Gideon Spilett walked one on each side of the cart, ready to answer to any attack. However, it was not probable that the convicts would have yet left the plateau of Prospect Heights.

Neb's note had evidently been written and sent as soon as the convicts had shown themselves there. Now, this note was dated six o'clock in the morning, and the active orang, accustomed to come frequently to the corral, had taken scarcely three quarters of an hour to cross the five miles which separated it from Granite House. They would, therefore, be safe at that time, and if there was any occasion for firing, it would probably not be until they were in the neighborhood of Granite House. However, the colonists kept a strict watch. Top and Jup, the latter armed with his club, sometimes in front, sometimes beating the wood at the sides of the road, signalized no danger.

The cart advanced slowly under Pencroft's guidance. It had left the corral at half-past seven. An hour after, four out of the five miles had been cleared, without any incident having occurred. The road was as deserted as all that part of the Jacamar Wood which lay between the Mercy and the lake. There was no occasion for any warning. The wood appeared as deserted as on the day when the colonists first landed on the island.

They approached the plateau. Another mile and they would see the bridge over Creek Glycerine. Cyrus Harding expected to find it in its place; supposing that the convicts would have crossed it, and that, after having passed one of the streams which enclosed the plateau, they would have taken the precaution to lower it again, so as to keep open a retreat.

At length an opening in the trees allowed the sea-horizon to be seen. But the cart continued its progress, for not one of its defenders thought of abandoning it.

At that moment Pencroft stopped the onager, and in a hoarse voice,—

"Oh! the villains!" he exclaimed.

And he pointed to a thick smoke rising from the mill, the sheds, and the buildings at the poultry-yard.

A man was moving about in the midst of the smoke. It was Neb.

His companions uttered a shout. He heard, and ran to meet them.

The convicts had left the plateau nearly half-an-hour before, having devastated it!

"And Mr. Herbert?" asked Neb.

Gideon Spilett returned to the cart.

Herbert had lost consciousness!

Chapter 10

Of the convicts, the dangers which menaced Granite House, the ruins with which the plateau was covered, the colonists thought no longer. Herbert's critical state outweighed all other considerations. Would the removal prove fatal to him by causing some internal injury? The reporter could not affirm it, but he and his companions almost despaired of the result. The cart was brought to the bend of the river. There some branches, disposed as a liner, received the mattress on which lay the unconscious Herbert. Ten minutes after, Cyrus Harding, Spilett, and Pencroft were at the foot of the cliff, leaving Neb to take the cart on to the plateau of Prospect Heights. The lift was put in motion, and Herbert was soon stretched on his bed in Granite House.

What cares were lavished on him to bring him back to life! He smiled for a moment on finding himself in his room, but could scarcely even murmur a few words, so great was his weakness. Gideon Spilett examined his wounds. He feared to find them reopened, having been imperfectly healed. There was nothing of the sort. From whence, then, came this prostration? why was Herbert so much worse? The lad then fell into a kind of feverish sleep, and the reporter and Pencroft remained near the bed. During this time, Harding told Neb all that had happened at the corral, and Neb recounted to his master the events of which the plateau had just been the theater.

It was only during the preceding night that the convicts had appeared on the edge of the forest, at the approaches to Creek Glycerine. Neb, who was watching near the poultry-yard, had not hesitated to fire at one of the pirates, who was about to cross the stream; but in the darkness he could not tell whether the man had been hit or not. At any rate, it was not enough to frighten away the band, and Neb had only just time to get up to Granite House, where at least he was in safety.

But what was he to do there? How prevent the devastations with which the convicts threatened the plateau? Had Neb any means by which to warn his master? And, besides, in what situation were the inhabitants of the corral themselves? Cyrus Harding and his companions had left on the 11th of November, and it was now the 29th. It was, therefore, nineteen days since Neb had had other news than that brought by Top—disastrous news: Ayrton disappeared, Herbert severely wounded, the engineer, reporter, and sailor, as it were, imprisoned in the corral!

What was he to do? asked poor Neb. Personally he had nothing to fear, for the convicts could not reach him in Granite House. But the buildings, the plantations, all their arrangements at the mercy of the pirates! Would it not be best to let Cyrus Harding judge of what he ought to do, and to warn him, at least, of the danger which threatened him?

Neb then thought of employing Jup, and confiding a note to him. He knew the orang's great intelligence, which had been often put to the proof. Jup understood the word corral, which had been frequently pronounced before him, and it may be remembered, too, that he had often driven the cart thither in company with Pencroft. Day had not yet dawned. The active orang would know how to pass unperceived through the woods, of which the convicts, besides, would think he was a native.

Neb did not hesitate. He wrote the note, he tied it to Jup's neck, he brought the ape to the door of Granite House, from which he let down a long cord to the ground; then, several times he repeated these words,—

"Jup Jup! corral, corral!"

The creature understood, seized the cord, glided rapidly down the beach, and disappeared in the darkness without the convicts' attention having been in the least excited.

"You did well, Neb," said Harding, "but perhaps in not warning us you would have done still better!"

And, in speaking thus, Cyrus Harding thought of Herbert, whose recovery the removal had so seriously checked.

Neb ended his account. The convicts had not appeared at all on the beach. Not knowing the number of the island's inhabitants, they might suppose that Granite House was defended by a large party. They must have remembered that during the attack by the brig numerous shot had been fired both from the lower and upper rocks, and no doubt they did not wish to expose themselves. But the plateau of Prospect Heights was open to them, and not covered by the fire of Granite House. They gave themselves up, therefore, to their instinct of destruction,—plundering, burning, devastating everything,—and only retiring half an hour before the arrival of the colonists, whom they believed still confined in the corral.

On their retreat, Neb hurried out. He climbed the plateau at the risk of being perceived and fired at, tried to extinguish the fire which was consuming the buildings of the poultry-yard, and had struggled, though in vain, against it until the cart appeared at the edge of the wood.

Such had been these serious events. The presence of the convicts constituted a permanent source of danger to the settlers in Lincoln Island, until then so happy, and who might now expect still greater misfortunes.

Spilett remained in Granite House with Herbert and Pencroft, while Cyrus Harding, accompanied by Neb, proceeded to judge for himself of the extent of the disaster.

It was fortunate that the convicts had not advanced to the foot of Granite House. The workshop at the Chimneys would in that case not have escaped destruction. But after all, this evil would have been more easily reparable than the ruins accumulated on the plateau of Prospect Heights. Harding and Neb proceeded towards the Mercy, and ascended its left bank without meeting with any trace of the convicts; nor on the other side of the river, in the depths of the wood, could they perceive any suspicious indications.

Besides, it might be supposed that in all probability either the convicts knew of the return of the settlers to Granite House, by having seen them pass on the road from the corral, or, after the devastation of the plateau, they had penetrated into Jacamar Wood, following the course of the Mercy, and were thus ignorant of their return.

In the former case, they must have returned towards the corral, now without defenders, and which contained valuable stores.

In the latter, they must have regained their encampment, and would wait on opportunity to recommence the attack.

It was, therefore, possible to prevent them, but any enterprise to clear the island was now rendered difficult by reason of Herbert's condition. Indeed, their whole force would have been barely sufficient to cope with the convicts, and just now no one could leave Granite House.

The engineer and Neb arrived on the plateau. Desolation reigned everywhere. The fields had been trampled over; the ears of wheat, which were nearly full-grown, lay on the ground. The other plantations had not suffered less.

The kitchen-garden was destroyed. Happily, Granite House possessed a store of seed which would enable them to repair these misfortunes.

As to the wall and buildings of the poultry-yard and the onagers stable, the fire had destroyed all. A few terrified creatures roamed over the plateau. The birds, which during the fire had taken refuge on the waters of the lake, had already returned to their accustomed spot, and were dabbling on the banks. Everything would have to be reconstructed.

Cyrus Harding's face, which was paler than usual, expressed an internal anger which he commanded with difficulty, but he did not utter a word. Once more he looked at his devastated fields, and at the smoke which still rose from the ruins, then he returned to Granite House.

The following days were the saddest of any that the colonists had passed on the island! Herbert's weakness visibly increased. It appeared that a more serious malady, the consequence of the profound physiological disturbance he had gone through, threatened to declare itself, and Gideon Spilett feared such an aggravation of his condition that he would be powerless to fight against it!

In fact, Herbert remained in an almost continuous state of drowsiness, and symptoms of delirium began to manifest themselves. Refreshing drinks were the only remedies at the colonists' disposal. The fever was not as yet very high, but it soon appeared that it would probably recur at regular intervals. Gideon Spilett first recognized this on the 6th of December.

The poor boy, whose fingers, nose, and ears had become extremely pale, was at first seized with slight shiverings, horripilations, and tremblings. His pulse was weak and irregular, his skin dry, his thirst intense. To this soon succeeded a hot fit; his face became flushed; his skin reddened; his pulse quick; then a profuse perspiration broke out after which the fever seemed to diminish. The attack had lasted nearly five hours.

Gideon Spilett had not left Herbert, who, it was only too certain, was now seized by an intermittent fever, and this fever must be cured at any cost before it should assume a more serious aspect.

"And in order to cure it," said Spilett to Cyrus Harding, "we need a febrifuge."

"A febrifuge—" answered the engineer. "We have neither Peruvian bark, nor sulphate of quinine."

"No," said Gideon Spilett, "but there are willows on the border of the lake, and the bark of the willow might, perhaps, prove to be a substitute for quinine."

"Let us try it without losing a moment," replied Cyrus Harding.

The bark of the willow has, indeed, been justly considered as a succedaneum for Peruvian bark, as has also that of the horse-chestnut tree, the leaf of the holly, the snake-root, etc. It was evidently necessary to make trial of this substance, although not so valuable as Peruvian bark, and to employ it in its natural state, since they had no means for extracting its essence.

Cyrus Harding went himself to cut from the trunk of a species of black willow, a few pieces of bark; he brought them back to Granite House, and reduced them to a powder, which was administered that same evening to Herbert.

The night passed without any important change. Herbert was somewhat delirious, but the fever did not reappear in the night, and did not return either during the following day.

Pencroft again began to hope. Gideon Spilett said nothing. It might be that the fever was not quotidian, but tertian, and that it would return next day. Therefore, he awaited the next day with the greatest anxiety.

It might have been remarked besides that during this period Herbert remained utterly prostrate, his head weak and giddy. Another symptom alarmed the reporter to the highest degree. Herbert's liver became congested, and soon a more intense delirium showed that his brain was also affected.

Gideon Spilett was overwhelmed by this new complication. He took the engineer aside.

"It is a malignant fever," said he.

"A malignant fever!" cried Harding. "You are mistaken, Spilett. A malignant fever does not declare itself spontaneously; its germ must previously have existed."

"I am not mistaken," replied the reporter. "Herbert no doubt contracted the germ of this fever in the marshes of the island. He has already had one attack; should a second come on and should we not be able to prevent a third, he is lost."

"But the willow bark?"

"That is insufficient," answered the reporter, "and the third attack of a malignant fever, which is not arrested by means of quinine, is always fatal."

Fortunately, Pencroft heard nothing of this conversation or he would have gone mad.

It may be imagined what anxiety the engineer and the reporter suffered during the day of the 7th of December and the following night.

Towards the middle of the day the second attack came on. The crisis was terrible. Herbert felt himself sinking. He stretched his arms towards Cyrus Harding, towards Spilett, towards Pencroft. He was so young to die! The scene was heart-rending. They were obliged to send Pencroft away.

The fit lasted five hours. It was evident that Herbert could not survive a third.

The night was frightful. In his delirium Herbert uttered words which went to the hearts of his companions. He struggled with the convicts, he called to Ayrton, he poured forth entreaties to that mysterious being,—that powerful unknown protector,—whose image was stamped upon his mind; then he again fell into a deep exhaustion which completely prostrated him. Several times Gideon Spilett thought that the poor boy was dead.

The next day, the 8th of December, was but a succession of the fainting fits. Herbert's thin hands clutched the sheets. They had administered further doses of pounded bark, but the reporter expected no result from it.

"If before tomorrow morning we have not given him a more energetic febrifuge," said the reporter, "Herbert will be dead."

Night arrived—the last night, it was too much to be feared, of the good, brave, intelligent boy, so far in advance of his years, and who was loved by all as their own child. The only remedy which existed against this terrible malignant fever, the only specific which could overcome it, was not to be found in Lincoln Island.

During the night of the 8th of December, Herbert was seized by a more violent delirium. His liver was fearfully congested, his brain affected, and already it was impossible for him to recognize any one.

Would he live until the next day, until that third attack which must infallibly carry him off? It was not probable. His strength was exhausted, and in the intervals of fever he lay as one dead.

Towards three o'clock in the morning Herbert uttered a piercing cry. He seemed to be torn by a supreme convulsion. Neb, who was near him, terrified, ran into the next room where his companions were watching.

Top, at that moment, barked in a strange manner.

All rushed in immediately and managed to restrain the dying boy, who was endeavoring to throw himself out of his bed, while Spilett, taking his arm, felt his pulse gradually quicken.

It was five in the morning. The rays of the rising sun began to shine in at the windows of Granite House. It promised to be a fine day, and this day was to be poor Herbert's last!

A ray glanced on the table placed near the bed.

Suddenly Pencroft, uttering a cry, pointed to the table.

On it lay a little oblong box, of which the cover bore these words:—"SULPHATE OF QUININE."

Chapter 11

Gideon Spilett took the box and opened it. It contained nearly two hundred grains of a white powder, a few particles of which he carried to his lips. The extreme bitterness of the substance precluded all doubt; it was certainly the precious extract of quinine, that pre-eminent antifebrile.

This powder must be administered to Herbert without delay. How it came there might be discussed later.

"Some coffee!" said Spilett.

In a few moments Neb brought a cup of the warm infusion. Gideon Spilett threw into it about eighteen grains of quinine, and they succeeded in making Herbert drink the mixture.

There was still time, for the third attack of the malignant fever had not yet shown itself. How they longed to be able to add that it would not return!

Besides, it must be remarked, the hopes of all had now revived. The mysterious influence had been again exerted, and in a critical moment, when they had despaired of it.

In a few hours Herbert was much calmer. The colonists could now discuss this incident. The intervention of the stranger was more evident than ever. But how had he been able to penetrate during the night into Granite House? It was inexplicable, and, in truth, the proceedings of the genius of the island were not less mysterious than was that genius himself. During this day the sulphate of quinine was administered to Herbert every three hours.

The next day some improvement in Herbert's condition was apparent. Certainly, he was not out of danger, intermittent fevers being subject to frequent and dangerous relapses, but the most assiduous care was bestowed on him. And besides, the specific was at hand; nor, doubtless, was he who had brought it far distant! And the hearts of all were animated by returning hope.

This hope was not disappointed. Ten days after, on the 20th of December, Herbert's convalescence commenced.

He was still weak, and strict diet had been imposed upon him, but no access of fever supervened. And then, the poor boy submitted with such docility to all the prescriptions ordered him! He longed so to get well!

Pencroft was as a man who has been drawn up from the bottom of an abyss. Fits of joy approaching delirium seized him. When the time for the third attack had passed by, he nearly suffocated the reporter in his embrace. Since then, he always called him Dr. Spilett.

The real doctor, however, remained undiscovered.

"We will find him!" repeated the sailor.

Certainly, this man, whoever he was, might expect a somewhat too energetic embrace from the worthy Pencroft!

The month of December ended, and with it the year 1867, during which the colonists of Lincoln Island had of late been so severely tried. They commenced the year 1868 with magnificent weather, great heat, and a tropical temperature, delightfully cooled by the sea-breeze. Herbert's recovery progressed, and from his bed, placed near one of the windows of Granite House, he could inhale the fresh air, charged with ozone, which could not fail to restore his health. His appetite returned, and what numberless delicate, savory little dishes Neb prepared for him!

"It is enough to make one wish to have a fever oneself!" said Pencroft.

During all this time, the convicts did not once appear in the vicinity of Granite House. There was no news of Ayrton, and though the engineer and Herbert still had some hopes of finding him again, their companions did not doubt but that the unfortunate man had perished. However, this uncertainty could not last, and when once the lad should have recovered, the expedition, the result of which must be so important, would be undertaken. But they would have to wait a month, perhaps, for all the strength of the colony must be put into requisition to obtain satisfaction from the convicts.

However, Herbert's convalescence progressed rapidly. The congestion of the liver had disappeared, and his wounds might be considered completely healed.

During the month of January, important work was done on the plateau of Prospect Heights; but it consisted solely in saving as much as was possible from the devastated crops, either of corn or vegetables. The grain and the plants were gathered, so as to provide a new harvest for the approaching half-season. With regard to rebuilding the poultry-yard, wall, or stables, Cyrus Harding preferred to wait. While he and his companions were in pursuit of the convicts, the latter might very probably pay another visit to the plateau, and it would be useless to give them an opportunity of recommencing their work of destruction. When the island should be cleared of these miscreants, they would set about rebuilding. The young convalescent began to get up in the second week of January, at first for one hour a day, then two, then three. His strength visibly returned, so vigorous was his constitution. He was now eighteen years of age. He was tall, and promised to become a man of noble and commanding presence. From this time his recovery, while still requiring care,—and Dr. Spilett was very strict,—made rapid progress. Towards the end of the month, Herbert was already walking about on Prospect Heights, and the beach.

He derived, from several sea-baths, which he took in company with Pencroft and Neb, the greatest possible benefit. Cyrus Harding thought he might now settle the day for their departure, for which the 15th of February was fixed. The nights, very clear at this time of year, would be favorable to the researches they intended to make all over the island.

The necessary preparations for this exploration were now commenced, and were important, for the colonists had sworn not to return to Granite House until their twofold object had been achieved; on the one hand, to exterminate the convicts, and rescue Ayrton, if he was still living; on the other, to discover who it was that presided so effectually over the fortunes of the colony.

Of Lincoln Island, the settlers knew thoroughly all the eastern coast from Claw Cape to the Mandible Capes, the extensive Tadorn Marsh, the neighborhood of Lake Grant, Jacamar Wood, between the road to the corral and the Mercy, the courses of the Mercy and Red Creek, and lastly, the spurs of Mount Franklin, among which the corral had been established.

They had explored, though only in an imperfect manner, the vast shore of Washington Bay from Claw Cape to Reptile End, the woody and marshy border of the west coast, and the interminable downs, ending at the open mouth of Shark Gulf. But they had in no way surveyed the woods which covered the Serpentine Peninsula, all to the right of the Mercy, the left bank of Falls River, and the wilderness of spurs and valleys which supported three quarters of the base of Mount Franklin, to the east, the north, and the west, and where doubtless many secret retreats existed. Consequently, many millions of acres of the island had still escaped their investigations.

It was, therefore, decided that the expedition should be carried through the Far West, so as to include all that region situated on the right of the Mercy.

It might, perhaps, be better worth while to go direct to the corral, where it might be supposed that the convicts had again taken refuge, either to pillage or to establish themselves there. But either the devastation of the corral would have been an accomplished fact by this time, and it would be too late to prevent it, or it had been the convicts' interest to entrench themselves there, and there would be still time to go and turn them out on their return.

Therefore, after some discussion, the first plan was adhered to, and the settlers resolved to proceed through the wood to Reptile End. They would make their way with their hatchets, and thus lay the first draft of a road which would place Granite House in communication with the end of the peninsula for a length of from sixteen to seventeen miles.

The cart was in good condition. The onagers, well rested, could go a long journey. Provisions, camp effects, a portable stove, and various utensils were packed in the cart, as also weapons and ammunition, carefully chosen from the now complete arsenal of Granite House. But it was necessary to remember that the convicts were, perhaps, roaming about the woods, and that in the midst of these thick forests a shot might quickly be fired and received. It was therefore resolved that the little band of settlers should remain together and not separate under any pretext whatever.

It was also decided that no one should remain at Granite House. Top and Jup themselves were to accompany the expedition; the inaccessible dwelling needed no guard. The 14th of February, eve of the departure, was consecrated entirely to repose, and—thanksgiving addressed by the colonists to the Creator. A place in the cart was reserved for Herbert, who, though thoroughly convalescent, was still a little weak. The next morning, at daybreak, Cyrus Harding took the necessary measures to protect Granite House from any invasion. The ladders, which were formerly used for the ascent, were brought to the Chimneys and buried deep in the sand, so that they might be available on the return of the colonists, for the machinery of the lift had been taken to pieces, and nothing of the apparatus remained. Pencroft stayed the last in Granite House in order to finish this work, and he then lowered himself down by means of a double rope held below, and which, when once hauled down, left no communication between the upper landing and the beach.

The weather was magnificent.

"We shall have a warm day of it," said the reporter, laughing.

"Pooh! Dr. Spilett," answered Pencroft, "we shall walk under the shade of the trees and shan't even see the sun!"

"Forward!" said the engineer.

The cart was waiting on the beach before the Chimneys. The reporter made Herbert take his place in it during the first hours at least of the journey, and the lad was obliged to submit to his doctor's orders.

Neb placed himself at the onagers' heads. Cyrus Harding, the reporter, and the sailor, walked in front. Top bounded joyfully along. Herbert offered a seat in his vehicle to Jup, who accepted it without ceremony. The moment for departure had arrived, and the little band set out.

The cart first turned the angle of the mouth of the Mercy, then, having ascended the left bank for a mile, crossed the bridge, at the other side of which commenced the road to Port Balloon, and there the explorers, leaving this road on their left, entered the cover of the immense woods which formed the region of the Far West.

For the first two miles the widely scattered trees allowed the cart to pass with ease; from time to time it became necessary to cut away a few creepers and bushes, but no serious obstacle impeded the progress of the colonists.

The thick foliage of the trees threw a grateful shade on the ground. Deodars, Douglas firs, casuarinas, banksias, gum-trees, dragon-trees, and other well-known species, succeeded each other far as the eye could reach. The feathered tribes of the island were all represented—grouse, jacamars, pheasants, lories, as well as the chattering cockatoos, parrots, and paroquets. Agouties, kangaroos, and capybaras fled swiftly at their approach; and all this reminded the settlers of the first excursions they had made on their arrival at the island.

"Nevertheless," observed Cyrus Harding, "I notice that these creatures, both birds and quadrupeds, are more timid than formerly. These woods have, therefore, been recently traversed by the convicts, and we shall certainly find some traces of them."

And, in fact, in several places they could distinguish traces, more or less recent, of the passage of a band of men—here branches broken off the trees, perhaps to mark out the way; there the ashes of a fire, and footprints in clayey spots; but nothing which appeared to belong to a settled encampment.

The engineer had recommended his companions to refrain from hunting. The reports of the firearms might give the alarm to the convicts, who were, perhaps, roaming through the forest. Moreover, the hunters would necessarily ramble some distance from the cart, which it was dangerous to leave unguarded.

In the afterpart of the day, when about six miles from Granite House, their progress became much more difficult. In order to make their way through some thickets, they were obliged to cut down trees. Before entering such places Harding was careful to send in Top and Jup, who faithfully accomplished their commission, and when the dog and orang returned without giving any warning, there was evidently nothing to fear, either from convicts or wild beasts, two varieties of the animal kingdom, whose ferocious instincts placed them on the same level. On the evening of the first day the colonists encamped about nine miles from Granite House, on the border of a little stream falling into the Mercy, and of the existence of which they had till then been ignorant; it evidently, however, belonged to the hydiographical system to which the soil owed its astonishing fertility. The settlers made a hearty meal, for their appetites were sharpened, and measures were then taken that the night might be passed in safety. If the engineer had had only to deal with wild beasts, jaguars or others, he would have simply lighted fires all around his camp, which would have sufficed for its defense; but the convicts would be rather attracted than terrified by the flames, and it was, therefore, better to be surrounded by the profound darkness of night.

The watch was, however, carefully organized. Two of the settlers were to watch together, and every two hours it was agreed that they should be relieved by their comrades. And so, notwithstanding his wish to the contrary, Herbert was exempted from guard. Pencroft and Gideon Spilett in one party, the engineer and Neb in another, mounted guard in turns over the camp.

The night, however, was but of few hours. The darkness was due rather to the thickness of the foliage than to the disappearance of the sun. The silence was scarcely disturbed by the howling of jaguars and the chattering of the monkeys, the latter appearing to particularly irritate Master Jup. The night passed without incident, and on the next day, the 15th of February, the journey through the forest, tedious rather than difficult, was continued. This day they could not accomplish more than six miles, for every moment they were obliged to cut a road with their hatchets.

Like true settlers, the colonists spared the largest and most beautiful trees, which would besides have cost immense labor to fell, and the small ones only were sacrificed, but the result was that the road took a very winding direction, and lengthened itself by numerous detours.

During the day Herbert discovered several new specimens not before met with in the island, such as the tree-fern, with its leaves spread out like the waters of a fountain, locust-trees, on the long pods of which the onagers browsed greedily, and which supplied a sweet pulp of excellent flavor. There, too, the colonists again found groups of magnificent kauries, their cylindrical trunks, crowded with a cone of verdure, rising to a height of two hundred feet. These were the tree-kings of New Zealand, as celebrated as the cedars of Lebanon.

As to the fauna, there was no addition to those species already known to the hunters. Nevertheless, they saw, though unable to get near them, a couple of those large birds peculiar to Australia, a sort of cassowary, called emu, five feet in height, and with brown plumage, which belong to the tribe of waders. Top darted after them as fast as his four legs could carry him, but the emus distanced him with ease, so prodigious was their speed.

As to the traces left by the convicts, a few more were discovered. Some footprints found near an apparently recently extinguished fire were attentively examined by the settlers. By measuring them one after the other, according to their length and breadth, the marks of five men's feet were easily distinguished.

The five convicts had evidently camped on this spot; but,—and this was the object of so minute an examination,—a sixth footprint could not be discovered, which in that case would have been that of Ayrton.

"Ayrton was not with them!" said Herbert.

"No," answered Pencroft, "and if he was not with them, it was because the wretches had already murdered him! but then these rascals have not a den to which they may be tracked like tigers!"

"No," replied the reporter, "it is more probable that they wander at random, and it is their interest to rove about until the time when they will be masters of the island!"

"The masters of the island!" exclaimed the sailor; "the masters of the island!..." he repeated, and his voice was choked, as if his throat was seized in an iron grasp. Then in a calmer tone, "Do you know, Captain Harding," said he, "what the ball is which I have rammed into my gun?"

"No, Pencroft!"

"It is the ball that went through Herbert's chest, and I promise you it won't miss its mark!"

But this just retaliation would not bring Ayrton back to life, and from the examination of the footprints left in the ground, they must, alas! conclude that all hopes of ever seeing him again must be abandoned.

That evening they encamped fourteen miles from Granite House, and Cyrus Harding calculated that they could not be more than five miles from Reptile Point.

And indeed, the next day the extremity of the peninsula was reached, and the whole length of the forest had been traversed; but there was nothing to indicate the retreat in which the convicts had taken refuge, nor that, no less secret, which sheltered the mysterious unknown.

Chapter 12

The next day, the 18th of February, was devoted to the exploration of all that wooded region forming the shore from Reptile End to Falls River. The colonists were able to search this forest thoroughly, for, as it was comprised between the two shores of the Serpentine Peninsula, it was only from three to four miles in breadth. The trees, both by their height and their thick foliage, bore witness to the vegetative power of the soil, more astonishing here than in any other part of the island. One might have said that a corner from the virgin forests of America or Africa had been transported into this temperate zone. This led them to conclude that the superb vegetation found a heat in this soil, damp in its upper layer, but warmed in the interior by volcanic fires, which could not belong to a temperate climate. The most frequently occurring trees were knaries and eucalypti of gigantic dimensions.

But the colonists' object was not simply to admire the magnificent vegetation. They knew already that in this respect Lincoln Island would have been worthy to take the first rank in the Canary group, to which the first name given was that of the Happy Isles. Now, alas! their island no longer belonged to them entirely; others had taken possession of it, miscreants polluted its shores, and they must be destroyed to the last man.

No traces were found on the western coast, although they were carefully sought for. No more footprints, no more broken branches, no more deserted camps.

"This does not surprise me," said Cyrus Harding to his companions. "The convicts first landed on the island in the neighborhood of Flotsam Point, and they immediately plunged into the Far West forests, after crossing Tadorn Marsh. They then followed almost the same route that we took on leaving Granite House. This explains the traces we found in the wood. But, arriving on the shore, the convicts saw at once that they would discover no suitable retreat there, and it was then that, going northwards again, they came upon the corral."

"Where they have perhaps returned," said Pencroft.

"I do not think so," answered the engineer, "for they would naturally suppose that our researches would be in that direction. The corral is only a storehouse to them, and not a definitive encampment."

"I am of Cyrus' opinion," said the reporter, "and I think that it is among the spurs of Mount Franklin that the convicts will have made their lair."

"Then, captain, straight to the corral!" cried Pencroft. "We must finish them off, and till now we have only lost time!"

"No, my friend," replied the engineer; "you forget that we have a reason for wishing to know if the forests of the Far West do not contain some habitation. Our exploration has a double object, Pencroft. If, on the one hand, we have to chastise crime, we have, on the other, an act of gratitude to perform."

"That was well said, captain," replied the sailor, "but, all the same, it is my opinion that we shall not find the gentleman until he pleases."

And truly Pencroft only expressed the opinion of all. It was probable that the stranger's retreat was not less mysterious than was he himself.

That evening the cart halted at the mouth of Falls River. The camp was organized as usual, and the customary precautions were taken for the night. Herbert, become again the healthy and vigorous lad he was before his illness, derived great benefit from this life in the open air, between the sea breezes and the vivifying air from the forests. His place was no longer in the cart, but at the head of the troop.

The next day, the 19th of February, the colonists, leaving the shore, where, beyond the mouth, basalts of every shape were so picturesquely piled up, ascended the river by its left bank. The road had been already partly cleared in their former excursions made from the corral to the west coast. The settlers were now about six miles from Mount Franklin.

The engineer's plan was this:—To minutely survey the valley forming the bed of the river, and to cautiously approach the neighborhood of the corral; if the corral was occupied, to seize it by force; if it was not, to entrench themselves there and make it the center of the operations which had for their object the exploration of Mount Franklin.

This plan was unanimously approved by the colonists, for they were impatient to regain entire possession of their island.

They made their way then along the narrow valley separating two of the largest spurs of Mount Franklin. The trees, crowded on the river's bank, became rare on the upper slopes of the mountain. The ground was hilly and rough, very suitable for ambushes, and over which they did not venture without extreme precaution. Top and Jup skirmished on the flanks, springing right and left through the thick brushwood, and emulating each other in intelligence and activity. But nothing showed that the banks of the stream had been recently frequented—nothing announced either the presence or the proximity of the convicts. Towards five in the evening the cart stopped nearly 600 feet from the palisade. A semicircular screen of trees still hid it.

It was necessary to reconnoiter the corral, in order to ascertain if it was occupied. To go there openly, in broad daylight, when the convicts were probably in ambush, would be to expose themselves, as poor Herbert had done, to the firearms of the ruffians. It was better, then, to wait until night came on.

However, Gideon Spilett wished without further delay to reconnoiter the approaches to the corral, and Pencroft, who was quite out of patience, volunteered to accompany him.

"No, my friends," said the engineer, "wait till night. I will not allow one of you to expose himself in open day."

"But, captain—" answered the sailor, little disposed to obey.

"I beg of you, Pencroft," said the engineer.

"Very well!" replied the sailor, who vented his anger in another way, by bestowing on the convicts the worst names in his maritime vocabulary.

The colonists remained, therefore, near the cart, and carefully watched the neighboring parts of the forest.

Three hours passed thus. The wind had fallen, and absolute silence reigned under the great trees. The snapping of the smallest twig, a footstep on the dry leaves, the gliding of a body among the grass, would have been heard without difficulty. All was quiet. Besides, Top, lying on the grass, his head stretched out on his paws, gave no sign of uneasiness. At eight o'clock the day appeared far enough advanced for the reconnaissance to be made under favorable conditions. Gideon Spilett declared himself ready to set out accompanied by Pencroft. Cyrus Harding consented. Top and Jup were to remain with the engineer, Herbert, and Neb, for a bark or a cry at a wrong moment would give the alarm.

"Do not be imprudent," said Harding to the reporter and Pencroft, "you have not to gain possession of the corral, but only to find out whether it is occupied or not."

"All right," answered Pencroft.

And the two departed.

Under the trees, thanks to the thickness of their foliage, the obscurity rendered any object invisible beyond a radius of from thirty to forty feet. The reporter and Pencroft, halting at any suspicious sound, advanced with great caution.

They walked a little distance apart from each other so as to offer a less mark for a shot. And, to tell the truth, they expected every moment to hear a report. Five minutes after leaving the cart, Gideon Spilett and Pencroft arrived at the edge of the wood before the clearing beyond which rose the palisade.

They stopped. A few straggling beams still fell on the field clear of trees. Thirty feet distant was the gate of the corral, which appeared to be closed. This thirty feet, which it was necessary to cross from the wood to the palisade, constituted the dangerous zone, to borrow a ballistic term: in fact, one or more bullets fired from behind the palisade might knock over any one who ventured on to this zone. Gideon Spilett and the sailor were not men to draw back, but they knew that any imprudence on their part, of which they would be the first victims, would fall afterwards on their companions. If they themselves were killed, what would become of Harding, Neb, and Herbert?

But Pencroft, excited at feeling himself so near the corral where he supposed the convicts had taken refuge, was about to press forward, when the reporter held him back with a grasp of iron.

"In a few minutes it will be quite dark," whispered Spilett in the sailor's ear, "then will be the time to act."

Pencroft, convulsively clasping the butt-end of his gun, restrained his energies, and waited, swearing to himself.

Soon the last of the twilight faded away. Darkness, which seemed as if it issued from the dense forest, covered the clearing. Mount Franklin rose like an enormous screen before the western horizon, and night spread rapidly over all, as it does in regions of low latitudes. Now was the time.

The reporter and Pencroft, since posting themselves on the edge of the wood, had not once lost sight of the palisade. The corral appeared to be absolutely deserted. The top of the palisade formed a line, a little darker than the surrounding shadow, and nothing disturbed its distinctness. Nevertheless, if the convicts were there, they must have posted one of their number to guard against any surprise.

Spilett grasped his companion's hand, and both crept towards the corral, their guns ready to fire.

They reached the gate without the darkness being illuminated by a single ray of light.

Pencroft tried to push open the gate, which, as the reporter and he had supposed, was closed. However, the sailor was able to ascertain that the outer bars had not been put up. It might, then, be concluded that the convicts were there in the corral, and that very probably they had fastened the gate in such a way that it could not be forced open.

Gideon Spilett and Pencroft listened.

Not a sound could be heard inside the palisade. The musmons and the goats, sleeping no doubt in their huts, in no way disturbed the calm of night.

The reporter and the sailor hearing nothing, asked themselves whether they had not better scale the palisades and penetrate into the corral. This would have been contrary to Cyrus Harding's instructions.

It is true that the enterprise might succeed, but it might also fail. Now, if the convicts were suspecting nothing, if they knew nothing of the expedition against them, if, lastly, there now existed a chance of surprising them, ought this chance to be lost by inconsiderately attempting to cross the palisades?

This was not the reporter's opinion. He thought it better to wait until all the settlers were collected together before attempting to penetrate into the corral. One thing was certain, that it was possible to reach the palisade without being seen, and also that it did not appear to be guarded. This point settled, there was nothing to be done but to return to the cart, where they would consult.

Pencroft probably agreed with this decision, for he followed the reporter without making any objection when the latter turned back to the wood.

In a few minutes the engineer was made acquainted with the state of affairs.

"Well," said he, after a little thought, "I now have reason to believe that the convicts are not in the corral."

"We shall soon know," said Pencroft, "when we have scaled the palisade."

"To the corral, my friends!" said Cyrus Harding.

"Shall we leave the cart in the wood?" asked Neb.

"No," replied the engineer, "it is our wagon of ammunition and provisions, and, if necessary, it would serve as an entrenchment."

"Forward, then!" said Gideon Spilett.

The cart emerged from the wood and began to roll noiselessly towards the palisade. The darkness was now profound, the silence as complete as when Pencroft and the reporter crept over the ground. The thick grass completely muffled their footsteps. The colonists held themselves ready to fire. Jup, at

Pencroft's orders, kept behind. Neb led Top in a leash, to prevent him from bounding forward.

The clearing soon came in sight. It was deserted. Without hesitating, the little band moved towards the palisade. In a short space of time the dangerous zone was passed. Neb remained at the onagers' heads to hold them. The engineer, the reporter, Herbert, and Pencroft, proceeded to the door, in order to ascertain if it was barricaded inside. It was open!

"What do you say now?" asked the engineer, turning to the sailor and Spilett. Both were stupefied.

"I can swear," said Pencroft, "that this gate was shut just now!"

The colonists now hesitated. Were the convicts in the corral when Pencroft and the reporter made their reconnaissance? It could not be doubted, as the gate then closed could only have been opened by them. Were they still there, or had one of their number just gone out?

All these questions presented themselves simultaneously to the minds of the colonists, but how could they be answered?

At that moment, Herbert, who had advanced a few steps into the enclosure, drew back hurriedly, and seized Harding's hand.

"What's the matter?" asked the engineer.

"A light!"

"In the house?"

"Yes!"

All five advanced and indeed, through the window fronting them, they saw glimmering a feeble light. Cyrus Harding made up his mind rapidly. "It is our only chance," said he to his companions, "of finding the convicts collected in this house, suspecting nothing! They are in our power! Forward!" The colonists crossed through the enclosure, holding their guns ready in their hands. The cart had been left outside under the charge of Jup and Top, who had been prudently tied to it.

Cyrus Harding, Pencroft, and Gideon Spilett on one side, Herbert and Neb on the other, going along by the palisade, surveyed the absolutely dark and deserted corral.

In a few moments they were near the closed door of the house.

Harding signed to his companions not to stir, and approached the window, then feebly lighted by the inner light.

He gazed into the apartment.

On the table burned a lantern. Near the table was the bed formerly used by Ayrton.

On the bed lay the body of a man.

Suddenly Cyrus Harding drew back, and in a hoarse voice,—"Ayrton!" he exclaimed.

Immediately the door was forced rather than opened, and the colonists rushed into the room.

Ayrton appeared to be asleep. His countenance showed that he had long and cruelly suffered. On his wrists and ankles could be seen great bruises.

Harding bent over him.

"Ayrton!" cried the engineer, seizing the arm of the man whom he had just found again under such unexpected circumstances.

At this exclamation Ayrton opened his eyes, and, gazing at Harding, then at the others,—

"You!" he cried, "you?"

"Ayrton! Ayrton!" repeated Harding.

"Where am I?"

"In the house in the corral!"

"Alone?"

"Yes!"

"But they will come back!" cried Ayrton. "Defend yourselves! defend yourselves!"

And he fell back exhausted.

"Spilett," exclaimed the engineer, "we may be attacked at any moment. Bring the cart into the corral. Then, barricade the door, and all come back here."

Pencroft, Neb, and the reporter hastened to execute the engineer's orders. There was not a moment to be lost. Perhaps even now the cart was in the hands of the convicts!

In a moment the reporter and his two companions had crossed the corral and reached the gate of the palisade behind which Top was heard growling sullenly.

The engineer, leaving Ayrton for an instant, came out ready to fire. Herbert was at his side. Both surveyed the crest of the spur overlooking the corral. If the convicts were lying in ambush there, they might knock the settlers over one after the other.

At that moment the moon appeared in the east, above the black curtain of the forest, and a white sheet of light spread over the interior of the enclosure. The corral, with its clumps of trees, the little stream which watered it, its wide carpet of grass, was suddenly illuminated. From the side of the mountain, the house and a part of the palisade stood out white in the moonlight. On the opposite side towards the door, the enclosure remained dark. A black mass soon appeared. This was the cart entering the circle of light, and Cyrus Harding could hear the noise made by the door, as his companions shut it and fastened the interior bars.

But, at that moment, Top, breaking loose, began to bark furiously and rush to the back of the corral, to the right of the house.

"Be ready to fire, my friends!" cried Harding.

The colonists raised their pieces and waited the moment to fire.

Top still barked, and Jup, running towards the dog, uttered shrill cries.

The colonists followed him, and reached the borders of the little stream, shaded by large trees. And there, in the bright moonlight, what did they see? Five corpses, stretched on the bank!

They were those of the convicts who, four months previously, had landed on Lincoln Island!

Chapter 13

How had it happened? who had killed the convicts? Was it Ayrton? No, for a moment before he was dreading their return.

But Ayrton was now in a profound stupor, from which it was no longer possible to rouse him. After uttering those few words he had again become unconscious, and had fallen back motionless on the bed.

The colonists, a prey to a thousand confused thoughts, under the influence of violent excitement, waited all night, without leaving Ayrton's house, or returning to the spot where lay the bodies of the convicts. It was very probable that Ayrton would not be able to throw any light on the circumstances under which the bodies had been found, since he himself was not aware that he was in the corral. But at any rate he would be in a position to give an account of what had taken place before this terrible execution. The next day Ayrton awoke from his torpor, and his companions cordially manifested all the joy they felt, on seeing him again, almost safe and sound, after a hundred and four days separation.

Ayrton then in a few words recounted what had happened, or, at least, as much as he knew.

The day after his arrival at the corral, on the 10th of last November, at nightfall, he was surprised by the convicts, who had scaled the palisade. They bound and gagged him; then he was led to a dark cavern, at the foot of Mount Franklin, where the convicts had taken refuge.

His death had been decided upon, and the next day the convicts were about to kill him, when one of them recognized him and called him by the name which he bore in Australia. The wretches had no scruples as to murdering Ayrton! They spared Ben Joyce!

But from that moment Ayrton was exposed to the importunities of his former accomplices. They wished him to join them again, and relied upon his aid to enable them to gain possession of Granite House, to penetrate into that hitherto inaccessible dwelling, and to become masters of the island, after murdering the colonists!

Ayrton remained firm. The once convict, now repentant and pardoned, would rather die than betray his companions. Ayrton—bound, gagged, and closely watched—lived in this cave for four months.

Nevertheless the convicts had discovered the corral a short time after their arrival in the island, and since then they had subsisted on Ayrton's stores, but did not live at the corral.

On the 11th of November, two of the villains, surprised by the colonists' arrival, fired at Herbert, and one of them returned, boasting of having killed one of the inhabitants of the island; but he returned alone. His companion, as is known, fell by Cyrus Harding's dagger.

Ayrton's anxiety and despair may be imagined when he learned the news of Herbert's death. The settlers were now only four, and, as it seemed, at the mercy of the convicts. After this event, and during all the time that the colonists, detained by Herbert's illness, remained in the corral, the pirates did not leave their cavern, and even after they had pillaged the plateau of Prospect Heights, they did not think it prudent to abandon it.

The ill-treatment inflicted on Ayrton was now redoubled. His hands and feet still bore the bloody marks of the cords which bound him day and night. Every moment he expected to be put to death, nor did it appear possible that he could escape.

Matters remained thus until the third week of February. The convicts, still watching for a favorable opportunity, rarely quitted their retreat, and only made a few hunting excursions, either to the interior of the island, or the south coast.

Ayrton had no further news of his friends, and relinquished all hope of ever seeing them again. At last, the unfortunate man, weakened by ill-treatment, fell into a prostration so profound that sight and hearing failed him. From that moment, that is to say, since the last two days, he could give no information whatever of what had occurred.

"But, Captain Harding," he added, "since I was imprisoned in that cavern, how is it that I find myself in the corral?"

"How is it that the convicts are lying yonder dead, in the middle of the enclosure?" answered the engineer.

"Dead!" cried Ayrton, half rising from his bed, notwithstanding his weakness.

His companions supported him. He wished to get up, and with their assistance he did so. They then proceeded together towards the little stream.

It was now broad daylight.

There, on the bank, in the position in which they had been stricken by death in its most instantaneous form, lay the corpses of the five convicts!

Ayrton was astounded. Harding and his companions looked at him without uttering a word. On a sign from the engineer, Neb and Pencroft examined the bodies, already stiffened by the cold.

They bore no apparent trace of any wound.

Only, after carefully examining them, Pencroft found on the forehead of one, on the chest of another, on the back of this one, on the shoulder of that, a little red spot, a sort of scarcely visible bruise, the cause of which it was impossible to conjecture.

"It is there that they have been struck!" said Cyrus Harding.

"But with what weapon?" cried the reporter.

"A weapon, lightning-like in its effects, and of which we have not the secret!"

"And who has struck the blow?" asked Pencroft.

"The avenging power of the island," replied Harding, "he who brought you here, Ayrton, whose influence has once more manifested itself, who does for us all that which we cannot do for ourselves, and who, his will accomplished, conceals himself from us."

"Let us make search for him, then!" exclaimed Pencroft.

"Yes, we will search for him," answered Harding, "but we shall not discover this powerful being who performs such wonders, until he pleases to call us to him!"

This invisible protection, which rendered their own action unavailing, both irritated and piqued the engineer. The relative inferiority which it proved was of a nature to wound a haughty spirit. A generosity evinced in such a manner as to elude all tokens of gratitude, implied a sort of disdain for those on whom the obligation was conferred, which in Cyrus Harding's eyes marred, in some degree, the worth of the benefit.

"Let us search," he resumed, "and God grant that we may some day be permitted to prove to this haughty protector that he has not to deal with ungrateful people! What would I not give could we repay him, by rendering him in our turn, although at the price of our lives, some signal service!"

From this day, the thoughts of the inhabitants of Lincoln Island were solely occupied with the intended search. Everything incited them to discover the answer to this enigma, an answer which would only be the name of a man endowed with a truly inexplicable, and in some degree superhuman power.

In a few minutes, the settlers re-entered the house, where their influence soon restored to Ayrton his moral and physical energy. Neb and Pencroft carried the corpses of the convicts into the forest, some distance from the corral, and buried them deep in the ground.

Ayrton was then made acquainted with the facts which had occurred during his seclusion. He learned Herbert's adventures, and through what various trials the colonists had passed. As to the settlers, they had despaired of ever seeing Ayrton again, and had been convinced that the convicts had ruthlessly murdered him.

"And now," said Cyrus Harding, as he ended his recital, "a duty remains for us to perform. Half of our task is accomplished, but although the convicts are no longer to be feared, it is not owing to ourselves that we are once more masters of the island."

"Well!" answered Gideon Spilett, "let us search all this labyrinth of the spurs of Mount Franklin. We will not leave a hollow, not a hole unexplored! Ah! if ever a reporter found himself face to face with a mystery, it is I who now speak to you, my friends!"

"And we will not return to Granite House until we have found our benefactor," said Herbert.

"Yes," said the engineer, "we will do all that it is humanly possible to do, but I repeat we shall not find him until he himself permits us."

"Shall we stay at the corral?" asked Pencroft.

"We shall stay here," answered Harding. "Provisions are abundant, and we are here in the very center of the circle we have to explore. Besides, if necessary, the cart will take us rapidly to Granite House."

"Good!" answered the sailor. "Only I have a remark to make."

"What is it?"

"Here is the fine season getting on, and we must not forget that we have a voyage to make."

"A voyage?" said Gideon Spilett.

"Yes, to Tabor Island," answered Pencroft. "It is necessary to carry a notice there to point out the position of our island and say that Ayrton is here in case the Scotch yacht should come to take him off. Who knows if it is not already too late?"

"But, Pencroft," asked Ayrton, "how do you intend to make this voyage?"

"In the 'Bonadventure.'"

"The 'Bonadventure!'" exclaimed Ayrton. "She no longer exists."

"My 'Bonadventure' exists no longer!" shouted Pencroft, bounding from his scat.

"No," answered Ayrton. "The convicts discovered her in her little harbor only eight days ago, they put to sea in her—"

"And?" said Pencroft, his heart beating.

"And not having Bob Harvey to steer her, they ran on the rocks, and the vessel went to pieces."

"Oh, the villains, the cutthroats, the infamous scoundrels!" exclaimed Pencroft.

"Pencroft," said Herbert, taking the sailor's hand, "we will build another 'Bonadventure'—a larger one. We have all the ironwork—all the rigging of the brig at our disposal."

"But do you know," returned Pencroft, "that it will take at least five or six months to build a vessel of from thirty to forty tons?"

"We can take our time," said the reporter, "and we must give up the voyage to Tabor Island for this year."

"Oh, my 'Bonadventure!' my poor 'Bonadventure!'" cried Pencroft, almost broken-hearted at the destruction of the vessel of which he was so proud.

The loss of the "Bonadventure" was certainly a thing to be lamented by the colonists, and it was agreed that this loss should be repaired as soon as possible. This settled, they now occupied themselves with bringing their researches to bear on the most secret parts of the island.

The exploration was commenced at daybreak on the 19th of February, and lasted an entire week. The base of the mountain, with its spurs and their numberless ramifications, formed a labyrinth of valleys and elevations. It was evident that there, in the depths of these narrow gorges, perhaps even in the interior of Mount Franklin itself, was the proper place to pursue their researches. No part of the island could have been more suitable to conceal a dwelling whose occupant wished to remain unknown. But so irregular was the formation of the valleys that Cyrus Harding was obliged to conduct the exploration in a strictly methodical manner.

The colonists first visited the valley opening to the south of the volcano, and which first received the waters of Falls River. There Ayrton showed them the cavern where the convicts had taken refuge, and in which he had been imprisoned until his removal to the corral. This cavern was just as Ayrton had left it. They found there a considerable quantity of ammunition and provisions, conveyed thither by the convicts in order to form a reserve.

The whole of the valley bordering on the cave, shaded by fir and other trees, was thoroughly explored, and on turning the point of the southwestern spur, the colonists entered a narrower gorge similar to the picturesque columns of basalt on the coast. Here the trees were fewer. Stones took the place of grass. Goats and musmons gambolled among the rocks. Here began the barren part of the island. It could already be seen that, of the numerous valleys branching off at the base of Mount Franklin, three only were wooded and rich in pasturage like that of the corral, which bordered on the west on the Falls River valley, and on the east on the Red Creek valley. These two streams, which lower down became rivers by the absorption of several tributaries, were formed by all the springs of the mountain and thus caused the fertility of its southern part. As to the Mercy, it was more directly fed from ample springs concealed under the cover of Jacamar Wood, and it was by springs of this nature, spreading in a thousand streamlets, that the soil of the Serpentine Peninsula was watered.

Now, of these three well-watered valleys, either might have served as a retreat to some solitary who would have found there everything necessary for life. But the settlers had already explored them, and in no part had they discovered the presence of man.

Was it then in the depths of those barren gorges, in the midst of the piles of rock, in the rugged northern ravines, among the streams of lava, that this dwelling and its occupant would be found?

The northern part of Mount Franklin was at its base composed solely of two valleys, wide, not very deep, without any appearance of vegetation, strewn with masses of rock, paved with lava, and varied with great blocks of mineral. This region required a long and careful exploration. It contained a thousand cavities, comfortless no doubt, but perfectly concealed and difficult of access.

The colonists even visited dark tunnels, dating from the volcanic period, still black from the passage of the fire, and penetrated into the depths of the mountain. They traversed these somber galleries, waving lighted torches; they examined the smallest excavations; they sounded the shallowest depths, but all was dark and silent. It did not appear that the foot of man had ever before trodden these ancient passages, or that his arm had ever displaced one of these blocks, which remained as the volcano had cast them up above the waters, at the time of the submersion of the island.

However, although these passages appeared to be absolutely deserted, and the obscurity was complete, Cyrus Harding was obliged to confess that absolute silence did not reign there.

On arriving at the end of one of these gloomy caverns, extending several hundred feet into the interior of the mountain, he was surprised to hear a deep rumbling noise, increased in intensity by the sonorousness of the rocks.

Gideon Spilett, who accompanied him, also heard these distant mutterings, which indicated a revivification of the subterranean fires. Several times both listened, and they agreed that some chemical process was taking place in the bowels of the earth.

"Then the volcano is not totally extinct?" said the reporter.

"It is possible that since our exploration of the crater," replied Cyrus Harding, "some change has occurred. Any volcano, although considered extinct, may evidently again burst forth."

"But if an eruption of Mount Franklin occurred," asked Spilett, "would there not be some danger to Lincoln Island?"

"I do not think so," answered the reporter. "The crater, that is to say, the safety-valve, exists, and the overflow of smoke and lava, would escape, as it did formerly, by this customary outlet."

"Unless the lava opened a new way for itself towards the fertile parts of the island!"

"And why, my dear Spilett," answered Cyrus Harding, "should it not follow the road naturally traced out for it?"

"Well, volcanoes are capricious," returned the reporter.

"Notice," answered the engineer, "that the inclination of Mount Franklin favors the flow of water towards the valleys which we are exploring just now. To turn aside this flow, an earthquake would be necessary to change the mountain's center of gravity."

"But an earthquake is always to be feared at these times," observed Gideon Spilett.

"Always," replied the engineer, "especially when the subterranean forces begin to awake, as they risk meeting with some obstruction, after a long rest. Thus, my dear Spilett, an eruption would be a serious thing for us, and it would be better that the volcano should not have the slightest desire to wake up. But we could not prevent it, could we? At any rate, even if it should occur, I do not think Prospect Heights would be seriously threatened. Between them and the mountain, the ground is considerably depressed, and if the lava should ever take a course towards the lake, it would be cast on the downs and the neighboring parts of Shark Gulf."

"We have not yet seen any smoke at the top of the mountain, to indicate an approaching eruption," said Gideon Spilett.

"No," answered Harding, "not a vapor escapes from the crater, for it was only yesterday that I attentively surveyed the summit. But it is probable that at the lower part of the chimney, time may have accumulated rocks, cinders, hardened lava, and that this valve of which I spoke, may at any time become overcharged. But at the first serious effort, every obstacle will disappear, and you may be certain, my dear Spilett, that neither the island, which is the boiler, nor the volcano, which is the chimney, will burst under the pressure of gas. Nevertheless, I repeat, it would be better that there should not be an eruption."

"And yet we are not mistaken," remarked the reporter. "Mutterings can be distinctly heard in the very bowels of the volcano!"

"You are right," said the engineer, again listening attentively. "There can be no doubt of it. A commotion is going on there, of which we can neither estimate the importance nor the ultimate result."

Cyrus Harding and Spilett, on coming out, rejoined their companions, to whom they made known the state of affairs.

"Very well!" cried Pencroft, "The volcano wants to play his pranks! Let him try, if he likes! He will find his master!"

"Who?" asked Neb.

"Our good genius, Neb, our good genius, who will shut his mouth for him, if he so much as pretends to open it!"

As may be seen, the sailor's confidence in the tutelary deity of his island was absolute, and, certainly, the occult power, manifested until now in so many inexplicable ways, appeared to be unlimited; but also it knew how to escape the colonists' most minute researches, for, in spite of all their efforts, in spite of the more than zeal,—the obstinacy,—with which they carried on their exploration, the retreat of the mysterious being could not be discovered.

From the 19th to the 20th of February the circle of investigation was extended to all the northern region of Lincoln Island, whose most secret nooks were explored. The colonists even went the length of tapping every rock. The search was extended to the extreme verge of the mountain. It was explored thus to the very summit of the truncated cone terminating the first row of rocks, then to the upper ridge of the enormous hat, at the bottom of which opened the crater.

They did more; they visited the gulf, now extinct, but in whose depths the rumbling could be distinctly heard. However, no sign of smoke or vapor, no heating of the rock, indicated an approaching eruption. But neither there, nor in any other part of Mount Franklin, did the colonists find any traces of him of whom they were in search.

Their investigations were then directed to the downs. They carefully examined the high lava-cliffs of Shark Gulf from the base to the crest, although it was extremely difficult to reach even the level of the gulf. No one!—nothing!

Indeed, in these three words was summed up so much fatigue uselessly expended, so much energy producing no results, that somewhat of anger mingled with the discomfiture of Cyrus Harding and his companions.

It was now time to think of returning, for these researches could not be prolonged indefinitely. The colonists were certainly right in believing that the mysterious being did not reside on the surface of the island, and the wildest fancies haunted their excited imaginations. Pencroft and Neb, particularly, were not contented with the mystery, but allowed their imaginations to wander into the domain of the supernatural.

On the 25th of February the colonists re-entered Granite House, and by means of the double cord, carried by an arrow to the threshold of the door, they re-established communication between their habitation and the ground.

A month later they commemorated, on the 25th of March, the third anniversary of their arrival on Lincoln Island.

Chapter 14

Three years had passed away since the escape of the prisoners from Richmond, and how often during those three years had they spoken of their country, always present in their thoughts!

They had no doubt that the civil war was at an end, and to them it appeared impossible that the just cause of the North had not triumphed. But what had been the incidents of this terrible war? How much blood had it not cost? How many of their friends must have fallen in the struggle? They often spoke of these things, without as yet being able to foresee the day when they would be permitted once more to see their country. To return thither, were it but for a few days, to renew the social link with the inhabited world, to establish a communication between their native land and their island, then to pass the longest, perhaps the best, portion of their existence in this colony, founded by them, and which would then be dependent on their country, was this a dream impossible to realize?

There were only two ways of accomplishing it—either a ship must appear off Lincoln Island, or the colonists must themselves build a vessel strong enough to sail to the nearest land.

"Unless," said Pencroft, "our good genius, himself provides us with the means of returning to our country."

And, really, had any one told Pencroft and Neb that a ship of 300 tons was waiting for them in Shark Gulf or at Port Balloon, they would not even have made a gesture of surprise. In their state of mind nothing appeared improbable.

But Cyrus Harding, less confident, advised them to confine themselves to fact, and more especially so with regard to the building of a vessel—a really urgent work, since it was for the purpose of depositing, as soon as possible, at Tabor Island a document indicating Ayrton's new residence.

As the "Bonadventure" no longer existed, six months at least would be required for the construction of a new vessel. Now winter was approaching, and the voyage would not be made before the following spring.

"We have time to get everything ready for the fine season," remarked the engineer, who was consulting with Pencroft about these matters. "I think, therefore, my friend, that since we have to rebuild our vessel it will be best to give her larger dimensions. The arrival of the Scotch yacht at Tabor Island is very uncertain. It may even be that, having arrived several months ago, she has again sailed after having vainly searched for some trace of Ayrton. Will it not then be best to build a ship which, if necessary, could take us either to the Polynesian Archipelago or to New Zealand? What do you think?"

"I think, captain," answered the sailor; "I think that you are as capable of building a large vessel as a small one. Neither the wood nor the tools are wanting. It is only a question of time."

"And how many months would be required to build a vessel of from 250 to 300 tons?" asked Harding.

"Seven or eight months at least," replied Pencroft. "But it must not be forgotten that winter is drawing near, and that in severe frost wood is difficult to work. We must calculate on several weeks delay, and if our vessel is ready by next November we may think ourselves very lucky."

"Well," replied Cyrus Harding, "that will be exactly the most favorable time for undertaking a voyage of any importance, either to Tabor Island or to a more distant land."

"So it will, captain," answered the sailor. "Make out your plans then; the workmen are ready, and I imagine that Ayrton can lend us a good helping hand."

The colonists, having been consulted, approved the engineer's plan, and it was, indeed, the best thing to be done. It is true that the construction of a ship of from two to three hundred tons would be great labor, but the colonists had confidence in themselves, justified by their previous success.

Cyrus Harding then busied himself in drawing the plan of the vessel and making the model. During this time his companions employed themselves in felling and carting trees to furnish the ribs, timbers, and planks. The forest of the Far West supplied the best oaks and elms. They took advantage of the opening already made on their last excursion to form a practicable road, which they named the Far West Road, and the trees were carried to the Chimneys, where the dockyard was established. As to the road in question, the choice of trees had rendered its direction somewhat capricious, but at the same time it facilitated the access to a large part of the Serpentine Peninsula.

It was important that the trees should be quickly felled and cut up, for they could not be used while yet green, and some time was necessary to allow them to get seasoned. The carpenters, therefore, worked vigorously during the month of April, which was troubled only by a few equinoctial gales of some violence. Master Jup aided them dexterously, either by climbing to the top of a tree to fasten the ropes or by lending his stout shoulders to carry the lopped trunks.

All this timber was piled up under a large shed, built near the Chimneys, and there awaited the time for use.

The month of April was tolerably fine, as October often is in the northern zone. At the same time other work was actively continued, and soon all trace of devastation disappeared from the plateau of Prospect Heights. The mill was rebuilt, and new buildings rose in the poultry-yard. It had appeared necessary to enlarge their dimensions, for the feathered population had increased considerably. The stable now contained five onagers, four of which were well broken, and allowed themselves to be either driven or ridden, and a little colt. The colony now possessed a plow, to which the onagers were yoked like regular Yorkshire or Kentucky oxen. The colonists divided their work, and their arms never tired. Then who could have enjoyed better health than these workers, and what good humor enlivened the evenings in Granite House as they formed a thousand plans for the future!

As a matter of course Ayrton shared the common lot in every respect, and there was no longer any talk of his going to live at the corral. Nevertheless he was still sad and reserved, and joined more in the work than in the pleasures of his companions. But he was a valuable workman at need—strong, skilful, ingenious, intelligent. He was esteemed and loved by all, and he could not be ignorant of it.

In the meanwhile the corral was not abandoned. Every other day one of the settlers, driving the cart or mounted on an onager, went to look after the flock of musmons and goats and bring back the supply of milk required by Neb. These excursions at the same time afforded opportunities for hunting. Therefore Herbert and Gideon Spilett, with Top in front, traversed more often than their companions the road to the corral, and with the capital guns which they carried, capybaras, agouties, kangaroos, and wild pigs for large game, ducks, grouse, jacamars, and snipe for small game, were never wanting in the house. The produce of the warren, of the oyster-bed, several turtles which were taken, excellent salmon which came up the Mercy, vegetables from the plateau, wild fruit from the forest, were riches upon riches, and Neb, the head cook, could scarcely by himself store them away.

The telegraphic wire between the corral and Granite House had of course been repaired, and it was worked whenever one or other of the settlers was at the corral and found it necessary to spend the night there. Besides, the island was safe now and no attacks were to be feared, at any rate from men.

However, that which had happened might happen again. A descent of pirates, or even of escaped convicts, was always to be feared. It was possible that companions or accomplices of Bob Harvey had been in the secret of his plans, and might be tempted to imitate him. The colonists, therefore, were careful to observe the sea around the island, and every day their telescope covered the horizon enclosed by Union and Washington Bays. When they went to the corral they examined the sea to the west with no less attention, and by climbing the spur their gaze extended over a large section of the western horizon.

Nothing suspicious was discerned, but still it was necessary for them to be on their guard.

The engineer one evening imparted to his friends a plan which he had conceived for fortifying the corral. It appeared prudent to him to heighten the palisade and to flank it with a sort of blockhouse, which, if necessary, the settlers could hold against the enemy. Granite House might, by its very position, be considered impregnable; therefore the corral with its buildings, its stores, and the animals it contained, would always be the object of pirates, whoever they were, who might land on the island, and should the colonists be obliged to shut themselves up there they ought also to be able to defend themselves without any disadvantage. This was a project which might be left for consideration, and they were, besides, obliged to put off its execution until the next spring.

About the 15th of May the keel of the new vessel lay along the dockyard, and soon the stem and stern-post, mortised at each of its extremities, rose almost perpendicularly. The keel, of good oak, measured 110 feet in length, this allowing a width of five-and-twenty feet to the midship beam. But this was all the carpenters could do before the arrival of the frosts and bad weather. During the following week they fixed the first of the stern timbers, but were then obliged to suspend work.

During the last days of the month the weather was extremely bad. The wind blew from the east, sometimes with the violence of a tempest. The engineer was somewhat uneasy on account of the dockyard shed—which besides, he could not have established in any other place near to Granite House—for the islet only imperfectly sheltered the shore from the fury of the open sea, and in great storms the waves beat against the very foot of the granite cliff.

But, very fortunately, these fears were not realized. The wind shifted to the southeast, and there the beach of Granite House was completely covered by Flotsam Point.

Pencroft and Ayrton, the most zealous workmen at the new vessel, pursued their labor as long as they could. They were not men to mind the wind tearing at their hair, nor the rain wetting them to the skin, and a blow from a hammer is worth just as much in bad as in fine weather. But when a severe frost succeeded this wet period, the wood, its fibers acquiring the hardness of iron, became extremely difficult to work, and about the 10th of June shipbuilding was obliged to be entirely discontinued.

Cyrus Harding and his companions had not omitted to observe how severe was the temperature during the winters of Lincoln Island. The cold was comparable to that experienced in the States of New England, situated at almost the same distance from the equator. In the northern hemisphere, or at any rate in the part occupied by British America and the north of the United States, this phenomenon is explained by the flat conformation of the territories bordering on the pole, and on which there is no intumescence of the soil to oppose any obstacle to the north winds; here, in Lincoln Island, this explanation would not suffice.

"It has even been observed," remarked Harding one day to his companions, "that in equal latitudes the islands and coast regions are less tried by the cold than inland countries. I have often heard it asserted that the winters of Lombardy, for example, are not less rigorous than those of Scotland, which results from the sea restoring during the winter the heat which it received during the summer. Islands are, therefore, in a better situation for benefiting by this restitution."

"But then, Captain Harding," asked Herbert, "why does Lincoln Island appear to escape the common law?"

"That is difficult to explain," answered the engineer. "However, I should be disposed to conjecture that this peculiarity results from the situation of the island in the Southern Hemisphere, which, as you know, my boy, is colder than the Northern Hemisphere."

"Yes," said Herbert, "and icebergs are met with in lower latitudes in the south than in the north of the Pacific."

"That is true," remarked Pencroft, "and when I have been serving on board whalers I have seen icebergs off Cape Horn."

"The severe cold experienced in Lincoln Island," said Gideon Spilett, "may then perhaps be explained by the presence of floes or icebergs comparatively near to Lincoln Island."

"Your opinion is very admissible indeed, my dear Spilett," answered Cyrus Harding, "and it is evidently to the proximity of icebergs that we owe our rigorous winters. I would draw your attention also to an entirely physical cause, which renders the Southern colder than the Northern Hemisphere. In fact, since the sun is nearer to this hemisphere during the summer, it is necessarily more distant during the winter. This explains then the excess of temperature in the two seasons, for, if we find the winters very cold in Lincoln Island, we must not forget that the summers here, on the contrary, are very hot."

"But why, if you please, captain," asked Pencroft, knitting his brows, "why should our hemisphere, as you say, be so badly divided? It isn't just, that!"

"Friend Pencroft," answered the engineer, laughing, "whether just or not, we must submit to it, and here lies the reason for this peculiarity. The earth does not describe a circle around the sun, but an ellipse, as it must by the laws of rational mechanics. Now, the earth occupies one of the foci of the ellipse, and so at one point in its course is at its apogee, that is, at its farthest from the sun, and at another point it is at its perigee, or nearest to the sun. Now it happens that it is during the winter of the southern countries that it is at its most distant point from the sun, and consequently, in a situation for those regions to feel the greatest cold. Nothing can be done to prevent that, and men, Pencroft, however learned they may be, can never change anything of the cosmographical order established by God Himself."

"And yet," added Pencroft, "the world is very learned. What a big book, captain, might be made with all that is known!"

"And what a much bigger book still with all that is not known!" answered Harding.

At last, for one reason or another, the month of June brought the cold with its accustomed intensity, and the settlers were often confined to Granite House. Ah! how wearisome this imprisonment was to them, and more particularly to Gideon Spilett.

"Look here," said he to Neb one day, "I would give you by notarial deed all the estates which will come to me some day, if you were a good enough fellow to go, no matter where, and subscribe to some newspaper for me! Decidedly the thing that is most essential to my happiness is the knowing every morning what has happened the day before in other places than this!"

Neb began to laugh.

"'Pon my word," he replied, "the only thing I think about is my daily work!"

The truth was that indoors as well as out there was no want of work.

The colony of Lincoln Island was now at its highest point of prosperity, achieved by three years of continued hard work. The destruction of the brig had been a new source of riches. Without speaking of the complete rig which would serve for the vessel now on the stocks, utensils and tools of all sorts, weapons and ammunition, clothes and instruments, were now piled in the storerooms of Granite House. It had not even been necessary to resort again to the manufacture of the coarse felt materials. Though the colonists had suffered from cold during their first winter, the bad season might now come without their having any reason to dread its severity. Linen was plentiful also, and besides, they kept it with extreme care. From chloride of sodium, which is nothing else than sea salt, Cyrus Harding easily extracted the soda and chlorine. The soda, which it was easy to change into carbonate of soda, and the chlorine, of which he made chloride of lime, were employed for various domestic purposes, and especially in bleaching linen. Besides, they did not wash more than four times a year, as was done by families in the olden times, and it may be added, that Pencroft and Gideon Spilett, while waiting for the postman to bring him his newspaper, distinguished themselves as washermen.

So passed the winter months, June, July, and August. They were severe, and the average observations of the thermometer did not give more than eight degrees of Fahrenheit. It was therefore lower in temperature than the preceding winter. But then, what splendid fires blazed continually on the hearths of Granite House, the smoke marking the granite wall with long, zebra-like streaks! Fuel was not spared, as it grew naturally a few steps from them. Besides, the chips of the wood destined for the construction of the ship enabled them to economize the coal, which required more trouble to transport.

Men and animals were all well. Master Jup was a little chilly, it must be confessed. This was perhaps his only weakness, and it was necessary to make him a well-padded dressing-gown. But what a servant he was, clever, zealous, indefatigable, not indiscreet, not talkative, and he might have been with reason proposed as a model for all his biped brothers in the Old and New Worlds!

"As for that," said Pencroft, "when one has four hands at one's service, of course one's work ought to be done so much the better!"

And indeed the intelligent creature did it well.

During the seven months which had passed since the last researches made round the mountain, and during the month of September, which brought back fine weather, nothing was heard of the genius of the island. His power was not manifested in any way. It is true that it would have been superfluous, for no incident occurred to put the colonists to any painful trial.

Cyrus Harding even observed that if by chance the communication between the unknown and the tenants of Granite House had ever been established through the granite, and if Top's instinct had as it were felt it, there was no further sign of it during this period. The dog's growling had entirely ceased, as well as the uneasiness of the orang. The two friends—for they were such—no longer prowled round the opening of the inner well, nor did they bark or whine in that singular way which from the first the engineer had noticed. But could he be sure that this was all that was to be said about this enigma, and that he should never arrive at a solution? Could he be certain that some conjuncture would not occur which would bring the mysterious personage on the scene? who could tell what the future might have in reserve?

At last the winter was ended, but an event, the consequences of which might be serious occurred in the first days of the returning spring.

On the 7th of September, Cyrus Harding, having observed the crater, saw smoke curling round the summit of the mountain, its first vapors rising in the air.

Chapter 15

The colonists, warned by the engineer, left their work and gazed in silence at the summit of Mount Franklin.

The volcano had awoke, and the vapor had penetrated the mineral layer heaped at the bottom of the crater. But would the subterranean fires provoke any violent eruption? This was an event which could not be foreseen. However, even while admitting the possibility of an eruption, it was not probable that the whole of Lincoln Island would suffer from it. The flow of volcanic matter is not always disastrous, and the island had already undergone this trial, as was shown by the streams of lava hardened on the northern slopes of the mountain. Besides, from the shape of the crater—the opening broken in the upper edge—the matter would be thrown to the side opposite the fertile regions of the island.

However, the past did not necessarily answer for the future. Often, at the summit of volcanoes, the old craters close and new ones open. This had occurred in the two hemispheres—at Etna, Popocatepetl, at Orizabaand on the eve of an eruption there is everything to be feared. In fact, an earthquake—a phenomenon which often accompanies volcanic eruption—is enough to change the interior arrangement of a mountain, and to open new outlets for the burning lava.

Cyrus Harding explained these things to his companions, and, without exaggerating the state of things, he told them all the pros and cons. After all, they could not prevent it. It did not appear likely that Granite House would be threatened unless the ground was shaken by an earthquake. But the corral would be in great danger should a new crater open in the southern side of Mount Franklin.

From that day the smoke never disappeared from the top of the mountain, and it could even be perceived that it increased in height and thickness, without any flame mingling in its heavy volumes. The phenomenon was still concentrated in the lower part of the central crater.

However, with the fine days work had been continued. The building of the vessel was hastened as much as possible, and, by means of the waterfall on the shore, Cyrus Harding managed to establish an hydraulic sawmill, which rapidly cut up the trunks of trees into planks and joists. The mechanism of this apparatus was as simple as those used in the rustic sawmills of Norway. A first horizontal movement to move the piece of wood, a second vertical movement to move the saw—this was all that was wanted; and the engineer succeeded by means of a wheel, two cylinders, and pulleys properly arranged. Towards the end of the month of September the skeleton of the vessel, which was to be rigged as a schooner, lay in the dockyard. The ribs were almost entirely completed, and, all the timbers having been sustained by a provisional band, the shape of the vessel could already be seen. The schooner, sharp in the bows, very slender in the after-part, would evidently be suitable for a long voyage, if wanted; but laying the planking would still take a considerable time. Very fortunately, the iron work of the pirate brig had been saved after the explosion. From the planks and injured ribs Pencroft and Ayrton had extracted the bolts and a large quantity of copper nails. It was so much work saved for the smiths, but the carpenters had much to do.

Shipbuilding was interrupted for a week for the harvest, the haymaking, and the gathering in of the different crops on the plateau. This work finished, every moment was devoted to finishing the schooner. When night came the workmen were really quite exhausted. So as not to lose any time they had changed the hours for their meals; they dined at twelve o'clock, and only had their supper when daylight failed them. They then ascended to Granite House, when they were always ready to go to bed.

Sometimes, however, when the conversation bore on some interesting subject the hour for sleep was delayed for a time. The colonists then spoke of the future, and talked willingly of the changes which a voyage in the schooner to inhabited lands would make in their situation. But always, in the midst of these plans, prevailed the thought of a subsequent return to Lincoln Island. Never would they abandon this colony, founded with so much labor and with such success, and to which a communication with America would afford a fresh impetus. Pencroft and Neb especially hoped to end their days there.

"Herbert," said the sailor, "you will never abandon Lincoln Island?"

"Never, Pencroft, and especially if you make up your mind to stay there."

"That was made up long ago, my boy," answered Pencroft. "I shall expect you. You will bring me your wife and children, and I shall make jolly chaps of your youngsters!"

"That's agreed," replied Herbert, laughing and blushing at the same time.

"And you, Captain Harding," resumed Pencroft enthusiastically, "you will be still the governor of the island! Ah, how many inhabitants could it support? Ten thousand at least!"

They talked in this way, allowing Pencroft to run on, and at last the reporter actually started a newspaper—the New Lincoln Herald!

So is man's heart. The desire to perform a work which will endure, which will survive him, is the origin of his superiority over all other living creatures here below. It is this which has established his dominion, and this it is which justifies it, over all the world.

After that, who knows if Jup and Top had not themselves their little dream of the future.

Ayrton silently said to himself that he would like to see Lord Glenarvan again and show himself to all restored.

One evening, on the 15th of October, the conversation was prolonged later than usual. It was nine o'clock. Already, long badly concealed yawns gave warning of the hour of rest, and Pencroft was proceeding towards his bed, when the electric bell, placed in the dining-room, suddenly rang.

All were there, Cyrus Harding, Gideon Spilett, Herbert, Ayrton, Pencroft, Neb. Therefore none of the colonists were at the corral.

Cyrus Harding rose. His companions stared at each other, scarcely believing their ears.

"What does that mean?" cried Neb. "Was it the devil who rang it?"

No one answered.

"The weather is stormy," observed Herbert. "Might not its influence of electricity—"

Herbert did not finish his phrase. The engineer, towards whom all eyes were turned, shook his head negatively.

"We must wait," said Gideon Spilett. "If it is a signal, whoever it may be who has made it, he will renew it."

"But who do you think it is?" cried Neb.

"Who?" answered Pencroft, "but he—"

The sailor's sentence was cut short by a new tinkle of the bell.

Harding went to the apparatus, and sent this question to the corral:—

"What do you want?"

A few moments later the needle, moving on the alphabetic dial, gave this reply to the tenants of Granite House:—

"Come to the corral immediately."

"At last!" exclaimed Harding.

Yes! At last! The mystery was about to be unveiled. The colonists' fatigue had disappeared before the tremendous interest which was about to urge them to the corral, and all wish for rest had ceased. Without having uttered a word, in a few moments they had left Granite House, and were standing on the beach. Jup and Top alone were left behind. They could do without them.

The night was black. The new moon had disappeared at the same time as the sun. As Herbert had observed, great stormy clouds formed a lowering and heavy vault, preventing any star rays. A few lightning flashes, reflections from a distant storm, illuminated the horizon.

It was possible that a few hours later the thunder would roll over the island itself. The night was very threatening.

But however deep the darkness was, it would not prevent them from finding the familiar road to the corral.

They ascended the left bank of the Mercy, reached the plateau, passed the bridge over Creek Glycerine, and advanced through the forest.

They walked at a good pace, a prey to the liveliest emotions. There was no doubt but that they were now going to learn the long-searched-for answer to the enigma, the name of that mysterious being, so deeply concerned in their life, so generous in his influence, so powerful in his action! Must not this stranger have indeed mingled with their existence, have known the smallest details, have heard all that was said in Granite House, to have been able always to act in the very nick of time?

Every one, wrapped up in his own reflections, pressed forward. Under the arch of trees the darkness was such that even the edge of the road could not be seen. Not a sound in the forest. Both animals and birds, influenced by the heaviness of the atmosphere, remained motionless and silent. Not a breath disturbed the leaves. The footsteps of the colonists alone resounded on the hardened ground.

During the first quarter of an hour the silence was only interrupted by this remark from Pencroft:—

"We ought to have brought a torch."

And by this reply from the engineer:—

"We shall find one at the corral."

Harding and his companions had left Granite House at twelve minutes past nine. At forty-seven minutes past nine they had traversed three out of the five miles which separated the mouth of the Mercy from the corral.

At that moment sheets of lightning spread over the island and illumined the dark trees. The flashes dazzled and almost blinded them. Evidently the storm would not be long in bursting forth.

The flashes gradually became brighter and more rapid. Distant thunder growled in the sky. The atmosphere was stifling.

The colonists proceeded as if they were urged onwards by some irresistible force.

At ten o'clock a vivid flash showed them the palisade, and as they reached the gate the storm burst forth with tremendous fury.

In a minute the corral was crossed, and Harding stood before the hut.

Probably the house was occupied by the stranger, since it was from thence that the telegram had been sent. However, no light shone through the window.

The engineer knocked at the door.

No answer.

Cyrus Harding opened the door, and the settlers entered the room, which was perfectly dark. A light was struck by Neb, and in a few moments the lantern was lighted and the light thrown into every corner of the room.

There was no one there. Everything was in the state in which it had been left.

"Have we been deceived by an illusion?" murmured Cyrus Harding.

No! that was not possible! The telegram had clearly said,—

"Come to the corral immediately."

They approached the table specially devoted to the use of the wire. Everything was in order—the pile on the box containing it, as well as all the apparatus.

"Who came here the last time?" asked the engineer.

"I did, captain," answered Ayrton.

"And that was—"

"Four days ago."

"Ah! a note!" cried Herbert, pointing to a paper lying on the table.

On this paper were written these words in English:—

"Follow the new wire."

"Forward!" cried Harding, who understood that the despatch had not been sent from the corral, but from the mysterious retreat, communicating directly with Granite House by means of a supplementary wire joined to the old one.

Neb took the lighted lantern, and all left the corral. The storm then burst forth with tremendous violence. The interval between each lightning-flash and each thunder-clap diminished rapidly. The summit of the volcano, with its plume of vapor, could be seen by occasional flashes.

There was no telegraphic communication in any part of the corral between the house and the palisade; but the engineer, running straight to the first post, saw by the light of a flash a new wire hanging from the isolator to the ground.

"There it is!" said he.

This wire lay along the ground, and was surrounded with an isolating substance like a submarine cable, so as to assure the free transmission of the current. It appeared to pass through the wood and the southern spurs of the mountain, and consequently it ran towards the west.

"Follow it!" said Cyrus Harding.

And the settlers immediately pressed forward, guided by the wire.

The thunder continued to roar with such violence that not a word could be heard. However, there was no occasion for speaking, but to get forward as fast as possible.

Cyrus Harding and his companions then climbed the spur rising between the corral valley and that of Falls River, which they crossed at its narrowest part. The wire, sometimes stretched over the lower branches of the trees, sometimes lying on the ground, guided them surely. The engineer had supposed that the wire would perhaps stop at the bottom of the valley, and that the stranger's retreat would be there.

Nothing of the sort. They were obliged to ascend the south-western spur, and re-descend on that arid plateau terminated by the strangely-wild basalt cliff. From time to time one of the colonists stooped down and felt for the wire with his hands; but there was now no doubt that the wire was running directly towards the sea. There, to a certainty, in the depths of those rocks, was the dwelling so long sought for in vain.

The sky was literally on fire. Flash succeeded flash. Several struck the summit of the volcano in the midst of the thick smoke. It appeared there as if the mountain was vomiting flame. At a few minutes to eleven the colonists arrived on the high cliff overlooking the ocean to the west. The wind had risen. The surf roared 500 feet below.

Harding calculated that they had gone a mile and a half from the corral.

At this point the wire entered among the rocks, following the steep side of a narrow ravine. The settlers followed it at the risk of occasioning a fall of the slightly-balanced rocks, and being dashed into the sea. The descent was extremely perilous, but they did not think of the danger; they were no longer masters of themselves, and an irresistible attraction drew them towards this mysterious place as the magnet draws iron.

Thus they almost unconsciously descended this ravine, which even in broad daylight would have been considered impracticable.

The stones rolled and sparkled like fiery balls when they crossed through the gleams of light. Harding was first—Ayrton last. On they went, step by step. Now they slid over the slippery rock; then they struggled to their feet and scrambled on.

At last the wire touched the rocks on the beach. The colonists had reached the bottom of the basalt cliff.

There appeared a narrow ridge, running horizontally and parallel with the sea. The settlers followed the wire along it. They had not gone a hundred paces when the ridge by a moderate incline sloped down to the level of the sea.

The engineer seized the wire and found that it disappeared beneath the waves. His companions were stupefied.

A cry of disappointment, almost a cry of despair, escaped them! Must they then plunge beneath the water and seek there for some submarine cavern? In their excited state they would not have hesitated to do it.

The engineer stopped them.

He led his companions to a hollow in the rocks, and there—

"We must wait," said he. "The tide is high. At low water the way will be open."

"But what can make you think-" asked Pencroft.

"He would not have called us if the means had been wanting to enable us to reach him!"

Cyrus Harding spoke in a tone of such thorough conviction that no objection was raised. His remark, besides, was logical. It was quite possible that an opening, practicable at low water, though hidden now by the high tide, opened at the foot of the cliff.

There was some time to wait. The colonists remained silently crouching in a deep hollow. Rain now began to fall in torrents. The thunder was re-echoed among the rocks with a grand sonorousness.

The colonists' emotion was great. A thousand strange and extraordinary ideas crossed their brains, and they expected some grand and superhuman apparition, which alone could come up to the notion they had formed of the mysterious genius of the island.

At midnight, Harding carrying the lantern, descended to the beach to reconnoiter.

The engineer was not mistaken. The beginning of an immense excavation could be seen under the water. There the wire, bending at a right angle, entered the yawning gulf.

Cyrus Harding returned to his companions, and said simply,—

"In an hour the opening will be practicable."

"It is there, then?" said Pencroft.

"Did you doubt it?" returned Harding.

"But this cavern must be filled with water to a certain height," observed Herbert.

"Either the cavern will be completely dry," replied Harding, "and in that case we can traverse it on foot, or it will not be dry, and some means of transport will be put at our disposal."

An hour passed. All climbed down through the rain to the level of the sea. There was now eight feet of the opening above the water. It was like the arch of a bridge, under which rushed the foaming water.

Leaning forward, the engineer saw a black object floating on the water. He drew it towards him. It was a boat, moored to some interior projection of the cave. This boat was iron-plated. Two oars lay at the bottom.

"Jump in!" said Harding.

In a moment the settlers were in the boat. Neb and Ayrton took the oars, Pencroft the rudder. Cyrus Harding in the bows, with the lantern, lighted the way.

The elliptical roof, under which the boat at first passed, suddenly rose; but the darkness was too deep, and the light of the lantern too slight, for either the extent, length, height, or depth of the cave to be ascertained. Solemn silence reigned in this basaltic cavern. Not a sound could penetrate into it, even the thunder peals could not pierce its thick sides.

Such immense caves exist in various parts of the world, natural crypts dating from the geological epoch of the globe. Some are filled by the sea; others contain entire lakes in their sides. Such is Fingal's Cave, in the island of Staffa, one of the Hebrides; such are the caves of Morgat, in the bay of Douarnenez, in Brittany, the caves of Bonifacio, in Corsica, those of Lyse-Fjord, in Norway; such are the immense Mammoth caverns in Kentucky, 500 feet in height, and more than twenty miles in length! In many parts of the globe, nature has excavated these caverns, and preserved them for the admiration of man.

Did the cavern which the settlers were now exploring extend to the center of the island? For a quarter of an hour the boat had been advancing, making detours, indicated to Pencroft by the engineer in short sentences, when all at once,—

"More to the right!" he commanded.

The boat, altering its course, came up alongside the right wall. The engineer wished to see if the wire still ran along the side.

The wire was there fastened to the rock.

"Forward!" said Harding.

And the two oars, plunging into the dark waters, urged the boat onwards.

On they went for another quarter of an hour, and a distance of half-a-mile must have been cleared from the mouth of the cave, when Harding's voice was again heard.

"Stop!" said he.

The boat stopped, and the colonists perceived a bright light illuminating the vast cavern, so deeply excavated in the bowels of the island, of which nothing had ever led them to suspect the existence.

At a height of a hundred feet rose the vaulted roof, supported on basalt shafts. Irregular arches, strange moldings, appeared on the columns erected by nature in thousands from the first epochs of the formation of the globe. The basalt pillars, fitted one into the other, measured from forty to fifty feet in height, and the water, calm in spite of the tumult outside, washed their base. The brilliant focus of light, pointed out by the engineer, touched every point of rocks, and flooded the walls with light.

By reflection the water reproduced the brilliant sparkles, so that the boat appeared to be floating between two glittering zones. They could not be mistaken in the nature of the irradiation thrown from the glowing nucleus, whose clear rays were shattered by all the angles, all the projections of the cavern. This light proceeded from an electric source, and its white color betrayed its origin. It was the sun of this cave, and it filled it entirely.

At a sign from Cyrus Harding the oars again plunged into the water, causing a regular shower of gems, and the boat was urged forward towards the light, which was now not more than half a cable's length distant.

At this place the breadth of the sheet of water measured nearly 350 feet, and beyond the dazzling center could be seen an enormous basaltic wall, blocking up any issue on that side. The cavern widened here considerably, the sea forming a little lake. But the roof, the side walls, the end cliff, all the prisms, all the peaks, were flooded with the electric fluid, so that the brilliancy belonged to them, and as if the light issued from them.

In the center of the lake a long cigar-shaped object floated on the surface of the water, silent, motionless. The brilliancy which issued from it escaped from its sides as from two kilns heated to a white heat. This apparatus, similar in shape to an enormous whale, was about 250 feet long, and rose about ten or twelve above the water.

The boat slowly approached it, Cyrus Harding stood up in the bows. He gazed, a prey to violent excitement. Then, all at once, seizing the reporter's arm,—

"It is he! It can only be he!" he cried, "he!—"

Then, falling back on the seat, he murmured a name which Gideon Spilett alone could hear.

The reporter evidently knew this name, for it had a wonderful effect upon him, and he answered in a hoarse voice,—

"He! an outlawed man!"

"He!" said Harding.

At the engineer's command the boat approached this singular floating apparatus. The boat touched the left side, from which escaped a ray of light through a thick glass.

Harding and his companions mounted on the platform. An open hatchway was there. All darted down the opening.

At the bottom of the ladder was a deck, lighted by electricity. At the end of this deck was a door, which Harding opened.

A richly-ornamented room, quickly traversed by the colonists, was joined to a library, over which a luminous ceiling shed a flood of light.

At the end of the library a large door, also shut, was opened by the engineer.

An immense saloon—a sort of museum, in which were heaped up, with all the treasures of the mineral world, works of art, marvels of industry—appeared before the eyes of the colonists, who almost thought themselves suddenly transported into a land of enchantment.

Stretched on a rich sofa they saw a man, who did not appear to notice their presence.

Then Harding raised his voice, and to the extreme surprise of his companions, he uttered these words,—

"Captain Nemo, you asked for us! We are here.—"

Chapter 16

At these words the reclining figure rose, and the electric light fell upon his countenance; a magnificent head, the forehead high, the glance commanding, beard white, hair abundant and falling over the shoulders.

His hand rested upon the cushion of the divan from which he had just risen. He appeared perfectly calm. It was evident that his strength had been gradually undermined by illness, but his voice seemed yet powerful, as he said in English, and in a tone which evinced extreme surprise,—

"Sir, I have no name."

"Nevertheless, I know you!" replied Cyrus Harding.

Captain Nemo fixed his penetrating gaze upon the engineer, as though he were about to annihilate him.

Then, falling back amid the pillows of the divan,—

"After all, what matters now?" he murmured; "I am dying!"

Cyrus Harding drew near the captain, and Gideon Spilett took his hand—it was of a feverish heat. Ayrton, Pencroft, Herbert, and Neb stood respectfully apart in an angle of the magnificent saloon, whose atmosphere was saturated with the electric fluid.

Meanwhile Captain Nemo withdrew his hand, and motioned the engineer and the reporter to be seated.

All regarded him with profound emotion. Before them they beheld that being whom they had styled the "genius of the island," the powerful protector whose intervention, in so many circumstances, had been so efficacious, the benefactor to whom they owed such a debt of gratitude! Their eyes beheld a man only, and a man at the point of death, where Pencroft and Neb had expected to find an almost supernatural being!

But how happened it that Cyrus Harding had recognized Captain Nemo? why had the latter so suddenly risen on hearing this name uttered, a name which he had believed known to none?—

The captain had resumed his position on the divan, and leaning on his arm, he regarded the engineer, seated near him.

"You know the name I formerly bore, sir?" he asked.

"I do," answered Cyrus Harding, "and also that of this wonderful submarine vessel—"

"The 'Nautilus'?" said the captain, with a faint smile.

"The 'Nautilus.'"

"But do you—do you know who I am?"

"I do."

"It is nevertheless many years since I have held any communication with the inhabited world; three long years have I passed in the depth of the sea, the only place where I have found liberty! Who then can have betrayed my secret?"

"A man who was bound to you by no tie, Captain Nemo, and who, consequently, cannot be accused of treachery."

"The Frenchman who was cast on board my vessel by chance sixteen years since?"

"The same."

"He and his two companions did not then perish in the maelstrom, in the midst of which the 'Nautilus' was struggling?"

"They escaped, and a book has appeared under the title of 'Twenty Thousand Leagues Under the Sea,' which contains your history."

"The history of a few months only of my life!" interrupted the captain impetuously.

"It is true," answered Cyrus Harding, "but a few months of that strange life have sufficed to make you known."

"As a great criminal, doubtless!" said Captain Nemo, a haughty smile curling his lips. "Yes, a rebel, perhaps an outlaw against humanity!"

The engineer was silent.

"Well, sir?"

"It is not for me to judge you, Captain Nemo," answered Cyrus Harding, "at any rate as regards your past life. I am, with the rest of the world, ignorant of the motives which induced you to adopt this strange mode of existence, and I cannot judge of effects without knowing their causes; but what I do know is, that a beneficent hand has constantly protected us since our arrival on Lincoln Island, that we all owe our lives to a good, generous, and powerful being, and that this being so powerful, good and generous, Captain Nemo, is yourself!"

"It is I," answered the captain simply.

The engineer and the reporter rose. Their companions had drawn near, and the gratitude with which their hearts were charged was about to express itself in their gestures and words.

Captain Nemo stopped them by a sign, and in a voice which betrayed more emotion than he doubtless intended to show.

"Wait till you have heard all," he said.

And the captain, in a few concise sentences, ran over the events of his life.

His narrative was short, yet he was obliged to summon up his whole remaining energy to arrive at the end. He was evidently contending against extreme weakness. Several times Cyrus Harding entreated him to repose for a while, but he shook his head as a man to whom the morrow may never come, and when the reporter offered his assistance,—

"It is useless," he said; "my hours are numbered."

Captain Nemo was an Indian, the Prince Dakkar, son of a rajah of the then independent territory of Bundelkund. His father sent him, when ten years of age, to Europe, in order that he might receive an education in all respects complete, and in the hopes that by his talents and knowledge he might one day take a leading part in raising his long degraded and heathen country to a level with the nations of Europe.

From the age of ten years to that of thirty Prince Dakkar, endowed by Nature with her richest gifts of intellect, accumulated knowledge of every kind, and in science, literature, and art his researches were extensive and profound.

He traveled over the whole of Europe. His rank and fortune caused him to be everywhere sought after; but the pleasures of the world had for him no attractions. Though young and possessed of every personal advantage, he was ever grave—somber even—devoured by an unquenchable thirst for knowledge, and cherishing in the recesses of his heart the hope that he might become a great and powerful ruler of a free and enlightened people.

Still, for long the love of science triumphed over all other feelings. He became an artist deeply impressed by the marvels of art, a philosopher to whom no one of the higher sciences was unknown, a statesman versed in the policy of European courts. To the eyes of those who observed him superficially he might have passed for one of those cosmopolitans, curious of knowledge, but disdaining action; one of those opulent travelers, haughty and cynical, who move incessantly from place to place, and are of no country.

The history of Captain Nemo has, in fact, been published under the title of "Twenty Thousand Leagues Under the Sea." Here, therefore, will apply the observation already made as to the adventures of Ayrton with regard to the discrepancy of dates. Readers should therefore refer to the note already published on this point.

This artist, this philosopher, this man was, however, still cherishing the hope instilled into him from his earliest days.

Prince Dakkar returned to Bundelkund in the year 1849. He married a noble Indian lady, who was imbued with an ambition not less ardent than that by which he was inspired. Two children were born to them, whom they tenderly loved. But domestic happiness did not prevent him from seeking to carry out the object at which he aimed. He waited an opportunity. At length, as he vainly fancied, it presented itself.

Instigated by princes equally ambitious and less sagacious and more unscrupulous than he was, the people of India were persuaded that they might successfully rise against their English rulers, who had brought them out of a state of anarchy and constant warfare and misery, and had established peace and prosperity in their country. Their ignorance and gross superstition made them the facile tools of their designing chiefs.

In 1857 the great sepoy revolt broke out. Prince Dakkar, under the belief that he should thereby have the opportunity of attaining the object of his long-cherished ambition, was easily drawn into it. He forthwith devoted his talents and wealth to the service of this cause. He aided it in person; he fought in the front ranks; he risked his life equally with the humblest of the wretched and misguided fanatics; he was ten times wounded in twenty engagements, seeking death but finding it not, but at length the sanguinary rebels were utterly defeated, and the atrocious mutiny was brought to an end.

Never before had the British power in India been exposed to such danger, and if, as they had hoped, the sepoys had received assistance from without, the influence and supremacy in Asia of the United Kingdom would have been a thing of the past.

The name of Prince Dakkar was at that time well known. He had fought openly and without concealment. A price was set upon his head, but he managed to escape from his pursuers.

Civilization never recedes; the law of necessity ever forces it onwards. The sepoys were vanquished, and the land of the rajahs of old fell again under the rule of England.

Prince Dakkar, unable to find that death he courted, returned to the mountain fastnesses of Bundelkund. There, alone in the world, overcome by disappointment at the destruction of all his vain hopes, a prey to profound disgust for all human beings, filled with hatred of the civilized world, he realized the wreck of his fortune, assembled some score of his most faithful companions, and one day disappeared, leaving no trace behind.

Where, then, did he seek that liberty denied him upon the inhabited earth? Under the waves, in the depths of the ocean, where none could follow.

The warrior became the man of science. Upon a deserted island of the Pacific he established his dockyard, and there a submarine vessel was constructed from his designs. By methods which will at some future day be revealed he had rendered subservient the illimitable forces of electricity, which, extracted from inexhaustible sources, was employed for all the requirements of his floating equipage, as a moving, lighting, and heating agent. The sea, with its countless treasures, its myriads of fish, its numberless wrecks, its enormous mammalia, and not only all that nature supplied, but also all that man had lost in its depths, sufficed for every want of the prince and his crew—and thus was his most ardent desire accomplished, never again to hold communication with the earth. He named his submarine vessel the "Nautilus," called himself simply Captain Nemo, and disappeared beneath the seas.

During many years this strange being visited every ocean, from pole to pole. Outcast of the inhabited earth in these unknown worlds he gathered incalculable treasures. The millions lost in the Bay of Vigo, in 1702, by the galleons of Spain, furnished him with a mine of inexhaustible riches which he devoted always, anonymously, in favor of those nations who fought for the independence of their country.

(This refers to the resurrection of the Candiotes, who were, in fact, largely assisted by Captain Nemo.)

For long, however, he had held no communication with his fellow-creatures, when, during the night of the 6th of November, 1866, three men were cast on board his vessel. They were a French professor, his servant, and a Canadian fisherman. These three men had been hurled overboard by a collision which had taken place between the "Nautilus" and the United States frigate "Abraham Lincoln," which had chased her.

Captain Nemo learned from this professor that the "Nautilus," taken now for a gigantic mammal of the whale species, now for a submarine vessel carrying a crew of pirates, was sought for in every sea.

He might have returned these three men to the ocean, from whence chance had brought them in contact with his mysterious existence. Instead of doing this he kept them prisoners, and during seven months they were enabled to behold all the wonders of a voyage of twenty thousand leagues under the sea.

One day, the 22nd of June, 1867, these three men, who knew nothing of the past history of Captain Nemo, succeeded in escaping in one of the "Nautilus's" boats. But as at this time the "Nautilus" was drawn into the vortex of the maelstrom, off the coast of Norway, the captain naturally believed that the fugitives, engulfed in that frightful whirlpool, found their death at the bottom of the abyss. He was unaware that the Frenchman and his two companions had been miraculously cast on shore, that the fishermen of the Lofoten Islands had rendered them assistance, and that the professor, on his return to France, had published that work in which seven months of the strange and eventful navigation of the "Nautilus" were narrated and exposed to the curiosity of the public.

For a long time alter this, Captain Nemo continued to live thus, traversing every sea. But one by one his companions died, and found their last resting-place in their cemetery of coral, in the bed of the Pacific. At last Captain Nemo remained the solitary survivor of all those who had taken refuge with him in the depths of the ocean.

He was now sixty years of age. Although alone, he succeeded in navigating the "Nautilus" towards one of those submarine caverns which had sometimes served him as a harbor.

One of these ports was hollowed beneath Lincoln Island, and at this moment furnished an asylum to the "Nautilus."

The captain had now remained there six years, navigating the ocean no longer, but awaiting death, and that moment when he should rejoin his former companions, when by chance he observed the descent of the balloon which carried the prisoners of the Confederates. Clad in his diving dress he was walking beneath the water at a few cables' length from the shore of the island, when the engineer had been thrown into the sea. Moved by a feeling of compassion the captain saved Cyrus Harding.

His first impulse was to fly from the vicinity of the five castaways; but his harbor refuge was closed, for in consequence of an elevation of the basalt, produced by the influence of volcanic action, he could no longer pass through the entrance of the vault. Though there was sufficient depth of water to allow a light craft to pass the bar, there was not enough for the "Nautilus," whose draught of water was considerable.

Captain Nemo was compelled, therefore, to remain. He observed these men thrown without resources upon a desert island, but had no wish to be himself discovered by them. By degrees he became interested in their efforts when he saw them honest, energetic, and bound to each other by the ties of friendship. As if despite his wishes, he penetrated all the secrets of their existence. By means of the diving dress he could easily reach the well in the interior of Granite House, and climbing by the projections of rock to its upper orifice he heard the colonists as they recounted the past, and studied the present and future. He learned from them the tremendous conflict of America with America itself, for the abolition of slavery. Yes, these men were worthy to reconcile Captain Nemo with that humanity which they represented so nobly in the island.

Captain Nemo had saved Cyrus Harding. It was he also who had brought back the dog to the Chimneys, who rescued Top from the waters of the lake, who caused to fall at Flotsam Point the case containing so many things useful to the colonists, who conveyed the canoe back into the stream of the Mercy, who cast the cord from the top of Granite House at the time of the attack by the baboons, who made known the presence of Ayrton upon Tabor Island, by means of the document enclosed in the bottle, who caused the explosion of the brig by the shock of a torpedo placed at the bottom of the canal, who saved Herbert from certain death by bringing the sulphate of quinine; and finally, it was he who had killed the convicts with the electric balls, of which he possessed the secret, and which he employed in the chase of submarine creatures. Thus were explained so many apparently supernatural occurrences, and which all proved the generosity and power of the captain.

Nevertheless, this noble misanthrope longed to benefit his proteges still further. There yet remained much useful advice to give them, and, his heart being softened by the approach of death, he invited, as we are aware, the colonists of Granite House to visit the "Nautilus," by means of a wire which connected it with the corral. Possibly he would not have done this had he been aware that Cyrus

Harding was sufficiently acquainted with his history to address him by the name of Nemo.

The captain concluded the narrative of his life. Cyrus Harding then spoke; he recalled all the incidents which had exercised so beneficent an influence upon the colony, and in the names of his companions and himself thanked the generous being to whom they owed so much.

But Captain Nemo paid little attention; his mind appeared to be absorbed by one idea, and without taking the proffered hand of the engineer,—

"Now, sir," said he, "now that you know my history, your judgment!"

In saying this, the captain evidently alluded to an important incident witnessed by the three strangers thrown on board his vessel, and which the French professor had related in his work, causing a profound and terrible sensation. Some days previous to the flight of the professor and his two companions, the "Nautilus," being chased by a frigate in the north of the Atlantic had hurled herself as a ram upon this frigate, and sunk her without mercy.

Cyrus Harding understood the captain's allusion, and was silent.

"It was an enemy's frigate," exclaimed Captain Nemo, transformed for an instant into the Prince Dakkar, "an enemy's frigate! It was she who attacked me—I was in a narrow and shallow bay—the frigate barred my way—and I sank her!"

A few moments of silence ensued; then the captain demanded,—

"What think you of my life, gentlemen?"

Cyrus Harding extended his hand to the ci-devant prince and replied gravely, "Sir, your error was in supposing that the past can be resuscitated, and in contending against inevitable progress. It is one of those errors which some admire, others blame; which God alone can judge. He who is mistaken in an action which he sincerely believes to be right may be an enemy, but retains our esteem. Your error is one that we may admire, and your name has nothing to fear from the judgment of history, which does not condemn heroic folly, but its results."

The old man's breast swelled with emotion, and raising his hand to heaven,—

"Was I wrong, or in the right?" he murmured.

Cyrus Harding replied, "All great actions return to God, from whom they are derived. Captain Nemo, we, whom you have succored, shall ever mourn your loss."

Herbert, who had drawn near the captain, fell on his knees and kissed his hand.

A tear glistened in the eyes of the dying man. "My child," he said, "may God bless you!"

Chapter 17

Day had returned. No ray of light penetrated into the profundity of the cavern. It being high-water, the entrance was closed by the sea. But the artificial light, which escaped in long streams from the skylights of the "Nautilus" was as vivid as before, and the sheet of water shone around the floating vessel.

An extreme exhaustion now overcame Captain Nemo, who had fallen back upon the divan. It was useless to contemplate removing him to Granite House, for he had expressed his wish to remain in the midst of those marvels of the "Nautilus" which millions could not have purchased, and to wait there for that death which was swiftly approaching.

During a long interval of prostration, which rendered him almost unconscious, Cyrus Harding and Gideon Spilett attentively observed the condition of the dying man. It was apparent that his strength was gradually diminishing. That frame, once so robust, was now but the fragile tenement of a departing soul. All of life was concentrated in the heart and head.

The engineer and reporter consulted in whispers. Was it possible to render any aid to the dying man? Might his life, if not saved, be prolonged for some days? He himself had said that no remedy could avail, and he awaited with tranquillity that death which had for him no terrors.

"We can do nothing," said Gideon Spilett.

"But of what is he dying?" asked Pencroft.

"Life is simply fading out," replied the reporter.

"Nevertheless," said the sailor, "if we move him into the open air, and the light of the sun, he might perhaps recover."

"No, Pencroft," answered the engineer, "it is useless to attempt it. Besides, Captain Nemo would never consent to leave his vessel. He has lived for a dozen years on board the 'Nautilus,' and on board the 'Nautilus' he desires to die."

Without doubt Captain Nemo heard Cyrus Harding's reply, for he raised himself slightly, and in a voice more feeble, but always intelligible,—

"You are right, sir," he said. "I shall die here—it is my wish; and therefore I have a request to make of you."

Cyrus Harding and his companions had drawn near the divan, and now arranged the cushions in such a manner as to better support the dying man.

They saw his eyes wander over all the marvels of this saloon, lighted by the electric rays which fell from the arabesques of the luminous ceiling. He surveyed, one after the other, the pictures hanging from the splendid tapestries of the partitions, the chef-d'oeuvres of the Italian, Flemish, French, and Spanish masters; the statues of marble and bronze on their pedestals; the magnificent organ, leaning against the after-partition; the aquarium, in which bloomed the most wonderful productions of the sea—marine plants, zoophytes, chaplets of pearls of inestimable value; and, finally, his eyes rested on this device, inscribed over the pediment of the museum—the motto of the "Nautilus"—

"Mobilis in mobile."

His glance seemed to rest fondly for the last time on these masterpieces of art and of nature, to which he had limited his horizon during a sojourn of so many years in the abysses of the seas.

Cyrus Harding respected the captain's silence, and waited till he should speak.

After some minutes, during which, doubtless, he passed in review his whole life, Captain Nemo turned to the colonists and said,

"You consider yourselves, gentlemen, under some obligations to me?"

"Captain, believe us that we would give our lives to prolong yours."

"Promise, then," continued Captain Nemo, "to carry out my last wishes, and I shall be repaid for all I have done for you."

"We promise," said Cyrus Harding.

And by this promise he bound both himself and his companions.

"Gentlemen," resumed the captain, "to-morrow I shall be dead."

Herbert was about to utter an exclamation, but a sign from the captain arrested him.

"To-morrow I shall die, and I desire no other tomb than the 'Nautilus.' It is my grave! All my friends repose in the depths of the ocean; their resting-place shall be mine."

These words were received with profound silence.

"Pay attention to my wishes," he continued. "The 'Nautilus' is imprisoned in this grotto, the entrance of which is blocked up; but, although egress is impossible, the vessel may at least sink in the abyss, and there bury my remains."

The colonists listened reverently to the words of the dying man.

"To-morrow, after my death, Mr. Harding," continued the captain, "yourself and companions will leave the 'Nautilus,' for all the treasures it contains must perish with me. One token alone will remain with you of Prince Dakkar, with whose history you are now acquainted. That coffer yonder contains diamonds of the value of many millions, most of them mementoes of the time when, husband and father, I thought happiness possible for me, and a collection of pearls gathered by my friends and myself in the depths of the ocean. Of this treasure at a future day, you may make good use. In the hands of such men as yourself and your comrades, Captain Harding, money will never be a source of danger. From on high I shall still participate in your enterprises, and I fear not but that they will prosper."

After a few moments' repose, necessitated by his extreme weakness, Captain Nemo continued,—

"To-morrow you will take the coffer, you will leave the saloon, of which you will close the door; then you will ascend on to the deck of the 'Nautilus,' and you will lower the mainhatch so as entirely to close the vessel."

"It shall be done, captain," answered Cyrus Harding.

"Good. You will then embark in the canoe which brought you hither; but, before leaving the 'Nautilus,' go to the stern and there open two large stop-cocks which you will find upon the water-line. The water will penetrate into the reservoirs, and the 'Nautilus' will gradually sink beneath the water to repose at the bottom of the abyss."

And comprehending a gesture of Cyrus Harding, the captain added,—

"Fear nothing! You will but bury a corpse!"

Neither Cyrus Harding nor his companions ventured to offer any observation to Captain Nemo. He had expressed his last wishes, and they had nothing to do but to conform to them.

"I have your promise, gentlemen?" added Captain Nemo.

"You have, captain," replied the engineer.

The captain thanked the colonists by a sign, and requested them to leave him for some hours. Gideon Spilett wished to remain near him, in the event of a crisis coming on, but the dying man refused, saying, "I shall live until to-morrow, sir."

All left the saloon, passed through the library and the dining-room, and arrived forward, in the machine-room where the electrical apparatus was established, which supplied not only heat and light, but the mechanical power of the "Nautilus."

The "Nautilus" was a masterpiece containing masterpieces with itself, and the engineer was struck with astonishment.

The colonists mounted the platform, which rose seven or eight feet above the water. There they beheld a thick glass lenticular covering, which protected a kind of large eye, from which flashed forth light. Behind this eye was apparently a cabin containing the wheels of the rudder, and in which was stationed the helmsman, when he navigated the "Nautilus" over the bed of the ocean, which the electric rays would evidently light up to a considerable distance.

Cyrus Harding and his companions remained for a time silent, for they were vividly impressed by what they had just seen and heard, and their hearts were deeply touched by the thought that he whose arm had so often aided them, the protector whom they had known but a few hours, was at the point of death.

Whatever might be the judgment pronounced by posterity upon the events of this, so to speak, extra-human existence, the character of Prince Dakkar would ever remain as one of those whose memory time can never efface.

"What a man!" said Pencroft. "Is it possible that he can have lived at the bottom of the sea? And it seems to me that perhaps he has not found peace there any more than elsewhere!"

"The 'Nautilus,'" observed Ayrton, "might have enabled us to leave Lincoln Island and reach some inhabited country."

"Good Heavens!" exclaimed Pencroft, "I for one would never risk myself in such a craft. To sail on the seas, good, but under the seas, never!"

"I believe, Pencroft," answered the reporter, "that the navigation of a submarine vessel such as the 'Nautilus' ought to be very easy, and that we should soon become accustomed to it. There would be no storms, no lee-shore to fear. At some feet beneath the surface the waters of the ocean are as calm as those of a lake."

"That may be," replied the sailor, "but I prefer a gale of wind on board a well-found craft. A vessel is built to sail on the sea, and not beneath it."

"My friends," said the engineer, "it is useless, at any rate as regards the 'Nautilus,' to discuss the question of submarine vessels. The 'Nautilus' is not ours, and we have not the right to dispose of it. Moreover, we could in no case avail ourselves of it. Independently of the fact that it would be impossible to get it out of this cavern, whose entrance is now closed by the uprising of the basaltic rocks, Captain Nemo's wish is that it shall be buried with him. His wish is our law, and we will fulfil it."

After a somewhat prolonged conversation, Cyrus Harding and his companions again descended to the interior of the "Nautilus." There they took some refreshment and returned to the saloon.

Captain Nemo had somewhat rallied from the prostration which had overcome him, and his eyes shone with their wonted fire. A faint smile even curled his lips.

The colonists drew around him.

"Gentlemen," said the captain, "you are brave and honest men. You have devoted yourselves to the common weal. Often have I observed your conduct. I have esteemed you— I esteem you still! Your hand, Mr. Harding."

Cyrus Harding gave his hand to the captain, who clasped it affectionately.

"It is well!" he murmured.

He resumed,—

"But enough of myself. I have to speak concerning yourselves, and this Lincoln Island, upon which you have taken refuge. You now desire to leave it?"

"To return, captain!" answered Pencroft quickly.

"To return, Pencroft?" said the captain, with a smile. "I know, it is true, your love for this island. You have helped to make it what it now is, and it seems to you a paradise!"

"Our project, captain," interposed Cyrus Harding, "is to annex it to the United States, and to establish for our shipping a port so fortunately situated in this part of the Pacific."

"Your thoughts are with your country, gentlemen," continued the captain; "your toils are for her prosperity and glory. You are right. One's native land!—there should one live! there die! And I die far from all I loved!"

"You have some last wish to transmit," said the engineer with emotion, "some souvenir to send to those friends you have left in the mountains of India?"

"No, Captain Harding; no friends remain to me! I am the last of my race, and to all whom I have known I have long been as are the dead.—But to return to yourselves. Solitude, isolation, are painful things, and beyond human endurance. I die of having thought it possible to live alone! You should, therefore, dare all in the attempt to leave Lincoln Island, and see once more the land of your birth. I am aware that those wretches have destroyed the vessel you have built."

"We propose to construct a vessel," said Gideon Spilett, "sufficiently large to convey us to the nearest land; but if we should succeed, sooner or later we shall return to Lincoln Island. We are attached to it by too many recollections ever to forget it."

"It is here that we have known Captain Nemo," said Cyrus Harding.

"It is here only that we can make our home!" added Herbert.

"And here shall I sleep the sleep of eternity, if—" replied the captain.

He paused for a moment, and, instead of completing the sentence, said simply,—

"Mr. Harding, I wish to speak with you—alone!"

The engineer's companions, respecting the wish, retired.

Cyrus Harding remained but a few minutes alone with Captain Nemo, and soon recalled his companions; but he said nothing to them of the private matters which the dying man had confided to him.

Gideon Spilett now watched the captain with extreme care. It was evident that he was no longer sustained by his moral energy, which had lost the power of reaction against his physical weakness.

The day closed without change. The colonists did not quit the "Nautilus" for a moment. Night arrived, although it was impossible to distinguish it from day in the cavern.

Captain Nemo suffered no pain, but he was visibly sinking. His noble features, paled by the approach of death, were perfectly calm. Inaudible words escaped at intervals from his lips, bearing upon various incidents of his checkered career. Life was evidently ebbing slowly and his extremities were already cold.

Once or twice more he spoke to the colonists who stood around him, and smiled on them with that last smile which continues after death.

At length, shortly after midnight, Captain Nemo by a supreme effort succeeded in folding his arms across his breast, as if wishing in that attitude to compose himself for death.

By one o'clock his glance alone showed signs of life. A dying light gleamed in those eyes once so brilliant. Then, murmuring the words, "God and my country!" he quietly expired.

Cyrus Harding, bending low closed the eyes of him who had once been the Prince Dakkar, and was now not even Captain Nemo.

Herbert and Pencroft sobbed aloud. Tears fell from Ayrton's eyes. Neb was on his knees by the reporter's side, motionless as a statue.

Then Cyrus Harding, extending his hand over the forehead of the dead, said solemnly, "May his soul be with God!" Turning to his friends, he added, "Let us pray for him whom we have lost!"

Some hours later the colonists fulfilled the promise made to the captain by carrying out his dying wishes.

Cyrus Harding and his companions quitted the "Nautilus," taking with them the only memento left them by their benefactor, the coffer which contained wealth amounting to millions.

The marvelous saloon, still flooded with light, had been carefully closed. The iron door leading on deck was then securely fastened in such a manner as to prevent even a drop of water from penetrating to the interior of the "Nautilus."

The colonists then descended into the canoe, which was moored to the side of the submarine vessel.

The canoe was now brought around to the stern. There, at the water-line, were two large stop-cocks communicating with the reservoirs employed in the submersion of the vessel.

The stop-cocks were opened, the reservoirs filled, and the "Nautilus," slowly sinking, disappeared beneath the surface of the lake.

But the colonists were yet able to follow its descent through the waves. The powerful light it gave forth lighted up the translucent water, while the cavern became gradually obscure. At length this vast effusion of electric light faded away, and soon after the "Nautilus," now the tomb of Captain Nemo, reposed in its ocean bed.

Chapter 18

At break of day the colonists regained in silence the entrance of the cavern, to which they gave the name of "Dakkar Grotto," in memory of Captain Nemo. It was now low-water, and they passed without difficulty under the arcade, washed on the right by the sea.

The canoe was left here, carefully protected from the waves. As additional precaution, Pencroft, Neb, and Ayrton drew it up on a little beach which bordered one of the sides of the grotto, in a spot where it could run no risk of harm.

The storm had ceased during the night. The last low mutterings of the thunder died away in the west. Rain fell no longer, but the sky was yet obscured by clouds. On the whole, this month of October, the first of the southern spring, was not ushered in by satisfactory tokens, and the wind had a tendency to shift from one point of the compass to another, which rendered it impossible to count upon settled weather.

Cyrus Harding and his companions, on leaving Dakkar Grotto, had taken the road to the corral. On their way Neb and Herbert were careful to preserve the wire which had been laid down by the captain between the corral and the grotto, and which might at a future time be of service.

The colonists spoke but little on the road. The various incidents of the night of October 15th had left a profound impression on their minds. The unknown being whose influence had so effectually protected them, the man whom their imagination had endowed with supernatural powers, Captain Nemo, was no more. His "Nautilus" and he were buried in the depths of the abyss. To each one of them their existence seemed even more isolated than before. They had been accustomed to count upon the intervention of that power which existed no longer, and Gideon Spilett, and even Cyrus Harding, could not escape this impression. Thus they maintained a profound silence during their journey to the corral.

Towards nine in the morning the colonists arrived at Granite House.

It had been agreed that the construction of the vessel should be actively pushed forward, and Cyrus Harding more than ever devoted his time and labor to this object. It was impossible to divine what future lay before them. Evidently the advantage to the colonists would be great of having at their disposal a substantial vessel, capable of keeping the sea even in heavy weather, and large enough to attempt, in case of need, a voyage of some duration. Even if, when their vessel should be completed, the colonists should not resolve to leave Lincoln Island as yet, in order to gain either one of the Polynesian Archipelagoes of the Pacific or the shores of New Zealand, they might at least, sooner or later, proceed to Tabor Island, to leave there the notice relating to Ayrton. This was a precaution rendered indispensable by the possibility of the Scotch yacht reappearing in those seas, and it was of the highest importance that nothing should be neglected on this point.

The works were then resumed. Cyrus Harding, Pencroft, and Ayrton, assisted by Neb, Gideon Spilett, and Herbert, except when unavoidably called off by other necessary occupations, worked without cessation. It was important that the new vessel should be ready in five months—that is to say, by the beginning of March—if they wished to visit Tabor Island before the equinoctial gales rendered the voyage impracticable. Therefore the carpenters lost not a moment. Moreover, it was unnecessary to manufacture rigging, that of the "Speedy" having been saved entire, so that the hull only of the vessel needed to be constructed.

The end of the year 1868 found them occupied by these important labors, to the exclusion of almost all others. At the expiration of two months and a half the ribs had been set up and the first planks adjusted. It was already evident that the plans made by Cyrus Harding were admirable, and that the vessel would behave well at sea.

Pencroft brought to the task a devouring energy, and would even grumble when one or the other abandoned the carpenter's axe for the gun of the hunter. It was nevertheless necessary to keep up the stores of Granite House, in view of the approaching winter. But this did not satisfy Pencroft. The brave, honest sailor was not content when the workmen were not at the dockyard. When this happened he grumbled vigorously, and, by way of venting his feelings, did the work of six men.

The weather was very unfavorable during the whole of the summer season. For some days the heat was overpowering, and the atmosphere, saturated with electricity, was only cleared by violent storms. It was rarely that the distant growling of the thunder could not be heard, like a low but incessant murmur, such as is produced in the equatorial regions of the globe.

The 1st of January, 1869, was signalized by a storm of extreme violence, and the thunder burst several times over the island. Large trees were struck by the electric fluid and shattered, and among others one of those gigantic nettle-trees which had shaded the poultry-yard at the southern extremity of the lake. Had this meteor any relation to the phenomena going on in the bowels of the earth? Was there any connection between the commotion of the atmosphere and that of the interior of the earth? Cyrus Harding was inclined to think that such was the case, for the development of these storms was attended by the renewal of volcanic symptoms.

It was on the 3rd of January that Herbert, having ascended at daybreak to the plateau of Prospect Heights to harness one of the onagers, perceived an enormous hat-shaped cloud rolling from the summit of the volcano.

Herbert immediately apprised the colonists, who at once joined him in watching the summit of Mount Franklin.

"Ah!" exclaimed Pencroft, "those are not vapors this time! It seems to me that the giant is not content with breathing; he must smoke!"

This figure of speech employed by the sailor exactly expressed the changes going on at the mouth of the volcano. Already for three months had the crater emitted vapors more or less dense, but which were as yet produced only by an internal ebullition of mineral substances. But now the vapors were replaced by a thick smoke, rising in the form of a grayish column, more than three hundred feet in width at its base, and which spread like an immense mushroom to a height of from seven to eight hundred feet above the summit of the mountain.

"The fire is in the chimney," observed Gideon Spilett.

"And we can't put it out!" replied Herbert.

"The volcano ought to be swept," observed Neb, who spoke as if perfectly serious.

"Well said, Neb!" cried Pencroft, with a shout of laughter; "and you'll undertake the job, no doubt?"

Cyrus Harding attentively observed the dense smoke emitted by Mount Franklin, and even listened, as if expecting to hear some distant muttering. Then, turning towards his companions, from whom he had gone somewhat apart, he said,—

"The truth is, my friends, we must not conceal from ourselves that an important change is going forward. The volcanic substances are no longer in a state of ebullition, they have caught fire, and we are undoubtedly menaced by an approaching eruption."

"Well, captain," said Pencroft, "we shall witness the eruption; and if it is a good one, we'll applaud it. I don't see that we need concern ourselves further about the matter."

"It may be so," replied Cyrus Harding, "for the ancient track of the lava is still open; and thanks to this, the crater has hitherto overflowed towards the north. And yet—"

"And yet, as we can derive no advantage from an eruption, it might be better it should not take place," said the reporter.

"Who knows?" answered the sailor. "Perhaps there may be some valuable substance in this volcano, which it will spout forth, and which we may turn to good account!"

Cyrus Harding shook his head with the air of a man who augured no good from the phenomenon whose development had been so sudden. He did not regard so lightly as Pencroft the results of an eruption. If the lava, in consequence of the position of the crater, did not directly menace the wooded and cultivated parts of the island, other complications might present themselves. In fact, eruptions are not unfrequently accompanied by earthquakes; and an island of the nature of Lincoln Island, formed of substances so varied, basalt on one side, granite on the other, lava on the north, rich soil on the south, substances which consequently could not be firmly attached to each other, would be exposed to the risk of disintegration. Although, therefore, the spreading of the volcanic matter might not constitute a serious danger, any movement of the terrestrial structure which should shake the island might entail the gravest consequences.

"It seems to me," said Ayrton, who had reclined so as to place his ear to the ground, "it seems to me that I can hear a dull, rumbling sound, like that of a wagon loaded with bars of iron."

The colonists listened with the greatest attention, and were convinced that Ayrton was not mistaken. The rumbling was mingled with a subterranean roar, which formed a sort of rinforzando, and died slowly away, as if some violent storm had passed through the profundities of the globe. But no explosion properly so termed, could be heard. It might therefore be concluded that the vapors and smoke found a free passage through the central shaft; and that the safety-valve being sufficiently large, no convulsion would be produced, no explosion was to be apprehended.

"Well, then!" said Pencroft, "are we not going back to work? Let Mount Franklin smoke, groan, bellow, or spout forth fire and flame as much as it pleases, that is no reason why we should be idle! Come, Ayrton, Neb, Herbert, Captain Harding, Mr. Spilett, every one of us must turn to at our work to-day! We are going to place the keelson, and a dozen pair of hands would not be too many. Before two months I want our new 'Bonadventure'—for we shall keep the old name, shall we not?—to float on the waters of Port Balloon! Therefore there is not an hour to lose!"

All the colonists, their services thus requisitioned by Pencroft, descended to the dockyard, and proceeded to place the keelson, a thick mass of wood which forms the lower portion of a ship and unites firmly the timbers of the hull. It was an arduous undertaking, in which all took part.

They continued their labors during the whole of this day, the 3rd of January, without thinking further of the volcano, which could not, besides, be seen from the shore of Granite House. But once or twice, large shadows, veiling the sun, which described its diurnal arc through an extremely clear sky, indicated that a thick cloud of smoke passed between its disc and the island. The wind, blowing on the shore, carried all these vapors to the westward. Cyrus Harding and Gideon Spilett remarked these somber appearances, and from time to time discussed the evident progress of the volcanic phenomena, but their work went on without interruption. It was, besides, of the first importance from every point of view, that the vessel should be finished with the least possible delay. In presence of the eventualities which might arise, the safety of the colonists would be to a great extent secured by their ship. Who could tell that it might not prove some day their only refuge?

In the evening, after supper, Cyrus Harding, Gideon Spilett, and Herbert again ascended the plateau of Prospect Heights. It was already dark, and the obscurity would permit them to ascertain if flames or incandescent matter thrown up by the volcano were mingled with the vapor and smoke accumulated at the mouth of the crater.

"The crater is on fire!" said Herbert, who, more active than his companion, first reached the plateau.

Mount Franklin, distant about six miles, now appeared like a gigantic torch, around the summit of which turned fuliginous flames. So much smoke, and possibly scoriae and cinders were mingled with them, that their light gleamed but faintly amid the gloom of the night. But a kind of lurid brilliancy spread over the island, against which stood out confusedly the wooded masses of the heights. Immense whirlwinds of vapor obscured the sky, through which glimmered a few stars.

"The change is rapid!" said the engineer.

"That is not surprising," answered the reporter. "The reawakening of the volcano already dates back some time. You may remember, Cyrus, that the first vapors appeared about the time we searched the sides of the mountain to discover Captain Nemo's retreat. It was, if I mistake not, about the 15th of October."

"Yes," replied Herbert, "two months and a half ago!"

"The subterranean fires have therefore been smoldering for ten weeks," resumed Gideon Spilett, "and it is not to be wondered at that they now break out with such violence!"

"Do not you feel a certain vibration of the soil?" asked Cyrus Harding.

"Yes," replied Gideon Spilett, "but there is a great difference between that and an earthquake."

"I do not affirm that we are menaced with an earthquake," answered Cyrus Harding, "may God preserve us from that! No; these vibrations are due to the effervescence of the central fire. The crust of the earth is simply the shell of a boiler, and you know that such a shell, under the pressure of steam, vibrates like a sonorous plate. It is this effect which is being produced at this moment."

"What magnificent flames!" exclaimed Herbert.

At this instant a kind of bouquet of flames shot forth from the crater, the brilliancy of which was visible even through the vapors. Thousands of luminous sheets and barbed tongues of fire were cast in various directions. Some, extending beyond the dome of smoke, dissipated it, leaving behind an incandescent powder. This was accompanied by successive explosions, resembling the discharge of a battery of machine-guns.

Cyrus Harding, the reporter, and Herbert, after spending an hour on the plateau of Prospect Heights, again descended to the beach, and returned to Granite House. The engineer was thoughtful and preoccupied, so much so, indeed, that Gideon Spilett inquired if he apprehended any immediate danger, of which the eruption might directly or indirectly be the cause.

"Yes, and no," answered Cyrus Harding.

"Nevertheless," continued the reporter, "would not the greatest misfortune which could happen to us be an earthquake which would overturn the island?

Now, I do not suppose that this is to be feared, since the vapors and lava have found a free outlet."

"True," replied Cyrus Harding, "and I do not fear an earthquake in the sense in which the term is commonly applied to convulsions of the soil provoked by the expansion of subterranean gases. But other causes may produce great disasters."

"How so, my dear Cyrus?'

"I am not certain. I must consider. I must visit the mountain. In a few days I shall learn more on this point."

Gideon Spilett said no more, and soon, in spite of the explosions of the volcano, whose intensity increased, and which were repeated by the echoes of the island, the inhabitants of Granite House were sleeping soundly.

Three days passed by—the 4th, 5th, and 6th of January. The construction of the vessel was diligently continued, and without offering further explanations the engineer pushed forward the work with all his energy. Mount Franklin was now hooded by a somber cloud of sinister aspect, and, amid the flames, vomiting forth incandescent rocks, some of which fell back into the crater itself. This caused Pencroft, who would only look at the matter in the light of a joke, to exclaim,—

"Ah! the giant is playing at cup and ball; he is a conjurer."

In fact, the substances thrown up fell back again in to the abyss, and it did not seem that the lava, though swollen by the internal pressure, had yet risen to the orifice of the crater. At any rate, the opening on the northeast, which was partly visible, poured out no torrent upon the northern slope of the mountain.

Nevertheless, however pressing was the construction of the vessel, other duties demanded the presence of the colonists on various portions of the island. Before everything it was necessary to go to the corral, where the flocks of musmons and goats were enclosed, and replenish the provision of forage for those animals. It was accordingly arranged that Ayrton should proceed thither the next day, the 7th of January; and as he was sufficient for the task, to which he was accustomed, Pencroft and the rest were somewhat surprised on hearing the engineer say to Ayrton—

"As you are going to-morrow to the corral I will accompany you."

"But, Captain Harding," exclaimed the sailor, "our working days will not be many, and if you go also we shall be two pair of hands short!"

"We shall return to-morrow," replied Cyrus Harding, "but it is necessary that I should go to the corral. I must learn how the eruption is progressing."

"The eruption! always the eruption!" answered Pencroft, with an air of discontent. "An important thing, truly, this eruption! I trouble myself very little about it."

Whatever might be the sailor's opinion, the expedition projected by the engineer was settled for the next day. Herbert wished to accompany Cyrus Harding, but he would not vex Pencroft by his absence.

The next day, at dawn, Cyrus Harding and Ayrton, mounting the cart drawn by two onagers, took the road to the corral and set off at a round trot.

Above the forest were passing large clouds, to which the crater of Mount Franklin incessantly added fuliginous matter. These clouds, which rolled heavily in the air, were evidently composed of heterogeneous substances. It was not alone from the volcano that they derived their strange opacity and weight. Scoriae, in a state of dust, like powdered pumice-stone, and grayish ashes as small as the finest feculae, were held in suspension in the midst of their thick folds. These ashes are so fine that they have been observed in the air for whole months. After the eruption of 1783 in Iceland for upwards of a year the atmosphere was thus charged with volcanic dust through which the rays of the sun were only with difficulty discernible.

But more often this pulverized matter falls, and this happened on the present occasion. Cyrus Harding and Ayrton had scarcely reached the corral when a sort of black snow like fine gunpowder fell, and instantly changed the appearance of the soil. Trees, meadows, all disappeared beneath a covering several inches in depth. But, very fortunately, the wind blew from the northeast, and the greater part of the cloud dissolved itself over the sea.

"This is very singular, Captain Harding," said Ayrton.

"It is very serious," replied the engineer. "This powdered pumice-stone, all this mineral dust, proves how grave is the convulsion going forward in the lower depths of the volcano."

"But can nothing be done?"

"Nothing, except to note the progress of the phenomenon. Do you, therefore, Ayrton, occupy yourself with the necessary work at the corral. In the meantime I will ascend just beyond the source of Red Creek and examine the condition of the mountain upon its northern aspect. Then—"

"Well, Captain Harding?"

"Then we will pay a visit to Dakkar Grotto. I wish to inspect it. At any rate I will come back for you in two hours."

Ayrton then proceeded to enter the corral, and, while awaiting the engineer's return, busied himself with the musmons and goats which seemed to feel a certain uneasiness in presence of these first signs of an eruption.

Meanwhile Cyrus Harding ascended the crest of the eastern spur, passed Red Creek, and arrived at the spot where he and his companions had discovered a sulphurous spring at the time of their first exploration.

How changed was everything! Instead of a single column of smoke he counted thirteen, forced through the soil as if violently propelled by some piston. It was evident that the crust of the earth was subjected in this part of the globe to a frightful pressure. The atmosphere was saturated with gases and carbonic acid, mingled with aqueous vapors. Cyrus Harding felt the volcanic tufa with which the plain was strewn, and which was but pulverized cinders hardened into solid blocks by time, tremble beneath him, but he could discover no traces of fresh lava.

The engineer became more assured of this when he observed all the northern part of Mount Franklin. Pillars of smoke and flame escaped from the crater; a hail of scoriae fell on the ground; but no current of lava burst from the mouth of the volcano, which proved that the volcanic matter had not yet attained the level of the superior orifice of the central shaft.

"But I would prefer that it were so," said Cyrus Harding to himself. "At any rate, I should then know that the lava had followed its accustomed track. Who can say that it may not take a new course? But the danger does not consist in that! Captain Nemo foresaw it clearly! No, the danger does not lie there!"

Cyrus Harding advanced towards the enormous causeway whose prolongation enclosed the narrow Shark Gulf. He could now sufficiently examine on this side the ancient channels of the lava. There was no doubt in his mind that the most recent eruption had occurred at a far-distant epoch.

He then returned by the same way, listening attentively to the subterranean mutterings which rolled like long-continued thunder, interrupted by deafening explosions. At nine in the morning he reached the corral.

Ayrton awaited him.

"The animals are cared for, Captain Harding," said Ayrton.

"Good, Ayrton."

"They seem uneasy, Captain Harding."

"Yes, instinct speaks through them, and instinct is never deceived."

"Are you ready?"

"Take a lamp, Ayrton," answered the engineer; "we will start at once."

Ayrton did as desired. The onagers, unharnessed, roamed in the corral. The gate was secured on the outside, and Cyrus Harding, preceding Ayrton, took the narrow path which led westward to the shore.

The soil they walked upon was choked with the pulverized matter fallen from the cloud. No quadruped appeared in the woods. Even the birds had fled. Sometimes a passing breeze raised the covering of ashes, and the two colonists, enveloped in a whirlwind of dust, lost sight of each other. They were then careful to cover their eyes and mouths with handkerchiefs, for they ran the risk of being blinded and suffocated.

It was impossible for Cyrus Harding and Ayrton, with these impediments, to make rapid progress. Moreover, the atmosphere was close, as if the oxygen had been partly burned up, and had become unfit for respiration. At every hundred paces they were obliged to stop to take breath. It was therefore past ten o'clock when the engineer and his companion reached the crest of the enormous mass of rocks of basalt and porphyry which composed the northwest coast of the island.

Ayrton and Cyrus Harding commenced the descent of this abrupt declivity, following almost step for step the difficult path which, during that stormy night, had led them to Dakkar Grotto. In open day the descent was less perilous, and, besides, the bed of ashes which covered the polished surface of the rock enabled them to make their footing more secure.

The ridge at the end of the shore, about forty feet in height, was soon reached. Cyrus Harding recollected that this elevation gradually sloped towards the level of the sea. Although the tide was at present low, no beach could be seen, and the waves, thickened by the volcanic dust, beat upon the basaltic rocks.

Cyrus Harding and Ayrton found without difficulty the entrance to Dakkar Grotto, and paused for a moment at the last rock before it.

"The iron boat should be there," said the engineer.

"It is here, Captain Harding," replied Ayrton, drawing towards him the fragile craft, which was protected by the arch of the vault.

"On board, Ayrton!"

The two colonists stepped into the boat. A slight undulation of the waves carried it farther under the low arch of the crypt, and there Ayrton, with the aid of flint and steel, lighted the lamp. He then took the oars, and the lamp having been placed in the bow of the boat, so that its rays fell before them, Cyrus Harding took the helm and steered through the shades of the grotto.

The "Nautilus" was there no longer to illuminate the cavern with its electric light. Possibly it might not yet be extinguished, but no ray escaped from the depths of the abyss in which reposed all that was mortal of Captain Nemo.

The light afforded by the lamp, although feeble, nevertheless enabled the engineer to advance slowly, following the wall of the cavern. A deathlike silence reigned under the vaulted roof, or at least in the anterior portion, for soon Cyrus Harding distinctly heard the rumbling which proceeded from the bowels of the mountain.

"That comes from the volcano," he said.

Besides these sounds, the presence of chemical combinations was soon betrayed by their powerful odor, and the engineer and his companion were almost suffocated by sulphurous vapors.

"This is what Captain Nemo feared," murmured Cyrus Harding, changing countenance. "We must go to the end, notwithstanding."

"Forward!" replied Ayrton, bending to his oars and directing the boat towards the head of the cavern.

Twenty-five minutes after entering the mouth of the grotto the boat reached the extreme end.

Cyrus Harding then, standing up, cast the light of the lamp upon the walls of the cavern which separated it from the central shaft of the volcano. What was the thickness of this wall? It might be ten feet or a hundred feet—it was impossible to say. But the subterranean sounds were too perceptible to allow of the supposition that it was of any great thickness.

The engineer, after having explored the wall at a certain height horizontally, fastened the lamp to the end of an oar, and again surveyed the basaltic wall at a greater elevation.

There, through scarcely visible clefts and joinings, escaped a pungent vapor, which infected the atmosphere of the cavern. The wall was broken by large cracks, some of which extended to within two or three feet of the water's edge.

Cyrus Harding thought for a brief space. Then he said in a low voice,—

"Yes! the captain was right! The danger lies there, and a terrible danger!"

Ayrton said not a word, but, upon a sign from Cyrus Harding, resumed the oars, and half an hour later the engineer and he reached the entrance of Dakkar Grotto.

Chapter 19

The next day, the 8th day of January, after a day and night passed at the corral, where they left all in order, Cyrus Harding and Ayrton arrived at Granite House.

The engineer immediately called his companions together, and informed them of the imminent danger which threatened Lincoln Island, and from which no human power could deliver them.

"My friends," he said, and his voice betrayed the depth of his emotion, "our island is not among those which will endure while this earth endures. It is doomed to more or less speedy destruction, the cause of which it bears within itself, and from which nothing can save it."

The colonists looked at each other, then at the engineer. They did not clearly comprehend him.

"Explain yourself, Cyrus!" said Gideon Spilett.

"I will do so," replied Cyrus Harding, "or rather I will simply afford you the explanation which, during our few minutes of private conversation, was given me by Captain Nemo."

"Captain Nemo!" exclaimed the colonists.

"Yes, and it was the last service he desired to render us before his death!"

"The last service!" exclaimed Pencroft, "the last service! You will see that though he is dead he will render us others yet!"

"But what did the captain say?" inquired the reporter.

"I will tell you, my friends," said the engineer. "Lincoln Island does not resemble the other islands of the Pacific, and a fact of which Captain Nemo has made me cognizant must sooner or later bring about the subversion of its foundation."

"Nonsense! Lincoln Island, it can't be!" cried Pencroft, who, in spite of the respect he felt for Cyrus Harding, could not prevent a gesture of incredulity.

"Listen, Pencroft," resumed the engineer, "I will tell you what Captain Nemo communicated to me, and which I myself confirmed yesterday, during the exploration of Dakkar Grotto.

"This cavern stretches under the island as far as the volcano, and is only separated from its central shaft by the wall which terminates it. Now, this wall is seamed with fissures and clefts which already allow the sulphurous gases generated in the interior of the volcano to escape."

"Well?" said Pencroft, his brow suddenly contracting.

"Well, then, I saw that these fissures widen under the internal pressure from within, that the wall of basalt is gradually giving way and that after a longer or shorter period it will afford a passage to the waters of the lake which fill the cavern."

"Good!" replied Pencroft, with an attempt at pleasantry. "The sea will extinguish the volcano, and there will be an end of the matter!"

"Not so!" said Cyrus Harding, "should a day arrive when the sea, rushing through the wall of the cavern, penetrates by the central shaft into the interior of the island to the boiling lava, Lincoln Island will that day be blown into the air—just as would happen to the island of Sicily were the Mediterranean to precipitate itself into Mount Etna."

The colonists made no answer to these significant words of the engineer. They now understood the danger by which they were menaced.

It may be added that Cyrus Harding had in no way exaggerated the danger to be apprehended. Many persons have formed an idea that it would be possible to extinguish volcanoes, which are almost always situated on the shores of a sea or lake, by opening a passage for the admission of the water. But they are not aware that this would be to incur the risk of blowing up a portion of the globe, like a boiler whose steam is suddenly expanded by intense heat. The water, rushing into a cavity whose temperature might be estimated at thousands of degrees, would be converted into steam with a sudden energy which no enclosure could resist.

It was not therefore doubtful that the island, menaced by a frightful and approaching convulsion, would endure only so long as the wall of Dakkar Grotto itself should endure. It was not even a question of months, nor of weeks, but of days; it might be of hours.

The first sentiment which the colonists felt was that of profound sorrow. They thought not so much of the peril which menaced themselves personally, but of the destruction of the island which had sheltered them, which they had cultivated, which they loved so well, and had hoped to render so flourishing. So much effort ineffectually expended, so much labor lost.

Pencroft could not prevent a large tear from rolling down his cheek, nor did he attempt to conceal it.

Some further conversation now took place. The chances yet in favor of the colonists were discussed; but finally it was agreed that there was not an hour to be lost, that the building and fitting of the vessel should be pushed forward with their utmost energy, and that this was the sole chance of safety for the inhabitants of Lincoln Island.

All hands, therefore, set to work on the vessel. What could it avail to sow, to reap, to hunt, to increase the stores of Granite House? The contents of the storehouse and outbuildings contained more than sufficient to provide the ship for a voyage, however long might be its duration. But it was imperative that the ship should be ready to receive them before the inevitable catastrophe should arrive.

Their labors were now carried on with feverish ardor. By the 23rd of January the vessel was half-decked over. Up to this time no change had taken place on the summit of the volcano. Vapor and smoke mingled with flames and incandescent stones were thrown up from the crater. But during the night of the 23rd, in consequence of the lava attaining the level of the first stratum of the volcano, the hat-shaped cone which formed over the latter disappeared. A frightful sound was heard. The colonists at first thought the island was rent asunder, and rushed out of Granite House.

This occurred about two o'clock in the morning.

The sky appeared on fire. The superior cone, a mass of rock a thousand feet in height, and weighing thousands of millions of pounds, had been thrown down upon the island, making it tremble to its foundation. Fortunately, this cone inclined to the north, and had fallen upon the plain of sand and tufa stretching between the volcano and the sea. The aperture of the crater being thus enlarged projected towards the sky a glare so intense that by the simple effect of reflection the atmosphere appeared red-hot. At the same time a torrent of lava, bursting from the new summit, poured out in long cascades, like water escaping from a vase too full, and a thousand tongues of fire crept over the sides of the volcano.

"The corral! the corral!" exclaimed Ayrton.

It was, in fact, towards the corral that the lava was rushing as the new crater faced the east, and consequently the fertile portions of the island, the springs of Red Creek and Jacamar Wood, were menaced with instant destruction.

At Ayrton's cry the colonists rushed to the onagers' stables. The cart was at once harnessed. All were possessed by the same thought—to hasten to the corral and set at liberty the animals it enclosed.

Before three in the morning they arrived at the corral. The cries of the terrified musmons and goats indicated the alarm which possessed them. Already a torrent of burning matter and liquefied minerals fell from the side of the mountain upon the meadows as far as the side of the palisade. The gate was burst open by Ayrton, and the animals, bewildered with terror, fled in all directions.

An hour afterwards the boiling lava filled the corral, converting into vapor the water of the little rivulet which ran through it, burning up the house like dry grass, and leaving not even a post of the palisade to mark the spot where the corral once stood.

To contend against this disaster would have been folly—nay, madness. In presence of Nature's grand convulsions man is powerless.

It was now daylight—the 24th of January. Cyrus Harding and his companions, before returning to Granite House, desired to ascertain the probable direction this inundation of lava was about to take. The soil sloped gradually from Mount Franklin to the east coast, and it was to be feared that, in spite of the thick Jacamar Wood, the torrent would reach the plateau of Prospect Heights.

"The lake will cover us," said Gideon Spilett.

"I hope so!" was Cyrus Harding's only reply.

The colonists were desirous of reaching the plain upon which the superior cone of Mount Franklin had fallen, but the lava arrested their progress. It had followed, on one side, the valley of Red Creek, and on the other that of Falls River, evaporating those watercourses in its passage. There was no possibility of crossing the torrent of lava; on the contrary, the colonists were obliged to retreat before it. The volcano, without its crown, was no longer recognizable, terminated as it was by a sort of flat table which replaced the ancient crater. From two openings in its southern and eastern sides an unceasing flow of lava poured forth, thus forming two distinct streams. Above the new crater a cloud of smoke and ashes, mingled with those of the atmosphere, massed over the island. Loud peals of thunder broke, and could scarcely be distinguished from the rumblings of the mountain, whose mouth vomited forth ignited rocks, which, hurled to more than a thousand feet, burst in the air like shells. Flashes of lightning rivaled in intensity the volcano's eruption.

Towards seven in the morning the position was no longer tenable by the colonists, who accordingly took shelter in the borders of Jacamar Wood. Not only did the projectiles begin to rain around them, but the lava, overflowing the bed of Red Creek, threatened to cut off the road to the corral. The nearest rows of trees caught fire, and their sap, suddenly transformed into vapor, caused them to explode with loud reports, while others, less moist, remained unhurt in the midst of the inundation.

The colonists had again taken the road to the corral. They proceeded but slowly, frequently looking back; but, in consequence of the inclination of the soil, the lava gained rapidly in the east, and as its lower waves became solidified others, at boiling heat, covered them immediately.

Meanwhile, the principal stream of Red Creek Valley became more and more menacing. All this portion of the forest was on fare, and enormous wreaths of smoke rolled over the trees, whore trunks were already consumed by the lava.

The colonists halted near the lake, about half a mile from the mouth of Red Creek. A question of life or death was now to be decided.

Cyrus Harding, accustomed to the consideration of important crises, and aware that he was addressing men capable of hearing the truth, whatever it might be, then said,—

"Either the lake will arrest the progress of the lava, and a part of the island will be preserved from utter destruction, or the stream will overrun the forests of the Far West, and not a tree or plant will remain on the surface of the soil. We shall have no prospect but that of starvation upon these barren rocks—a death which will probably be anticipated by the explosion of the island."

"In that case," replied Pencroft, folding his arms and stamping his foot, "what's the use of working any longer on the vessel?"

"Pencroft," answered Cyrus Harding, "we must do our duty to the last!"

At this instant the river of lava, after having broken a passage through the noble trees it devoured in its course, reached the borders of the lake. At this point there was an elevation of the soil which, had it been greater, might have sufficed to arrest the torrent.

"To work!" cried Cyrus Harding.

The engineer's thought was at once understood. It might be possible to dam, as it were, the torrent, and thus compel it to pour itself into the lake.

The colonists hastened to the dockyard. They returned with shovels, picks, axes, and by means of banking the earth with the aid of fallen trees they succeeded in a few hours in raising an embankment three feet high and some hundreds of paces in length. It seemed to them, when they had finished, as if they had scarcely been working more than a few minutes.

It was not a moment too soon. The liquefied substances soon after reached the bottom of the barrier. The stream of lava swelled like a river about to overflow its banks, and threatened to demolish the sole obstacle which could prevent it from overrunning the whole Far West. But the dam held firm, and after a moment of terrible suspense the torrent precipitated itself into Grant Lake from a height of twenty feet.

The colonists, without moving or uttering a word, breathlessly regarded this strife of the two elements.

What a spectacle was this conflict between water and fire! What pen could describe the marvelous horror of this scene—what pencil could depict it? The water hissed as it evaporated by contact with the boiling lava. The vapor whirled in the air to an immeasurable height, as if the valves of an immense boiler had been suddenly opened. But, however considerable might be the volume of water contained in the lake, it must eventually be absorbed, because it was not replenished, while the stream of lava, fed from an inexhaustible source, rolled on without ceasing new waves of incandescent matter. The first waves of lava which fell in the lake immediately solidified and accumulated so as speedily to emerge from it. Upon their surface fell other waves, which in their turn became stone, but a step nearer the center of the lake. In this manner was formed a pier which threatened to gradually fill up the lake, which could not overflow, the water displaced by the lava being evaporated. The hissing of the water rent the air with a deafening sound, and the vapor, blown by the wind, fell in rain upon the sea. The pier became longer and longer, and the blocks of lava piled themselves one on another. Where formerly stretched the calm waters of the lake now appeared an enormous mass of smoking rocks, as if an upheaving of the soil had formed immense shoals. Imagine the waters of the lake aroused by a hurricane, then suddenly solidified by an intense frost, and some conception may be formed of the aspect of the lake three hours after the eruption of this irresistible torrent of lava.

This time water would be vanquished by fire.

Nevertheless it was a fortunate circumstance for the colonists that the effusion of lava should have been in the direction of Lake Grant. They had before them some days' respite. The plateau of Prospect Heights, Granite House, and the dockyard were for the moment preserved. And these few days it was necessary to employ in planking and carefully calking the vessel, and launching her. The colonists would then take refuge on board the vessel, content to rig her after she should be afloat on the waters. With the danger of an explosion which threatened to destroy the island there could be no security on shore. The walls of Granite House, once so sure a retreat, might at any moment fall in upon them.

During the six following days, from the 25th to the 30th of January, the colonists accomplished as much of the construction of their vessel as twenty men could have done. They hardly allowed themselves a moment's repose, and the glare of the flames which shot from the crater enabled them to work night and day. The flow of lava continued, but perhaps less abundantly. This was fortunate, for Lake Grant was almost entirely choked up, and if more lava should accumulate it would inevitably spread over the plateau of Prospect Heights, and thence upon the beach.

But if the island was thus partially protected on this side, it was not so with the western part.

In fact, the second stream of lava, which had followed the valley of Falls River, a valley of great extent, the land on both sides of the creek being flat, met with no obstacle. The burning liquid had then spread through the forest of the Far West. At this period of the year, when the trees were dried up by a tropical heat, the forest caught fire instantaneously, in such a manner that the conflagration extended itself both by the trunks of the trees and by their higher branches, whose interlacement favored its progress. It even appeared that the current of flame spread more rapidly among the summits of the trees than the current of lava at their bases.

Thus it happened that the wild animals, jaguars, wild boars, capybaras, koalas, and game of every kind, mad with terror, had fled to the banks of the Mercy and to the Tadorn Marsh, beyond the road to Port Balloon. But the colonists were too much occupied with their task to pay any attention to even the most formidable of these animals. They had abandoned Granite House, and would not even take shelter at the Chimneys, but encamped under a tent, near the mouth of the Mercy.

Each day Cyrus Harding and Gideon Spilett ascended the plateau of Prospect Heights. Sometimes Herbert accompanied them, but never Pencroft, who could not bear to look upon the prospect of the island now so utterly devastated.

It was, in truth, a heart-rending spectacle. All the wooded part of the island was now completely bare. One single clump of green trees raised their heads at the extremity of Serpentine Peninsula. Here and there were a few grotesque blackened and branchless stumps. The side of the devastated forest was even more barren than Tadorn Marsh. The eruption of lava had been complete. Where formerly sprang up that charming verdure, the soil was now nothing but a savage mass of volcanic tufa. In the valleys of the Falls and Mercy rivers no drop of water now flowed towards the sea, and should Lake Grant be entirely dried up, the colonists would have no means of quenching their thirst. But, fortunately the lava had spared the southern corner of the lake, containing all that remained of the drinking water of the island. Towards the northwest stood out the rugged and well-defined outlines of the sides of the volcano, like a gigantic claw hovering over the island. What a sad and fearful sight, and how painful to the colonists, who, from a fertile domain covered with forests, irrigated by watercourses, and enriched by the produce of their toils, found themselves, as it were, transported to a desolate rock, upon which, but for their reserves of provisions, they could not even gather the means of subsistence!

"It is enough to break one's heart!" said Gideon Spilett, one day.

"Yes, Spilett," answered the engineer. "May God grant us the time to complete this vessel, now our sole refuge!"

"Do not you think, Cyrus, that the violence of the eruption has somewhat lessened? The volcano still vomits forth lava, but somewhat less abundantly, if I mistake not."

"It matters little," answered Cyrus Harding. "The fire is still burning in the interior of the mountain, and the sea may break in at any moment. We are in the condition of passengers whose ship is devoured by a conflagration which they cannot extinguish, and who know that sooner or later the flames must reach the powder-magazine. To work, Spilett, to work, and let us not lose an hour!"

During eight days more, that is to say until the 7th of February, the lava continued to flow, but the eruption was confined within the previous limits. Cyrus Harding feared above all lest the liquefied matter should overflow the shore, for in that event the dockyard could not escape. Moreover, about this time the colonists felt in the frame of the island vibrations which alarmed them to the highest degree.

It was the 20th of February. Yet another month must elapse before the vessel would be ready for sea. Would the island hold together till then? The intention of Pencroft and Cyrus Harding was to launch the vessel as soon as the hull should be complete. The deck, the upperworks, the interior woodwork and the rigging might be finished afterwards, but the essential point was that the colonists should have an assured refuge away from the island. Perhaps it might be even better to conduct the vessel to Port Balloon, that is to say, as far as possible from the center of eruption, for at the mouth of the Mercy, between the islet and the wall of granite, it would run the risk of being crushed in the event of any convulsion. All the exertions of the voyagers were therefore concentrated upon the completion of the hull.

Thus the 3rd of March arrived, and they might calculate upon launching the vessel in ten days.

Hope revived in the hearts of the colonists, who had, in this fourth year of their sojourn on Lincoln island, suffered so many trials. Even Pencroft lost in some measure the somber taciturnity occasioned by the devastation and ruin of his domain. His hopes, it is true, were concentrated upon his vessel.

"We shall finish it," he said to the engineer, "we shall finish it, captain, and it is time, for the season is advancing and the equinox will soon be here. Well, if necessary, we must put in to Tabor island to spend the winter. But think of Tabor island after Lincoln Island. Ah, how unfortunate! Who could have believed it possible?"

"Let us get on," was the engineer's invariable reply.

And they worked away without losing a moment.

"Master," asked Neb, a few days later, "do you think all this could have happened if Captain Nemo had been still alive?"

"Certainly, Neb," answered Cyrus Harding.

"I, for one, don't believe it!" whispered Pencroft to Neb.

"Nor I!" answered Neb seriously.

During the first week of March appearances again became menacing. Thousands of threads like glass, formed of fluid lava, fell like rain upon the island. The crater was again boiling with lava which overflowed the back of the volcano. The torrent flowed along the surface of the hardened tufa, and destroyed the few meager skeletons of trees which had withstood the first eruption. The stream, flowing this time towards the southwest shore of Lake Grant, stretched beyond Creek Glycerine, and invaded the plateau of Prospect Heights. This last blow to the work of the colonists was terrible. The mill, the buildings of the inner court, the stables, were all destroyed. The affrighted poultry fled in all directions. Top and Jup showed signs of the greatest alarm, as if their instinct warned them of an impending catastrophe. A large number of the animals of the island had perished in the first eruption. Those which survived found no refuge but Tadorn Marsh, save a few to which the plateau of Prospect Heights afforded asylum. But even this last retreat was now closed to them, and the lava-torrent, flowing over the edge of the granite wall, began to pour down upon the beach its cataracts of fire. The sublime horror of this spectacle passed all description. During the night it could only be compared to a Niagara of molten fluid, with its incandescent vapors above and its boiling masses below.

The colonists were driven to their last entrenchment, and although the upper seams of the vessel were not yet calked, they decided to launch her at once.

Pencroft and Ayrton therefore set about the necessary preparations for the launching, which was to take place the morning of the next day, the 9th of March.

But during the night of the 8th an enormous column of vapor escaping from the crater rose with frightful explosions to a height of more than three thousand feet. The wall of Dakkar Grotto had evidently given way under the pressure of gases, and the sea, rushing through the central shalt into the igneous gulf, was at once converted into vapor. But the crater could not afford a sufficient outlet for this vapor. An explosion, which might have been heard at a distance of a hundred miles, shook the air. Fragments of mountains fell into the Pacific, and, in a few minutes, the ocean rolled over the spot where Lincoln island once stood.

Chapter 20

An isolated rock, thirty feet in length, twenty in breadth, scarcely ten from the water's edge, such was the only solid point which the waves of the Pacific had not engulfed.

It was all that remained of the structure of Granite House! The wall had fallen headlong and been then shattered to fragments, and a few of the rocks of the large room were piled one above another to form this point. All around had disappeared in the abyss; the inferior cone of Mount Franklin, rent asunder by the explosion; the lava jaws of Shark Gulf, the plateau of Prospect Heights, Safety Islet, the granite rocks of Port Balloon, the basalts of Dakkar Grotto, the long Serpentine Peninsula, so distant nevertheless from the center of the eruption. All that could now be seen of Lincoln Island was the narrow rock which now served as a refuge to the six colonists and their dog Top.

The animals had also perished in the catastrophe; the birds, as well as those representing the fauna of the island—all either crushed or drowned, and the unfortunate Jup himself had, alas! found his death in some crevice of the soil.

If Cyrus Harding, Gideon Spilett, Herbert, Pencroft, Neb, and Ayrton had survived, it was because, assembled under their tent, they had been hurled into the sea at the instant when the fragments of the island rained down on every side.

When they reached the surface they could only perceive, at half a cable's length, this mass of rocks, towards which they swam and on which they found footing.

On this barren rock they had now existed for nine days. A few provisions taken from the magazine of Granite House before the catastrophe, a little fresh water from the rain which had fallen in a hollow of the rock, was all that the unfortunate colonists possessed. Their last hope, the vessel, had been shattered to pieces. They had no means of quitting the reef; no fire, nor any means of obtaining it. It seemed that they must inevitably perish.

This day, the 18th of March, there remained only provisions for two days, although they limited their consumption to the bare necessaries of life. All their science and intelligence could avail them nothing in their present position. They were in the hand of God.

Cyrus Harding was calm, Gideon Spilett more nervous, and Pencroft, a prey to sullen anger, walked to and fro on the rock. Herbert did not for a moment quit the engineer's side, as if demanding from him that assistance he had no power to give. Neb and Ayrton were resigned to their fate.

"Ah, what a misfortune! what a misfortune!" often repeated Pencroft. "If we had but a walnut-shell to take us to Tabor Island! But we have nothing, nothing!"

"Captain Nemo did right to die," said Neb.

During the five ensuing days Cyrus Harding and his unfortunate companions husbanded their provisions with the most extreme care, eating only what would prevent them from dying of starvation. Their weakness was extreme. Herbert and Neb began to show symptoms of delirium.

Under these circumstances was it possible for them to retain even the shadow of a hope? No! What was their sole remaining chance? That a vessel should appear in sight of the rock? But they knew only too well from experience that no ships ever visited this part of the Pacific. Could they calculate that, by a truly providential coincidence, the Scotch yacht would arrive precisely at this time in search of Ayrton at Tabor Island? It was scarcely probable; and, besides, supposing she should come there, as the colonists had not been able to deposit a notice pointing out Ayrton's change of abode, the commander of the yacht, after having explored Tabor Island without results, would again set sail and return to lower latitudes.

No! no hope of being saved could be retained, and a horrible death, death from hunger and thirst, awaited them upon this rock.

Already they were stretched on the rock, inanimate, and no longer conscious of what passed around them. Ayrton alone, by a supreme effort, from time to time raised his head, and cast a despairing glance over the desert ocean.

But on the morning of the 24th of March Ayrton's arms were extended toward a point in the horizon; he raised himself, at first on his knees, then upright, and his hand seemed to make a signal.

A sail was in sight off the rock. She was evidently not without an object. The reef was the mark for which she was making in a direct line, under all steam, and the unfortunate colonists might have made her out some hours before if they had had the strength to watch the horizon.

"The 'Duncan'!" murmured Ayrton—and fell back without sign of life.

When Cyrus Harding and his companions recovered consciousness, thanks to the attention lavished upon them, they found themselves in the cabin of a steamer, without being able to comprehend how they had escaped death.

A word from Ayrton explained everything.

"The 'Duncan'!" he murmured.

"The 'Duncan'!" exclaimed Cyrus Harding. And raising his hand to Heaven, he said, "Oh! Almighty God! mercifully hast Thou preserved us!"

It was, in fact, the "Duncan," Lord Glenarvan's yacht, now commanded by Robert, son of Captain Grant, who had been despatched to Tabor Island to find Ayrton, and bring him back to his native land alter twelve years of expiation.

The colonists were not only saved, but already on the way to their native country,

"Captain Grant," asked Cyrus Harding, "who can have suggested to you the idea, after having left Tabor Island, where you did not find Ayrton, of coming a hundred miles farther northeast?"

"Captain Harding," replied Robert Grant, "it was in order to find, not only Ayrton, but yourself and your companions."

"My companions and myself?"

"Doubtless, at Lincoln Island."

"At Lincoln Island!" exclaimed in a breath Gideon Spilett, Herbert, Neb, and Pencroft, in the highest degree astonished.

"How could you be aware of the existence of Lincoln Island?" inquired Cyrus Harding, "it is not even named in the charts."

"I knew of it from a document left by you on Tabor Island," answered Robert Grant.

"A document!" cried Gideon Spilett.

"Without doubt, and here it is," answered Robert Grant, producing a paper which indicated the longitude and latitude of Lincoln Island, "the present residence of Ayrton and five American colonists."

"It is Captain Nemo!" cried Cyrus Harding, after having read the notice, and recognized that the handwriting was similar to that of the paper found at the corral.

"Ah!" said Pencroft, "it was then he who took our 'Bonadventure' and hazarded himself alone to go to Tabor Island!"

"In order to leave this notice," added Herbert.

"I was then right in saying," exclaimed the sailor, "that even after his death the captain would render us a last service."

"My friends," said Cyrus Harding, in a voice of the profoundest emotion, "may the God of mercy have had pity on the soul of Captain Nemo, our benefactor."

The colonists uncovered themselves at these last words of Cyrus Harding, and murmured the name of Captain Nemo.

Then Ayrton, approaching the engineer, said simply, "Where should this coffer be deposited?"

It was the coffer which Ayrton had saved at the risk of his life, at the very instant that the island had been engulfed, and which he now faithfully handed to the engineer.

"Ayrton! Ayrton!" said Cyrus Harding, deeply touched. Then, addressing Robert Grant, "Sir," he added, "you left behind you a criminal; you find in his place a man who has become honest by penitence, and whose hand I am proud to clasp in mine."

Robert Grant was now made acquainted with the strange history of Captain Nemo and the colonists of Lincoln Island. Then, observation being taken of what remained of this shoal, which must henceforward figure on the charts of the Pacific, the order was given to make all sail.

A few weeks afterwards the colonists landed in America, and found their country once more at peace alter the terrible conflict in which right and justice had triumphed.

Of the treasures contained in the coffer left by Captain Nemo to the colonists of Lincoln Island, the larger portion was employed in the purchase of a vast territory in the State of Iowa. One pearl alone, the finest, was reserved from the treasure and sent to Lady Glenarvan in the name of the castaways restored to their country by the "Duncan."

There, upon this domain, the colonists invited to labor, that is to say, to wealth and happiness, all those to whom they had hoped to offer the hospitality of Lincoln Island. There was founded a vast colony to which they gave the name of that island sunk beneath the waters of the Pacific. A river there was called the Mercy, a mountain took the name of Mount Franklin, a small lake was named

Lake Grant, and the forests became the forests of the Far West. It might have been an island on terra firma.

There, under the intelligent hands of the engineer and his companions, everything prospered. Not one of the former colonists of Lincoln Island was absent, for they had sworn to live always together. Neb was with his master; Ayrton was there ready to sacrifice himself for all; Pencroft was more a farmer than he had ever been a sailor; Herbert, who completed his studies under the superintendence of Cyrus Harding, and Gideon Spilett, who founded the New Lincoln Herald, the best-informed journal in the world.

There Cyrus Harding and his companions received at intervals visits from Lord and Lady Glenarvan, Captain John Mangles and his wife, the sister of Robert Grant, Robert Grant himself, Major McNab, and all those who had taken part in the history both of Captain Grant and Captain Nemo.

There, to conclude, all were happy, united in the present as they had been in the past; but never could they forget that island upon which they had arrived poor and friendless, that island which, during four years had supplied all their wants, and of which there remained but a fragment of granite washed by the waves of the Pacific, the tomb of him who had borne the name of Captain Nemo.

www.ingramcontent.com/pod-product-compliance
Lightning Source LLC
Chambersburg PA
CBHW030918020726
47498CB00001B/20